DARKSONG RISING

BOOK THREE OF *THE SPELLSONG CYCLE*

L. E. MODESITT, JR.

TOR®
fantasy

A TOM DOHERTY ASSOCIATES BOOK
NEW YORK

To and for the sorceress
who made this all possible—Carol Ann

....

This is a work of fiction. All the characters and events portrayed in this book are either products of the author's imagination or are used fictitiously.

DARKSONG RISING

Copyright © 1999 by L. E. Modesitt, Jr.

Edited by David G. Hartwell

A Tor Book
Published by Tom Doherty Associates, LLC
175 Fifth Avenue
New York, NY 10010

www.tor.com

Tor® is a registered trademark of Tom Doherty Associates, LLC.

ISBN 0-812-56668-8

First edition: October 1999
First mass market edition: January 2001

Printed in the United States of America

0 9 8 7 6 5 4 3 2 1

CHARACTERS

Anna *Regent of Defalk and Lady of Loiseau [Mencha]*
Jimbob *Heir to Defalk, and Lord of Falcor and Synfal [Cheor]*
Hanfor *Arms Commander of Defalk*
Dythya *Counselor of Finance*
Essan *Lady and widow of Lord Donjim*
Herene *Younger sister of Lady Gatrune [Pamr]; warder of Dinfan, heir to Suhl*
Herstat *Saalmeister of Synfal [Cheor]*
Menares *Counselor*

LORDS OF DEFALK

Jecks *Lord of Elheld [Elhi], Lord High Counselor to the Regent*
Birfels *Lord of Abenfel; consort is Fylena*
Clethner *Lord of Nordland*
Dannel *Lord of Mossbach; consort is Resengna*
Dinfan *Underage daughter of late Lord Sargol; heir to Suhl*
Ebraak *Lord of Nordfels*
Fustar *Lord of Issl*
Gatrune *Lady of Pamr*

Geansor *Lord of Sudwei*

Genrica *Lord of Wendel*

Gylaron *Lord of Lerona, consort is Reylan*

Hryding *Lord of Flossbend [Synope]; consort is Anientta*

Hulber *Lord of Silberfels*

Jearle *Lord of Denguic*

Klestayr *Lord of Aroch*

Mietchel *Lord of Morra, brother of Lady Wendella of Stromwer*

Nelmor *Lord of Dubaria; consort is Delyra; eldest son and heir is Tiersen*

Tybel *Lord of Arien*

Vlassa *Lord of Fussen; heirs are twin sons, Ustal and Falar*

Vyarl *Rider of Heinene*

Wendella *Lady of Stromwer*

FOSTERLINGS AND PAGES

Alseta *Daughter of Chief Player Liende*

Barat *Page*

Birke *Heir of Lord Birfels [Abenfel]*

Cataryzna *Daughter and heir of Lord Geansor [Sudwei]*

Cens *Page*

Clayre *Younger daughter of Lord Birfels [Abenfel]*

Hoede *Youngest son of Lord Dannel [Mossbach]*

Kinor *Son of Chief Player Liende*

Lysara *Daughter of Lord Birfels [Abenfel]*

Resor *Page*

Secca *Daughter of Lord Hryding [Flossbend]*

Skent *Page*

Tiersen *Son and heir of Lord Nelmor [Dubaria]*

Ytrude *Daughter of Lord Nelmor [Dubaria]*

DEFALKAN ARMSMEN

Alvar *Overcaptain*
Himar *Overcaptain*
Jirsit *Undercaptain*

DEFALKAN PLAYERS

Daffyd *Viola; first chief player*
Liende *Woodwind; second chief player*
Delvor *Violino*
Duralt *Falk-horn*
Hassett *Violino*
Palian *Violino*
Yuarl *Violino*

OTHERS OUTSIDE DEFALK

Ashtaar *Spymistress of Nordwei*
Bertmynn *Lord of Dolov, Ebra*
Hadrenn *Lord of Synek, Ebra*
Konsstin *Liedfuhr of Mansuur; heir is Kestrin; eldest daughter is Aerlya*
Maitre of Sturinn *Leader of Sturinn; master of the Sea-Priests*
Matriarch *Head of State, Ranuak; consort is Ulgar*
Nubara *Overcaptain of Lancers, Mansuur, stationed in Neserea as Regent*
Rabyn *Prophet of Music, Lord of Neserea; regent is Nubara*
Siobion *Widow of Lord Ehara; Regent of Dumar*
Tybra *Leader, Council of Wei, Nordwei*

I

LIEDFALSCH

1

Anna readjusted her floppy brown hat and shifted her weight in the saddle. Beneath her, Farinelli, the big palomino gelding, continued his quick walk eastward along the dusty road that ran south of the Chean River toward the former ford at Sorprat. Anna glanced sideways at Himar, the sandy-haired captain—overcaptain now—whose mustache drooped more than usual—perhaps from the road dust . . . perhaps from sweat. Two of her personal guards flanked them—Rickel on her left, and beyond and slightly back of Himar, Lejun. An overcaptain, personal guards—sometimes it was still hard to believe that she was Regent and Sorceress of Defalk, and Lady of Mencha.

Less than two years earlier, she had been Anna Marshall, struggling assistant professor of voice in Ames, Iowa, a divorcée mourning the death of her eldest daughter. Then, a spell sung in Defalk and her own ill-uttered wish to be anywhere but Ames had thrown her into the intrigues and battles of Liedwahr, both colored by the ever-present male chauvinism, a chauvinism that so often she seemed the only one to recognize, even after she'd survived three attempted rapes. Because the world of Erde was governed by the harmonies—and song magic that worked—those struggles she faced were more deadly than the faculty politics of Ames. *But only slightly,* Anna reflected as she thought of the fate of untenured and discarded junior faculty members at the universities where she had taught over the years.

The late-summer sun had burned the back of her neck, despite her ever-present felt hat, and the sweat that oozed from her hair added to the stinging. In her green trousers and shirt, and floppy brown hat, she scarcely looked like a regent. Only the gold-trimmed purple vest betrayed the slightest indication of rank—that and her position at the head of the column that stretched a good hundred yards behind her.

An older-looking woman with red hair liberally streaked

with white rode up alongside Himar, clearing her throat to announce herself.

Anna turned toward her chief player. "Yes, Liende?"

"Lady . . . the players are tired . . . especially young Delvor."

Anna glanced at the road ahead, rising slowly to a crest perhaps a dek away—roughly a kilometer in earth terms—then back to Liende. "I suspect all the armsmen are tired, too," Anna temporized, blotting the sweat from her forehead. "Everyone can rest a little when we get to Sorprat. I mean, this side of the river. I think it should be only two or three deks from here."

"Four at the most," added Himar.

"It won't be that long," Anna promised.

"As you say, lady." The woodwind player nodded, then let her mount drop back.

The air was still, so hot that the browned grasses to the south of the road hung limply in the heat. Road dust coated the legs of the horses, and a finer film covered the riders' legs. Anna rubbed her nose, gently, wondering why she had ended up breathing so much road dust. *Because there wasn't any other way?*

Himar eased his mount closer to Anna, his eyes on the pair of scouts nearing the rise in the road almost a dek ahead. "I will be glad when you have completed this task, lady," the overcaptain said in a low voice, "and you can return to Falcor."

Anna nodded. Lord Jecks would also be glad when she returned, since the white-haired and still-young-faced lord of Elheld had questioned the need for her mission, even though he was the grandfather of young Jimbob, the heir to Defalk, for whom Anna ruled as Regent. *Regent for a youth not always grateful. Yet you've used your sorcery for Jimbob when you can't even use it to see your own children.*

She swallowed, her throat even drier than from road dust alone. Would she ever be able to use the mirrors and her song magic to see Elizabetta again? Or Mario?

"Lord Jecks was concerned about this task," Himar added, unnecessarily.

The blond-haired Rickel—head of her personal guard—smiled, if briefly, before the professional indifference again masked his amusement at Himar's acknowledgment of Jecks' protectiveness of the sorceress.

Anna hadn't realized how much she missed Jecks, but she'd

insisted that he remain in Falcor to heal from his wounds. In their efforts to drive the Sturinnese out of Dumar, to save Anna he'd thrown himself into the enchanted javelin hurled by the Sea-Priest of Sturinn. She still wasn't sure that she would have been able to do something like that to save someone else—not the immediate and selfless way Jecks had done to save her. She moistened her lips at the memory.

Jecks had not been happy with her decision to leave Falcor—especially for the ten days it would take, and he had been quite forceful. "I do not see why you insist on riding out to Sorprat . . . you do not need a ford there. Not this year. What crops there are come from the lower valley, and the peasants and farmers can use the bridge at Pamr. For another year or so, there will be little enough trade with Ebra. What there is can take the old road on the south side of the Chean River."

Except that the old road adds almost two days travel to Mencha—and Ebra—and you may need those days all too soon. In fact, her own journey to repair the ford was on the old road, and even pushing, it would take a day more—but she knew she needed to be on the south side to see what she could do to undo the mess she'd made of the ford when she'd created a giant sinkhole to swallow the Ebran invaders. And she *felt* that repairing the ford was necessary. She ignored solid gut feelings at her own peril, and the ford's destruction had been nagging at her for well over a year.

As she rode across the high bluff on the south side of the river, Anna glanced to her left, northward out across the river, across the green valley that—everywhere away from the irrigation ditches—had been brown and dusty little more than a year earlier. She did not look forward to revisiting the site of the battle with the Dark Monks of Ebra—except that it had been more of a slaughter than a battle. Even under the hot sun of late summer, she shivered, recalling the screams and the terrible grinding of the earth as her song-sorcery had churned the muddy waters of the Chean River over the trapped soldiers.

The column crossed the low rise in the road and started on the gentle downgrade toward the point on the south bank of the river opposite the town of Sorprat—or what of it had been rebuilt after the destruction wrought by Anna's magic. It still astounded her that "good" or harmonic song magic—Clearsong—could create such massive destruction, often with not too great a side effect on Anna. Yet the smallest of Darksong spells—even those which would have obviated the need for destructive Clearsong—could prostrate her, possibly threaten her life. *Another unfairness that you can do nothing about . . . because that's the way this world operates. Period.* She put that thought aside and concentrated on the spell she would have to use shortly.

Before long, she reined up Farinelli short of where the high grassland ended—abruptly. Himar gestured, and a trumpet signal echoed through the early afternoon. Behind them, the column slowed and halted. Anna patted Farinelli on the shoulder, and the gelding nodded ever so slightly as if to suggest that he indeed deserved some thanks.

Where the plateau ended, what had once been a sinkhole was now a circular and placid lake, smaller than it had been, and cut off from the Chean River by a low muddy rise barely three yards above the lake's surface. The water was still brownish. Below the sorcery-cut bluffs, between the base of the bluffs and the water's edge, instead of beaches, mud slopes angled into the murky lake.

"It is peaceful now," said Himar quietly. "One would hardly know that thousands perished there."

Anna nodded. Ten thousand Ebrans. *Dark Monks*, she added mentally. "We're close enough."

Himar turned his mount and stood in the stirrups. "Stand down!"

As she thought about the Ebrans, Anna almost wanted to shake her head. Hadrenn, the Ebran Lord of Synek, had beseeched her to accept his fealty. She had, and in making him one of the thirty-three lords of Defalk, thereby effectively added a quarter of Ebra to Defalk. *And probably ensured another war in Ebra.* One way or another there would have been war in Ebra, she reminded herself, between Hadrenn and Bertmynn, the noble who had taken the title of Lord of Dolov and sought to unite all Ebra under his rule. The difference was that Hadrenn had a legitimate claim to lands that had been seized from his father, and sought only those lands, while Bertmynn was willing to sell out to the Liedfuhr of Mansuur and the Sturinnese to rule all of Ebra. *And the Sturinnese chain their women.*

Anna dismounted. For a moment, as she grasped the cantle of the saddle with one hand, she wasn't sure if her legs would hold. After she took the bottle that still held water, she drank slowly. She recorked the bottle and replaced it in the holder before walking slowly in the open road before Farinelli to stretch her legs. Next came the vocalises, to clear her cords of dust, and the mucus from allergies that Brill's youth spell had done nothing to remedy.

"Holly-lolly-pop. . . ."

Behind her, horses sidestepped, and the armsmen murmured in voices so low that the sound was more like locusts than men. She shook her head, then began another vocalise, hoping that getting her cords clear would not take forever.

"Quiet!" snapped Himar, and the murmuring died away.

When Anna felt her cords were clear, she walked back to the gelding and extracted from the left saddlebag the sketch of the ford she had drawn from memory back in Falcor. Once she unrolled it, her eyes flicked from the drawing to the terrain before her and back to the drawing, comparing the two.

The sketch showed almost a wide and flat stone shelflike structure that would spread the river into a shallow and wide expanse, similar to the clay flats and gravel shallows that had existed before Anna had destroyed the bend in her efforts to annihilate the Ebran forces. She'd also sketched out what amounted to a gradual spillway that would funnel the river back into the deeper channel that existed below where the ford had been.

While she could have used sorcery to construct another bridge, the ford had worked before, and she was reluctant to change what had worked, especially since the northern side of the river was so much lower than the south and there was little enough stone beneath the bluffs.

Finally, Anna lowered the scroll, turned, and motioned to Liende, who stood before the players. Anna waited until the red-and-white-haired woodwind player eased forward.

"If you would bring the players up here. Face them toward the river, not the . . . lake," the sorceress said. "We'll use the

long building spell. Warm up and run through it a few times
while I finish getting ready."

"Players to position, here." Liende motioned for the others to
gather in a semicircle.

Anna walked forward a few steps, before stopping and looking
at the sketch of the ford and attempting to reconcile it to the real-
ity of crumbling bluffs and mudflats split by a turbid river perhaps
thirty yards wide in a deep channel.

While the falk-horn, the woodwinds, and the strings tuned
behind her, she sang the notes of the spell, using "la" instead of
real words, and worked at visualizing the ford.

"We stand ready," Liende announced.

Anna turned to the chief player. "I'd like one run-through to
fix the spell and words, please."

"At my mark," Liende ordered. "Mark!"

Anna tried to mesh the visual image, the words, and the
melody, all without actually singing the spell itself. Halfway
through, she stopped and shook her head. "I'm sorry. Could we
try that again?"

After the second run-through, Anna took another sip of
water, squared her shoulders, and nodded once more at the
chief player.

"The long building song—for the spell," commanded
Liende. "At my mark. . . . Mark!"

Anna concentrated on just the spell and the image of the
stone-footed ford the spell was designed to form, ignoring the
heat, ignoring the fivescore armsmen mounted and ranked
behind the players, using full opera voice to set the spell.

> . . . replicate the blocks and stones.
> Place them in their proper zones. . . .
> Set them firm, and set them square
> weld them to their pattern there. . . .
>
> Bring the rock and make it stone. . . .

The bluff underfoot shivered, and kept shivering. Anna had
to step sideways, but managed to keep her voice open, strong,
and clear. The lightning marking her use of the harmonies, and
unseen to any but her, or so it had seemed, flickered in the

bright blue southern sky. The haze that formed would turn into clouds, clouds that would dissipate within a few hours—glasses, she corrected herself mentally.

As the song ended and the shimmering haze lifted, Anna smiled raggedly. The bluff to her right had been trimmed into a stone-paved inclined road down to the river, and the murky waters of the Chean formed a glistening sheet nearly a hundred yards wide across the newly created stone ford. On the far side, a second stone causeway rose out of the ford to join the road through the dozen huts that represented the rebuilding of Sorprat.

"Most amazing, Lady Anna," offered Himar.

Murmurs from the armsmen ranked behind the players were louder.

"See?"

". . . not many others who can do that."

"Not many, Nirweit? How about none?"

". . . hope the peasants appreciate it."

The dizziness that accompanied strenuous songspell-casting again left Anna light-headed, but she stood firmly on the ground that shifted under her. Every spell she cast—or so it seemed—left her weak, if for varying periods. That she had to eat like a glutton to maintain her strength was something she still had trouble accepting.

Rickel handed her the water bottle and a hard biscuit.

Anna took both, murmuring, "Thank you." *Will you ever do a songspell without feeling drained?* Her eyes blurred, and she grasped at the saddle to steady herself, holding on until the dizziness subsided.

The near-dozen players stood drained, their shoulders drooping, as they also sought water and biscuits.

Anna stepped toward them. "Thank you all." She had to make an extra effort to ensure her voice carried, that it was steady. She nodded to Liende, and offered a smile. "Everyone was together."

"We have been practicing," Liende acknowledged, her eyes dark with fatigue.

"I can tell. Thank you."

Liende bowed slightly, and Anna took another swallow from her water bottle.

Even after drinking and eating several biscuits, she remained light-headed, and might until the next day. But she remounted Farinelli, offering a smile to Himar. "Shall we try the ford?"

"As you wish, Regent," responded the overcaptain gravely. "As you wish."

Once the column was remounted, Anna urged Farinelli toward the stone causeway that sloped down to the Chean River, toward the ford only she thought was necessary. *Was it really for faster travel to Mencha—and Ebra? Or because you destroyed the old ford? To redress the wrongs your sorcery has created?*

Her gut feeling remained that she had done the right thing, but the uncertainty as to why remained, long after the column had passed through Sorprat and the Chean River sheeted near silently over the newly wrought stones of the ford.

2

WEI, NORDWEI

With the knock on the door, Ashtaar sets aside the polished black agate oval and straightens herself behind the wide table of a Counselor of Wei. "Enter."

Gretslen bows as she enters, and again as she approaches the table where the dark-haired spymistress waits.

Ashtaar nods toward the chair, but remains silent behind the table as the younger woman seats herself.

After a moment of silence, Gretslen begins to speak. "As you requested, your mightiness, we have scried the waters of harmony and dissonance. Both the Sturinnese and the Liedfuhr are assisting Bertmynn's efforts to conquer the freewomen of Elahwa. He is gathering barges at the river quays on the south side of Dolov. Three Sturinnese ships are skirting the Shoals of Discord now. Earlier, they anchored off the northern coast."

"Has the Liedfuhr sent any assistance in recent weeks?"

"The seers have found none."

"What of the sorceress?"

"The sorceress has sent some golds to Hadrenn, but neither armsmen nor arms. Hadrenn has sworn fealty to Defalk and the Regency. The sorceress did use Clearsong to repair the ford on

the Chean where she massacred the Ebrans. That will reduce
the time of travel to the east of Defalk and to Ebra. She is
returning to Falcor, but she has done nothing about the darksinger in Pamr. It is possible she does not know of his efforts,
local as they are."

"And the Maitre of Sturinn?"

"The high forests of the Ostisles are being cut to build more
ships to replace those lost in Dumar," replies the blonde seer.
"Near-on half a score already rise from the ways at Yular and
almost as many at Puertoclaro."

"Has the situation changed in Neserea?"

"The fiftyscore Mansuuran lancers remain in Esaria, but our
sources indicate that they will soon be posted to Elioch. Even
so, it is unlikely they will ride near the West Pass. No Neserean
lancers or armsmen will accompany them."

Ashtaar nods—once. "Watch Esaria and Elahwa most
closely."

"Not the sorceress?"

"She has never moved without provocation, and you have
told me how strained your seers are. Once there is provocation . . . then, it will be time to watch her more closely."

Before Ashtaar speaks again, Gretslen asks, her voice deferential, "Will the Council do anything to assist the freewomen?"

"Earlier the Council sent food and tools to help rebuild
Elahwa from the floods loosed by the sorceress when she
destroyed the Evult. There may have been some weapons and
golds in those ships, and it is possible that there could be additional assistance to the people of Elahwa." Ashtaar's voice is
level.

"It is possible," Gretslen repeats, her voice equally level.

"Do not press, Gretslen." Ashtaar stands. "You may go."

3

The white and scattered puffy clouds of morning had thickened and darkened throughout the early afternoon until a nearly unbroken stretch of gray filled the sky. A cool breeze blew out of the northeast and across eastern Defalk, fueled by the chill of the distant icy peaks of the Ostfels. Anna enjoyed the break from what had seemed a steamy and unending ride back from Sorprat toward Pamr. She'd been happy to pull off the floppy brown hat and let the light breeze blow through her neck-length hair, scarcely longer than that of some of the armsmen. Hair any longer than that was hardly suited to riding, or washing in a half-medieval culture, and she had far more to worry about than her hair. *Like how to build an effective national army so that you don't have to resolve every border problem with song-sorcery or the threat of it.*

The road through the green fields and the river valley were both flat—flatter even than Iowa—and the air was humid, despite the breeze. Even the road dust was heavier, coating only a span or two of the horses' legs.

Thrummmm. . . . The muted and distant thunder rolled out of the northeast.

"We'll see rain before we reach Pamr." Himar glanced to Lejun, the guard to his right, as if for confirmation.

Anna studied the clouds for a moment, shifting in the saddle, and absently patting Farinelli on the neck. "A light rain. Maybe not that much." She looked at Rickel, riding to her left. "You're from around here, aren't you? What do you think?"

The broad-shouldered Rickel cocked his head, but his eyes continued to survey both the road and the waist-high bean plants that flanked the road behind the irrigation ditch filled with muddy water. "I'm from Heinene, but I'd agree with you, Lady Anna. The clouds aren't dark enough. Not by half."

Heinene? He does look like one of the grassland riders . . . .

At the sound of a muted hail, all four looked westward along the dusty road.

"That would be the messenger." Himar pointed toward the rider who neared after passing the scouts riding nearly a dek ahead of the main column. "There's another rider with him, in blue livery."

"I hope that Lady Gatrune is at home," Anna said.

"You would be welcome even if she is not," pointed out the overcaptain.

"That might be, but it would be less awkward if she is." *And it would be seen as less of an imposition by the more hostile lords of the Thirty-three.*

The young-faced messenger reined up short of Anna and Himar, as did the second rider. The grizzle-bearded older man wore the Prussian blue livery Anna recalled from when she had first met Lord Kysar before the old lord had died at the battle of the Sand Pass, before his consort Gatrune had taken over running his lands for their son and heir, before Anna had ever even thought about becoming a regent.

"Regent . . . Overcaptain," offered the older armsman, "the lady Gatrune expects you and bids you welcome."

Anna concealed a frown. The armsman looked familiar. She repressed a sigh. The name wouldn't come. Finally, she offered a smile. "I should know you, armsman, but I'm tired, and your name escapes me."

"Meris . . . I asked to come, Regent."

Meris? Anna could feel the broader smile with her recognition of the man. "You were the one who made it easy for me to see Lady Gatrune after the Sand Pass battle—on my way to Falcor. It's good to see you."

Meris beamed. "Thank you, Regent. Like I told Beyless when you came to Pamr . . . I owe you my life for that."

Anna fumbled with the wallet at her belt, then extended a gold. "Meris . . . I promised you once I wouldn't forget you. I couldn't recall your name, and you did a service that I couldn't repay you for then. Words are fine, but golds help with getting on with life."

Meris took the gold slowly. "Wouldn't as I came for that . . ."

"I know that, but when a regent promises . . ." Anna offered another smile.

"Thank you, lady. Thank you, and Eniabel will thank you, too." He bobbed his head. "Like as she will, seeing as she's said words like that often enough." Meris offered a grin.

Anna nodded at Meris, then Himar. "We'd better keep riding, or we will get caught in the rain. And so will the armsmen."

Meris guided his mount into the column somewhere behind Anna and beside the messenger as the force resumed the ride toward Pamr. Shoulder-high maize graced the fields ahead, still green in the late summer. Anna glanced at a hut, smoke circling from its chimney, recalling when most of the small dwellings between Mencha and Pamr had been abandoned because of the drought caused by the Evult's spells. Then she turned her attention to the problem Jecks had set her before she had left Falcor. What should she do about Neserea? Could she do anything about the Liedfuhr's buildup of armsmen and lancers in his grandson's realm? Or did she need to wait until Konsstin acted? *Probably . . . or the lords of the Thirty-three will get even more upset. . . .*

That didn't include the thousand golds she still owed the Ranuan Exchange, golds her predecessor had borrowed to pay for the armsmen to fight off the Ebrans. Or the golds she needed to build her own national army so that Defalk wouldn't always be at the mercy of its adventurous neighbors—and of the fractious nobles of its own Thirty-three. She took a deep breath.

As the first houses of Pamr appeared, Anna forced herself into a more erect and regal position in the saddle.

A gray-haired woman looked up from the basket she carried, saw the horses, and the Regent's banner, then bowed her head to Anna. A door opened on the porch of the next house, but no one stepped out. The old woman quickly lifted her basket of laundry and struggled into a scurry toward the back of the nearer house.

The dusty main street of Pamr remained empty, all the way to the center of the town. There, as Anna guided Farinelli to the right onto the street that would become the north road to Lady Gatrune's holding, her eyes went to the chandlery on the street leading westward out of the center of town. She found herself shaking her head ever so slightly, recalling how Forse the chandler had tried to rape her—and she'd scarcely been that provocative, not in trousers and shirt and vest and covered with road dust. All she'd wanted had been directions, and she'd ended up turning him to ashes when he'd barred the door and turned a bow on her after she'd refused his advances.

Anna looked back over her shoulder, realizing that the entire town had been quiet, that outside of a dog and the older woman carrying laundry, she had seen no one. The rain?

She frowned, then straightened in the saddle and looked ahead along the road. It would be good to see Lady Gatrune's friendly face.

The day was darkening into twilight, and sprinkles of rain had begun to fall a good half-glass before Anna's force and her players rode slowly through the stone gates a dek or so north of Pamr. The duty guards rang a bronze bell by the gates—an innovation since Anna's last visit—and Captain Firis was waiting by the stables. Even in the dim light of late twilight, Anna could tell that Firis' salt-and-pepper beard was even whiter than it had been a year before, although his face remained almost as young-looking as ever, despite the few additional lines around his eyes.

"Regent and lady." Firis bowed as Anna reined up. "More beautiful than ever."

"Captain Firis, bold as ever." She couldn't help grinning at the man's effrontery. "It's good to see you."

"I but follow your example as Regent and leader."

Anna shook her head and dismounted, trying not to stagger as her legs took up her weight, and holding the raised cantle of the saddle for a moment before stepping a pace or so away from Farinelli.

"You will groom him? Before you go to meet Lady Gatrune?"

"It won't take long." Anna nodded. Farinelli suffered only Tirsik in Falcor, Quies in Mencha, and a handful of other grooms in all Defalk to approach him except to feed him. *One of the drawbacks of a raider beast.* "Is there some sort of shelter for my players—and armsmen?" She beckoned. "Liende?"

The chief player eased her mount forward, stopping beside Himar.

"Himar is my overcaptain," Anna explained, "and Liende my chief player. You may recall Liende. She was with us at the Sand Pass battle."

"The players—Lady Gatrune said that they would be quartered in the main house, as would your officers. Lady Gatrune asked me to join you and . . . the senior members of your party for dinner, once you have all refreshed yourselves." Firis paused. "You have fivescore . . . ?"

"Armsmen, yes."

"It will be crowded, but between the hall in the west barracks and the few empty caserns in the older barracks, we can shelter all of them. I would be pleased to show Overcaptain Himar . . ." Firis nodded again. "The front large stall has been swept and cleaned for you."

"Thank you. If you would show Himar . . ." Anna said tiredly, beginning to lead Farinelli out of the light rain and toward the stable.

"I would be pleased."

"This way . . ." said Firis to Himar.

While Lejun unsaddled and groomed both guards' mounts, Rickel stood watch as Anna began to groom Farinelli. Before Anna knew it, Firis had returned. He peered over the stall wall. "It amazes me to see a regent grooming her mount."

"Why? He's saved my life more times than I can count." The discomfort of the remark, almost like a faint sense of Darksong, prompted Anna to add, "A good handful of times, at least." After setting aside the brush, she left the stall, carrying the lutar that had been strapped behind her saddle. Lejun carried the saddlebags with her few changes of clothes and limited toiletries.

"How are you doing in training the lady's forces?" Anna asked the captain, as she stepped out of the stable into the light rain.

Firis smiled. "The training here goes well." His smile faded.

"There's a problem." Anna glanced around. "Perhaps you should come and see me later."

Firis frowned, then smiled wryly. "Almost, Lady Regent, I would have deferred. Yet I recall our first meeting. After you are refreshed, and we dine, I will attend you at Lady Gatrune's will."

"That might be best." Anna was glad Firis had suggested consulting Gatrune. *You've got to get out of the habit of saying what comes to mind when you're tired and hungry. People listen to every word.* With a faint smile, Anna nodded, recalling her first meeting with Firis. She'd been tired and not thinking clearly, and Firis had suggested sorceresses were worse than useless. She'd almost turned Firis into a bonfire—targeting his goblet instead of him, before apologizing. Then, after the near-disastrous Sand Pass battle, he'd gathered Lord Kysar's armsmen after the lord's death, and returned the forces to Pamr, where he'd become the chief armsman for Lady Gatrune.

Anna lifted the leather-cased lutar, and the two began to walk across the nearly flat ground toward the dwelling. Rickel and Lejun followed them through the misting rain.

The tall and big-boned Gatrune was waiting on the wide stone steps for Anna. In the light of the lamps beside the double doors, her smile was wide and genuine. "All of Pamr welcomes you, lady, sorceress, and Regent." Lady Gatrune bowed deeply. Beside her, her son bowed, if a trifle after his mother.

Anna struggled to remember the boy's name.

"As do Kyrun and I," the Lady of Pamr added smoothly, as if she had sensed Anna's inability to remember the heir's name.

"I am most glad to be here, Lady Gatrune, in the hold that was the first to welcome and support me, and for that I will always be truly and deeply grateful." Political as her words had been, Anna still meant them. "Both to you and Kyrun."

"What brings you so far east? Will you stay long?" Gatrune stepped back and gestured toward the entry hall beyond the doors.

Anna laughed. "We're returning from Sorprat . . . I finally managed to find time to repair the ford there . . . the one I destroyed more than a year ago." *Just a year ago . . . it seems like it's been two or three.*

"Let me offer you the guest chamber—and a bath—before we eat."

"That would be wonderful." Anna didn't have to feign gratitude for the offer as she followed Gatrune down the side corridor.

Kyrun and Firis remained in the entry hall, as did Lejun, but Rickel followed his Regent, eyes flicking from side to side along the dim-lit corridor.

The Lady of Pamr stopped perhaps fifteen yards down the passage and opened the heavy dark-oak door. Beyond the door was a bedchamber, a room large enough to hold not only the oversize bedstead, but a love seat before the yellow-brick hearth, and a small writing desk with a chair. Two wall candles lit the room.

The older-looking blonde led the way to the second door—one that led to a combined dressing room and bathchamber. The copper-enameled tub was already filled, and the doors of the wardrobe against the inside wall lay open. "I know you travel light—like an armsman. There are several gowns in the wardrobe, should you find one you like."

"Thank you." Still holding the lutar, Anna smiled. "I won't be long."

"We await you, lady, and look forward to what you may say." Gatrune bowed and eased out of the chambers.

Once the doors closed, with Rickel stationed outside them, Anna uncased the lutar and tuned it, then accompanied herself on the water-heating spell.

> Hot and steaming, clean and clear,
> now make this water to appear. . . .

Setting aside the lutar, she peeled off her dusty riding clothes and slipped into the copper-enameled tub, where she luxuriated in the hot water for a time before rousing herself and dressing in a green dress from the wardrobe—possibly the same one she had worn the year before. She also borrowed a pair of sandals. Then she opened the chamber door and walked back down the corridor, hoping she hadn't delayed dinner unduly for the others.

Both Himar and Gatrune bowed as Anna approached. A moment later, so did Liende. As if the big-boned, but rangy Lady of Pamr had been waiting but a few moments for Anna, Gatrune gestured toward the open double doors of the dining hall.

Anna did not argue, but took the seat at one end of the table. Gatrune took the other end, and Firis and Himar sat on the side to Anna's right, Liende to her left. Two sets of twin-branched candelabra provided the light.

Gatrune glanced at Anna.

Anna recalled a grace greeting from somewhere and spoke

slowly. "In the name and spirit of harmony, may we be blessed and may this food pass our lips."

"That was nice. I've never heard it quite that way," said Gatrune, as a serving girl offered the large platter to Anna.

Perhaps you didn't recall it quite so well as you thought. "Thank you." Anna speared two large slabs of meat with her knife and eased them onto her plate, knowing she would probably need a third or fourth, just to keep her weight up, especially after the effort she'd made at Sorprat. She took an entire potato coated with cheese as well, and broke off a large chunk of crusty bread before passing the willow basket to Liende. "This looks wonderful."

"Especially after days of travel," added Himar.

A third serving girl filled the heavy crystal goblet before Anna with an amber wine. Anna took a small sip. "This is good, too."

"You did not say why you chose to repair the ford now. I would not pry . . ." Gatrune let her words trail off.

"That's simple enough," Anna replied dryly. "I've worried about it ever since I destroyed it when we defeated the Evult's forces. This was the first opportunity I've had to do anything about it. Even so, we'll have to hurry back to Falcor."

"Did you build a bridge, as we heard you did across the Fal?" asked Firis.

"No. I replaced the ford with one made of stone, but wider and shallower than before. It should be solid enough for wagons, except when it floods."

Firis nodded.

"That will speed travel to the east," observed Gatrune.

"Indeed," mumbled Firis, swallowing quickly.

"It may last longer than Defalk," suggested Liende. "When the Regent creates a sorcery, it is powerful indeed."

"Not always," replied Anna. "There was this dam——"

"The flood was powerful . . . was it not?" countered the chief player. "And the dam remains, a third cataract on the Falche."

"This was the dam that tilted and started the flood that swept away most of Dumaria and Narial?" asked Firis.

Anna nodded as she took another mouthful of the beef, dry beneath the brown gravy. The dam she'd created across the

Falche near Abenfel had drained her energies for weeks, and it had almost been a relief when it had slipped loose from the canyon walls and tilted forward—except for the wall of water that had swept through Dumar, killing thousands, and precipitating the Spellsong War with Lord Ehara.

"They say that it created a new lake leagues long. Is that true?"

"There's a new lake there," Anna answered. "How long it is, I don't know." *A good reminder of how trying to do too much with spellsong can create an even worse mess.*

"Will Dumar keep the agreement?" asked Gatrune bluntly.

"Lady Siobion serves as regent for her son. Her armsmaster serves me. If she fails to keep the agreement, I could let the dam at Abenfel fail completely." Anna took two more slices of beef, as delicately as she could. *But how can you be delicate when you have to stuff yourself to maintain the energy you need for spellsinging?*

Gatrune nodded. "It is good that you do not rely just upon faith."

Necessary, but not good. "I've discovered that." Anna paused, then asked, "How does the harvest look?"

"Better than in years, but now we must worry about late rains." Gatrune shook her head. "In past years, we could count on dry weather for harvesting what little survived the dry and heat. Now the fields are high and full—but we could have too much rain."

"Let us hope not." Anna took another sip of the amber wine. "Have you heard from your sister lately?"

"Herene has written often. She is well, but she finds herself . . . less sure than she will admit."

Anna smiled at the wry tone. "She asks for advice?"

The white-and-blonde-haired Lady of Pamr laughed, openly and without rancor. "Truly, it is amazing how matters change."

"I thought she would be a good warder for Sargol's heirs."

"You were most gracious to allow them to retain their sire's lands, after his treason," pointed out the Lady of Pamr.

"He didn't see it as treason," Anna pointed out. "I am a woman, and from another world. Women with power are not easily accepted in Defalk."

"That is true, but you are the Regent for the heir to Defalk, and you were confirmed by the Thirty-three. Attacking such a regent is treason." Gatrune's voice was firm as she added. "You were gracious."

"Not quite so gracious," Anna admitted. "I have indicated that Dinfan will be the heir. She's the oldest."

Gatrune's laugh was almost raucous. "And Herene is her warder, and the armsmaster is beholden to you. Even my own brother found that morsel hard to swallow. Yet, he finds his sisters with as much power as he—thanks to you, Regent."

"I'm not trying to replace men with women." Anna took a sip of the amber wine, a very small sip. "I'm just trying to have the best people do the job. If a woman is better . . ." She shrugged.

"Some of the older lords find that thought disturbing."

"I know. Some have made it very clear."

As the serving girl took Anna's empty plate, the Regent wanted to shake her head. Once, if she'd eaten four huge slabs of gravied beef, an enormous potato, and half a loaf of bread, she would have gained who knew how many pounds. Now she worried that she might not have eaten enough for the sorcery she had performed and might be called on to perform daily.

"We have but white cheese and melon," Gatrune apologized.

"That's fine," Anna said. "We didn't give you much warning, and you've been very gracious."

The serving girls set melon—a half melon—before each guest at the table, accompanied by a thick wedge of the white cheese.

"Most gracious," affirmed Liende.

"How do you find your quarters?" asked Gatrune.

"Comfortable . . . and dry," answered the chief player. "All the players appreciate that, and the food."

"You and the Regent deserve far more than that, but we provide what we can." The Lady of Pamr smiled.

"We are grateful," replied Liende.

"So am I," Anna said.

When all had finished the cheese and melon, Firis inclined his head toward Anna, then toward Gatrune. "If we might be excused, ladies? There are a few matters we must consider for the Regent's armsmen."

"And I also?" asked Liende. "I should see to my players."

Anna accepted the excuse and smiled. "Of course. I had not realized we had kept you."

"Would that we were kept so more often," answered Firis.

Liende offered the slightest of wry headshakes, and even stolid Himar cracked a smile at the younger overcaptain's brazen gallantry.

Once the doors closed behind the officers, Anna inclined her head toward the older-looking woman.

"Let us repair to my study," suggested Gatrune, rising.

The study was similar to many Anna had come to visit in Defalk—wood-paneled, with a wall of shelves only partly filled with books, and with a working tablelike desk, several chairs, and two side tables between the three chairs facing the desk. The two candles in the wall sconces barely flickered, but also provided but dim illumination. The Lady of Pamr took one of the armed wooden chairs before the desk. This time, Lejun stood outside the doors, presumably to let Rickel get something to eat.

Anna took the one farthest from Gatrune's, leaving a chair vacant between them.

"Firis has indicated you wished to speak with him." Gatrune's eyebrows lifted ever so slightly.

Firis has learned a lot . . . Anna smiled. "I'm neither here to recruit your captain, nor to use him as a spy. But I need to know what people think . . . how his men feel. Would you like to sit in?"

"I think Firis will speak more freely without me, and you will find our views are similar."

"Then, tell me," Anna suggested, "what he will say."

"He will try to be tactful, and he will be charming." Gatrune laughed, but the sound died almost hollowly. "He worries, and so do I. In the past two seasons, many of the tradespeople in Pamr have become less friendly. Yet none has said a hostile word, not that they would. Several of the serving girls and cooks' helpers have begged to move onto my lands, yet none could explain why."

Anna frowned, feeling a coldness grip her stomach, recalling the deserted feeling of Pamr when she had ridden through the town.

"I cannot tell you how candid he may be, but"—Gatrune

frowned—"the armsmen that he holds and trains have become most skilled. And their consorts and children have asked to live here upon the lands, even unto offering to pay rents, rather than remain among the townsfolk."

"That hasn't happened before? People begging to move onto a lord's lands?"

"Not that I recall." Gatrune stood. "Best you talk to Firis. I will tell him that you await him."

"Thank you." Anna rose as well.

"Thank you, my lady. You concern yourself about my problems, and that is more than any Lord of Defalk in memory did."

Anna did not wait long in the dimness of the private study.

Firis bowed as he entered. "As you requested, Regent. These days I no longer question the worth of sorceresses." His face remained somber, but a hint of amusement lay behind the words.

Anna stood beside the broad table, then gestured toward the carved straight-backed chair before taking a seat behind the table. "I don't question the value of captains and armsmen either," she replied after sitting. "I wish we had more good ones."

Firis sat on the edge of the chair. "I am most pleased to be in the service—"

"I'm not recruiting you, Firis. From what I've seen and heard, and from what Lady Gatrune has said, you've done a good job here." Anna paused. "Something here is bothering you, and, as Regent, I need to know that sort of thing." She waited.

"It is most difficult . . ." After a moment, the overcaptain added, "The town of Pamr . . . it was not this way when I became Lady Gatrune's captain. At first, I thought the strangeness I felt was because I was an outsider, but many of the armsmen have lived all their lives in the demesne of Pamr, and most of those have even moved their families to the lands." Firis snorted. "Most times, armsmen will keep their women and consorts as far as they can from a lord's holding."

"It sounds strange," Anna said. "Do you know why?"

"Would that I did, lady. Would that I did. Many feel as I do, yet none has heard or seen anything that would give voice to the cause of those feelings."

"Well . . . I would appreciate it if you or Lady Gatrune would let me know if anything happens . . ." Anna held in a yawn. The day had been all too long.

"By your leave, Regent?"

Anna stood. "By my leave, Firis."

After Firis left, Gatrune appeared in the open study doorway.

"You were right," Anna admitted, stifling a yawn. "He was gallant and tactful, and he's worried." *So are you, but what exactly can you do?*

"We will watch and inform you of what we discover."

Anna couldn't stop the next yawn. Lord, she was tired.

"You are tired. We can talk more in the morning." Gatrune waited for Anna.

Lejun followed the two down the corridor to the guest chambers.

When Anna finally stretched out on the big bed—lumpy as most were in Defalk—tired as she felt, her mind continued to race. Both Firis and Lady Gatrune felt something was wrong in Pamr. *Is it because of what you did to the chandler?* Anna sighed. *Why do you have to pay for everything you do? Pay more for it than others do?*

Still . . . she wasn't sure that was the cause. She only felt that. *How often are your feelings wrong?*

There was no answer to that—not one she liked.

4

ESARIA, NESEREA

Rabyn glances at his own image in the heavy gilt-framed mirror that dominates the dressing room off his bedchamber. Light green eyes survey his high-cheeked, narrow-faced visage. He nods and brushes damp and freshly washed hair back over his left ear. After fingering his beardless chin, he frowns, then readjusts the green cloak of the Prophet of Music.

His eyes drop to the miniature portrait on the long dressing table, and he smiles at the dark-haired woman centered in the gold frame. "I am being patient—as you taught me. But, Nubara, all of them, they will find out who is Prophet."

As he leaves the dressing room, his eyes go to the bedchamber where the blonde girl shivers under the silks, pretending to be asleep, and his lips curl into a smile of pleasure—momentarily—before he turns and walks down the short hall, stepping through the double doors from his chamber. The Mansuuran lancers stiffen. So do the guards who flank the lancers, the pair who wear the cream-and-green of the Prophet's Guard.

Rabyn ignores all four and walks not-quite-briskly along the corridor to the stairs, and thence up to the scrying pool. The two guards in green and cream follow, four paces back.

From the door Rabyn studies the three players who have risen and then bowed to him.

"The scrying song. Now!"

"It will take a moment, Prophet, to check the tuning," explains the older violino player, bowing again.

"Then best you do so. Quickly."

As the trio of string players tune, Rabyn studies them, his eyes going from the graying and heavyset lead violinist to the balding man, and then to the thin-faced strawberry blonde. He studies the blonde, then looks back to the leader.

"We're ready, Prophet."

"Play." Rabyn clears his throat and nods, then waits for the melody before starting the spell.

> Show me the sorceress of Defalk,
> what she does and where she may walk . . .
> and who stands by her side and hand. . . .

The scrying pool silvers, revealing a slender blonde woman about to mount a palomino—one of the oversized beasts from the grassland raiders of the north. She swings up into the saddle with an ease born of practice and settles herself quickly, then nods to the officer in Defalkan purple beside her. They ride from the stables toward a column of waiting armsmen.

Rabyn studies the image, nodding abruptly. He sings the release couplet, and ripples cross the silvered water. The image vanishes, and the pool is but a pool. He turns to the three players, his eyes on the center woman, a heavy figure with graying brown hair. "You did not hold the tone clearly. Best you do better next time."

The violino player swallows. "Yes, Prophet and Seer."

Beside her, the thin and younger strawberry blonde player conceals a silent gulp.

Rabyn turns and leaves the scrying room. The two Prophet's Guards again follow as he makes his way down the stairs and along a shaded and columned walkway toward the open-columned hilltop chamber that serves as the summer receiving room. Out beyond the palace of the Prophet, the Bitter Sea is calm and flat under the morning sunlight. Barely a breeze penetrates the columns of the chamber.

"Greetings, Lord Rabyn." The overcaptain in the maroon uniform of a Mansuuran lancer who awaits Rabyn stands from behind the small desk to the side and below the dais on which the throne is set.

"Good day, Nubara." The latest Prophet of Music, Lord of Neserea, and Protector of the Faith of the Eternal Melody fixes his eyes upon his regent. "What have you heard about the sorceress?"

"She is said to be visiting the eastern lands of Defalk." Nubara shrugs.

"What might she be doing there?" Rabyn's voice turns lazy, close to indolent, as he steps onto the dais and settles himself into the throne.

"Almost certainly essaying to enlist greater support among the Thirty-three. Possibly visiting Lady Gatrune. She did not venture so far as her own holdings on the border."

"Is it not strange that she has yet to visit her own lands in more than a year?"

"She cannot obtain support from her own lands, and, as your sire had planned, those lands are among the more distant from Falcor." Nubara inclined his head, waiting.

"I would see Eidlon later in the day. We should hear of his progress in assembling and training the Prophet's Lancers."

"You should, indeed," answers Nubara smoothly.

"I should. For once they are ready for battle, then Overcaptain Relour can move his lancers to Elioch. They will be in position to counter any schemes of the sorceress."

"And well away from Esaria, as well."

"That, too," agrees Rabyn, smiling. "Today is the day for petitions. Which is the first?"

"The rivermen on the Salya River are asking for a copper more for each passenger from Nesalia to Esaria."

"Boring." Rabyn nods. "But necessary. And after that?"

"A civil dispute between two cloth factors . . ."

5

"The day will be hot," ventured Himar from where he rode to Anna's right.

"Too hot," she agreed, glancing toward the houses ahead, where the town of Pamr began. Under a clear sky, the morning air was still and moist, yet the lingering dampness of the road was the only sign of the previous night's rain. To her left, Rickel nodded, but his eyes, like those of Lejun, studied the road and the fields that flanked it—and the houses they neared.

"Zechis won't be that long a ride—late midafternoon, eighth or ninth glass," suggested the overcaptain.

"Tomorrow is the long ride," she replied, readjusting the floppy brown hat, "but the sooner we get back to Falcor the happier everyone will be." Anna frowned as a motion from the house they approached caught her eye. Had someone closed a shutter? A door? She turned her head, but the first house remained silent.

At the back of the third house Anna passed, a gray-haired woman stood bent over a washtub, shielded from the already strong sun by a sagging porch. As the sound of horses reached her, she straightened. Then she stiffened, but made no other move as the column passed her and continued toward the center of Pamr.

Anna's eyes narrowed, and she concentrated on studying each dwelling or shop they neared, wondering if she should uncase the lutar. *In your own land? In a town held by your strongest supporter?*

A bearded man peered out of the open window of what looked to be a cabinetry shop, then jerked his head inside as he caught sight of Anna. Firis was right, she decided, more than right, but there was little she could do about mere chilliness toward the Regency, especially when she could only speculate about the cause. *The chandler?* Her killing of the man who had tried to assault and kill her hadn't raised any coldness the year before.

Anna took a deep breath. She needed to know more, but she still didn't know enough to use her scrying glass to find it out. The problem with asking questions was always that you needed to know a good part of the answer before you could frame a decent question.

At the junction of the road from the north with the unnamed main street of Pamr, Anna turned Farinelli right—toward the bridge over the Chean River that lay more than a dek beyond the west end of town.

On the left side of the street was the inn—the Green Bull—and the well-endowed animal on the sign was portrayed graphically in green. On the right side . . . Anna stiffened slightly as she saw the repainted blue and white of the chandlery—the one where she'd been forced to incinerate Forse. In the doorway stood a figure in brown. As the dark-haired youth or young man—somehow familiar—met her glance, Anna wanted to shiver at the coldness in his eyes.

She held her eyes firmly on him until he lowered his gaze. Only then did she blink, for the building almost appeared to have two images—as though she'd used Darksong magic. One image appeared deep brown and brooding black, shadowed, the other a bright white and deep blue and weathered. She blinked again and studied the chandlery. There were still two images.

"Rickel—do you see the chandlery there? Do you notice anything strange about it?"

The blond-haired guard frowned as he looked to the right. "The wood has been painted recently, and the door looks to be new."

Anna wanted to sigh, but only answered. "Thank you. The door has been painted in the past year. They had a fire there."

"That young fellow—he's watching you," added Himar.

"I imagine he is. I had to kill the chandler last year. He might be his son." *And he probably hates you.* "Before I became Regent. He tried to kill me." *When he couldn't rape me.*

"Not a wise idea," observed Himar.

"I didn't have much choice." *At least, you didn't think you did then.*

Anna glanced at the houses on the left side of the street, but no one appeared outside, unlike the year before, when a girl had brought her a basket of gifts in thanks. She thought she could see figures—women—watching from the windows, but no one appeared outside.

"Quiet town," suggested Himar.

"Too still by far." The murmur from Liende was barely audible, and Anna agreed with the chief player's words.

The unnatural quiet remained for the last dek out of the town. It almost seemed to Anna that not even the birds sang until she had almost reached the stone bridge that spanned the Chean River. Two things bothered her about Pamr. Of those who had watched her, none had come out to see the Regent, and most were women. The handful of men had looked away. Not spit or expressed open dislike, but just looked away. Then, there had been the feel of the chandlery—something like Darksong—and the man who had watched. She knew the face was familiar, and that she should have recognized him. But she hadn't, except for knowing that he had to be some relative of the late Forse.

Does that lack of recognition come from having to meet and remember too many people in too short a time? Should you have stopped and investigated?

Anna knew she couldn't stop and deal with everything that felt wrong, but there was that nagging sense that she should have recognized something about the son of Forse, that she knew him from somewhere. Clearly, there was something about Pamr, despite Lady Gatrune's hospitality, that felt wrong. *Then . . . what doesn't these days?*

6

PAMR, DEFALK

The two young and bearded men watch as the column passes along the main street westward, back toward Falcor, one in the doorway of the chandlery, one from the window beside the door, half-hidden by the shutters.

Once the last armsman rides past the chandlery, and then past the coppersmith's porch, the older of the two men steps back into the store. "The bitch sorceress! Our beloved Regent. With such a pretty face, so innocent-looking, as if she had no evil on her soul." He snorts as he looks at his brother. "So evil! She is evil, and none see it. But they will . . . they will. Oh . . . they will."

"Then, why did you nothing, Farsenn?" asks the younger. "You have spoken against the sorceress. There she was. But a handful of armsmen rode between you and her, and you did nothing. I had most of my drums ready."

"Now is not the time, my brother." Farsenn smiles. "She has not suffered enough, and she will suffer."

"You mean that you are not yet skilled enough to stand against her?" Giersan raises his eyebrows. "When then? She will be back in Falcor, Farsenn. Her power grows daily. Even the Liedfuhr of Mansuur has acknowledged her Regency." Giersan rubs his forehead, then uses the maple mallet to tap the single drum that rests on the wooden floor beside him. He cocks his head and listens to the sound.

"Do you not see? Do you not care? I saw the blazing pyre she made of our father! A man, a worthy man, our father, and she turned him to ashes! A woman, a lowly bitch from beyond dissonance, and she destroyed him on a whim!" snaps the chandler in brown. His voice rises almost into a screech. "We suffered from the fire that burned half the merchandise. Did she offer a coin? A condolence? Did she even look back?"

"I wasn't there," points out the drummer.

"You didn't have to be. I was, and I saw, and she will suffer!" Giersan shrugs. "As you say."

"I do say. I will say." Farsenn glares at his younger brother. "And she will suffer."

The drummer nods, then looks at the wooden floor. The silence between them lengthens.

"How are the other drums coming?" asks Farsenn, long after the sound of hoofs has died away.

"They are almost ready. But even with eight, I can only play simple melodies." Giersan runs his fingertips over the wood of the drums.

"Simple will be enough." The young chandler in brown smiles, and his eyes fix on an image none can see but him. "More than enough. Far more than she will expect."

7

Still dusty from the ride, Anna sank into the upholstered wooden armchair beside her bedchamber's small working desk table. The room was dim, lit but by the single taper on the desk and one candle in the wall sconce inside the heavy oak door. Her stomach growled, and she wondered which she wanted more—food or a hot bath.

Her eyes flicked to the wall, and the black rectangle etched there. A different, deeper pain burned through her. *How long . . . how long before you can try to see Elizabetta again? Tomorrow? It's been almost a season, and Brill said you could look across the mist worlds occasionally.* The last time she'd tried to use her sorcery to see her youngest child, the mirror had exploded. Anna had been most fortunate that the knife-sharp glass fragments had not killed her. *But you have a pool now . . . water doesn't explode the way glass mirrors do.*

Her eyes flicked to the door as she heard the rap on the wood and Lejun's announcement.

"Lord Jecks is here, Lady Anna."

"Have him come in." Anna straightened in the chair. *Tomorrow . . . when you're more rested, then you can see about Elizabetta.*

The white-haired and clean-shaven Lord of Elheld smiled as

he stepped into her chamber. "You returned sooner than I thought, my lady Regent."

"A certain lord suggested that if I had to repair a ford, I had better do it quickly and get back to the important business of being Regent." She gestured to the other straight chair, the one beside the writing desk.

"I do not recall being so incautious as to say anything such as that." Jecks raised his eyebrows as he settled gracefully, if slightly gingerly, into the chair. The pallor had left his face, although his outdoor tan had faded and a trace of gauntness had left his face five years older than it had been. The smile he bestowed on Anna was as devastating as always, but she managed to avoid swallowing or overtly betraying the attraction she felt.

"My dear lord Jecks, you didn't need to voice a word." Anna rose. "I'm dusty and tired and hungry. I'm going to take a bath. Would you like to join me for dinner in a while? I won't be long."

"I would be most pleased. Then I can tell you what has transpired in your absence."

"Not much, I hope."

"You may have been correct in feeling that the time was right to repair the ford at Sorprat." His lips quirked into another smile.

"Things are getting worse someplace. I can tell that." She gestured toward the door. "Let me get cleaned up. I'll see you in the small dining hall." She paused. "You wouldn't mind sending a message to the kitchen, would you? I don't think I did." She offered a rueful smile. "It's been a long day."

"I would be most happy to ensure we are fed, my lady." Jecks rose and bowed.

Once the heavy door closed, Anna slid the bolt and walked to the bathchamber adjoining her bed and work chamber. The water— lukewarm—was already in the tub. Slowly, she tuned the lutar, then sang.

> Water, water, in the bath below,
> both hot and soothing flow. . . .

Once she had the water not quite steaming, and a headache from doing the spell on an empty stomach, she replaced the lutar in its case and plopped into the high-sided tub, spilling water onto the stone floor of her bathchamber. "Damn . . ." slipped from her lips.

Anna pushed away the irritation at her clumsiness and concentrated on washing her face with the square of rough cloth. When she'd been a student in Europe, washcloths had been hard to find, and they weren't exactly common in Defalk, necessary though she found them for removing road dust and other grime—especially since deodorants weren't in the primitive chemical repertoire of Erde, and perfume was hard to come by, even for a regent.

Then, everything was hard to come by in impoverished and beleaguered Defalk, although it was getting slightly less difficult, thanks to the golds she'd added to the treasury through subduing a few unruly lords—and Dumar. The battles in Dumar might well have been easier than the problems she still faced. Jecks' very presence upon her arrival indicated his concern for her—and his concern for Defalk and the Regency for his grandson Jimbob. What was the problem? Something wrong in Dumar? Or with the lords of the Thirty-three? Or Neserea? Or . . . the list of possibilities was all too depressingly long. *Probably some Defalkan lord . . .*

She washed and dressed quickly—choosing a plain green gown, since all but one of her limited workday clothes— trousers, shirts, and vests—were filthy. *Amazing that you're the ruler of a land and your wardrobe is less than when you were an assistant professor of music.*

Jecks was waiting outside the door, talking to Giellum and Kerhor—the two duty guards.

". . . and it's still spouting flaming rock . . ." The white-haired lord broke off his words as he saw Anna. "Lady . . ."

"Yes, I look almost human without the road dust all over me, Lord Jecks." She inclined her head to the guards in turn. "It's good to see you both. Did you get some rest while I was gone?"

"Ah . . . some, Lady Anna," admitted the black-haired Kerhor. "Except Lord Jecks and Arms Commander Hanfor had us drilling every day."

"Many glasses," added Giellum, his voice mock-mournful.

"They needed the practice," Jecks said, "and they don't have the time when you're around."

"I hope you worked hard and learned something," Anna temporized.

"Both Lord Jecks and Arms Commander Hanfor strike hard."

Anna winced. She doubted Jecks had any business teaching arms yet. "You were out there with a blade?" she asked him, as they turned the corner and headed down the stone stairs to the lower floor and the small dining hall. "You're not—"

"I am mostly healed, my lady, thanks to your sorcery, and I will not sit around the liedburg and be thought a useless old dodderer."

"Even when you were barely moving you were worth more than a dozen men who can't do anything but swing those blades."

"That is not the way the young ones see it." Jecks laughed sardonically.

The way Defalk was, Anna suspected he was all too right. "Do I work them too hard? Should we recruit some more?"

"That might be wise, especially if you insist on traveling all over Liedwahr."

The small dining hall was set for two—with two three-branched candelabra providing the light. Jecks waited for Anna to sit. Courtesy in Defalk did not extend to seating women, merely allowing the highest or most noble to sit first.

A serving girl Anna did not recognize hurried in with a basket of fresh-baked bread, followed by a figure she did. "Dalila!"

The once-stocky and now-petite brunette smiled as she set the crockery casserole dish on the pottery tile serving as a trivet, then bowed. "Regent."

"I didn't expect you . . ." Anna had worked out the arrangements for Daffyd's sister to teach the younger children in the liedburg and to help Meryn in the kitchen, but that had been before she had left Falcor to deal with the uprising in southern Defalk and the attack from Lord Ehara of Dumar. *Lord . . . you lose track of things . . .* Sometimes, Anna felt she couldn't keep track of half of what was going on.

"Meryn was feeling ill, but Assolan is watching Ruetha and Anadra."

"How are you getting along with Meryn?"

"Very well," answered Jecks. "We're getting some new

dishes, I've noticed." He inclined his head toward the casserole. "Is that one of them?"

"Yes, ser. This is the stew you liked, Regent."

Anna could feel her mouth water. "That's wonderful." She smiled at Jecks. "You'll like it."

"I've liked all the new dishes. It was one of the few pleasures left for a time."

Anna looked at Dalila. "Are you sure you're doing all right?"

"Oh, yes. Dythya has me teaching letters to some of the smaller children in the liedburg." The pert brunette offered Anna another smile, then turned and slipped from the dining hall.

"That one . . . she's another that would lay her life in front of a charger for you."

Anna didn't argue, only nodded. *You took refuge in her home, and after you rejected the forceful advances of her consort, he left her penniless and friendless, and his brother took everything because Dalila was a woman unable to hold property. You made her brother your chief player, and he died fighting the Evult. And now, because you pay her for cooking and teaching, she thinks you're wonderful.* Defalk needed more feminism than one sorceress and Regent could ever supply.

Anna poured herself some of the maroon wine, then filled Jecks' goblet.

"Thank you, lady. It is unusual to be served by a ruler."

"Just remember that." Anna broke off a chunk of bread, then served two huge ladlefuls of the stew. "What was so urgent that you were waiting for me?"

"I would not say it was terribly urgent, and it should wait until you have eaten. You are most pale," Jecks said.

"It has been a while since I ate. Midday, I think."

"What if you had to sing a spell?"

"I'd have been in trouble." Anna took a mouthful of the stew, the spices muting the taste of the strong mutton. The second mouthful she accompanied with a chunk of the dark bread. Dark bread—they had it, and that meant someone was indeed getting molasses from Dumar—or had recently. Did that mean that Lady Siobion was keeping the agreement? And that all was well with Alvar, the captain Anna had made over-captain and armsmaster of Dumar both to aid Siobion's regency and to ensure Dumar's compliance with the terms of surrender, even if Anna had been careful not to call them precisely that.

"You carry provisions," he said gently, not quite suggesting that she was a fool not to have eaten them. "What happens to those who travel with you if you cannot protect them?"

"I know. I should have eaten more." She continued to eat the stew and bread, also slicing a peach, and thin wedges of white cheese. When she had cleared her plate—twice—she looked up. "Now . . . what's the problem?"

"It is not a . . . difficulty . . . yet. Not all of them." Jecks held the wine goblet but did not take a swallow.

"All of them?" Anna's stomach tightened. "Start with the worst."

"None is pressing, yet . . ."

"Go on."

"All of the Mansuuran lancers in Neserea will soon be sent to Elioch. Those are the reports."

"How many is that?" *You need to get busy with your scrying pool.*

"Fiftyscore. And either young Rabyn or Nubara has formed a new force—the Prophet's Lancers. According to Arms Commander Hanfor, the new Prophet can muster at least another two-hundred–score lancers and armsmen."

A trained Neserean army of more than five thousand men—and she had perhaps three hundred pledged to her, plus the levies of the Defalkan lords—if they heeded the call. Still, she'd destroyed more than that in the war with Dumar. *And look what it did to you and Jecks.* "There's more."

Jecks shrugged, almost apologetically. "The SouthWomen have sent arms to Elahwa, and Lord Bertmynn is assembling men and boats on the River Dol, as if he will be using the river to ferry men there."

"The Ranuans wouldn't sell us arms, but they'll send them to Elahwa?"

"To the freewomen there. They revolted."

"That's a good way to get slaughtered." *Especially in this world . . . and you're supposed to support Hadrenn to pull them out?* "How did we find that out?"

"Menares received a message from Wei."

"The last message from Wei led to the problems with Dumar," Anna said slowly.

"I thought you might see it that way."

"We can't afford to do much for Hadrenn."

"If you do not . . ." Jecks let the silence drag out.

"I know. Then we'll be back to having unfriendly neighbors on both the east and the west borders, with the inscrutable traders of Wei breathing down on us from the north. I suppose the Ranuans will be unhappy if we don't support these . . . freewomen."

"That I could not say."

"What else?" Anna asked, knowing there had to be more bad news.

"The Rider of Heinene has asked for aid. The wet spring caused the grass to grow far higher than in past years, and there was a fire that swept half the grasslands."

"So they have no forage?"

Jecks nodded.

"You bring such cheerful news, my lord. I take it you've got more of the same?"

"You recall Lord Vlassa?"

"He was the Lord of Fussen, the one whose twin sons were fighting over the lands?"

"Ustal and Falar have both raised armsmen, and each has sent a scroll requesting that you recognize him. You did say I should read scrolls. . . ."

"I did. Go on."

"Falar is the younger by a fraction of a glass, and he wrote that, should you not support him, and should he prevail, he will consider seeking support for his 'just' claim elsewhere."

"Let me guess," Anna hazarded. "Ustal has the . . . traditional right to the lands, and he's some sort of idiot, or wastrel, or something?"

"Ah . . . why do you suggest such?" Jecks raised his eyebrows.

"Because, for a younger son to go to such lengths would mean he's either an idiot or he has a just claim. If he can raise armsmen, that means people are putting themselves on the line for him, against tradition. Most folks won't. That suggests that Ustal has more than a few faults—of some sort." Anna took a bigger sip of wine than she'd intended before asking, "Can Menares or Dythya or someone find out what Ustal's faults are? In the meantime, *you* send back a scroll to each saying that I'm returning from Pamr and will look at the claims as soon as I return."

Jecks smiled. "You will gain two weeks by that."

"If that."

"Oh . . . and the weapons smith, the one who was a wheelwright, he was killed in a tavern brawl."

"And we're back to having no one in Falcor who can forge weapons?" Anna refilled her goblet, knowing she shouldn't be drinking so much so quickly, but she'd taken a little over a week to repair something that needed to be fixed, and the moment she'd left, things had started to get worse. She paused. "Was the brawl an accident?"

Jecks shrugged. "I would say so, but one could not rule out foul play."

"No . . . not when we need an armorer to hold off enemies on half our borders." Anna forced herself to take a small sip of the wine.

"Hanfor has suggested you create the position of Armorer of Defalk and offer a ten-gold bonus for an experienced smith."

"Twenty," said Anna. "Ten to be paid after the first two weeks, and ten after the first year. Send scrolls everywhere."

"Tomorrow, I will talk to Hanfor."

"Well . . . since we're discussing problems, there's one more."

Jecks waited.

"There was this youth . . . at the chandlery . . ." Anna swallowed. *The one in the pools in your seeking spells, the one who wants your destruction . . .* "Shit!"

Jecks' mouth dropped open.

"It's hard to explain. Come with me." She pushed back her chair and started for the door, and Jecks rose, following.

Lejun and Kerhor followed them back up the stairs, first to Anna's chamber, where she grabbed the lutar, and then to the scrying room, the room that had once been a guest chamber and now held only a mirror pool and a writing desk—and candles in wall sconces. The two guards stationed themselves outside the door, while Jecks lit the candles and Anna tuned the lutar.

"You think you will see something now?" Jecks gestured toward the darkness beyond the closed shutter.

"Enough," grunted Anna, struggling with the tuning pegs.

A single vocalise was enough to clear her cords, enough for the simple spell she sang, at least.

> Of those with power of the song
> seek those who'd do me wrong
> and show them in this silver cast
> and make that vision well last.

As it had been the last time she had used the spell—there were three images, but one was different. The blonde seer from Nordwei was in one silvered circle. The second contained a dark-haired and thin-faced youth in an ornate cream-and-green tunic, lounging at a table beside a less than fully clothed young woman. His face was familiar, though Anna had never seen it, and so were the cream and green.

"Neserean colors there . . ." murmured Jecks.

"That has to be Rabyn," concluded Anna. "He looks more like his mother."

"He's acting like his sire." Jecks' voice was dry.

"It's the other one—the one in brown." Anna gestured toward the young man at the battered-looking writing table. "He was watching me in Pamr, and I knew I'd seen him. I just couldn't place where I'd seen his face."

"A chandler's son?"

"He's the chandler's son. He has to be. You remember? The one who tried to kill me with a bow in Pamr when I was on my way to meet Behlem?"

"That was before you became Regent," Jecks pointed out.

"He uses Darksong. The whole chandlery felt twisted when I looked at it, but I thought it was me." Anna sang the release couplet.

> Let this scene of scrying, mirror filled with light,
> vanish like the darkness when the sun is bright. . . .

Jecks tilted his head sideways. "He uses Darksong, and he's opposing you, but he's only a chandler."

"Until I became a sorceress, I was only a teacher and a singer," she replied.

Jecks shook his head. "You were always a sorceress and a Regent."

Anna frowned. *Does that mean what you think it does?*

"He is only a chandler who would be a darksinger."

"We—I—still have to do something about him."

"You can't do anything about it tonight," Jecks pointed out reasonably. "Tomorrow, you can send a messenger to Lady Gatrune and have her people find out the man's name and what they know about him."

That made sense, but she knew it wouldn't be enough. Once again, it was looking like what she could do wouldn't solve the problem. "Tomorrow," she agreed. "And I'll have to look for Bertmynn and see what he's doing . . . and those Mansuuran lancers . . ."

Tomorrow . . . will every tomorrow always be filled with more tasks than you started yesterday with?

8

As the sunlight poured through the liedburg window, Anna struggled up into a sitting position in the bed. Her eyes were gummy, and her head ached. *Too much not very good wine last night. Not a good idea, either, with more problems today.*

As she took a slow deep breath and swung her feet to the side of the bed, the black-etched rectangle on the wall—the visual representation of the last time she'd been able to see her daughter through her sorcery—strobed at her. She closed her eyes again and just sat on the edge of the bed. *You can kill, and create great bridges, and rule a country, but you can't use sorcery to see your daughter.*

After a moment, she found herself correcting that thought. *You weren't able to see her for a while, but it's been more than a season since you tried. Brill said it could be done across the gap between the mist worlds and Erde infrequently—not never.*

She padded to the bathchamber, where she washed up and then dressed in her remaining clean green working trousers and shirt. After pulling on the brown-leather boots, she trudged to the door and opened it. Blaz and Rickel were the guards.

"If you would . . . please . . . have someone bring me some breakfast."

"Yes, Lady Anna," Rickel answered.

"Thank you." She closed the door and went to the writing desk, rummaging around until she found a sheet of parchment.

What do you say to a daughter a world away, a daughter growing up without you. . . . She dipped the quill carefully, and began to write.

"No . . . that's not . . ." She scratched through the words, knowing she couldn't afford to crumple the parchment. She'd just have to use one sheet for drafting, and then recopy.

A second beginning wasn't any better. Nor was a third, and she set the parchment aside at the knock on the door.

"Dalila, Lady Anna, with your breakfast."

"Come on in." Anna stood as the brunette brought in the tray—on which were piled a wedge of yellow cheese and fresh bread, a lopsided peach, and a large pitcher of water.

"We didn't cook anything, lady. If you want more . . ." Dalila waited.

"This is fine." Anna smiled. "How are the children?"

"Ruetha is doing well. I am letting her learn letters with the older bairns. I hope you do not mind. . . ."

"That's fine. When she's older, she can learn numbers from Dythya as well."

"You would let her . . . ?"

"Of course." Anna wanted to frown. "Dythya doesn't come from lordly blood. She got where she is because she's able. I want the same to be true for Ruetha and Anadra and all the young girls in the liedburg." *And throughout Defalk—as much as possible.*

"I would want that. Yet . . ." Dalila left the question unvoiced.

"How long will that be possible?" asked Anna. "So long as I'm Regent, and if I'm a good one, a long time after that."

"You will be Regent for many years."

"We'll have to see." *Right now, it doesn't look all that promising.*

"You will." Dalila bowed, turned, and slipped out the door.

Before eating, Anna did take the precaution of taking out the lutar and orderspelling the water. She found she finished everything, even gnawing the peach down to the pit. As she sipped another goblet of water, the headache faded, then vanished. *Dehydration or low blood sugar or both.*

After setting aside the tray, Anna wrote out the letter to Elizabetta, slowly, carefully, then wrapped the four golds she took from her wallet in old parchment and placed them in the crude envelope.

With a deep breath she stood. Carrying the lutar and envelope, she walked to the door, opened it, and stepped out. "I'll be working across the hall."

"Yes, Lady Anna." Rickel nodded, and he and Blaz followed her, resuming a guard position around the scrying room's door.

Anna closed the door, stepped forward, and glanced at the silvered waters of the pool. She set the envelope on the worktable. After retuning the lutar, and running through two vocalises, she lifted the lutar, and began to sing.

> Bertmynn, Bertmynn, Lord I'd see,
> show his forces now to me. . . .

The image in the silvered waters of the pool was that of a quay, where several barges were tied, and where men in brown carried barrels toward the barge in the foreground. At the side were several armsmen, almost lounging. The fact that there were buildings and greenery in the distance beyond the gray of the water confirmed to Anna what Jecks had said about Bertmynn loading on the River Dol.

After a time, she lifted the lutar again.

> Rabyn, Rabyn, Lord who'd be,
> show his grandsire's lancers now to me. . . .

The second image was less useful than the first, showing a column of lancers garbed in maroon and riding along a dusty road. Still, the length of the column indicated the lancers were on the move, possibly toward Elioch, and probably confirming the information that Jecks and Menares had gathered.

Now what? Anna released the second image and took a deep breath. *First, you do something for you.* After a moment, she lifted the lutar a third time.

> Silver pool, silver pool, it's scrying time for my child
> silver pool, silver pool . . .

Even before she strummed the last chord, the silvered waters wavered into an image—her red-haired Elizabetta driving in a green car Anna didn't recognize, a faint smile on her face. Anna smiled in return. *She's all right.*

Then the water of the pool began to boil, and gouts of steam burst upward.

Anna jumped back, forcing the release couplet. Even after the image faded, the pool continued to boil and bubble, the roiling subsiding slowly.

Elizabetta is all right, though . . . that's what's important. But the tears that rolled down Anna's cheeks contradicted her words as she slumped against the heavy oak door, sobbing silently. *Why . . . why? Why can't you even get a look at your daughter for more than an instant without the whole universe striking back at you . . . why?*

She picked up the envelope with the unsent letter and stepped out of the heat and humidity of the scrying room into the hallway, half carrying, half dragging the lutar with her. The eyes of both Rickel and Blaz widened as the steam and water vapor swirled out behind her.

"Lady . . . Regent?" stammered Blaz.

"I'll . . . be . . . all right." She walked across the hall and slipped quickly into her own chamber, sliding the bolt behind her, then dropping the unused envelope on the writing desk.

In the bathchamber, she looked into the mirror. Red face—blotchy as if burned—probably from the steam, wet cheeks . . . "You look like shit . . ." *Then . . . you feel like shit, too. You couldn't even send the letter . . . not even one small letter.*

She looked back into the mirror, into the too-thin face, at the golden silver-blonde hair that belonged to a teenager and framed blue eyes that had seen too much. She blotted her face with cool water, and kept blotting. There were times when having makeup would have still been a help, youth spell or not.

Finally, she returned to the writing desk and tucked the envelope into the drawer. *Just try to send it . . . with another note . . . maybe you can tell her to write something and that you'll try to recover it with sorcery in a few weeks . . . would that work?* Who knew what would work? Even all of Brill's books offered little and rather incomplete guidance.

She gathered herself together, then stepped back into the corridor and headed down to the receiving room, and the business of the day. Based on what Jecks had already offered the night before, a long week awaited her. *Another long year . . . more likely.* She reclaimed the lutar case and carried the cased instrument down the stairs.

Once in the receiving room, already warm, with its single high window, Anna looked at the pitcher of murky water. After a sigh, she took out the lutar and orderspelled the water. Without water—clean water—she wouldn't get through the day. Then, she poured a goblet, and took a swallow, before settling into the chair behind the table. She lifted the bell and rang it.

A dark-haired page—Skent—peered in. "Yes, Lady Anna?"

"Skent . . . it's good to see you. Ah . . . will you see if Counselor Dythya is free to meet with me?"

"Yes, lady." The door closed.

Anna picked up the first scroll in the pile. It was from Lord Birfels of Abenfel. She began to read.

> . . . You may recall when you were in Abenfel, Lady and Regent, that we had discussed the possible consorting of Lysara with Hoede, the son of Lord Dannel of Mossbach . . .

"In short," Anna murmured to herself, "we intend to marry off Lysara to Hoede immediately unless you come up with a better match. And better means someone with more lands and golds, not brains." She wondered if Dannel was as thickheaded as his youngest son. The problem was simple enough, but simple didn't mean solvable. Anna had started a school for fosterlings in the liedburg, which functioned as a combination capital and administrative center. Many of the lords of the Thirty-three regarded the fostering school as more of a matchmaking opportunity. Lysara was beautiful and bright, and would be totally miserable consorted to the stubborn, arrogant, and thickheaded Hoede. Unfortunately, Anna didn't have the faintest idea of who might be a better match. *You mean you haven't had time to think about it.*

What could she say? She set aside Birfels' scroll and picked up the next one—from Vyarl, the Lord and Rider of Heinene. She read quickly, but the scroll said little more than what Jecks had told her the night before about the grasslands and the fires.

The next scroll was from Hadrenn, the self-styled Lord of Synek, whom she'd made one of the Thirty-three earlier in the year, effectively expanding Defalk's borders a good hundred and fifty deks eastward and probably increasing the territory under the Regency by close to twenty percent. *If he and you can hold it against Bertmynn.*

Hadrenn's words were to the point.

> . . . the golds you have sent have allowed me to increase my armsmen by tenscore, but the usurper Bertmynn receives many more golds from both the Maitre of Sturinn and the Liedfuhr of Mansuur. . . . Already, Bertmynn's forces move south to take Elahwa from the Council of the Freewomen. . . .

That meant that Ebra was split into three factions—the freewomen apparently held the port city of Elahwa and at least some of the surrounding area; Bertmynn held the northeastern third; and Hadrenn the western third. Who or what the freewomen were was another question to which she needed an answer. Anna nodded and set the scroll in the pile that required her to do something . . . when she could figure out what.

The next scroll was from Ustal, the elder son of the late Lord Vlassa of Fussen. Anna began to read, then winced, and forced herself to continue.

> The Regent in Falcor,
> Greetings from Ustal, the son and sole heir of Lord Vlassa of Fussen. For many years, Fussen has paid liedgeld it could sore afford, and received nothing in return, save drought, disruption, and the loss of levies at the Sand Pass. Thus, as heir to Lord Vlassa, I must insist

that the Regency use all its powers to ensure the rightful and traditional succession in Fussen.

If the Regency feels it cannot adjudicate and enforce the rightful succession, then I further must insist that Fussen be allowed to determine its own affairs. . . .

Anna shook her head as she finished the scroll. After Ustal's scroll, Jecks or Dythya had set the one from Falar, the younger son of the late Lord Vlassa of Fussen. Anna began to read it, gingerly.

To the Regent of Defalk, Sorceress of the Land, and Lady of Mencha,
Your graciousness, with heavy heart and burdened conscience I send this missive. Because you have sacrificed much for Defalk, and will doubtless sacrifice more in the years to come, your heart may also be heavy with the news of dissension about the succession in Fussen. Unlike others, I have been reluctant to address you, yet address you I must, not for my sake, but for the sake of the people of Fussen. . . .

Anna smiled. Young Falar or his advisors were far from stupid.

. . . my elder brother has abused the trust of the people and squandered the substance of Fussen, so much so that the merchants and freeholders have requested that I seek the succession and pledged their lives and coins to that end. . . .

Anna's lips tightened. If . . . if what the scroll said was indeed true, matters were a mess in Fussen. Behind Falar's scroll were Jecks' responses—identical to each brother—stating that the Regent was returning from repairing the ford at Sorprat and would be addressing the concerns of the succession upon her return. Anna nodded. She never had to tell Jecks anything twice. *He's told you things twice . . . that he shouldn't have had to*. Anna winced at the thought.

"Counselor Dythya," announced another page—Resor.

"Have her come in." Anna set down the scrolls, for the moment.

"Lady Anna." The gray-haired and stocky Dythya bowed as she entered the receiving room.

Anna nodded to the seat across the small conference/worktable from her. "Where do we stand with our golds?"

"I thought you might wish to know." Dythya smiled and extended a single sheet of parchment. "Those show what the liedstadt has received, and what remains in the treasury."

Anna looked at the precise black script numbers: six thousand golds from Cheor, three thousand from Suhl, two thousand from Stromwer, and two thousand from Dumar. . . .

"Dumar owes another four thousand golds," Dythya pointed out.

"And we owe the Ranuan Exchange a thousand."

"Not until harvest."

"Have it sent now. We could use the goodwill."

"My lady . . ." Dythya cleared her throat. "About the accounts . . ."

Anna skipped to the bottom line . . . barely a thousand more than what her expeditions of submission and conquest had brought in. "You're going to tell me that we're spending more golds and that we're spending them faster than we planned?"

"Yes, lady."

"How much faster?" Anna's voice was wary. She took another swallow of the water. Already the room felt stifling, despite the open window behind her.

"Almost four thousand golds more." Dythya eased a sheet of parchment across the table.

Anna scanned the listing. Nearly a thousand golds more in supplies for the liedburg—to replace food stocks and other things that Barjim had not. Anna had authorized that. Four hundred golds for wrought-iron stock for the weapons smith—whom they had to replace. Nearly a thousand golds in silvers paid to the armsmen who had followed and supported Anna in her campaign to subdue the rebellious Suhlmorran lords of Defalk and Lord Ehara of Dumar. Eight hundred golds for replacement mounts . . . Anna took a deep breath. She'd authorized most of the expenditures. "But after we pay everything, we still should have almost seven thousand more than at the beginning of summer."

"Six thousand if you pay the Ranuans, and you cannot count on the liedgeld being paid on time," Dythya pointed out.

"Only from Cheor, Elheld, and Mencha," Anna replied, adding after a pause, "and Stromwer, Suhl, Lerona, Abenfel, and Pamr."

A surprised look crossed Dythya's face, as if a quarter of the lords paying on time were a novelty. "That is true."

"But you're right," Anna replied. "We will be cutting it close. I still want to pay the Ranuans, though. If we or any of the lords have to borrow from them in the future, it might make it easier. We also may need allies, and a land that repays its debts is a better ally than one who doesn't." She paused. "If you would draft a scroll and make the arrangements with Arms Commander Hanfor to ensure the repayment reaches Encora safely?"

"Yes, lady."

"Also . . . perhaps you could draft a scroll to go with that party, and copies that could be sent elsewhere. We'll offer a twenty-gold bonus for weapons smith. Five golds after examination of his work, five golds after the first month, and ten golds after the first year."

Dythya nodded.

"How is the schooling going for the pages and fosterlings?"

"Well enough for most . . ." Dythya's voice was cautious.

"Except Hoede is becoming impossible?"

"He has difficulty with numbers. He has little interest in them, and less in learning them from a woman."

Anna shook her head sadly. "How about the others? What about Nelmor's heir—Tiersen, is it?"

"After the first weeks, he is fine. His sister had a word with him, I believe." A smile crossed Dythya's lips.

Anna smiled as well. Had the timid Ytrude actually had the nerve to advise her brother? "Any other problems?"

"No. The others learn well. Some, like Cataryzna and Lysara, know as much as I do already, and even young Secca has begun to do complicated sums like the others. Skent is the best of the young men, but Jimbob works hard."

That the heir of Defalk worked hard was good, but Anna hoped at least some of the motivation was internal, rather than provided by his grandsire externally.

"Lord Jecks, lady," announced Resor.

Anna motioned for the white-haired lord to enter.

"Will that be all?" asked Dythya, standing.

"Just for now," Anna said. "I wanted to know how things stood before I started thinking about spending golds."

"Would that more rulers thought such, my lady," Jecks offered as he bowed to Anna.

Dythya bowed and slipped out of the receiving room. With Anna's gesture, Jecks took the seat the counselor had vacated.

"How am I supposed to deal with the mess in Fussen?" she asked him.

"As Regent, you must reach a decision about which will inherit—and quickly."

"I don't know either one."

Jecks smiled. "Yet, my lady."

"I think, you schemer, that you're saying I need to go to Fussen and meet the two young men."

"How else will you know them? How else will the Thirty-three feel at ease with your decision? You have not been to the west of Defalk, my lady."

"If I upheld the older male, no one would say anything So . . ."—she dragged out the word—"that means that you think something's rotten in Fussen, or at least with Ustal, and you think my presence will reassure such stalwarts as Nelmor—"

". . . and Lord Jearle."

Anna looked and felt blank at the last name. She took another swallow of water and blotted a forehead that had become damp as the midmorning heat had begun to build in the receiving room.

"Lord of Denguic," Jecks explained.

The name was vaguely familiar, but probably only from the liedgeld lists. "We haven't heard much from him."

"He is the Lord of the Western Marches," Jecks explained. "He was supposed to defend the approach from Neserea."

"He didn't do much to stop Behlem."

Jecks nodded. "He sent a scroll claiming that he had lost tenscore men and would have lost all had he not surrendered. He relinquished the title and the one-third exemption from liedgeld."

"Whom did he send it to?" Anna asked. "Behlem didn't march into Defalk until after Lord Barjim was killed at the Sand Pass."

"It was addressed to Barjim and was waiting at the liedburg for Lord Behlem. Menares found it and brought it to me sometime back."

"No wonder he paid his liedgeld on time," Anna muttered. Barjim and his consort Alasia had risked everything and borrowed from the future to raise arms to fight off Ebra.

"Jearle saw no point in dying when he could not stop the Prophet's armsmen and lancers," Jecks said dryly.

"I don't think we'll restore his title or his duties, and especially not his exemption from paying the liedgeld," Anna said.

"There has always been a Lord of the Western Marches."

"There may be again," Anna conceded. *But not anyone that slippery.* She looked meaningfully at the pile of scrolls. "We have a few other matters to discuss."

"I feared such."

Anna wanted to laugh at the rueful tone of his voice. Instead, she nodded. "So do I, but remember, you thought my being Regent was a good idea."

"My life was simpler before I thought so much . . ."

Anna did laugh before she picked up the next scroll. She jotted down a quick note on the back of a used piece of parchment to talk to Menares about sending a scroll to Gatrune about the young chandler—and learning his name. At times, especially when she returned to Falcor from somewhere, she wondered if she would ever be able to juggle all the problems.

9

ESARIA, NESEREA

The workroom is large, light, and airy. Dark woods ranging from flat planks to narrow timbers are stacked against one of the inner walls. A woodworker's bench is set out from the other inner wall, and on a set of wooden shelves beside the bench are set planes, chisels, saws, clamps, wood knives, several jars with stoppers, clean rags, and other implements.

Three dark circular frames fill much of the open floor space. Each is man-high, and a stocky but bent and gray-haired man carefully smooths a rib of the frame closest to the door. The door opens, revealing that the outside is guarded by two of the Prophet's Guards. The craftsman steps back from the frame on which he was working and straightens, waiting.

The Prophet Rabyn steps into the workroom, followed by an older Mansuuran officer who accompanies him. Rabyn pauses by the smooth and polished frame. His fingers caress the nearly black wood, before his eyes go to the gray-haired craftsman, who glances from the young Prophet to Nubara.

"You know what I want?" demands the youth.

"Yes, most honored Prophet. I have studied the scrolls you gave me, and I will do as they show." The crafter gestures to the three frames. "These are to the requirements of the scrolls."

"There must be no imperfections. Do you understand?"

"There will be none, honored sire. None at all." The woodworker lowers his head.

"Good." Rabyn studies the second frame and then the third. With an abrupt nod, he turns and departs.

Nubara follows hurriedly. The door closes, and the two walk along the outer corridor back toward the columned audience chamber.

The Mansuuran officer glances from Rabyn back toward the guarded door. "How do you know he will do as you say?"

"He has a daughter, Nubara. Right now, she is in the south villa, with her mother."

"Her mother?" Nubara frowns.

"Of course. That way, he will know no one has abused her." Rabyn's laugh is cold. "I have not touched either. No one has. She is not that attractive, but he does not know that. Besides, I could turn her over to the lowest of the Westfels Foot, and he knows that. Or"—Rabyn smiles, and his face appears almost serpentlike—"I could think of something."

"Yet you will reward him if he builds these . . . these devices?"

"Even I know, Nubara, that a ruler must keep his promises." A second laugh follows. "You might notice how few I make, and how careful I am with my words." Rabyn looks toward the audience chamber. "The glass has come for me to appear concerned and caring for the welfare of my people." He lifts his eyebrows. "Are you ready?"

"Yes, honored Prophet."

Rabyn does not look at the Mansuuran officer before stepping through the door that a servant has opened for him.

Behind him, Nubara shivers, then follows.

10

Anna stepped out of the receiving room and nodded at the two guards, Lejun and Rickel. "I'm going to observe the lessons."

The two followed her as she turned into the small service hall. Three sets of boots echoed on the stone floor of the narrow passage until Anna stopped at the back door of the large hall that continued as the working classroom for the pages and fosterlings. *Until you can figure out something better . . . like everything else.*

She eased open the narrow door and slipped behind the tapestry arras, simultaneously listening and attempting to keep from sneezing in the narrow and dusty space.

". . . Sturinn is not a land nation, such as Mansuur or Defalk. It is but a collection of large and small isles set in the Western Sea. These isles are held together by great fleets, by a form of Darksong magic, and by the largest numbers of armsmen in our world. The Maitre of Sturinn lost more than forty great vessels and two hundred–score armsmen when the Regent unloosed the Falche River. These were but as a handful of ships and men to the Maitre . . . yet the loss of the same number of armsmen ruined Dumar and left it prostrate."

Anna shook her head as the heavyset and gray-haired Menares droned on.

"Now . . . see this map. You can see how many deks lie between Mansuur and the nearest isles of Sturinn. Those are the Ostisles, and five years ago they were free. Likewise, fifteen years ago, Buerann was governed by the young lord Zuerien."

"Buerann?" asked a voice Anna did not recognize.

"The large island here, in the corner, north of Pelara."

At least he's using maps. . . . Anna slipped out from behind the arras, as silently as she could.

The red-haired Lysara saw the sorceress, and the girl's mouth formed an O. Anna smiled, and put a finger to her own lips. Lysara quickly looked back toward the graying tutor.

"What matters it," asked the sandy-haired Hoede, his tone verging on insolence, "how far lies Sturinn? The Sturinnese cannot sail their ships to Defalk."

"Their ships . . . do not just affect Nordwei or Mansuur," replied Menares. "Had the sorceress not stopped them in Dumar, Stromwer would now belong to Sturinn, and all the trade that goes through that road would either pay tribute to the Maitre or travel a far longer way to Ranuak, and that would cost the lords of the south many golds. . . ."

"They're all Suhlmorrans anyway," mumbled Hoede. "Weak women . . . all of them."

Anna tightened her lips, deciding that she could not wait much longer to deal with Hoede. *But here is not the place or time.*

The blonde Cataryzna—the object of Skent's affection— glanced toward the back of the hall, then looked quickly back to Menares. Beside Cataryzna, Secca sat almost at the end of the table, the redheaded and youngest of the fosterlings and pages, and very much the smallest.

Looking at Secca, Anna was reminded of several things. She had yet to resolve the rather mysterious nature of the death of

Lord Hryding, the little redhead's father. The red-haired child, an echo of her own redheads, prompted her resolve to rewrite the letter to Elizabetta—or write a cover note—and just try to send the envelope without looking at her daughter, and ask Elizabetta to write a letter in return—and leave it someplace where it would be undisturbed and somewhere that Anna could visualize—like under the stairwell at Avery's lake house.

"Oh . . . Lady Anna . . ." Menares looked up from the map on the easel.

"I'll only be a moment." Anna studied the fosterlings and pages slowly, her eyes resting on each in turn before she finally spoke. "There are neither Suhlmorrans nor northern lords in Defalk, not if you wish to have your children remain under the banner of Defalk, and not that of Sturinn or Mansuur or Neserea." Her eyes fixed on Hoede, but the stocky blond refused to meet her eyes.

"There's another reason why ships are important," Anna said after another pause. "It costs less to carry grains and cargoes for long distances by ship. That is why Nordwei is powerful and how the Ranuans manage to get so much gold for their Exchange."

Seeing the confusion on both Tiersen's and Hoede's faces, Anna added, "Some of you wonder what golds have to do with power. How do we get the weapons for armsmen? We have to buy iron and pay a weapons smith to forge them. What do you pay armsmen with? If the Regency has to use levies for more than a few weeks, they must be paid, and even if they aren't, their food costs money. Coins," she added. It was still hard to recall that not all English terms translated into Defalkan German/Old English.

Tiersen, Skent, and Kinor nodded. Hoede continued to look blankly at Menares, as if he didn't even want to acknowledge the Regent's presence.

"You may continue, Menares." Anna nodded at the older tutor before slipping out the main door, Rickel before her and Lejun behind her.

Why are the young men such knuckleheads? Does all that swordplay and honor nonsense knock every bit of the ability to think out of their skulls? That couldn't be it. Jecks was reputed as one of the best blades of Defalk, and the white-haired lord could certainly think.

As she slipped back into the receiving room, she slowed, and said to the duty page—Cens—"Find Lord Jecks for me, if you would."

Cens bowed and scurried off. Anna picked up yet another scroll, another petition from the rivermen for a reduction in their permit taxes. *How can you say "no" in another and different way?*

Before she had finished, there was a rap on the door.

"Yes, lady?" Jecks bowed deeply as he entered the receiving room.

"How would you suggest we get rid of that idiot Hoede? Or will that cause another great uproar among the distinguished northern lords?"

Jecks' face blanked at the bite in the phrase "distinguished northern lords," but he replied smoothly, "Ah . . . his sire might be somewhat displeased . . . but you are the Regent."

"Can't we just tell the good lord Dannel that Hoede is better fitted for direct instruction on his father's lands? Or that he seems to have more ability with weapons than with a quill? Or something like that?"

"He has little ability with a blade," Jecks pointed out. "Even Lysara, slight as she is, would kill him, although they have never sparred." He paused. "Well you might talk to Lady Essan. She has seen much about consorts and joinings."

Thinking about Lady Essan, the white-haired widow who remained in the liedburg, brought a smile to Anna's lips. Essan had ridden to battle, although the lords of the Thirty-three would scarcely have wanted to admit that a woman and consort of the Lord of Defalk—even two generations back—had done so.

Anna nodded. She'd had all the fosterlings tutored with weapons, but she and Jecks had decided that in the beginning, the young women would only practice with other women or with the armsmen or officers designated as instructors. Anna had informed all the lords of daughters that she was requiring that the young women understood arms in the unlikely event that they were required to defend their lands in the absence of their consorts. Then she'd told Jecks to make sure that the girls got as tough a course of training as they could handle.

Some, like Cataryzna, whose father had been crippled in battle years before, understood immediately. Others, like the shy Ytrude, had had to be coaxed through everything in the beginning.

"Well," Anna reflected, "I will talk to Lady Essan, but Hoede still has more ability with a blade than a quill or a book."

"Best you tell his sire that, then, since it is the truth. And since you think so poorly of northern lords."

"Oh, my dear lord Jecks, I'm not angry at you. I'm angry at the situation. Lord Birfels' consort Fylena wants Lysara consorted out immediately, and that knothead Hoede is the only one available. . . ."

"What about Tiersen?"

"Even that would be better, but I have no idea whether the two would even talk to each other. Or whether Nelmor would consider it." Anna wondered why she hadn't thought of Tiersen. *Is it because you've disliked Nelmor's attitude toward women and the Regency?*

"Nelmor needs a consort for Tiersen. That is true—save he would set his lance on Geansor's daughter."

"Cataryzna? She's off-limits."

Jecks' eyes twinkled. "I know that. You have plans for young Skent. Perhaps you should bring him with you to Fussen."

"That's not a bad idea. What about Jimbob?"

"He should remain here."

"You don't want his name tied up in the succession mess?"

Jecks shrugged. "Is there reason for him to be so immersed?"

"No," Anna admitted.

"When would you leave for Fussen, my lady?"

"How about the day after tomorrow? This isn't going to go away, and it will only get worse if we don't do something." Anna sighed. "Do you think we should take a few more days and visit Lord Nelmor?"

"That could not hurt." Jecks flashed the warm smile that crept into Anna's heart.

Why do you lash out at him? He's always stood by you. "You are coming, you know, High Lord Advisor?"

"I had hoped so." The second smile was even warmer, then faded. "I know you do not have a high opinion of Lord Jearle . . . but it would not hurt to stop there as well, and his keep is but a few deks off the road from Fussen to Dubaria."

Anna nodded reluctantly. "And it will help make the western lords feel better."

"It will not harm you."

"What do I tell him about being Lord of the Western Marches? Or not tell him?"

"Say there is much to be considered, and that is why you are planning to visit his keep." Jecks smiled. "Besides, if you dislike him, you can ask for more grain and supplies for your travels. Supplying such is his duty to the Regency."

"We'll consider that part. Will you have Menares write some flowery scrolls to Ustal, Jearle, and Nelmor, announcing that we will be visiting them?"

"I will so instruct Menares."

"Good. He writes flowery scrolls well." Anna took a sip of the spell-cleaned water. "Then there's the problem in Ebra. Hadrenn is practically begging for more coins we don't have, or armsmen." She took a deep breath. "I wonder if Ebra will always be a problem."

"What would you do?"

Anna frowned. "I can't do anything about it, except for sending him a few more golds, but I worry about the mess in Ebra. Menares said something about Bertmynn sending troops to Elahwa to take over the city from the people. I tried to find out something in the scrying pool the other day. He's loading barges with armsmen, but I don't even know who holds Elahwa." Anna looked at Jecks.

"There are rumors . . . you recall the blades you tried to purchase?"

"Yes. Some trader bought them."

"They were sent to Elahwa—by the SouthWomen."

Anna sighed. "So the Matriarch is trying to grab some territory, too?"

"No. The SouthWomen and the Matriarch—"

"Oh . . . Lady Essan told me something about that. The SouthWomen are the radicals. . . ." Anna wanted to smile at the puzzled look that crossed Jecks' face when she used political terms from Earth. "And they sent the blades . . . to these free-women that Hadrenn wrote me about in his scroll? Does that mean they're trying to set up a land for themselves?" *Lord, all you need is a bunch of Liedwahran radical feminists with blades starting another conflict to complicate things.*

"I do not know." Jecks frowned. "The SouthWomen keep matters to themselves."

Anna nodded. "Another thing to keep track of. We ought to send a few golds to Hadrenn. How many, do you think?"

"A hundred, if you can spare them."

"Will you take care of that before we leave for Fussen?"

"That I will."

"Thank you." Anna didn't have to force the smile.

11

DOLOV, EBRA

What news, Ceorwyn?" The blond man in the burgundy tunic smiles warmly as the gray-haired figure in battle leathers steps across the time-polished stones of the north wall of Castle Dolov.

"What we expected, Lord Bertmynn," answers Ceorwyn. "A Ranuan trader slipped past the Shoals of Discord, and ported in Elahwa. The cargo was grain from Encora—grain and blades supplied by the SouthWomen to the freewomen. The free-women now hold both the north and south sides of the river—and perhaps three leagues west along the river."

"The Matriarch, for all her talk of peace and harmony!" Bertmynn's smile vanishes with his snort. "Yet she sends cold iron to arm those rebel women."

Ceorwyn shakes his head. "No . . . your seer—Lessted . . ."

"Lessted. What says he?" asks Bertmynn, an ironic cast slid-ing across his smile.

"The arms came against the will of the Matriarch. The old woman struggles with her own Mercantile Exchange as well as with the SouthWomen. That is why she will throw what support she can into allowing the Sorceress of Defalk generous terms in repaying the debts incurred by Defalk in years past."

"Better yet if the bitches of the south are disunited. Still, I like it less that the Matriarch speaks well of the . . . sorceress."

Ceorwyn nods.

Bertmynn turns and rests his elbows on the sun-warmed stone of the rampart, looking westward and downhill across the city to the wharves that line the eastern shore of the River Dol. He fingers his curly blond beard before asking, "Are the barges ready?"

"Not before weekend, sire," replies the armsmaster. "Or perchance later."

"I had thought as much. Promises come easy, but actions lag those promises." Bertmynn stretches, and his near-two-yard height becomes more apparent, even beside the tall and muscular Ceorwyn.

"The bargemasters would not act until they received the advance golds you promised."

"We have enough golds to take the city before winter. Hadrenn cannot wage a winter war, and both the Sturinnese and the Liedfuhr will supply us." A wry smile crosses Bertmynn's lips, and even his clear blue eyes smile. "Especially now that cousin Hadrenn has thrown in with the sorceress."

"He would claim you left him no choice," points out Ceorwyn.

"I would have left him Synek and even Vult. . . ."

"All that is left of Vult is the Zauberinfeuer—and it continues to spread its lava across what was once a fertile valley."

"Proof enough that the Regent-sorceress is evil, do you not think, Ceorwyn?"

"I am loath to call any ruler who has saved her land evil, sire. Best you know that." Ceorwyn looks up as he faces his lord, but his dark brown eyes are clear and steady.

"Yet you serve me."

"I owe you, sire. But owing you and following you does not mean I should abandon my judgment." Ceorwyn smiles ironically. "By overthrowing the Evult, the sorceress has granted you the chance to reclaim the lands of your great uncle. She has also freed her own people, and retained the old succession by choosing to act as Regent for young Jimbob. It is also said that she avoids the use of Darksong, though she has the power to call upon it. Few of power such as hers would act so."

"Ceorwyn . . . honest and forthright." Bertmynn smiles broadly, shaking his head as he does. "Yet you serve me. What other cautions have you?"

"Beware the Sturinnese. You saw how they promised friendship to Lord Ehara of Dumar. Yet they risked no more ships when the sorceress destroyed their fleet and hounded Ehara to his death. Nor did they send armsmen or ships against Defalk in retribution. Best you be most careful, sire. Lord Ehara thought the Sturinnese were his allies also. He lies dead in the ruins of Envaryl, and Dumar pays tribute to Defalk, and Sturinn does not act."

"The Sturinnese will aid us. Who else will they aid?"

"They will aid you so long as the coins are few, and you make life unpleasant for the sorceress . . . and no longer. Should you defeat Hadrenn early on, you will see no more coins from either the Liedfuhr or the Maitre of Sturinn."

Bertmynn laughs. "You would counsel me against attacking my posturing cousin?"

"I would not counsel you against attacking him, sire. I would counsel you against doing so until you have no other pressing concerns. But before the sorceress learns of what you may plan."

The blond-haired lord gestures southward, toward where the river vanishes between the green hills. "That is our plan. I am glad it pleases you. I intend to hold Elahwa—freewomen or no. The sorceress will do naught about that. Nor will the Ranuans."

"The Ranuans will not act." Ceorwyn touches his iron gray beard. "That is true. The sorceress is less certain. It is said that she marched on Dumar when Ehara declared that he would put every woman in Dumar in chains before he would pay damages to Defalk."

"I believe in women in their place, well in their place, Ceorwyn, but I'm not fool enough to suggest chains for them. Even in the most discreet of talks or . . . anything." Bertmynn straightens and walks back from the battlement. "The sorceress is astute. She will scarcely attack us while Hadrenn lies between the borders of Defalk and our forces. Not with the Liedfuhr and his grandson and the lancers of Mansuur threatening her western border. And not with the older lords of the Thirty-three chafing against the rule of a woman."

Ceorwyn nods. "Best it should remain so."

"It will. It will. Let us attend the barges."

The north wall of Castle Dolov continues to soak in the heat of the summer sun long after the sounds of two sets of boots taking the narrow stone steps have died away.

12

In the early-morning light that but seeped through the west window of her scrying room, Anna looked at the envelope on the desk beside the pool, an envelope containing another envelope within it. *Parchment is supposed to be fire-resistant . . . they bake filet of sole in it . . . and you have two heavy layers around the letter.*

After three vocalises, and after coughing up more mucus than she had in a while, Anna strummed through the chords of the spell twice. She glanced at the envelope on the writing desk once more, then at the blank waters of the scrying pool. Finally, she began to sing the spell with lutar accompaniment.

> Bring this to my daughter in her land,
> Deliver it safely to her hand,
> Intact and without a burning flame
> Bring it whole in word and frame. . . .

As she finished the song, Anna concentrated on visualizing the letter at Elizabetta's fingertips, and upon making the words and melody and visualization match.

The entire scrying pool exploded in steam even before Anna struck the final chord and finished the last note. Small geysers erupted upward into the dim white plaster of the ceiling and sprayed in all directions. The heat radiating from the water turned the air into a steam bath, and large bubbles of steam burst from the vanishing water of the pool.

But the envelope was gone!

Lutar in hand, Anna wrenched open the heavy door with the other and staggered out of the steam and boiling water and into the liedburg's wide stone-walled corridor. Her back was soaked with near-boiling water.

"My lady!" Lejun reached out and dragged her farther away from the cascading steam.

Anna stared down, dumbly, at her reddened right hand. Her face felt hot, almost burning. Beside her, Blaz and Lejun looked from her to the thick, smokelike steam pouring from the half-open door and the puddles of steaming water on the floor stones outside the scrying room.

Jecks appeared from somewhere, his hazel eyes wide as he surveyed the slowly subsiding steam. Then his gaze snapped to Anna,

Anna took a slow breath. She *thought* she hadn't inhaled any of the steam. *You hope not.* She'd read about what live steam did to lungs. "I need cold water! Quickly."

Lejun dashed down the corridor.

Jecks' eyes followed Lejun, then snapped back to Anna. "Mighty sorcery, my lady. Mighty indeed. Are you well?" Was there the faintest quiver in that firm voice?

"I think so." Her knees were rubbery, and her eyes blurring slightly. Anna found that she was clutching the lutar all too tightly. *All you tried to do was send a letter! One letter to your daughter. Just one!*

She walked quickly, but almost mechanically, into her own chamber, where she dropped the lutar on the bed as she lurched toward her bathchamber. There she began to splash cool water across her face for several moments before groping for the washcloth and holding it across her forehead until it warmed.

She had almost run through the water in the pitcher when Lejun reappeared with a full bucket.

"Thank you." She plunged her hands into the bucket.

After a time, she could tell the cold water had helped, although her forearms and the back of her hands were still blotchy and red. She walked slowly into the main chamber, where she sank into the chair behind her writing desk, knocking off a scroll she didn't bother to pick up as it rolled across the worn rug.

After bending and replacing the scroll on the desk next to the others, Jecks sat down in the other straight-backed chair, his warm hazel eyes on her. "Might I ask . . ." Jecks inclined his head toward the closed chamber door, in the direction of the scrying pool.

"I was sending a letter . . . a scroll . . . to my daughter."

"Across to the mist world?"

"Yes." Anna nodded. She could feel the tears welling up, but held them back, back behind the invisible barriers she'd learned to erect so many years before. Rather than try to say more, she nodded.

"Are you most certain that you are well?"

"I feel all right. Except I'm burned a little." She looked down at her hands.

Jecks shook his head slowly. After a time of silence, he said, "You are not what you seem. I see a woman who looks young, but has children nearly so old as mine and who is wiser than I am. I see a lady who speaks well, and appears beautiful, yet who can wreak greater destruction than this Erde has ever beheld." He laughed, not quite ruefully. "Just when I can tell myself that you are not that different from the women of this land, then . . . you prove otherwise."

Anna wasn't sure that she wanted to prove otherwise. "I'm a woman like many others."

"No. You are not like any others. There is none close to you. And for that, I am most grateful, if sometimes startled."

Does it have to be this way? Can't I be reassured and be held and still be strong? "I'm still a woman," Anna insisted, "and all I wanted to do was send a message to my daughter." *Like any other mother.*

"Do you know if . . . she received your scroll?"

"I can't tell. I sent the letter *somewhere*." Anna reached for the half-full goblet of water on her writing desk and swallowed it in two quick gulps. "I'll try to summon her answer in a few weeks. Then I might know. After that"—she gestured toward the closed door and the scrying room beyond—"it's clear I can't try it often."

Jecks nodded somberly. "You best might wait longer . . . after such as today."

Anna refilled the water goblet and took another swallow. "We'll see."

"Do you still wish to leave for Fussen on the morrow?"

"We might as well. The burns won't be that bad. They're not

forming welts. Maybe I can do something about the succession in Fussen, and reassure Nelmor and Jearle, and . . . whatever else will help the western lords." Anna stood slowly. "I need to put myself back together. We still have a lot to do before we go. If you'd meet me in the receiving room in a bit . . . ?"

"Of course." Jecks rose as she did.

Anna looked at the back of the door as it closed. *Are you pushing him away again? Why? Or is it just because you're a sorceress?* She took another deep breath as she walked toward the bathchamber. Her legs were still rubbery, and she probably should eat before long.

When she had blotted and combed and straightened herself, and checked her face again to ensure that it was not blistering, she left her room, stepping past her guards, and started for the receiving room. Then she turned and headed back along the stone tiles of the corridor, past the door to her own room, striding purposefully until she reached Lady Essan's door.

Giellum and Lejun trailed her, then set themselves on each side of the door as Anna knocked, and then stepped inside.

As Anna entered, the white-haired lady turned in her seat. Her eyes flicked to the middle-aged woman who had started toward the door. "You may go, Synondra." The firmness in her voice reminded Anna that Lady Essan had once been the consort of the strongest ruler of Defalk in the generations before the unfortunate Lord Barjim.

"Welcome, Regent." Synondra bowed to Anna, and then to her mistress. "Yes, Lady Essan." The maid stepped out of the chamber and closed the door behind her.

"Lady Essan, I'm afraid I've been neglecting you." Anna slipped into the straight chair across from the carved and upholstered rocker that held the older woman.

"Aye . . . a while it's been, sorceress and near-daughter. . . ." Essan nodded.

"Yes," Anna admitted. "It never seems like there's enough time."

"Donjim, always he said that. Said it while he was dying, too." Essan's laugh was both harsh and rueful.

"I'll try to keep that in mind." Anna bent forward and took a handful of the salted nuts in the small circular dish. They'd help her falling blood sugar.

"Do that, daughter-who'd-be." Essan smiled momentarily. "And what bit of gossip or history might you wish today?"

Anna couldn't help grinning at Essan's knowing tone. "You know Lysara? Lord Birfels' oldest daughter?"

"The stately young redhead . . . aye. Courteous . . . and well-spoken. She visits me at times. A good head on those shapely shoulders."

Anna nodded. She hadn't known that Lysara visited Lady Essan, but then, there was probably all too much she didn't know. "Did she tell you that her parents are pushing for a consort for her?"

Essan frowned. "That she did not. We had talked of her mother. Lady Trien was quite young when she died, and young Lysara wished to know more of her. The daughter is much like her lady mother, I fear."

"You fear?"

"Lady Trien was like you—fearless and far brighter than the men around her. Birfels took her against his family's wishes. With him, she was almost happy. With another she might have perished."

The sorceress nodded slowly. That figured. "Lysara's step-mother wants to consort her to young Hoede."

"That Lady Fylena would, for should aught happen to Birke or the other boy, none would wish Abenfel to fall to Lysara's consort, were he young Hoede." Essan laughed harshly.

"I'm opposing it, but all I've promised is to look for a suitable consort." Anna shook her head before helping herself to another handful of nuts.

"Finding such may be difficult."

"Almost anyone would be better than Hoede, but I'd like to find someone to complement her."

"Lord Dannel be a proud man, and one not to cross lightly."

"His son's proud, too, but there's nothing between his ears except pride." Anna snorted. "Lysara deserves better."

"Ah . . . well she might, but the old lords will be turning in their graves even afore they are laid in them, and you may have to lay some in those graves, would you support a woman's cares." Essan arched her eyebrows. "Would you do such?"

"I'd rather not, but I might have to," Anna said. "What would you suggest?"

"Find her the proper consort, and tell none of her family or his until you tell all, and decree it to be so, and that way all will blame you—as they would anyway."

"You're so encouraging."

"You would wish an old lady to deceive?"

Anna laughed. "You know better."

Essan nodded. "Now . . . what lies ahead for you? You have that restless demeanor."

Anna stood. "I have to get ready for the trip to Fussen."

"Lord Vlassa's brats? They still squabble over the lands?"

"Not exactly squabble. The older one demands I recognize him: the younger suggests that the high-handed style of his brother will ruin all the craftsmen."

"Like as both be right. You needs must recognize the older, and if he be like his father, he will ruin the lands. Donjim had to lean an axe against young Vlassa's face—he was young in those years. We all were." Essan smiled. "I prattle on. Go and tend your work, near-daughter, and thank you for remembering me."

Anna returned the smile, wishing she'd been able to do that more often with her own mother. Then she slipped out of the chamber and turned back toward the receiving room where Jecks doubtless waited—Jecks and all the scrolls and details she still hadn't ironed out.

She took a deep breath. Behind her near-silent steps echoed the heavier boots of her guards.

13

Thrap. A knock . . . more of a tap . . . sounded on Anna's chamber door.

Anna looked up from the seemingly endless pile of scrolls, rubbing her eyes, in the pool of candlelight that fell across the writing desk. Outside, the sky had not quite faded from deep purple into the darkness of night, although she could see the small bright disc of the larger moon—Clearsong—through the window. Darksong, the smaller red moon associated with the ill-regarded and self-destructive sorcery that affected living things, had not risen or had already set. Anna still hadn't exactly figured out the moons' periods.

Who could it be at the door? The guards normally announced anyone, except, sometimes, Jecks, who would announce himself. "Yes?"

"It's Secca, Lady Anna. Might I please come in?"

"Please do." Anna stood.

The small redheaded girl peered around the door, then stepped forward past Kerhor, bowed, and shut the door behind her. "I heard you burned your hand and face this morning." Secca looked at the floor, then extended a small jar. "It's an ointment. It helps. It helped me when I picked up the kettle from the fire, and I brought it all the way from Flossbend."

"Thank you." Anna took the jar and unstoppered it.

"Just a little," Secca advised.

The Regent dabbed the oily ointment on the reddest part of the back of her right hand, and then at the spot on her cheek that felt tender. She restoppered the jar, and handed it back to the girl. "Thank you. You'd better keep this. I'll let you know if I need some more."

"Sorcery doesn't work on you when you're a sorceress. Anyway, you said that sorcery on people is Darksong. So I thought the ointment would help."

"It does." Anna eased herself onto the wide bed and motioned for Secca to climb up as well.

"This is like Father's big bed." Secca sat cross-legged beside Anna, patting the gold-and-green comforter. "Except his is . . . it was . . . red and blue."

"I'm glad you like the bed. You miss him, don't you?"

"I miss him awfully, Lady Anna."

"He was a good man. He was good to me." Anna recalled how Lord Hryding had insisted on supplying an escort to take her to Falcor when she had still been learning sorcery and struggling to understand the strange land that was Defalk. *You're still struggling, and it's still strange.*

"He was good to lots of folks," Secca confided. "Sometimes, Mother was not pleased."

"I'll remember that he helped me when no one knew that I would be a regent." Anna patted the redhead's shoulder.

"Did you really use sorcery on Calmut? To put cold water on

him?" Secca smiled broadly, as though she knew the answer, but wanted to hear the story.

"I didn't want to, but he wasn't going to let me see your father," Anna admitted. "I didn't think he'd get so angry." She fingered her chin. "I should have known, but I wasn't thinking. That water was cold."

Secca giggled. "I wish I could do that someday."

"Perhaps you can. We'll see when you're older."

"I'd like that." Secca nodded. "You're leaving tomorrow? For Fussen, Lysara said."

"That's right. We'll leave early. It's a long ride."

"What are you going to do about poor Lysara? She doesn't want to be Hoede's consort."

"How did you hear about that?"

"She told me. Her sister Clayre sent her a scroll telling her."

"She doesn't? Has she said anything?"

"Lysara's nice. She doesn't say anything bad about anyone. But I can tell." Secca squirmed closer to Anna.

The sorceress put an arm around the girl. "I suppose you can. You watch a lot, don't you?"

"She likes Tiersen; I think he likes her, but he's shy." Secca yawned. "I like Lysara. Maybe that's because we both have red hair." Secca yawned. "She's nice."

"You're tired. I'll walk back to your room with you," Anna said.

"You don't have to." The redhead yawned again.

"I'd like to." *It's been too long since someone wanted you to walk them to bed, or tuck them in.*

"You're the Regent," protested Secca, stifling a yawn.

"That means I can walk you to bed if I want to." Anna smiled as she slipped off the bed and took Secca's hand. The two walked out into the stone-floored corridor, and with the padding of Secca's feet, Anna realized the girl was barefoot. Behind them, discreetly, followed Rickel and Kerhor.

"You . . . the guards . . . follow . . . everywhere . . ." Secca said, trying not to yawn.

"That's part of being a regent."

"Father . . . he said . . . you'd be good. . . ."

"You're too tired." With a smile, Anna reached over and

swept up Secca, carrying her up the stairs, amazed at how little the ten-year-old weighed.

"Father . . . he did that."

Anna swallowed as she concentrated on the steps. Secca's room was in the south tower, one level up, little more than a single-windowed cube with a bed, a chest, and a narrow armoire. Anna set Secca on the bed.

"It's not very big, but it's big enough for me, and it's all mine," the girl said as she pulled back the coverlet on the narrow bed. Another yawn followed. "It is, isn't it?"

"So long as I'm Regent, and, if I'm not, you can come to Loiseau with me."

"Good."

Anna eased the covers around the little redhead. "Good night, Secca."

"Good night, lady. Thank you for thinking of Lysara." The small voice was sleepy. "Tiersen's nice, you know. He just doesn't want anyone to know."

"Sleep tight," Anna managed to say softly, holding back the tears. "Sleep tight."

Rickel's and Kerhor's footsteps echoed dully on the floor stones as Anna made her way back to her room—her lonely room.

For a time, she stood by the window, looking out in the darkness toward the Falche River, her eyes resting on Clearsong, glad, absently, that the red point of light that was Darksong was not in that night's sky. The faint murmur of insects rustled out of the darkness, and a light breeze ruffled her short hair.

With a sigh, she turned and walked to the desk. She sat and dipped the quill, beginning to write.

My dear lord Birfels,

I have received your scroll about Lysara, and I deeply appreciate your concerns, and those of your consort, about your daughter. She is attractive, intelligent, and most perceptive, and she is the daughter of a most noble and respected house. For these reasons, and many others, I do not believe that a match between Hoede and Lysara would be in Lysara's interests, in your interests, or in the interests of the Regency. True to my word, as I promised in Abenfel, I am pursuing a more suitable union, and one with which I trust you will find no fault. Because this will take several weeks, I ask for your patience and forbearance. . . .

Anna paused. What of the other daughter—Clayre? She didn't deserve Hoede, either, and Anna had no doubt that Fylena would transfer the match to Clayre, if only to push Anna into finding a better consort for the younger daughter of Lady Trien. After a moment, she continued writing, the quill scratching in the puddle of light thrown by the candles in the midst of the growing darkness of her chamber.

> Because Lysara will soon be consorted, I also offer an invitation for Clayre to come to Falcor, where she will be most warmly received. As I am doing for Lysara, I will also pursue available opportunities for Clayre, once she has had a chance to learn more about Falcor and what the future holds for Defalk.

Anna couldn't threaten, but hopefully, by making the offer, she could remove Clayre from Abenfel. Fylena might not be quite so eager to pair off her second stepdaughter to whoever might be available at the moment, not with the suggestion that Hoede was unsuitable and the promise of a better match.

When Anna had added more compliments and flowery language, she signed the second scroll, leaving it unsealed for Dythya to have Skent copy it. The dark-haired page could be trusted to keep matters to himself. That she had learned and was glad for. *Then, Skent's like you. He doesn't come from a long line of prickly nobles.*

She would have liked to have had the equivalent of a trusted secretary, but Skent and Dythya were the only two besides Jecks who could write and she could fully trust. *Secretaries, now?*

Anna laughed softly and blew out the candle on the writing desk, trying not to think too much about a small redhead in a small tower room. And an older redhead worlds away.

But her eyes still burned.

14

With the midmorning sun on her back and a light breeze in her face, Anna absently patted Farinelli and glanced along the dusty road that led westward, toward Denguic—and Fussen. Jecks rode to her right, smiling and cheerful as he had been since dawn.

You would be attracted to one of those morning people. . . .

Immediately behind her rode Skent and Himar. Behind them rode Liende and the players, and then a solid tenscore lancers, spaced loosely enough that the column stretched back toward Falcor for close to half a dek.

"The next town is Ciola," Skent told the overcaptain in a low voice. "That's where Tirsik used to get horses for my father. It's been a while since I've been there."

"What kind of horses did your father prefer?" Himar's tone was polite.

"He liked steady mounts, ser. He said that too many young lancers were more interested in proving themselves to the horse than being lancers."

Himar laughed. Beside Anna, a smile crossed Jecks' face.

"The trip will do him good," Jecks said. "Especially if he doesn't try to use that blade at his side."

"How good is he with it?" Anna kept her voice low.

"Better than most his age, and not half so good as he thinks. He's a shade better than Tiersen, and much better than Kinor and Jimbob. But Skent has three years on Jimbob, and Kinor, for all his height and strength, hasn't handled a blade before."

"How is Jimbob doing? I haven't talked to him much lately. Dythya and Menares say that he does his lessons, but that he's quiet. That bothers me."

"He wanted to come. I told him he couldn't go everywhere, and that there were reasons why it would be best that he did not accompany us this time." Jecks shrugged. "He was not pleased. He worries too much about what the other young people think."

"They all do at that age. He'll get over it." *You hope . . . it took a long time for Mario, and Avery never did.* "If people think he has anything to do with whatever I decide . . ." Anna let the words trail off.

"Then the hard feelings will rest on him. That is one reason why he should not be here. Also, we would have to worry about him. Feelings will run high in Fussen."

"Do you know if any lords have declared support for one or the other of Vlassa's sons?" Anna half stood in the stirrups, then settled back into the saddle.

"No one has told me." Jecks offered a crooked smile. "These days they tell me far less than they once did."

"Because you're close to me?" Anna readjusted the floppy brown hat before continuing. "Or because Jimbob is the heir?"

"Both, I would say."

"Tell me about Fussen . . . anything you know." Anna reached down for her water bottle.

Even without the parching dryness of previous years, she still needed more water than most people to keep from getting dehydrated.

Jecks cleared his throat before speaking. "Vlassa was a hard man. All said he was fair, but hard. It was said that he never spoke well or ill of Rylenne. She was his consort, but no one else was ever allowed a single ill-chosen word about her. He was a man of few words on the handful of times I saw him."

"Lady Essan suggested that he was hard to handle as a young lord—at least for Lord Donjim."

"That may well have been, but I did not know him when he was first lord. Later, under Barjim, he paid his liedgeld and sent his levies, but always under a captain." Jecks fingered his chin. "The same captain. Lorensil, I believe. A firm arms-leader, but he smiled, unlike Vlassa . . . the lands around Fussen are hilly, and only the valleys are good for cropping. There's a sawmill, and much of the timber for Falcor came from there . . ."

Anna nodded and listened.

15

MANSUUS, MANSUUR

"What reports have we from Elahwa?" Standing behind the empty silver chair, his large hands resting on its back, Konsstin's eyes narrow as he studies the raven-haired officer who waits before him in his private study.

"Your seers believe that Lord Bertmynn's barges are loaded and ready to depart for Elahwa. Three Sturinnese ships anchored off the coast close to Dolov—"

"I told you Sturinn would appear again in Liedwahr, just like a clipped copper. Did I not?"

"Yes, sire," Bassil answers formally.

"What about the dissonant traders of Wei?" The Liedfuhr straightens and steps back, turning toward the open window. The silver cloak swirls, revealing the close-fitting sky-blue-velvet tunic and trousers with the silver piping that nearly matches the silver that has begun to dominate his once-brown hair and beard.

"Nothing has changed. Their seers watch the sorceress, the freewomen, the Ebrans—"

"—and us! Do not forget that they study us as well. They watch all of Liedwahr." Konsstin turns back toward Bassil.

"Yes, sire." The lancer officer bows again.

"And do not be so deeply and insolently respectful, Bassil. We have talked about this before, you and I."

Bassil straightens and continues. "The SouthWomen sent that one cargo of blades and arms to Elahwa, but no ships or armsmen or armswomen followed. The Matriarch has yet to issue any proclamations or take any action."

"She never does, yet matters change all the same from her interest." Konsstin clears his throat. "Has Bertmynn requested more assistance?"

"No, sire."

"We have supplied him near-on five hundred golds and ten-score well-forged blades, and little have we received but polite scrolls of thanks." Konsstin snorts. "I scarce expected more, yet when the other lordlet pledged fealty to Defalk . . ." The Liedfuhr paces toward the wide windows to his right. "This wouldn't have happened, Bassil, not if we had a true Empire of Harmony. And what have we?" His lips purse for a moment. "You have heard me talk of this before. So have many. Most think I spout nonsense about an Empire of Music. I am not stupid. I see what lies behind the polite eyes of those who watch. The sorceress destroyed twoscore ships of Sturinn. Twoscore, and yet more ships and gold find their way past the Shoals of Discord to Ebra, as if the Maitre had lost nothing. My grandson builds his lancers for a vain attack on the sorceress. Nubara believes he can control Rabyn, as his sire believed he could control my daughter." Konsstin's laugh is half-ironic, half-rueful.

"You think Nubara will fail to rein in the young Prophet?"

"I know he will fail. We can but hope that he will not fail too soon. Nor fail too completely."

"Perhaps you should reconsider . . . and send another fiftyscore lancers to support Nubara." Bassil moistens his lips.

"Sooner or later, Rabyn would only use them against the sorceress, or Nubara would use them to defend himself against Rabyn. The lancers would be lost . . . wasted, as would the coins to pay them and feed them." Konsstin turns, flings open the windowed door, and steps out onto the sunlit balcony, where he looks out at where the rivers join, the silver cloak hanging limply from his broad shoulders.

Bassil follows. When Konsstin does not speak, the lancer officer finally asks, "Would they be wasted if the sorceress were elsewhere—say in Ebra?"

"You think she would go to Ebra to support Hadrenn?" From the balcony of the bluff-top palace, the Liedfuhr looks westward, beyond the ancient walls of the fort below to where the Ansul and the Latok Rivers merge. "She has made no move, even with the freewomen in danger."

"Sire? Does she even know about the freewomen? Remember, while her leanings would support them . . . who would have told her of them and their cause?"

"She could scry what is happening."

"If she knew for what she looked," Bassil points out.

"Hmmmm . . . she is still new to Liedwahr."

"Exactly. Perhaps you should so inform her. That would give her two reasons to be in Ebra."

"That assumes you are correct, Bassil." Konsstin turns on one bootheel and studies the lancer officer. "Even given her inclinations, why would she do that? Defalk still must contend with Nordwei to the north and Neserea and my grandson to the west. She must placate or control thirty-three stiff-necked and feuding lords. Her strength is sorcery, and she has no standing army. Not one to call such. She can only be in one place at a time. Oh . . . and of her thirty-three lords, perhaps two-thirds doubt her powers, for they have not met her, nor have they seers to follow her." Konsstin clasps his hands, then unclasps them and stretches. "With such constraints, why would she risk herself in Ebra?"

"What if you sent her a message, supported with golds?"

"You suggest treachery? That I tell her I have no designs on Defalk?" Konsstin shakes his head. "Even I would not stoop so low as that, Bassil. Not even for an Empire of Music."

"Do you have designs on Defalk, sire? Now?"

"Not realistic designs."

"Then you have no designs. It is not treachery to state the truth." Bassil swallows, waiting.

"You are suggesting that I encourage the sorceress to support Hadrenn in Ebra, after all the golds we have sent to Bertmynn?"

"You yourself said last year, sire, that you did not want Sturinn in Liedwahr. You also said that Mansuur could not send armsmen into other parts of Liedwahr, except for Neserea. Who, then, do you propose will be the one to defeat the Sturinnese?"

"But . . . if she goes to Ebra, Rabyn, in his anger, may well attack Defalk. With our lancers, no less."

"If Nubara does not restrain him."

Konsstin fingers his well-trimmed and mostly silver beard. "If Nubara does away with Rabyn, would the sorceress oppose my taking Neserea?"

"She would not like it, but . . . you could always propose splitting the land. You could take the Great Western Forest and the Westfels and the mines, and leave Defalk the lands of the east and south."

"Rabyn may well remove Nubara. Then the sorceress would have to defend Defalk . . . and she may or may not triumph, but as matters now stand she would destroy Rabyn and the armsmen and lancers of Neserea—and our good lancers."

Bassil nods. "That is true. The worst that could happen would be that Liedwahr would be dominated by three lands. And the sorceress would be hard-pressed to unify what she held for the heir for years." He shrugs. "And if she fails, then who could blame Mansuur for stepping in to unify the remains of Neserea and Defalk? Bertmynn need not know that you have also supported the sorceress."

"So that if she does fail, he will owe me fealty—and if he does not provide such, who will stand behind him?"

"Certainly not Ranuak or Nordwei." Bassil inclines his head slightly. "In one case, Mansuur will hold all of Liedwahr, except Wei and Ranuak, and in the other, there will be three powers, instead of having seven squabbling ragtag states."

"Bassil . . . you do know how I dislike having my own words used against me?"

"Yes, ser."

"There is Nordwei. Let us not forget the cautious traders. Cold silver flows in their veins." Konsstin frowns, then leaves the balcony and the view of the two rivers that form the Toksul, the great river of Mansuur that flows westward to Wahrsus and the ocean. Back in his study, he closes the windowed door. "So I should send a large gift to the Regent of Defalk and explain that the additional fiftyscore lancers going to Neserea are there to restrain my grandson?"

"Would that not be true? One way or another? And it is far less costly than another war of unification. Even if you lose all one hundred–score lancers."

Konsstin takes a deep breath. "Draft the scrolls . . . and propose a way to inform the sorceress about the freewomen, without our quill strokes upon it. I will think upon this, but draft them for me by tomorrow."

Bassil bows. "As the Liedfuhr commands."

"I will be riding with Aerlya in the morning. That is something I promised her, and to deny a daughter who is both sweet and stubborn . . ." Konsstin shakes his head. "That is almost as bad as provoking a sorceress." He pauses again. "And to think that before long I will have to find her a consort—a suitable one, no less."

"I will have them in the early afternoon," Bassil promises.

16

Some ten deks west of Borteland, another village in Defalk Anna had never heard of until traveling through it, the dusty road wound out from between two hills to reveal both a dek-stone and a valley containing a much larger town. The dek-stone read: "Fussen: 1 d."

"That must be Fussen," announced Skent from where he rode behind Anna.

Anna smiled, thinking of how often her son Mario had announced the obvious, even when he'd been well over sixteen—like Skent.

As with most of the other mountain or hill towns in Defalk Anna had visited, the keep of Fussen sat on a hill, just to the west of the town itself, a dark mass outlined by the late-afternoon sun. Beyond the shadowed structure rose another line of hills, and beyond those, the true peaks of the Mittfels.

Anna squinted, but could only make out the general outline of walls rising above a clear grassy slope that separated the keep from the town below. To the left of the road, a stream burbled generally southward, apparently coming from the hills to the north of Fussen.

"Break out the Regent's banner!" announced Himar.

The armsman riding behind Blaz unfurled the purple banner with the golden crossed spears and the crown, with the *R* beneath. The banner billowed for a moment in a sudden light breeze as the lancer rode to the head of the column, then drooped limply around the staff as the armsman set the base in his lanceholder.

"Tell me again why I'm doing this," Anna said to Jecks.

"You will show that you care about the lands to the west."

"You want me to support Ustal?"

"I would hope that you could, my lady, but I know as little about the man as you. Less perhaps, for I do not see all that you do."

"Flattery—that's another danger of being Regent."

"Only if you heed it, my lady." Jecks smiled.

Anna enjoyed the smile. "How do you think Ustal will feel?"

"From the words he used in his scrolls, he will believe you have to come to confirm his claim. He will be angry if you do not."

"I've been afraid of that," Anna admitted. "If I don't, what will he do?"

"That is why you have armsmen and players, is it not, though he will not go that far, I think."

You think? Ah, yes ... once more into the breach, dear friends, with flame and fire and sorcery—the sorceress' universal answer to each problem. Anna's lips curled into a sardonic, self-mocking smile. "I hope we don't have to use them. The mirror showed no danger."

"That was *before* you decide," Jecks reminded her. "Hope you do not need sorcery, but prepare yourself to use it."

Anna nodded. Then she turned in the saddle and motioned for Skent and Himar to ride closer to her.

Jecks said nothing, but eased his mount back on the dusty road to allow the two others to ride beside the Regent.

"I will be talking," Anna began, "to Lord Ustal. Skent, I think you will see some of the younger folk. I would ask that you talk to them. Do not talk about Falcor or me, or as little as you can. Try to get them to talk to you. Ask about Fussen, about its prosperity, about the old lord, and only then about Ustal. Do not ask about any of the lord's family except him and his father." Anna glanced at Himar. "If you would do the same ... and if there are one or two senior armsmen of ours that you trust totally, if you would ask them to do the same."

"We can do that, Lady Anna," affirmed Himar.

"Yes, Lady Anna," said Skent.

Anna then called for Liende, and went through her explanation with the chief player.

Liende smiled. "Players do talk, and we will hear what we can hear."

When Liende had dropped back, and Jecks rode up beside Anna, he said in a low voice, "You did not ask me." His tone was not plaintive, but even, almost flat.

For a moment, Anna missed the twinkle in the hazel eyes. Then she laughed. "You! You'll be with me most of the time. Besides, you have the brains to do that anyway."

A faint smile creased Jecks' lips. "You honor me too much."

"Enough of the false humility, you . . ." She shook her head.

Jecks said nothing, but his eyes were warm.

They had ridden no more than a half-dek closer to Fussen when the road curved slightly north. Less than fifty yards after the curve was a bridge that spanned a narrow rocky gorge less than ten yards wide. The bridge was wooden, heavy planks barely wide enough for a wagon and a single horse abreast, with flimsy-looking sides composed of two planks set sideways and fastened to posts attached to the planks and the two heavy timbers that formed the roadbed. Below the plank roadbed, the stream foamed through the narrow defile less than three yards below. The narrow bridge flexed noticeably as the scouts crossed, one after the other.

"A moment, Lady Anna." Himar eased his mount past Anna and Jecks and onto the bridge. Then he turned and rode back. "No more than two mounts on the bridge at once."

He motioned for Anna's guards—Kerhor and Blaz—to cross first.

Once the two were on the far side, Anna and Jecks followed. Farinelli's hoofs echoed on the heavy worn planks of the bridge. Anna could feel the narrow bridge flex. She glanced at Jecks.

"The bridge planks should be replaced," Jecks affirmed. "It would be dangerous for an ironmonger's wagon." With a quick look at Anna, he added, "and it should *not* be replaced through sorcery, my lady and Regent."

"Not now, at least," Anna agreed.

Lord Jecks snorted. "You would replace every bridge in Defalk, could you do so."

"And every major road that's dirt," she said pleasantly.

Less than a hundred yards beyond the bridge, the road curved back through fields of maize that had grown saddle-high toward its previous course. A redstone wall a yard high and extending but five yards on either side of the road marked the eastern boundary of the town proper. At the wall, the maize ended, and beyond the gateless entry, the road was paved with slabs of red stone.

An inn stood on the left, its signboard portraying a pitcher tilted upside down with a single drop of ale clinging to the lip. Beyond the Last Drop Inn was a chandlery, also of red stone.

Anna shivered as she saw the emblem of the crossed candles, thinking about Forse's son, and the Darksong with which the young man in Pamr had infused his chandlery. Would Gatrune be able to shed more light on his actions?

Two men stood on the porch of the inn, their pale gray tunics tinged red by the light of the sun low above the western hills.

". . . has to be the Regent. . . . Regency banner there."

". . . looks young, like a boy . . ."

". . . sorcery . . . what you expect from a sorceress . . ."

". . . no good of her being here . . ."

"Better a Regent deciding than having house fight house. . . ."

Anna strained, but she was already too far away to hear more.

Red stone—that was the predominant building material in the town of Fussen. Redstone walls and dark-slate roofs. A few dwellings were of wattle and plaster, and some of wood, but Fussen was mainly solid stone and square.

Only a handful of people were on the streets or in the main square, and all studied the Regency banner and Anna, silently, unlike the two men at the Last Drop. She was almost relieved when she and Jecks reached the gateless walls at the west side of the town. There, beyond the town buildings, the road, its paving stones newer, angled up the slope to the keep, its entire length exposed to the parapets above.

Two lancers in maroon-and-green livery waited there. Both inclined their heads.

"Regent Anna?" asked the more slight and gray-haired armsman.

"She is the Lady Anna." Himar had edged his mount alongside Farinelli.

"Yes, I'm Anna," the Regent confirmed. "This is Lord Jecks of Elheld. He is head of the Council of Lords advising the Regency, the Lord High Counselor."

"Your grace and your honor, if you would but follow us."

Anna nodded, and the two armsmen turned their mounts.

"I am pleased to know that I am Lord High Counselor. I would that you had let me know such earlier." Jecks laughed softly.

"That's what you've been doing all along. I just thought you needed a title to go with the work." Anna grinned.

The oiled wooden gates overlooking Fussen were bound with heavy strap iron and swung wide. Two rows of eight lancers in green and maroon formed an honor guard and an entry corridor that led to the back of the courtyard. As Anna and Jecks and Himar rode through the gates and neared the honor guard, a short fanfare—off-key—echoed from three trumpeters standing in the corner behind the lancers of Fussen.

A tall figure in green and maroon stepped forward toward Anna, even before she had reined Farinelli up. Ustal was tall for someone from Liedwahr, almost a head and a half taller than Anna, and a head taller than Jecks. His shimmering blond hair was square-cut level with his jaws, and his green tunic was spotless—and displayed his well-developed muscles effectively.

"A blond Prince Valiant," Anna murmured to herself, squaring herself slightly in the saddle.

"Fussen welcomes the Regent and the Lord Counselor!" Ustal's voice was a strong baritone, true in tone. "Welcome to Fussen!" He bowed, then looked expectantly up at Anna.

Anna inclined her head. "We are most pleased to be here, and look forward to learning more about Fussen and meeting with you all." She offered a wide smile, hoping it wasn't too forced. "Lord Jecks, the Lord High Counselor. Overcaptain Himar. My chief of players, Liende, and one of our pages, Skent." As she finished the introductions, Anna wondered whom she'd forgotten.

"All of you are most welcome." Ustal extended a hand, as if to offer Anna assistance, but Anna swung out of the saddle, easily, hoping that after the long ride her legs wouldn't cramp when her boots touched the stones of the courtyard. She managed standing erect without hanging on to the saddle, and got a low *whuff* from Farinelli, as if the big gelding were happy she had dismounted.

"It feels good to stand," she said, to cover the silence, "and to be here, Lord Ustal."

"We are pleased that you saw fit to visit Fussen, humble as it may be."

Anna just smiled once more, aware that Ustal could out-"please" her. He'd been raised on courtly nothings.

"Might I escort you . . . ?"

"After I stable Farinelli." She nodded toward the gelding.

Ustal took a long look at the palomino. "Ah . . . it is true. He is a raider beast, and only you can . . . approach him?" The lord stepped toward Farinelli, as if to test what Anna had said.

The gelding snorted, edged back.

So did Ustal, nodding. "I will await you at the entrance there. Giesil will show you the guest stable." He smiled, formally, bowing again.

"Thank you. I won't be long." Anna returned the smile and followed the sour-faced armsman in maroon.

Even with Rickel and Blaz taking the saddle, blanket, saddlebags, and lutar from her, and leaving her to deal directly with Farinelli, stabling and grooming the gelding took Anna longer than normal. Her hands felt clumsy, and she knew she was too hungry and dehydrated to function well.

Finally, she gave Farinelli a last pat and picked up the lutar case. Rickel lifted off the saddlebags, and Blaz the mirror. Kerhor and Lejun remained empty-handed. All remained close behind Anna as she recrossed the courtyard in the fading light of day.

Standing inside the entrance, Ustal glanced from the four guards to Anna to Jecks, and back to the Regent. "You are cautious."

"I've learned that nothing in Defalk is quite what it seems, Lord Ustal, and since I am a stranger, I must be more cautious than you might be in my position." Anna forced another smile.

"I understand. With Neserea so close to the west, we also have learned caution, if of a different type."

"I was not aware that the new Prophet had created trouble. Is this something I should know?"

"We know little here, save that Mansuuran lancers have been posted to Elioch, or somewhere near there."

"That's not surprising," Anna said. "The new Prophet is increasing his armsmen, and he would prefer the Mansuurans be as far from Esaria as possible."

"We should talk of such *after* you are refreshed. For you to have ridden here in four days is remarkable."

For a woman? Anna nodded. "It was a pleasant ride."

"Let me show you to the guest chambers, such as they are."

Ustal turned. Anna and Jecks followed through a set of heavy oak double doors, along a corridor, and up one set of stairs.

"There is the dining hall," said Ustal as he turned up the second set of redstone stairs.

The guest chamber was moderate in size, a single room with a tub shielded by a screen, and a large and ornate armoire in the corner by the tub. The bed was set under a headboard decorated with carved hunting scenes, and a settee rested at the footboard. Under one open window was a writing desk.

A small alcove led to a curtained jakes set against the outer wall.

"This is very pleasant." Anna smiled and inclined her head to Ustal.

"I will send up the servants with hot water. Once you are refreshed, we look forward to seeing you at dinner and showing you the cooking of Fussen."

"I also look forward to that." Anna inclined her head.

Ustal bowed and eased out of the chamber. Rickel and Blaz deposited her mirror and saddlebags, then slipped out to station themselves outside her door.

Anna looked at Jecks and smiled. "I'll see you in a bit."

He smiled back and bowed.

While waiting for the servants and the water, Anna took the mirror from where Blaz had set it on the settee and eased it from its case, setting it on the writing table. Then she took out the lutar and tuned it. Next came the vocalises, and more coughing and mucus than she would have liked. Finally, she was ready for the spell.

> Show from Fussen, danger to fear,
> Ustal's threats to me bright and clear. . . .

When the mirror remained blank silver, Anna tried a second spell.

Mirror, mirror, in your frame,
Show me young Ustal in his fame,
Where'er he may stand or be,
Show him now to me.

The mirror silvered, then showed Ustal in a sitting room, pacing before a dark-haired and pale young woman, who was seated on a low couch at the foot of a large bedstead. Ustal stopped and leveled an index finger at her accusingly, almost violently. The woman, wearing a tentlike dress, seemed to cringe from each motion of the pointed finger offered by the young lord. Anna realized the woman was pregnant, and nodded to herself, quickly singing a release couplet to cut off the image in the glass. *So . . . Ustal is not the pleasant soul in private.*

Anna's lips tightened as she set the lutar on the bed and sank into the straight-backed chair, waiting for the servants with the water.

Once the servants arrived—three young girls, each with two large buckets—Lejun accompanied them in, standing between Anna and the servants.

When the chamber was clear again, Anna slipped the iron bolt and bathed, after using another spell to clean and reheat the water—and getting a throbbing headache with the third spell. After bathing, and after massaging her forehead, she slipped into the single green gown she had brought, and into the green slipper shoes, and studied herself in the mirror.

The figure looking back from the glass had blonde hair cut short, shorter than a bob. The fine features were those of a more mature woman than would have belonged to the almost girlish figure below—trim and muscular, with lightly tanned and flawless skin and clear blue eyes that looked like those of an eighteen-year-old—except for the darkness behind them. Even without makeup and jewelry, she looked nearly regal. *Careful . . . don't flatter yourself. Regal is as regal does.*

After a last look in the glass, Anna turned and left the guest chamber. As she stepped through the heavy oak door, she found Jecks waiting, standing beside Lejun. Clean-shaven and washed, in the blue of Elheld, he bowed.

"You look most handsome, my lord," Anna said. *Incredibly handsome . . . and what am I to do with you . . . with us?*

"You are . . . more than beautiful, my lady. You always surprise me." The slight huskiness in his compliments discomfited
Anna, and she spoke quickly to cover her vulnerability. "Thank
you. Shall we see what we can discover about Lord Ustal?"

Jecks looked at Anna. "You are worried."

"Shouldn't I be? Ustal looks like the perfect Defalkan lord.
He's handsome, probably as strong as a bull. He says the right
things, and he expects to get his way."

"So it would seem . . . yet his brother has garnered some support." Jecks smiled and stopped speaking as he looked down
the steps, where Ustal was waiting.

The lord-claimant's eyes widened as he saw Anna in the
green gown. The lord frankly surveyed the Regent, clearly surprised at her appearance. "I had not expected . . ."

"A Regent who appeared so young?" Anna smiled politely.
"You must have heard the story of what happened at the Sand
Pass." *How couldn't he? All of Liedwahr must have heard it by
now.*

"I had heard, much later, but . . . the story does not do you
justice." Ustal offered a broad smile and a second bow, with a
gesture toward the hall, before leading the way into the dark
and high-ceilinged room, lit both by wall sconces, and a series
of five-branched wrought-iron candelabra set at intervals along
a table that stretched nearly ten yards.

Anna could tell that the others had been waiting, and felt
guilty for the time it had taken her to dress. *Will you ever get
over feeling guilty, even for little things?*

"This is my consort, Yelean." Ustal inclined his head in the
direction of the pale dark-haired woman in green that Anna had
observed through the glass.

"I am pleased to meet you," Anna answered.

"And I, you, your grace." Yelean's smile was shy, almost
frightened.

Ustal rattled off a series of names, the only one of which
Anna fixed in her mind being that of Weyrt, the chief of arms-
men, who was seated directly across the long table from
Himar.

*Again . . . you've let your blood sugar get too low . . . and
you're probably dehydrated.* Once seated, Anna took a sip, a
very small sip, of the red wine from her goblet, wondering

whether it would be the swill she'd first tasted at Mencha or the polished vintages of Lerona. It was neither, merely an acceptable red table wine. "The wine tastes good, Lord Ustal."

"Not so fine as those of Lerona or Abenfel I fear, but good for accompanying a meal."

"It is far better than comes from my lands in Mencha," she managed.

A puzzled expression flitted across the blond lord's face.

"Lady Anna is not only Regent, but sole holder of Mencha as well," Jecks said, his voice almost melodious. "She finds herself in the odd position of both paying and receiving liedgeld. She was Lady of Mencha before she became Regent."

As the white-haired lord spoke, Anna heaped her platter with the fowl and with the cheese-clotted potatoes.

"Ah . . . so she knows some of the troubles of a holder," suggested Ustal.

"My lands are not so rich as yours," Anna said, after swallowing her first mouthful, "and I see them seldom these days. Mencha is farther from Falcor than Fussen is. And your wine is better."

A faint smile crossed Yelean's face.

Ustal's eyes widened as he watched Anna eat everything on the platter and then finish a second helping.

"I'm sorry, Lord Ustal, but it has been a long ride, and I was more hungry than I'd thought." Anna broke off another small chunk of bread, and nibbled on it. *Amazing what sorcery does to your appetite and metabolism.*

"I had heard that sorceresses required . . . much sustenance. . . ."

"It's true." Anna took another sip of wine. For the first time in days, she was beginning to feel she wasn't running on the edge of hunger and fatigue. *You've been undereating again. . . . Won't you ever learn that being overweight isn't your problem? The sorceress' equivalent of anorexia is.* Except old patterns were hard to unlearn. Anna wanted to snort, or something. If she were in a novel, she'd have no problems unlearning old habits. Just recognize them, and they'd be gone. *Time to get this back on track.* "I did not have the pleasure of meeting your sire. Would you say that you are much like him? Or different?"

There was the slightest of pauses before Ustal set down his

goblet. "My sire was well-known for being honorable and for caring for his lands. The vineyards were his doing as a young man. So was the sawmill . . ."

Anna listened intently, trying to sort out what the words revealed of Ustal and what they told of Lord Vlassa.

". . . my younger brother . . . let us just say that Falar and I differ."

"You would be a lord more like your sire?" suggested Anna.

"Is that not why you are here, honored Regent—to offer your sanction to my succession." Ustal bowed, offering a dazzling smile of perfect white teeth, rare indeed in Defalk.

"I have come to see Fussen," Anna replied, "and to meet you."

"You should also meet Falar," Ustal said politely. "That way, you will understand why it is best that matters remain as they are."

"That is a wise suggestion, Lord Ustal," Jecks said smoothly. "But where might one find this brother of yours? Surely, he would not be so foolish as to take quarters close to you?"

A frown flickered across the handsome lord's face and vanished as he turned toward Jecks. "Your prowess in the past struggles of Defalk is well known, Lord Jecks, and we are pleased to see that you remain in good health and wit." The lord paused. "There is a house, an old hold, in Sudborte, which he claims as his. It once belonged to my mother's grandsire, many years ago." Ustal shrugged. "It could be mine as well as his, but I have suffered to let him claim it. One might find him there."

Anna kept smiling. *Careful . . . arrogant he may be, but he's no fool.* "Indeed Lord Jecks has remained most wise and powerful, Lord Ustal, as many younger have discovered. I would that all lords of Defalk were so able with arms and so devoted to maintaining the succession. We will consider your suggestions most carefully."

"I commend him, and you, my Regent, for ensuring that succession. As Lord of Fussen, I, too, support the Regency and hope that the day will not be too distant when Lord Jimbob takes his place in his sire's seat." Ustal frowned. "I had hoped he might grace us with his presence." A smile followed. "Though such is certainly not necessary with your beauty and ability."

"Lord Jimbob visited Cheor earlier this year and will be visiting other holds in the seasons to come," Jecks offered. "He also must learn what any wise ruler must, and study both arms and strategy, and how best to use coins and men."

"And his thoughts," Anna added.

"Has he—or you—considered a match for his lordship?"

"Several have been considered," Anna replied, "and I would hope to see him with a consort before he becomes lord." *For lots of reasons . . .*

"So would we all." Ustal paused. "And would you then advise him and his successors?"

Anna made sure her laugh was gentle. "Lord Ustal . . . a youth spell may allow me to live a few more years, but I don't think I'll be around for very long by the time Jimbob's children are ready to rule." *Assuming Jimbob is up to it in the first place.*

Ustal flushed. "I did not know."

"It isn't that widely known." Anna decided against telling Ustal anything that wasn't fairly common knowledge. He was the type to decide he was more fit to rule than Jimbob, or anyone else. She turned to Yelean. "Has it been hard, carrying this child?"

"It would seem hard, lady, but since he is my first, I do not know."

"Usually, the first are the hardest, but my second was."

"You have children?" Yelean barely managed to keep her mouth closed after her question.

"They're all grown, but they're in the mist worlds. My oldest would have been several years older than Lord Ustal, but she was killed in a magic-carriage accident just before I was summoned to Liedwahr. . . ." Anna continued with a very abbreviated version of how she had come to be Regent.

When she finished, Ustal nodded. "So . . . to keep your powers, you will have no children and support Lord Jimbob."

"No," Anna corrected him. "The youth spell stopped my ability to have children, and it seemed far better to support the current succession than to create even more fighting over who would found a new line. This way, at least some of our neighbors, such as Nordwei and Ranuak, have indirectly provided assistance, rather than tried conquest."

"You have received assistance from both?" Ustal's voice was not quite incredulous.

"Yes. As well as most useful information." Anna smiled. "Now . . . if you would tell me what you know about Neserea that is not widely told. You must, with your experience and living so close."

Anna hoped Jecks wouldn't burst out laughing at the blatant flattery and the warm smile she offered.

Her white-haired and handsome lord merely nodded sagely, and added, "And anything your sire may have passed down would also be most helpful."

Ustal squared his shoulders ever so slightly. "It is true that we in Fussen see the Nesereans more closely. . . ."

Anna nodded for him to continue, while quietly stifling a yawn, and hoping she could continue to avoid making a direct pronouncement on the succession.

17

After glancing at the mirror on the guest chamber's writing desk that earlier had held her breakfast of an early-ripened apple, bread, and cheese, Anna cleared her throat, then began to sing the spell, accompanying herself with the lutar:

> Show from Fussen, danger to fear,
> Falar's threats to me bright and clear. . . .

The mirror did not even flicker, remaining a bright blank silver. So Anna tried the follow-up spell.

> Mirror, mirror, in your frame,
> Show me young Falar in his fame,
> Where'er he may stand or be,
> Show him now to me.

The mirror silvered, then showed a beardless and slender figure in blue bent over a table writing something. As Anna watched, he pushed back a lock of hair and seemed to sigh before he dipped the quill into the inkwell once more. The small room was empty and lit only by the shaft of early-morning sunlight through the single narrow window.

Anna sang the release couplet, then slowly recased the lutar and the traveling mirror, noting that the finish of the wood framing the glass was beginning to discolor from the heat created by her scrying spells. The discoloration reminded her again of the difficulty she had in even seeing Elizabetta. *You have to be patient . . . she might not even be able to get to the lake house now . . . even if it is summer.*

After a time, she lifted the lutar case and opened the door, stepping out into the keep's corridor in order to make her way down to the courtyard. Blaz and Kerhor followed her closely, with Rickel trailing.

She had entered the courtyard and almost reached the stable when Ustal appeared, bowing. "Lady Anna."

"Good morning, Lord Ustal."

"And to you. I trust you slept well."

"I did, and I appreciated the breakfast tray. You have been most kind and hospitable."

"One owes one's Regent respect and hospitality." Ustal bowed. "Charming as you are, I could not help but notice that you did not comment on the succession," offered the blond as he straightened.

"You suggested I meet with your brother." Anna smiled. "After I do so, I will make a decision. Then I will inform you."

"Caution wars with your image as the decisive and powerful Regent." Ustal laughed lightly.

"Power and caution go hand in hand, Lord Ustal." Anna paused, wondering how she could end the discussion without conflict and get Ustal off her back. Then she almost nodded. "If you have real power, you'd better use it with caution, and if you don't, it pays to be twice as cautious." She smiled. "So, you see, I would have to be even more cautious if I weren't Regent."

A ghost of a frown flicked over Ustal's face, as if he were unsure whether he'd been reprimanded. "You do not offer a direct answer, my Regent."

"I will," Anna promised. "As a lot of people have found out, I can be *very* direct . . . especially if I'm pushed."

Those words did bring a frown, but, again, Ustal seemed to push the expression away. "I look forward to your decision."

"Thank you, Lord Ustal."

"And I will not detain you, but wish you a safe journey, both to Sudborte, and then to Dubaria. If you would convey my regards to Lord Jearle and Lord Nelmor?" Ustal offered another bow. "Fussen respects and honors its Regent."

"Thank you, and I would be most happy to carry your greetings to Lord Nelmor and Lord Jearle." Anna did not move until Ustal bowed a third time, and slipped away.

Then she lifted the lutar case. Rickel's and Kerhor's boots echoed hers as they walked through the hazy early-morning light toward the stable. The ostlers slipped away when she headed toward the gelding's stall.

Farinelli *whuffed* as she quickly brushed her mount before saddling him.

"I know. It's clean, but it's not home." She tightened the girths, then checked them again. The last thing she or Farinelli needed was a loose saddle.

Jecks appeared at the end of the stall, and Himar stood behind the white-haired lord.

"Lady Anna," asked Jecks, "if you are near-ready . . ."

"You can tell everyone to mount up. I'll be right there."

Himar vanished silently, and in moments, Anna could hear the echo of orders in the courtyard, then the sounds of boots and hoofs.

After accepting the saddlebags from Jecks, who in turn had taken them from Kerhor, Anna fastened them behind the saddle, then strapped the traveling mirror and lutar in place before leading Farinelli out into the courtyard, where she quickly mounted.

"The road to Sudborte runs south from the main square of Fussen," offered Jecks, riding his mount up beside Anna and Farinelli.

Himar glanced at the sorceress, and Anna nodded, then flicked the reins gently. Anna and Jecks led the way out of the keep.

The sorceress waited until the column was well out of Fussen and in good order on the south road before she turned in the saddle and beckoned for her chief player to ride beside her.

Liende eased her mount next to Farinelli, looking at Anna for direction.

"Could you tell how Lord Ustal's players feel about him?"

Liende looked back toward Skent and Jecks, then toward Anna, lowering her voice. "He has but three, a flute player, who is barely that, an old violinist, who is as good as Kaseth was, and a younger violinist, who is better than Delvor . . . and might someday be adequate. They said little, but their words would convey that Lord Ustal is to be preferred to his sire . . ." Liende let the words hang.

"That sounds like Lord Vlassa was not to be preferred at all," suggested Anna.

"He whipped a cooper to death who protested when his armsmen brought the cooper's consort to Vlassa's bed."

Anna winced. "He wasn't exactly beloved. Anything else?"

"The lady Yelean was promised to Ustal's brother Falar, until Lord Vlassa took to his bed with his last illness."

Worse and worse . . . "And . . . ?"

Liende shrugged. "None knew . . . or would say."

"What else?"

"Lord Vlassa could not sing, even the simplest of spells, and so had young Ustal sing them for him." Liende's shrug was expressive. "Many lords have neither seers nor players, you must understand. Only the powerful lands like Fussen."

Anna refrained from wincing. *So Ustal has a much longer experience with sorcery, and with his father's cruelties. . . .* "Did anyone say anything else about Ustal's brother?"

"Nay, Lady Anna, save the young violino player, who mentioned that Falar rode out of Fussen a half year ago, a week after Lord Vlassa's death, and none in the keep had seen him since."

"Thank you." Anna nodded, and the chief player eased her mount back toward her position at the head of the players.

After a moment, the Regent beckoned for Skent to join her.

The dark-haired page nodded to Himar and urged his mount forward. "Yes, Lady Anna?"

"Did you find out anything about Lord Ustal . . . or Fussen . . . that would be good for me to know?"

"Begging your pardon, Lady Anna . . ." Skent glanced at his mount's mane. "There were not many who'd speak at my end of the table, and what they said . . ."

"Tell me what you did hear."

"Lord Ustal spends much of his time flying his falcons. The mews is bigger than some folks' cots."

Anna reflected. The stable had also been clean, well swept, and the horses she had seen well fed and groomed. "He cares for his animals, then."

"That he does, and the armsmen's quarters are good. My room was there."

"How did the girls behave?" Anna asked. "Were there any serving girls or others you saw?"

Skent frowned. "Few enough, and most were quiet. They said nothing, and slipped away as quick as they could."

"Thank you, Skent." Anna definitely didn't like the picture she was getting.

"I tried, my lady."

"In something like this, that's all I can ask."

Skent dropped back to where he had been riding beside Himar, and, at Anna's gesture, the overcaptain rode forward.

"Can you add anything?"

Himar smiled ironically, the expression lifting his drooping mustache. "He has spent over a hundred golds on having new blades forged for his personal guard, and has sent a farrier and the second-in-command of his armsmen to Heinene to see what beasts the grassland folk will sell."

"Shrewd—they would have to sell with the grass fires," Anna said. "Anything else?"

"He spars only with the foremost of the armsmen, and can best them all—and he had one whipped for not striving to his best against him."

"Did they say anything about Falar?"

"Not in so many words." Himar tugged on the right end of his mustache before continuing. "Lord Ustal has recently hired twoscore of armsmen, yet it appears that he has but the same number as his sire, and Jirsit heard tell that a serving girl had consorted with one of the newer armsmen . . . he *thought* that her first consort had been killed in a skirmish, yet . . . there has been no talk of brigands or raiders, or of Nesereans . . ." The overcaptain shrugged.

"So . . . there have been some hidden battles between the brothers?" Anna nodded slowly.

"That . . . that is what I heard." With a nod, Himar dropped back.

Anna rode silently for a time.

"You are quiet, my lady," Jecks said.

"Ustal is going to be a problem." The difficulty Anna faced was simple. While everything she'd seen and heard indicated that Ustal was generally pleasantly despicable, his actions were within what most Defalkans would have considered acceptable behavior for a lord—and certainly within the bounds of acceptability as defined by most members of the Thirty-three.

"Many lords are like Ustal," observed Jecks. "Perhaps wiser in some ways, perhaps more discreet, but not that different."

"That's why he's a problem." Anna frowned, then glanced at Jecks. "Liende said that not that many lords could use a glass or scrying pond. . . ."

Jecks smiled. "I could not, for I cannot hold a tune, and never had I players until Liende and the others fled to Elheld."

Anna frowned. So . . . perhaps many lords knew far less about what occurred than she had thought. Messengers cost coins, and that meant communications were not exactly that frequent or speedy in Defalk. "I have to think about this." *And a lot of things.*

Jecks nodded slowly, but did not speak as they continued southward.

Sudborte itself was scarcely more than a hamlet, with a single row of stores, including a single-storied chandlery that could not have been more than five yards wide and not that much deeper.

A red hound sat on the narrow porch of the chandlery, tied to one of the posts. His eyes followed the horses, but he did not howl or bark. Anna wasn't sure whether the dog might not have offered the slightest pleading moan, as though he would have liked to follow the riders. While Anna could sense someone observing her, no one stepped onto the porch. The single street of Sudborte remained deserted, at least until well after the Regent's force had passed through the town itself.

The keep was on the west side of Sudborte, a square structure less than twenty-five yards on a side, with rough-quarried, redstone walls six or seven yards high. There was only one tower, rising another two yards above the parapets of the walls and set to the right of the single wooden gate. Several outbuildings of wood, including what appeared to be a stable, had clearly been constructed later.

A pair of armsmen stood on the parapets above the open gate, but neither had a weapon at hand as the column rode toward the keep.

"Lady . . ." Himar cleared his throat.

Anna nodded. "You can take some men and check it out."

Himar looked puzzled for a moment, and Anna almost grinned. Sometimes, Earth colloquialisms did not translate even though the languages were similar. "Make sure it's safe," she added, reining up. Jecks and the players reined up as well, while Himar took a score of armsmen and proceeded.

"At times, my lady, you do trust too much," Jecks murmured quietly.

He was probably right, although she had trusted not so much in Falar's goodness as her own sorcery. *But sorcery isn't always that precise . . . or your spells aren't.*

"That's why I listen to you and Himar." She smiled impishly. "I did wear that breastplate, you remember, and I did enchant those shields."

"That you did, my lady, and for that all of us are grateful." A hint of a smile flickered in the hazel eyes of the white-haired lord, but not upon his lips.

Shortly, Himar rode back. "It appears safe enough. There are but a handful of armsmen, but we will keep watch." He glanced toward Liende, suggestively.

Anna smiled wryly and called, "Chief player! Have the players standing ready. When we dismount, have them run through the short flame song." *They need to be in practice for that sort of thing anyway.*

"Yes, Regent."

Anna turned in the saddle and unfastened the lutar case, then extracted the instrument, holding it while Jecks leaned over and refastened the empty case in place. Then, they followed Himar toward the small redstone keep.

A red-haired young man stood by the open gate, with but two armsmen beside him. As Anna reined up, he bowed deeply. "Regent, welcome to Sudborte. I am Falar." He stood, waiting, almost as if Anna might order his capture or death.

"This is the Regent," Jecks announced.

"And that is Lord Jecks, High Lord Counselor of Defalk," Anna said, "Overcaptain Himar, and Chief of Players Liende."

Falar paled ever so slightly, even as he bowed to each figure.

"I wanted to talk to you," Anna said.

"I had hoped for that, Regent and sorceress." Falar bowed again. "I can but offer meager hospitality, far less grand than can my brother, Lord Ustal." Unlike his brother, Falar was red-haired, with a pale freckled complexion, and barely taller than Anna. He was slender and lacked the overt muscular toughness displayed by Ustal or even the wiriness of some armsmen. Yet, he offered a smile that held a hint of roguishness.

Himar deployed lancers both outside the keep and within the courtyard, some mounted, and some on foot. Liende set the players to practicing in a shaded corner on the east side behind the open gate.

Anna dismounted, carefully, still holding the lutar, and Falar led them to a hall—less than ten yards long and half that in width—where he gestured to the single chair at the head of the table flanked by benches. "If you would, Regent?"

Anna sat. Rickel and Lejun stationed themselves behind her, while Jecks sat on the bench to her left, leaving the one on the right for Falar.

"You wished to tell me . . ." Anna began gently.

"Lady, Regent, sorceress, I am not a powerful-looking man. My brother is. He looks like a lord should look. He believes he is a lord, but he is not the lord for Fussen."

"Why do you believe you should be the heir to Fussen?" Anna asked bluntly.

"Because Ustal will ruin Fussen. He has already begun. I do not believe I would be the best lord, but I will not ruin the land and its people." Falar cleared his throat. "I do not speak well of myself, but I have waiting some folk, in hopes you would come. If you would but hear their words?"

"Who are these folk?" asked Jecks, his voice even.

"Tradespeople, crafters, Lord Jecks. I would have the Regent hear each in turn, if that would be acceptable."

Jecks glanced toward Anna. She nodded.

Falar gestured toward the slim youth who stood in the door-way of the hall. The youth ducked out of sight, then returned with a stooped figure who walked to the foot of the table—a good four yards from Anna.

"This is Gheratt," Falar explained. "He is the millwright at the sawmill."

Gheratt was a wiry man, slightly taller than Jecks, slightly stooped with gray-and-brown hair. He wore a clean brown tunic, dark blue trousers, and battered brown-leather boots. "My sire built the mill to the west of here, on the Eisig River. Then Lord Vlassa told him that a tenth part of what he took in would go to Fussen. Lord Ustal has sent a scroll demanding a fifth part."

"Did he offer a reason?" asked Jecks.

"Nay, ser. Not excepting that he expected a reckoning in writing . . . and who would keep that?" asked Gheratt. "I be a miller, not a scribe."

"He claimed you weren't paying what you owed and asked for twice that?" asked Anna.

"Aye . . ." Gheratt said, "and his men said he'd take the mill iffen I didn't pay, either in coin or timber."

Falar gestured again. Gheratt stepped back, replaced by a younger, burlier, black-haired man wearing coarsely woven gray-linen trousers and shirt. "This is Reytal, the smith in Sudborte."

"Lady . . . Regent . . ." the smith stammered. "It be . . . like . . . always . . . My tariff to the lord's . . . been four blades a year . . . one each season. . . ."

Anna kept her nod to herself. From what she'd heard, even a cheap blade was worth half a gold, and that meant the smith was paying the equivalent of between two and six golds a year.

"At summer turn, the armsmen came . . . told me . . . Lord Ustal . . . said that I must provide eight blades now. . . ."

After the smith came a cooper, and then a weaver, and a fuller, and each had a similar tale to tell, and Anna listened to each.

When the fuller had left the small hall, Falar looked to Anna. "They were all I could gather when I heard you might be coming, but others would say the same. If you wish, you could talk to any crafter. . . ."

"They seem to tell the truth," Jecks said, "but all tell the truth as they see it."

"That is true, but all tell of vastly increased tariffs, tariffs they can scarce pay," responded Falar. "You saw the armsmen. I had to hire such, for my dear brother sent his after me, and yet I raised neither blade nor word against him then."

"You do now," pointed out Jecks.

"Would you not . . . after this?" asked Falar, his eyes turning to Anna once more. "Might I ask your inclinations on the succession?"

"You can, but it's something I'll have to think about," Anna replied, as she stood and glanced at Jecks.

"Will you stay?" asked Falar. "We have but little, yet it is yours to command."

"I appreciate your hospitality, Falar, but much as we would like to do so, we need to be on our way," Anna demurred. *And well out of Lord Ustal's lands . . . if only for my peace of mind.*

"I cannot say how grateful I am that you even heeded my plea and came to hear what I would say for the folk of Fussen."

"Falar . . . I will always listen." Anna forced herself not to say more beyond that promise. "And I will let you know my decision after I return to Falcor."

"More than that can no man ask." The younger son of Vlassa bowed, offering his charming smile.

After inclining her head in return, Anna followed Jecks back to the courtyard, flanked by her guards, where she mounted Farinelli.

When the column was northbound, a good dek from the keep, Anna turned toward Jecks. "What do you think, my lord Jecks?"

"I would suggest prudence. If you remove Ustal now, none will understand why, save a handful of tradesmen."

"And the Thirty-three will be upset."

"Some would be most upset; others would defer to your judgment."

Anna nodded slowly. *So you have to let things get bad enough that everyone can see the reasons for your actions . . . and all the time, people will suffer.* She shook her head, sadly.

"Think you that I am mistaken, my lady?"

"No, my lord. I think you're right. That's why I'm bothered." Anna stared blankly at the dusty road ahead, and the long afternoon of riding to come. "That's also why we have to visit Lord Jearle in Denguic."

18

···

Jecks took Anna's arm as they neared the great hall of West-fort, where Lord Jearle waited, smiling broadly, several paces from the open doors of the hall. On each side of the doors stood an armsman in red and black.

"You make a striking appearance, my lady," Jecks whispered. "Lord Jearle has not taken his eyes from you."

Striking? In simple green gown with a costume, gold-plated link necklace, and green slippers? "I don't think Lord Jearle's eyes are on me for my appearance, Lord High Counselor. I'm so thin I look more like a boy."

"No one would ever mistake you for such," Jecks replied, his voice low. "You even take away this old warhorse's breath."

Anna could feel her heartbeat speed up at the words, knowing how much it cost Jecks to offer any admission. "You're not old, and I'm glad to see I still have some effect on men." She paused, then added, "Particularly men of judgment and experience."

Is there a slight blush there? Good! Anna smiled.

"Some have questioned that judgment. . . ."

"I wouldn't." Anna broke off as Jearle stepped forward.

"Regent Anna, Lord High Counselor Jecks . . . one would scarcely know that you had ridden from Falcor so recently," said Jearle in a resonant baritone. The Lord of Denguic bowed, deeply and dramatically and declaimed, "We are honored, mightily honored." He smiled even more broadly. "When you were announced by my messenger, I must say that I was most pleased to learn that you had made Lord Jecks your chief counselor."

"Lord Jecks has always been my chief advisor," Anna replied. "The title merely affirms that."

"The magnificence of Westfort has restored us from the rigors of the journey," offered Jecks, with a hearty laugh following his words, clearly trying to move the conversation away from his title.

"And the hospitality of its lord," Anna added sweetly, keeping a smile on her face. *Remember . . . Mother always said you'd catch more flies with honey than vinegar . . . except Jearle's more like a cockroach.*

The graying Lord of Denguic made a sweeping gesture to the woman standing to his left and back two paces, almost between the armsmen in red and black. "Might I present my consort, Livya. My dear, the Regent, the lady Anna, and Lord High Counselor Jecks."

"It's good to meet you," Anna said, inclining her head. "Westfort is both imposing and charming."

"We are so honored that you have come to grace Westfort." The white-haired and thin-faced woman in the loose and dark red gown smiled and offered a gesture of respect somewhere between a curtsy and a bow.

"And my heir, Brellyt." Jearle beckoned for a broad-shouldered and red-bearded and red-haired man to step forward.

"I am honored, Regent. Most honored." Brellyt bowed.

Anna would have been impressed by the shy nature of the young man's smile, except for the seeming contradiction of the hardness of his eyes.

"If you would lead the way, Regent. . . ." Lord Jearle gestured toward the open double doors flanked by the armsmen.

"Thank you." Anna inclined her head ever so slightly, then swept through the door, careful to keep a dazzling smile in place as she and Jecks walked toward the seat at the head of the long table.

She stood there, surveying the long and dark table, on which gleamed silvery cutlery and shimmering crystal. Seven-branched candelabra, set at intervals on the polished dark wood, lit the hall and the table, which was set for more than twenty people. After waiting for her entrance, others followed Jearle into the hall. Anna stood and waited, as if holding court, until people gathered at places around the table.

Realizing that she was in a situation where no one would sit until she did, Anna seated herself. So did everyone else.

As soon as he sat to Anna's right, the gray-haired Jearle smiled broadly once more, revealing teeth remarkably even and white for Defalk. "Regent and sorceress of power . . . I cannot tell you how greatly your message and your decision to visit Denguic and Westfort has cheered all of us."

Anna wanted to shiver at the oiliness she sensed in Jearle's words, but replied with the phrase she had rehearsed, "A regent must know those in power in the land she serves, and you are most gracious to receive us all so warmly." *You sound as false as he does, but that's politics . . . or diplomacy . . . or something.*

Jecks sat across the table from Jearle, with Jearle's consort Livya to his left. Brellyt sat to his father's right. Anna could see Liende, Himar, and Skent farther down the table, interspersed with those who had to be Jearle's retainers or relatives.

A serving girl filled Anna's goblet with a ruby liquid, then those of Jearle, Jecks, Livya, and Brellyt.

"The Mylelot, that comes from the Guereck Valley—it is at least as good as the Neserean vintages from Ferantha." Jearle smiled again, revealing his teeth once more.

Anna returned the smile and took a small sip, admitting to herself that the wine was good. Not great, but good, and certainly better than many she had tasted in Defalk. "Excellent, and far better than any I have tasted recently."

"That is why I made sure we had an ample supply for your visit, honored Regent, and Lord High Counselor. . . ."

As Jearle talked, and Anna smiled, unbidden, Henry Higgins' words from *My Fair Lady* slipped into her mind . . . *Oozing charm from every pore . . . he oiled his way across the floor . . .* Was Jearle that bad? She wanted to nod.

"Have you visited any other lords before coming to Denguic?" asked Jearle.

"We have just come from Fussen, where we met Lord Ustal," Anna said. *You hope the news won't upset him too much, but he'll find out sooner or later. . . .*

"The succession, I imagine. Difficult situation, there, most difficult." Jearle took a modest swallow of the ruby wine, then gestured for Anna to serve herself from the platter heaped high with slabs of meat and held by a serving girl. "Our most tender lamb, lady."

"Thank you." Anna took three slabs, sensing young Brellyt's eyes open as she did.

"Have you any thoughts on the succession?" asked Jecks.

"Ha . . . you jest, of course. A lord had best not comment on the affairs of his neighbor." Jearle laughed, and the sound was as oily as his words.

"His sire was not known to have been the most accommodating of souls," Jecks pursued.

"Accommodating, Lord Jecks? I don't know as I'd ever heard that word in the same sentence as Lord Vlassa's name before." Jearle shrugged, still smiling. "They say the son is quite accomplished, in arms and elsewhere."

"He presents a fine appearance," Anna said.

"As did his sire, years back . . . but none of us present the appearance now as we did then . . . save for you, Regent. And you, the stories say, paid most dearly for your youth." Jearle paused, then added. "That is what one hears."

"The Regent has taken more wounds than most," Jecks affirmed. "Two crossbow bolts, a knife, and possibly others I know not of."

"Lord Jecks is modest," Anna interjected. "My wounds came through . . . unfamiliarity. He has exhibited far greater bravery and skill."

"Begging your pardon, Regent, but it is said that you took Dumar with but twentyscore lancers." Jearle raised his eyebrows.

"That's about right. We started with fifteen, I think, and Lord Sargol and Lord Birfels offered some aid as well."

"And how many armsmen did you face?" asked Brellyt.

Anna tried to remember. "About five thousand . . . two hundred fifty–score . . . that's about how many we killed in battle." She didn't want to think too long about the innocents killed in the flooding or in the destruction of Envaryl.

Brellyt's gulp was audible.

"She destroyed almost five hundred–score of the Evult's lancers and armsmen," Jecks added.

"The strongest ruler of Defalk in generations," Jearle observed, "and a regent." He laughed humorously. "Would we had had more such."

Although Anna trusted the man less and less, she smiled and took another sip of wine, and another helping of the heavy-cheesed potatoes.

"Have you any news on the new Prophet?" inquired Jearle.

"Very little except that the Liedfuhr has sent fiftyscore Mansuuran lancers in his support," Anna answered politely.

"The lord Behlem brought well over three hundred–score

armsmen through the West Pass before you vanquished him. So thick they were that one could not see the road," Jearle said. "Far more lancers and armsmen there were than ever seen or gathered in Defalk."

Anna understood where Jearle was taking the conversation, but only said, "There were so many that they could not be quartered within the liedburg at Falcor."

"Yet the lady Anna vanquished them and their Prophet," Jecks pointed out, "and without assistance."

"Ah, yes . . . sorcery, was it not?" Jearle beamed. "Most welcome indeed. And what a sight it was when they marched back, their packs and tails dragging." He smiled.

"Many things are called sorcery," observed Jecks mildly. "At times, entire forces of armsmen have vanished, and there have been no sorcerers within deks. Other times, bridges have been built without masons."

Livya's eyes clouded, and she coughed gently. "There are many tales about the Regent, and how she came from the mist worlds. Alas, we have never been privy to them, and if it would not be too wearisome to repeat that tale, Regent, I for one would be most pleased to hear it from the one who lived it." A warm smile crossed her face.

Anna didn't trust Livya's smile any more than her consort's, and she had a good idea that the Lady of Westfort was more than either ornament or broodmare. Whether Jearle had gotten Jecks' point or not, the lady Livya certainly had. "If you don't mind hearing an old tale, I would be more than pleased to tell you. . . ."

Anna launched into the tale of how she had come to Liedwahr, all too conscious of Jecks' eyes upon her as she spoke— and of the assessing speculation of both Jearle and Livya.

19

L ord Nelmor." Anna inclined her head, then took the armchair on one side of the table in the private study, so that Nelmor and Jecks would have to sit on the other side. Anna hoped that might give the Lord of Dubaria the impression, subconscious or otherwise, that he and Jecks were on the same side. The dark-paneled walls of the room reminded her vaguely of Jecks' study, although she recalled Jecks' study as being and smelling far cleaner.

"You are most kind to visit Dubaria. I do not believe any from Falcor have come so far north and west since before the time of Donjim," replied Nelmor as he seated himself. "It may have been even longer."

Jecks slipped into the other armchair slightly after Nelmor was settled.

"We were persuaded to go to Fussen, and since we were there, we wished to show support for those who supported the Regency from the beginning." Anna smiled warmly. "We also wished to inform you about the successes and the challenges ahead."

"I think I would hear of the successes," said Nelmor. "I face challenges enough each week."

"So do we all," said Jecks.

"We have managed to pay off the debts Lord Barjim ran up to the Ranuan Exchange," Anna began. "That should make it easier for the Thirty-three to trade there. We have repaired the ford on the Chean River to restore the road to Ebra. We have received the fealty of Lord Hadrenn of Synek. . . ." Anna paused at the expression on Nelmor's face. "You had not heard that the western third of Ebra had asked to become part of Defalk?"

Nelmor shook his head. "Ah . . . truthfully, no, my Regent."

"The armsmaster of Dumar is our appointment, and we are expecting golds from Dumar by harvesttime. Most of the damages of the Evult's flood have been repaired in Falcor, and if the weather holds . . ." Anna continued with every promising scrap she could remember, ending with, ". . . and many holdings are expecting far better crops than in recent years."

"Better news than I have heard in many years." A sardonic smile crossed the tall lord's face. "And the news that is less promising?"

"There is another war brewing in Ebra, between Lord Bertmynn of Dolov and the freewomen of Elahwa—"

"Freewomen?"

"The local women. They took the city and started to rebuild it after the flood. They have received blades from the South-Women of Ranuak," Anna explained. "Lord Bertmynn does not appear pleased."

"Ah . . . that explains Lord Hadrenn's desires."

"Better to have a third of Ebra behind us, than none at all in these times," suggested Jecks.

Nelmor nodded slowly.

"A number of the merchants and crafters in Fussen have petitioned the Regency to replace Lord Ustal with his younger twin brother," Anna said.

"And what has the Regency decided, if this lord might ask?"

"The Regency does not feel," Anna said carefully, "that the Regency should act unless many lives are in danger or unless Defalk itself is in danger. Or unless a lord defies the Regency," she added. "None of those has happened."

Nelmor pulled thoughtfully at his left earlobe. "Wise guidelines, I would say. Yet you seem less than pleased."

"I think that there will be trouble unless things change," Anna said bluntly. "Lord Ustal is far too hard on his people and his crafters."

"Lord Vlassa was said to be hard," Nelmor pointed out.

Anna merely nodded.

"Other troubles? Surely, Defalk faces more difficulties than those?"

"Ebra seems to be the problem. The Sturinnese could be sending golds to Lord Bertmynn. They did to Lord Ehara, you might remember."

"I had heard such."

"There were twoscore ruined Sturinnese hulls in the bay at Narial," Jecks said mildly, "and some hundred and fifty–score Sturinnese lancers that Lady Anna destroyed."

And one Lord Jecks was most unhappy about at the time, Anna recalled. She also remembered how she'd exploded at Jecks, and how they'd barely spoken for over a week.

"You saw these?" asked Nelmor.

"I did."

"Lord Jecks was also wounded with an enchanted Sturinnese javelin," Anna pointed out. "That's why we're concerned about Sturinn sending golds to Bertmynn."

"Has this yet occurred?"

"Only in small amounts so far," Anna fudged.

Nelmor nodded. "And what of the new young Prophet of Music—*our* nearest threat? Have you heard aught promising or less so?"

"He has fiftyscore Mansuuran lancers to add to his armsmen," Anna replied, "and a regent who is an officer sent by his grandsire. Right now, he has sent some of his grandsire's armsmen to Elioch, but none of his own armsmen."

"That bears watching, but it would be good if no other lancers near Elioch." After a silence, Nelmor asked, "How do you find Tiersen and Ytrude?"

"They have not sent you scrolls?"

"Alas, I have not sent a messenger. How would they? They would not have imposed upon you, your grace, and even had they, I would just have received such."

"Ytrude seems to be settling in at Falcor," Anna observed. "She is shy, but she seems bright."

"Bright she has always been." Nelmor cleared his throat. "And what of Tiersen?"

"He seems thoughtful, but I have not had as much time to observe him."

"You are like my sister, Lady Anna. And yet you are not." Nelmor shrugged.

What that meant, Anna suspected, was that Gatrune was direct, and Nelmor thought Anna was, but that he was reluctant to admit anything, since he was a lord, and lords admitted nothing. At least, Defalkan lords of the old style didn't.

"You were most supportive to send Tiersen to Falcor," Anna

began slowly, "but he will learn more about those who will be his peers in years to come, before he must make decisions about them and their families. He has also begun to learn other skills."

"It is said that you are instructing the fosterlings in another way in which to keep the accounts of their lands. Why would you find this necessary?" Nelmor's expression was that of a quizzical frown.

"I have already learned, Lord Nelmor, that not all those who keep the accounts of their lords are as honest as they profess. The accounts and figures Dythya is teaching them will allow them to check those accounts quickly. This will give them greater control—and they will have to spend less time on accounts." She smiled. "That way, Tiersen can devote more time to those matters you feel are most important without leaving his fate in the hands of others."

"And Lord Dannel has said that some who instruct them are lowborn," Nelmor added cautiously.

"I was not born into a lordly family of Defalk." *In fact, they'd have called your grandparents peasants, since they worked a farm in an Appalachian holler.* "Nor was Arms Commander Hanfor. Nor Tirsik the stablemaster. Yet we all do certain things better than others. I felt that your son and daughter should learn about the uses and limits of blades from the best and how stables should be run from a good stablemaster. Sometimes, the best instructor is a lord, such as Lord Jecks here. Sometimes, they are not."

"Your words are wise, Regent, yet Lord Dannel is not pleased."

"Lord Dannel is not pleased, Lord Nelmor, because his son is not as quick-witted nor as skilled in arms as his sire. He is not pleased because his son refuses to learn and blames it upon his instructors." Anna forced another smile. "As Arms Commander Hanfor has told me," she fibbed, "it is a poor lancer who blames his blade or his mount."

Surprisingly, Nelmor laughed. "True. Has he not wit enough to find better mount or blade, or to use what he has, soon enough he will be dead." The laugh died away. "Yet Lord Dannel has suggested a match between Lord Birfels' eldest daughter and his youngest."

"That match is not suitable." Anna looked straight at Nelmor.

"Your son, or the son of another lord, would be far better. That is, if those involved like each other." Based on her past meetings with the proud lord, that was as much as she dared suggest to Nelmor, and the not-quite-direct approach would give him the opportunity to consider such a match without the impression of pressure.

"Why should their likes matter?" asked Nelmor, his tone curious.

"I did not say 'love,' my lord Nelmor," Anna pointed out. "But I have observed the poisoning of one lord by a consort who was ill suited and the abuse and treachery of another lord who refused to heed his consort. Defalk cannot afford that kind of scheming. I would prefer that matches have some acceptance by both parties." Her tone turned dry. "It is easier upon all the rest of us."

A smile crossed Jecks' face, and after a moment, Nelmor chuckled. "You appear so young that sometimes I forget that you have seen far more than that lovely face displays."

"You would not wish to have seen all she has seen," Jecks added ironically. "I've seen but a fraction of it, and I have little wish to see more."

Nelmor glanced sideways, almost abruptly, then back at the Regent. "Lady Anna . . . there is one other matter. I would not trouble you . . . yet I must bring this up." A trace of a smile flitted around Nelmor's face, at odds with the seriousness of his words.

"Yes?"

"I hope you do not mind, but Lord Klestayr had prevailed upon me . . . and requested most urgently that he be allowed to join us for dinner. . . ." Nelmor broke off and offered a shrug.

"Just how urgently?" Anna kept a straight face and arched her eyebrows.

"Urgently enough that he rode in not too far in advance of you, his mounts lathered."

"The more at dinner the better, and I look forward to meeting Lord Klestayr under your most gracious hospitality." Anna almost wanted to gag at the syrup she'd put in her voice. "And I'm even more glad that we met before dinner."

"I appreciate your informing me before others at table, and

for your many courtesies, Regent Anna, and for yours as well, Lord High Counselor." Nelmor remained seated.

Anna realized that she had to end the meeting, and stood. "You have always been most supportive, and we would not wish to have you surprised in any way." *That's the last thing you need, especially with this touchy lord.*

The Lord of Dubaria waited for Jecks to rise before standing and speaking, "If you would like some air before supper, you might wish to view the side garden. It is Delyra's pride, and quite beautiful." Nelmor smiled.

"We look forward to seeing it." *Is that the royal "we," or are you including Jecks?* Anna didn't like the idea of the royal "we," but was beginning to understand its necessity.

Nelmor bowed again as the two left his private study.

As Anna and Jecks stepped through the double doors into the small garden, perhaps twenty yards on a side, graced by what appeared to be a boxwood hedge surrounding a small fountain, Anna glanced at Jecks, handsome in his royal blue tunic. "We need a postal service." *Among a good many other things.*

Behind them followed Blaz and Lejun, each with a hand upon his blade.

"What sort of service might that be?" asked Jecks. "You have few enough golds as it is."

Anna took a deep breath as she walked slowly toward the hedge. She had as many problems dealing with Defalk that came from her own assumptions. How would people communicate? Scrolls from the lords—but only if they had something to say. "I think I have an idea. When we get back to Falcor, I'll draft a long scroll with all sorts of news in it. Big stuff and little stuff . . ." She glanced at Jecks, and could see the blank expression crossing his face. "You saw that Nelmor didn't know about Hadrenn or about the freewomen or even about what his own children were doing in Falcor?"

"That is true."

"So I draft one scroll. Each fosterling copies, say, five. We figure out how many lancers it will take to travel to each lord."

"But that costs golds . . ."

"Bear with me, my dear lord Jecks. Anyone who wants to send a scroll, including fosterlings—a one-sheet scroll—pays a silver to send a message to father and mother." She smiled. "Or anyone else. Anyone except the lord who wants to send a return message also pays a silver."

She pulled at her earlobe. She'd always had little earlobes, and Brill's youth spell had done nothing to change that. "If I send out those scrolls two or three times a year . . . the lords will know more than they do now—and they'll hear some things the way I want them said. We might even get enough silvers to pay for it."

Jecks fingered his chin. "Some would not trust such."

"It doesn't matter. We tell the truth, and they'll hear it some-where else. In time, they'll accept it. And some might also decide to send fosterlings to Falcor when they find out who else's offspring are there."

Jecks laughed. "For that alone they might!"

Anna enjoyed his laugh, and the moist and garden-fresh air in the early twilight, for the few moments before they faced the strain of yet another dinner with more skeptically inquisitive lords and consorts.

20

ENCORA, RANUAK

Alone at the table, the Matriarch stands and smiles as the dark-haired and thin-faced woman enters the small hall.

The newcomer wears a sea-blue tunic and trousers, the sole ornamentation being a gold pin on her collar. The fine gold wires of the pin represent two sheaves of grain, crossed. She bows, a movement barely more than perfunctory. "I am here at your request, Matriarch."

"It is good to see you, Abslim. I know it is early, and you must soon be on your way to preside over the opening of the Mercantile Exchange, but I appreciate your taking the time to come and see an old woman." The Matriarch stands, slowly, deliberately.

A tight smile precedes Abslim's reply. "With such compli-ments, Matriarch, I fear the words that will follow."

"Nonsense. The harmonies will protect you. They have protected us all." The round-faced Matriarch absently smooths back her gray hair, then straightens her own faded blue tunic before reseating herself at the table and gesturing to the chair across from her.

"Your wish?" asks Abslim.

"When I visited the Exchange earlier this year, you expressed a certain concern that Defalk might not make good on the debts of the previous Lord of Falcor." The Matriarch pauses, then adds when she perceives that Abslim is not ready to respond. "At least, that was what I perceived."

"The Exchange was concerned about the unrest in Defalk." Abslim's words are tight.

"All Defalk now acknowledges the Regent. I would assume that this would greatly reassure the Exchange."

"There remains the matter of over a thousand golds."

"And were those golds repaid?"

Abslim forces a shrug. "That would be up to the traders."

"I think not." The Matriarch's contralto voice is both rich and commanding. "Once the golds are received, you will ensure that Defalk and its lords and merchants receive the treatment accorded our friends and most valued customers."

"That will be after harvest, Matriarch. At least six weeks."

The gray-haired woman laughs. "The sorceress' messenger and guards arrived here last night. With eleven hundred golds. I persuaded them to wait until I spoke to you."

Abslim remains silent. "The traders who support the South-Women will not be pleased."

"Have I been right in judging the sorceress and Regent of Defalk, Abslim? Or has the Exchange been right?"

"The Exchange will defer to the Matriarch."

"No." The word is cold, yet menacingly melodic. "You will grant those terms, of your own accord, with no word about deference to the Matriarch. You will treat Lord Bertmynn as you have treated the sorceress in the past." A gentle, but cold, smile suffuses the round face. "Is that clear, Mistress of the Exchange?"

"There will be muttering, Matriarch . . . and unhappiness."

"You *will* ensure that there is none." The Matriarch rises.

Abslim rises as well, her face pale. "As you command. As you command, and may the harmonies protect us all."

"I trust the harmonies, Abslim, even when they appear in dissonance. Best you do as well."

The Matriarch remains standing until well after the Mistress of the Exchange has left the small hall.

21

The afternoon sun beat down on Anna's back as Farinelli carried her eastward, back toward Falcor. While Anna's floppy hat blocked much of the sun, she could feel the lower part of her neck beginning to burn.

Beyond the wooden rail fence on the north side of the road, men with scythes were cutting the golden wheat, and behind the reapers, women were bundling the grain and loading it onto flat wagons. Puffs of dust rose from Farinelli's hoofs, but the light road dust settled quickly in the still and warm air. Anna readjusted her hat and glanced over her shoulder, past Lejun and Blaz toward Skent and Liende, riding side by side. Behind them rode the rest of the players, led by Palian and Yuarl. The column of lancers following the players stretched back past the wheat field and past the woodlot that lay farther west along the road. Farther back, dust was rising high enough that the lancers in the rear were breathing and eating dust.

Anna turned her attention back to the lord riding easily on her right.

"A far better harvest than in many years." Jecks gestured toward the field and the workers.

"Is that true on your lands?" Anna asked.

"I would hope so, but I have not seen such, nor heard." Jecks smiled. "Being Lord High Counselor keeps one away from those lands."

"I'm keeping you from your duties? Is that what you're telling me?" Anna parried lightly.

"My duties are with my Regent." Jecks' voice took on a deep and ponderous tone.

"Oh . . . such devotion to duty . . ." Anna grinned broadly, but tried to keep from laughing. She failed and laughed gently.

"I would hear you laugh more," the handsome lord said.

You wish you could . . . but why aren't you? It's a beautiful day, and there's nothing else you can do until you return to Falcor—except worry. "I should . . . sometimes it's hard to put things aside."

"The careworn Regent . . ." Jecks chuckled. "She should care for herself, as well as her subjects."

"Look!" Anna pointed to the hawk that was diving into the corner of the field.

"The reapers have disturbed a rodent."

"They're awesome. Hawks."

Jecks nodded. "I prefer the black falcons of the north, the wild ones."

"I'll bet they're spectacular."

"They can stun a coney with their dive."

Anna paused, recalling the time she'd seen a falconer with an eagle. Where had that been? At that Shakespeare Festival in southern Utah? "Do you have many eagles here?"

"Only in the Ostfels. They say there are fish eagles on the cliffs of Nordwei, but I have never been there."

"I never saw any eagles the one time I was in the Ostfels." *Then, you were worried about the road and the Evult.*

"Watch ahead," Jecks cautioned, pointing to a wagon coming westward along the road.

The driver pulled on the reins until he had slowed the two-horse team and halted the empty wagon on the north side of the road. Himar gestured for the lancers in the vanguard to ride the road's south shoulder. The wagoner, a middle-aged man with a brown beard, watched impassively as the first of the lancers rode past.

Rickel eased his mount up to flank Anna on her left as she eased Farinelli onto the south shoulder of the road to pass the wagon and the pair of chestnut horses in the traces. The driver bowed his head as Rickel, Anna, and Jecks passed. "Best to you, Lady Regent."

"And to you," Anna called back as she guided Farinelli back onto the road.

Rickel dropped back slightly with a nod to the Regent.

"Thank you," she said.

The head guard nodded in return.

For some reason, the wagon reminded Anna of a Wells Fargo wagon, though there was not the slightest resemblance. "We do have to do something about a postal service—the couriers to lords, I mean," Anna reflected. "People don't know enough about what's going on, and that makes it hard for them to understand."

"That blade bears two sharp edges," Jecks said. "Do you want all the Thirty-three to know that you share some sympathies with the Matriarch?"

"They'll find out sooner or later. . . ."

"Best later, when you are in a stronger seat."

"Maybe." Anna cleared her throat, thinking. After a moment, she asked, "What should I do about Ustal? Send a scroll declaring that he is the Lord of Fussen? Then wait until his lands rise in revolt?"

"If he tariffs his crafters as he is, within two years he will not have the coins to pay his liedgeld." Jecks smiled sadly. "And for that, you can remove a lord."

"Won't some of the lords of the Thirty-three be upset about my removing a lord merely for golds? Especially if I remove the lordly and noble-looking Ustal, who treats horses and falcons well?"

"You do not like Ustal? I would scarce have guessed."

"Let's hope it was not too obvious to him. He treats his falcons and mounts better than his consort. She shrinks away from him, even in public."

"The older lords might say that was a sign of respect." Jecks' laugh was ironic. "They will have to change."

"Are you saying that to placate me?" Anna arched her eyebrows.

"No. I am saying such because it is true. They will change, or they will not long last under the Regency." Jecks shook his head. "Had Barjim lived, Alasia would have changed that. Even under Lord Behlem some would have changed. The times change, but men change more slowly." He shrugged and offered a broad and warm smile. "Some of us essay such change before it is demanded."

"You're doing quite nicely, thank you, Lord High Counselor. I am most appreciative—and thankful." *You're more than thankful. Why can't you say so? Why do you keep backing away? Because you don't want to lose your independence after working so long to get it? Because every man has tried to tie you down?*

Jecks inclined his head. "For that, I am grateful."

Anna smiled warmly, hoping he would understand, hoping she could work out her own tangled emotions.

22

Anna stepped out of her chamber, hurrying, and feeling as though she were already behind, even though she'd arrived in Falcor but the night before. She made it to the corner that led to the stairs when she stopped abruptly at the sound of voices—loud voices. The sorceress froze just before the corner of the corridor and held out her hand to halt the guards who followed her from her scrying room down to the receiving room where she was to meet with Jecks, and then Dythya and Menares.

"You . . . and the Regent, you let that . . . commoner . . . go to Fussen, and I'm the heir." Jimbob's voice carried. "You've dishonored me. My own grandsire, and you let *her* dishonor me by letting a mere stable boy go to Fussen while I was kept in Falcor . . . like an infant."

And you're behaving like one! Anna shook her head, but gestured at Rickel and Giellum for silence.

"That . . . commoner, as you would call him, works hard. He is worth two of you at the moment." Jecks' voice carried an amount of contempt and scorn Anna had never heard. "You are fortunate even to be alive. A woman who has no reason to care for you has had the *honor* to put her life in danger time after time to preserve your patrimony. That is honor, *Lord* Jimbob. She has saved your honor and your face. She has added to your lands and patrimony so that you will not face the problems your sire did. Talk not to me of honor."

"You love her. That's all it is."

"You are so blind, grandson, that you cannot see what is honorable. Not for all that it is laid before you with trumpets and harmony."

"You love her, and you don't understand honor anymore. You've been turned to a weak old man because you love her."

"You're not worthy to be in the same liedburg as she is." Jecks' voice turned tight.

"Oh, spare me your talk of honor, grandsire. Spare me when you're rutting like an old goat. . . ."

Crack!

There was a dull thud.

"You hit me. . . ."

Anna glanced sideways. Rickel nodded approvingly, then turned his face blank as he realized Anna was watching him.

"I am the Lord of Defalk and you hit me . . . spit on you . . ."

Crack!

"The first one was for ignorance. The second is for insolence. You will go on the punishment detail for all the lancers this afternoon, and you will work and be whipped as necessary. You have allowed your pride to blind you to your duties. You are a self-centered brat, and you will learn some respect."

"You can't do this . . . I'm the heir. I'll go to the Lady Anna . . . she won't let you hurt me."

Anna stepped around the corner.

Jimbob stood with his back against the wall, pinned there by Jecks' large hand around his neck. The heir's face was flushed.

"You don't have to go to the Lady Anna, Jimbob. I'm right here. What did you want to say?"

"You see what he's doing to me. . . ."

"I think it's long overdue," Anna said quietly. "Your grandfather and I have tried to show you how to be a good ruler, and what you have to learn. All you seem to care about is what others think and how you look."

"But . . . I'm the heir. . . ."

"You are the heir. But you're not acting like one. You're acting like a spoiled brat. I'd hoped you'd have more sense."

Jecks released his grasp on Jimbob. Jimbob lurched forward. The imprint of the older lord's hand was outlined in red on the youth's cheek.

"I'll tell the Thirty-three . . . you'll see!" gasped Jimbob.

Anna shook her head slowly. "That would be stupid. You'd put yourself in their hands? You'd go whining to them? What would they do? You don't seem to understand. The perceptions your lords have of you matters. This will have the armsmen and lords saying you're spoiled and willful, and lords won't follow a spoiled and willful leader, especially a young one." *They won't even follow a good leader unless coerced. . . .*

"*Lord* Jimbob . . ." Jecks drawled out the word "lord" sardonically, "You might recall that more than half the lords of Defalk are beholden to the Regent. You might also recall that she is a sorceress and that she has the only professional armsmen in Defalk—except for those who serve me and Lady Gatrune."

"You're all against me. . . ."

"Jimbob," Anna said coldly, "if we were against you, you'd already be dead."

Jimbob's eyes traveled from Anna, then to Jecks, and then across the faces of the two guards. His shoulders slumped.

"You are my grandson, but if you are not worthy to become Lord of Defalk, I will work with the Regent and the Thirty-three to find another who is. After this, it will take a great deal of proving for us to find you worthy of more than mucking out stable stalls." Jecks lifted the boy by one arm. "Stand up. You're going to take your punishment like a man."

"There is one other matter, Lord Jimbob," Anna said. "Defalk is more important than your vanity, and both your grandsire and I have worked to preserve this land. When you try to play us against each other, you're showing contempt for what we have worked for, and you're also showing how unsuited you are. Do you honestly think we don't talk to each other about you and your skills and abilities?" Anna could feel the withering scorn in her voice that infused her last sentence.

Jimbob paled. Then he actually bowed his head, but he did not speak.

Anna had the feeling the youth was so angry and yet so humiliated that he was unable to find words. "I tried to be gentle with you so you wouldn't be humiliated when I went to Elheld and you questioned me. I guess that was a mistake. I guess you'll have to learn everything the hard way." She looked at Jecks. "I'd suggest that you have Arms Commander Hanfor work out his punishment. But make sure Hanfor knows that we're both serious. If Hanfor has any questions, he can come to me." Anna paused. "Once you have that taken care of, I'd like to see you and then the counselors in the receiving room."

"Yes, Regent." Jecks' voice was formal.

Knowing the pain of a child's ingratitude, Anna wanted to reach out and hug Jecks, but she merely nodded. *What if this doesn't work? What if Jimbob's so spoiled that he won't see? What can you do . . . who else is there?* Anna waited until Jecks and Jimbob started down the wide stone steps before she began to walk in the same direction. She did not look at either guard who followed her, her mind on Elizabetta, almost always grateful, and on Jecks, saddled with an ungrateful grandson.

Outside the receiving room, Resor was the page waiting. "Good morning, Lady Anna."

"Good morning, Resor." Anna smiled, briefly, at the cheerful greeting, before slipping into the receiving room.

There, waiting for Jecks, she took the top scroll from the pile, one she hadn't seen, a scroll bound with intertwined crimson and blue ribbons. *From Dumar?* She broke the seal and began to read, still standing behind her working table.

> My Lady and Regent,
>
>   I said I would write. I am poor at words, but I will report on what I know. We had some trouble at first with the City Patrol in Dumaria. Now, matters are fine, and I have heard some say that the city is safer than ever.
>
>   We have reclaimed the golds from the ruins of Envaryl. Some were stolen before we found them. We erected the small memorial to Lord Ehara, as you instructed. I have sent five thousand golds under guard, and they will follow this scroll. Lady Siobion has said that for your mercy you deserve the extra thousand for your own use. I leave that to you. She said that few conquerors would have destroyed but one city after all the insults offered by Lord Ehara. . . .

After noting Alvar's signature, Anna set down the scroll. Destroying Envaryl when Ehara had refused to face her—that had bothered her at the time, and it still did. Hanfor had said that such destruction had been necessary. Necessary to leave the mark of Anna's power, necessary to ensure that all Dumar respected the sorceress and Regent of Defalk.

But you still deliberately killed innocents. . . . She frowned. All the other times, either she had killed armsmen or rebels, but she had not directed her sorcery at innocents and armsmen alike. Even the disaster created when her damming of Falche had failed had not been directed at innocents. *Does that make a difference? Did you accept Hanfor's advice because it was easier? Because you were tired and angry? Or because power corrupts, even when you try not to be corrupted? Or because no one respects anyone without power? But needing that respect . . . isn't that a form of corruption? Except, that without respect, as you've learned, even greater use of force is required. As with Jimbob?*

She took a deep breath.

"Lord Jecks," Giellum announced.

Anna turned toward the door, waiting until it shut behind the haggard-looking Lord of Elheld. "My lord Jecks . . ." she said softly, "I'm sorry. I didn't mean to walk in, but I didn't want him to put us against each other." She reached out and touched his arm, then squeezed his hand.

"For your words . . . there . . . my lady, I am most grateful, I do admit." A wintry smile appeared.

"You were right that he shouldn't have gone to Fussen," Anna said quietly.

"I did not mean for this . . ." Jecks looked down, not meeting her eyes. "I have not taken enough time with him."

"The fosterlings play up to him too much, I think," mused Anna, "especially Hoede, I'd bet. The sooner we send Hoede home to daddy, the better."

"Lord Dannel will not be pleased."

"I'm sure he won't, but I need Lord Nelmor more than Dannel, especially with that weasel Jearle still trying to suggest, politely, that he get back his title as Lord of the Western Marches. Geographically, it should be Ustal, Jearle, or Nelmor. Who would you have?"

"You can trust Nelmor, for you have his heirs, and his sister's support, but none knows how well he can command. Jearle can neither command nor be trusted, and the same is true of Ustal."

Sorry mess that is. . . . "We can wait, but my inclination is to name Nelmor when we have to name someone."

"Of the choices you have, he would be the best."

But certainly far from ideal. "Alvar is sending five thousand golds, including a thousand as a tribute from Lady Siobion to me personally." Anna handed Jecks the scroll.

"You have golds enough to run your lands now. You might consider a saalmeister of your own."

"Halde—the young assistant from Cheor?"

"You could do worse, far worse."

"Could you send Herstat a message and ask for his thoughts about Halde?" asked Anna. "I think he would be more open with you." She smiled. "After all, he was your saalmeister."

"He might be less open for that," replied Jecks.

"Not if you tell him that his judgment is for my saalmeister." Anna paused. "I could also ask Dythya to write him. He might be more honest with his daughter."

"Then you have Dythya write, and I will write, and we will see." Jecks chuckled, before reading the scroll slowly. After he finished he looked at Anna. "You chose wisely to leave Alvar in Dumar."

"Too bad I don't have more choices in Defalk." She took a sip of the orderspelled water.

"You have more power than any Lord of Defalk in generations, perhaps ever, my lady."

"Power doesn't always allow any better choices. Sometimes, all the time, anymore, it seems, sorcery is the only real tool I have."

Thrap. At the rap on the door, both turned.

"Counselor Menares," announced Resor.

"Come on in, Menares. Dythya should be here in a few moments." Anna turned to Jecks. "Somehow, it always gets back to that," Anna said. "Which lords fear my power as a sorceress enough to do as requested, and which don't. If I don't exhibit power, then none want to honor their obligations. If I do, they complain about my being high-handed."

"All lords respond to power, and little else," Jecks pointed out. "Your being Regent does not change that."

"But I can't ignore their complaints, because—" She broke off as there was a second rap on the door.

"Lady Anna, the counselor Dythya."

"Have her come in." Anna glanced at Jecks, then Menares. "Time to go over the accounts and the obligations."

Dythya bowed as she entered, carrying a stack of scrolls under each arm. "I have the accounts as you requested, Regent."

Anna nodded. "Thank you." It was going to be a long, long day. Even patient Jecks rolled his eyes.

23

With the late-afternoon sun shining through the high window behind her, Anna rubbed her forehead and looked down at the conference table and the stacks of scrolls and accounts that surrounded her. Slowly she reached for the pile that held the expenditures for armsmen and lancers—Hanfor's accounts.

"Lady Anna?"

Anna looked up as Menares peered around the door, "Yes, Menares?"

"Lady Anna . . . if I might have a word . . . ?" The gray-haired advisor's head bobbed up and down as he stood inside the double doors.

What does the old schemer want? "Of course, Menares." She gestured to the chair across from her, and Menares closed the door behind him.

"Thank you, lady . . ." As he took the proffered seat, the heavy and gray-haired counselor cleared his throat, once and then again. "Ah . . . uhm . . . what I have to say might be considered presumptuous, and I do not mean it to be taken such in the slightest . . . but I have had some modest experience in observing the ways of rulers in Liedwahr. . . ."

Anna nodded for the older man to continue.

"It is just . . . Lady Anna . . . that I overheard your words to Lord Jecks about . . . about the lords of Defalk . . . and at that time . . . it would not have been my place to offer any words . . . not in public . . . but I have reflected . . . and I trust . . . that in revealing my observations in private . . ."

Roundabout as Menares often was, seldom had he been so indirect. Anna caught herself managing to keep from clicking her nails in impatience. "I will keep your observations between us."

"Ah . . . thank you." Menares cleared his throat again. "You had remarked that you felt that few listened to you, except to obviate the threat of magical force which you could bring against them . . . and you offered some words about how many of the Thirty-three and even lords throughout Liedwahr responded but to the power of your sorcery."

"I did." Anna wondered where Menares was headed, but tried to keep her eyes off the stack of paper that represented what she needed to spend on armsmen. *And what you really don't have, even with the golds coming from Dumar . . . if they arrive.*

"You may recall that Lord Jecks pointed out that all men respond to power. You said that you yet need worry about their complaints. . . ." Menares paused, glancing at the Regent for a moment before going on. "Yet the real complaint to which they will not give voice is that your power is greater than theirs. Even Lord Behlem had once told me that the lords of Defalk revered their customs only insofar as those customs and traditions enhanced their power." Menares gave a wry smile. "I doubt that much has changed since his death."

"I doubt it," Anna acknowledged.

Menares continued, speaking more smoothly, "Men are willful. Women may also be willful, but there are few in power, save you and the Matriarch of Ranuak. Lords and rulers talk about reason, and about the need to solve disputes without the use of force, but they require such methods not because they admire them, but because all forms of power are limited, and the use of force must be reserved for times when no other method can be employed. They are jealous, my lady, because you are not bound by their limitations.

"They cannot match the force you can muster with your song magic . . . so they will try to weaken your resolve to use it, and thus weaken you and Defalk, by claiming that you rule but by force of magic. Yet all rulers maintain their reign by force. They cloak their force and call its differing manifestations by various terms. Some, as do the Norweians, talk of the necessity of trade. Others, such as the Sturinnese, talk of the freedom of the seas. Lord Behlem insisted he was but the manifestation of the will of harmony. The Ranuans purchase their power with golds. . . ."

He's right . . . money is a kind of force—economic force. So is trade . . . so even is the ability to logically persuade—you could call that intellectual force. Avery was great at that. . . . Anna found her nails clicking together and clasped her hands under the table to stop the mannerism.

"The great lords talk of harmony and of the need for agreement and peace, but all the words and the maneuverings—they rest on the armsmen and the golds they control."

Politics is really only a system for legitimizing the use of force in the minds of the people—or in the minds of the lords of the Thirty-three. . . . "You've thought about this," Anna said. "But I must worry about whether the people feel there is truth in what they've charged. I have used force. I've used a lot of force. They know I have this power. So why do they require me to use force?"

"Force is distasteful to the people," Menares replied. "To some people. If you always use force, then some of the lords believe that you will be less popular with the people."

"That could happen. Easily," Anna said. "I worry about it."

"Worry you must, but worry most about not using your powers, my lady. Few powerful rulers lose their lives and kingdoms, but many have failed for lack of use of their powers."

Was life that brutal—or that direct—when you stripped away the façades of society? She nodded. Almost all people wanted things their own way. Societies developed because the weaker needed protection against the strong. Ruling elites developed ways to attain their goals without unnecessary brutality. She laughed, almost bitterly. Dowries and marriage—a bartering of women—little more than economic coercion . . . the indirect use of force to reduce women to commodities by male power brokers.

Menares swallowed. "I have spoken more . . . perchance than I should. . . ."

"No . . . you haven't. I'm glad to have your words, Menares. I really am. You've reminded me of some pretty basic truths, and regents and rulers sometimes need reminding." She offered a smile. "Even we forget what we shouldn't." *Or never had to think about except in political science classes years ago.*

"Thank you, my lady."

Anna rose. "Thank *you*, Menares."

After the old counselor left, Anna sat, looking down at the stacks of accounts. Her lips tightened. *When I became Regent, there were no coins: so that form of power wasn't available. Nor was the power of politics, because I'm a woman, and most lords disliked or distrusted women with power, and insisted on my proving that I had power and knew how to use it. They were the ones who required I use force. They wouldn't do anything except bicker among themselves until I did—and then they complained.*

Why was it always different for women when they got power? Dieshr had schemed her way to being chair of the music department at Ames, and the moment she retired, the men would be at her throat. Of course, there, position and control of funds had been power. Anna tightened her lips. Someone like the Liedfuhr of Mansuur could use coins instead of force. The Norweians had trade, and fleets of ships. As Regent of a land that had yet to recover from nearly a decade of drought, what resources did she have? None—except her powers as a sorceress—and every time she used them, some lord or another whined or whimpered that all she could do was destroy something.

No one talked about the bridges she'd built, or the drought she'd ended, or the peace she'd brought to Defalk itself.

If this were a book, male readers would be complaining that all this sorceress does is fry people . . . but it's not, and I haven't been able to come up with any better alternatives—and neither have my male advisors. So . . . the only sin of which I'm really guilty is a failure to use my power in differing ways? Anna laughed, but the sound was hollow in the receiving room.

24

Leaning over the conference table that served as her working desk, Anna rubbed her forehead and her eyes. She wasn't sleeping that well . . . wondering about what was happening in Ebra, in Pamr, in Neserea, and with who knew how many lords of the Thirty-three. She couldn't keep up with it, even with scrying sorcery, not without being totally exhausted all the time. And there was the underlying strain of wondering whether she'd waited long enough before trying to retrieve any message Elizabetta might have written. *If you try too early . . . you'll destroy anything she has written with fire . . . too long, and she'll lose hope . . . faith . . . whatever . . . .*

Anna took a deep breath and glanced toward the woman sitting across the table—Dythya—waiting patiently for Anna to refocus her attention on the problems involved with governing Defalk itself. The accounts for the liedstadt—what passed for a national government—were her responsibility—and a general disaster. Even with the four thousand golds sent from Dumar, the treasury didn't hold really enough golds to do more than scrape by.

"How much will it cost to arm and maintain another tenscore lancers?" Anna asked.

"Almost a thousand golds for arms and mounts, and another thousand each year for wages and food," answered Dythya. "That is, if the weather is good, and food is not dear, and if there is no horse fever."

"We'll still have to spend several hundred each year for replacement arms and mounts. . . ." mused Anna. "Yet the Liedfuhr can casually send fiftyscore lancers to Neserea. That has to cost him as much as us . . . say something like five thousand golds a year or more." *That's like a quarter of your total budget . . . and you think you can build Defalk into an independent power?*

Anna massaged her forehead again before a thought struck her, and she pulled a gold coin from her belt wallet and examined it, slowly. The image struck on the coin was that of a woman, and the lettering, though worn, read "Mutter Harmonie." Anna smiled, wondering if Mansuuran coins held the legend "Vater Harmonie," except that "harmonie" was feminine. She shook her head. *Stop woolgathering . . .* "Defalk doesn't make . . . mint . . . its own coins, does it?"

"Not for generations. It's said Lord Jecks has a gold piece that was struck by the last Corian lord, and Lord Mietchel has several Suhlmorran pieces."

Anna fingered the small heavy coin for a time, then nodded, looking at the gray-haired counselor, "Dythya . . . ?"

"Yes, Lady Anna?"

"Do you know if there was ever any place in Defalk where gold was once mined?" Anna knew that no such mines existed now, but that didn't mean that there hadn't been mines at some time.

"Gold?" Dythya raised her eyebrows.

"Or silver, but gold would be better." Anna reached for the water goblet.

"There were mines near Nordland," answered the counselor slowly. "Lord Clethner would know."

Anna had to concentrate. Nordland? She shook her head. Nordland was practically in Nordwei. "Is there anywhere east of Falcor?"

"Lord Hulber of Silberfels once told Lord Jecks that his great grandsire found nuggets of gold, small ones, in the Chean, but there were no mines, not in recent memory."

Silberfels? Then Anna laughed. Silver rocks? That was what the name meant in German. Except she couldn't recall where Silberfels was. "Is that far from Mencha?"

"One, perhaps, two days' ride north of Mencha. Silberfels is a small holding, and very old. It was there even before the Corian lords ruled the north."

After a knock on the receiving-room door, Menares slipped inside, bowing, then extending a scroll toward Anna. "Lady and Regent, you have a scroll from Lady Gatrune."

"Thank you." Anna read though the missive, skipping over the compliments.

> ... As you requested, Regent and Lady, Captain Firis had discreet inquiries made. Some unknown magics have been reported in the chandlery of Farsenn, the son of Forse, and some say that his brother Giersan has constructed a strange assemblage of drums ... few would answer anyone from my lands, and this is troubling. That is why some indirection was required and why I have been so long in responding to your request. ...
>
> ... you might also be interested to know that Herene sent a messenger asking for clothing for her wards, or a skilled seamstress, and since we have several I dispatched one to Suhl.... Herene is working hard to

instruct the children, both on their letters and figures and
on other matters as well. . . . The daughter is most bright,
but Herene has some doubts about the sons. . . .

So did you. Anna reflected, then stopped as the receiving
room door opened yet again.

Jecks slipped inside and hurried toward Anna. "My lady
Anna, there is an emissary from the Liedfuhr of Mansuur—an
overcaptain of lancers with some sort of gift."

"A gift . . . more like a Trojan horse . . ?" murmured Anna.

Jecks and Dythya exchanged glances at the unfamiliar term,
but Anna didn't bother to explain.

"Have them come in, with the guards." Anna smoothed her
hair back, almost unconsciously, and stepped back onto the
dais, where she stood by the high-backed and heavy carved
chair she used to receive people on a more formal basis.

Jecks slipped from the receiving room, to return moments
later with Rickel and Blaz. The Lord High Counselor gestured
for the two to flank Anna on the dais. As the guards stepped into
place, the receiving room doors opened.

"The emissary of the Liedfuhr of Mansuur," Skent
announced.

Flanking Anna, Rickel and Blaz stiffened, easing forward
slightly as two lancers in maroon carried in a chest and set it on
the receiving-room floor before the dais. The lancers were
accompanied by Kerhor and Lejun, who watched not Anna, but
the lancers.

The two lancers withdrew, leaving the single officer in
maroon. He bowed, deeply, almost reverently. "Regent, Sorceress of Power, Lady of Mencha . . . we are here to convey a message from the Liedfuhr and to bring his greetings and best
wishes."

Anna inclined her head slightly to the lancer officer. "You are
most welcome, and I appreciate the effort you have made to
come so far."

The officer extended a scroll, but Jecks stepped forward,
took it, studied it, and then passed it to the Regent.

"How did you come here?" asked Anna as she took the scroll.

"We took one of the Liedfuhr's fastest ships to Narial, and
then rode through Dumar to Stromwer and thence to Falcor."

Anna glanced at the maroon and gold ribbons that twined the scroll. "And how long did it take?"

"More than two weeks at great speed," admitted the lancer with a smile. "Mansuus is not close to Falcor."

"I appreciate your effort. If you would wait for a moment . . ." Anna broke the seal and began to read through the scroll.

Regent of Defalk, and Sorceress of Power,
    Greetings from Mansuus and from the people of Mansuur to those of Defalk and to their most wise and puissant Regent . . .

Anna skimmed over the paragraph of flowery praise and formality, her eyes settling on the next lines.

Many have speculated about what actions may be taken by Mansuur in the days and years to come. . . . You have shown, by your actions in Dumar, that the Maitre of Sturinn is the greatest threat to all Liedwahr. You have also risked greatly for all those who wish Liedwahr's destiny to be controlled by its peoples, and not those who would chain us to traditions that are not ours. . . .

He definitely has an idea who you are. Anna's lips crinkled slightly at the blatantly veiled reference to the chains of adornment used by the Sturinnese on their women.

    . . . As Liedfuhr, I wish to assure you that Mansuur has no designs upon the lands of Defalk, nor of Dumar, now that Dumar has declared its allegiance to Defalk. To assure you that these words are written in honesty and honor and not empty, I have sent a chest to demonstrate both my gratitude for your actions in opposing the Maitre of Sturinn, and the strength of my word that no forces of Mansuur under the command of officers loyal to the Liedfuhr, will be brought against the forces of Defalk. . . .

Anna frowned at the wording, then smoothed her face and continued.

. . . I must, regretfully, inform you that Mansuur cannot be held responsible for any actions taken by the Prophet of Music of Neserea, since the Prophet has renounced any guidance from Mansuur . . . I will be dispatching shortly fiftyscore lancers to Neserea in an effort to ensure restraint by the Prophet in dealing with Defalk and to attempt to assure continuing peacefulness between Neserea and Defalk. Knowing how your powers have destroyed hundreds of scores of lancers, I trust that you will not regard these fiftyscore lancers as a reason to distrust my pledge and honor. . . .

The scroll concluded with more praise and formality, and was signed: "Konsstin, Liedfuhr of Mansuur."

As she looked up from the scroll, Anna did not look at the chest, but she could see from its size that it had to contain more than a thousand golds. *A thousand . . . and he's sending another fiftyscore lancers to Neserea?*

"We thank you, Overcaptain . . ."

"Captain Gislhem, Regent." Gislhem bowed.

". . . and we thank the Liedfuhr for his wisdom and his warm gestures. I will have a response for you to take back tomorrow, and we look forward to seeing you at dinner. I hope you will be able to tell us about your journey."

"You are most kind."

Anna glanced at Dythya. "If you would ensure that the captain is conveyed to Arms Commander Hanfor and that arrangements are made for him and his men . . . ?"

"Yes, Regent." Dythya bowed.

"And then you'd better come back. We've a lot more to do." Anna smiled crookedly. "And send in Skent, if you would."

Once the door closed, Anna looked at Jecks, then started toward the chest.

"Regent . . ." Lejun coughed.

Anna nodded and stepped back.

Lejun opened the chest lid, gingerly. His swallow was more than audible in the silence of the receiving room. A single gold coin slipped from those heaped in the chest and clanked on the stone floor.

Anna swallowed as well. *There have to be thousands of them* . . . "You can close it for now, Lejun."

The guard replaced the single missing coin and closed the chest's lid.

Anna looked at the four guards and smiled. "It looks like everyone will get paid."

The faintest trace of a smile appeared on Rickel's face. Giellum looked puzzled. Lejun and Blaz nodded, if barely.

Anna stepped off the dais and lifted the bell off the conference table, ringing it once.

"Lady Anna?" The dark-haired Skent peered into the receiving room.

"Would you find Arms Commander Hanfor and tell him that I would like to see him once he has settled his business with the Mansuuran lancers?"

"Yes, Lady Anna." Skent flashed a smile before departing and closing the door.

Anna looked at the guards, each in turn. "Thank you all. Lord Jecks and I have some things to discuss." She handed Jecks the Liedfuhr's scroll as the guards walked from the receiving room.

Jecks read the scroll, slowly.

"What do you think?" Anna asked when he had finished.

"I think that the Liedfuhr is most sincere." Jecks laughed. "Or he is most willing to spend coins on allaying your concerns."

"We'll have to use the scrying pool to see what we can over the next few days."

"That would be wise."

Anna wasn't certain what the pool would show, or if it would show anything. She'd already discovered that the Mansuuran lancers in Neserea were somewhere in eastern Neserea, but how close they were to Elioch—and Defalk—was another question. Even with the scrying pool, hard information was difficult to come by. But if they had in fact finally reached Elioch, as reported, were they there to help with an attack on Defalk—or to prevent it?

"Arms Commander Hanfor," announced Skent, his words spaced with heavy breathing.

"That was quick," said the Regent, as Hanfor entered the chamber.

"I had Undercaptain Jirsit settle Captain Gislhem and his men." Hanfor bowed, then nodded. His quick eyes flitted from Anna to Jecks to the chest.

"A gesture from the Liedfuhr," Anna explained. "Several thousand golds, it appears."

Hanfor's eyes narrowed.

The Regent glanced at Jecks. "He should read the scroll."

Jecks extended the message to the weathered senior officer.

Hanfor took longer to read the message, but finally he looked up. "I cannot say. The Liedfuhr may mean what he says, or he may wish to deceive you. Yet he could deceive with far less than such." Hanfor pointed to the brass-bound chest.

Anna cleared her throat. "But what if . . . *if* he says what he means? Why would he go to such lengths?"

"He has no great fleet, as does Sturinn, or Nordwei," mused Jecks.

"If he must fight you, lady, he would have to move his forces far from Mansuus," pointed out Hanfor. "It would take him weeks to return them, more time than it would take the Sturinnese to send a fleet to invade Mansuur."

"Is he that worried about Sturinn?" Anna wondered. "And why would the lancers he sent earlier be in Elioch if he is so worried about the Sturinnese?"

"Perhaps he tells the truth, but wishes that you act otherwise in a manner that will benefit him?" suggested Jecks. "The lancers, they are not under his command, but under his regent's command."

"That's still Nubara, and I trust him less than the Liedfuhr." Anna shook her head, then pulled out her chair at the conference table and sank into it.

"Mayhap . . ." began Hanfor slowly, ". . . you should decide what is best for Defalk first."

Far easier said than done. What will benefit Defalk? More war? She snorted. *More sorcery?* "Best?"

"Each of the Thirty-three would have an answer different from his peers. . . ." suggested Jecks.

His peers? What about "her peers"? "What if I take a few companies—tenscore—and the players, and lead Hadrenn's forces in support of the freewomen?" asked Anna, her tone almost idle.

"That would be most dangerous, my lady Anna," offered Jecks.

"More dangerous than doing nothing?"

Hanfor offered an apologetic shrug. "Perhaps not, but you have said that young lord Rabyn has placed fiftyscore lancers in Elioch. If he and the Liedfuhr know that you are in Ebra—or making your way there—then they also know that nothing will stand between them and Falcor."

"And if they take Falcor, and I return . . . then what?"

Jecks smiled wryly. "No one doubts your ability to defeat them, my lady." Jecks smiled wryly. "Many of the Thirty-three might feel that you had sacrificed their lands and crops on behalf of Ebra."

"So if I neutralize Ebra—"

"A year ago, you destroyed the Evult," Jecks replied. "Many thought that would end the threat from the east."

Does each fight lead to another? How do you stop that? "How many levies can we call up after harvest?" Anna turned to Jecks.

"If you call them all, perhaps one hundred fifty-score."

"And what if they all were assembled in Deguic? Would Rabyn attack them?"

"He can muster twice that," ventured Hanfor.

"But would he?"

"You have something in mind, my lady?"

"Well . . . I really should go tend to my own lands, in Mencha." Anna smiled. *And try something else along the way.* "Perhaps I should do that, soon, before the Mansuuran lancers reach Elioch."

Hanfor and Jecks exchanged glances, but Anna decided against explaining. *Yet . . . until you decide for certain.*

25

A nna served herself her usual heaping platter of food—three slabs of meat, plus early potatoes, as well as bread and cheese—then waited for Jecks and her guest as Dalila carried the meat platter to them.

"Are you from Mansuus, Captain Gislhem?" Anna asked.

"Ah . . . Regent . . . no. I'm from Aleatur, at the foot of the Westfels." The balding Gislhem limited himself to two slabs of the lamb.

"As you must have heard," Anna continued, "I'm not from Liedwahr, and I don't know a great deal about Mansuur. What is Aleatur like? Is it dry or hot? Or wet?"

"It's high, Regent, and it rains but infrequently. Most folk are herders, and Aleatur is the market town where they sell their sheep and goats, and they're shipped downriver from there. I couldn't see being a herder. . . ." Gislhem shrugged. "So I learned something about arms from the trade guards, and then made my way to Robur and joined the lancers there. Must have been ten years ago."

"Dry . . ." Anna nodded. "Those are like my lands." She took a sip of the amber wine sent to Falcor by Lord Gylaron of Lerona and nodded. It was much better than anything else in the cellars of Falcor, not that there was that much of anything.

"Defalk is green once more," ventured Gislhem.

"Most of Defalk is," Anna agreed pleasantly, "but I was talking about Loiseau. Those are the lands I inherited from Lord Brill."

"The Lady Anna," Jecks added, "is not only Regent, but one of the Thirty-three in her own right."

"I see." Gislhem looked puzzled.

"It's all very confusing, but a Regent—or a lord—of Defalk rules with the consent of the lords and ladies of Defalk, and there are thirty-three of them. So I only have to get agreement from the other thirty-two." Anna laughed, then asked, "Do you get back to Aleatur often?"

"No, lady. I have not been back since I left."

"It is hard to get to places when you're required to be else-where. I'm hoping to go to Loiseau in a few days, and that will be the first time in more than a year. I won't be able to stay long." She offered a crooked smile. "It's hard to be a Regent and a lady at the same time."

"I wouldn't know . . . Lady Anna. I'm happy enough being a lancer."

"Better than being a herder in Aleatur?"

"Much better," affirmed the captain.

"I don't know," mused Anna. "There are times I wish I could stay in Loiseau, but we can't always do what we like. Still, I will get to see it for a few days." She hoped she wasn't being too trans-parent, but she needed the captain to carry back the message that she was going to Loiseau to look after her lands, not because it was on the way to Ebra. She turned to Jecks. "Do you miss Elheld?"

Jecks laughed, and it was clear he understood. "Lady Anna, I often miss Elheld. But someone made me Lord High Coun-selor, and that means I must stay in Falcor more than I might wish were matters otherwise."

Anna laughed in return, then glanced at Hanfor, sitting beside Jecks. "Arms Commander, was not your story similar to Captain Gislhem's?"

"Much the same," affirmed the grizzle-bearded arms com-mander. "My father wished that I follow him. . . ."

Anna took another sip of wine and listened.

26

The single scene in the scrying pool wavered, then split into two distinct images, each half-superimposed on the other, although each clearly depicted the front of the chandlery in Pamr. One image was darker, almost sinister, the other brighter, more sunny.

Anna released the spell-image immediately, then walked to the door. "Blaz?" She peered out of the scrying-room door into the corridor.

The guard jumped, and so did Cens, the duty page.

The sorceress repressed a brief smile. She continued to forget that while she was in the room, it seemed empty to anyone looking in. So when she looked out, it appeared to the guards as though she had appeared from nowhere.

"Yes, Regent Anna?" asked Blaz.

"Actually, Cens is the one I need." Anna turned to the youngster. "Would you find Lord Jecks and ask him to join me as quickly as he can?"

Anna left the door open and walked back to the table against the wall, where she stood and lifted a goblet of water, drinking deeply before taking a solid bite out of the chunk of crusty bread that sat in the basket. She had finished the bread before Jecks appeared, following Cens.

Jecks paused outside the open door, his eyes squinting as he peered into the room.

Anna almost laughed at the quizzical expression on the face of the white-haired lord, but walked to the door and stepped into the hall. "I somehow spelled the room when I created it," she explained. "When I'm inside, no one can see anything except the room itself."

Jecks offered a wry smile. "Never will I cease to be amazed, even at the smallest of matters involving you, my lady. You summoned me?"

"Yes." Anna inclined her head toward the pool, and stepped into the room.

Jecks followed. "I can see you."

"That's because you're here with me," Anna explained. "Ever since I got the message from Lady Gatrune, I've been trying to scry the chandlery as often as I can. This is the first time when something was happening."

She picked up the lutar, checked the tuning, then chorded her own accompaniment as she sang the spell.

> Mirror, mirror, in your frame,
> Show me the chandler in his fame,
> Where'er he may stand or be,
> Show him now to me.

The pool silvered, then shivered and turned a deep black, before an image swam into place. The view of a single room in the chandlery wavered, almost to curling in on itself, except it didn't. *Darksong?*

"It looks . . . wrong," Jecks said slowly.

"Wait." As Anna watched, the view split again into two images of the interior room that contained the drummer and the chandler and two other men. The darker and more sinister image also showed the statue of a naked blonde woman, extraordinarily beautiful and lifelike. The brighter image depicted the same scene except with a crude clay figure.

Jecks swallowed. "Drums . . . the obscenity . . ."

"Darksong, I think," Anna said. *Or worse.* She sang a release couplet, and the pool returned to its blank silver state.

"Never has good come from drums," Jecks murmured.

"I think we should stop in Pamr."

"How would you deal with this chandler?" asked Jecks. "Turn him to flame like his sire?"

"You don't think that would be a good idea? Why not?"

"Did not Lady Gatrune tell you what difficulty she and Captain Firis had in obtaining any information?"

Anna nodded. "You think that this Farsenn has used Darksong like the Evult . . . to turn the town against me?"

"The men, I would guess." Jecks gestured at the pool. "Would women be ensnared by the statue of a woman?"

"I'd doubt it."

"And if this Farsenn discovers you are coming to Pamr? Would he use Darksong to raise the men of the town against your armsmen? Will you then destroy Pamr—or the men in it? Will you leave the lady Gatrune without the means to pay her liedgeld?"

Anna winced. "That wouldn't make me any better than the Evult, would it? Or Behlem? Or Sargol? But if I sent a force to bring him back to Falcor, wouldn't he just use Darksong on them?"

"I would think so. Anyone who would use drums . . ." Jecks shook his head.

Another impossible situation. If Farsenn has spelled all the men, or even most of them, and you use sorcery against Farsenn, then you destroy Lady Gatrune. If you don't, sooner or later, you'll have bigger problems.

"You do not have to decide now," Jecks pointed out. "You can do nothing until you reach Pamr. If you insist on going to Mencha . . . and onward."

"We're going. If I let others decide what happens, then I know things will be worse." Long experience had already taught her that, well before she had come to Liedwahr. Anna tried to ignore the bleakness in her own voice.

27

The sun had barely cleared the horizon when Anna entered the receiving room and sat down at the conference table and began to write. She'd awakened early, unable to sleep with all the thoughts and ideas for what she had to do running through her mind.

First, she had to finish her newsletter so that the fosterlings and pages could start making versions for each of the Thirty-three. And she needed to get Hanfor to make plans for lancers to act as couriers. She picked up the quill, then looked for the penknife to scrape the nib and sharpen it. Then she had to stir the ink, and then clean the quill again when the first attempt deposited a black blob on the brown paper. Finally, she began to write.

After a time, Anna glanced down at the rough paper that tended to soak the ink and turn her letters into fat blobs . . . but she didn't want to use parchment or the good paper for drafting the first of her scrolls to the Thirty-three. She scanned the words remaining from what she had crossed out and rewritten.

> . . . Fighting may soon take place in Ebra. As you may have heard, the Lord Bertmynn of Dolov is sending arms-men against the freewomen of the city of Elahwa. . . . Lord Hadrenn of Synek has pledged fealty to the Regency, placing himself and his lands between Defalk and Lord Bertmynn. Bertmynn is receiving golds from the Maitre of Sturinn. . . .

She slashed out part of the line and changed the wording to read "appears to be receiving."

"A newsletter sent as a scroll and written for bureaucrats," she muttered as she continued. "Don't forget the fosterlings, either."

> ... the liedburg of Falcor is now home to more than a dozen fosterlings and pages from across Defalk, who are receiving tutoring in a wide range of subjects. Some fosterlings come from as far as Abenfel, Sudwei, and Dubaria. ...

She set down the quill. What else? After a moment, she began to write again.

> ... the Regency continues to receive information from the Council of Wei ... the Liedfuhr of Mansuur has pledged that he will respect the lands of Defalk and has backed that pledge with a token gift to the Regency ... has also indicated that he will support his grandson as the new Prophet of Music of Neserea. ...

How long it had taken her, she wasn't certain, but the room had warmed considerably by the time Jecks eased through the door.

"Lord Jecks . . ."

"My lady." Jecks bowed. He wore a padded brown doublet, stained in several places, and rudely mended in others. "Lejun says that you have been here since dawn. Have you eaten?"

"I had some cheese and bread." Anna thrust the ink-spattered and much-corrected missive text at the hazel-eyed and handsome Jecks. "If you would read this . . ."

Jecks took the heavy brown paper and began to read, then looked up. "This . . . this is what you would have the fosterlings and pages copy and send to all of the Thirty-three?"

"Sort of. Each one will start off with a personal note to each lord or lady, then this part will be in the middle, and then the closing will be personal."

Jecks nodded and went back to reading. After a time, he looked up. "Perhaps . . . I would not suggest . . ."

"Go ahead," Anna replied with a smile.

"You might mention that the tribute from Dumar arrived before it was due, and that the debt to the Ranuan Exchange has been paid, so that lords might have greater freedom to borrow there."

"I'd meant to mention the Exchange debt . . . but it slipped my mind when I was writing. The coins from Dumar—that will make some happy, and have some asking to have their liedgeld reduced." She snorted and picked up the quill, absently sharpening it before dipping it into the ink. "They ought to have it increased."

"You are not considering such?"

"It's not acceptable, but the liedgeld doesn't bring in enough coins to defend Defalk, or build bridges and roads . . . or much of anything. It's fine, except if you have enemies, droughts, or problems, and from what I've seen Defalk's never been without most of those. So . . . next year, we'll inch up the liedgeld, and mine will go up more than anyone else's, and you can tell everyone that."

"Some will not be pleased. . . ." he observed.

The Thirty-three will never be pleased . . . not until Defalk returns to a time that never was, that exists only in their memories. "They may not be." She smiled. "So you should be thinking of ways to convince them that they're better off under the Regency with a higher liedgeld. For one thing, they've all held their lands—except for Lord Arkad—and that wouldn't have happened under either the Evult or Lord Behlem. Maybe . . . a reminder from the Lord High Counselor?"

"Do you still intend to go to Ebra?"

"I am only going to Mencha for certain. . . ."

"Why . . . if I might inquire? Your lands do not require attention that urgently." The hint of a smile crossed the lips of the white-haired lord.

"I have an idea, one that might help Defalk a lot." *If it works.* "And it won't put anyone in danger."

"You are not sure it will work?" Jecks raised his eyebrows.

"If it doesn't, it won't hurt anyone."

"Saving you." Jecks frowned. "Defalk needs its Regent. Do not hazard yourself."

"I'll try." Anna paused. "What do you know about Lord Hulber? Of Silberfels?"

"Less than most of the Thirty-three. The line is old, older than even the Corians, and Hulber has always paid his liedgeld and answered the calls for levies—but never offered more . . . or less. I have never met him, nor had Barjim or Donjim. Not to my knowledge."

"Hmmmm . . . what about his lands?"

"He is said to have one fertile valley on the Chean, and the rest fit for little but forage for sheep. His consort is the youngest daughter of Lord Clethner's sire, perhaps ten years younger than Clethner. You recall him?"

"Lord Clethner? I met him at Elheld before I went to Vult."

"He was impressed with you, and he may have written his sister. How close they are, I would not hazard." Jecks paused, then added, "If you will excuse me . . . this morning Himar and I are instructing both the lancers in the penal detail and the fosterlings."

"The doublet. I should have realized," Anna said. "Don't let me keep you." Then she asked, "How is Jimbob responding?"

Jecks shrugged. "He is doing as I expected."

"Not quite sullen, and going through all the motions without being overtly rebellious."

"You understand."

"Unhappily, yes."

Jecks bowed again, then turned and left the receiving room.

Jimbob—what could she do about the spoiled brat he had apparently become? Or had always been? Despite taking the punishment of a lancer penal detail, the youth wasn't listening to Jecks . . . and had clearly withdrawn more into himself.

The problem was that there really wasn't anyone else to inherit Defalk—the acceptability of everything Anna and the Regency were doing rested on the idea that she was doing it to preserve and enhance the succession. Without Jimbob, there was no succession, and without the succession . . . She didn't even want to think about the mess that would occur. *Not now.*

She took a long and slow deep breath, and set aside the draft message to the Thirty-three. Next she needed to work on the spell for mining or refining—through sorcery. She reached for another sheet of the rough paper and dipped the quill pen, ignoring the blot of ink that dropped on one corner of the brown paper even before she began to write.

After what seemed more than a glass, Anna looked at the draft spell . . . or what was the beginning of it.

> Search, search, search the ground
> deeply all around,
>
> verily, verily, verily,
> gold will here be found. . . .
>
> Bring, bring, bring the gold,
> straightly to the mold,
> verily, verily, verily. . . .

But how would she end the spell? She took a deep breath and then a sip from the goblet.

"You need a break."

Finally, she stood, and made her way out of the chamber and up the stairs to the south wing . . . and Lady Essan's chamber. Lejun and Kerhor followed her, stationing themselves outside Essan's door when Anna entered.

The white-haired woman sat erect in the sunlight falling through the window, then turned her head at Anna's presence. Anna still found it hard to believe that she was the widow of the man who had ruled Defalk before Jimbob's father.

"Lady Essan, I'm sorry. It's been longer than I'd have liked since we last talked." Anna turned the straight chair across from the ancient rocker where Essan sat, then seated herself, looking straight at the older woman.

"You are the sorceress-Regent, my dear near-daughter. . . ." Essan smiled faintly. "This be a hard land that asks much of those that rule, and most of the glasses of their lives."

"There isn't much time," Anna admitted. "It always seems that way."

"Synondra tells me that you and Lord Jecks put Barjim's brat on a punishment detail. Be it true that he spat at your Lord High Counselor?"

"Yes," Anna admitted.

"Donjim would have flayed the skin off his back, and considered that merciful."

"Jecks had him whipped."

"Good! Feared your Lord High Counselor was getting too soft on the brat." Essan squinted through the sunlight at Anna. "Know ye that young Jimbob has been talking about sending you off to Mencha once he's old enough?"

"No . . . but I can't say I'm surprised."

"Boy doesn't know what strong is . . . or what he owes you." Essan shook her head. "Enough of ungrateful young wretches. You need more like that young Skent. Proper and dutiful fellow he is . . . make him an undercaptain, you should, then a captain if he has it in him. Then when you consort him to Cataryzna . . . he'll have the experience and the reputation to hold the lands."

Anna laughed. "Is there anything that doesn't come to you?"

"Leave an old woman her secrets. 'Sides, that be so obvious that I'd have told you if you were not already minded to do so." Essan took a sip of the ever-present apple brandy. "Is there any other gossip or tidbit that this old brain of mine can offer?"

"You do know more about the past than anyone else I've met in Defalk," Anna smiled.

"That be because the hard times took all the other old folk." Essan sniffed.

"What have you heard about Lord Hulber of Silberfels?"

"There were always rumors . . . that lineage is strange . . . mountain folk from before the Corians . . ." Essan said, almost as if musing to herself.

Great . . . gnomes out of Oz burrowing under the mountains in a world where music creates magic. Anna merely nodded, waiting.

". . . been said once that the old folk were miners . . . but none have seen such . . . nor much of their lords . . ."

28

Rabyn slips into the light and airy workroom. Nubara follows. Both stand and study the three polished drums, each not quite as tall as is Rabyn. The floor has been swept spotlessly clean, and all the tools removed from the workbench and polished before having been set on the shelves adjoining the bench.

Beside each drum is a high stool, and a pair of wooden mallets is laid on the seat of each stool.

The gray-haired crafter bows. "They are finished, sire. As you requested. Exactly as you requested."

"We will be the judge of that." Rabyn barely looks at the older man as he steps around him and stops by the first drum. His fingers stroke the polished wood, now so smooth that it reflects the dark-haired Prophet's image as if the drum were a mirror.

Nubara sees his own reflection beside that of the Prophet and smiles, belatedly.

"I saw that, Nubara," Rabyn says easily.

The crafter steps back involuntarily.

"Let us see how these sound." Rabyn takes the mallets from the stool of the drum closest to the workroom door, then seats himself on the stool. He taps the stretched hide that covers the drum frame. A low rolling boom fills the workroom. He nods and slips off the stool, replacing the mallets. After repeating the process with both of the remaining drums, Rabyn returns to the second drum and reseats himself on the stool with a sly, serpentlike smile.

Nubara frowns, his eyes going from the Prophet to the crafter, who remains standing by the workbench, his head bowed.

Lifting the mallets, the young Prophet tries one rhythm, then a second. Finally, after several other attempts, he nods to himself, and a driving and thundering, rolling beat fills the workroom. Rabyn begins a chant, not exactly a song, but more than a simple refrain, with a thin tenor that is clear and rises above the thunder of the massive drum.

> Heed, heed, heed, the beating of the drum;
> break, break, break the heart whose end has
> come . . .

The crafter's eyes widen and he swallows, then drops to his knees, clutching at his chest, gasping for air.

> . . . turn, turn, the body into dust!

The rolling thunder that has filled the room dies away, and Rabyn carefully climbs down from the stool and replaces the mallets. "You will have the workbench and the woods removed, will you not, Nubara? And you *will* make sure that no one touches the drums."

"Ah . . . yes, honored Prophet." The Mansuuran officer licks his lips. "I . . . did not know you could do . . . such." He looks at the heap of dust on the workroom floor. He swallows. "Did you not promise . . . ?"

Rabyn laughs. "I promised to pay him well, and in gold. For his dislike of me, I have paid him. The golds will go to his ugly daughter, and she will be freed. So will her mother. You will tell them that he developed the bloody flux and a pox, and we had to burn his body. I promised him five golds. Give them ten . . . with great care."

"Yes, honored Prophet."

"Remember, Nubara, I am a ruler who keeps his promises." The serpentlike smile follows. "All of them." Rabyn strokes the side of the drum, lovingly. "A most wonderful drum, and *it* will do exactly as I wish."

Nubara looks down at the pale paving stones of the workroom floor, then lifts his eyes to the Prophet, meeting the younger man's glance evenly. "With drum and Darksong, best you be most careful of what you wish, Prophet."

"I always am sure of that, Nubara. Just like my mother was. Always."

29

Anna slowed as she heard voices in the side corridor leading to the receiving room. She glanced back at Lejun and Rickel. The taller blond Rickel nodded and slowed.

The Regent listened. A small high voice reached her ears—Secca's.

". . . she's not like that. She worries about everyone. You just worry about you. Lords can't do that. They have to worry about everyone."

Anna waited.

"You're too young to say things like that, Secca." The older youth's voice held a sneer. "You're being silly."

Anna wanted to slap Jimbob for the patronizing tone, but instead remained silent, waiting to see how Secca would handle the heir.

"You're like all boys. When someone's right, and you don't like it, you tell them they're silly. Or you hit them."

Anna couldn't help but grin.

"I do not," replied Jimbob.

"You would," Secca insisted. "You're afraid of Lady Anna and your grandsire."

There was silence in the corridor.

"A lot *you* know," Jimbob finally answered.

"You could be nicer. You should be if you want to be the lord like your father was."

"I'll be lord. It doesn't matter what you think."

"It matters what Lady Anna thinks, and if you don't get nicer, you'll never be lord."

"Nice people don't win battles," snapped Jimbob. "Lady Anna isn't always nice. She's killed scores and scores of people. You just see her here in Falcor. It's different in battle. All the lancers say so."

Have you become two people . . . nice when it suits you and ruthless the rest of the time? Anna frowned. *If you wanted to survive, did you have any choice?*

"She's only nasty when people like you make her that way! I don't have to talk to you." The sound of small footsteps headed toward the corner.

Anna waited and let Secca run almost into her. "Secca! Where are you going in such a hurry?"

Secca stopped, and looked up. Her eyes were bright, but not tearing. "Lady Anna." She bowed. "I have to get my scrolls for figures. Dythya said we had to bring them every day."

Anna smiled. "Don't let Jimbob get to you. He's having trouble understanding that just because he's the heir doesn't mean that the rules are any different for him."

"He said . . . you weren't always nice."

Anna looked straight into the redhead's amber eyes. "Sometimes, I've had to do things that weren't what I wanted. You will, too. We all do the best we can. When you can do something better—or nicer—and you don't, that's when you get in trouble." *Like you have . . .*

Secca smiled shyly, then bowed again. "I should go, Lady Anna."

Anna watched as the redhead scurried down the corridor. Then she turned and headed toward the staircase. The receiving room was empty when she reached it, except for another pair of guards, Kerhor and Blaz—and the dark-haired Skent, who waited as the duty page.

"Skent? Would you see if Lord Jecks and Arms Commander Hanfor could meet with me shortly?"

"Yes, Lady Anna."

Once inside her de facto office, Anna sorted through the scrolls that represented what she needed to do, beginning with the last draft of her proposed "newsletter" scroll. After reading it and nodding, she set it aside for the copying she had to set up by the fosterlings. *Before you go off anywhere.*

Her thoughts drifted to young Farsenn and his drums, and she shook her head before she finally picked the scroll that held the summary of accounts. She scanned Dythya's latest summary—not so bad as previously, not with the three thousand golds from the Liedfuhr and the four thousand from Dumar. *Almost enough to do what you'd planned . . .* Except that there were more needs—like forage for the grasslands people, or what seemed like the tenth petition for lower taxes on the merchants of Falcor, and the fifth for lower tariffs on the rivermen.

Then . . . she needed to do something about Secca's mother, the lady Anientta, who had probably poisoned her consort . . . and about the succession in Fussen . . . or did she? *You're becoming like all those bureaucrats on Earth . . . stalling because any decision is worse than none.*

She took a deep breath and reached for the water pitcher. After filling her goblet and taking a deep swallow, she sharpened the quill and began to add to the list of tasks that she needed to address.

Anna was still adding to that list when Jecks and Hanfor arrived. She set aside the quill and waited until the two men were seated across the conference table from her. "I'm thinking of taking tenscore armsmen and going to Mencha . . . and if nothing happens while I'm there, going on into Ebra."

Hanfor nodded slowly. "You remain worried about the Sturinnese?"

"I'm worried about someone like Bertmynn, who'll accept Sturinnese coins." *And having to pick up the pieces later, at a higher cost.*

"What have you seen in your pool?" Jecks asked.

"Bertmynn is about to head downriver toward Elahwa, if he hasn't already. It looks like he wants to take over the city and port there."

"Would it not be wiser to wait . . . to see the results in Ebra?" questioned Hanfor. "Or do you wish to call a hundredscore levies now?"

Anna shook her head. "I don't think so. Calling the levies before Rabyn does anything will only reduce their useful time of service. We can't wait on Ebra, either. Dolov wasn't affected by my sorcery against the Evult. Synek was more than half-destroyed, and Elahwa was partly destroyed. The freewomen are trying to do something in Elahwa, and Bertmynn's against that. I'd like to stop him, or if I'm too late, attack him before he gets more arms and armsmen from Sturinn."

"You cannot defend all of Liedwahr," Hanfor said slowly.

It does sound like that's what you're trying to do, doesn't it? Anna paused, then reached for the goblet. It was empty.

Jecks refilled it from the pitcher, then looked at Hanfor. The grizzled veteran nodded, and Jecks filled all three goblets.

"Let us say you are successful," Hanfor finally continued after a swallow from the goblet before him. "You destroy Lord Bertmynn. You are two weeks or more at a hard ride from Falcor. If the Nesereans attack? What would you have me do without levies?"

"I think we should call up some levies, preferably enough to make up a force for you to train . . . perhaps somewhere near Dubaria or Denguic. Not too many, though."

"And?"

"If we do so, then . . ." Anna paused, thinking, before concluding, "then Rabyn will have to move more armsmen to Elioch or the West Pass, and that will take time."

"You still may not return that quickly," Jecks pointed out. "What would you have your arms commander do if the Nesereans do cross into Defalk?"

"Defend Defalk." Hanfor offered a half smile. "Preferably with some effect."

"If you can manage it, Hanfor, have Rabyn attack Fussen," Anna said dryly. "And put Lord Ustal in charge of an attack on their center . . . or wherever. If that doesn't work, try to slow them down without losing too many levies. Give up territory rather than men. We can get the territory back, but not the armsmen."

Jecks laughed. "That will not make your western lords pleased."

Nothing will please them except the world not changing. "It may not come to that." *Except it will, because most men in Liedwahr instinctively believe that over time no woman can keep defeating men.*

"I think I will draw up plans for a retreat through Fussen." Hanfor's lips quirked. "I doubt not that you will succeed in Ebra, but success takes time."

"I leave the details to you," Anna acknowledged, turning her eyes to Jecks. "Lord Jecks, in the next day or so, you and Hanfor should discuss which levies to call up . . . and how many. Then I'll draft the scrolls."

Both men nodded.

"Oh . . . and I think I'd like some of the lancers who can handle bows to come with me."

"That would be best, lady," Hanfor said with a grin. "Most can only get the shafts into the air and pointed in the direction of the enemy without you and your spells."

Anna was afraid that still might have been the case.

"Do you wish me to accompany you in Mencha . . . and beyond?" asked Jecks.

"I had thought of it," Anna replied. "I also thought that we might bring Lord Jimbob along."

Hanfor nodded. "Words mean little to him."

"His father had trouble with them as well," Jecks answered dryly. "The peach falls not far from the tree, alas."

Anna frowned. "What about bringing one of the older students, too?"

"You would not wish Hoede, and Skent went to Fussen. There are no other fosterlings, only pages."

Anna ignored Jecks' unconscious chauvinism. "What about Kinor? Liende's son? I think they all need to see what Defalk faces."

"Best you ask your chief player," Jecks suggested.

"I will. If she's reluctant, we can bring Resor." Anna took a sip of water. "Oh . . . what do you think about making Skent an undercaptain? And bringing him?"

Jecks frowned.

Hanfor nodded slowly. "I would have him work with Jirsit, beginning this day. He has the sense, and you have need that he become experienced in arms and battle."

Abruptly, Jecks smiled. "I will work with him, as well. But he should not sit with you at table until after he proves himself."

"You mean, wherever we go?"

Jecks nodded.

"If you two would tell Skent, and let him know that this is an opportunity for him?"

"Best I do this," said Hanfor.

"We'll also need some wagons and some armsmen to leave at Mencha . . . another score or so. I'll explain later." Anna smiled. "We may have some . . . goods to bring back to Falcor."

"Derived through sorcery?" asked Hanfor.

"Or battle," suggested Anna. She looked down at the list before her—the long list. "Now . . . you know Lord Vyarl, Lord Jecks . . . how many coins should we send him to buy forage . . . ?"

She didn't want to think about all the other problems they needed to address before she dared leave for Mencha, like sending a message to summon Halde to Falcor once she returned. *That's assuming you return.* Or reworking the accounts with Dythya . . . or preparing the levy notices for Hanfor or making sure that her de facto postal system was launched . . . or . . . the list seemed endless.

30

The midafternoon, preharvest sun warmed the back of Anna's vest as the column neared the western bank of the Chean River. Several of the old oaks flanking the road were bare-leaved—dead—or graced with yellow leaves well before fall's turn. The air was so still that the afternoon seemed as hot as midsummer.

"River's running higher than in years," Jecks observed to Anna, before turning in the saddle to glance at Jimbob and Kinor—two redheads riding abreast before the second set of Anna's guards and before the players.

Behind the players rode the majority of lancers, ninescore or so. Somewhere back in the dust rode a new and determined undercaptain, Skent. The other score of lancers served as the vanguard and had already crossed the ancient stone bridge that lay slightly more than a hundred yards ahead of Anna.

"That's good." Anna patted Farinelli, then glanced at the bridge ahead, leading over the Chean and then into Pamr. "Maybe it will help some of the trees."

"For those, it's too late. It will be years before the forests begin to grow back."

Farinelli's hoofs clicked on the stones of the bridge. Anna glanced down at the brownish blue water, swirling past and through the brush that had grown up during the dry years of the Evult's drought.

". . . always talking about the drought . . ." Jimbob's voice was barely audible.

"Wasn't it that bad in Falcor? We lived in Mencha," Kinor replied, "and some days when the wind blew, you couldn't even see the fields for the dust. Once Lord Brill had to use sorcery to move big piles of dust out of his keep, and half the trees in his apple orchard died, even with the sorcery he used to bring water to them."

Anna smiled. Perhaps bringing Kinor would have advantages beyond those she and Jecks had discussed. She pulled off her floppy hat for a moment to try to let her short hair dry from the sweat beneath, then replaced it.

". . . never really saw much outside of Falcor . . . my sire . . . mother . . . were gone . . . more than they were there in the last years . . ."

"I suppose they didn't have much choice," offered Kinor. "The lady Anna doesn't seem to. There's always a problem somewhere."

Jimbob's reply was inaudible.

As Anna realized she was nearing Pamr—and the chandler who used Darksong—she twisted in the saddle and reached for the lutar, half-wrestling, half-easing it from the leather case. She fumbled to tune the instrument, and began a vocalise, "Holly-lolly-pop. . . ."

"Arms ready!" snapped Jecks and Himar almost simultaneously.

The hazel-eyed lord's blade was clear of his scabbard before he finished the command.

Anna could sense that both Jimbob and Kinor had drawn steel as well, but she hoped neither would have to use a blade. As she tried to clear her throat and cords, Anna surveyed the houses that led toward the crossroads in the middle of Pamr, her eyes shifting from one to the next as the blond gelding carried her eastward. At the fourth or fifth house, she thought she saw a woman's face, but the shutters closed quickly.

Pamr was still, the streets empty, too empty for a midweek afternoon. *Again.* The only sounds were those of the lancers' murmuring, mounts breathing, and hoofs striking the dusty clay of the street.

She let the second vocalise die away, and holding the lutar ready, continued to survey the dwellings and buildings on both sides of the street.

At the creak of a door the Regent turned in the saddle toward the inn—The Green Bull—but the shaded porch remained empty. Her eyes went to the chandlery across the street.

The bearded brown-haired man—the drummer Anna had seen in the scrying pool—glanced at the column of riders, then darted back inside the building, closing the door with a *thud*.

"Not good," Anna murmured. "Listen for drums . . ."

"Drums?" Jecks' face clouded. "Vile things."

Despite the ominous silence and the vanishing drummer, the column passed through the center of town and out along the north road without encountering anyone and anything—except a stray black dog that slunk away behind a browning hedgerow on the north side of Pamr.

Anna frowned as Pamr dropped behind her. She would have liked to do something about the young chandler—but what? She didn't really even have any proof that he was using Darksong—only her own visions in a scrying pond, and she had more than enough problems in Defalk without imprisoning or killing someone who hadn't actually done anything.

Still . . . Anna did not relax her guard until she reined up in the open area below Lady Gatrune's mansion—or keep, where the black-bearded captain Firis stood with a smile.

"Welcome, Lady Anna." Firis bowed. "Your presence is always welcome." He turned toward Jecks. "And yours, Lord Jecks."

Anna gestured toward the two redheads. "Captain Firis, this is Lord Jimbob, and Kinor, one of my students in Falcor." Student was as good a term as any, since Kinor was neither fosterling nor page. "And you remember Overcaptain Himar and my chief player Liende."

"Greetings and welcome," Firis responded. "Lady Gatrune awaits you . . . once you take care of that beast."

Farinelli tossed his head, if gently, as though to suggest to Anna that he needed to be brushed and fed.

"Yes, I know." Anna patted the gelding's neck, then dismounted. She looked at Jimbob and Kinor, then Liende. "Once we have the mounts stabled, we'll go up to the main house together." As she finished, she caught a glimpse of Skent leading his company toward the rear stable area.

Her words brought nods, and she turned and began to follow Firis toward the stable. Behind her came Rickel and Lejun.

Once at the stable, Lejun took both guards' mounts, while Rickel remained within a few steps, his hand on the hilt of his blade as Anna led Farinelli into the large stall clearly reserved for the big gelding.

Firis stood for a moment at the end of the stall as Anna loosened the girths, and then swung the saddle onto the rack above the stall wall.

"You still amaze me, lady."

"Why? Because I take care of Farinelli?" She slipped off the blanket and found the brush.

Firis laughed. "That . . . and many other things."

"Pamr seemed . . . quiet. . . . What have you heard?"

Firis' smile died away. "It is far too quiet, my lady. No one in the town talks to us, any of us, except when they must." He shrugged. "Yet . . . one cannot punish folk for silence."

"Is anyone forging arms or anything?" Anna patted the gelding and began to brush out the dust and road dirt. "Easy, there, fellow."

"We have seen nothing. We have heard nothing. More of the men's consorts have come here to live. Few live in town any longer."

As she continued to groom Farinelli, Anna pursed her lips, silently pondering the situation in Pamr. *Should you have done something? What?*

Firis stepped back. "Best I see that quartering is going well."

Anna smiled and nodded. As Firis stepped away, from farther inside the stable, Anna heard some murmurs.

". . . doesn't even bring a lancer to groom her mount . . ."

". . . you want someone to groom your mount?" Kinor's voice was loud enough for Anna to identify.

"Not . . . seemly . . ."

"It's more than seemly," answered Jecks, not quite sharply. "And it is effective, Lord Jimbob. Your sire and your mother groomed their own mounts as well. When rulers do such, then lancers and others do not complain and are more willing to heed orders."

Anna nodded, wondering how long—if ever—it would be before Jimbob understood the power of example. *And the finer points in using guilt?* She laughed to herself. Not all people could be guilt-tripped, especially not all men.

Rickel and Lejun returned, and Rickel picked up the cased mirror, and Lejun Anna's saddlebags.

"Are you ready, my lady?" Jecks appeared at the end of Farinelli's stall as Anna stepped away, carrying her lutar.

"More than ready. I'm hungry and filthy."

Lejun and Rickel flanked Anna and Jecks as they left the stables. Kinor and Jimbob—and Liende and Himor—followed the four, if several paces back. Again, Anna felt as though she led a parade of sorts.

"Young Captain Firis . . . is somewhat . . ." Jecks shook his head.

"Familiar?" Anna grinned. "Why . . . Lord Jecks . . . you sound almost jealous."

"Me?"

Despite Jecks' denial, Anna could see the flush under the tanned skin of the older lord. She touched his arm gently. "If I should choose to be . . . familiar . . . with anyone . . . it would not be Firis. He's far more like a fresh younger brother who sometimes needs a scolding."

"My lady . . . I did not . . ."

Anna squeezed his shoulder again. "You don't need to apologize." She smiled. "Your . . . I'm glad you care." Her boots clicked on the stones of the lower outer landing leading to the steps up to the house. She glanced up to see Lady Gatrune and several others standing under the portico, waiting. "Ready for more pleasantries, Lord High Counselor?"

Jecks squared his shoulders. "A quiet dinner with you, even with piles of scrolls, would be more to my taste."

"Mine, too . . . but that's not in the cards."

Again, as a puzzled expression flitted across Jecks' face, Anna was reminded of how idioms didn't translate, even in similar languages. *Like George Bernard Shaw or whoever it was that said the Americans and British were divided by a common language.*

"Regent, Lord Jecks." A broad smile crossed the face of Lady Gatrune, whose blonde-and-white hair was drawn back into a bun of sorts, and bound with silver-and-purple cords. "You remember my son Kyrun?"

Kyrun retained the short blond hair Anna vaguely remembered, and the cowlick she clearly recalled. "Lady Regent, Lord Jecks." He bowed, then straightened.

"Lady Gatrune, Kyrun," Anna inclined her head to the taller Gatrune, then to her son.

Jecks repeated the salutations.

"We are glad to see you, but will not trouble you until you are refreshed and we can talk at dinner." Gatrune offered another smile.

"Thank you. It's always good to be here," answered Anna. "I don't know if you knew, but Lord Jecks is also now Lord High Counselor."

"Defalk could scarcely do better," replied the rangy lady. "My brother speaks highly of you, Lord Jecks, and he seldom speaks highly of anyone."

Anna half-turned, gesturing to those who followed. "Lord Jimbob, Kinor, my chief of players, Liende, and Overcaptain Himar."

"I am pleased to welcome you all to Pamr," Gatrune said. "We will settle you in your rooms, first."

After following Gatrune down one corridor and up a set of wide stairs and down a second corridor, Anna found herself in the largest guest suite, one with an oversize and netted four poster bed and a separate bathing chamber—with the tub already filled. Jecks had the adjoining chamber on one side, and Jimbob on the other. *I suppose Jimbob will be irked that he doesn't have the chamber of honor, too.*

Careful . . . he might not be thinking that at all. Right . . . Anna glanced at the bolt on the dark-stained oak door, then set the lutar on the bench at the foot of the bed, beside the mirror and the saddlebags.

While she bathed, Anna sang a set of vocalises to warm up her voice. Then, after dressing in the single all-purpose green gown she carried everywhere, Anna took out the lutar and tuned it. Setting it aside, she went to the door of the second-floor guest chamber and opened it.

"Kerhor . . . if you would, could you see if someone could find Lord Jecks for me?"

"Yes, Lady Anna."

Anna walked back into the chamber and extracted the lutar, running her fingers over the wood so carefully crafted by young Daffyd. She shook her head. Poor Daffyd. All he'd wanted was revenge for his father's death, and yet he'd changed all Defalk by summoning Anna, and never lived to see all the changes.

"Lady Anna?" Jecks' voice followed the *thump* on her door.

"Come in." Anna laid the lutar on the bench and uncased the traveling mirror, propping it up on the straight-backed chair before reclaiming the lutar.

"You summoned me?" Jecks wore the blue tunic and white shirt beneath, the outfit in which he appeared so handsome.

"I didn't summon you." Anna smiled. "I hoped you'd be free. I didn't like the way Pamr felt this afternoon." She took out the lutar and began to tune it. "I wanted you to watch the mirror with me."

Jecks nodded. "You continue to fret about the chandler."

"There's a lot to fret about." Anna finished tuning the instrument and turned to face the mirror, clearing her throat before starting the spell.

> Mirror, mirror, now let us see,
> young Farsenn as he may be,
> within the chandlery. . . .

The mirror remained blank.

"He's not in the chandlery, then."

"Can you see that chamber?" asked Jecks.

"I'll need to change the spell for that." Anna thought, then strummed the lutar and sang.

> Mirror, mirror, now let us see,
> the chandlery's place of sorcery,
> where Farsenn and the drums did bring. . . .

The back room of the chandlery was empty. Even the clay statue had vanished, as had the set of drums.

"They're afraid of you," Jecks said.

"Not afraid enough," Anna replied. "They took everything, and that means that they're still planning something." She lifted the lutar once more.

> Mirror, mirror, let us now see
> Farsenn the chandler where he may be.
> Show the image bright and clear. . . .

Farsenn appeared, along with his brother, in a cellar of some sort, with the clay statue set in a dim corner. The two men appeared to be arguing, with strong gestures.

Anna and Jecks watched, but the argument continued, and Anna sang a release couplet. Then she tried three other spells, to see if she could locate the pair. The first image revealed a square house set on a dusty road. Anna sighed. They'd passed dozens of dwellings virtually identical.

The second image showed farmlands and the Chean River, but the location could have been anywhere in a hundred deks to either side of Pamr. The third image was blank.

Anna swayed.

Jecks caught her, and eased her into the chair that did not hold the mirror. "You can do no more."

Anna sat quietly for a moment, then leaned forward and laid the lutar on the bench at the foot of the bed. "Now . . . what do I do? I can't think of any better way to find him, and he can wait longer than we can."

"He cannot believe he can stand against you, not if he fled so precipitously," Jecks pointed out. "Best you deal with your task at Mencha and then determine what you must do."

"You're not excited about going into Ebra, are you?"

"No, my lady, but I was not eager to enter Dumar, or for you to attack Vult, either." Jecks laughed sardonically. "You managed well despite my fears."

"I only made it through Dumar because of you," she pointed out, finally standing. "We need to eat, and I shouldn't keep everyone waiting any longer."

The two walked down the corridor, Rickel following, Kerhor remaining to guard her chamber.

Lady Gatrune stood at the door to the long hall on the second level. Beside her in the hallway waited Jimbob, Kinor, Kyrun, Firis, Liende, and Himar, as well as two men and a woman who were unfamiliar to Anna.

The Lady of Pamr extended an arm toward the three strangers. "Lady Anna, might I present Lord Kysar's younger sister Je'elasia and her consort Dvoyal, and Dvoyal's brother Zybar? They are returning to Arien."

"I'm so pleased to meet you." Anna smiled. *Are they related to Anientta, Secca's mother? With Anientta's father the lord of Arien, that would be just your luck.*

"And we you, Lady Anna," replied Dvoyal smoothly, so smoothly that Anna felt her guard rising.

"Indeed," added Je'elasia.

"I apologize for delaying supper." Anna felt herself flushing as she inclined her head to Gatrune. "There was a pressing matter . . . involving . . ." She shook her head. "I'll explain after everyone gets a chance to eat."

"Then let us eat." Lady Gatrune nodded toward Anna.

Anna led the way into the dining hall, and, once more, Anna found herself at the head of the table, with Gatrune on her right, and Jecks on her left. Jimbob sat beside Gatrune, and Je'elasia beside Jecks. Zybar sat beside Jimbob, and Dvoyal beside his consort. Then came Kyrun, Liende, Himar, Firis, and Kinor. Anna almost felt sorry for the redheaded student at the bottom of the table, except that he was across from Firis, who was always animated.

The dinner was simple—a heavy lamb stew laden with potatoes and vegetables, accompanied by dark rye bread. Anna took her normal huge helping, ignoring the glances from Dvoyal and Zybar.

Gatrune poured an amber wine into Anna's goblet, and then Jecks', before passing the pitcher down the table. Once the wine had reached Kinor, the Lady of Pamr lifted her goblet, "To the Regent, and a good dinner."

"To the Regent."

Anna, feeling slightly light-headed, ate several mouthfuls of stew before stopping and looking at Gatrune, and speaking to the lady, directly and softly, under the louder voices from the lower end of the table. "I mentioned . . . sorcerous work. You remember the chandler? He and his brother fled the town after we rode through. He's been working Darksong, and one of the reasons why we came to Pamr was to look into what he was doing . . . except he's disappeared."

"You cannot scry him with your sorcery?" murmured Gatrune.

"I can, but all the mirror shows is a simple house like dozens of others. I'll try more later. . . ." Anna shrugged apologetically. "He is working Darksong. I'd have Firis strengthen your walls and gates."

Gatrune nodded. "I will talk to him."

Anna lifted her voice toward the three from Arien. "Perhaps you could tell me something about Arien. I haven't had the chance to visit there."

Dvoyal and Zybar exchanged glances before Dvoyal, who appeared to be the older sibling, replied, "Arien lies in the most fertile valley to the west and north of where the Ostfels turn west toward Synope. Lord Tybel has worked long and hard to ensure that peace and prosperity are the lot of the people of Arien."

"Are you related to Lord Tybel?" asked Anna with what she hoped was apparent ingenuousness. "Forgive my ignorance, but, as you must know, I do not come from Liedwahr."

"Lord Tybel is our uncle."

"Oh . . . so your mother or father is related to Lady Anientta of Flossbend."

"Anientta is our father's younger sister."

Anna nodded politely. "And your father is?"

"Beltyr," replied Zybar.

"It sounds as though your father and Lord Tybel are close."

"Indeed they are, as brothers should be," emphasized Dvoyal.

Tybel's requests to consolidate his holdings with those of Anientta made a great deal more sense. "Brothers should be close and respect each other. They do not, always, unfortunately, even in Defalk."

Dvoyal frowned, almost quizzically, while Zybar looked as though he were about to nod before catching himself.

Interesting difference between the brothers. "You two are brothers, but do you always agree?" asked Anna.

"Family must always agree," answered Dvoyal smoothly, but quickly. "If we do not, there will always be others who would put us at each other."

Zybar gave a slightly ironic smile that vanished quickly.

"I don't know that outsiders are always the problem. I've already been requested to deal with problems involving brothers and their inheritances." Anna smiled faintly. "So it's good to hear that your father and Lord Tybel get along well. Who might be Lord Tybel's heirs? You might know that if they're younger, I'd be pleased to invite them to Falcor."

"He has two sons," answered Dvoyal. "Altyr is near-on thirty, but Reralt is but fourteen."

"Well . . . there are a number of fosterlings at Falcor, and your uncle might well consider the possibility." Anna smiled, then pitched her voice toward young Kyrun, who was trying to squelch a yawn. "Kyrun . . . would you like to come to Falcor when you're older? If your mother approves, of course."

Kyrun offered a wide-eyed look, as if to say that he'd never considered the matter.

Anna laughed gently. "You have a few years to think about it."

"You are headed . . . if I might inquire?" asked Lady Gatrune.

"To Loiseau . . . my holding at Mencha," Anna replied. "I haven't been able to get there in more than a year, and I'm afraid there's more to be done than I'll have time to accomplish."

"Your holding?" asked Zybar.

"Mine." Anna smiled, feeling her face would drop off from all the semifalse smiles she had already offered. "I received it from Lord Brill . . . in a manner of speaking, after his death. . . ." Anna went on to recount how she had gained the lands and the keep of Loiseau, careful to keep eating between fragments of the story, knowing she would need the food and the energy in the days to come.

31

As the sun cleared the eastern horizon, Anna stood on the portico steps and turned a last time to Lady Gatrune. "Please keep an eye out for the chandler."

"You have warned us, and Captain Firis will ensure we are well kept, lady. You must take care of your own lands." The rangy white-and-blonde-haired lady smiled. "And whatever else is needful for Defalk and the Regency." Her eyebrows lifted. "I will not pry, but knowing you, you would not have come all this way with so many lancers merely to set your lands in order. Few others would know, and I will not speak of it, but be there anything we can offer . . ."

"The provisions and the food and shelter and company were all very welcome." Anna returned Gatrune's smile warmly. "What means the most to me is your friendship from the beginning, when no one knew who I was."

"That you have continued to accord us that friendship, after many more glorious in Defalk have sought you . . . that, Lady Anna, is why you are Regent, and why we always look to your visits." Gatrune inclined her head. "May your journey prove fruitful."

"Thank you. Thank you very much." Anna leaned forward and lifted the cased lutar, then turned and walked down the paved way toward the stables. Jimbob, Kinor, and Jecks had already said their farewells and were down readying their mounts.

Firis stood by Farinelli's stall as Anna entered the stable, followed as always by her guards, this time Rickel and Blaz. "Good day, Lady Regent."

"Good day," Anna replied, despite feeling slightly queasy. Early rising had always done that to her, and being on Erde hadn't changed that. She slipped into the stall and patted the gelding, then slipped the blanket in place, followed by the saddle.

Farinelli *whuff*ed.

"There are rumors, Lady Anna . . . that you might stray east of Mencha." Firis looked at Anna as she stood beside Farinelli. "I would that some of our armsmen—and I—might serve you again."

"Rumors are only rumors, Captain Firis." Anna smiled, looking straight at the dark-haired Firis. "I would like to take some of your armsmen, and you, Firis, but they might be needed here."

"Here?"

Anna nodded. "I have told Lady Gatrune. The chandler Farsenn has been trying Darksong, and I do not think he will be friendly to any lord or lady. My sorcery cannot locate him, and the needs of Defalk mean that I cannot remain here. Farsenn has been using Darksong to convert men to follow him. If you weakened your force to strengthen mine . . ."

"A chandler?" Firis laughed.

Anna smiled gently. "Once, Firis, I was only a teacher."

The dark-haired captain's face sobered. "From any but you, Lady Anna, I would still laugh. When you say such, my soul chills. . . ."

"You have a task, Firis. It may not be glorious, but it remains solid and important." She bent to fasten the girths.

Firis laughed. "You would protect me from my own nature, yet again."

"I just want you to protect Lady Gatrune." Anna took the saddlebags from Blaz and eased them up in place behind the saddle, tying the leather thongs quickly, but firmly. Then came the mirror and lutar, heavier by far than the few garments she carried.

"I hear, and I will do so. Even with my life." After a moment, Firis added, "Not that I do not worry about your adventures."

"You can worry. Just keep Gatrune and the hold safe." Anna checked the bridle.

After leading Farinelli out to join Jecks and the others—already horsed—Anna mounted and offered a wave that she hoped would do for a salute and farewell before guiding Farinelli to the head of the column.

"I worry about leaving them without dealing with the chandler," she finally murmured to Jecks as they approached the gate.

"You worry too much, my lady," offered Jecks. "You have frightened off the chandler, and you have warned the lady and her captain. As you said, you cannot be everywhere, and you have determined that the eastern borders must be secured."

"I brood. You know that, my lord Jecks." *And you know that jobs left undone are always worse when they have to be done later or redone. Yet a relatively new Regent cannot kill even a chandler—if you could locate him—merely for suspicion of Darksong—not without creating even more unrest among the lords of the Thirty-three.*

Anna squinted into the sun, wondering what she would find at Loiseau, hoping the mess would not be too great, and that the staff had managed to keep things in some semblance of order. As they passed beyond the gate, she inclined her head to Meris, the armsman who had first eased her way into seeing Lady Gatrune and whom she'd failed to recognize a year later. "Take care, Meris."

"You, too, Lady Anna." The older man smiled.

Anna glanced back at the house on the rise, hoping that she wasn't making too much of a mistake in leaving Pamr. *Yet what can you do? You don't know Defalk well enough to find the chandler, and you can't be away from Falcor too long, or Rabyn will have armsmen running from the West Pass all the way to Falcor. You're standing before two doors, and they both say "damned."*

With a sigh, she pulled her floppy hat forward on her head to try to shield her eyes from the morning sun.

32

OUTSIDE OF PAMR, DEFALK

Outside the small cot, the road is empty, and the dust of the riders has settled, long settled, before the dark-bearded man goes to the window and opens the shutters just enough to peer between them. "She has departed . . . and left no armsmen behind to bother us."

"They did not bother us. They did not seek us or leave lancers," says Giersan. "Why would they?"

"The sorceress has sought me in her glass. I have sensed that. Lady Gatrune's lackeys have inquired after us, but they did not find us." The dark-haired Farsenn nods, almost to himself as he steps back. "We have much to do . . . now."

Giersan stares at Farsenn, almost disgustedly. "Why did we run this time? What excuse will you offer?"

"I was not prepared. Nor were you."

"When will you be prepared, O great master of Darksong?" Giersan snorts, rudely. "You have promised and promised. I had thought I was the cautious one. She would have seen nothing. One would think you were a mouse and not a sorcerer."

"She had the lutar in her hand, and it was broad daylight," counters Farsenn.

"She could come in daylight next time, or the time after."

"She rides eastward. She must ride back through Pamr to Falcor. My brother, we will ensure that it matters not whether she comes in darkness or in full light. I have a plan. When she returns, then we will be prepared . . . more than prepared."

Giersan raises his eyebrows, but says nothing.

33

After three long days of travel from Pamr, dust coated the lower legs of both riders and mounts, and Anna had gone through three of her four daily water bottles by the time the bluish-tinged, off-white walls of Loiseau appeared on the eastern horizon above the low houses of Mencha. Even as Anna watched, the low sun at her back began to turn the stone parapets the sorcerer Brill had once raised with his skills from blue-white to a rosy twilit color that spread above the late-afternoon shadows.

Although almost a year had passed since Anna had returned the rains to Defalk, the road into Mencha remained as dusty as Anna had recalled it when she had first ridden Farinelli around Loiseau.

"Break out the banner!" Himar ordered. "Even up the column! Undercaptain Skent . . . bring up your laggards!"

"Smerda, Bius . . . move it up!"

Anna smiled at the tone of firmness in Skent's voice. Perhaps she had kept him as a page too long. *For his sake, probably . . . but he's young. Then . . . everyone does things young here.* She straightened herself in her saddle, recalling that she was the Lady of Mencha.

Small as Mencha was, more than a score of people watched, most smiling, some even waving, as Anna rode through the dusty streets toward Loiseau. Their words were open, not at all hushed.

"See . . . did come back . . . and there's the banner, sure as you can see . . ."

"Just a visit, Armal . . ."

"When . . . ever have a ruler of Defalk from Mencha . . . I ask you?"

"Rightly . . . is she ours?"

"Whose else? First place she came . . . almost like being born . . . stop asking foolish questions, Vernot . . ."

"Regent-sorceress?"

Anna turned toward the girl who called, a stocky brunette not even as old as Secca, and smiled.

"Thank you for the rains."

"You're welcome. Take care of yourself," Anna called back, not quite sure what to say, but not wanting to appear too aloof.

"You are truly theirs," murmured Jecks.

"I don't know why," she replied in a low voice.

"Because you changed little, perhaps," he speculated. "Perhaps because few return who have gained fame and position, and you have . . ."

Whatever the reasons, the sorceress enjoyed the short ride through the center of Mencha, perhaps more than any ride since she'd come to Liedwahr, especially after the experience in Pamr. Just past the store that was half-chandlery, half–dry goods, in the center of the small town, Anna turned Farinelli south toward the hill on which Loiseau rested.

A dek out of town, they neared the apple orchard where she had been ambushed by the Dark Monks. The trees had more leaves than in previous years, and apples filled the branches, most of the fruit already turned red. Large patches of grass dotted the space beneath the trees, and the hum of insects filled the air.

"The orchard looks better. It was close to dying," she told Jecks. *So were you, on that day, then, even if you didn't know it.* She patted the gelding on the neck, recalling how he had carried her back to Loiseau with a war arrow through her upper chest and shoulder.

As Farinelli started up the sloping road toward the walled hold, Anna's eyes turned toward the low-domed building on the lower ridge where she had learned how to turn earthly singing into Erdean sorcery—and first struggled through Brill's books on sorcery. Not a single hoofprint stood out in the dust of the lane from the main road to the silent dome.

The road was steep enough that even the big gelding was breathing more heavily by the time his hoofs rang on the paving stones that led to the open gates of Loiseau.

"... don't understand ... they waved to her ... I'm the heir ..." Jimbob's plaintive comment to Kinor was barely audible.

"It may be because she is *their* lady. Or it might be that you haven't risked your life for them," suggested Kinor dryly, with a wit that Anna hadn't suspected of the lanky redhead. "People do remember little things like that, once in a while."

"You were born here. . . ."

"So I was told," answered Kinor. "I don't remember." He laughed gently.

Jecks glanced at Anna and caught her eye. "Mayhap we should keep young Kinor around Lord Jimbob," he murmured as he leaned toward her.

"Only until Jimbob is of age," Anna replied wryly. "Besides, Kinor might make a good captain—or consort for a hold without sons . . . or both."

Jecks laughed.

Blaz and Kerhor rode into the courtyard first, and Anna could hear voices before she passed the gates.

"The Regent's here!"

"There's the banner!"

"Where is she?"

"There's Liende, and her boy Kinor."

The figures by the doors were few, but Anna recognized all seven—all those she'd actually met when she'd first come to Loiseau: Serna—the white-haired cook and head of household—and her diminutive dark-haired daughter Florenda; Albero, the armorer, who had taught Anna the little she knew about using a knife—and that had saved her life in Falcor; and his father Quies, the stablemaster; Gero, Brill's young aide; and Wiltur, the grizzled armsman, and his younger companion Frideric.

The Regent reined up short of the steps and the mounting block, turning Farinelli gently so she could address the immediate staff. "I'll talk to you all later, but I wanted to thank you for everything you've done here at Loiseau when I couldn't be here. You've seen the lancers and the players, but I've also brought Lord Jecks, the Lord High Counselor of the Regency, and Lord Jimbob, the heir to Defalk." Anna gestured toward the redheaded Jimbob. "You all may recall Liende. She is chief of the Regent's players, and some of you know Kinor, her son. And the officer there is Overcaptain Himar." Anna cleared her throat, then smiled. "It's good to be back."

Serna stepped forward, looking up at the sorceress. "We are glad to have you back, Lady Anna."

"I hope you can manage, Serna. With Liende and my players and tenscore armsmen . . . there are a lot of mouths to feed."

"We are ready, and we will feed them all." Serna offered a wide grin. "Welcome home, Lady Anna."

"Thank you." Anna was afraid she would choke up if she said much more. "Thank you all." Slowly, she eased Farinelli around the north wall of the main hall and toward the stables. Quies left the group that had greeted her and walked beside Anna and Farinelli until they reached the stable doors.

Anna dismounted, holding on to her saddle for a moment until she was sure her legs wouldn't buckle or cramp. Then she led Farinelli toward his stall.

As he followed, Quies glanced from Anna to Farinelli. "You been taking good care of each other, you and the beast."

"He probably takes better care of me." Anna loosened the girths, but let Quies take the saddle. "We've been through a lot." She paused, glancing to the adjoining stall where Jecks had already unsaddled his own mount. "How have you managed here? Did I send enough coin and clear enough instructions to you and Serna?"

"More than enough coin, Lady Anna. We have some saved in the lower chest room. Could use a few more mounts, if you'll be coming back here more often."

"I don't know, but that's probably a good idea anyway. We need to talk . . . but not now. It's been a long ride, and I'm not thinking too well."

Quies nodded. "Always . . . Albero and me, we're here to do what you need, lady. Best I check with the overcaptain, see what he might need. Always a lame mount or something."

"Don't let me keep you . . . but thank you . . . again."

"My pleasure, lady." Quies offered a bow, and a surprisingly shy smile before slipping away.

After unsaddling and grooming Farinelli, Anna walked across the stone-paved courtyard, noting how even and how clean the area was, although a thin layer of dust coated the stones wherever the hoofs of her party's mounts had not scuffed it away. As Jecks joined her, her eyes went to the low parapets—unguarded—and then to the long blue-tinted windows on the upper level of the keep itself and the metal louvers beneath each window. No wonder Brill had wanted to stay at Loiseau. It was a work of art, from the well-proportioned walls to the graceful sweep of the keep itself.

Behind her echoed the boots of her guards, carrying everything she had brought except the lutar she held.

"You are thinking, my lady," Jecks said quietly from beside her.

"Yes . . . I was thinking about how beautiful Loiseau is."

"It is a small hold, but gracious. It will barely hold the tenscore lancers you brought."

"I won't always need tenscore lancers," Anna pointed out.

Jecks laughed. "You will need them for near-on another six–seven years. Jimbob will not reach his score until then."

"I won't need so many if we can make Liedwahr more peaceful."

"I wish you luck."

"You, too," she pointed out, turning beside the mounting block and starting up the half dozen low wide stone steps into the entry hall.

Brill's former assistant Gero stepped forward even before Anna was through the main doorway. "My lady Anna, I have waited. I know I cannot be a sorcerer . . . but what can I do?"

Anna wanted to shake her head. She definitely needed Halde—or someone—to sort everything out. "You can stay, Gero. Don't worry about that. I'll be talking to everyone, probably tomorrow."

The youth bowed, deeply. "Thank you, Lady Anna. Thank you."

Anna paused, to take in the three-storied entry hall that she hadn't seen in over a year. The space was warm, but far cooler than the courtyard outside. Her eyes went up to the brass chandelier that dominated the space overhead, then down to the black-and-white interlocking triangles of polished stone, embellished with inlaid strips of curlicued brass. The purple twilit sky was barely distinguishable through the high translucent skylights of milky blue glass set in the angular trapezoidal cupola that topped the entry foyer.

A faint gasp came from the youths behind. Jimbob, Anna guessed, since Kinor had been raised in and around Loiseau. A wry smile crossed Anna's lips. She'd almost forgotten the half-Moorish feel of the entry hall.

"Your hall is most impressive, my lady." Jecks' eyes twinkled. "More impressive from within than without."

"You hadn't been here?"

"Lord Brill never invited me," Jecks admitted.

"He should have." Anna smiled. "Then, maybe he shouldn't have. This way, you see the hall as mine."

"Yours it is and will always be."

Serna and her daughter Florenda stepped through the stone arch at the back of the entry foyer, both pausing to bow before stepping forward, then drawing closer to Anna. "All the chambers are ready, my lady."

As Anna stepped through the second archway and approached the grand staircase, Anna drew Serna aside. "I have to confess . . . I really don't know how many chambers we have."

"Six on the second level, besides your master chamber, lady. There are five vacant chambers on the lower level beyond the dining hall. They are smaller, but hold two beds each."

Anna nodded. "The players will go there, except for Liende. She, Lord Jecks, Lord Jimbob, Himar, and Kinor can have chambers upstairs, then."

"Very good, Lady Anna." Serna smiled. "All are in readiness, and we can serve your immediate party in the grand dining hall in a glass, or a trace beyond. As we have done before, I summoned Unana from Mencha and her daughters to prepare food for the armsmen." Her voice lowered. "We will need three golds a meal to pay her. That includes the provender as well, for we do not carry that much in our larder."

"We need to carry more, and I did bring some golds for you to keep running the household," Anna said.

Serna beckoned before Anna could turn away. "Some things . . . they still work. There is water, because Lord Brill set that up to always run, but it is but cool, and not heated, and the air comes through the window ports unchilled. . . ."

Anna nodded. "It may have to do for now. I have not had the time . . ."

"We understand, Lady Anna, but . . ." Serna's head inclined toward Jecks, Liende, and the others who followed.

"They will be happy with what we have."

"Then, Florenda"—Serna nodded to her daughter—"she will assist you while I return to my stoves."

"Thank you."

Florenda led the way up the grand staircase to the second level. "While you were gone, Lady Anna . . . I hope you don't mind . . . but we moved your clothes to the master chamber . . . and set aside Lord Brill's things until you could decide what to do with them. We had no instructions. . . ."

"I should have thought of that," Anna said, trying to put the young woman more at ease.

"I would suggest the chamber here on the left for Kinor," Florenda whispered to Anna, "and the one you had for Lord Jimbob. The one beyond Kinor's for your chief player, and beyond that is the great lord's chamber . . . perhaps Lord Jecks . . ."

"That would be fine."

"And the overcaptain should take the chamber by the back stairs."

Anna nodded and relayed the information, trusting Florenda and wanting to shake her head. Mistress of Loiseau, and she'd never even set foot in the master bedchambers of the holding—or any beyond the one she had occupied.

As the others took their chambers, only Jecks and her guards followed Anna and Florenda to the end of the upper corridor. There, Florenda opened the door—a single door, just as the door to her own chambers at Loiseau had been—an eight-paneled door, but the panels were diamond-shaped and blue-lacquered, not rectangular as on Earth, and framed in blond wood. Anna stepped inside, followed by Jecks and her guards.

Surprisingly, at least to Anna, Brill's chambers had not been that much larger than the one that had once been her bedchamber. The main chamber in the master suite was nearly ten yards long and two-thirds of that in width. The north wall contained the same almost-floor-to-ceiling, clear, but blue-tinted, windows, with the metal louvers beneath. The bedstead was of the same blue-lacquered metal, as were the delicate-looking chairs set around a blue-lacquered table below the foot of the bed. An open archway led into a bathchamber.

The difference was that on the south wall was a second, wider archway that led into a small study with a full wall of built-in bookcases on the east wall, and an ancient table-desk and chair backed up to the west wall. The south wall boasted more windows, with a view of the domed sorcery workshop beyond the hold walls.

"Impressive, your hold," observed Jecks.

"It gets more impressive, the more I see."*But when will you ever be able to spend much time here?* She turned to Jecks with a smile. "I need to get washed up and ready for dinner."

"I stand dismissed, my lady." The twinkle in his hazel eyes belied the formality of the words.

"Excused . . . never dismissed, my lord Jecks." Anna smiled. "Never dismissed."

"For that I have come to be most grateful."

Anna wanted to reach out and touch him for a moment, but the moment passed, and, instead, she smiled gently. "So am I. I'll see you shortly."

The hazel-eyed lord bowed and turned, leaving with Rickel

and Lejun, who stationed themselves outside the closed door. Anna stood alone for a time in the unfamiliar chamber, before turning back to the bathchamber and jakes area.

As the cold water filled the capacious stone tub, Anna wandered back to the study, letting her eyes range across the volumes on the bookshelves. Many had no titles at all on their spines, and the titles she did see encompassed a variety of subjects: *Historie of Wei, NordAphorisms, Reisefuhr Botanisch, Kunstmusik.* She shook her head slowly—nearly two hundred leather-bound volumes—a fortune of sorts in a world where books were copied and bound by hand.

She picked up the saddlebags as she headed back to the bathchamber, although she knew that she would wear one of the gowns Florenda had transferred into the master suite. Tonight, she would eat and rest. Tomorrow—it would be another day—and a long one.

34

After breakfast the next morning, Anna stood on the fourth step of the central stone staircase and glanced out at the hold's key staff. Quies stood in front, with his redheaded son Albero by his side. Serna and Florenda stood a few paces back, while Frideric and Gero stood to the right of the women.

Rickel and Lejun stood behind Anna, but a step up and several paces to each side. Wiltur stood to the right of Lejun. Despite the older guard's grizzled appearance and his silver hair, the steady eyes, the blade in the well-worn scabbard, and the long scar across his cheek marked him as perhaps more to be feared than the two younger men.

"You all know I have not been able to come home to Loiseau as much as I would have liked," Anna began. "That isn't likely to change soon. I cannot maintain the hold with sorcery when I am not here." She looked around. "But I do want Loiseau maintained. You were all helpful when I knew nothing about Defalk and Liedwahr, and for that I thank you. I will only be making one large change . . . and one I make reluctantly." Anna scanned the group, but no one's face seemed to fall or appear displeased. "Sometime after harvest, I will be bringing in a saalmeister who has run a much larger holding. He will probably have to bring in more people to make sure Loiseau remains well kept, because I cannot use sorcery from a distance, as much as I am gone. But I will make sure that all of you will remain here, if you wish, and that you are rewarded for your loyalty, both to me and to Lord Brill. Also, Serna, Quies, Albero . . . Wiltur . . . you will all, if you wish, and I hope you will, continue to do as you have. You will lose no responsibilities. Halde is young, but has much experience, and I have cautioned him to heed your knowledge. He will be here to do some of those things which otherwise I would do, not to do what you all have done so well." Anna offered a sad smile. "I cannot be here to do them, and I do not wish to see Loiseau ill served."

She paused once more, then added, "I'd like to meet with each of you individually in my study upstairs, starting with Quies in just a moment." With a smile, Anna turned and went up the stairs. While using her personal chamber was not perfect, there were no private rooms—that she knew of—on the main level of the hold.

As she had suggested, Quies was the first to step into the chamber, looking around, as if he had never been there.

"Over here," called Anna, standing by the ancient table-desk, on which rested a leather pouch.

The stablemaster stepped through the archway.

Anna took two golds from the pouch and pressed them on the older stablemaster. "Quies, I appreciate all you've done to hold things together . . . and for finding Farinelli for me."

The short and wiry Quies bowed his head. "I wasn't sure . . . Lady Anna . . . but Serna, she said you'd be back . . . and when the scrolls and the coins came . . . well . . . she was right."

"If I can come back, I will, as often as I can."

"We know that, lady." Quies smiled.

Next was Gero, the former assistant to Brill.

Anna offered him a gold. "Just keep the workrooms and pool in shape." She paused. "Are they prepared now?"

The youth nodded. "Yes, Lady Anna . . . when the messenger arrived, I cleaned it and set it up just as Lord Brill always instructed me." He bowed.

"I'll be going there shortly . . . and thank you."

"Thank *you*, lady." Gero looked down, then slipped away.

The white-haired Serna was third in the line, accompanied by her daughter Florenda. Serna bowed twice, once as she entered the chamber, and once as she came through the archway to the study area. "Lady and Regent."

"I understand you were the one who really kept people together. . . ."

"Lady . . . I did what any houseminder would do—"

"Lady . . . she did all that and more," interjected the diminutive Florenda. "Mum . . . she wouldn't admit anything."

Anna couldn't help grinning. "The loyal daughter."

"That she be," admitted Serna.

"She's also right, I'll bet." Anna offered three golds to Serna, and two to Florenda. "For keeping the house together, and," she added to Florenda, "for all the altering and extra food."

Serna's mouth opened as she realized the coins were golds. "My lady . . . never . . ."

"I cannot be here to tell you how much I value you and your work." Anna shrugged. "Gold's a poor substitute, but all I can do."

The two women bowed deeply.

Albero was next, and the hold armorer smiled shyly.

"I owe you more than you realize, Albero, especially for teaching me about knives." She slipped him two golds. "Thank you."

"Lady . . . I did what . . ."

"You did well." She smiled.

Frideric and Wiltur came in together, and each of the hold guards received two golds. As had the others, they bowed reverently.

"Said you don't forget . . . good or evil," offered Wiltur. "Good thing." He grinned briefly.

"I try not to," Anna answered. "We'll be going to the workroom building in a bit, after I finish."

"I'll be waiting by the stables, lady," Wiltur confirmed.

After the two left, Anna retrieved the lutar before heading back down the hallway and then down the stone steps to the main level, followed once more by her guards. At the base of the stairs, she looked through the stone arch to the front entry hall, but the hall remained empty. *Where is Jecks? Or did he mention something about blade lessons for Kinor and Jimbob?*

Anna walked to the stables, followed once more by the guards. As she crossed the north courtyard, her glance went to the rear of the courtyard, where Jecks was instructing Kinor and Jimbob in some aspect of using a blade, while several of the younger lancers watched. Anna wondered if Jimbob was really paying attention.

"Lady Anna?"

Her head turned back toward the stables. Outside the open doors in the already hot morning sunlight stood Quies.

"Yes, Quies?"

"If I might ask, Lady Anna, from where does this Halde hail?" inquired the stablemaster.

"He's been the saalmeister at Synfal, Lord Arkad's hold at Cheor," Anna answered. "When Lord Jimbob received those lands, he also decided to replace the saalmeister with someone from Lord Jecks' lands."

Quies nodded.

"I thought Halde had done an excellent job in the weeks after Lord Arkad's death and the death of the head saalmeister, and I've had him working under Herstat. I believe he will do a good job. He's fair, and he works hard." Anna looked at Quies. "If he has any fault, it is that he may not praise good work enough, but those who have worked with him for years say he does not bully or cheat, but expects the best out of each person."

Quies pursed his lips before speaking. "You won't be here long, will you, lady? And you won't be here that much."

"No," Anna admitted. "I can't be. Not now. I might be here for a week, or less, and I don't know when I'll be back."

"Lady . . . ?"

"Yes, Quies." Anna smiled.

"I'd not be the youngest stablemaster . . . and the horses are not Albero's love . . ."

"You want to train someone else to help you?"

"Aye . . . my sister's bairn Vyren. A bit young, not twelve, but he loves the horses, and they love him."

"Can he learn the rest of running a stable?"

"That young, I'd not be knowing for sure, but I'd send him home if he could not." A crooked smile appeared on the stablemaster's face. "With two . . . we could build up the stable more."

"Then have him come to work for you . . . you tell Serna and anyone else who needs to know."

"Thank you, lady."

"Thank *you*. You do the work, and Farinelli's shown me that you do it well, Quies."

A nervous smile appeared.

"I meant it." Anna stepped into the comparative cool of the always-clean stables and toward the front stall where the big gelding greeted Anna with a *whuff*, as if to ask why she'd taken so long.

"Business, fellow, business." She slipped into the stall and brushed him briefly, not all that necessary since she'd groomed him thoroughly the night before, tired as she'd been.

The ride out to the workshop buildings was almost too short, except for the heat, and, again, almost a parade, Anna felt, with Wiltur and two of her guards following her.

Wiltur insisted on checking the building before she entered. Then, as Anna carried the lutar, a water bottle, and a sheaf of her notes into the building, Wiltur stationed himself by the door, joining Rickel and Blaz as guards.

After closing the door behind her, the sorceress and Regent wandered through the dusty workrooms, then through the larger room where Brill's players had practiced, and where hers would later.

After checking the last of the three workshop rooms, she stopped by the pool in the scrying room, pondering. *It's been long enough . . . do you dare? Besides, when and where else can you try?* She nodded and took out the lutar, beginning her vocalises, as she tuned the instrument. When she was ready, she faced the pool, not that she needed it, and sang the simple spell.

> Bring to me the letter I desire,
> from my daughter, safe from fire
> across the void from Earth to here,
> let all words from her appear. . . .

A column of flame exploded beside the scrying pool, forcing Anna to lurch backward—then died abruptly, leaving a steaming oblong lump of blackened matter on the stones beside the pool. Her eyes went to the object. She swallowed.

"Shit . . ." Then, as she continued to study the object, she smiled, realizing that the black was a heavy black fabric. Once the steaming subsided, she set aside the lutar, laying it on the small worktable behind her, and bent down.

Her fingers brushed the heavy cloth—almost like a stage curtain.

Within the crude bag was an envelope of some sort of synthetic material, and within that were two envelopes. The first contained a small pencil sketch of Elizabetta, and the second a thick letter. Anna looked at the sketch for a long time before she opened the letter and began to read.

Mom—

Your letter arrived. It just popped into the passenger seat of my car. The outer envelope was pretty charred, and there's a brown spot on the upholstery now, and it reminds me of you. I'm leaving this under the stairs like you said, but I found pieces of an old stage curtain, lined with asbestos or something, in the back rooms at PSC. One of my friends goes there, and I made a pouch out of it for this. I hope it works.

The sketch is because I don't know if a modern picture would get there. The sketch of you got here, so I was pretty sure this would. Cortland was happy to do it, and I didn't tell him why.

Anna took a deep breath, looking at the black blot of soot on the stone floor. She turned to the careful script and kept reading.

I decided not to show Dad the coins. Mr. Asteni paid me by their weight, cause he says there isn't any speculative market for private mint coins. He thinks they were minted by those creative anachronism folks, and I'll bet he's keeping a few for himself. I told Mario you'd left money hidden in the jewelry case I brought back from Ames, and I just found it. I tried to give him half that way, but he wouldn't take it. He said he had a job, and I'd need the money more.

I'm headed back to school. Because you're "missing"—and Dad thinks you're dead because even he

admits you would stay in touch, that means you're pre-
sumed to be dead. The insurance people said it could be
years, but the school gave me full tuition and room and
board. So don't worry about that.

You can't be dead. Ghosts don't send messages on real
parchment or whatever it is, and funny gold coins. Especially not coins worth that much. I worry about you, and
I was really glad to get your last letter. When I come back
to the lake house for Christmas, if this one is gone, I'll
leave another letter there, and I hope you can use your
sorcery or whatever to pick it up. It sure is weird to write
each other this way, but it helps to know you're all right
somewhere. It'd be really hard if you had just vanished
into nowhere. I don't know how people stand that.

By the way, my grades did go up second semester, and I
made the honors list. German was easier than I'd thought
it would be, but I barely scraped out a B+ in theory. You
said it would be hard, and it was. My voice teacher
sounds like you, always talking about keeping the sound
free. . . .

The police in Iowa haven't closed the case, but they're
not actively investigating anymore. I think they think you
just adopted a new identity. You did, but not the way they
think. . . .

Anna blotted her eyes, and cleared her throat, then blotted
once more. She had trouble swallowing, but she looked back at
the letter, reading quickly, almost as if she were afraid it would
turn to dust in her hands . . . or disappear.

. . . still hard to think of a world or a place like you
describe. Somehow, I can see you running things, though.
You never got a chance here, not taking care of us, and
always being there and picking up all the messes . . .

Anna had to set the letter down . . . letting the sobs come.
After another interval, she sniffed, blotted her eyes once

more, and continued reading the rest of the long and chatty letter, collapsing into sobs with the closing lines.

> . . . Wherever you are, even if you can't ever write again, I love you.

A good half-glass or more passed before Anna was ready to tackle scrying again. She'd also finished off most of the water in the bottle she'd brought out to the domed building.

Finally, she stood before the pool, lutar in hand, and began the next spell.

> Silver pool, show me now and as you can
> where near Mencha sorcery by this woman
> will find gold to mine and gold to coin. . . .

The pool showed three images. Anna took a deep breath and studied them.

One depicted a low hill covered with scattered pines with mostly bare ground around each short tree. The second showed a narrow gorge that appeared almost impassable, so steep that only a few straggly junipers sprouted out of the reddish rock. The third site was a river flat under a bluff with evergreens in the background.

None was familiar, but Anna had expected that. That there were sites was encouraging. *Now all you have to do is find them.* Her head was throbbing, and every muscle in her body felt tight. *After you eat . . . and try to relax a little.*

35

A nna turned in the saddle, looking out against the early midmorning sun across the river flat toward the hills that led eastward to the Ostfels, past the lancers and the six heavy wagons that she had optimistically rented from various crafters and farmers around Mencha. She and Jecks had finally decided against driving wagons all the way from Falcor.

On the south side of the small river whose name she did not know, but which flowed westward toward the Chean, were grasslands and scattered herds of sheep. She suspected that the herders owed her rents, but that was something Halde would have to look into, once he arrived. *Once that's been worked out with Herstat* . . . .

According to the scrying pool at Loiseau, the site was a good thirty deks northeast of Mencha, a bit less than halfway to Sil-berfels, and according to the maps in Brill's study at Loiseau, definitely on Anna's lands.

Anna dismounted on a knoll a good thirty yards east of the river, and the players followed her example. Jecks, Himar, and the lancers remained mounted.

The white-haired lord stood in his stirrups, then settled down. "There is no one else in sight."

"Worried?" asked Anna.

"If you succeed . . . yes, I will be worried. Gold-bearing wagons far from a hold are scarce little to sneeze at."

"There aren't any armsmen near," she pointed out as she handed Farinelli's reins to Kerhor, who had remained mounted. "I checked that before we left Loiseau."

"For that I am glad."

"So am I." Anna offered a crooked smile as she turned and began a last series of vocalises as the players tuned.

When the tuning died away, Liende glanced toward the Regent.

"The searching song," Anna nodded to Liende.

"The searching song. On my mark . . . Mark!"

Anna stood on the knoll, thinking, *Just a hundred bars or ingots.* She concentrated on visualizing those bars, stacked on the open ground to the right of the players, as she began the spell.

> Search, search, search the ground
> deeply all around,
> verily, verily, verily,
> gold will here be found. . . .

The ground shivered, noticeably, and several horses *whuff*ed uneasily, even before Anna started into the second stanza of the spell.

> Bring, bring, bring the gold,
> straightly here to mold,
> verily, verily, verily. . . .

As she neared the end of the spell, the ground began to heave, and she forced herself to concentrate on finishing while struggling to maintain her balance. A series of strobelike lights flashed overhead and seemed to knife into the ground near the players, lights so bright that the fall sun seemed dim. After the strobes came a hot wind, nearly blistering.

Then, the unseen harp of harmony strummed the chords of the afternoon with an intricate chording that only Anna sensed and heard—that she'd discovered from experience. In the sky to the east, over the Ostfels, clouds appeared where none had been, quickly expanding and darkening as they rose even higher into the heavens.

Thurummmm . . . Thunder rolled across the sky and rumbled over the river flat.

Anna sank onto the hot ground, barely sitting up, and only marginally conscious of the rising wind and the lightning and thunder to the east. Her eyes burned, and her head throbbed. She looked up dully as Jecks eased his mount beside her and handed down a water bottle.

"You must drink," he insisted.

She took the bottle . . . and a long swallow . . . before speaking. "Did we get any gold?"

"Look there." Jecks laughed and gestured beyond the players, most of whom were sitting in positions similar to Anna's. "More than enough. You have mayhap a hundred bars or so."

"A hundred," Anna said, half-wondering. "Would you go see . . . if they're gold."

Nodding, Jecks eased his mount away from Anna. She took another long swallow from the water bottle, and the worst of the headache faded ever so slightly. *Not only does spellsinging drain you, but it dehydrates you as well.*

She found she had almost drained the water bottle by the time Jecks again reined up beside her.

"There are indeed a hundred," he announced quietly, bending down from the saddle. "Each of the bars weighs more than a stone, and yet they are barely two spans long. It will take all six wagons to carry them."

Gold was heavy, Anna recalled, but how heavy had eluded her. She wanted to shake her head, but tried to keep her mind on the necessary. "If you would have them start loading the wagons . . . ?"

"I have already. I have young Skent watching the loading and counting. We should make prudent haste for Loiseau." Jecks frowned. "You will need a strongroom there."

"There is one, I think." Anna slowly stood and walked toward Liende.

The chief player, cleaning her horn, glanced up. "Regent?"

"Good work. There will be a special bonus of two golds for each of them, and five for you."

"Ah . . . two golds?" Liende swallowed.

Doesn't anyone reward anyone around here? "Isn't that fair?" asked Anna, adding guilelessly, she hoped, "A lot of this will have to pay for roads and armsmen, but the players should have some."

"Never have any players received golds such as that," Liende pointed out.

"Good. If you would tell them . . . but they won't get them until after we get back to Loiseau."

Liende smiled. "I would be most happy to tell them."

Anna took Farinelli's reins from Kerhor and slowly mounted the gelding, her legs so wobbly that she had to pull herself up as much as use her legs. Once mounted, she eased the gelding up beside Jecks.

"Never would I have suspected such use of sorcery. . . ." Jecks frowned. "Yet . . . one cannot pay in bars of gold."

"No . . . but if I can drag gold out of the ground, I can turn bars of gold into coins." After a moment, she added, "I hope." *Always hoping . . . but someday that hope won't work out. Just trust that it won't be too soon.*

Would the hundred bars or ingots be enough? Sitting limply in the saddle as the ten lancers loaded the bars into the wagons, Anna hoped so . . . and that she could indeed turn bars into coins. *More hope . . .*

36

Anna forced herself to finish the loaf of bread and the last wedge of cheese set on the wooden platter beside her in what once had been Brill's scrying room. That left one loaf of bread. The spell to mine and refine the gold had cost her weight—and strength—that she couldn't afford to lose.

Feeling the pressure of the food she needed and didn't want, she burped quietly, instinctively looking around. She had to smile at her foolishness, but she'd been brought up to believe that ladies *never* burped. *Even when they're stuffing themselves with heavy food to survive.*

She took another swallow of cool water, welcome in the warmth of the scrying room, then set the mug down on the table.

Her eyes went to the scroll that had just arrived by messenger from Lord Dannel of Mossbach. She picked it up again, her eyes going over the words.

"... understand you have done much for Defalk ... but you must understand that you have treated my son less kindly than I would treat a serving maid. You have dismissed him because he cannot master numbers he will never employ and because he would not defer to those of lower birth. You have denied him the right to an honorable consort. ... Such actions may hold beyond the mist worlds, but no lord of Defalk would gainsay my right to withhold liedgeld for such unacceptable behavior. I will not do so, in recognition of your efforts on behalf of the Thirty-three, but I would like the honored customs of Defalk restored and respected. ..."

Lord Dannel was angry—but angry enough to suggest withholding liedgeld—because of a spoiled and thickheaded idiot who was his son? Anna shook her head. Almost all parents were protective, but Dannel's actions reminded her of the worst of those she had encountered as a teacher. *The chauvinistic worst.*

She'd have to draft some sort of placating response that suggested that Hoede was the honorable son of an honorable father whose talents did indeed lie elsewhere, but that honor on the part of Mossbach and honor on the part of Abenfel did not necessitate drawing two youngsters into a consortship both would regret. . . .

She sighed. "Or something like that," she murmured, looking down at the ten bars of gold stacked beside the table, and she studied the blocks of gold—or bars—or ingots. Then she bent and lifted the topmost. That took two hands, even though the bar was only two spans long. After holding it briefly, she eased it back onto the small pile.

With a deep breath, she looked at the two sketches on the table. The circular designs were simple—the crossed spears with the *R* beneath on the drawing that represented one side of a coin, and the simple word "Defalk" imposed on simple outlines of the liedburg at Falcor. Anna then picked up the Neserean gold coin and compared it to the second gold, one minted in Wei. From what she could tell, both weighed the same. In a strange way, it made sense. Underlying Liedwahr was the idea of harmony, and it would have been unnecessarily disharmonious to have coins of different weights. Dissonance was reserved for weightier matters.

She snorted and stood, easing the lutar from its case and beginning to tune it, as she went through another vocalise.

After several more vocalises, she straightened and concentrated on the first spell, and on the set of designs on the table.

> Coin, coin, by this my own design,
> a coin figured round and fine,
> weighted like all others here of gold,
> signifying the Regency as strong and bold.

Clink! As the last note died away, a single coin rested on the table, next to the drawing. Anna reached for it, then stopped. Her fingers could feel the heat radiating from the metal. She bent down and looked. The coin, not even quite the size of an American nickel, bore on the upper side the emblem of crossed spears.

"Now all you need is a few thousand more," she murmured, setting aside the lutar and reseating herself at the small worktable. She refilled the mug from the pitcher and took another healthy swallow.

She brushed her index finger over the surface of the small coin, but it was merely warm. She picked it up and studied it, noting that the inscriptions and design matched those she had drawn. With that, a smile crossed her lips, then faded. *You only need a few thousand more like this one.*

Shouldn't you bring in the players? Anna shook her head. Some things were better not seen . . . if she could make the spell work at all for larger numbers of coins, then she should do it with the lutar.

She stood once more, checking the lutar's tuning and clearing her throat before beginning the revised spell.

> Coin, coin, by this my own design,
> a thousand coins both round and fine,
> weighted like all others made of gold,
> signifying the Regency as strong and bold.

This time, a wave of heat, steamy and metallic, filled the workroom, and Anna backed out into the hallway. As she retreated, awkwardly closing the door, the clink of metal striking the floor sounded almost like heavy rain.

With her right hand still holding the lutar, she blotted her steaming forehead with her left sleeve, listening. The pattering *clinking* had stopped. After what seemed forever, she eased open the door, stepping back as warm metallic air puffed from the scrying room. Finally, she stepped inside. Gold coins lay strewn across the polished stones of the floor, hundreds of them. *Probably a thousand.*

Anna slipped into the room and closed the door. After she set the lutar on the table, she began to stack the warm coins on the table in stacks of ten. In time, she had exactly one hundred stacks. Her eyes dropped to the stack of bars on the floor. She swallowed. Exactly one bar was missing. She looked again . . . less than one bar, since a small oblong of gold lay in the right-hand upper corner of the stack of gold bars.

She tried to figure it out—with more than a thousand coins a bar, and one hundred bars stored below Loiseau—ninety below the hold and nine before her . . . The Regent shook her head slowly. What dared she do with all that gold? She had the equivalent of more than ten years' liedgeld. If she spent it too quickly . . . she'd generate the local equivalent of inflation . . . and if anyone knew exactly how much there was . . . she'd have thieves and who knew what else prowling through Mencha and Loiseau.

She needed a concealment spell—or something—after she converted another bar or two to coins to pay for her coming campaign. Then she laughed. Once she had all the gold in the storeroom, she could weld it into a stack with sorcery and then conceal it. No one had the technology to move that mass—not quickly—and that would be if they could find it.

She went to the door of the domed building and peered out. Frideric, Blaz, and Lejun all stiffened.

"If one of you could find Lord Jecks and ask him to join me . . . if you would?" She smiled as pleasantly as possible.

"Ah . . . I will, Lady Anna," offered Blaz.

"Thank you. Tell him I'll be in the room with the pool, please." She slipped out of the early-fall heat and into the somewhat cooler hallway, walking slowly back to the scrying room. Then she sat down and forced another swallow of water and more of the bread before she got back to work.

Anna was making a list—of everything that needed to be handled in one way or another before she left Loiseau—when Jecks knocked on the door.

"Come on in."

Jecks' eyes widened as he looked at the stacks of coins on the worktable.

"What do you think?" asked Anna. "There are a thousand there."

The older lord picked up one of the golds, then turned it over, noting the milled edges, and the emblems. "It should bear your image."

"No. The crossed spears and crown with the *R* are enough. If

I mint coins with my image, just how long will your beloved lords of the Thirty-three keep believing in a Regency? Or how long before one of them gets to Jimbob?"

"These are yours," Jecks said slowly. "The gold came from your lands by your sorcery. They do not belong to the Regency or to Jimbob."

"We need them, though," Anna pointed out.

"Then use them to add to the liedgeld fees collected by the Regency, but do not allow the Thirty-three to think that they will always be there."

"As a Lord of Defalk might use coins from his own lands to help support the realm?" she asked.

"As such," Jecks answered. "I would also transfer some of the armsmen and perhaps Himar into your personal force, and pay them yourself, now that you can."

Anna nodded. That definitely made sense, because it established her as a power independent of being Regent—and as a power without having to use sorcery. "Won't that upset some of them?"

"They need not know exactly how you obtained the gold."

"I could keep it secret?" Anna snorted.

"There are so many tales about you," Jecks pointed out, "that it becomes difficult for those who know you not to determine which may be true and which false. If you do not speak . . . who will know for certain. Your players will not speak, nor will most armsmen. That is why young Skent's company has guarded the gold most closely." Jecks laughed. "And if some armsmen speak . . . well, who will believe such?"

Anna nodded. Her players understood well enough that any alternative to playing for her was probably worse. *You hope they do.* She took a deep breath. She'd have to watch them, if only because she'd learned that most people didn't know when they were well off.

Jecks fingered the coin he held. "It is softer, I think."

"How could you tell?"

The white-haired lord smiled, almost sheepishly. "I cannot. But I know that pure gold is softer than coin gold, and the gold you created—"

"I gathered it. I didn't create it."

"That gold must be pure," Jecks finished.

"It's pure. Will people take it? As golds, I mean?"

Jecks smiled again. "They will take it, and they will save those of your coins they can, and spend the coins of others. Yours are worth more, especially to merchants. If you had paid the Ranuans with such, you would have had even less difficulty."

"I don't know . . ." answered Anna musingly. Then she looked up. "Now . . . we can see about going to Ebra." Anna handed the list to Jecks. "If you would read this . . . see if there's anything on it we shouldn't do . . . and what I might have forgotten." She paused, then added, "and please sit down. We also need to talk about Lord Dannel."

"I feared he would be less than pleased."

"He is less than pleased. I'll try to draft some sort of response to say he's honorable, but Lysara's not going to be his consort."

"You will not reconsider? Many of the northern lords . . ."

Anna met Jecks' eyes. "If I give in to him, then where do I stop?"

"That may be, my lady, but he is a man who never relinquishes a grudge."

The Regent nodded. "I understand, but even if Nelmor agrees to a match between Tiersen and Lysara, Dannel would never accept it. Besides, he has to know that Defalk won't survive if things don't change." She looked at the rest of the scrolls. "Even here, things keep piling up."

Jecks laughed ruefully. "So said my daughter."

Anna picked up the second scroll. "The rivermen . . . again . . ."

37

Anna, Himar, and Jecks stood beside the scrying pool in the domed sorcery work building outside the hold at Loiseau. At midday, even despite the thick stone walls, the room was hot and still, and a trace steamy. The two men watched as Anna finished tuning the lutar.

"First," she said, "we need to find out where Bertmynn's

forces are." She glanced at Himar, then at Jecks. "And what they're doing."

"They must be nearing Elahwa," hazarded Jecks, "if they are not already there and attacking the city. They were loading the barges weeks ago."

"Not all leaders move so quickly as the Regent," countered Himar. "The roads may not be so good, either."

"We'll have to see, won't we?" Anna took a moment to clear her throat, then hummed, trying to ensure she was ready, before beginning the spell and concentrating on the idea of Bertmynn's forces.

> Bertmynn, Bertmynn, Lord I'd see,
> show his forces now to me. . . .

Upon the silvered waters of the scrying pool shimmered an image. Lancers rode along a muddy road through what appeared to be a drizzle. On the right side was a levee or a riverbank, Anna thought, and low field to the left. Behind the group of lancers in the image slogged several score of armsmen, and behind them was another dark mass that might have been more lancers. The rain was heavy, because large puddles had formed on the road, and the horses' hoofs were churning up large globules of mud.

Anna glanced at Jecks and Himar. Jecks was frowning, pulling at his clean-shaven chin, while Himar continued to study the image, his mustache drooping as he also fingered his chin and watched the image in the pool.

Anna could feel the perspiration building on her forehead, and, rather than hold the image longer, sang the release couplet. The water of the pool rippled slightly, then returned to its transparent state.

"They have not reached Elahwa," said Himar slowly.

"They have to be close with that rain," replied Anna.

Both men frowned.

"Most of Ebra is higher ground, except the plains near Elahwa or the Sand Hills, and they're south and west of Elahwa. So there's going to be more rain near the coast or at the piedmont." She still remembered Sandy's lectures on the effect of orographic factors on rainfall distribution.

That got another set of blank looks.

"Never mind. They're not at Elahwa, but they're close. So it will take us . . . what? Ten days, two weeks, to reach Elahwa? Or three weeks?"

"I do not see how it could be done in less than two weeks," offered Himar.

"You do not wish to be tired when you reach Bertmynn's forces," Jecks pointed out.

Anna nodded slowly. *We'll see about who's tired.* "We also have to see what young Rabyn is doing."

She lifted the lutar again.

> Rabyn, Rabyn, Lord who'd be,
> show his grandsire's second lancers now to me
> and his own lancers and armsmen strong. . . .

This time the image split, the first showing Mansuuran lancers riding along a road that could have been anywhere, with golden fields to one side, and what looked to be vineyards on the other, bounded with stone walls. The second image was that of a parade ground overlooking a city . . . with what looked to be the ocean in the background.

"I would guess that to be Esaria," suggested Jecks. "No other city in Neserea is close to an ocean or even a large lake."

"It is Esaria," confirmed Himar. "There is the Prophet's Palace, the west wing . . . there." The overcaptain gestured.

Anna sang the release couplet, then set down the lutar and blotted her steaming forehead, wondering if the sorcery effectively heated the pool and boosted the humidity in the room. She touched a finger to the water in the pool and nodded. It was almost warm enough to bathe in. Another spell soon, and it would be.

"So the second set of lancers are on their way somewhere, probably to Elioch or our borders, but Rabyn's own troops haven't left Esaria." Anna nodded. "Let's take a look at Hadrenn." She lifted the lutar and sang once more.

> Hadrenn, Hadrenn, Synek's lord for me,
> show him clear and close to me. . . .

The silvered waters of the pool showed a heavyset brown-haired man in a stained green tunic. The left side of his face bore a long reddish scar. Hadrenn stood in a courtyard, apparently resting from practicing or sparring with a blade. The smile he offered the other figure was open, yet rueful.

Anna concentrated, trying to remember Hadrenn's face, before she released the image. "I'll keep checking on him from time to time."

"You trust him not? Yet you would consider going into Ebra?" asked Jecks.

"I trust him more than most people I haven't met, but it can't hurt." She looked toward Himar. "We leave tomorrow. You'll need to send a messenger to Hadrenn telling him we're coming."

"Tomorrow?"

"Why not? If Rabyn decides to attack, it's better we go into Ebra before he starts to move his troops. It's farther from Esaria to Elioch than from Mencha to Elahwa, isn't it?"

"Maybe three or four days farther, a week if they do not make haste."

"Tomorrow," Anna reiterated. *And you hope this isn't a big mistake, but it's better to act than react, and you've always had to react before.*

38

WEI, NORDWEI

The Council Chamber is empty except for the five figures seated around the long black table, a table that shimmers like a perfect black gem in the dim light cast by the oil lamps set in sconces on the dark stone walls.

"Counselor Ashtaar . . . junior Counselor Ashtaar . . . has some information to share with us," announces Tybra. The black-and-silver seal that hangs from her neck casts darts of light randomly. "You may begin." The dark-haired council leader nods at Ashtaar.

"The sorceress has employed her skills to lift gold from the earth and to turn a small portion of it into coins. She has not made that knowledge known. She is now marching her forces toward Synek, presumably to meet with Hadrenn, and thence to deal with Bertmynn."

"She will support Hadrenn?" asks a smooth-shaven man in dark green to Tybra's right.

"It is more likely that Hadrenn will support her when she defeats Bertmynn, Counselor Virtuul." Ashtaar's voice is even, and her eyes remain on Tybra.

"You seem to think that Bertmynn's defeat is the likely outcome. Is that not a . . . hasty . . . assumption?"

"Unless she attempts sorcery that will kill her, or unless she is killed by those close to her, I do not see anyone in Ebra defeating her. Those of great talent left when the Evult took power, or served the Evult and died at the sorceress' spells."

"A very careful statement, Ashtaar, regarding Ebra. See you other possibilities, then?" asks Tybra.

"There is a darksinger in Pamr who has twice evaded her. He is far stronger than she knows, and he has rediscovered the use of the thunder-drums. . . ."

"Truly barbaric," comes a whisper from the left side of the table.

". . . and young Rabyn is not only building thunder-drums, but he is equally adept with poison and treachery. The young Prophet is training and marshaling large forces. He will doubt-less attack the west of Defalk when he discovers the sorceress is engaged in Ebra."

"What of his regent, the wily Nubara?"

"We doubt that Nubara will prevail, but should he, then the sorceress would be free to act at leisure in Ebra."

"Has she made no provisions for a possible attack from the west?" asks Virtuul, his tone almost idle.

"She has called up some levies, and her arms commander is quietly mustering forces to move to Denguic . . . we think. Rabyn can bring almost three hundred–score armsmen and lancers, with the hundredscore from Mansuur. Defalk could not muster half that, even were all levies called, and they have not been." Ashtaar waits for the next question.

"Yet the sorceress is far from stupid," points out Tybra. "Far from that. Has she not scried what is occurring?"

"It is difficult to ascertain what she has scried, but she has done much scrying. That we know. And she left many indications with the Liedfuhr's envoy that she would finally visit her own lands in Mencha. She took but tenscore lancers there."

"So she grows cunning as well," remarks Virtuul. "No one would suspect she would begin an attack into Ebra with but tenscore lancers."

"She took but fifteen when she headed south toward Dumar," notes Ashtaar.

"But she picked up additional forces from Lerona, Abenfel, and Stromwer," counters Virtuul.

"And she will use Hadrenn's forces as well," suggests Ashtaar. "What choice has he, but to follow her?"

"She is not so much cunning as bold," declares Tybra. "She gambles that she can defeat Bertmynn quickly and then return to destroy Rabyn, if he should attack."

"If she does . . ." comes the whisper from the left side of the table.

"If she does, the Liedfuhr will have to decide whether to reach terms with her or hazard his forces against her."

"He has pledged not to act."

"Has that made any difference before?" asks Tybra dryly.

II

LIEDFINSTER

39

With the late-afternoon sun at their backs, Anna and Jecks rode eastward along the narrow road, leading the players and the tenscore lancers. Each hoof that struck the ground lifted dust out of the fine soil that had drifted across the road from Mencha to the Sand Pass. Ahead, looming on the horizon, lay the Ostfels.

Anna blotted her forehead before taking another long swallow from her water bottle. "It's hard to believe that it could have been hotter here."

"It was, my lady," replied Jecks dryly. "It was, as we both know."

"Maybe I didn't want to remember." Anna laughed and took another swallow from the bottle before replacing it in the holder.

The ground on each side of the road was covered with intermittently spaced brown grass. Almost level, it rose gradually for several deks to a low hillcrest. As Anna recalled, beyond that crest, the land dropped into the shallow bowl-like valley below the Sand Pass, and in that valley, against the base of the Ostfels and the beginning of the Sand Pass, lay the fort raised by the sorcerer Brill for Lord Barjim—the fort and the now-drained defense reservoir. The fort had been built to guard the Sand Pass—the gateway to southern and eastern Ebra—and it had been the site of Anna's first battle in Defalk. *Not exactly a resounding victory, either.*

The Regent could see tracks in the ground between the clumps of grass, tracks left by fleeing armsmen and pursuing Ebrans a year earlier, tracks that would not vanish anytime soon in the still-dry lands of eastern Defalk, lands dry despite the return of seasonal rains.

"It will be years before these grasslands recover," said Jecks.

"If ever," Anna replied.

"If the rains continue, they will. When I was a boy, the grass here was shoulder-high on my mount. I would see that again."

"So would I." Anna blotted sweat out of her eyes once more.

"You sent that scroll to Lord Dannel?" asked Jecks, somewhat later.

"I did. I tried to be gentle, but . . ." Anna shrugged. "If I waited or stalled him, he would be angry because I put him off, and if I don't change my mind, he'll be angry."

"He will not be pleased."

"I know. No one's ever pleased around here. Save us, but don't upset anything, and don't change anything, even if the reason why we got in trouble was because we wouldn't change."

"Lady . . . you are hard on them. Change comes not easily to any man."

"I know." She took a deep breath. "But it's the same everywhere. I had to dismiss the granary attendant because he wouldn't clean out the granary before it was filled. I destroyed a family because I wouldn't submit to a man's advances. Yet these people think it's my fault. I allow a young woman some little choice in whom she will spend her life with, and you'd think I'd . . . I don't know what . . ."

Jecks looked away, clearly uncomfortable, and Anna closed her mouth. The handsome lord was still from Defalk, and nothing she said would change matters.

For another three or four deks, they rode in comparative silence, Anna shifting her weight in the saddle occasionally, and hoping that the Sand Pass fort did lie beyond the hillcrest they approached, and not one even farther along the road.

"How far does the Sand Pass stretch through the Ostfels?" Behind the sorceress, Kinor's voice rose over the murmurs of the lancers and the muted thumping of hoofs.

"If one can believe the maps, we will need to ride almost fifty deks from the fort before we clear the eastern hills of the Ostfels," responded Himar, "and then more than a hundred to reach Synek."

"A long journey with but tenscore lancers," added Jimbob.

Does he think lancers grow on trees? Anna tightened her lips, but forced herself not to reply.

Jecks glanced at Anna, rolling his eyes.

They both laughed.

". . . and the Regent took all of Dumar with but fifteenscore lancers," Himar finished. "That was against more than a hundredscore."

Jimbob did not reply, not audibly.

A few moments later, they reached the gentle hillcrest, and, as Anna had hoped, the shallow valley ahead was the one that held the Sand Pass fort, the redstone-and-brick structure almost blending with the red rock that framed the entrance to the pass itself.

"Not much farther," Himar said, adding, "The Regent's banner to the fore!"

The walls of the Sand Pass fort had indeed been repaired, although the irregular lines of mortar showed the damage inflicted by the Evult's dark magic on the stones and brickwork created by Brill's sorcery, and Anna doubted that the structure could withstand much more than attacks by brigands.

The gates had been returned to place and were swung back to welcome the Regent. A score of armsmen in leathers and the purple of Defalk were formed up just inside the gateway into the fort. A gray-bearded figure stood before them.

Although she remembered Hanfor and others talking about the veteran armsman who had come from Mencha once and who was in charge of the fort, Anna had never met him, and she struggled to remember his name.

"Jerat," whispered Himar from behind the Regent.

"Thank you," Anna murmured.

"Welcome, Regent and sorceress!"

"Thank you, Jerat. I am glad to see you and to offer my gratitude for all the efforts you and your men have made to repair the fort. The last time I saw it, it was in ruins." *That's certainly true.*

Jerat bowed, then looked up. "Regent . . . we have done the best we can, and we continue to labor."

"You have done much," Anna affirmed. *More than enough for a fort that's outlived its usefulness . . . you hope.*

"Repairing the fort has helped us add some armsmen as well, Lady Anna. Did you know that we have over twoscore here, and a score could go with you . . . should you need additional forces."

"You have done well, Jerat, and we appreciate that." Anna managed not to wince at her own words. *You're sounding like royalty . . . or a politician.* She nodded and turned to Himar. "Once everyone's quartered and settled, perhaps you could review these armsmen with Jerat and see whether it would be better to have them accompany us . . . or whether they might best be held in reserve to follow us later. I imagine you'll have to look into the question of supplies and mounts . . . and other matters."

"Jerat and I will discuss this," Himar said. "And perhaps the Lord High Counselor?" He glanced toward Jecks.

Jecks smiled politely. "I am at your disposal, Overcaptain."

"The stables are on the southeast wall . . . the ones left. We didn't try to rebuild the others, collapsed like they were." Jerat turned and began to walk toward the remaining stables.

Anna looked over the armsmen as she rode past. They looked like any others she had seen. "He found more than a score of men to train here in the middle of nowhere . . ." she murmured to Jecks.

"So it would seem . . . though some might be Ebran deserters or from our forces."

"Still . . ." Anna mused, "in little more than a season . . ."

"If others did as well, you would have a greater force," agreed Jecks.

"Maybe we need to do recruiting in the outlying lands," suggested Anna. *Yet another task and job . . . even if you survive the battles, you'll be buried by the bureaucracy you'll have to create to run this place.*

She tried not to groan as she reined up outside the stable, keeping a smile firmly in place.

40

ESARIA, NESEREA

The dark-haired Rabyn slips from the audience chair without looking at the Mansuuran overcaptain and makes his way into the smaller chamber behind the receiving hall, where he steps to a serving table. There he lifts a pitcher and pours a goblet of wine, looking up as Nubara walks slowly into the chamber.

"Audiences are done for the day," the youth says. "For that, I am pleased. A charade, but a necessary one, you know?"

"I understand," offers Nubara. "Charades are useful to rulers. Most useful, if one would gain the support of the people."

"Ah, yes, the people, the dear people." Rabyn takes a second goblet from the back of the table, set slightly apart from two others, and fills it, then extends the goblet. "You look thirsty, Nubara, even if I did all the speaking."

"That is your role as Prophet." Nubara takes the goblet.

Rabyn smiles across the small chamber and lifts his glass, drinking. After a moment, he replies. "The Prophet of Music has many roles."

"All rulers do." Nubara takes a sip from the wine goblet, then frowns, looking at the dark liquid.

"One of those roles is to make sure they continue to rule," Rabyn says easily, setting his goblet on the back of the table.

Nubara's hands begin to shake, and he barely manages to set the goblet on the serving table.

"You see . . . Nubara . . . you should pay attention to me." Rabyn's smile is hard, almost dispassionate.

The officer pales, trying to speak before his knees buckle, and he slowly collapses into a heap on the polished white tiles of the floor. Rabyn watches, seemingly waiting, until the lancer overcaptain convulses. Then the youth kneels and rolls Nubara onto his back. Rabyn takes a small vial from his wallet and lets several drops ooze into the Mansuuran officer's mouth.

The convulsions slow, and Rabyn stands, stepping back and watching, his dark eyes cold and intent.

After several convulsive movements, Nubara slowly sits up. Then he stands, if shakily. "What . . . you serpent . . . what have you done?"

"Careful, Nubara." Rabyn steps back, holding up the vial. "This will only last a week . . . and none but I know the way to formulate more."

"If you would explain . . . Prophet . . ." Sweat begins to pour from Nubara's forehead, and he shudders.

"I did not trust you, Nubara . . . so I took steps to introduce . . . certain ingredients into your diet . . . they have damaged your body. You will die within a day without the antidote. The damage is forever; the antidote is temporary."

Rabyn's smile is hard. "You will need several drops every few days."

"You are truly your mother's son," Nubara's voice is rasping. "Truly . . ."

"I am indeed, and do not ever forget that. You will not forget, not if you wish to live. Nor will that bitch sorceress." Another smile crosses Rabyn's youthful face, a countenance that suddenly appears far older, far more cruel. "Now . . . shall we plan the attack on Defalk?"

Nubara looks down, if momentarily, before he raises his eyes. "I believe such an attack is most unwise, Prophet."

"Will you assist me? Or do you wish to die?"

Nubara takes another deep breath. "I will assist you."

"I thought you would see reason, Nubara." Rabyn smiles once again.

41

"Come in." Anna stepped back from the pine-planked door to let Jecks and Himar enter the chamber that had once been meant for Lord Barjim. It was larger than the room she had once occupied at the Sand Pass fort with three other women, but spare, containing little more than a large bed, whose frame had been roughly repaired with pine splints over the light oak, a few chairs, a wash table with bowl and pitcher, a small writing table with a single stool, a chamber pot, and a plank with hanging pegs nailed to the brick wall.

The traveling scrying mirror rested upon the writing table, and the uncased lutar lay across the lower corner of the bed.

"You wished to see us?" A humorous glint tinged Jecks' hazel eyes.

"I did." Anna let Himar close the door before she asked, "We still have two companies of bowmen, right?" *We'd better . . .*

"They can shoot arrows. Most would be useless without your spells to guide the arrows," Himar said. "Years it takes to make an archer."

"We'll need their arrows, though." Anna pursed her lips. "Before we talk, we need to see what's happening in Ebra." *If we can.* She motioned toward the mirror on the table, then turned and reclaimed the lutar. She checked the tuning, cleared her throat, and began what she hoped would be the last vocalise.

Her cords clear, she began the scrying spell.

> Bertmynn, Bertmynn, Lord I'd see,
> show his forces now to me . . .

As the last notes of the spell died way, the mirror silvered over, and then presented an image of armsmen in leathers and burgundy tunics advancing across a recently harvested grain field. One armsman staggered, flailed as an arrow went through his neck, then slowly crumpled. Those behind and beside him continued to trot forward with bared blades.

"They are fighting. Whether it is the beginning or the end . . ." Jecks shrugged.

"The beginning," offered Himar. "Bertmynn's armsmen still hesitate."

Without waiting, Anna tried a second spell.

> Show me now, and as must be,
> any fighting near Elahwa city. . . .

Anna tried not to wince at the rhyme, but the mirror image shifted, this time to show what seemed to her a pitched skirmish between figures in blue and others in burgundy. To the side of the blue figures with blades were others in blue with bows. Abruptly, a squad of lancers in burgundy appeared, slashing at both archers and armsmen afoot. Anna could tell that most, if not all, of those in blue were women.

As it became clear that few of the freewomen shown by the glass would survive, Anna sang a release couplet, then slowly laid the lutar on the bed.

"It may be different elsewhere near Elahwa," offered Jecks.

"It might be, but . . . is it likely?" asked Anna. "I'll check again before we leave in the morning."

"The morning?" Himar's eyebrows rose.

"We should march before Bertmynn can recover. We can't reach Elahwa before he takes over the city, anyway," Anna said. *You couldn't reach the other side of the Sand Pass. . . .*

"You should not," returned Himar. "Let the freewomen weaken him, and let young Hadrenn understand the danger. Your support will be worth more to him."

"And it will be less costly for you and for our lancers," added Jecks.

The Regent nodded slowly. What both men said made sense. So why did she feel guilty about not being able to attack Bertmynn before he reached Elahwa? *Because women are dying, and they have no one else?* Her lips tightened, but she nodded once more. "We leave in the morning."

42

The Ostfels and the eastern end of the Sand Pass lay a good ten deks to the west and behind the column of Defalkan lancers. On the north side of the narrow road were grasslands, similar to those around Mencha, but more lush. A half dozen deks or so to the south of the road lay a long beige ridge of sand—the westernmost part of the Sand Hills. The air above the dunes shifted and shimmered, sometimes reflecting the sun or something else.

Anna could almost feel the heat radiating from the dunes, and she took another long swallow from the water bottle as she studied the Sand Hills. According to Brill, at one point years earlier the sand had actually blocked the entrance to and the use of the Sand Pass, effectively isolating Ebra from Defalk. Then the Evult had shifted the dunes and begun his plans to invade and subdue Defalk.

Anna frowned. Without the Evult, would the sands shift again?

"What is the worst mistake a lancer can make in battle?" asked Kinor, his voice drifting forward to Anna and Jecks.

"Trying too hard to kill people," answered Himar.

Anna found herself listening, wondering what the overcaptain would say next.

"Aren't you supposed to kill the enemy?" interjected Jimbob.

Himar laughed. "If you must and if you can—easily. If your blade skills are good, it is best to let others make mistakes." There was a pause, as if the former Neserean officer had shrugged. "If you cannot, then by all means attack vigorously so that none will know how little skill you have."

". . . doesn't make sense . . ."

Anna thought the words were Jimbob's, but she wasn't sure.

"Perhaps one lancer in fivescore is strong enough and skilled enough to beat down another's blade. In all other cases, lancers die from their mistakes, and the biggest mistake is being too hasty in trying to kill another."

Jecks smiled and murmured to Anna. "His words are true."

"They make sense," she replied. *They're true in everything . . . but it's so hard to be patient when everyone is flailing at you.* She wished Skent had heard Himar's words . . . or that someone had conveyed them to the all-too-young undercaptain. *Another mistake? Another case of haste on your part? Because you need trusted and intelligent officers so badly?*

Her eyes went back to the shimmering expanse of the Sand Hills, then to the road ahead, the long road to Synek . . . and the longer road to bloody Elahwa.

43

"There's someone riding toward us," observed Rickel, checking his blade and glancing toward Blaz, who rode on Anna's left, away from the River Syne, a narrow and placid strip of brown water winding between intermittent low hills. The hills were covered mostly with a mixture of brown and green grass with patches of trees that represented woodlots for the cots that appeared at irregular intervals.

"In a hurry," suggested Blaz, as both guards reached for the large shields they carried to protect Anna for enough time to allow her to use her spellcasting.

Anna squinted into the low, late-afternoon sun, looking to see if she could discern any sign of Synek, but all she saw was the rider, and a good dek farther up the road, on a hillcrest to the west, another group of riders, two of whom appeared to be the scouts Himar had sent out ahead of the main column. She readjusted the floppy brown hat, but the sun was too low for the hat to help much.

"Ready arms!" ordered Himar. "Bowmen, first squad!"

Jecks drew his blade and eased up beside Anna.

Anna turned in the saddle and slipped the lutar out of its case. She glanced back at Jimbob and Kinor, both of whom had drawn steel, and then at the small round shield in the open-topped case at her knee, spelled against weapons directed toward her—an idea Jecks had forced upon her when they had begun the campaign in Dumar, but one that had proved its value more than once. Then she began to check the lutar's tuning as Rickel and Blaz eased forward so that they could lift the shields to protect her.

A rider in a green tunic neared, one hand on his mount's reins, and a second empty hand held clear of mount or the long blade he bore in a shoulder harness. "Greetings!" came the call as he reined up. "Regent and sorceress . . . Lord Hadrenn sent us to escort you to his hold." The black-haired lancer gestured. "My squad waits with your scouts." He paused, looking flustered, then extended a gold ring to Rickel. "My master's seal ring . . . to . . . so that . . ."

Anna took the ring from Rickel. "I will be happy to return it to Lord Hadrenn."

As Hadrenn's escort turned his mount, Anna slipped the ring into her wallet, but kept one hand on the lutar as they rode uphill and westward. Below, along the river, those few trees not uprooted or buried in piles of clay were bent over, almost touching the uneven ground on the lower riverbanks. The leaf patterns were uneven, with some trees having but few leaves at all, and one or two having full leaves, although touches of red and yellow were beginning to appear.

When the riders reached the hillcrest on the packed-clay road, Anna finally saw Synek on the far bank and to the northwest. At the next dip in the road, a crude timber bridge spanned the narrow river—the only bridge Anna could see looking either up or down the river, and clearly placed there because of its location on the narrowest part of the Syne.

"We must cross here," announced the guide. "Perhaps some of your force, then my squad, and then the Regent and players, and then the remainder of your lancers . . ."

Anna touched the shield at her knee, but it remained still, without vibration.

"Two companies first," suggested Jecks.

Anna nodded.

"Purple and gold companies to the fore!" ordered Himar.

Anna, Jecks, Jimbob, Kinor, and Liende and the players gathered to one side of the clay-packed causeway leading to the bridge as the two companies crossed and formed up on the northern side. Then Jecks and Blaz started across, and it was Anna's turn.

The bridge flexed, alarmingly to Anna, under Farinelli's weight, even as they took it in single file with no more than two mounts on the structure at a time. On the north side, as she waited for the remainder of the long line of lancers, Anna retuned the lutar, her eyes flicking along the north river road every few moments. Except for her escort and her own force, both roads remained empty.

Skent led his company—the cyan company—across the bridge with a show of confidence. Anna just hoped the young man was not too confident.

Once all had crossed, and they rode slowly back westward toward Synek, Anna studied the southern riverbank, the one that showed the most damage—more than half the area within a hundred yards of the water had not been repaired or rebuilt, and pile after pile of bricks and debris filled the ground. In a few places, dwellings and shops, seemingly rebuilt from the yellowish bricks, rose in clumps.

Anna swallowed. While she had not meant to visit such destruction on Synek . . . she had. *The most damning obituary, someone said, is: "She meant well." You meant well, and did worse.* Yet what else could she have done?

"There is Lord Hadrenn's hold." The guide gestured to a structure built of tan stone and yellow brick, not even so large as Loiseau, set on a hilltop perhaps a dek to the north of Synek. "We take the next lane."

An effort had been made to fill in the worst of the potholes on the side road, and to cut back trees and bushes, some of the saw cuts so recent that Anna could smell the odor of pine resin and other saplike odors.

The hold itself lacked a separate wall for fortification, but the windows on the lowest level were infrequent, small, and iron-barred. Otherwise, the mansion appeared more like an English country estate, but without either lawns or gardens. Several out-buildings flanked the dwelling hall, and one was newly built of old yellow bricks.

Armsmen's and lancers' quarters, no doubt.

"This is Lord Hadrenn's family home and birthplace," explained the guide.

The man who rode out alone down the road from the man-sion toward them was stocky, almost overweight, for all that he was probably less than thirty years old, Anna estimated. He was already mostly bald, and a scar ran from the side of his nose to below his right ear. Anna recognized him from her efforts at scrying him.

"Regent and sorceress?" His voice was surprisingly uncer-tain.

"Yes, Lord Hadrenn. I'm Lady Anna, Sorceress and Regent of Defalk." Anna gestured. "This is Lord High Counselor Jecks; Lord Jimbob, heir to Defalk; Liende, my chief of play-ers; and Overcaptain Himar."

Hadrenn inclined his head deeply. "To bring such . . . you honor me. You honor Synek." When he looked up, Anna noted that his eyes were deep and brown, almost cowlike except for the intentness and concentration they held.

"There is much to do," Anna temporized.

The young lord bowed again. "Lady Regent, I cannot say I expected you to come to my aid . . . even after your messenger arrived."

Anna smiled politely. "I am here . . . and we need to talk about what we should do. After we are settled and somewhat refreshed."

At her shoulder, Jecks nodded.

44

The blonde woman taps on the study door, a door slightly ajar.

"You may come in, Alya," responds the Matriarch.

Alya slides through the door and closes it behind her, if gently and nearly silently. "You have heard, Mother?" Her eyes focus directly on the round-faced Matriarch, who wears gray and black, not the usual garb of brighter colors.

"About the fate of the freewomen in Elahwa?" The Matriarch looks up from the sheet of parchment on the table-desk and nods somberly. "Your sister still lives. Beyond that, I do not know."

"Did you . . . have to . . . send her?"

The Matriarch looks up at her older daughter with eyes that are reddened, and ringed with black. "What would you have me do? Should my own daughter not follow the rules of harmony, the laws of Ranuak?"

"Why . . . why didn't Veria listen?"

"Because she could not accept that harmony is paid for again and again, endlessly. Or that harmony requires what it will and not what we wish. You see this. Even the sorceress from the mist worlds understands this." The Matriarch offers Alya a sad smile. "She does not know how dearly she will pay."

"She will pay . . . most dearly," interjects Ulgar from the corner of the study. He has been so still that Alya had not even noted her father's presence. "Even now, the young Prophet of Music gathers his forces to assault the western lords of Defalk."

"He is proving more cunning than his sire . . . and less perceptive," says the Matriarch. "All too many will suffer for that."

"The Regent of Defalk will turn back, then? When she has barely begun to march into Ebra?" Alya's voice is almost flat.

"Since young Hadrenn has pledged to her, she remains in Defalk," explains the silver-haired Ulgar. "And she will not turn back."

"Father . . . you know what I meant."

"Yet your father is correct," answers the Matriarch, "for what was western Ebra is now Defalk, as well may be all of Ebra."

"Why did the sorceress wait so long?" asks Alya plaintively. "Why did she stop to use sorcery to wrench gold from the ground?"

"Without that gold, daughter, the sorceress could not afford to march to Elahwa. Who would lend her the coins? Certainly not the Exchange. And how would she guarantee them? Nor could she let the Thirty-three know of such resources before she marched, or they would demand that she use the coins to reduce their liedgeld."

"Men . . ." Alya's voice is close to a sigh.

"Women are no better. Consider Abslim. Like those of the Defalkan Thirty-three, she considers the weight of coins first and sees what she will see, and not what is there to see."

"Still . . . I would that the sorceress could have reached Elahwa before the dog of the north."

"Your sister could not expect to be rescued by the very ruler she condemned," points out Ulgar. "Not even by the twisted laws of Darksong."

Alya draws a long, slow, and silent breath.

45

Anna smoothed the green traveling gown into place, checking the cinches at her waist, far smaller than she had ever thought to see again, centered the link necklace, wiggled her toes in the loose sandals, then glanced around the guest chamber—a single large room without bathing facilities, although an older brass tub had been dragged in and hurriedly polished, then surrounded by screens. A pair of ancient porcelain chamber pots glazed with a faded rose pattern rested in the far corner of the room away from the tub, the writing desk, and the four-postered bedstead and its array of netting.

The windows bore no glass, only heavy outer shutters and

louvered inner ones, both sets oiled at some time in the distant past, but not recently.

No wonder Hadrenn needs help. She couldn't help but consider the wisdom of her decision to support the young lord of Synek. *Except, as always, the alternatives appear worse, especially with Ebra under the heavy male thumb of Bertmynn . . . so you will accept the lighter thumb of Hadrenn?*

She winced as she considered the scenes of Elahwa she had called up in the mirror. *You couldn't have gotten there in time, even if you'd gone straight from Pamr. But if you'd decided earlier . . .* As she opened the door, she shook her head. *You can't live on "ifs."*

Four guards were stationed in the brick-floored and dusty hall outside Anna's door—Rickel, Lejun, Kerhor, and Blaz. Anna raised her eyebrows.

"This hold is less secure," answered Rickel. "Both Lord Jecks and the overcaptain agree."

"I wouldn't dispute either on that." Anna offered a short, wry laugh, then managed to contain a sneeze. She'd definitely need a bit of sorcery before she slept in the guest bed, or she'd be so allergenic she'd spend the entire night sneezing, and that would weaken her voice for days. That was something she certainly couldn't afford.

"I am gladdened that you would not." Jecks stepped from the door down the hall, wearing the blue dress tunic that served the same purpose as Anna's gown. He bowed, then smiled as he straightened. "As always, you are most beautiful."

"Beautiful?" Anna's lips curled, and she leaned forward and murmured almost into his ear. "I look more like a boy than a woman."

"No one would mistake your beauty for other than it is—"

"What? That of a tightened bow, of a woman most solitary and stern?" Anna couldn't resist the paraphrase of Yeats, though she doubted she was any Maude Gonne. *Or Helen. Then . . . do you really want to be?*

A momentary frown crossed the white-haired lord's face, then vanished. "Lord Hadrenn will be most astonished."

"He might be, but for all the wrong reasons."

Followed by both Rickel and Kerhor, Anna and Jecks

descended the main staircase, its wooden balustrade rails polished by generations of hands, toward the central foyer. Before they reached the wide steps below the landing, the stocky Hadrenn hurried toward them, now wearing a green-velvet jacket of sorts over a mostly white-silk shirt. He stood, waiting as the two descended, his eyes taking in all of Anna, just a fraction short of pure lechery. "Ah . . . Lady Anna."

"Remember, Lord Hadrenn," she said, lightly, "I have children of your age."

"One . . . would never know that." The scar on the left side of his face turned pinkish, then faded. "You are an ornament to any company, any land, any table." He gestured toward the age-darkened double doors of the dining hall. "The hall . . . and the poor best we have . . . await you and your company."

Anna managed not to wince at the thought of being an ornament as Jecks slipped beside her, not quite possessively, offering his arm. She took it, squeezing his muscled forearm, if lightly and briefly, before leading the way toward the dining area. Again, both Rickel and Kerhor flanked them.

The dining hall, while large for a private home, was smaller than the main dining hall at Loiseau. Anna stood behind the seat at the end of the table, with Jecks to her left, and waited for Jimbob, Kinor, Himar, and Liende to join them.

Hadrenn arrived first, smiling. "I had thought that Gestatr might join us, as my commander."

"That would be good," Anna said, smiling and turning as the dark-haired and square-faced Gestatr neared. "I'm glad to see you again, Gestatr. Frideric and Markan send their best."

The man who had been Lord Hryding's captain nodded. "Lady Anna . . . it appears that we both have come far since last we met."

Anna could sense the puzzlement from Jecks and some of the others. "Overcaptain Gestatr . . . or arms commander . . . he was the lead armsman for Lord Hryding of Synope during the years when the Evult ruled Ebra. Because his family had served the previous lords of Ebra, his first allegiance has always been to his homeland, and he returned when he had the chance." Anna looked at Gestatr. "I hope I got that right . . . but that's what I heard."

Gestatr inclined his head and returned the smile. "Lord Hryding had said you would not forget much, and you have not. My grandsire was the arms commander for Lord Julenn, Lord Hadrenn's grandsire."

As the well-muscled Gestatr slipped into place beside Jecks, Anna noted that his once-jet-black hair was shot with white. *Or didn't you notice that in Synope?* She sat down, ignoring the frown from Jimbob as the youth realized that Gestatr sat above him at the table. Anna suspected Jecks had managed that . . . somehow.

A serving girl poured pale, amber-tinged wine into the silver goblets.

"A toast!" Hadrenn lifted his goblet. "To the Regent!"

"To the Regent."

Anna lifted her goblet in acknowledgment, but did not drink. When the goblets were lowered, she responded, "To Lord Hadrenn and his hospitality."

Everyone but Hadrenn drank to her toast, but the young lord lifted his goblet in response.

Large platters of beef covered in a brown sauce appeared, as did casserole dishes of sliced and roasted potatoes. Anna took her usual enormous helping, forcing herself to wait until most had a chance at being served before she took the first bite. Despite the sauce, the meat was dry, but she was hungry enough that it didn't matter too much.

"Perhaps . . . Regent Anna," suggested Hadrenn, "you could begin by telling us how you came to be Regent."

Anna took another mouthful of potatoes before she replied, ignoring the glance at her less-than-supremely-endowed chest, still glad that the gown was comparatively high-necked. "It's rather simple, Lord Hadrenn, but I'll be happy to tell that story. A rather strange combination of spells on both the mist world and on Erde combined to bring me to Mencha, near the hold of the sorcerer Brill . . ." Anna cut down the tale to close to the bare essentials, concluding with, ". . . and I found myself Regent of Defalk."

Hadrenn pulled at his thick, but short-trimmed brown beard. "It is said that you have killed men, not only with sorcery, but with a blade."

"One," Anna answered. "With a dagger." *Because you were stupid and careless . . .*

"And that you have been wounded innumerable times, but saved by sorcery . . ."

Anna laughed. "I've been wounded badly twice, and no sorceress can save herself through sorcery. I had to heal the hard way."

"She took a war arrow in one shoulder, and iron crossbow bolts in the chest and arm," interjected Jecks.

Hadrenn shook his head. "Most do not survive one such wound."

"I'm a survivor," Anna replied. *A better survivor than a fighter, still . . .*

"And you are here . . . surely not merely to visit," suggested Gestatr.

"No . . . we're not here just to visit." Anna nodded toward Jimbob. "I also thought Lord Jimbob should meet you, Lord Hadrenn."

"I still find it hard to believe that you brought the heir with you." Hadrenn's bushy eyebrows rose.

"Lord Jecks and I felt he should experience matters more directly. That's hard to do with a tutor in Falcor."

"Ah . . . I could see that." Hadrenn refilled his silver goblet.

Anna took a sip of the wine, which had begun to taste metallic. Wine was better in glass, even poor wine—much better.

"If I might inquire about Markan and Frideric . . ." ventured the black-haired Gestatr after another silence.

"Markan is now the lead armsman at Suhl . . ." Anna began, after finishing the rest of the beef on her platter, then taking a sip of the amber wine. She explained how the two had left Flossbend after Lord Hryding's death. ". . . and Frideric was overseeing the stables and mounts and arms supplies of the hold. Lady Herene is there to serve as the guardian of the heirs."

Hadrenn frowned. "Sargol revolted, and you let his children keep the lands?"

"The oldest child is eight, Lord Hadrenn. Their guardian and tutor is indebted to me." Anna shrugged. "You would have me disinherit every lord who questions? How then would I be different from the Evult?"

Gestatr laughed, easily. "You see, my lord, why many would have her as Regent for the years to come. Lord Hryding entrusted her with his daughter." He turned toward Anna.

"Secca is well. She's with the other fosterlings in Falcor, and has made friends with several. She is a very determined young lady," Anna said, without looking at Jimbob, "and believes, as did her father, in doing right." After a moment, she continued, "Markan said that Stepan had joined you here."

"He has, and he is captain over the levies of the north."

Anna nodded. "And how have you found Ebra since you returned?"

"Ebra was once rich, with the most fertile of lands. Now . . . farming is a struggle, and none are rich. Here . . . the lands have held their strength. . . ."

Anna finished her meal as first Gestatr, and then others, talked. She spoke seldom, and only to ask a question that prompted another's stories.

When it was clear all had finished, Anna turned to Hadrenn. "We have some things to discuss," she said pleasantly. "Himar, Lord Jecks and I, and you, and Gestatr. A more private meeting."

"You have just arrived . . ."

Anna's eyes were cool. "Lord Hadrenn . . . your hospitality and your greetings are most welcome . . . and generous. But much as I appreciate your hospitality and the beauty of Ebra, it's best that we do what needs to be done quickly."

Hadrenn swallowed, as if he were trying to hold back a flush of anger.

"I am here to aid you. I wouldn't be here otherwise, but we must work quickly." Anna smiled warmly.

After only a momentary hesitation, Hadrenn rose, as did Anna, and the group followed the Lord of Synek down the corridor, boots and shoes scuffing the hollowed and worn yellow bricks in the dim light of candles in scattered wall sconces. The private study was small, the green carpet laid over the yellow-brick floor faded and worn.

Rickel and Kerhor stationed themselves at the study door.

"You are not . . . as others . . . of Defalk." Hadrenn said slowly, standing by the small carved desk, glancing toward the closed door.

"I'm not like either the lords of the Thirty-three, nor like most women of Liedwahr," Anna acknowledged. "If I were, you'd be facing Bertmynn alone, and you'd lose. From what the mirrors tell me, he lost almost as many armsmen in taking Elahwa as you have." Anna knew she was being too blunt, but her guts told her that flattery and indirection would have been lost on Hadrenn.

"That is doubtless true." Gestatr nodded. "When Bertmynn's strength became known, I suggested, and Lord Hadrenn agreed that an alliance . . . a fealty to Defalk . . . was our only hope."

"I understand that Bertmynn slaughtered almost all the free-women." Anna's voice was flat.

"Many escaped into the marshes, and they say that some are gathering in the northern part of the Sand Hills to await forces from Ranuak," suggested Gestatr smoothly.

"I doubt there will be any forces from Ranuak," Anna answered. "There do not appear to be any lancers or armsmen moving northward. There are no more ships in the harbor at Encora, either."

"I see . . ." murmured Hadrenn. After a moment, he added, "Still . . . Regents do not risk their sorcery and their forces for naught. . . ."

"No . . . they don't," Anna agreed, forcing herself to wait, meeting Hadrenn's deep brown eyes, but making sure that her eyes did not waver and that they promised nothing.

"What do you wish? The fealty of all of Ebra?"

"That's a start," Anna agreed.

"This land is poor, and you have already ravaged it once, lady. That was justified, but there is little left to take."

"Beyond liedgeld, I don't want any more golds," Anna said. "I want some other conditions."

"That is good." Hadrenn gestured around the ancient room. "As you can see, golds are not plentiful."

"What might Defalk wish?" asked Gestatr.

"Let's talk about what you'd like first," suggested Anna. "What do you want?"

"To hold and restore my family's lands and patrimony. Is that not obvious?"

"You could have pledged to Bertmynn and received that." Anna waited.

"I think not. Long has there been a sharpened blade between our houses."

Anna nodded. "So you wish to have all of Ebra, if it is possible."

The round-faced lord chuckled, uneasily. "I would not hazard so much. . . ."

"You have the right of it," said Gestatr. "Lord Hadrenn would like the position his grandsire held. He cannot hold that without your aid. What would you have us do to obtain such assistance?"

Hadrenn looked hard at his arms commander.

"My lord, one does not deceive this lady. Not if one wishes her aid." Gestatr's voice was matter-of-fact.

"Gestatr and his family have seldom steered us wrong," Hadrenn said slowly. "What must I do?"

"First, you have been constant in what you have said. When matters are settled in Ebra, I would like to confirm you as the Lord of Ebra—except I'd prefer a title more along the lines of High Counselor."

Hadrenn nodded slowly. "And you want Ebra's friendship for the harmony of the ages." A faint smile crinkled his lips.

"That, too, but there are a few other conditions," Anna said.

The smile vanished.

"Once Bertmynn is defeated, I think Ebra should be organized into three lands under you—the demesne of Synek, the demesne of Dolov, and the demesne of Elahwa. Third, I want Elahwa to be rebuilt as an open-port city—under the rule of the freewomen, but they must acknowledge you as their high counselor. Fourth, I require a thirty percent surtax on all goods from Sturin. Half the tax goes to Falcor, and half to you. And last, I require that Ebra honor and extend the post-courier system we have adopted in Defalk to carry scrolls throughout the land."

Hadrenn pulled at his short, square-cut beard. "All your . . . conditions . . . save one . . . are well within reason."

"You have trouble with the freewomen," Anna said. "I understand that. However, if you want my support, and if you want trade and grain and coins from Ranuak, you must allow the freewomen to rule Elahwa as a sanctuary for women who do not wish to be bartered as goods."

Hadrenn shifted his weight from one foot to the other. "That will not sit well with some."

"I'm sure it won't." Anna's smile was hard. "Do you want me to remove Lord Bertmynn?"

"How . . . how can I accept a demesne . . . even one acknowledging me . . ."

"How about pointing out that it cost Bertmynn something like fifteenscore armsmen to take Elahwa, and that you'd be facing rebellion there every generation? How about suggesting that it might be better to have a place for women who don't fit than having both the Matriarch and the sorceress angry at Ebra?"

"Those thoughts might be most convincing, my lord," suggested Gestatr. "And who else would oppose more strongly any attempts at invasion by the Sea-Lords?"

"There is that . . ." mused Hadrenn.

"You can tell a few trusted supporters that I strongly urged you to do this . . . strongly enough that you had no choice."

"Why?" The brown eyes conveyed puzzlement. "You would allow me to say such?"

Jecks smiled. "It is to your advantage. As Gestatr has said, do you think the freewomen will allow another land to use Elahwa as a port for conquering Ebra? Do you not think that you will obtain better trading terms from Ranuak?"

Hadrenn shook his head, then smiled ruefully. "I cannot but accept your terms, sorceress and Regent. Not all will be happy, and even though I order such for Elahwa, all will know whence came the idea."

"That may be," answered Anna, "but in time the credit, and the benefits, will be yours." *Now . . . all you have to do is win battles and get back to Defalk before Rabyn decides to march through Denguic.* She held back a yawn. It had been a long day, just one of many to come.

46

ELAHWA, EBRA

You *will* answer my questions." Bertmynn smiles as he looks down at the figure tied and spread-eagled on the broad dark wooden table in what had recently been an inn. Slowly he draws the dagger and studies it.

The figure bound to the table is a woman, who wears a blue undertunic, her dirty sandy hair cut short as any armsman's of Bertmynn's. The pattern of sweat, dirt, and blood on the fabric indicates she had once worn some type of plastron. A narrow cut, scabbed over, runs from below the corner of her mouth to a point short of her left ear.

"Where did you bitches find archers?"

". . . can't answer what . . . don't know . . ."

"Those archers . . . where did they come from?" Bertmynn fingers the knife suggestively.

". . . don't know . . ."

Bertmynn bends over slightly, easing aside fabric with the sharpened tip of the short blade, pressing firmly, then twisting. Blood wells around the point. "Where do you think they came from? Defalk?"

". . . don't know . . . didn't know we had archers . . ."

"Come now . . . do not take me for a simpleton." Bertmynn's smile turns crooked, and he twists the blade.

The woman's body twitches, but she does not speak.

The Lord of Dolov lifts the dagger and wipes it on her tunic, before leaning forward once more to part the fabric. He stops and straightens at the rap on the door, watching as it swings open to reveal a gray-haired man in a stained burgundy tunic, who stands waiting in the half-open doorway.

"Yes, Ceorwyn?"

"I have discovered what you sought."

"Then tell me."

Ceorwyn glances at the bound woman.

"It does not matter. She thinks she will not talk. So I will turn her over to the First Foot for their pleasure. They lost the most men. They should enjoy themselves." Bertmynn sheaths the dagger. "Well?"

Behind him, the woman's eyes turn cold, then fill with hatred.

"Ser . . . your seers report that the Regent of Defalk is marching down the river road from Synek, and that lancers and armsmen loyal to Hadrenn accompany her." The gray-haired Ceorwyn bows slightly to Bertmynn.

"Are the drums ready?"

"Two are prepared. She is four days ride to the west . . . or five." Ceorwyn's eyes avoid the bound figure on the table.

"How many lancers and armsmen?"

"She has perhaps fifteenscore lancers, and another fifteenscore armsmen in green."

"Those are Hadrenn's." Bertmynn frowns. "Fifteenscore is less than half of what he has raised."

"It is said, ser, that she took but fifteenscore lancers into Dumar. She returned with fourteen score, and Ehara and the Sturinnese lost twenty times her force, and every city on the Falche River."

"Ebra is not Dumar. I am not that dunce Ehara." Bertmynn snorts. "No woman will prevail in Ebra." He turns and his eyes go to the bound woman. "As you will discover."

The faintest smile crosses the captive's lips.

"You will not mock me." Bertmynn's hand crashes against the woman's cheek. The captive remains silent, and her face becomes impassive, but rage pours from her eyes.

"Yes . . . rage if you will, but rage you will but against the dying of the light." Bertmynn laughs. "No sorceress will save you . . . or your frail deeds. Or your freewomen—those few that remain uncaptured."

The Lord of Synek strides out of the room and out onto the porch that overlooks the river quays of Elahwa. Ceorwyn follows silently.

"Twentyscore armsmen lost here . . . who would have thought it . . ." Bertmynn mutters. "Who possibly would have thought a gaggle of geese, of untrained women, of green archers . . . twentyscore?"

"The sorceress' forces are well trained, and all have seen battle," Ceorwyn says.

"No . . . they have seen her battle," corrects Bertmynn. "And how the lords of Defalk could let a woman . . ." He shakes his head. "They have betrayed their own heritage and will indeed suffer."

Ceorwyn does not respond, but remains in the shadow cast by the overhanging eaves.

"Dissonance . . . that I should be required to call upon Darksong to hold my own lands." Bertmynn's lips tighten, and he looks northward at the calm and nearly still waters of the river. "But better Darksong than a woman ruling over Ebra. Better anything than that."

47

The River Syne wound through the sun-splashed rolling hills of mid-Ebra, and the road to Elahwa followed the slightly higher hills on the south side of the river, though there was a lane or dirt track on the north side that she could see occasionally across the river. The air was moist, and Anna had felt as though her tunic and trousers were perpetually soaked, half-steamed. She blotted her forehead, then reached for the water bottle, looking at the winding road before her. Riding ahead of the main body—if behind the scouts—were the two standard-bearers, one bearing the purple banner of Defalk, with the crossed spears with the crown and the *R* beneath, and the other bearing a green banner with gold blades crossed over a sheaf of grain.

Hadrenn rode to Anna's right, a large hand-and-a-half blade in a shoulder harness, and a shortsword in a scabbard. Rivulets of sweat streamed down his round face, and his tunic was splotchy with the dark stains of sweat.

Behind Hadrenn and Anna, crowded stirrup to stirrup, rode Jecks, Jimbob, and Kinor. Behind them rode Himar and Stepan.

". . . problem with lances . . . one-time weapons . . . get

under a lance, or knock it aside, and your lancer's chopped meat . . . can't carry that many lances anyway . . . what do you do once you break the first lance, or it lodges in some other armsman or lancer?" Jecks laughed, almost sardonically. "Lances and heavy armor work well against peasants or ill-equipped foot without a pike—if your heavy cavalry doesn't have to ride far . . . and if you can find enough peasants to carry all the baggage . . ."

Anna nodded, almost to herself, as she listened to Jecks' voice carrying forward. She'd often wondered about lances and knights, about what earthly use a lance was except in a joust or a pitched battle in a small area. She'd heard Avery give all the arguments, but most of those arguments were what she'd have called Eurocentric chauvinism. In Earth's history heavily armed knights had been an expensive and costly rarity useful only in limited circumstances, and mainly in European settings by barons and others able to amass large amounts of wealth. No empire of any great size or extent had ever been held through the armored knight . . . for all the romanticization about knights. *And of course, neither Avery nor Mario had ever listened to your observations.*

Anna snorted to herself. Some things didn't change across worlds. Lord Dannel and Avery would have gotten along fairly well. She shook her head. *That's too cynical, even for you. Avery wasn't near that bad.*

Hadrenn glanced toward the Regent. "You said that the usurper's forces were still in Elahwa?"

Anna blinked, reorienting her thoughts. "According to the mirror, that's where he was this morning." She took another long swallow of water. In some ways, the steamy fall heat of Ebra was as bad as the drought-created heat of Defalk had once been. "You think it will take another two days to reach where the rivers join?"

"Two, if it does not rain." The stocky brown-haired lord glanced to the east, and the intermittent thunderclouds forming there.

"Good."

"You feel that Bertmynn will meet us there, and that he will fight. What if Bertmynn retreats to Dolov?"

Anna thought. *What if he does?* Then she shrugged. "Then

we will free Elahwa, and you will set up a free state ruled by
the freewomen, but under your protection. Bertmynn will
return. Quickly, I'd bet."

"That's a wager I'd not take." Jecks laughed from where he
rode behind Anna and beside Jimbob.

"I yield to your judgment, Lord High Counselor," Hadrenn
responded, wiping his damp brow with the back of his forearm.

"Bertmynn, indeed all Liedwahr, knows that Lady Anna's
sympathies lie with women who have been ill-treated. For that
reason alone," Jecks continued, "I would doubt that he would
allow you two to ride unmolested to Elahwa."

"You are certain that Bertmynn is near Elahwa?" asked
Hadrenn.

"The mirror hasn't misled me that way yet," Anna answered.
"Unless he can cover two days' ride in half a day, he can't be far
from Elahwa or where the rivers meet north of there."

"He will wait for us," Jecks said. "We should take three days,
if necessary."

Anna understood that, but she worried. Even though the mirror indicated that Rabyn and his forces had just left Esaria, the
ride from Elahwa back to Denguic was farther than from Esaria
to Denguic. *Lord, every military strategist ever quoted by Avery
or Sandy talked about not fighting wars on two fronts, and
you've gotten into one?* Was she acting out the old adage about
fools rushing in?

She pursed her lips and shifted her weight in the saddle.

48

Anna's tent was set up without the sidewalls, more as an
awning to offer some shade for the group that gathered in
the late afternoon. She glanced at Jecks, then let her eyes travel
across Hadrenn, Stepan, Jimbob, Kinor, and Liende. Liende
brushed back hair that showed less and less red and more white,
but offered an amused smile to Anna.

Himar stood before the group, and his voice was raspy as he
talked. ". . . likely that we will meet with Bertmynn's forces on

the morrow. He brings near-on eighty score, though some are foot levies from Dolov . . . with little experience or training. His own lancers are well seasoned, and they will be at the fore. . . ."

The faintest of breezes carried a hint of coolness from the river to the north then faded, leaving the group sweating in the unseasonably sultry heat.

"Lady Anna has studied Bertmynn's forces with her glass, and they are here." Using a whittled length of pencil wood, Himar pointed to a spot on the crude map just south and east of where the River Syne and the River Dol joined. "Where he now waits is perhaps a ride of three glasses."

Hadrenn looked at the maps and then toward Anna before speaking. "We could circle south of him, cross at one of the lower fords, and then go downriver and take Elahwa from behind. We would not have to face Bertmynn. . . ."

Anna shook her head, without even thinking about getting opinions from Jecks or Himar. "That's not the reason I'm here. I want it set up so that all of Bertmynn's armsmen are in one battle."

"You risk all of your armsmen as well," countered Hadrenn, "and much of my forces."

"Yours are at risk in any eventuality, Lord Hadrenn," suggested Jecks. "You cannot raise the numbers he has, nor can you count on assistance from the Liedfuhr or the Sturinnese."

"Well we know that," answered the brown-haired lord of Synek. "Well we do."

Himar cleared his throat, and the others looked at the mustached overcaptain. "Ah . . . also, if we circled south, Bertmynn could well be between us and either Synek or Defalk, and then we would have to fight more in a place of his choosing." Himar addressed Hadrenn. "Also, should aught go amiss, you can return to Synek more easily if we fight more to the north."

Jecks nodded. After a moment, so did Hadrenn.

"We'll have to move slowly in the morning," Anna said. "We can't afford to attack from lower grounds—"

"Or be attacked from higher ground," added Jecks.

"And we'll need time to set up the players." Anna glanced

toward Liende, who nodded. Then she inclined her head to Himar.

"The Regent and Lord Hadrenn have explained our aims," Himar said. "It is now time for you to tell your subofficers and those men who will carry them out. Remember that the task of all the lancers is to protect the sorceress and the players first. If we succeed in that, Bertmynn will fall."

As the others hurried away, in the burnt orange of twilight, Jecks and Anna remained under the awning tent, with Kerhor and Blaz a dozen paces away.

"You do not wish Ebra to be like Dumar," Jecks offered in a low voice.

"That's partly it."

"You could take Ebra, and none would gainsay that." The white-haired lord's eyes flicked in the direction where, a hundred paces away, Hadrenn was speaking with Stepan. "You would likely rule better than young Hadrenn, even from Falcor."

"I can't rule Defalk very well," Anna said. "The last thing I need . . . anyone needs . . . is another set of lords to argue with. This way, the women of Ebra who don't like the old ways have somewhere to go. Those who like the old ways can keep them, and outside of complaining about the free state, and me . . ." She shrugged. "Whatever."

"You do not wish to leave a trail of fire and spells," Jecks suggested.

"No. In Dumar, I ended up destroying a whole city of innocents—or mostly innocents. That was because I let myself get backed into a corner."

"You backed Ehara into a corner, most would say."

"No. In losing, he forced my hand. Or I let him, because I worried about spending too much time in Dumar with the Thirty-three machinating in Defalk. And . . . I was trying to be merciful, and it didn't turn out that way. This time . . ."

"Is that why Gestatr remains in Synek?" Jecks' eyes twinkled.

"Yes. He's more valuable to Ebra than Hadrenn."

"And so, to Defalk," Jecks affirmed.

Anna nodded. *Except nothing works out the way you plan it, not the details or the costs, anyway.*

49

Bertmynn runs a hand through his thick blond hair, then glances at the scroll on the folding camp table. He picks up the scroll once more, squinting to read it by the light of the candle. "She travels the Syne River road . . . she is camped less than a half day's ride from here." He drops the scroll and stands, stretching, before he looks at the older man, who is the only other one in the tent with him.

"We could swing northward, through Nuvann, and then strike at Synek. . . ." Ceorwyn lines a general path on the map pinned to the battered board set on a makeshift easel of lashed branches beside the table.

Bertmynn picks up the scroll once more, studies it, and sets it back on the table. He shakes his head. "No . . . we have kept the drums hidden from her, and we cannot do that for long. Nor dare we use Darksong too often. We must ensure that her forces are concentrated in one place, where we hold the high ground. She must be destroyed all at once. Otherwise, we will fight and fight and fight, and neither the Liedfuhr nor the Sea-Marshal will send us golds week after week, season after season."

"The sorceress cannot linger long in Ebra, my lord," counters the gray-haired warrior. "Many of the lords of the Thirty-three are less than pleased with her, and should she stay in Ebra too long, she risks an attack from the mad young Prophet of Music. He, too, is building Darksong drums to use against her, and he can call upon near-on a hundredscore Mansuuran lancers, and two hundred–score of his own lancers and armsmen. You have far more armsmen than does Hadrenn. You can afford to wait. She will have to leave, and soon."

"No . . . I cannot afford to wait. I cannot defeat the bitch without Darksong, and I cannot long use it and still see my way across a room, let alone to a mount. And I must use it while she suspects it has not yet been raised."

"Do not use it . . . wait. Harry Hadrenn's forces, and avoid the sorceress. She cannot linger," counsels Ceorwyn. "She cannot, and have a land to return to."

"Hadrenn can retreat back to the hills. He sent but half his forces down the river. The sorceress can send him golds. Then . . . what will I do when Elahwa rises again, or the South-Women send more golds and blades? Or when the Sturinnese send more than a mere three ships? Will I be forced to follow Lord Ehara of Dumar's example? Then, the Thirty-three might well unite behind her, and even the bitches of the south might send the sorceress golds. So I would then be fighting half of Liedwahr and Hadrenn—"

"Hadrenn is an inexperienced young lord."

"He is, but his force leaders are not, and he has the wit to listen to them, the dissonant young puppy." Bertmynn coughs and spits on the ground in the corner of the tent. "So I would be fighting Hadrenn, the freewomen and the SouthWomen, and the sorceress again. Or I would submit to being a counter for the Sea-Lords."

"Those may not happen."

Bertmynn looks hard at Ceorwyn. "Think you not?"

After a time, Ceorwyn's eyes drop.

50

Anna stepped into a patch of shade to get out of the already warm morning sun, then glanced around the group—Jecks, Himar, Hadrenn, and Liende, with Stepan, Jimbob, and Kinor standing farther back. Behind them were her guards, and a full score of lancers surrounding the shaded grove where she had laid out the traveling scrying mirror on a fallen tree trunk. To the west, along the Syne River road, the column was forming, preparing for the ride eastward, to meet Bertmynn's forces.

Finally, after a vocalise, she swallowed and cleared her throat, then lifted the lutar and sang:

Show me now and show me clear
a road to Bertmynn with no armsmen near,
Like a vision, like a map . . .

The mirror displayed an image, almost a topographical map with a light brown line that appeared to be the river road they traveled—until just short of the juncture of the two rivers, when the path veered south and around a line of hills.

Ulpp.

Anna suspected the gulp belonged to Hadrenn, but she continued to concentrate on the image. Himar was sketching rapidly on a sheet of crude brown paper, his eyes flicking from the mirror to the paper.

"If the glass is correct," Anna said, "that will bring us out on the higher south side of the valley."

"The last part of the way is narrow." Himar kept sketching. "There are trees on both sides. We would not see any lancers until they were upon us."

"Let me know when you have it drawn out." Anna could feel the heat building around her, and within the mirror and its frame. After a short time, Himar lifted his head. "I have enough."

Anna sang the release couplet, and then took a long swallow from the water bottle Jecks handed her. She thought about waving away the biscuit that followed, but took it instead and munched through it. *Have to keep your energy levels up.*

"Let's see if Bertmynn has planned any surprises." She cleared her throat and raised the lutar.

Danger from Bertmynn, danger near,
show me that danger bright and clear. . . .

The image showed a line of armsmen, arrayed on a hillside. There was a smaller group, barely a handful of figures, behind the armsmen, higher on the hillside.

"Are those archers?" asked Jecks. "Or players?"

"They don't have as many players as we do, if they're players, and less than a score of archers won't change things." Anna frowned. "Whatever danger there is . . . it looks like it will be when we meet."

"I worry about those folk . . ." Jecks gestured toward the mirror, speaking in a voice meant only for Anna's ears.

"So do I, but we can't just ride away because we don't feel things are quite right." She forced a light laugh.

Jecks tightened his lips.

"I need to talk to Liende." Anna motioned to the chief player, and then to Himar, and to Stepan, waiting for them to approach more closely before continuing. "As soon as we can get within vocal range of Bertmynn's forces, we'll use the long flame song—that's the one for weapons that might be spelled against us."

"The long flame song," Liende repeated.

Anna looked at Himar. "Do you think his lancers will attack quickly?"

"Either quickly, or they will wait for us to attack." Himar fingered his chin. "They would have to come down from higher ground and then charge uphill. I would wait, were I in their position."

"Does it look like our bowmen can lift arrows far enough to reach their position? If we form on the southern ridge?"

"I cannot tell." Himar shrugged apologetically.

"Well . . . we'll hope so." Anna looked back at Liende. "We'll plan on the arrow song second. If the arrows reach them, we'll do it several times."

"The arrow song for the second spell," Liende confirmed.

"And I may need the short flame song, almost at any time."

A frown crossed Liende's face, then vanished.

"And possibly the short arrow song, the one I used against Sargol." *Not that it did any good there.* She turned to Himar. "Are we ready to ride?"

"Yes, Lady Anna."

Anna nodded, and recased the lutar, then looked toward the mirror, but Jecks had already packed it and was strapping it to Farinelli.

Hadrenn took a long, thoughtful look at Anna, before turning to follow Himar.

Liende glanced at Anna as the others moved through the dappled shadows of the grove toward their mounts, then asked the sorceress, "You will not let Kinor ride with the lancers?"

"No . . . I told him and Jimbob that they had to help my personal guards. There's some danger there, but . . . less, I would judge."

"Kinor . . . he would prove he is worthy."

"I know. But he has to see what happens in battles, I think. People die, and most battles . . ." *Don't have to be fought? Except they do, because people's beliefs aren't the same, and someone always wants to force other people to believe differently.* After a moment, Anna found the question coming back. *Are you any different? Aren't people dying because you want to force this world to treat women better?*

"You are silent, lady."

Anna sighed. "I'd like to think I'm different from others who rule, but I'm not. I fight for what I believe in, and so do they. I just have to hope that what I believe in is worth the deaths."

"Life is not what we wish, lady, but I believe you do the best you can. That is why I ride with you." Liende smiled sadly.

"Thank you," answered Anna softly. "I try." As Liende turned, Anna carried the lutar toward Farinelli, and Jecks.

"Can you bring your spells against the players—if that is what they are?" The hazel eyes of the white-haired lord radiated concern.

"You're worried, aren't you?"

"For you, my lady, not for me."

Anna reached out with her free hand and squeezed his shoulder, firmly but gently. "I'll try to think of something as we ride." *You'd better . . . when he's worried, he's usually right.* She strapped the lutar behind her saddle, then patted Farinelli, and mounted.

51

Anna brushed a strand of silver-blonde hair out of her eye. A cooler breeze blew out of the east, and although high gray clouds had appeared on the horizon a glass or so earlier, they seemed no nearer than when Anna's force had resumed the ride along the River Syne. The sorceress eased back her brown hat and glanced ahead at the scouts on the road, then at the vanguard waiting at the junction to a lane that sloped down and to the south.

Anna touched the spelled shield at her knee, but there was no energy, no sense of sorcery there.

"We should head south here." Himar glanced back past Rickel and Lejun, who had their shields out and now rode directly before Anna, while Blaz and Kerhor rode behind Jecks, Jimbob, and Kinor.

"I'd like to take a last look in the mirror," Anna said, reining up. "Before we get too close to where Bertmynn is."

After Anna dismounted, Jecks laid out the mirror on the browning grass by the shoulder of the river road, and she tuned the lutar. Her guards and Jimbob and Kinor remained mounted, providing a circle of protection.

She sang the danger spell . . . but the only dangers that the shimmering glass showed were Bertmynn's armsmen and the handful of figures behind them. *Why are they a danger?* Yet if she didn't know more, sorcery would offer no answers.

Anna released the image quickly. The less energy she spent on looking, the better, but she also didn't want to ride into an ambush.

"Still those players," Jecks said. "Have you a spell? Can you use an arrow spell?"

Does he think you've got endless spells memorized? Anna wanted to scream, but forced a long, slow breath instead. "I'm thinking about it."

What could she use . . . something along the line of "Heads of arrows, shot into the air . . . strike Bertmynn's players there . . . ?" She needed more, more time, more armsmen, more everything. *And just whose idea was this expedition?*

Anna recased the lutar and fastened it behind her, but where she could reach it easily. Then she looked back at Liende, past Jimbob and Kinor. "How are the players?"

"Ready for what calls," Liende replied.

"Good." Anna remounted. *You just hope you are.* Then she guided Farinelli down the narrow road after the vanguard. Rickel and Lejun looked nervously from side to side, as did Jecks. Kinor and even Jimbob were studying the road ahead.

Before long, Himar's first scouts were far out of sight, and the second group more than a dek ahead along the rutted and narrower south road that ran through what seemed to be potato fields. At least Anna thought the low green almost vinelike plants were potatoes. They looked like what Papaw had grown in the marshy lower field by the creek. Sometimes, it was hard to believe that a girl raised in the hollers of the Appalachians had ended up as Regent of Defalk. *If you don't concentrate on what's ahead... and come up with a spell against Darksong, you won't be anything much longer.*

Jecks had eased his mount beside Anna, and Hadrenn had dropped back to ride easily beside Himar. Fragments of their conversation drifted back to Anna and Jecks.

"... travels light ..."

"... she's a warrior, Lord Hadrenn ... say Lord Barjim's consort was like that ... and Lady Essan years before ..."

Anna smiled, even as she wondered how Himar had picked up the information on Essan and Alasia.

"... women in Defalk ... different ..."

"... comes from the mist worlds ... you'll see ... fine iron 'neath that young face ... seen what being a sorceress is ... glad to be an overcaptain."

Anna shut out the conversation, still working on some form of the arrow spell. "How about ..." she murmured to herself,

> Heads of arrows, shot into the air,
> strike Bertmynn's players, straight through there,
> rend the spells and those who play ...

She needed a last line. Her eyebrows furrowed. Then she nodded, repeating the words and cadences to herself as she rode. When she *hoped* she had them, she cleared her throat, deciding she'd better start warming up, since she guessed the rest of the ride would take less than a glass, and she needed to be ready. She began on the first vocalise, wondering if she'd waited too long.

"Holly-lolly-lolly-pop ..." She had to stop and cough out mucus. *Another day when getting clear isn't going to be that easy.* "Mueee ... mueee ..."

Anna coughed again, but by the time they'd gone several hundred yards, she wasn't cutting out on every fourth syllable. *But you're not that clear ...*

Farinelli *whuff*ed once, and then again, as if to comment on the quality of her warm-up.

"I know . . . I sound like hell." She patted the gelding absently, and to reassure him, not that he needed reassurance as much as she did.

A scout rode out from where the road had turned eastward into the low trees, an orchard of some type, Anna thought, although the fruit was green. Once he had cleared the orchard by a few hundred yards, he reached the north–south part of the narrow road. From there he brought his mount into a quick trot on the way back north, toward Himar and the main section of Anna's and Hadrenn's forces.

Himar signaled for the column to halt, and the orders rippled back along the line of men and horses that extended nearly a dek back toward the River Syne.

Anna edged Farinelli forward, and Jecks kept his mount beside her, until they reined up beside Himar and Hadrenn. Despite the light breeze, Anna found herself blotting a damp forehead to keep perspiration out of her eyes.

"Sers . . . Regent . . . they're drawn up on the hills, to the east here . . . except we'll be south of them the way the road goes, and they're just waiting."

"Waiting? They don't have any scouts out?"

"They have some. They are but a dek or so out from the others."

"Archers?" asked Jecks. "Or crossbows?"

"Didn't see none, ser. Could be, but not up front or where we'd see 'em."

"Were there any players tuning?" Jecks persisted.

"No, ser."

"How far is it to the ridge that faces the enemy?" asked Himar.

"Dek and a half . . . maybe two deks."

The overcaptain nodded, then stood in his stirrups. "Four Defalkan companies to the fore! Green, gold, purple, and orange!" Himar ordered. "Two more from Lord Hadrenn's forces."

"Nortenn company! Fosternn company!" ordered Stepan.

Anna was glad that Skent's cyan company hadn't been called

forth, but Himar was only being a good commander, by not putting a green subofficer forward in his first true battle.

"Be ready to hold the hillside there, the front of the ridge,
should the enemy attack before all our forces are assembled,"
declared Himar.

Anna turned. "Liende, have the players ready to dismount
and play." The words felt dry in her mouth. "Once we get to the
slope opposite the enemy."

"Yes, Regent."

The sorceress turned back to study the lane leading to the
orchard, her eyes lighting on the fruit. Something she didn't
recognize . . . were they greenages? Or just green plums? Or
were they the same? *Back to vocalises.*

"Mueeee . . . oueeee . . . oueeee." She coughed again, but by
the time they resumed their ride and passed the last of the plum
trees—where the road ended—and started across the browning
grass on the eastern end of the long orchard, she'd stopped cutting out and could concentrate more on warming up without
worrying about choking.

"Be ready to dismount and play," ordered Liende from
behind.

"Remember," Jecks ordered Jimbob and Kinor, "you are to
remain with the guards to protect the Regent. She is Defalk."

"Yes, ser. . . ."

"Yes, ser."

Anna continued to warm up even as she studied the ridgeline
along which they rode eastward toward a shallow depression
too small to be a valley—a depression covered with browning
grasses bending slightly in the crisp fall breeze. Beyond the
ridge they traveled and across the expanse of golden brown
grasses, the burgundy tunics of Bertmynn's lancers and armsmen stood out like fresh blood against the grass and the green
of the trees behind the far hill on which those lancers and armsmen were arrayed.

"Still, he waits," said Jecks quietly.

"Somebody has to wait." *Why . . . why are you so edgy?*

The sound of mounts died away as Himar and Stepan finished arranging their companies on the low ridgeline.

Anna estimated the distance—less than a third of a dek—a
shade over three hundred yards, and the air was almost still.

Her spells would carry that far. *And the spells of his players, if they are players, will carry back, too.*

Her eyes rested on the burgundy tunics, and then on the purple tunics and those in green on her side of the field. *They're going to die . . . some of them—many of them—if you're successful. And why? Because you don't want to keep fighting and because Bertmynn wants power? Are you any different?* Anna pushed that thought away.

"Set up to play as close to the front here, as you can." The sorceress swung out of the saddle and handed the reins to Blaz, stepping forward onto a slight knoll that would give her a bit more height.

Behind her, players scrambled out of their saddles, and into position, as they prepared instruments and began to tune. Anna blinked in the noon sun, trying to take in Bertmynn's forces on the rolling rise while the familiar cacophony built, and then began to subside.

A slow drumbeat rolled across the space between the two forces . . . long and dull, and the tone seemed to freeze the day for a moment.

"Drums!" Jecks' voice hissed across the distance between them. "Not players . . . but drummers. Battle drums!"

Anna frowned, worried as much by Jecks' tone and the disgust and horror he conveyed as by the low drumrolls. *Can you adapt that spell to drums? Do you need to? How soon?*

"You must spell against the drums," Jecks insisted.

"We stand ready, Regent," Liende called.

You can do only one thing at a time. Anna shook her head, pulled her thoughts away from the slow rhythm of the drumbeats, and tried to make sense of the burgundy lancers and armsmen moving down the opposite hillside and across the shallow depression—less than two hundred yards east and perhaps three yards lower than the rise on which Anna and her players stood.

"Ah . . ." *Why is it so hard to think?* "The flame song!"

"The flame song," Liende repeated. "On my mark."

"Go!" Anna tried to ignore the sounds of trumpets, the dull clang and clunk of weapons, and the continuing roll of the drums from behind Bertmynn's forces. She concentrated instead on the spell she would have to use.

"Mark now!" called Liende.

Anna waited for a moment, then began.

> Fill with fire, fill with flame
> those weapons spelled against my name . . .
> Fill with fire, fill with flame . . .

Lines of fire crisscrossed the eastern part of the field, yet the lancers and armsmen in burgundy continued to advance, despite perhaps a third of them falling under the spell fires.

"Why don't they stop?" muttered Jimbob.

Why don't they . . . so many are dying . . . but they keep coming . . . Anna shook her head, trying to clear her thoughts, trying to escape the feeling of walking through mud—or quicksand.

Anna squinted. Was there a haze covering the grass? Was the grass burning somewhere?

Next, the burgundy armsmen marched forward, armsmen alone, without lancers, their steps seemingly matching the two- . . . or three-toned . . . drumbeats. The lack of horse bothered Anna, though she knew she was no military strategist.

Himar stood in the stirrups, his voice loud and clear. "Bowmen! To the east, to the lancers in red. Nock your arrows."

The volume of Himar's orders shook Anna, like cold water, and she turned and gestured to Liende. "Once through—the first arrow song."

As the music rose, in tune, Anna began to sing, each word a terrible effort against the very air that seemed to congeal around her.

> These arrows shot into the air,
> the head of each must strike one armsman there
> with force and speed to kill them all,
> all those who stand against our call!

Anna dropped her arm, half-conscious of the *thrum*ming of shafts released. Her limbs felt as though they were clad in lead.

> These arrows shot into the air . . .

As her words ended, she looked at Himar, but the overcaptain continued to study the field, where fifty or so more red-clad Ebrans had fallen.

"We have not enough archers, Regent. Shall we loose shafts again?"

"Again!" Anna commanded. She blinked, as for a moment, she had seen double. *But you're not using Darksong.* "The arrow song! Again!"

The players began the spell tune once more, and Anna forced her thoughts and visualization, concentrating on the image of arrows striking burgundy-clad figures, but even the images seemed to skitter out of her mind. Drawing on the years of recitals, she slowly reinforced her concentration with each word.

> These arrows shot into the air,
> the head of each must strike one armsman there. . . .

Anna finished the spell, finding herself almost gasping. *That shouldn't happen . . . what's happened to your breathing? You never had problems breathing.*

Jecks seemed to be guiding his mount toward her, but his progress was slow, as if something were holding him back.

The drums sounded louder, heavier, reverberating across the shallow valley, building and echoing, and the ground seemed to shiver with each drumroll. A smokelike pall rose out of the grass, like a ground fog rolling toward Anna and her forces— and the first line of burgundy armsmen reached within yards of the Defalkan lancers.

"Stop the drums, lady!" Jecks called. "The drums . . ."

A single trumpet burst rose from somewhere beyond the fog. Anna looked stupidly into the growing grayness. Adding to the drumbeats were the thundering hoofs of lancers.

Anna squinted and blinked, her eyes trying to focus, to make sense out of the conflicting images that assaulted her.

Out of the grayness charged burgundy lancers, sabres slashing at the near-motionless Defalkan lancers. Each blow struck by the burgundy-clad lancers seemed to fell a lancer of Defalk or Synek.

"The drums! Use a spell to direct shafts to the drumskins. . . ." yelled Kinor, riding toward Anna, yelling, blade out
in a guard position. Yet even the young man's progress
appeared glacial, as he called again, "A spell to the drums!"

Kinor's words fell around Anna, as she struggled to compre-
hend what he meant. Anna felt as though she were dragging
herself out of a pit. *What do you have to lose?* Each word was
labored as she forced it out, deliberately. "Liende, the arrow
spell! Now! Himar, have them loose more arrows, any
arrows!"

The players' first notes were almost cacophonous, but by the
end of the first bar they joined, and the grayness that had covered the field began to shred.

> Heads of arrows, shot into the air,
> strike the drumskins, straight through there,
> rend the drums and those who play . . .
> for their spells and Darksong pay!

As the last notes of the spell shimmered in the heavy air, the
drumbeats from the far hillside wavered, faltered, and then died
away.

Even without the support of the drums, the burgundy lancers
had already fought their way through two ranks of Anna's and
Hadrenn's lancers before the effects of the Darksong lifted and
the defenders began to raise blades.

Kinor and Rickel abruptly appeared before Anna, mounted,
to head off a single burgundy lancer who had broken through
and charged toward the Regent. Blaz and Lejun converged as
well, and bright blades slashed.

Anna dropped back several paces, turning toward Liende.
One player lay sprawled on the ground.

"Another set of arrows . . . the arrow spell again . . . !" Anna
demanded.

Anna timed the music and lifted her voice toward the east.

> These arrows shot into the air,
> the head of each must strike Lord Bertmynn there—

Anna dropped her hand, and sensed the release of the arrows.

—with force and speed to kill him dead,
for all the treachery he's done and led.

Light-headed and off-balance, she did not move as the dozen
or so arrows flew eastward, but tried to catch her breath,
watching.

A single pillar of fire flared just forward of the smoldering
ashes that had been drums.

Abruptly, a trumpet blast sounded, and the front section of
the burgundy lancers lurched forward.

Anna swallowed. There were still twice as many lancers in
red as those in purple and green. Or more. She blinked. There
were still two groups of burgundy lancers—or was one group
turning, disappearing over the back of the ridge? Her eyes
burned.

"The flame song!" She tried to keep her voice calm, but her
remaining lancers could not hold against twice their numbers—
or more.

"The flame song, at my mark! Mark!" Liende's voice was
ragged, hoarse, and the agony in her words tore at Anna.

Yet, from somewhere, a spell melody rose—true and clear,
but thin, as if carried by less than half the players. Even so, the
first bars were ragged, before the clarity of the strings lifted the
horn and woodwind into a fusion.

Anna forced her full concentration into the spell itself, while
trying to make her voice open and free with full concert projec-
tion.

> Those of Ebra who will not be
> loyal to the Defalkan Regency,
> let them die, let them lie,
> struck by fire, struck by flame. . . .

This time, as had happened at Envaryl, the chords of harmony shivered the sky, and the ground. The wailing that should
have been a counterpointed chord followed, except that
strangely harmonic as the wailing felt, once more, nothing
matched, not intervals, not key or scale or *anything*—the second time Anna had heard harmony that approximated pure dissonance, again a sound that no one else seemed to hear.

She wanted to cover her ears, but the sound knifed through her like a series of needles that burned every nerve in her body. Behind her, there were screams, and she knew that awful sound had struck through the players as well.

Before she could turn, she could feel her legs collapsing, could sense figures moving toward her, and she wanted to tell them, *I'll be all right.*

When she woke, she lay on the narrow cot under her tent, and Jecks sat on the stool facing her, his face barely illuminated by the single candle.

"Oh . . ." A line of pain knifed through her eyes.

"My lady . . . how long must you do this?"

As long as it takes . . . Anna turned her head to look at Jecks, turned it without lifting it. Even that gentle movement sent additional stabs of pain through her skull.

"You need to drink . . . and eat." He extended the water bottle.

Some of the stabbing pain abated after several swallows. "Dehydrated . . . I guess."

"You will need to eat in a time." Jecks' voice was soft, caring. *Thank heavens there's only one image of him. . . .* "In a moment . . . more water, please . . . if you would."

Jecks eased the bottle to her lips again.

After several more small swallows, she coughed slightly, wincing, then asked, "Did we win?"

"None who remained on the field and wore the burgundy live. Some half-score of Hadrenn's lancers died also from the last spell."

"The players?" Anna asked, her voice fearful.

"Some fell . . . like you—Liende . . . the young one, Yuarl . . . but they awakened earlier and have eaten. They are resting. Some may be sleeping."

Anna let out her breath, and stars sparkled before her eyes. Then the full import of what Jecks had said earlier struck. "Those on the field?"

"Ah . . . Just before your last spell, many score of Bertmynn's lancers turned and fled."

"How many?"

"We could not tell, but perhaps twentyscore or thirtyscore.

The Lord Bertmynn had brought more than eightyscore."

Anna took a deep breath. Thirtyscore lancers loose—that wasn't good, especially the way she felt. *What about the fiftyscore you killed . . . is that good?*

"How many . . . how many did they kill?" she asked fearfully.

"Almost fivescore," Jecks admitted. "Three from Defalk, two from Synek. Less than in many battles, far less than at the Sand Pass."

". . . shouldn't have been that many."

"Against battle drums? Without you, all would have perished."

". . . should have thought faster . . ."

"Himar has gathered all the blades and lances," Jecks added, as if to change the subject. "I suggested that you might be willing to make a gift of them to Lord Hadrenn . . . to defer the expense he will incur in raising the additional forces he will need."

"He'll need them."

"More than he now knows."

"How did Kinor and Jimbob take it? The battle." She knew the question was inane as she asked it, but did not try to take it back.

"Jimbob was white, and he shivered, but said nothing and kept to his post. You saw Kinor; he would give his life to save you. He was not injured, but when the final spell fell, he wept, but still lifted his blade as though to smite any Ebrans who might be left." Jecks' crooked smile warmed Anna. "I took the precaution of having the purple company guard young Hadrenn closely, for his protection, of course. With that, and with your friend Stepan in charge of the green forces, I thought that might ensure that Hadrenn had no second thoughts."

"Probably a good idea," Anna whispered, taking another swallow of water, and then reaching for the hard biscuits. "Skent?" she asked.

"He acquitted himself well, though his company was the last Himar threw into the melee."

Anna moistened lips that were still dry. ". . . got to stop doing this . . ."

"I believe I suggested that, my lady."

"You're not sorry I used the flame spell?" Anna had to know.

"Against drums and Darksong?" Jecks laughed. "Would that you had done so earlier, but we did not know how low Bertmynn would stoop or that they would be so used."

"But I suspected something . . . so did you." *But you couldn't think . . . was that the spell Bertmynn was casting, or something that slowed everything?* ". . . didn't think fast enough."

"No one thinks fast enough in battle. You thought well enough to save most of your forces."

In spite of herself, Anna found the yawns coming. Her eyelids were heavy, far too heavy. ". . . stupid . . . really stupid . . ."

"All is well now. You must sleep."

Anna wanted to protest, but couldn't as her eyes closed in spite of her wanting to say more, to hear Jecks' comforting voice.

52

Anna found herself shaky the next morning, even after washing as best she could in the bucket of water the guards left by the tent entrance, until she'd eaten enough hard cheese and biscuits for three people. Even after that, she was tired, and she retained a faint, but dully throbbing headache. Her neck and shoulders were also sore. She hadn't noticed the stiffness or the pain the night before, but she hadn't noticed much of anything.

"Good morning, my lady." Jecks looked at her as she stepped out in front of the small tent in the morning light—not dawn, but not all that late, either.

Rickel and Blaz nodded greetings, but neither guard spoke.

"It's morning," Anna admitted, her eyes taking in the day. The sky was gray, and she suspected it had been since her excessive use of sorcery the day before. *Maybe that's just the way you think it should be.* She shook her head at the thought, and winced. Headshaking didn't go with headaches. The trampled brown grass was covered with dew, and the damp breeze out of the northeast was cold, but the high gray clouds didn't seem to promise rain, not too soon.

"Lady Anna?" inquired two voices, almost simultaneously. She turned. "Good morning, Jimbob, Kinor."

"Good morning, lady." Jimbob inclined his head, not deeply, but more than perfunctorily.

So did Kinor, but not before Anna saw the stark darkness in the redhead's eyes.

"Thank you both." She paused, then asked, "You see why I need guards?" Her voice was dryly humorous. "Nowhere in a battle is necessarily safe."

"I had heard such, lady," Kinor replied.

Jimbob nodded, almost fearfully.

"Kinor," Anna said gently. "Thank you for your thought about the drums yesterday. It was a good suggestion. A very good suggestion. Without you and Lord Jecks, matters might have turned out differently."

Kinor glanced at the white-haired lord, and Jecks looked at Kinor.

"You both suggested a spell against drums," Anna explained, "but I probably wouldn't have been able to act and come up with a spell had you both not reminded me. So thank you both."

In retrospect, the idea made sense. Even Darksong couldn't both cast a spell and protect an object made of wood and skin against a spelled arrow. She just hadn't thought about it at the time. Then, she hadn't had that much time, not as she considered the battle in retrospect.

Jimbob looked sideways at his grandsire, appraisingly. Anna hoped they'd all survive the youth's practical education.

Too many spells . . . she'd used too many spells, that was also clear in hindsight. *Does that mean that you should just go out and use the most destructive spells and clear the battlefield? And if you don't, you risk losing, or dying of a spell overdose?* It wasn't fair. Every time she tried to limit the damage, it seemed, the end result was worse. Close to sixtyscore dead, and what would happen in Ebra was still unresolved.

"You need not ride today," Jecks said.

"With thirtyscore of Bertmynn's lancers somewhere?" She raised her eyebrows.

"Himar's scouts say that they rode perhaps ten deks, but that their mounts could carry them no farther yesterday." Jecks nodded to Kinor, who walked quickly away from Anna's tent.

"They're still there?" asked Anna, massaging her forehead and neck.

"That I do not know," admitted Jecks.

"It looks like Bertmynn wanted a big battle and someone else didn't," suggested the sorceress, walking toward where Farinelli was tethered on a tieline. She stopped as she caught sight of Himar striding toward her.

The overcaptain twisted the end of his mustache nervously as he stopped. "Lady Regent."

"Thirtyscore of Bertmynn's lancers—Jecks says they got away." *And you nearly killed yourself and didn't get them all.* "How did that happen?"

"When Bertmynn fell, the reserves turned," Himar said slowly. "They galloped over the ridge, as though dissonance were after them. The stragglers fell under the fires. Hadrenn's men say that they were likely led by his arms commander, for the one who commanded them to turn was a tall gray-haired officer, and so was this Ceorwyn. . . ."

Anna wondered how Hadrenn's men were close enough to see, and yet had done nothing to stop the retreat. Then they'd have been outnumbered two to one. She took a deep breath. That just pointed out that she'd have to defeat—*destroy*—another thirtyscore armsmen for Hadrenn to have any real chance of holding all of Ebra.

And what will that make you?

Jecks stepped up beside her. "Their mounts were spent, and they could not go far." He looked at Himar. "Was that as your scouts found?"

The overcaptain nodded. "Yes, ser, Lady Regent."

"We need to follow those armsmen, and, in a day or two, strike at them," Anna insisted. "Otherwise, we'll have more trouble here in Ebra."

"Not today and not tomorrow," insisted Jecks.

"Not today," Anna half agreed, looking at Himar.

The overcaptain nodded. "I will send out the scouts once more."

Anna kept her glance level until Himar looked away, then turned.

Seeing Anna unoccupied, Liende approached from the fire ring to the south where the players had gathered.

"How is everyone?" asked Anna.

"Yuarl and Delvor are most tired, and weak." Dark circles ringed Liende's eyes. "They cannot play, and may not for several days. The others are tired."

"So am I. I don't have plans for any spells for a while." Anna paused. "Not for another day or so, anyway." Should she tell Liende about her gratitude to Kinor? No . . . better that Kinor tell his mother. "We will have to ride today. It may be a shorter day, but we need to follow the last of the armsmen so that we can hurry back to Defalk."

"I understand."

"Liende . . . you and the players did very well. Without you, without them . . . well, yesterday could have been very bad." *Just how bad you don't even want to consider right now.* "Thank you, and tell them that I'm very grateful and pleased."

"Thank you, Regent. They played well, and it was hard to play against the Darksong drums."

"I know. You . . . and they . . . will be rewarded."

Liende bowed slightly. "We will make ready, Regent."

"Thank you." How long could she call upon the players for such destruction? *As long as you need them . . . and you can.* She sighed to herself.

53

In the cool sunlight and long dawn shadows outside her tent, Anna stretched. Her neck was still stiff, and her shoulders ached, but not so much as the day before. The pungent odor of the wood fueling cookfires drifted to her, and she rubbed her suddenly itching nose, then tried to clear a dry throat.

On the lower rise to the south, lancers were beginning to form up, and behind her Kerhor and Blaz were beginning to strike her tent.

She glanced at Rickel. "If we . . . if I . . . let those armsmen return to Dolov, battles will go back and forth across Ebra for years. That will be an invitation to the Sturinnese. With the maybe twentyscore lancers we have, we cannot stop them without sorcery." Anna shrugged, unsure if even she were willing to spell out the conclusion.

"My lady," Rickel offered cautiously after a short silence, "armsmen have choices. We do. We are not slaves. That is why many remained with Hanfor and Himar. That is why some captains have but butchers and fresh-faced boys. We have followed this Ceorwyn for two days, and none of his armsmen have left. They will fight . . . and fight—unless you stop them." The blond guard offered an embarrassed smile. "Some armsmen are going to die. Might be Hadrenn's, probably will be if you don't do something, and it might be ours if the Sea-Priests do like they did in Dumar. . . ." He broke off as Jecks walked toward Anna from the back side of the tent.

"Best you not slaughter those armsmen without some gesture," Jecks said. "Ceorwyn did leave the field." The white-haired lord looked toward Rickel. "Would you not say so, Rickel?"

"Folk like that . . . they'd never take terms from . . . a sorceress."

"You mean, from a woman," Anna replied.

Jecks laughed, easily. "Always the truthful Regent."

"So I should offer terms," asked the sorceress, "knowing that they won't accept them." *If they do, they'll just lie about it, and you'll have to come back.*

"They may not, but do you wish all Ebra to know you killed armsmen without offering any chance of surrender? Or some of the Thirty-three to know that?"

"No." Anna glanced toward her small camp table and the saddlebags on the cot, standing under just the roof canopy since her guards had removed and begun to roll up the sidewalls. "There's some parchment . . . I'd better draft them on the rough paper first." She laughed, knowing that she'd make a mess with a quill.

"I will tell Himar that we needs must send a parley messenger to Ceorwyn." Jecks gave a brisk nod before turning.

Anna pulled the camp stool toward the table, and took out the quill to sharpen it.

The drafting was as laborious as she had feared, and Jecks had returned and was standing at her shoulder long before she finished. All too conscious of his presence, she found herself scratching out phrases and rewriting them, seemingly in every line of what she penned.

Her forehead was damp when she finally finished what she thought were the last words.

Then, with a deep breath, she forced herself to read over the oft-corrected terms, skipping from line to line.

... continue as arms commander of Dolov, as regent for the heirs of Bertmynn ...

... acknowledge Lord Hadrenn as Lord High Counselor of Ebra, under the protection of the Regency of Defalk ...

... acknowledge, accept, and protect the free state of Elahwa established by the freewomen ...

Finally, she handed the terms to Jecks.

He took the rough draft and read slowly before finally stopping and looking up. "He will not agree to the women in Elahwa."

"I know that. But those are my terms. What's the point of agreeing to another lord just like the last one? All sorts of people get killed, and nothing changes? No, thank you." Anna snorted.

"You have offered terms, and you do not ask for executions or slaves." Jecks offered a broad shrug.

"Your tone of voice suggests that those might be more acceptable."

"For some, perhaps," Jecks agreed. "I would prefer your terms, but, then, I have come to know you." His hazel eyes offered the slightest hint of a twinkle.

Anna responded with a crooked smile before she pulled out one of the few sheets of parchment and began to write, far more carefully, the final draft. Jecks nodded, then walked out of the half-disassembled tent, and toward Kinor and Jimbob, who stood waiting with Kerhor and Lejun.

"... will not be long ... she drafts terms for Ceorwyn ..."

"He should ask for terms," said Jimbob.

"He will not," countered Kinor. "He cannot."

Anna pushed away the conversation and concentrated on the scratchy quill and the draft, laboriously transferring one word after another. She ignored the muted clamor from the camp as mounts were saddled, cookfires banked, and as her guards disassembled and packed her tent around her, leaving but the table she worked on and the stool.

It took a good glass before she had completed the short document. When she looked up from writing her signature and title, Jecks was waiting, patiently. So was Himar. Behind them, in the cool harvesttime sunlight, stood the two young redheads.

"I have told Himar that you were near-finished, and he has the lancers ready to ride." The white-haired lord smiled sadly. "No Ebran can accept terms and remain as a leader. So we must arrive most close to Ceorwyn's forces. We must be prepared for battle when he sees them and rejects them."

"You still believe he will attack?" asked Himar. "After the last . . . battle?"

Jecks offered a wintry smile. "He may choose to retreat, in order to preserve his forces. Or to obtain days or seasons to rebuild. But . . ."

Anna understood the pause. *You can't afford to spend days or weeks chasing Ebrans northward along the river—not with Rabyn poised to invade Defalk as soon as he learns you're in Ebra—if he hasn't already.* Except the glass had only shown Rabyn on the march, and not clearly in Defalk. Not yet.

Anna stood, and Blaz stepped forward to take the stool, while Kerhor glanced at the quill and inkstand.

"You can pack them," Anna said, extending the scroll to Himar. "I'll get Farinelli ready, and . . ." She shrugged. *You'll use more sorcery because no one seems to respond to anything besides sorcery and armsmen . . . and armsmen will die needlessly because Ceorwyn will not accept terms from a woman or women as people.*

"We are ready to ride, lady." Standing on the trampled grass, with the ends of his mustache drooping, Himar inclined his head, portraying almost a caricature of the professional soldier knowing that politics would result in armsmen being killed. *Unnecessarily killed.* But how necessary were so many killings?

"I'll be ready as soon as I can be." Anna turned, looking toward the tielines, where Kinor and Jimbob stood by mounts already saddled and packed. Liende and the players stood by their mounts as well, to the right of the two young men.

Anna stepped toward the chief player. "Liende . . . Lord Jecks thinks that this Ceorwyn will reject my terms. We're only asking that Hadrenn be a regent over Ebra. Lord Bertmynn's heirs will retain most of their lands, but I will insist that the freewomen hold Elahwa."

"I fear Lord Jecks is right, lady." Liende's voice was level.

"If he is, we will need the flame song as soon as he rejects those terms."

"We are your players, lady. We will be ready with the flame song."

"I'm sorry." Anna paused, then added, "Thank you."

Liende bowed.

As Anna turned and walked toward Farinelli, the gelding *whuff*ed and tossed his head. "I know. Everyone else is getting saddled and ready to go. You afraid you'll get left? Or just telling me to get on with it?" She patted his shoulder.

After saddling Farinelli, Anna folded her jacket and wedged it under the straps of the saddlebags. As she mounted the big gelding, she realized that all the others still wore jackets, while she had on but her shirt and vest. It was cool under the clear sky, but not that cool.

"How far?" Anna eased Farinelli up beside Himar's mount, half-amused as her guards and the two young men jockeyed their mounts around behind her.

"Five deks. They have not broken camp. Not a glass ago." Himar offered a lopsided smile. "I sent a scout as messenger saying to say that you were readying a message for arms leader Ceorwyn. Best that we not have to chase them, if it be possible."

"Thank you. That was a good idea." Anna nodded. She should have thought of something like that. Even after more than a year, there were so many aspects of being a regent she still had not grasped.

The sorceress-Regent turned Farinelli and rode back to where Liende sat upon her mount. "Chief player . . . ?"

"We are ready, lady."

"When we reach Ceorwyn's forces, we'll ask for terms. If he

rejects them, I may need the players immediately. The flame song," Anna reminded Liende.

"As you said, lady, the flame song."

"Thank you." Anna nodded and turned Farinelli back toward the head of the column. She felt stupid, reminding Liende again, but she knew that when the time came, she'd need the song immediately.

As Anna rode toward Himar, the overcaptain raised his hand, and a double trumpet blast rolled out into the midmorning air. Anna flicked the reins, and Farinelli carried her forward.

Like the road they had already traveled, the road eastward curved around hills, following the River Syne, with the higher ground to the north, on their left. In the shadows cast by hedgerows and the scattered clumps of trees bordering the fields, dew still glistened on the browning grass and the greener weeds.

Anna cleared her throat and began a vocalise. Or started to begin one, because the first note triggered a coughing attack. Her struggle against the asthma continued for almost a glass, and perhaps four deks before she managed to clear her lungs and throat.

"Being a sorceress is not so easy as most would suppose," Jecks offered.

"No. Being anything with power isn't, I guess."

Both looked up as a scout in Defalkan purple rode toward the column, slowing and stopping as Himar urged his mount forward to receive the report. After several moments, the overcaptain rode toward Anna and Jecks.

"The forces of Ceorwyn hold the next rise," Himar announced. "They await us, and their blades are bright."

"Will they attack when we appear?" asked Anna.

"I do not know." Himar shrugged apologetically. "They would have seen our scouts."

"He will wish you to ask for terms," Jecks predicted. "He will expect that, and then he will attack or hold fast. He will not turn from you."

Anna glanced back, but the players were close, and Liende nodded, as if to signify that they were ready. The sorceress looked forward. "The players will have to dismount quickly, in case Ceorwyn does attack. Can the lancers hold them for that long?"

"We will hold." Himar stood in his stirrups, and ordered, "Blades and lances ready!" A triplet from the trumpet echoed his words.

As Anna rode over the crest of the hill and looked eastward, she could see the burgundy surcoats, set in formation on the hillside opposite her. She reined up, then turned Farinelli back. Jimbob and Kinor pulled their mounts aside to allow her to reach the chief player.

"Liende, have the players come to the front where I am and dismount and tune. If Ceorwyn rejects our terms, they'll need to be ready with the flame song at once."

"The flame song . . . Yes, Regent."

Why doesn't anyone see? Anna rode forward and to the left of the road toward a flat section of grass that gave her an unobstructed view of Ceorwyn's three-deep formation—less than half a dek away. In the depression between the two forces, except for where the road lay, was a line of bushes that marked a sometime stream.

Rickel and Lejun, the big shields out, eased their mounts before her, and Jecks slipped his mount to the right of Farinelli as Anna reined up. Himar appeared on her left. Behind them, the players dismounted. Soon, the all-too-familiar near dissonance of tuning began to rise.

Himar looked at Anna. So did Jecks.

"Might as well send the herald."

Both glanced quizzically at her.

"The messenger—with the terms I wrote out."

The overcaptain nodded, then turned his mount.

As Himar rode toward the center of the Defalkan formation, Jecks guided his mount closer to Anna. "Best you remember that twice you have offered terms, and that before that the Ebrans invaded Defalk."

"You're telling me that I'm being reasonable." *Reasonable for Liedwahr, anyway.*

"You would let most of Ebra be ruled as it once was. You exert but a light hand, my lady."

Anna glanced up at the sound of the trumpet.

The messenger or herald in purple, one hand steadying the blue parley flag, the base of its staff set in his lanceholder, rode forward. Shielded by Rickel and Lejun, but still mounted, Anna watched from the hillside. To each side, behind the guards, watched Jecks, Jimbob, and Kinor.

The Defalkan lancer reined up in the depression between the two rises, waiting.

Shortly, a lancer in burgundy rode down from the formation and halted opposite the Defalkan. The Defalkan lancer extended the scroll. The lancer in burgundy took the document and then rode to the far hillside, disappearing through the line of Ebran lancers reined up in formation.

The sorceress-Regent blotted her forehead, glancing sideways at Jecks, but the lord's eyes were fixed on the opposite hill. A single fly buzzed past Anna. Then Farinelli swished his tail, several times.

Another horse, somewhere behind Anna, *whuff*ed, momentarily breaking the tension and the stillness.

The lancer in burgundy appeared from the formation, riding slowly back downhill toward the waiting Defalkan scout and the blue parley flag. Ceorwyn's lancer spoke for a time to the Defalkan, and then the two separated, and the Defalkan lancer rode back uphill toward the spot where Himar and Stepan waited, both mounted.

In turn, the messenger spoke to Himar.

Anna watched the lancers in burgundy, but there was no movement among them.

Stepan and Himar rode slowly back toward Anna. Himar reined up and looked steadily at Anna. "Ceorwyn will acknowledge you as sovereign, but not Hadrenn. And he will fight to the death, even though he be slaughtered by your sorcery before he will allow women to rule in Ebra."

"That's what he wants, that's what he'll get!" snapped Anna, turning in the saddle. "Chief player, the flame song!"

"My lady . . . why will you not accept his fealty?" asked Jecks.

Anna had almost begun to dismount. She stopped and looked at the white-haired lord. "You know why. Because I can't hold Defalk . . . let alone hold Ebra. I've got so many dissonant lords at home that I'll spend years pacifying them after this. And I can't leave some idiot who's as bad as the Sea-Priests in charge of the eastern coast of Ebra. They've already visited Bertmynn, and this Ceorwyn certainly knows them. I let him take over without a free state in Elahwa, and there'll be a revolt here the moment I die—and that's pretty optimistic. There might be one long before that. Either way, and a season after that the Sturin-nese will be pouring troops through Elahwa—if they wait that long." Anna looked at Jecks. "Is that what you want for your grandson?"

She could see Jimbob wince, even twenty yards away, and she realized she shouldn't have spoken so loudly.

"You would kill thirtyscore because their commander is a fool?"

"No," Anna said softly, "I will kill thirtyscore because they follow a commander who is a fool and because we can't afford to lose any more lancers to sort it out." *And because you're tired of everyone else expecting to get their way and for you to be the reasonable one?* Except using sorcery to try to kill thirtyscore lancers wasn't reasonable. Necessary, but not reasonable.

Jecks's eyes flicked away from meeting Anna's eyes directly. "You are Regent, and, again, I thank the harmonies that I am not." Abruptly, his eyes met hers again.

Anna could see the sadness in his hazel eyes, a sadness for which she had no real answer, except that she knew that compassion on her part now would be far more costly later—and that was no answer. Perhaps that was Jecks' weakness—that he could not do what needed to be done when there was the faintest chance that he might be wrong and many would die. *And yours? That when you get cornered and pushed, you lash out?* Without speaking, she dismounted.

"Again," Jecks said, turning to Jimbob and Kinor, "you will guard the Regent. She is Defalk."

"Yes, ser," the two affirmed.

Anna wasn't certain she liked Jecks' tone in referring to her as Defalk, but she did not look back as she strode to the space that the guards had opened facing the other hill and the bur-gundy-coated lancers of Dolov.

The lancers on the other—higher rise—made no movement,

either to charge or retreat. Anna swallowed. *Must you do this?* She swallowed again. *What choice do you have? You didn't ask for the moons of this forsaken world. You asked for limited allegiance and a place women could go and not be slaves.*

The sorceress cleared her throat and took a last solid look at the line of doomed lancers less than half a dek from her. *Idiots . . . male idiots . . . and you're a female idiot for not finding a way out.*

"We stand ready, Regent," Liende called.

"The flame song!" Anna forced coldness into the command.

"The flame song . . . Mark!" Liende's voice was hard, the hardness of discipline forced over emotion, but the spell melody was solid.

The sorceress put her concentration on the image of flames falling across the three-deep lines of the burgundy-clad lancers—and especially on Ceorwyn—and on keeping her voice open and full.

> Those of Ebra who will not be
> loyal to the Defalkan Regency,
> let them die, let them lie,
> struck by fire, struck by flame. . . .

Once more, the chords of harmony shivered the sky, and the ground.

As Anna watched lines of fire fall across the opposite hillside—and a single huge firebolt sear the center, she could sense a tension . . . something underlying the spell, almost like an overstrained and fraying string on a too-tightly strung harp or violin.

Because you know it's wrong—unharmonious . . . dissonant?

With the muted screams that rose from the wall of fire less than half a dek away, that unseen string broke—and slammed into her.

Darkness rose around her on her hillside as the fires died on the slopes opposite her, and she could feel herself toppling forward under the backlash of overstressed harmonies that centered on her.

54

Nubara stands in the corner of the stone-floored room that had once been a workroom, as the thunder of the drums buffets him. Reflections glitter off the smooth finish of the drums, reflections showing the motions of the three drummers, and the timekeeping motions of the Prophet of Music who directs the three who sit on the high stools, a pair of mallets wielded by each.

The three drummers with their mallets watch Rabyn, and their motions follow his direction, yet each drum has a different voice, and the three separate voices combine in a thunder that seems to shiver the plaster-covered stone walls of the Palace of Music.

The Mansuuran officer squints, shakes his head, for a shimmering, and barely visible blue nimbus surrounds the blue-clad Prophet of Music.

Craccck! A floor stone splits, and a wavering line runs for several yards around and through the solid paving stones of the workroom.

Rabyn does not even turn his head. "Heavier! Drum three! Faster, like I showed you! Don't make anyone wait!"

Sweat pours down the face of the drummers as they follow the tempo set by the Prophet who is no longer youth, but not yet man.

Sweat darkens the blue tunic worn by Rabyn, and his face glistens with perspiration. His eyes are hard.

The gray of morning seeped into the silk tent, then the brighter light of dawn itself. Anna slowly pried open her eyes. Jecks lay under a single blanket, snoring lightly, practically against the tent wall.

At his snoring, Anna found herself smiling—until she tried to raise her head. While she didn't have the double images engendered by the use of Darksong, a flash of lightning with the impact of a sledge drove her back onto the rolled blanket that served as a pillow, and tears streamed from her eyes.

"Shit . . ." she murmured under her breath. *They can murder thousands of women who just wanted to be free and not even get a headache, and you do the same thing to those who did it and you can't even sit up. And you even offered them terms, if they'd just let the women who survived rule themselves.*

"Lady?" At her slightest word, Jecks rolled out of his blanket and stood by the cot.

"I'm here." Her voice was raw, hoarse.

The white-haired lord brought her the water bottle from the narrow camp table and held it to her lips, watching as she did.

"Today . . . you must rest," he said.

". . . don't think I have much choice, do I?"

"You cannot use so much sorcery so often, my lady," Jecks said.

Tell me about it. "I can see that." *But it wasn't the sorcery, but the guilt . . . the backlash . . . or something.* "Why . . . why . . . wouldn't they accept terms . . . not as though . . . I was going to make anyone a slave . . ."

"You are a woman, and they have not seen your power."

Anna took another long swallow of water.

"In time, they will understand," Jecks insisted.

How much time and how many deaths? And will anything really have changed once you're gone?

Anna closed her eyes again.

The next morning, Anna sat on the edge of her cot for a long time, her head in her hands, before she dared to stagger up and retrieve the water bottle. Finishing off the water bottle helped some, as did eating too much of the hard cheese and biscuits. Finally, ignoring the dull and throbbing headache, she stepped out of the tent into a morning that felt far too bright for her physical condition.

Jecks turned quickly, but his smile was professional enough to tell her that she looked about the way she felt—like horse droppings flattened by a long column of lancer mounts. "Good morning, my lady."

Lejun and Kerhor both nodded, and a half dozen yards to their right, Kinor and Jimbob watched warily.

"It is morning." Anna admitted, "I think." The sky was a hazy white, not quite gray. *Another result of sorcery . . . or guilt about sorcery?* She stopped herself from shaking her head, knowing it would fall off. At least, it felt like it might.

The matted grass was damp, and the acrid odor of the cook-fires drifted toward her on the light breeze. Her stomach turned at the scent of something cooking. Cheese and biscuits had been better, but even they had settled uneasily.

"You should not ride today," Jecks said.

"With Rabyn probably at Elioch?" She raised her eyebrows. "I couldn't ride yesterday. That cost us a day already."

"You cannot do anything if you reach Denguic exhausted." Jecks met her eyes with concern in his own hazel orbs.

"I know, but we can shorten today's ride and the next day's if I get tired, but we can't push the horses to make up that distance once I get recovered, not if the lancers need to fight." She snorted. "No matter what I try, it seems that we still need men with sharp blades and strong arms."

A greater hint of cookfire smoke and the fainter odor of burned grass filled Anna's nostrils, and with those reminders of the impact of her sorcery, her stomach turned and churned even more as she stood before her little tent. *Another set of battles ... thousands more men dead ... will it ever end? Can it ever end?*

She took a deep breath. "We need to talk to Hadrenn. There's no point in dragging this out."

Jimbob and Kinor slipped back and toward where Liende had gathered with the players a good fifty yards to the south.

"Now?" Jecks looked at her, then nodded. "I will have him summoned." The white-haired lord slipped past the tent and walked swiftly toward another tent with a green pennant set before it.

Anna started after Jecks, then stopped, and shrugged. She hadn't meant to have Jecks chase down the young lord of Synek.

It seemed but a few moments later when Jecks returned with Hadrenn beside him. Both men stopped well short of the Regent.

"Sorceress and Regent." Hadrenn inclined his head. "You have destroyed Bertmynn. What can I say to express my gratitude?"

"We all did what needed to be done. I'm glad we could help you." Anna forced a smile she didn't really feel.

"All Synek is grateful. . . ." Hadrenn let his words slide into silence.

"And that will help erase some of the unpleasant memories of last year?" Anna offered an ironic smile.

"It cannot but help, and I will ensure all know."

"Does Bertmynn have a son or daughter?" asked Anna.

A look of puzzlement appeared in Hadrenn's deep brown eyes. "I have heard he has two sons . . . but those are words on the wind."

"Fine. You need to declare that his son—or other heir—will hold the lands around Dolov . . . but only there. And you need to proclaim that as widely as possible. You also need to proclaim that you have accepted the protection of the Regent and Sorceress of Defalk for all of Ebra to assist in repelling any who would strike at your land . . . or some words like that. And you need to send someone to Elahwa . . . saying that you will recognize a government by the freewomen." Anna paused.

"They may not believe you. You might ask for the Matriarch to send a representative—but make sure it's a representative of the Matriarch and not of the SouthWomen."

Hadrenn's eyes contained the expression of an ox stunned with a heavy hammer. Behind the younger lord's shoulder, Jecks shook his head gently, and mouthed, "Be gentle . . . be gentle."

Anna nodded that she'd heard. "Let me explain," she addressed Hadrenn patiently. "The SouthWomen started this mess by shipping blades to Elahwa. You don't want them in this. You do need someone outside of Ebra whom the women of Elahwa can trust. If you do that, the Matriarch and their grain factors will look on you more favorably, and you won't have another revolt on your hands in ten years. You—and Ebra—can't afford that. Neither can I."

"You do not sound as though you are fond of Ebra." Hadrenn's voice contained the hint of a querulousness.

"In my shoes . . . boots, would *you* be? My lands have been invaded by Ebra once, and I have to fight battles again a year later in Ebra in hopes of getting a just and peaceful ruler as a neighbor. However," Anna added, "I will recompense you slightly. Send a score of lancers with me, and I will send them back with golds to help you rebuild Synek—and Elahwa."

Hadrenn looked down. "You are generous."

You may be a damned fool. "Hadrenn, I want a peaceful neighbor strong enough to ensure that the free state of Elahwa survives and powerful enough that Ebra can keep the Sturinnese out of Liedwahr. I'm not after an empire like the Liedfuhr seems to be. Most empires don't last, and those that do aren't places most people would like to live."

Another puzzled look crossed Hadrenn's face, but he did not speak.

"The mist worlds have had more empires than Erde has ever dreamed of—or should." Anna glanced toward the west. "Do you have any questions? We need to be leaving."

"Leaving?"

"Leaving. There are no forces left in Ebra, except yours. You have my support, and, once you proclaim the free state of Elahwa for the freewomen, you'll have some support from the Ranuans. At the very least, they won't oppose you. You have

Gestatr, and his judgment is sound. What else do you need?" *If Hadrenn can't handle it now, he'll never handle it.*

"Gestatr said that you would be fair . . . no matter what it cost you. I was not certain." Hadrenn bowed his head. "Synek and Ebra will stand before and behind you, Regent and sorceress, for none could have a better ally nor a worse enemy." Hadrenn looked up, his eyes upon Anna. "I will not keep you, but I will also tell Stepan your words of wisdom, and we will begin." He paused. "Can I offer you an escort? You lost lancers, and you brought few enough."

"Just the score you'll need to bring back the golds I'll send. And an officer or suboficer you trust."

"You shall have them." Hadrenn bowed again.

As the younger lord turned, Anna drew Jecks toward her. "I didn't mean for you . . ."

"Who else, my lady?"

"Thank you." Anna smiled. "I don't say that enough. Especially to you. Without you . . . without you, I wouldn't be here."

"I think not, my lady. Without you, Defalk and Elheld would yet lie under Behlem's boots and I in an unmarked grave."

Anna shook her head. "I won't argue this one, but I don't agree. We'd better get ready."

Now . . . all you have to do is march across two countries and figure out how to defeat another madman without losing any more lancers—and that doesn't even count all the problems you don't know about.

57

Under a gray and misting sky that had threatened a full rain all morning, the green banner of Synek and the purple-and-gold banner of Defalk headed the column of lancers riding toward the eastern end of the river town whose name Anna did not know.

Rickel and Kerhor had brought out the heavy shields as they neared the town and had moved up to flank Anna. Jecks surveyed the small daub-and-wattle dwellings at the edge of the town, and then the wood-and-brick ones nearer the center of the hamlet.

Several figures peered out of open windows, and the column slowed as someone from the town called something to the Ebran lancers.

Anna glanced over her shoulder at the distant rumble of thunder, but the gentle mist did not intensify.

Sylvarn—the subofficer in charge of Hadrenn's lancers—replied loudly. "The sorceress and Lord Hadrenn defeated Bertmynn, and Lord Hadrenn is now Lord High Counselor of all Ebra, thanks be to the Regent and Sorceress of Defalk, his ally and supporter."

". . . who will rule Dolov?"

"Lord Bertmynn's heirs will hold his lands, and the freewomen will hold Elahwa—at the sorceress' insistence—but both pledge allegiance and fealty to Lord Hadrenn."

A low murmur, not entirely friendly, followed Sylvarn's second response. Rickel and Kerhor edged closer to Anna, their shields higher.

"The sorceress is returning to her demesnes . . . for her assistance is no longer necessary, but Defalk and Ebra have pledged friendship, and there will be peace between them." Sylvarn blurted out.

". . . peace . . . after the fire flood . . ."

". . . peace . . . why not?"

"Better peace than war . . ."

In the time it took Anna to ride the hundred yards to the small square, people poured from the buildings and stood, watching as the cavalcade made its way along the damp clay of the road, past, first, a small chandlery, and then past a cooper's.

"That's her!" whispered a high voice, either a young boy or girl. "The evil sorceress!"

"I don't want to hear it. She's not evil now," answered a woman. "She slew the war-dog of the north."

"But the man said . . ."

"The officer said," repeated a stronger voice.

"The sorceress slew the war-dog; young Hadrenn could not have done so himself."

"But she made the mountain of fire . . ."

"Hush . . ."

Abruptly, the girl ran to the front of the cooper's porch and called, "Sorceress . . . did you slay the war-dog of the north?"

Anna wanted to sigh, but she turned in the saddle to face the smudged-faced child and answered. "Yes. He used Darksong, but Clearsong was stronger. He died in fire."

"Darksong . . ."

"Darksong . . ." The word passed through the small crowd of perhaps forty souls, repeated again and again. Some seemed to shudder at the word itself.

"Well put," murmured Jecks.

Luckily put was more like it, Anna thought, but she kept a smile on her face all the rest of the way through the town—a smile on her face, but eyes that looked everywhere.

Neither Rickel nor Kerhor lowered their shields until the entire column was through the town and well along the River Syne on the road leading to the Sand Pass.

58

MANSUUS, MANSUUR

So . . . Bassil . . . she has vanquished Bertmynn, and placed young lordlet Hadrenn as her puppet over all Ebra." The Liedfuhr's hazel eyes flash, seemingly turning black momentarily, and he leans forward, putting his large hands on the polished walnut of the desk standing before the open windows of his private study. "And she has given the Matriarch a foothold in Ebra, without the slightest of requests and without any concessions from Ranuak."

"Yes, sire." The raven-haired lancer officer bows. "She also lost near-on a third of the lancers accompanying her, and she must return to Defalk, traverse the entire land, and meet with the overwhelming forces of your grandson."

"And most probably a hundredscore of my own lancers—as you recommended, Bassil."

"If she loses . . . then you bring all your forces into Neserea and Defalk because of the instability, and you will control all of Liedwahr. Neither Lady Siobion nor Lord Hadrenn can stand against you, and the Ranuans will remain as they always have. The Sturinnese will have to look elsewhere, and you have the beginnings of your empire of magic, sire. And you will not have to offer Aerlya to Rabyn."

"That . . . that . . . even I would never do, and I do not wish to hear aught of that again." The Liedfuhr's tone is like the ice of the polar caps south of Pelara.

"Yes, sire."

"Now . . . how does your logic run, if the sorceress wins—again?" questions Konsstin.

"Then you hold by your bargain and offer her half of Neserea. The Council of Wei will not move against her. Nor will the Matriarchy, and in all events she will take the rest of her long life to settle the internal affairs of what she holds in Defalk and Neserea. You will consolidate your hold on western Neserea, and Mansuur will be the most powerful land in Liedwahr."

"You make it sound so easy—for both me and the sorceress."

"For you, sire, there is little risk. The sorceress gambles much, in everything that she ventures. She attempts to remake a land that has undone everyone who has tried such. She will anger the Matriarchy and the SouthWomen because she does too little for their taste, and the old lords of Ebra and Defalk because she changes too much. Your grandson understands neither, nor will he, even when he perishes, and that will not be long, even should he defeat the sorceress."

"Now you are a prophet?"

Bassil laughs at the Liedfuhr's ironic tone. "No, sire. He schemes openly. He has poisoned wenches and innocent girls alike because they displease him, and he will soon take those goods and women he wants. With each taking, more will hate him, until there are so many against him that he will have no supporters. Even should he defeat the sorceress, he cannot take Defalk. Who has the lancers to wage thirty-three separate campaigns a land away?"

"The sorceress has taken Defalk."

"No, I must differ, sire. She has improved the lot of perhaps half the lords, and cowed the others into submission. Some of those cowed will rebel, or plot, or both, for they detest a woman of power, and it will take years for her to deal with them all in order to truly unite Defalk. And she acts to restore the old line, which gains her much of her appeal. Rabyn would not have the support of any lords."

"We shall see, Bassil."

"Yes, sire."

"Best you are right."

Bassil nods. He does not wipe his damp forehead, a forehead that has perspired despite the cool breeze from the open windows of the Liedfuhr's study.

59

Anna glanced into the low sun, squinting through the dust to see if she could make out the outlines of Loiseau, but all she saw was a flock of sheep to the right of the road and a half a dek north.

"Sheep—there wasn't anything out here last year," she said to Jecks, holding off a cough from the dust until she finished her words.

"So long as they do not graze too many," he said.

Anna had to nod at his words. That was something else she needed to discuss or leave a scroll about for Halde—the condition of the land and to watch that it wasn't overgrazed. She shook her head. She didn't even know when Halde was leaving Synfal. Even using the scrying mirror, there was so much she didn't know, and half the time she ended up with headaches from trying to find out too much through scrying.

Her legs were sore, and assorted aches permeated muscles she'd not been aware she had. At least, not since the last long trip. Harvest had probably come in most of Defalk while she'd been gone, and the days were shorter, and the nights definitely cooler than when they had departed.

". . . there be the sorceress' holding . . ." called someone from the vanguard.

Anna squinted again, trying to see Loiseau against the glare of the near-setting sun. After more than a week of travel back from the battle north of Elahwa, she was riding up to the gates of her own hold. And it would take nearly another two weeks, if not longer—assuming the roads remained dry—before she reached the area west of Defalk where Rabyn's forces were chasing Hanfor. She just hoped the wily veteran could keep from losing too many armsmen until she could get there. *Though, Lord knows, you've lost too many even with sorcery.*

Thoughts and speculations of how she might better have planned things preoccupied her, and she kept riding, straightening in the saddle when Farinelli's hoofs struck the stone causeway leading to the open gates of Loiseau.

"It's the Regent!" called one of the lancers on the wall, part of the detachment Anna had left to guard both the hold and the spell-concealed gold in the strongroom beneath it, although she had told no one, except Jecks, her personal guards, and Skent and a few of his men most trusted by Himar, all of whom had helped move it, that the gold was there. And none of them could see it now. *Not while you live . . . anyway . . . and after that . . . who cares?*

"The Regent!"

Anna plastered a smile in place, nodding as she rode into the courtyard, and guided Farinelli to the right.

The white-haired stablemaster Quies was waiting as Anna reined up beside the smaller personal stable inside the walls on the north side of the hold. "Welcome back, Lady Anna."

"It's good to be here, if only for a short time." *And it'll be better to sleep in a bed, get a bath and clean clothes without sorcery.* She dismounted gingerly, holding to the saddle for a moment until her legs adjusted to her weight.

"That raider beast of yours, he could use a mite bit more grain," Quies said, eyeing Farinelli as Anna led the big gelding into his stall. "Other'n that, he looks good."

"Are you trying to say that he looks better than his rider, Quies?" Anna grinned.

"Ah . . . no . . . beggin' your pardon, Lady Anna."

"He probably does." Anna laughed tiredly. She unstrapped the lutar, and then the mirror, then handed the saddlebags to Kerhor, then bent and loosened the girths.

Farinelli shook himself slightly and *whuff*ed once Anna had the saddle and blanket off.

"I know. It feels good, I'm sure." She picked up the brush and took it to the palomino's coat.

"He still comes first," offered Jecks from the end of the stall.

"Only when it comes to grooming and feeding," she replied. "He deserves it."

When she finished with Farinelli, Quies filled the feeding box, then cleared his throat.

Anna looked at the old ostler.

"Lady . . . I'd a been mentioning Vyren to you . . . and you said . . ."

"I said you could start to train him."

"I thought as you'd like to meet him. . . ."

"Of course." Anna smiled in spite of her tiredness. "Is he around?"

Quies gestured, and a thin black-haired youth stepped shyly forward. "This is Vyren, Lady Anna." He looked at the boy. "And this be the lady Anna, Lady of Mencha, and Regent of all Defalk, and the most powerful lady in all Erde."

"Ah . . . that's . . ." Anna flushed. No matter what she said, it would be wrong. "I'm sure there are others . . ."

"Not many, likewise." Quies grinned, then tapped Vyren on the shoulder. "Manners, lad."

Vyren bowed, his eyes not quite meeting Anna's. "Lady . . . Regent . . . thank you . . ."

"Just learn everything Quies can teach you, Vyren." Anna smiled again.

Vyren looked down, then stepped back.

"Thank you, Quies," Anna said.

"Being my pleasure, lady."

Anna and Jecks walked across the paved stones toward the main hall. Anna carried the lutar, Jecks the mirror and his saddlebags, while Kerhor carried her saddlebags, and Lejun surveyed the darkening courtyard. She marveled again at the comparative airiness and beauty of Loiseau. No wonder poor Brill had never wanted to leave it. The more she saw of Liedwahr, the more a compact marvel her own holding seemed to be.

"You are deep in thought," Jecks ventured.

"Just appreciating Loiseau. I forget how elegant it is." *And how clean.*

"As is its holder."

"You're gallant . . . very gallant." She smiled, warmly, in spite of her fatigue.

"It is easy to be so with you."

"Flattery . . ."

"Truth," corrected the white-haired and handsome lord, leaning forward and gesturing for Anna to enter through the front double door.

Serna, Florenda, and Gero were waiting in the entry foyer.

"Your messenger came early," Serna began immediately. "Dinner will be ready for your party, Lady Anna, within the glass, as you wish. The folk I brought on from Mencha, as you asked, lady, they are already serving the armsmen and the regular players in the rear barracks hall."

Anna nodded. "I may take a bit . . . almost a glass."

"We will be ready." Serna nodded, then added, "There were many scrolls. I put them on the writing desk in your chamber, Lady Anna."

Many scrolls? Of course . . . scrolls from Dythya, Menares, Hanfor, and who knew who else. Perhaps Birfels, or that insufferable pain in the ass, Lord Dannel. "Thank you." Anna nodded and walked through the foyer, then trudged up the stairs and back to her chambers.

Jecks walked beside her, and once inside her rooms, set the mirror on the side table in the study alcove, and Anna took the saddlebags from Kerhor. "Thank you." She added, "Make sure you get something to eat, you and Lejun."

"Yes, Lady Anna." The dark-haired Kerhor smiled as he closed the door to take up his post outside.

Anna turned to Jecks. "I'll try to hurry, but . . . the way I feel I just can't eat." Her stomach growled.

He raised his eyebrows.

"I'll hurry."

Jecks smiled broadly, then bowed slightly. "As will I, my lady." He slipped out, leaving Anna alone, really alone for the first time in days.

She turned to the desk and looked at the pile of scrolls stacked neatly there. She shook her head. A bath and a full stomach came before she even wanted to get near all those scrolls. Turning, she went straight to the bathchamber, carrying the lutar.

It took only a short spell to heat the water, and Anna slipped into the steaming warmth with a sigh. Dinner could wait. Not long, because the others were hungry, but for a few moments. *Only a few,* nagged a small voice within her. After too short a time, she sat up with a second sigh and quickly washed, then got out and dried, donning a loose gown from the open closet and the slipperlike shoes. She squared her shoulders as she walked to her chamber door.

The scrolls could wait until after dinner.

60

Sylvarn, the lancer subofficer from Synek, bowed in the saddle. "Lady Anna, you have been most generous, and Lord Hadrenn will be most thankful for the golds we carry."

Seated on Farinelli, on the north side of Loiseau's courtyard, Anna inclined her head in return. "I am most certain that you will carry them safely to him and that he will use them wisely."

"Indeed, lady and Regent. Our thanks for all you have done, and may the harmonies always be with you." Sylvarn bowed even more deeply, before turning his mount.

Anna and Jecks watched as the Ebran lancers rode out through the gates of Loiseau, eastward toward Synek.

"There are advantages to being a sorceress," Jecks observed. "All those lancers saw you destroy armsmen with a spell. They will return the golds to Hadrenn."

"They would scarce do otherwise," added Himar.

Anna hoped so, but wasn't so sanguine as Jecks or Himar, even though she had given each lancer three golds personally, with the strong suggestion that failure for the remaining golds to reach Hadrenn would result in dire consequences. Once the lancers in green were well clear of the gates, she flicked the reins and guided Farinelli out through them and along the lane to the domed work building. "We need to see what's happening with Hanfor and Rabyn before we leave."

"I fear we know already," answered Jecks, glancing back as if to ensure that Anna's guards followed the three of them.

They did, as did Frideric and Wiltur.

Anna wasted little time once she reached the work building,

only waiting for Wiltur to check the domed structure before she
slipped the lutar from behind the saddle and hurried in, the lutar
in one hand and a handful of scrolls under the other arm. Jecks
and Himar followed, but the guards took up posts outside the
door.

The scrolls went on the small table against the wall in the
scrying room, and she began to tune the lutar. She'd already
warmed up when she had dressed so that once the lutar was
ready, she launched into the spell.

> Show me now and show me there
> Hanfor's forces and how they fare. . . .

The image in the scrying pool showed Hanfor's forces riding
southward—at least the position of the early-morning sun and
shadows indicated that.

"He is up earlier, in the cool of the day," noted Himar. "He
will let the Nesereans weary their mounts in the heat."

Anna didn't recognize the landscape and looked at Jecks,
then Himar.

"I cannot say where he is," admitted the overcaptain.

"We can't do much, and he seems to have all the lancers he
left with." Anna released the first spell, then sang again.

> Show me now and show me clear
> Rabyn's forces that any might fear,
> near any hold or castle strong. . . .

The silvered waters of the pool revealed a line of lancers in
the blue and cream of Neserea posted along a ridgeline, with
Westfort in the background—its gates closed.

"Rabyn has left enough lancers there to keep Jearle within
his walls," suggested Himar.

"No . . . enough lancers there for Jearle to claim he was kept
within his walls," countered Anna.

Jecks nodded agreement with Anna. After a moment, so did
Himar.

"Still . . . those can't be all the armsmen Rabyn has out
there." Anna sang the release couplet and thought, then tried
again.

Show me now and show me bright
where Rabyn's forces may go to fight. . . .

The next image that wavered up in the pool showed a field beginning to catch fire, with Nesereans in uniform carrying torches.

Anna winced.

"That is good," Jecks suggested. "They have not won any battles, so that they must stoop to firing crops."

"There are no Mansuuran lancers there, either," suggested Himar.

Anna wanted to shake her head. Instead, she pursed her lips, then let the image go and tried another spell, one that mentioned the Mansuuran lancers.

The image was similar to the first, except the riders were in maroon.

"So the Mansuurans released to Rabyn chase us, while the Nesereans burn fields and lay siege," offered Jecks. "That speaks ill of Rabyn's forces."

"Mayhap . . ." Himar's response was slower. "The Mansuurans may have refused to burn fields."

"It doesn't matter." *Except it does . . . and there's a reason why.* Anna frowned, but she couldn't remember what that might be. Finally, she took a deep breath, released the image, and replaced the lutar in the case. "We need to get moving. That's what it shows." She glanced at Himar. "If you would have everyone ready to ride in a glass. . . ."

Himar inclined his head. "We will be ready. By your leave?"

"You may go. We won't be long." As the overcaptain left, Anna walked to the side table. "All of the scrolls can wait, except these. We need to go over them—quickly. Then I need to write what replies are necessary, and then we leave." Anna picked up the first of those she had culled; the others were packed to be taken back to Falcor and considered when necessary—and if necessary. "Herstat reports that he thinks Halde can leave Synfal, and would like our permission." She handed the scroll to Jecks.

After reading it, he nodded. "Herstat is cautious, but you need not have asked . . ."

"Jimbob is your ward, and I'd prefer to ask about things involving him."

"Thank you."

"I also thought if I sent off an answer with a fast messenger, Halde might be able to get to Falcor by the time we're there." Anna picked up the second scroll, then passed it to Jecks. "Lady Anientta is suggesting, ever so politely, that I make some sort of proclamation to Lord Tybel about how Lord Hryding's lands will go to his heir Jeron. That sounds to me like she's trying to stop a power grab by Tybel." Anna's smile was wry.

Jecks nodded more slowly after reading Anientta's missive. "Must you act now?"

"That was my thought," Anna admitted. "We already have problems with Lord Dannel, but he hasn't sent me a protest, and that bothers me as much as if he had. Unless I go to Synope or Arien, nothing will change. It might be better if Tybel did try something. . . ." Anna let her words die away.

"That way you could replace both?" Jecks raised his eyebrows.

"After meeting some of her shirttail relations in Pamr, I don't know that there's anyone in Tybel's whole family that could be trusted with lands."

"Then you should wait until you return from the Western Marches."

Anna lifted another scroll. "Lord Hulber of Silberfels wishes me well, and would like to remind me that the lands of Loiseau were once of Silberfels until graciously granted to Lord Brill's grandsire. He is most confident that I will manage all that is on and below them well." Anna snorted. "He must have a seer, or be able to do it himself. In short, he'd like a little of the gold as a gesture."

Jecks shook his head.

"I'll write him and thank him and tell him that I appreciate his wishes, and that I'll find some way to repay the graciousness of his family once Defalk is rid of the immediate threat from Neserea."

A wide grin lit Jecks' face.

"Only two more," Anna said. "Your neighbor, Lord Clethner, expresses concern about the deteriorating state of Wendell with

Lord Genrica's long illness, since Genrica's offspring are all daughters, and since Lord Fustar of Issl has numerous sons. That's a warning of another land grab that may be coming. Do we wait and beat up on Fustar . . . or try to head it off?"

"When you face a mountain cat, do not go out of your way to trample on a viper."

"Wait. All right." Anna rummaged for the last scroll. "We don't have to do anything on the next one, not until we get to Falcor, but it's the rivermen. Menares says that they are threatening to lay up their barges unless I reduce their tariffs." Anna offered a falsely bright smile. "Some days, I just love being Regent."

Jecks nodded slowly as Anna packed away the scrolls and then picked up the lutar.

61

With Farinelli's reins in her left hand, Anna rubbed her forehead and temples with her right, trying to massage away the residual headache that had started soon after they had ridden out of Loiseau. Something in the air? Worry about how long it would take to reach western Defalk? *Who knows?* She tried to concentrate on riding, on the river ahead.

The road from Mencha to Pamr sloped slowly upward to the bluffs on the south side of the Chean River, then swung abruptly northward around the steep-walled, sinkhole lake that was the remnant of Anna's destruction of the Evult's forces. She glanced to the west, noting the lake's now-blue waters sparkling in the sunshine, sunshine that had come and gone all morning with the scattered clouds. The low mudflats were now covered with bushes and clumps of grass, and the crumbling clay walls had become less steep. The lake itself did not appear any smaller to Anna than when they had traveled past it on the way to Loiseau. "It is hard to believe that so many died there," Himar said, turning in his saddle to look at Anna. "Alvar . . . he . . . never had he seen anything like it."

"I wish I hadn't," Anna replied.

"People do not learn," Jecks interjected. "She destroyed the Evult's lancers and armsmen—all of them—and yet he raised more lancers."

Anna shook her head. Were people really like that? Did she have to annihilate any opposition . . . or fight them endlessly? Or just individuals like the Evult or Lord Ehara?

"Some are like that." Himar turned and guided his mount around the wide curve back toward the river. "Some will not believe what they have not seen, and some will not credit their own eyes if what they have seen does not accord with what they wish."

Like about half of the Thirty-three.

At the top of the bluffs, before the road cut down to the ford, Anna slowed Farinelli. She continued to study the rock base of the ford set by her sorcery as the palomino gelding carried her down to the river.

When she reached the edge of the river, she could see the water sheeting evenly across the line of stone, so smoothly that it seemed like flowing glass. She couldn't help but nod. *You did do a good job replacing the ford.* After a moment, the qualifying thought popped into her mind. *More than a year later.*

Farinelli stepped into the water without hesitation, following Himar's mount along the rock shelf of the ford. The sound of splashing replaced the dull thud of hoofs on clay, and drops of water left small blotches on the lower legs of Anna's dusty riding trousers.

". . . one of the holding armsmen at Pamr called it . . . Sorceress' Ford . . ." Kinor's voice drifted forward from where the lanky redhead rode beside Jimbob—a smaller redhead.

". . . stone like that . . . last forever . . ."

Forever? Will you be remembered by things like fords and bridges . . . or by the number of bodies you've left strewn across Liedwahr?

Beyond the ford, the first fifty yards of road were dark and damp from the river water carried there by the mounts, but beyond that the dust resumed—as did the conversations behind Anna. The low fields were brown and cut to stubble, or in the case of those that had held beans, brown-dappled green plants stood in the noon sun ragged and wilting.

"Be late by the time we get to Pamr," Jecks said, glancing at the flat road that stretched through the fields toward the north-west.

"I know . . . but Gatrune and Firis will take care of us. I worry about Hanfor."

"Best you worry about yourself," Jecks suggested, his hazel eyes twinkling. "My lady."

He said that like he wished it were so. Lord . . . you wish this were all over. Then maybe there'd be time for you. But then, even on Earth, there had never been, what with job demands, Avery's demands, those of the kids. Now . . . there were the demands of spoiled lords, the need to fight off invaders, and endless demands for her time to deal with situations that shouldn't have been problems. Not to mention the worries—from the big ones like whether it had been stupid to go into Ebra to the littler ones like whether she should have pushed Hanfor and Himar into accepting Skent as an untried undercaptain.

That's life anywhere. She took a deep breath, looking at the still-long road to Pamr, and beyond.

62

Once more, Anna found herself massaging her neck, trying to reduce the growing throbbing in her skull, an ache that had increased with every dek she had ridden from almost the time she had left the gates at Loiseau. *Too much sorcery? Or had she used Darksong and not even known it?*

But how? She glanced back along the column, past Kinor and Jimbob. She'd left with two hundred lancers—tenscore—and eight players. Now she had eightscore, and that included the score of newer lancers half-trained by Jerat at the Sand Pass fort and the cyan company under Skent. Himar had put two veterans as senior lancers beside Skent and told the young man to heed them.

Anna hoped Skent would. *Then . . . that's what he has to learn if he wants to get Cataryzna as a consort . . . with your support.*

She winced. *Are you any better than Dieshr was in using*

people? The sorceress continued to scan the column until her eyes came to rest on the red-and-white hair of the chief player. Not looking up toward Anna, Liende rode slowly, apparently lost in her own thoughts. *She's doing this for her children ... not for you, not for Defalk.*

On each side of the road, the bare and harvested fields stretched out until they merged with twilight of what had turned into a gray day with dull low clouds. Ahead, off the right shoulder of the road, was a squat stone column. Anna squinted to make out the numbers chiseled there, finally reading the number and the single letter. Another two deks to Pamr, and perhaps another two beyond that to reach Lady Gatrune's holding.

The Regent and sorceress yawned, then absently massaged her neck again.

"You are tired," said Jecks, easing his mount closer to her.

"I don't know why. Riding isn't *that* exhausting."

"Riding and thinking, mayhap?" The bushy white eyebrows lifted. "And fretting about what may come. You have not reckoned what the battles cost you, either."

"It was a gamble to go to Ebra ... but I wanted to settle things there without worrying about Rabyn and the Liedfuhr."

"Nothing is ever settled in Liedwahr," suggested Jecks. "Had you not defeated those of Ebra once, and those of Neserea?"

"Not really the Nesereans. I killed their leader and his consort."

"Did you not spell some of them?"

"I did." Anna wanted to shake her head, except she had to stifle a yawn. *That* could be why some of Rabyn's forces were standing siege duty in western Defalk. Before she'd fully understood—or been forced to understand—the limits of Clearsong, she'd spelled the Neserean forces remaining in Falcor to be loyal to her. Did Rabyn even know that? Nubara wouldn't. He'd fled Falcor well before that. "But how many of those are in the forces attacking Defalk ... I don't know."

The sorceress looked through the dim twilight toward the indistinct shapes that had to be the outlying dwellings of Pamr. She blinked. Surely, there should be some light, some torches or lamps in some windows. The clouds made the early evening darker, although it would have been dark enough, since Darksong was the only moon visible at dusk in the weeks after harvest.

A faint clanging or tinkling of a distant bell echoed through the night from somewhere up ahead, going on and on.

She stiffened. What on earth—or Erde—was she thinking? They were entering Pamr, and she was so tired that she was woolgathering. *Lord!*

"Himar!" Anna turned in the saddle and tried to fumble the lutar free from its straps.

"Yes, lady?"

"It's Pamr, and that chandler! We need arms ready."

"Arms ready!" snapped Jecks, belatedly understanding Anna's concerns, and relaying her order. "Arms ready!"

"Arms ready!" echoed Himar.

As Farinelli carried Anna past the first darkened dwelling, Anna heard a dull rumble and glanced skyward toward the clouds that had been getting lower with every glass that had passed since midday at the Sorprat ford. She glanced up to see if it had started to rain, but she could feel nothing.

She began to try to tune the lutar in the dimness, but her fingers were clumsy. Her eyes strained to catch sight of the inn and the chandlery near the center of town. Yet all the buildings were dark. *Dark?*

"That is not thunder," Jecks said abruptly.

Anna swallowed. He was right. The sound was that of drums, and the pounding of those drums rumbled through Anna like the thunder she had first thought the drums had been.

"Now! Men of Pamr! Strike!"

The words floated in Anna's ears for a moment. Then, torches flared up beside the packed-clay road, and arrows whistled past her guards.

A good score of bearded men wielding spears and axes and other odd weapons charged out of the near darkness, directly toward Anna.

Shit! You're so tired you didn't even think . . . dumb!

"Blaz! Kerhor! Take them!" bellowed Rickel, as he and Lejun lifted the heavy shields, quickly, despite the deks of travel, while Anna bent, turned in the saddle, and tried to wrestle the lutar free.

Jecks had his blade free, as did Kinor, and a moment later,
Jimbob. The three blades joined those of Blaz and Kerhor.

The evening was filled with grunts, and the dull sounds of
metal on metal, metal on wood, wood on flesh and bone, but
not a single yell or shout issued from the lips or throats of the
attackers. The only sound from the attackers and the town, the
one that seemed to shiver both the air and ground alike, was
that of the deep triple-toned drums.

Anna's fingers fumbled over the lutar strings, and she sang a
few syllables, seeking a pitch. *Any pitch!* Her voice cracked,
and she attempted to clear her throat, trying somehow to force
dust and mucus out.

Somewhere in the darkness a horse screamed.

More arrows sleeted past, and there was a dull *thunk* and a
gasp from one of the guards, and Anna glimpsed an empty saddle even while she tried to sort out a spell, any spell.

You need a spell. . . . The thought pounded at her.

63

PAMR, DEFALK

A man races through the twilight and onto the porch of the
chandlery. On the porch, one brown-haired figure straightens from behind the largest of the drums arrayed there. The run-
ner looks past the drummer to the taller bearded figure of the
chandler standing in the darker shadows. "She returns, mighty
Farsenn. And her players have not even their instruments out."

"She returns to Pamr . . . but never to Falcor." Farsenn
laughs in his deep bass voice and looks to Giersan. "Ready
your drums." Then he turns back to the bearded messenger.
"Summon our mighty warriors. The archers go behind the
hedges near the first trees—as we practiced. Keep them in the
shadows. Have no torches lit until you hear the drums. Then
the torches and the arrows."

"As you command, mighty Farsenn." The man turns and hur-
ries into the darkness, ringing the handbell that he carries.

"Yes . . . yes . . . Today and tonight will be long remembered in Pamr," Farsenn says as he looks along the main street, toward the east and the approaching sorceress.

"Best we finish the task, or it will not be recalled as we wish," suggests Giersan.

"Taking down the bitch Gatrune was scarce a task at all. None had seen the power of Darksong." Farsenn strains as he looks eastward.

Shutters close, and lights and lamps vanish. Seemingly within moments, the town of Pamr is dark and silent, and even the ringing of the handbell is gone. Shadowy figures move toward the eastern side of the town, arranging themselves in the dimness behind the hedges.

"Now?" asks Giersan.

"No. They have not reached the hedges." Farsenn waits silently, then raises his hand. Finally, he drops it. "Now!"

The drummer's mallets caress the skins of the drum set, and a low rolling thunder rumbles out.

"The muddling song. Three, two . . . mark!"

The rolling sound of thunder switches into an almost-staccato beat to accompany Farsenn's dark and deep voice.

> Take their wits and hold them fast,
> so their actions cannot last.
> Take their eyes and make them slow,
> so they know not where the time may go. . . .

From somewhere to the east a torch flares, then another.

"Now! Men of Pamr! Strike!" With the command, the bearded figures surge from the hedges toward the line of riders.

The triple-toned drums shake the ground around the chandlery, seemingly more intense than thunder.

Against the clang of metal, the intermittent whir of arrows, and the grunts of men fighting, the single scream of a mount pierces the night air.

"Now!" calls Farsenn. "The death song."

The big drums shift their rhythm again, and the tones form a simple melody that melds with the darksinger's deep voice.

> Clearsong, sorceress, fall to the old,
> bright voice still and songs grow cold.

Darksong, darksong, strike with might,
put the sorceress to death this night. . . .

Farsenn glances up as he finishes the spell, sweat streaming down his face, while the triple-toned drums roar out yet another pattern.

The night sky blurs, then shudders, as if the clouds are being shaken by an unseen hand, and then a tinkling, yet penetrating chord blankets the land.

"No! NO!!!!" screams Farsenn, shaking his fist upward. "No!"

Silvered arrow-notes fly from somewhere east of the chandlery, arching into the dark sky and then falling . . . and with each of those silver notes, the thunder-rumble of the drums is muffled, more and more. Yet Giersan labors over the drums, even as their sounds die away.

"Dissonance! Clearsong cannot prevail! Never!" Farsenn's bass is hoarse, as though the words had come from a raw throat.

More of the silver-arrowed notes fall—striking bearded forms running westward, away from the remaining riders, away from the silvered and shimmering figure that is the sorceress, away from a voice whose clarity shivers through the shuttered town.

Farsenn looks up once more. His mouth opens, but he cannot speak before the silver arrows strike.

The drums blaze into flame, so quickly, and so violently that they might have been the driest of tinder soaked in oils, but the drums do not blaze so brightly as the briefly shuddering forms that topple from the porch of the burning chandlery.

64

Arrows kept sleeting past Anna, striking armsmen, and in the background the heavy multitoned and ominous rumbling thunder of the drums continued.

Sluggish as Anna continued to feel, with eyes sometimes almost feeling like she were looking through a fog, with her armsmen dying around her, Anna had to act. She had lost the time to think. All she could do was sing the one spell she knew . . . knew cold, changing but a few words, for she knew her attackers were not armsmen in the regular sense:

> Turn to fire, turn to flame,
> those weapons spelled against my name
> turn to ash all those spelled against my face
> who seek by spell or force the Regency to replace.

> Turn to fire, turn to flame . . .

Almost harplike, the night sky shivered . . . and Anna could not help but look skyward as visible silver notes cascaded like arrows down across Pamr. Where each struck, a silver flame seared like a flare, and with the sonic collision of drumbeat and harp note, silent screaming bolts of sound shivered the town.

"Dissonance!" The single exclamation rode over the irregular hissing of the fire arrows.

For the first time, screams filled the darkness—short agonizing screams that ended almost as they began.

Then . . . the night was silent, except for the panting of lancers, and the moans of wounded Defalkan armsmen.

"Lady?" Jecks addressed Anna, but his eyes surveyed the darkness, going from one fallen torch to another.

Anna's stomach turned, for by those torches were charred figures, and each had been a man, some woman's consort, some girl's brother, some child's father. And all had been set against her because, more than a year earlier, she had turned a chandler into ashes to stop him from raping her. When he had tried to force her over her violent objections, and then kill her when she had used gentler sorcery to dissuade him, she reminded herself. *You didn't use violence first . . . you didn't . . .*

"My lady?" Jecks asked again.

"I'm here. . . ." She looked at the guards who surrounded her, seeing again the empty saddle. After checking faces, she asked, "Kerhor?"

Kinor, blood splashed across his dusty tunic, reined up

beside Jecks, answered slowly. "He took an axe, Lady Anna, and an old halberd."

"I'm sorry," she whispered to no one in particular. "I'm sorry."

Behind her, a crackling sound began to grow. Turning, she saw the dwelling next toward the center of Pamr had begun to burn. More than a hundred yards farther away, the chandlery was already a bonfire reaching skyward toward the low clouds.

Anna and Jecks slowly surveyed the burning town . . . and the bodies strewn everywhere.

Unbidden, one of the stanzas from Britten's *On This Island* song cycle pounded through Anna's mind:

> Starving through the leafless wood
> Trolls run scolding for their food;
> And the nightingale is dumb,
> And the angel will not come.

"The nightingale is dumb . . ." Anna whispered hoarsely.

"Lady Regent?" asked Himar. "We have lost near-on another twoscore lancers. What would you have of us?"

"We'll go on to Lady Gatrune's. There's no one left here to harm us." Anna's voice sounded as dead as she felt inside.

"Bodies across their saddles! Leave no man who fought," ordered Himar. "Then mount up and ride out."

Anna continued to hold the lutar with her right hand as she flicked Farinelli's reins, her eyes scanning the darkness to the west and north.

The sound of hoofs and the heavy breathing of mounts and tired lancers began to rise over the crackling of dwellings burning and the scattered low moans of wounded men. Rickel and Lejun continued to flank Anna, their shields held high.

Behind the Defalkan lancers, as they reached the center of Pamr and turned their mounts northward on the road to Lady Gatrune's hold, flames hissed and built to a roar, casting flickering shadows across charred bodies left on the bloodstained clay.

Anna swallowed and moistened her lips. "I should have spent the time to find them." She wanted to shake her head. *To think that . . . all those people dead because one oversexed chandler wouldn't take no for an answer. Or because you couldn't find another way out of the situation. Were you just stupid, not realizing just how much Defalkan men regard women as property? And too tired because you were pushing too hard to reach Denguic?* "I should have."

"I would wager that last spell of yours did so," suggested Jecks. "Could you tell such?"

"I think so . . . but I don't know. I'll check when we get to Lady Gatrune's," Anna answered, looking into the darkness ahead. *If you can . . . if you can sing another spell tonight.*

"Torches! To the van!" ordered Himar. His voice lowered as he let his mount drop back, and as he addressed the Regent. "I like this not. Were the holding not close, I would ask that you have us make an encampment."

"Should we stop? I'd rather have friendly walls around us," Anna replied, "but I probably caused this by wanting to go on." *Probably? Definitely . . . it's all on your head.*

"I have sent scouts out, as if the land were not ours," Himar said, "but I would press on, so short is the distance, but with care. Great care."

Anna decided to continue keeping the lutar ready.

"I also," said Jecks. "Still, it is an ill night, without the bright moon."

Anna scarcely would have called the small white disc of Clearsong bright, not compared to the bright moon of earth. "We couldn't see it anyway."

"Mayhap not, but the clouds oft roll in under the evil moon when it rises."

Could that be? There's still so much you don't know. Darksong rising . . . pitted against sorcery . . . and where are the stars, the army of unalterable law? Her laugh was hoarse.

The torches shed only minimal light, and with Clearsong not in the sky, and the heavy low clouds blocking even starlight, the column moved slowly northward.

Even after perhaps half a glass, no lights betrayed the hold, although Anna knew it was but a few deks out the north road from Pamr. The air still smelled smoky despite the breeze out of the north.

Smoke drifted toward the Defalkan riders, reaching them in

waves, waves Anna could smell more than see. The smoke came from dying fires, but with an odor both similar to and different from that she had created in Pamr.

"Oh, no . . ." murmured the sorceress. "No . . ."

"Torches forward! Ready arms!"

There won't be any need for arms.

Anna was right. The holding was silent as death, and the dim light of the torches revealed the first bodies at the gates, bodies savagely hacked into near unrecognizability, mercifully cloaked in the dimness of the dark night.

"An ill night, indeed, my lady," Jecks said. "I am sorry. Most sorry, for I know the ties and gratitude you bore all who were here."

Anna held the lutar ready, though she knew she would need it no longer. *Not tonight. Then, you really didn't think you'd need it coming into Pamr, either.*

More bodies lay along the lane to the hold, a hold that had burned, leaving the stone-and-brick shell. From the ruins glimmered but faint coals.

"Purple company, check the stables. Green company, Yujul—check the barracks, over there. The rest of you search the grounds. By company now . . ." When he finished directing the lancers, Himar turned toward Anna. "Wait, if you would, Lady Anna."

Anna reined up and waited in the darkness barely broken by the torches, surrounded by guards in the ruins of a hold she had thought friendly and strong.

When the lancers confirmed that the grounds were indeed empty, Anna finally dismounted and walked up the ash-strewn steps toward what had been the entry to Gatrune's hall. At the threshold, as if he had tried to hold back the horde, lay a dark-haired, dark-bearded figure. Within the light of the torch held by Kinor, sprawled more than a half-score of figures. Others lay farther away from Firis.

"Most would not die so well," murmured Himar.

Anna swallowed. The dashing captain had always claimed Anna had brought him fortune. *Not this time.*

"Lady . . . if you would abide, with your guards," Jecks suggested.

The sorceress and Regent nodded, knowing what he had in mind. "I'll wait here. You won't find anyone alive."

Jecks' lips curled, but he did not speak as he and Himar stepped gingerly through the ruined doors.

"Was this the work of the rebels?" asked Jimbob, his voice simultaneously puzzled and deferential.

"They weren't rebels," Anna said slowly, finding she still clutched the lutar. "They were deluded men spelled with Darksong by a young man who didn't understand, and who didn't want to."

"Peasants . . ."

"No." Anna kept her voice level. "Your grandfather was right about the evil that can be done with drums. Two men did evil, and the others died because of it."

"Could you have done aught—" Jimbob's question halted with the jab to the ribs from Kinor.

"If I had . . . then we couldn't have gone into Ebra, and we'd be facing another enemy to the east." *You hope your judgment was correct.* Enough people had already paid.

The returning glow of the torch showed Jecks and Himar as they walked slowly back through the ruined doors toward Anna and the others.

"Both the lady . . . and her son . . ." Jecks' voice was flat, emotionless.

"I should have acted before." Anna could feel the dampness on her cheeks.

"You could not . . . not if you wanted to ensure that Ebra remains an ally," pointed out Jecks. "Even you, mighty as you are, can do but what you can." Jecks paused, then asked more gently, "Would you have wished to kill men who had done nothing then, suspecting only that they *might* do ill?"

Anna winced at the question. *You had thought about it.*

Was that another part of being Regent? Choosing when no action was without negative consequences? Letting things happen because there was no proof of evil that could justify action? Or was that just the lot of Defalk?

"You can do no more until first light," Jecks said gently.

Anna wished he could hold her, if but for a moment. Instead, she stiffened. "We will have much to do tomorrow." *Too much . . . like every other day.*

65

A nna stood beside the ash-dusted steps that led to the ruined main dwelling. She looked down the slight rise toward the half-ruined stables and barracks and the meadow beyond where her lancers had camped. Blaz and Lejun stood perhaps a yard behind her, with Jecks beside her. A raw cool wind blew out of the east, in surging gusts, as if presaging a cold rain, but the clouds were thin and high.

In the light of a gray morning, the hold looked even worse than the night before, and Anna didn't feel as though she had slept either well or long enough. Her eyes burned; her head still ached, even after forcing herself to eat; and her nose itched from something, perhaps from grooming and saddling Farinelli, or from the fine ash that was everywhere, so much that she almost wanted to tear at her face. Her riding clothes bore spots of blood that she hadn't noticed before. She moistened her lips as she watched her chief player walk slowly up the lane toward her.

Jecks did not speak, though his eyes also surveyed the devastation, and far larger patches of blood stained his tunic.

Liende stopped and bowed. "Lady Anna?" The chief player straightened, her tunic smeared with ash, one sleeve bearing a splotch of blood.

"How are you doing this morning?"

"We were fortunate. Delvor has a bruise on one leg, and Duralt and Palian have small cuts on their arms. They can still play."

"How about you?"

A wintry smile appeared, and Liende's freckled face appeared younger for a moment. "I have seen worse."

Anna nodded. "Could you and the players manage a spell this morning? After last night?"

"One . . . that we can do . . . or two, if it be the same spell."

"Depending on how they feel, we might repeat it for the stables and barracks. If everyone feels strong enough."

"Players play." Liende bowed slightly. "I will gather them."

Just like you . . . she's another woman who had no idea where things would lead, but she's not exactly happy about it all. Then, in Liende's shoes—or boots—Anna wouldn't have been all that happy either.

"You must rebuild it now?" asked Jecks once Liende was beyond earshot.

"Yes."

"There is no lord to hold it."

"Lady Herene will take it and refurnish it to her taste. I think one of the older fosterlings, perhaps Ytrude, can replace her at Suhl."

"Lady Herene?" Jecks frowned, as if attempting to recall the name.

"I don't think you ever met her. She was Gatrune's sister. She's the ward for Sargol's heirs, but she's the only relative of Gatrune I'd trust here, and a lady will be replaced by a lady. Especially here." Anna found her voice getting harsh, and she softened it. "I'm not angry at you."

"You are angry," Jecks pointed out.

"I am angry," she admitted. "But that won't change anything."

"You wish to change Defalk within seasons, and most do not wish change. Yet you are angry that they will not accept such."

"They want to live, don't they? They'd rather not be under the Evult's iron fist. Or Behlem's." Anna shrugged, feeling how tight her shoulders were from all the tension she carried. "They'd have to change one way or the other. This way would be easier."

"My lady, they do not see it. Nor do most of the lords."

"I know." Anna sighed. "I know."

"You must do what you can," Jecks added. "Some have come to see, and others will."

"We need to talk to Himar." Anna looked toward Blaz. "Would you please ask Overcaptain Himar if he could spare a moment?"

"Yes, Lady Anna."

Anna looked at Jecks. "I'm going to ask him who should remain here—I'd like Skent to do it . . . but he'd need an experienced senior armsman or undercaptain with him."

"Young Skent . . . that would be good. He is loyal, and he will live longer here."

Anna tried not to wince. Was anyone who followed her doomed to injury or death? Was it that bad?

"My lady . . . in this world, any who must bear arms risk death. You save more than other leaders, but you cannot expect to preserve them all."

Why not?

Himar walked briskly up from the stable area, followed discreetly by Blaz.

"You had inquired after me, Regent?"

"Himar, before we leave this morning, I'm going to use a spell to try to rebuild the hold here, and then the stables and barracks. We'll need to leave a company to hold it and support the next lady when she arrives."

Himar nodded. "You would suggest young Skent and some other undercaptain he can rely upon?"

"I had thought so, but I haven't told anyone because I wanted to talk to you first." Anna's eyes went to Jecks. "Except Lord Jecks."

The overcaptain smiled. "Again, Lady Anna, I am glad of what you understand."

"After last night?" Anna almost snorted.

"Regent," Himar said soberly, "in all lands in Defalk there are uprisings. Without you and your sorcery, many more would have died. Armsmen live with death, but we do not welcome it. Those who have seen battles would have you over any ruler in Liedwahr."

"About Skent?" Jecks prompted, clearly sensing Anna's discomfort.

"I would spare Jirsit to advise him. He has seen every battle since you became Regent, and has served well."

Anna understood. Jirsit could stand a respite, and Skent listened to Jirsit.

"I would also like to move some lancers between companies—a few older men for stability, and a few who might best serve with more training from them."

"I'll leave the arrangements to you, Himar."

"Thank you, Regent." Himar inclined his head. "By your leave?"

"Thank you, Himar." She turned to Jecks. "What do you think?" Then she laughed, softly. "That's backwards. I should have asked before I acted."

"You do what you think will be best, not always what will be easily accepted at first." Jecks smiled crookedly, but warmly. "Those who have followed you still remain willingly, and few rulers who fight battles can say such."

"Thank you. I hope they won't be too disappointed." She tried to clear her throat. "I need to warm up before the players get here, or I'll be the one holding things up."

"I will see that all is ready for our departure, my lady."

"Thank you," she repeated.

Warming up took Anna a long time. Jecks had returned, accompanied by Jimbob and Kinor. All three stood back to give her space, and the players were all gathered and tuning when Anna was finally warmed up. She looked toward Liende.

"We stand ready," replied the chief player.

The sorceress nodded, then began to sing as the melody and simple harmony rose from the gathered players.

> Replace all stones and set them new and strong
> so this hold will stand both firm and long.
> Replace what once was timber with steel to last,
> leaving but doors and shutters. . . .

Silvered mist seeped up from the ground or coalesced from somewhere, shrouding the ruined hall even before Anna had completed the second line of the spell. In the back of her mind, she could tell the players were tired, because the accompaniment was hanging on the edge as she finished the spell.

Then, after a rumbling and a shuddering of the ground, the faintest chord of harmony shimmered and echoed from somewhere, vanishing as the mist dissipated and left a pristine-appearing hall that replaced the burned-out walls and fallen roof. Anna blinked, then smiled, hoping that her visualization of the hall and the idea of girders or I-beams or whatever they were would suffice over the years ahead, but she couldn't afford anything that verged on Darksong, not the way she felt.

Kinor nodded in approval, but Jimbob's face was pale, and

the heir swallowed as he looked from Anna to his grandsire's impassive features.

Liende lowered the clarinetlike woodwind and stepped toward the Regent.

"How do you feel?" asked the sorceress.

"We could do another, Regent." A faint smile cracked the chief player's lips. "We will do it better."

"Then we should turn and face the ruins of the stable," Anna suggested.

The second spell was smoother, and resulted in an immaculate stable and a barracks standing where the former structures had been.

Despite the cool wind, Anna found herself blotting her forehead, and gratefully accepting the water bottle that Jecks extended. After drinking almost half of it, she returned it. "Thank you."

"That was better," Liende informed the players. "Much better. Now . . . prepare to ride. We leave shortly." She stepped toward Anna.

"It was better, but Lady Herene will have to rebuild the rest of the holding herself."

"Most lords would not begin with so impressive a hold," Jecks observed with a laugh. "She will have no cause to complain."

"I hope not." *And you hope she doesn't blame you for her sister's death.* "Thank you, Liende." She raised her voice. "Thank you all."

As the players slipped away to pack up instruments, Anna turned back to Jecks. "You made sure the messengers took those scrolls to Lady Herene and to Dythya and Menares? Ytrude will need to get to Suhl before Herene can leave."

"Both riders left before you began the first spell. I sent an escort with each."

"Thank you. I should have thought of that." But there was always something she should have thought about. Anna looked to the gray clouds that rumbled out of the north. "We need to get back to Falcor . . . and then to Denguic . . . or Dubaria."

"Perhaps we shall be able to go to Fussen," Jecks said.

Anna raised her eyebrows.

"You did suggest to Arms Commander Himar that it would not hurt to involve Lord Ustal." Jecks smiled ironically. "Your glass showed Hanfor riding south."

Anna laughed. "Maybe he can. If anyone could . . ."

They began to walk down the steps, still ash-dusted, from the new and silent hold, which Anna had no desire to inspect, toward their waiting mounts.

Once she had mounted Farinelli, she eased the gelding aside to where Skent and Jirsit stood. "Undercaptain Skent, as Overcaptain Himar has told you, you and Undercaptain Jirsit will hold these lands until the Lady Herene arrives, and then you will serve her bidding until she has determined her own staff and holdings."

"Yes, Regent." Skent nodded, a calm expression that reassured Anna.

Anna smiled and looked at Jirsit. "Himar thinks highly of you, and I appreciate your willingness to advise and assist Skent." Her eyes went back to the younger undercaptain. She lowered her voice, pitched only so the two could hear. "Skent, I charge you with learning everything you possibly can from Undercaptain Jirsit, from improving your skill at arms to every detail about training and leading lancers and armsmen."

To his credit, Skent did not pale or flush. "I know I still have much to learn, and I will do my best."

"Good." Anna paused. "You may be here some time." She paused. "You have the golds necessary for supplies?"

"Yes, lady." Both undercaptains nodded.

"Thank you both." Anna looked at Skent. "Learn everything you can from Jirsit, Skent. Everything."

"Yes, Lady Anna." Skent met Anna's eyes, then added, "If you would explain . . . in Falcor."

"I will, and try not to worry." Anna smiled, knowing exactly what worried Skent, or rather who worried him. *Still . . . he's come a long way from the worried page whose father had just been killed.* She turned Farinelli back toward Himar and Jecks.

"Scouts, forward!"

With Himar's first command, Anna and the fivescore or fewer of her party began the ride back to Falcor and whatever awaited her there.

66

ENCORA, RANUAK

The Matriarch looks from the vanishing silver image in the black-tiled pool to the four players on the far side and nods. Each of the four bows, then turns and slips out of the scrying room.

The waters of the pool remain serene as the Matriarch turns her head and addresses the younger woman. "You see, daughter? No unnecessary sentimentality, and no overreaction. Some rulers, as did the Evult, would have leveled all of that town. The Regent punished the guilty and the rebellious, then rebuilt the hold with sorcery, set a guard, and now continues westward to deal with Rabyn."

"There was not much left for overreaction," points out the silver-haired Ulgar, who stands at the Matriarch's other shoulder. "That spell of hers killed every man enchanted with Darksong, and that was almost every able-bodied man in Pamr."

"Does she have a heart, Mother?" asks Alya. "Or was Veria correct that she is a cold seeker after power?"

"She risks death every time she attempts to send a missive across the depths to the mist worlds, and all of Erde can feel the strain on the harmonies. Yet she continues those efforts. I believe they must be to her children."

"You don't know?"

"How would I? Except as a mother?" The Matriarch shrugs. "She has taken in those she did not have to take in. She allowed the Lady of Stromwer to live, and her first act upon taking that hold was to restore her child. She has returned Dumar to the old line, and after defeating Bertmynn, she has returned to her own land. She has tried to use Darksong to avoid killing, and she has tried, far from successfully, to use spells that would kill fewer souls. She does not act like a Bertmynn or an Evult. The lords of the Thirty-three fear her already, but now they will respect her, for she has shown that she will not tolerate disrespect from either those above or below the salt—or the table itself." The Matriarch laughs, sardonically. "And she has just begun to know the pain of justice in ruling."

Alya presses her lips together. "She fought but two battles and did not even march into Elahwa."

"She destroyed the war-dog who would not let any woman lift her head. She has supported the only lord that all of Ebra will accept in these days. And your sister lives. That we know, and she will recover from the wounds she has suffered. The sorceress has prevented Bertmynn from further abusing the city. I would gather that the sorceress has also prevailed upon young Hadrenn to treat Elahwa gently. In that, we shall see, but whatever the outcome, it is far better than what would have happened without her intervention."

"We shall see," avers Alya.

"Do not be so doubtful, daughter," chides Ulgar. "Has not your mother been proved wise in each event?"

Alya nods, if slowly.

"I am not infallible, Ulgar," replies the Matriarch. "Far from it. Only the harmonies are infallible. That they have reminded me, and that they will remind all who employ their powers, even the sorceress."

"Even the sorceress," Ulgar murmurs.

67

Anna wiped the dampness off her forehead, moisture from the cool mist that was not quite heavy enough to be even a drizzle, then shifted her weight in the saddle. Even the Chean River, to the right of the road that followed the river bluffs, looked gray in the early-morning light that filtered through the low and formless clouds.

After turning in the saddle, as if to check how closely Jimbob and Kinor followed, Jecks observed, "You are distressed, my lady."

"I'm not distressed. I'm worried. Right now, it's not raining enough to get the roads really muddy. But it could. What if it starts to rain before we can head out to help Hanfor?"

"Hanfor will carry out his orders," Jecks replied, easing his mount closer to Anna's. "He will not risk his lancers. You have ordered him to harry and delay Rabyn, and that he will do." Jecks offered both a smile and a shrug. "If it should rain, then Rabyn will have even more difficulty than Hanfor, and you will have more time to reach them."

"I hope so." The Regent glanced up at the featureless gray clouds hanging over the road that stretched westward along the river toward Falcor, still more than a day's ride away. *If it doesn't start to pour.*

"You will need that time. You cannot rush off to Denguic or Dubaria or Fussen," Jecks said slowly. "Spend one day in Falcor. One day to set right what you can."

"I'll think about it," Anna promised. One day didn't sound like much, but a day here and a day there, and pretty soon . . . There was already so much to worry about—whether Hanfor could continue to elude Rabyn and keep the Nesereans from going farther into Defalk; whether Hadrenn would be able to unite Ebra and whether he would keep his word; whether Skent would work out as the custodian of Gatrune's lands; whether Herene would be strong enough to reunite Pamr and hold the lands; whether Jimbob would learn from all that was happening; how long the Liedfuhr would honor his promise not to attack Defalk.

All that didn't include the worries over the mistakes she had already made, mistakes someone more experienced might have avoided.

She moistened her lips and looked at the road ahead once more. *One day at a time . . . that's all you can do . . . one day at a time.*

68

The clouds that had threatened rain during the entire ride from Pamr remained low and formless, continuing to drizzle mist across Anna and the others as they rode through the late-afternoon gloom. Ahead lay the imposing stone bridge that spanned the Falche just below where the Fal and Chean Rivers joined. Beyond and to the south of the bridge lay the northern part of the city of Falcor, on the higher part of the bluff. The liedburg lay across the bridge and even farther to the south.

Anna's eyes strayed to the north, past the wall on her right that was part of the wide causeway leading to the eastern end of the bridge. Both causeway and bridge she had erected with sorcery right before spring—and prostrated herself for nearly a week because she'd done it with a lutar for accompaniment, rather than using players. *Just three seasons ago?* She shook her head. Only a few weeks beyond half a year? It seemed far longer . . . more like years, years spent on horseback trying to repel invaders and deal with men who wanted to make every woman back into a slave. Or so it seemed, at times. *Except so often, no one sees it but you. They see a Lord Dannel as a protective father, or a Farsenn as an avenging son, or a Bertmynn as an ambitious lord, or a Ustal as a proud young lord. . . .*

"Regent?" Himar eased his mount around Jimbob's and up beside Farinelli.

"Yes, Himar?" Anna focused on the overcaptain.

"You should know . . . the scouts reported that several armsmen were watching from the north bank of the river. They wore dark leathers and no livery, but when the scouts crossed the bridge and rode after them, they were gone."

"Dark leathers . . . free-lance mercenaries?" Jecks frowned. "Why would such be here? The Regent put out no call for lancers-of-opportunity."

"Because they know I have to fight Rabyn and I pay well?" asked Anna. "That can't be much of a secret."

"Mayhap, but to travel so far . . ." mused the white-haired

lord. "They could not have come from nearer than Nordwei, and mercenaries are less than welcome there."

"Tomorrow will tell," suggested Himar. "Mercenaries are not shy about asking for golds. If those were mercenaries, they will be at the liedburg not much after dawn tomorrow, boasting of their prowess with blade and lance." He laughed. "They will ask for more gold each than a captain receives, and claim they are worth even more."

"Will any of them be any good?" Anna wondered if some might be skilled enough to hire to replace those men lost in Ebra and in Pamr.

"We will see." Himar shrugged. "It cannot hurt to listen and to look."

Farinelli's hoofs echoed on the hard stones of the bridge, and Anna looked over and down at the sorcery-created gorge that held the Falche River. Even though it was well into fall, the river had continued to rise over the summer, and now filled entirely the lowest level of the riverbed, more water than she'd ever seen there. Maybe Defalk had once been a truly green land, the way Jecks had said, and perhaps it would be once more.

As Anna rode down the western causeway into Falcor itself, she looked at the pedestal in the roundabout just beyond the causeway, a marble-and-brick foundation that had lost the statue that had once stood there long before she had come to Defalk. The marble base had no inscription or clue as to whose monument might have stood there. *If whoever had it erected had even ruled long enough to have had it completed.*

Fifty yards in front of Anna, the standard-bearer turned his mount southward, and the smell of roasted fowl drifted along the avenue that sloped downhill slightly and would lead them to the liedburg. The streets seemed to have people on them, unlike in years previous; but those who were out stepped clear from the paving stones as they saw the purple banner.

Rickel and Blaz rode forward of Anna and more toward the edges of the street, their eyes constantly moving, studying the scattered handfuls of people as the column continued southward.

"Hail the Regent!" called a tall man in innkeeper's brown from the narrow front step of the Golden Lutar.

"Best wishes to you, innkeeper!" Anna called back.

"Thank you, Regent and sorceress!"

"He'll tell everyone who'll listen that he talked to the Regent," murmured Jecks.

"It can't hurt, can it?" she asked.

"Not with those who will listen to him," Jecks answered with a laugh.

Ahead, another two hundred yards past the inn, past the last of the more affluent three-storied dwellings on the north side of the open ground that circled the liedburg, she could see the liedburg, with wisps of smoke curling above the walls and through the gray and damp air.

The gates stood wide open, as they always had since she had become Regent, and the pair of duty armsmen in Defalkan purple raised their arms in a form of salute as Anna neared the gates. She inclined her head in response as she and Jecks rode through the gate.

". . . good to be back . . ." said Jimbob from behind them.

". . . won't be here more than a day or two . . . just enough to get supplies and give the mounts a breather," answered Kinor.

". . . wouldn't mind a clean tunic . . ."

There's a lot you wouldn't mind, but you won't have much time to appreciate it. Anna glanced toward the side courtyard. Was Menares waiting for them? She frowned.

"If you have no need of me, lady," Himar said, easing his mount closer to Anna, "I will be setting the lancers and seeing what supplies we will be needing for the journey westward. You still plan on the day after tomorrow?"

"It won't be any earlier." Anna nodded. "There's too much for me to do, and I suppose the men and their mounts could use the rest."

"They could use more," Himar reminded her.

"Talk to me tomorrow. If you really think it's necessary, maybe we can add another day."

"Best I check on all the mounts, then." The overcaptain urged his mount toward the rear courtyard and the lancer barracks and stables.

The gray-bearded Menares was indeed standing ten yards ahead of Anna, against the inner wall of the liedburg's side courtyard, just outside the stable doors, clearly assuming that

Anna would unsaddle and groom Farinelli. The gray wool cloak he wore could not conceal the fact that Menares, while still remaining an impressively broad figure, had become considerably less corpulent. Dark circles ringed the intent but seemingly colorless eyes that dominated his round face.

Anna guided Farinelli to the stable door before dismounting, trying to leave space for the riders in the column behind to pass on their way to the main barracks and stables. For a moment, as always, Anna held to the saddle while her legs adjusted. Then she stepped out of the mist and into the dryer dimness of the stable.

Menares followed Jecks and Anna and Farinelli into the stable.

"He looks good, lady," offered Tirsik the stablemaster, stepping forward toward Anna, "except I'd like the farrier to check his shoes."

"If you would—" Anna stopped and sighed. "Let me know when you need me." She'd have to be there if Farinelli needed reshoeing.

"That I will, lady." The stablemaster looked at Jecks. "And your mount, lord?"

"It would not hurt to check his shoes, though he is less . . . choosy about shoeing." Jecks grinned at Anna.

She grinned back.

"Yours carries not the future of Defalk," countered Tirsik. "Merely a high and most noble lord."

"Were you my stablemaster, master Tirsik . . ." Jecks mock-threatened.

"You'd have my head, Lord Jecks, if I did not worry about the Lady Anna." Tirsik bowed.

Jecks laughed. "You are a scoundrel."

"Aye, and I'm too ancient to be other 'n that." Tirsik bowed to Lady Anna. "Beggin' your pardon, Regent."

"You're pardoned, Tirsik."

Anna had her gear and the saddle off Farinelli and had begun to brush the gelding before she noticed Menares standing beside Rickel at the end of the stall. "What is it, Menares?" Anna was almost afraid to ask, but Menares wouldn't have come out to the stable if he weren't concerned. She kept grooming Farinelli while she spoke.

"Lord Dannel, Lady Anna. He sent his son here to inquire when you would return. The young man was most rude."

"Hoede?"

"No. This be an older man."

"An older son of Lord Dannel? Did he leave a scroll or anything?" Anna ducked and slipped to the gelding's other side.

"No, Lady Anna. I asked, but the young fellow said that his sire would deliver his message in person."

"Those are the worst kinds," Jecks said, stepping up beside Menares. "Did he say when this might be?"

"No, Lord Jecks. That was yesterday, and no one saw him today."

"I'll have to tell him no. I can't back down just because he's upset. Then, I'd have to back down for every lord in Defalk, I suppose."

"Some have," Jecks said. "They lasted but a season or so."

"I haven't been Regent for much more than a year." Anna set the brush aside and gave Farinelli a last pat on the neck. "Tirsik will feed you, fellow."

"Aye, and I will." The stablemaster appeared with a wooden bucket containing grain.

Anna picked up the lutar, leaving the saddlebags and the mirror case to the guards. After she left the stable, Jecks at her side, she crossed the courtyard and stepped into the lower corridor that led toward the receiving room.

"I must check on Jimbob and Kinor," Jecks said.

"When you're done, would you meet me in the receiving room to review the damage . . . all the scrolls piled there?"

"I will be there after I settle the young scamps." With a smile, Jecks turned.

As she started toward the receiving room, she stopped, cocking her head, wondering if she heard rain on the roof—or horses coming across the open ground to the liedburg. *You imagine too much.* She shook her head and kept walking, carrying just the lutar. Much as she wanted a hot bath and clean clothes, she had the feeling that she'd better see just what had piled up in the way of scrolls and messages before she even thought about bathing.

Rickel handed the saddlebags to Giellum, who bowed and started for the stairs.

"Thank you, Giellum," Anna said.

"My pleasure, Lady Anna. We are all glad to see you back safe." With a smile, the youngest guard started up the side staircase to the second level.

Rickel and Blaz stationed themselves outside the receiving room, and Anna slipped through the door, and stopped—looking at the stack of scrolls that seemed to cover the worktable. "Lord . . ."

After a moment, she set the lutar against the wall, then slowly picked up the first scroll—something from the rivermen. *Not again . . .* She glanced at the first lines.

> Regent and sorceress, Savior of Liedwahr, Restorer of Defalk, Protectoress of Harmony, and Lady of Mencha,

> The Guild of Rivermen has approached your ministers, and has requested, time upon time. . . . We cannot plead too strongly that the tariff levied upon us will force all of us from the waters of the rivers that have nourished us and fed our families since from before the days of the Corian lords. . . .

The receiving-room door burst open, and Menares panted into the room, shouting, "Lady Anna! Your lutar! Your spells! Lord Dannel has attacked the liedburg with scores of armsmen and lancers! They are everywhere, killing everyone!"

Anna dropped the scroll and scrambled for the lutar case, flicking the leather straps away as quickly as she could. Shouts came through the half-open door, and the sound of metal against metal, followed by grunts.

"She's in there! Get to the bitch!"

Clunk. . . .

A dull thud followed as some armsman fell against a wooden door.

Anna shook herself, and pulled the lutar from the case. She fumbled with the tuning pegs and the strings, but moved toward the open door to the hallway as she began to sing, managing to get out words to the spell she knew all too well.

> Turn to fire, turn to flame . . .
> all those to strike—

She found herself coughing, choking on mucus that had come from somewhere. She managed to clear her throat and spit out the garbage that had come from her lungs. *Would happen now . . .* With a deep breath, she stood just back of the open side of the doorway and began the chording and singing a second time.

> Turn to fire, turn to flame . . .
> all those to strike against my name.
> Turn to ash, turn to dust,
> these enemies as I must. . . .

The hissing of fire whips mixed with screams that died quickly. Anna found herself coughing once more and reached out to steady herself on the doorframe, then stepped out into the corridor where Rickel and Blaz stood with bloodied blades. Lejun and Kinor came hurrying down the corridor, stepping over blackened corpses, their blades also bare and stained.

The muffled sound of arms and yells elsewhere was not ending, but continuing, and Rickel and Kinor glanced toward Anna, their eyebrows rising in puzzlement.

Why? Anna wanted to bang her head against the wall. *Because they can't hear your voice through all the walls.*

"Lady Anna?" asked Kinor.

"We need to get to the north tower. So I can sing out over the whole liedburg," she added after a pause. "Quickly." *Before too many people die.*

"To the north tower!" ordered Rickel, raising his blade. "Blaz, follow the lady so none slip behind us."

Holding the lutar, Anna followed Kinor and her guards, past a half dozen charred corpses. She tried not to gag on the smell that was all too similar to burned meat, coughing her throat clear. When they turned at the end of the corridor, moving toward the stairs to the upper levels, Kinor, and Rickel stopped, finding a half-score of armsmen lurching toward them. Another group was attacking four armsmen in purple who held the base of the stairs, able to keep off the invaders only because of the comparative narrowness of the staircase.

Anna began the chording and the spell, again.

Turn to fire, turn to flame . . .

The all-too-familiar whips of fire cleared both the corridor and the lower steps, leaving more blackened figures, and the sickening odor of burned meat. Anna coughed more secretions out of her throat, but kept moving, holding tightly to the lutar.

"The north tower! The sorceress needs to spell the liedburg," Kinor yelled through the smoky air. "Hold the stairs," he added to the four regular armsmen as Rickel and Anna raced past, followed by Lejun and Blaz. Kinor then sprinted up the steps after the others.

The second-floor corridor was empty, but Kinor and Anna's guards hurried northward toward the steps to the tower, quickly checking each corner, but finding no invaders.

At the sound of boots on the stone, coming from behind them and from the direction of her chambers, Anna lifted the lutar, but the two figures were those of Jecks and Jimbob.

"The north tower," Kinor explained as the white-haired lord glanced toward the Regent.

"Good. She can spell from there," Jecks said.

The sound of fighting continued to rise from the liedburg courtyard, sounding louder by the time Anna reached the north tower steps.

Anna winced as Kinor sprinted up the steps without waiting for any of the others.

"Blaz . . . follow him . . . you as well, Lejun," Rickel ordered.

"We will hold here," Jecks said to Rickel, "Jimbob, you follow the sorceress and guard her rear." Then Jecks raised his voice to Anna, "Lady, sing your worst upon them!"

Anna glanced up the narrow stone steps, but could hear nothing but the sound of boots on stone. She hurried after Blaz, lutar in her left hand, using her right for balance as she hurried upward, trying to breathe deeply, knowing she would need every bit of oxygen she could muster once she reached the open parapets of the tower. The tower steps were empty, and each door on every level had been flung open—none of the apartments, including the small one in which she had once lived, and the larger quarters that had briefly imprisoned Lady Essan, held anyone.

Lejun stood on the landing nearest the top. "They have cleared the tower, lady."

"Thank you," she gasped out. Riding had been good for her legs, but it clearly hadn't helped her breathing. She took two deep breaths, then started up the last dozen or so of the stone steps. She was still panting by the time she reached the open space of the tower's uppermost level. Kinor and Blaz—blades bare—waited for her.

"Do what you must, lady," Kinor said. "We will guard the steps."

Without speaking, Jimbob stepped up beside Kinor and Blaz.

"Jecks and Rickel are guarding the bottom." Anna forced herself to take several more deep breaths, breaths which led to another round of coughing. *Shit! You wouldn't think you'd need vocalises coming back to your own liedburg.* She coughed her throat clear and began to check the lutar's tuning before she walked to the chest-high parapet overlooking the courtyard and the liedburg building itself. Then she tried for full concert voice with the spell.

Turn to fire, turn to flame . . .

The liedburg shuddered, each stone seeming to glow in the twilight. Then, a long and low rumble of thunder, nearly subsonic, shook the air, and the liedburg towers shivered. Streaks of flame streamed from somewhere below the gray clouds that darkened as Anna watched.

For long moments, the entire liedburg was ringed with fire—or so it seemed. Then screams echoed from the open courtyards and from the space to the north of the open gates.

Another shudder of the ground was followed by silence.

Anna leaned against the stones of the parapet, half-stunned, exhausted, doubting that she could sing another spell. She could barely hang on to the lutar and her breath rasped hoarsely through her throat.

After a time, she peered into the twilit gloom and the courtyard below where figures still moved. But the yells and the clangor of metal on metal had ceased, as had the awful screams of men being flayed alive by fire.

Jecks stepped out onto the tower.

Anna turned.

"You have destroyed them all, my lady." Jecks had sheathed his blade. "Himar sent a messenger. Even Lord Dannel and his sons fell under your fire whips." He paused. "Young Giellum fell defending us." Jecks' eyes flickered to Jimbob.

Anna understood. Giellum had died protecting Jimbob. She nodded dumbly. *Lord ... all this because I blocked Dannel's son from taking Lysara as a consort?* After a moment, she straightened and made her way down the stone steps of the tower—carefully. It wouldn't do to trip and break her arm or neck after surviving an attack on the liedburg.

In the upper main corridor, the guards—as well as Kinor, Jimbob, and Jecks—formed almost a phalanx around her as she walked toward the steps that would take her down to the lowest level.

"Lady Anna!"

The sorceress looked down the dim corridor—the candles in the wall sconces had never been lit that evening, understandably.

A small red-haired figure ran down the corridor, dodging the dead bodies and then throwing her arms around Anna. "You're safe! Oh, Lady Anna." Abruptly, Secca stepped back and straightened, looking up at the sorceress.

Behind Secca, three other young women appeared, striding briskly toward the Regent—Alseta, Cataryzna, and Ytrude. All held bared blades.

Secca addressed Anna. "Resor ... Cens ... Tiersen ... they fought, but there were so many."

Anna wanted to hold Secca, but she could sense that the little redhead wanted to look strong. So the Regent looked at the three young women still holding shortswords. Ytrude's blade was streaked with blood. "How are they? Resor and Cens and Tiersen, I mean?"

Ytrude smiled crookedly. "Tiersen had gone to the stables. He fought his way back. He has not a scratch."

"Cens ... Liende is treating him with your elixir ... and Barat as well," replied Cataryzna. The blonde's eyes were cold, carrying a bottled rage, Anna suspected, something beyond the attack, but what that might have been Anna had no idea. "Lysara—they tried to attack her."

Anna turned cold. "Where is she? Is she all right?"

"She was as good with a blade as Cens, and Liende used the last of the elixir for her. Tiersen—he is standing guard."

Sorcery-distilled alcohol, and it's an elixir, as magic as your sorcery in this land. "How is she?"

"Lysara may recover, as may Barat and Cens." Ytrude paused and swallowed. "Resor put himself first, and for that Lysara and Secca are alive." The tall blonde looked at the blade she held, almost as if surprised that she still carried it.

"Resor is dead?"

"Yes, Lady Anna."

Anna tightened her lips.

"Barat was wounded as well . . . he joined the fosterlings holding the south tower. None of the armsmen could reach us." Ytrude looked down at Secca, then back at the sorceress-Regent. "They were almost overwhelmed. So we picked up blades."

Anna glanced at the streak of red on the brown-eyed blonde's sleeve. "What about your arm?"

"A long scratch. Liende cleaned it and coated it with your elixir."

Cataryzna looked at Anna, a question in her eyes. Anna smiled. "Undercaptain Skent is holding the lands of Pamr. He did not return with us."

Anna marked the slow exhalation.

"Lady?" Cataryzna asked.

"Yes, Cataryzna?"

"The armsmen came to the south tower seeking Secca and Lysara. I heard one yell about getting the two redheads, and not to forget the little redhead."

"Their words were not that polite," Alseta said dryly.

Anna could understand Dannel's grudge against Lysara, but why had Dannel's armsmen been seeking Secca? She had two older brothers who were the heirs.

"Lord Dannel was angered," Jecks said mildly. "He must have known that you are fond of Secca."

Anna clamped her lips together, finding herself shuddering

with rage. She forced herself to take a long and deep breath.
"I . . . am . . . we *will* talk about it tomorrow. Tonight . . . we
need to clean up this mess, and make sure that the gates are
closed against the northern lords."

Jecks stepped back. "As you wish, my lady."

Doesn't he understand? Will he ever really understand? "It's
been a long day, Lord Jecks, and armsmen and a lord have died.
I killed most of them. In a sane land, I shouldn't have had to kill
them."

She turned toward Kinor and Rickel. "I want to see the fosterlings who were wounded, and then Himar, and then I will
inspect the liedburg." *You need to know just how bad the damage is . . . and to avoid talking to one Lord Jecks right now. You
might say something you'd really regret.*

She took yet another long and deep breath.

69

It wasn't much past dawn when Anna paused by the door
where Tiersen and an armsman Anna did not know stood
guard. The armsman stiffened. "Yes, Regent?"

"I'm just here to see how she's doing." Anna glanced from
the armsman to the young heir of Dubaria. Dark circles ringed
Tiersen's eyes, and he wore the same blood-smeared tunic he
had worn the night before, when he had also been guarding
Lysara's door. "Have you been here all night?"

"Mostly, Lady Anna," admitted the tall and muscular blond.

"I'll get someone from my guard to relieve you. You need
some rest, too." Anna asked in a lower voice, "How is she this
morning?"

Tiersen inclined his head. "She seems better. The healer says
she is."

Anna hoped so. She set the lutar case beside the door, then
opened the door and stepped into the small south tower room.
Lysara lay propped up slightly, dressings across her left shoulder, her eyes closed. The sorceress could smell the faint odor of

alcohol, and she wondered if Liende had poured some onto the dressing . . . and how much.

The redhead opened her eyes. "Lady . . . Anna . . ."

"Just be quiet. I came to see how you were doing." Anna touched her forehead, but Lysara didn't seem to be running a fever. *Not yet.*

"Hurts more today."

"That's usually what happens."

"Tell Tiersen . . . sleep." The redhead seemed to have to force the words out.

"I have, but he won't leave until I send one of my guards to relieve him."

Lysara offered a faint smile. ". . . sweet . . ."

"He cares for you."

"I know . . . care for him."

Anna put a hand on her forehead again. "Try to rest."

Lysara closed her eyes even before Anna left the room and gently shut the door behind her.

"What do you think, Regent?" whispered Tiersen.

"So far, she's all right. I think Liende got the alcohol through the entire wound. That's probably one reason she's tired. It had to hurt, but . . . it might do the job." *You hope . . .*

Tiersen swallowed. "The healer said . . . most don't live with a cut that deep. She said you did, though."

Anna patted his shoulder. "We'll have to see." *Is there anything else you could do . . . any sorcery? That isn't Darksong?* "I'll send someone up. She told me to tell you to get some sleep. You can come back later."

"I wasn't there," Tiersen mumbled. "I tried."

Anna touched his shoulder. "You did what you could. That's all any of us can do." *And that sort of rationalization doesn't help much at all.* After a moment, she picked up the lutar and headed back down the stairs to the main level. *So much for the safety of fosterlings in Falcor.* She was lucky . . . so far . . . that the children of the various lords were still alive. The pages and Lysara had taken the worst of it, and Lysara looked better than she had a right to, especially in Defalk.

Anna made a mental note to use the spell to distill more alcohol.

She stopped outside the receiving room and looked at the strawberry blond guard. "Rickel . . . I have a favor to ask. Could you spare either Blaz or Lejun to relieve young Tiersen? He's been standing guard outside the door of Lord Birfels' daughter's room since last night." Anna paused, then added, "Lysara was one of the targets of the raid."

Rickel nodded. "I have already asked Overcaptain Himar for some men he would trust as guards for you, and I would have to work with them at first anyway."

Blaz smiled. "The young lord fought his way across the courtyard, they said, like a wild man. I would be happy to let him rest."

"We will take care of it, Lady Anna," Rickel affirmed.

"Thank you both." Anna offered a heartfelt smile.

As she stepped into the receiving room, carrying the lutar in her left hand, Anna looked at the blackened lines on the walls and then down at those etched on the floor stones. She supposed they could be removed by sorcery, but that wasn't exactly her highest priority—not with injured lancers and even fewer armsmen than ever—and an invader ravaging the western part of Defalk. *And whose fault is that?*

Her stomach growled, the result of eating too much, too quickly, and under too much tension, yet knowing that if she did not eat, the results could easily be worse, especially if she had to do more sorcery. Recently, she'd had to sing more spells than she'd anticipated, and not under the best of conditions.

That recalled something else. If she were to confront Rabyn, that meant sorcery, and she couldn't afford to keep getting caught off guard. She made a mental note to ensure that she always had bread and hard crackers in a small pouch beside her saddle so that her blood sugar didn't totally crash—and to drink lots of water whether she felt like it or not. The only problem with those ideas was that medieval-style nutrition wasn't conducive either to carbohydrate loading or to quick and heavy sugar intakes.

She picked up the quill, dipped it and jotted down the idea of a food pouch. *Maybe if it's handy . . .*

Surprisingly, after the turmoil of the last day, the scrolls lay where she had left them, and after she replaced the lutar in its case, she bent and retrieved the one she had dropped the afternoon before. She did not read the rivermen's petition again, but set it back on the table with the others.

The morning rain beat on the shutters. Would it pass, or would it rain for days and leave the roads a mess? *A mess . . . the way things have been going lately*.

She glanced at the scrolls. They could wait a moment, perhaps longer, because there was no way, with the rain, the injuries, and the attack, that she was leaving Defalk on the next day. According to what she and Himar had figured out, in the glass or so of fighting, Lord Dannel's surprise attack had killed another twoscore of Anna's armsmen and lancers, one of the cooks, a stable boy, probably a dozen townspeople, Giellum, and Resor. Cens and Barat would recover, and hopefully, Lysara. Ytrude had a shallow slash on one arm. The toll on Lord Dannel's forces was complete—more than tenscore bodies, plus Dannel and three others—presumably Hoede and his two older brothers.

On the positive side, if it could be called positive, Tirsik and the stable boys had rounded up over a hundred mounts, and most of the lances and blades of the invaders had been recovered as well. *Now . . . if you had armsmen and lancers to wield them*.

She looked at the scrolls again. They weren't going away. Perhaps she could deal with some of them. She pulled up the chair. Setting aside the rivermen's petition, she lifted the next scroll and began to read.

Nearly a glass had passed, and her eyes were watering when Anna stood, made her way to the doors, and peered out of the receiving room. "Do we have any pages or messengers?"

Besides Rickel and Lejun, three young women stood there—Alseta, Cataryzna, and Ytrude.

"We thought we could do it, Lady Anna," announced the blonde Cataryzna. "Kinor's really almost a subofficer now, and Tiersen is still guarding Lysara."

Anna smiled. She should have seen that one coming. "Fine. But only within the liedburg for right now."

The three nodded. So did Lejun, standing beside the door.

Then she paused. "Is Tiersen still up there?"

"Oh, no . . . Blaz took his place," answered Cataryzna. "Tiersen was so tired that he didn't protest."

"Not more than a half-score of times, anyway," quipped Alseta.

"Oh . . . will one of you—beside Ytrude—ask Lord Jecks to meet me outside the scrying room in half a glass—if he can. If he can't, please let me know." Anna looked at Ytrude. "I'd like to talk to you, Ytrude." At the look of concern that crossed the face of the tall and gangly blonde, Anna added, "It's nothing bad."

"I'll find Lord Jecks," offered the strawberry blonde Alseta, her thin face revealing the animation that once had marked her mother Liende's face, Anna suspected.

Anna gestured for Ytrude to enter the receiving room.

The tall blonde shivered as she stepped inside. "What do you wish of me? Have I offended you, my lady? Even if I have, don't send me back to Dubaria."

After closing the door, Anna held up a hand. "Wait. Listen to me before you jump to conclusions . . . and sit down. And no, you haven't offended me in any way." The Regent took the seat behind the table, not the gilt chair on the dais where she formally received people.

Slowly, Ytrude eased herself into one of the straight-backed chairs that matched the one in which Anna sat. Her eyes did not meet the Regent's.

"First, I have some news. It's not very good." Anna paused, studying the tall blonde girl across the table from her.

Ytrude swallowed. "Father?"

"No . . . so far as I know, your father is fine. So is Tiersen, other than being exhausted from staying up worrying about Lysara."

"Lysara? Will she be all right?"

"I think so . . . but I don't know," Anna replied honestly. "It's about your aunt, the lady Gatrune. There was a rebellion in Pamr. It was led by a darksinger. He and his followers killed about twoscore of my lancers. We couldn't reach your aunt's holding in time. They killed her and Kyrun, and everyone else. I'm sorry. I wish I didn't have to be the one to tell you." Anna paused briefly, then added, "None of the rebels survived."

Ytrude looked down. "She was good. Everyone said she was. Why? Why would they kill her?"

"For the same reason that Lord Ehara sent armsmen into Defalk or Lord Bertmynn slaughtered hundreds of freewomen in Elahwa." Anna knew her answer wasn't strictly and factually true, but in spirit, it was. Neither Farsenn nor his father had been able to accept women as any more than objects, and both were willing to kill to preserve their belief. And both had died, along with a lot of other innocents.

"Does . . . father know?"

"I don't think so. We returned as quickly as possible. I had meant to send a messenger, but then Lord Dannel . . ."

Ytrude nodded.

"After we finish, I will be sending a scroll to him." Anna paused, then added, "In a way, the other thing I wanted to talk over with you is tied up with your aunt. I have a task for you—if your father consents, and if you're willing."

The shy blonde forced her eyes from the floor stones and raised her head so that she looked down at Anna. "Yes, Lady Anna?"

"You recall that the lady Herene was acting as guardian for Lord Sargol's heirs?"

"Oh, yes. Is she ill or . . . ?" Ytrude shook her head. "Of course . . ."

"She's your father's youngest sister, isn't she?"

"Kylera was, but she died of the flux two years ago, and she never consorted. I'm glad you're not considering Je'elasia. She was only a half sister to Lord Kysar."

"Lady Herene is the only heir to Pamr." *The only one you'll consider.* "She needs to return there as soon as possible. I need someone I can trust to run the holding at Suhl and ensure that Dinfan and her brothers are tutored and cared for. Would you be interested?"

"Me?" Ytrude looked down again, then forced her eyes to meet Anna's. "I am honored . . . but why would you ask me?"

"I had already thought of you, but after yesterday and today, I'm even more certain you'd do a good job. If you are willing, I'll send a scroll to your father, saying that I will send you to Suhl, unless he voices any objection."

"He will not," Ytrude said with a surprising smile that faded with her next words. "He will be most upset at my aunt's death. He will say not a word, but he will grieve. He will like my being a tutor in Suhl. Such a task would show you find favor with me and make me more attractive as a consort."

Is that all these girls think about? "Do you want to be someone's consort?"

Ytrude looked down again for a moment, her posture recalling the extreme shyness she had shown when she had first come to Falcor. "I would like to find favor in a consort's eyes." Her eyes slowly lifted. "If he found favor in mine."

"You do not have to accept the first offer," Anna said. "Or any offer."

"Thank you, Lady Anna." Ytrude moistened her lips. "It is said that Lord Dannel attacked you because you would not allow Lysara to consort with Hoede. Is that so?"

Anna nodded. "Yes. Lysara did not wish to be Hoede's consort."

Ytrude licked her lips again.

"I can't promise you a true love, Ytrude," Anna said. "But I will stand behind you if you cannot abide someone proposed as consort for you."

The tall girl nodded slowly. "Thank you. We all thank you."

"That's all I wanted to tell you," Anna said, standing.

Ytrude rose quickly. "By your leave, Regent."

"By my leave," Anna replied softly. "I will send the scroll to your father by tomorrow."

Once the door closed, she seated herself at the table and began to draft the scroll that would contain the news of Gatrune's death and Anna's request for Ytrude to Lord Nelmor. Each word was difficult. *How do you tell someone that his sister died?* Anna wasn't about to take the total blame for it, even if it had occurred at least indirectly because Anna had killed Farsenn's father in defending herself. And she couldn't say to the touchy Nelmor that part of the problem was that men in Defalk had an excessively exaggerated self-esteem. *Don't most men anywhere? Even on Earth?* She snorted. Most people did. She decided to concentrate on Gatrune's efforts and the resentment held against women in power by the chandler, and she added words about her actions in destroying all those associated with Farsenn. Nelmor would want to know what Anna had done to avenge his sister—that Anna did know. She took a deep breath.

Then she smiled, thinking about Lysara and Tiersen. *Please let it work out for them.* She wasn't even sure to whom or what she addressed the short prayer.

She dipped the quill again and resumed the draft to Nelmor. Then she began the second draft, the one to Herene. After it was completed, and laid out to dry beside the one to Nelmor, she stood and picked up the lutar case and opened the receiving-room door.

"I understand the pages"—Rickel grinned without looking at either Ytrude or Cataryzna—"let you know that Blaz has relieved young Tiersen." Rickel's smile dropped as he gestured to the swarthy and stocky man at the other side of the receiving-room door. "This is Fielmir. He was in the purple company. Overcaptain Himar thinks highly of him."

"I'm pleased to meet you, Fielmir."

The black-haired guard bowed. "I will do my very best, lady."

"We all do," Rickel said.

"I'm sure you will."

The two followed her up to the scrying room where, outside the door, Jecks waited.

"You requested my presence, Regent." Jecks' voice was cool.

Anna supposed she deserved the chill. "I did. I wanted you to help me when I use the pool to see what I can discover about scheming before we decide what to do about Rabyn. And how quickly I need to leave Falcor." As she opened the door and stepped into the room that held the scrying pool, she gestured vaguely toward the unseen sky. "If this rain continues, I may not have much choice."

"The rain will pass. One can see the lighter clouds to the east."

"I hope you're right." She let Jecks close the door. "I'm going to try to see if the pool will tell me who else might be scheming against us. Before leaving Falcor."

"After yesterday, that would be wise."

Anna eased the lutar from the case and began to tune it. "What about your neighbors?"

Jecks frowned before he spoke. "Clethner will not scheme

against you, nor will Vyarl. I would not trust Genrica so far as one could hurl a mount with one hand, although it is said he is most ill. Fustar . . . I do not know well."

"Well . . . we'll see." Anna took another deep breath before launching into the scrying spell.

> Those in the Thirty-three
> who plot and scheme against me,
> show them now and show them clear. . . .

Six separate images appeared. Anna just looked. *Six! Was she that poor a Regent?*

Even Jecks scowled.

"Do you recognize any of them?" asked Anna.

"That . . . that is Lord Fustar, and there is Lord Genrica of Wendell, and Lord Tybel . . . there, I think . . ."

"That's Jearle, and there's Ustal. And Klestayr." Anna paused to study the images before adding, "I think you're right about that being Lord Tybel. . . ." She pointed to the image of a man with frizzy hair that was half henna brown and half gray. "He looks like Anientta."

"I have not met the woman, and Tybel but once when he was far younger."

"Six of them." Anna shook her head. "I'm trying to make this country safe for everyone, including the lords. They don't seem to care. I'm attacked in the country's liedburg, and there are six more lords standing in line to do something else." *The way Defalk operates . . . there won't be any Magna Carta . . . no privileges for the lords . . . except you're sounding like a tyrant yourself.* She turned to Jecks. "What am I supposed to do—replace every fucking son-of-a-bitching lord in the entire land?"

At the vehemence of her words, perhaps its obvious crudity, even Jecks swallowed.

"I'm risking my life, your life, the heir's life, and all people like Dannel and Genrica—yes, I've heard the stories—all they want to do is screw every available woman in sight . . . and grab every piece of land they can, and they'll do it even if it means that it will tear the country apart. . . ."

"Men are not . . ."

"No! It's not just men. There are just more of them in power," snapped Anna. "Anientta's every bit as bad, poisoning her consort, and probably trying to do the same to her father. You people deserve a frigging tyrant! An Evult or a Liedfuhr! You deserve the Wicked Witch of the West." She found herself glaring at Jecks. She didn't like that, and she sighed. "It's not you."

"Mayhap . . ." Jecks drawled out the word. "Yet . . . if you would change Defalk, best you understand why Dannel attacked."

Anna forced herself to take another deep breath. "Go ahead. Tell me."

"You destroyed all hope for his son." Jecks held up a hand. "Hoede is the third or fourth in line to hold Mossbach . . . under the old way of inheriting. If he consorts with Lysara, there would always have been the chance for him to hold Abenfel. It would not be a great chance, but a better chance than becoming Lord of Mossbach. You removed that chance, and struck at Dannel's pride by suggesting that a woman was more to be considered than Hoede." Jecks shrugged. "That is the way the lords of the north think—or many of them."

"It's that important . . ." Anna shook her head. "I'm not sure I'll ever understand. He'd rather kill me and have Defalk under that creep Rabyn than accept that his son is an incompetent thick-skulled dunderhead?"

"He can accept that," Jecks replied. "He cannot accept that you would place the good of any woman above that of his son."

"My son the dunderhead, right or wrong . . . is that it?"

After a moment, Jecks smiled sadly. "Yes . . . you have the right of it."

Anna looked down at the still waters of the scrying pool. She shook her head. "All right . . . I'll send a scroll to each of those idiots, suggesting that I *know* they're plotting against me, and suggesting that my rule is that their lands will stay in their families—unless there's treason . . . but that I will consider their daughters on the same terms as their sons . . . and that they had best accept it."

"I would suggest that you send those scrolls *after* you deal with Rabyn." Jecks' voice was sardonic.

Anna laughed harshly. "Deal with the more important problems first? You're right." She sighed once more, conscious that she was sighing all too much. Was that Defalk—or her? "What about Lord Dannel's lands and heirs? Do I send out a proclamation? Or confiscate them?"

Jecks offered a grim smile. "Do nothing. Let all of them wonder. You have destroyed all of his heirs—his sons. If you explain, they will think you weak. If you seize the lands and hand them to another, you must enforce that at this moment."

The Regent nodded. "You're probably right about that . . . and about Lord Dannel. It's just so hard for me to believe that people believe that crap." She shook her head. "Lady Essan rode to battle with Lord Donjim. Women run the entire land of Ranuak; and probably half the counselors of Nordwei are women. How can these . . . *idiots* . . . believe that women are less capable? So much that they would die rather than accept it?"

Jecks shrugged. "Mayhap once I did, but a daughter I had, and stronger than her consort."

"I liked Alasia," Anna said quietly. Then she stepped forward and hugged the handsome white-haired lord. "I'm sorry. You've been good to listen to me."

Jecks squeezed her back, then gently released her. "I would listen to aught you say."

She looked into the warm hazel eyes. "Thank you. You know . . . I do listen to you, too. It's just hard, sometimes." *Especially in this crazy place.*

The smile she received took all the chill out of the damp scrying room.

70

In the dampness of late morning, Anna stood on the old raised stone platform that backed up to the outside of the south wall of the liedburg, looking out at Jecks, Jimbob, and the pages and fosterlings to her right—except for Lysara—and to the lancers and officers arrayed to her left. Behind the lancers waited nearly two dozen older men and women—and perhaps three young women—sisters or consorts of the slain. Before her were the newly filled graves, almost fifty of them set behind the five rows of far older graves. Behind her were all her guards, each wearing a black sash.

Anna herself wore a black vest, instead of the green or purple of her office as Regent. While she had vaguely known there was a cemetery behind the liedburg, she certainly hadn't wanted to find out more about it, not so soon nor for so many.

She'd consulted with Himar and Jecks, as well as Tiersen, who, as the oldest of the fosterlings, had some experience with death in Defalk, to find out what sort of ceremony would be appropriate. For so many deaths in the liedburg itself, there had to be a ceremony, both for the dead and for the living.

After surveying those before her, Anna began to speak. "These brave men died in the cause of harmony. They died fighting to defend what was dear to them and to us . . . and they helped to preserve harmony and restore and maintain order and peace in Defalk. Because of their sacrifice, we are here. Because of their skill, we can go on to build a better land for all of us.

"I wish their sacrifice had not been necessary, but prosperity and harmony have always required dedication and hard work, and sometimes armsmen and even ordinary people die to maintain harmony. For doing what needed to be done, they will be remembered. For their sacrifice, they will be remembered. And for their inspiration, we must and will go forward with the gift of life they gave the rest of us.

"In the name and the cause of harmony, now and ever."

The last part was more than true. Had the guards and lancers not held off the treacherous surprise attack, then Anna would never have had time to turn her sorcery against the attackers.

Anna turned to the chief player and nodded.

"The dirge," ordered Liende in a low voice.

The usually cocky Duralt was somber and, wearing a black tunic, stepped forward and lifted the falk-horn to his lips.

The long and mournful notes filled the stone-walled cemetery and drifted beyond, to the liedburg, and to the town itself.

Duralt lowered the horn.

"Order out!" called Himar. "By files."

Anna remained facing the freshly packed earth that covered more than fifty men, as the lancers filed silently past her and through the baileylike gate and back into the liedburg.

"Old . . . style . . ." murmured someone. "The lord is the last to leave."

"Good to see . . . traditions . . . especially from a sorceress . . ."

". . . only right . . ."

Anna hoped so.

71

Anna lowered the lutar and studied the image in the scrying pool—clear enough to see that Jearle remained behind the walls of Westfort, and that more than twentyscore Neserean lancers patrolled the heights across the valley.

"That has not changed in a week," murmured Jecks.

Himar merely nodded.

"But why would they leave twentyscore at Westfort?" asked Anna. "A third or half of that would be more than enough to keep Jearle inside his walls."

"They would keep you from avoiding the main body of Rabyn's forces and going straight into Neserea."

The sorceress frowned.

"With the Mansuuran lancers, the Nesereans have more than one hundred fifty–score elsewhere in Defalk. Twentyscore is not that many for them," pointed out Jecks.

Anna doubted she could have raised twentyscore in real armsmen even if she had stripped Loiseau, Pamr, the Sand Fort, and Falcor. Lifting the lutar, she tried a second spell, one seeking Hanfor. This brought a picture of Hanfor reined up on a hillside road, looking westward, or so it seemed, with the morning sun falling on the backs of the arms commander and the lancers behind him.

The third spell called forth a troop of Mansuuran lancers who had dismounted beside a stream running through a deep and narrow gorge. The image in the pool shivered once, then again, as if being vibrated. Abruptly, timbers and planks lay beside the stream and pillars of steam rose from blackened soil where the stand of pines had been. Armsmen scurried forward on foot and began to lift the timbers and carry them toward the gorge.

"Darksong . . . the whelp is using Darksong," muttered Jecks.

The way things had been going for the last few weeks, that didn't surprise Anna at all. Eventually, Rabyn would have to cut back on Darksong, or it would kill him, but she doubted that he'd live long enough to worry about that, one way or the other. *You might not, either.*

As Anna, Jecks, and Himar watched, the armsmen began to place the timbers across the gorge.

"They are yet chasing Hanfor, and Rabyn grows impatient," Jecks said. "He would use sorcery to hurry his lancers across the gorge."

Anna nodded and sang the release couplet.

> Let this scene of scrying, mirror filled with light,
> vanish like the darkness when the sun is bright. . . .

"Should the Nesereans get too close to Hanfor . . . I like that dark spell not," Himar said slowly.

"Nor I," admitted Jecks.

"Can we leave tomorrow?" asked Anna, looking at Himar. "I'd like to get to Hanfor before Rabyn does."

"Aye, but we will not have so many lancers."

"How many lancers do we have?" Anna bent and eased the lutar into its case.

"There were fivescore left here, and you brought near-on six back. Dannel killed twoscore and eight," answered the overcaptain.

Another thought struck Anna. *You should have thought about that earlier.* She pulled the lutar from the case, quickly checking the tuning. "There's one other thing." She concentrated on trying to find the words she wanted.

> Show me now and as bright as may be
> other lords who fight to keep us free,
> those from Defalk who lift a blade and lance. . . .

The mirror offered a single image—that of a tall blond man at the head of a column riding down a narrow lane.

"Nelmor," Anna said quietly. "Of all the western lords, he has the least to offer."

"He has honor and courage," Jecks pointed out.

Anna was more impressed with the courage, but she nodded, and sang the release couplet, then replaced the lutar in its case.

"Let's go down to the receiving room," she suggested, lifting the lutar case. "We can finish planning there." She opened the door and stepped into the corridor to find three guards there.

Rickel bowed. With him was another man in the purple and green of a Regent's guard. "Lady Anna, this is Bersan."

"Lady Regent." Bersan bowed. His deep-set black eyes were even darker than the short-cut black hair and the trimmed short black beard.

"It's good to meet you, Bersan."

The new guard bowed again, then stepped back.

The three guards followed Anna, Jecks, and Himar down the corridor toward the steps to the main level.

"Sorcery . . . one would swear . . . not a soul in that room," Fielmir murmured to Rickel and Bersan.

"The Regent is a sorceress," Rickel replied mildly. "Best you both recall that."

Anna couldn't contain a brief smile, but it faded quickly as she thought of all those—like Gatrune and Lysara and more than fourscore lancers who had paid for her sorcery.

Lejun waited outside the receiving room with Alseta, who had clearly appointed herself the duty page for the day.

"Good day, Lady Anna." Alseta bowed.

"Good morning, Alseta . . . Lejun."

Lejun and Fielmir stationed themselves outside the doors, while Alseta reseated herself on the page's stool. Himar let Anna and Jecks enter the receiving hall, then followed and closed the door.

Anna gestured to the chairs around the conference table and sat down, knowing neither man would until she did. Then she filled three goblets with orderspelled water. "You said we had tenscore or elevenscore lancers. We can't take them all. That would leave the liedburg defenseless." Anna frowned. "What if I take fivescore?"

Jecks winced.

The Regent took a long swallow of water.

"Ninescore," suggested the white-haired Lord High Counselor.

"Seven," countered Anna, with a smile. "I can use sorcery." *Thrap!* The three looked up at the knock.

"A scroll . . . the messenger said it was urgent." Fielmir half stepped in and bowed. "Oh . . . and a young fellow by the name of Halde awaits you."

Anna could see Lejun behind the new guard, and motioned for Fielmir to bring the scroll. "Tell Halde to wait. I'll see him after I finish with Lord Jecks and Overcaptain Himar."

"As you wish, Regent." Fielmir bobbed his head and handed her the scroll.

Before the door closed, Anna had broken the seal on the rolled parchment and had begun to read the heavy black script.

Honored Regent and Sorceress,
    I am deeply saddened to inform you that sickness has indeed taken its toll here at Flossbend. My beloved younger sister Anientta has breathed her last, as have her sons.

    For the moment, awaiting your decision, I am administering the hold and lands on behalf of my brother Tybel. . . .

The Regent's eyes skipped over the rest of the polite words to the signature at the bottom—Beltyr. "So that was why . . . Tybel and Dannel were plotting this together. Probably some of the armsmen were Tybel's. Shit . . ."

Jecks raised his eyebrows. "You are distressed, my lady."

"Read this and tell me if you wouldn't be?" Anna handed him the scroll. *Shit! Now Secca's the only heir to Flossbend, not that Tybel and his brother intended it. Secca may not have been that well treated by her mother, but she doesn't need this. Not now. Not ever.* Anna waited as Jecks read.

When he was done, he looked up. "They are as bad as was Arkad."

"Worse." She motioned for Jecks to hand the scroll to the

overcaptain. "Arkad didn't run around killing children." *That really messes things up. If Secca and Jimbob are consorted, he'll end up owning half of Defalk, and you'll never shrink his head down to size. Plus . . . all the lords of the Thirty-three will believe you're going around doing them out of their lands to hand over to the heir. Shit . . .*

Himar returned the scroll to Anna, and his eyes flicked from the Regent to Jecks and back again.

"Another thing I put off dealing with, and it's just gotten worse."

"You could have done nothing," Jecks said.

"It doesn't matter; I didn't, and I can't. Not now. If I don't go and fight off Rabyn, there won't be much of Defalk left to worry about. . . ."

Himar's head bobbed in affirmation.

"Has this always happened?" asked Anna.

"Has what always occurred?" replied Jecks, a wariness in his voice.

"When the Lord of Defalk was occupied trying to save the country, the Thirty-three played games and tried to grab more lands behind his back."

"It has occurred more often than not," conceded the white-haired lord of Elheld.

"Was that another reason why you were worried about my going into Ebra?"

"I had not thought any would move so swiftly. I expected some such once you were occupied with Rabyn."

"So I can count on this infighting to get worse?"

Jecks shrugged. "Mayhap."

"All right. It will get worse. That's because they all know I can't deal with them while I'm fighting Rabyn. Will you hold Falcor for me?"

Jecks swallowed. "I had hoped . . ."

"I can't leave Falcor unarmed. Not now. If I leave Himar here, anyone can attack and claim that Himar's only a hired gun."

Jecks frowned in puzzlement.

"A hired blade," Anna explained. "If they attack you, they attack one of their own, and one who is the grandsire of the heir. That should stop some of this nonsense."

"What of Jimbob?"

"He still gets that puzzled look on his face. I think he should come with me. With Kinor, I think."

Jecks nodded slowly. "As do I."

Himar's eyebrows rose.

"She can protect him better than can I," Jecks said. "And I can summon some of my own armsmen here from Elheld, enough that you need leave but twoscore. Or three." The white-haired lord shrugged. "Only the Regent can hold Defalk together in these times. Being here will not help Jimbob, and he should see with his own eyes how perilous is the life and conduct of a ruler."

"I'll take sevenscore, and leave you three," Anna said, "if you send out a message today summoning armsmen from Elheld."

Jecks' lips quirked. "Sevenscore for you . . . but try not to have them fight. They should but protect you so that you may deal with Rabyn and his evil Darksong."

"I can't afford to have them fight any real battles." Anna grinned ironically. "I won't have any lancers left at all if I do." *Not against forces twenty times yours.*

"See that you hold to that resolve, my lady."

"I will." She turned to Himar. "Tomorrow?"

"Tomorrow, before the turn of the day's second glass." The overcaptain glanced toward the receiving-room doors.

"You may go . . ." Anna laughed gently. "I haven't left you much time."

Himar eased back the straight-backed chair and rose. He bowed. "I will have most of the experienced lancers accompany us." He looked at Jecks. "Would you not agree, Lord High Counselor?"

"I would insist . . . but that is the Regent's decision."

Anna had to laugh at the mock-seriousness in both men's voices. "All right. All right. You've made your points."

Himar bowed, a twinkle in his eyes. "We will be ready."

As the receiving-room door closed behind the overcaptain, Anna's eyes went to Jecks. "You have a scroll to write."

"Alas . . ." He shook his head "I would be with you."

"You can ease my worries more by holding Falcor."

"That I can accept, but I do not like it."

From somewhere, half-familiar words came to her, and she

murmured them, "Too long a sacrifice can make a stone of the heart." *Will your heart be stone . . . if you even survive?*

Jecks did not speak, and Anna reached out and touched his arm. "I know. I don't like it either."

Jecks rose, gracefully as ever, muscular and competent, and bowed. "I will send the scroll, and then inform young Jimbob and Kinor of their duties."

"Thank you."

After Jecks had left, Anna looked at the stack of scrolls and groaned. Too much to do . . . but if she didn't get moving to deal with Rabyn, she'd have even greater problems. And she needed to look in on Lysara again . . . and . . .

She took a swallow from the goblet before reaching for the bell to summon Halde.

"Yes, Regent?" Alseta peered into the receiving room.

"Is Halde still there?"

"He awaits your pleasure."

"Have him come in."

Halde stepped into the room, then immediately bowed. "I rode as quickly as I could, Regent."

"You did fine, Halde." Anna motioned to the chair across from her. "I don't have much time. So this will be quick. Are you willing to be my saalmeister?"

"Yes, lady. Herstat has told me much."

"Loiseau has never had a saalmeister, not in years and years, anyway. I have told everyone there to expect you. Serna is the housekeeper, and she has a chest of five hundred golds for your use in maintaining the place. Those must last until spring—at least . . ." Anna quickly ran through brief backgrounds on the older and more experienced staff members. Then she looked at the dark-haired and dark-bearded young man. "Do you understand?"

Halde bowed and nodded. "I trust I do, Regent. If I mark your words, your holding almost does not need a saalmeister, saving that you will be there seldom, and my task is to make sure that all goes well with those who already do their jobs well, to ensure it is guarded, because there has always been a sorcerer to guard before, to make the rounds to collect the rents and to refrain from collecting the rents where there has been death or trouble, and to discover ways to manage those aspects of the hold once handled by sorcery."

"And anything else that you feel should be done and isn't being done—after you discuss it with Serna and Quies." Anna paused. "I am not saying that their judgment should override yours, but I do not want you making a decision—except where there is no time—without talking it over with them so that you know how it will be received and can adjust your plans for implementing things, if necessary."

"A light but gently firm rein?" Halde offered a smile.

"Yes . . . and I will expect a scroll from you every two weeks, sooner if you think necessary. The armsmen there know they will have to act as couriers on occasion."

Halde bowed again.

"If you have any questions later . . . send me a scroll. Lord Jecks will know where to find me." Anna stood. "Oh . . . one other thing." She grinned. "What is a good saalmeister paid?"

Halde swallowed . . . for the first time. "Ah . . . I know not. I received two silvers a week as the assistant at Synfal."

"All right. Let's start at twice that, with an initial bonus of five golds for taking the job, and if either of us thinks you should get more . . . then we'll talk about it."

Anna fumbled with her belt wallet, glad she'd filled it before leaving Loiseau, and then extended seven golds. "That's your bonus plus your pay until close to spring. You tell me when I'm supposed to pay you again."

Halde's eyes widened as the words sank in. Then he shifted his weight from one boot to the other, uneasily.

"I operate on trust, Halde." Anna's eyes fixed on the saalmeister. "If I can't trust someone . . . they leave. I don't have time to do your job and mine, and if you aren't doing yours, I'll know soon enough. Understood?"

"Yes, Regent. You . . . are most generous."

"I hope you'll always feel that way. Now . . ." She gestured toward the pile of scrolls. "I have to read those before I leave tomorrow."

Halde bowed again.

Once Halde had left, Anna glanced at the piles of scrolls and reached for the one closest to her. *Lord . . .*

72

A fter setting aside the scroll from the Rider of Heinene, Anna sat in the pool of candlelight behind the writing desk in her own chamber, massaging her forehead. Lord Vyarl's missive had been one of the few she had received not asking for anything, but merely thanking the Regent for her kindness and generosity in seeing that grain had come to the grasslands people after the fires of summer. She'd liked Vyarl when she'd met him the summer before, and the scroll reinforced the impression of honesty and dignity she had gotten then. *Too bad there aren't more like him.* But there were few enough in any society, from what she'd seen on two worlds.

Though it was still comparatively early in the evening, not much past what would have been eight o'clock on Earth—the second glass of the night on Erde—she was tired, and had to repress a yawn.

Maybe it had been the de facto memorial service . . . or all the details that kept inundating her . . . or . . . or . . . Who knew? All she knew was that it was early, and she had more scrolls to read, and she was tired.

Maybe some cheese and bread would help—that was something she had to concentrate on remembering. She broke off a chunk of the crusty bread and used the knife on the side of the small wooden platter to cut a sliver of white cheese. After eating both slowly, she massaged the back of her neck, then looked out through the open shutters into the purpled darkness. A cool, not quite chill, breeze slipped into the chamber.

Thrap!

"Yes?" Anna glanced toward the closed door.

"The lady Secca," Fielmir announced.

"She can come in." Anna stood, leaving the pile of scrolls on the writing desk, lit by the pair of candles with polished-brass reflectors. Better lighting at night—that she did miss about Earth.

Secca slipped into Anna's chamber and bowed. "Are you all right, Lady Anna?" One hand remained behind her back.

Anna couldn't help smiling, warmed by the little redhead's question. "Are *you* all right? Yesterday and today have been hard days for you."

"I cried a lot. I couldn't help it." Secca sniffed. "I tried not to, but I really couldn't . . ." The redhead sniffed again.

"You're allowed to cry after things like that happen—even when you're a lady." Telling Secca earlier in the day about her mother's death had been hard enough for Anna.

"Why is everyone calling me 'Lady'? Is that because . . . ?" Secca looked almost as if she were going to break down and cry again. "I didn't want anything like that to happen. Not even to Kurik."

"I know." The sorceress nodded somberly. "But you are the Lady of Flossbend."

"It seems funny. Jeron was going to be lord after Papa. Or Kurik. Even Lysara's older, and she's not a lady." Secca tilted her head to the side, then straightened. "I'm sorry about Resor and Cens. I'm sorriest about poor Lysara, though. Tiersen looks awful. I think he loves her, you know."

"He does," Anna said.

"Do you think someone will love me like that?"

"Yes. When you're older." Anna smiled. *How could they not love you, child?*

"Will you let me show you something?" Secca stepped sideways and looked down at the floor stones. "And you won't get angry? It can't wait; it really can't."

"Secca . . . I won't get angry. Not at you."

"I was going to wait; but I heard Kinor say you were leaving tomorrow." The little redhead eased a small mandolin from behind her back. "Don't say anything yet." Then she took a stick of pencil wood and walked to the cold hearth, laying the wood in the iron grate. After she drew herself erect, Secca cleared her throat, almost as if in an unconscious imitation of Anna, and her fingers gripped what seemed to be a pick, drawing it over the mandolin's strings, as if to check the sound. Her voice was clear and on key.

> Fire, fire, burn so bright
> burn well and warm and light. . . .

A tongue of flame wrapped around the stick of wood, flickered, and died to almost nothing, before seeming to catch.

Anna swallowed.

"You used a bigger spell, but I couldn't make my fingers work right for that long, so I used just part of your spell . . . it's shorter." Secca bit her lip, lowering the mandolin slowly. "And I used a piece of copper—it was a part of a mirror—to pick at the strings."

"Secca . . . you sang that right on key."

A faint smile crossed the girl's lips. "It was hard. I had to practice the tones without words, the way you do, and . . . it was hard."

"Singing is always hard, if you do it right."

"Will you . . . can you teach me?"

Anna nodded slowly. "If you promise not to try any more spells without showing me the words first."

"I haven't tried any more. I used yours because I saw you do it."

"You remembered that spell from last winter?"

"It was almost spring," Secca pointed out.

Anna laughed softly, wonderingly. "You are a special child . . . a special young woman."

That brought another smile. "Papa was right to send me here."

"Yes, he was." *If not for the reasons he thought.*

Secca glanced at the still-burning stick of wood. "Will you let me light the fire sometimes when we play Vorkoffe?"

"Sometimes," agreed Anna, with a smile. "Who taught you to play the mandolin?"

"I asked Palian. She helped me. I made her promise not to tell anyone. She's teaching me how to play the violino, too. When she's here. I didn't tell her why. I didn't tell anyone."

"I'll tell Liende that Palian is to help you learn to play the violino. It can't hurt for a lady to know some sorcery."

"I don't want to be a lady. I'd rather be a sorceress like you."

"I'm both a sorceress and a lady. I don't see why you can't be both—if you work hard." Anna paused. "It works better that way."

"Will you teach me sorcery?"

"Not at first. First, you have to learn how to control your

voice all the time. You shouldn't do sorcery—or not much—
until you're as old as . . . say, Clayre. That's Lysara's younger
sister. She may be coming to Falcor." *If Birfels will let her after
this mess.*

"That long?"

"That long. You have a lot to learn if you want to do sorcery
right." Anna nodded slowly. *Will you get to see this redhead
grow up? First, Irenia, and then the separation from Elizabetta,
and now Lysara nearly being killed . . . all redheads.* Anna
wondered how Elizabetta was doing, in a world that seemed
increasingly distant.

Yet, for all the differences between Earth and Erde, she was
seeing more clearly how similar the two worlds were behind
their superficially different façades. *Was it that you didn't want
to see—or didn't have to?*

She pushed the thought away, stepping forward to hug the
one little redhead she could . . . while she could.

73

WEI, NORDWEI

Only a fraction of the bright afternoon sunlight penetrates
the nearly closed heavy green draperies that frame the sec-
ond-story window of Ashtaar's Council office. The counselor
looks at the polished black agate spheroid on the shimmering
surface of her table-desk. She does not reach out to touch it, but
forces her eyes to the blonde seer sitting in the straight-backed
chair across from her. "You were saying, Gretslen?"

Gretslen leans forward. "The Sorceress of Defalk has overreached herself. The harmonies could only have fated it to
occur."

The dark-haired Ashtaar continues to look at the head seer.
"How has she overreached herself? If you would explain . . . ?"

"When she left Defalk to meddle in Ebra once more, the
peasants in Pamr revolted. She put down the revolt, but it cost
her two parts in ten of her lancers, and another score to remain
and guard the hold. The lord of the north also rebelled, and his
efforts took another threescore of the sorceress' lancers. Rabyn

and the Mansuurans now hold much of the Western Marches of Defalk, and the Regent has but half the lancers and armsmen she possessed but a season ago, while young Rabyn has begun to use the drums of Darksong."

"That may be," points out Ashtaar, "but you have told me that Hadrenn has sworn allegiance to Defalk, and that the sorceress-Regent extracted some condition from him regarding Elahwa, for his armsmen have gone to Dolov, but not to the port city. That would seem to ensure that she faces trouble with neither Ebra nor Ranuak."

"She paid a high price for such peace," counters the seer. "More and more of the lords of Defalk have come to despise the sorceress. Lord Jearle has not so much as sent a single armsman against the Neserean invaders. Nor has Lord Ustal. Only Lord Nelmor, and he has been most careful but to harry them, and seems not minded to blunt their advance."

"From this you would conclude what?" asks the spymistress.

"The sorceress is greatly weakened, and she will fail." A slow smile creeps across the seer's face.

Ashtaar frowns, and she finally picks up the agate oval, letting its coolness suffuse her without speaking.

"You have doubts?" questions Gretslen.

"She has gambled, but she is not that weakened yet. We shall see," says Ashtaar politely. "Please keep observing Rabyn and his drums."

"You have doubts . . . when her land is in revolt and her Western Marches have fallen? She is powerful, but this is the first time she has faced all that a ruler of Defalk must face. No one can rule Defalk. No one ever has."

"You are correct in your second statement. We will see about the truth of the first." Ashtaar sets aside the black agate. "Be certain that you and your seers scry all that there is to see and not just those events which would support your wishes."

"Yes, Counselor Ashtaar." Gretslen bows her head, as if to conceal a smile. "We shall follow your orders."

"You may go." Ashtaar waits until the door shuts before she sighs.

74

The paving stones of the liedburg courtyard—wet from the predawn rain—glistened even in the shadows cast by the early-morning sun. Anna strapped the lutar behind the saddle, then patted Farinelli on the neck before mounting. "Easy, fellow. We've got a long way to ride."

"You have the shield enchanted?" asked Jecks.

Anna leaned forward in the saddle and touched the open-topped leather carrier that held the small round shield—without straps. The metal rim tingled her fingers. She looked down at Jecks, standing by the stable door. "It's ready." *Not that it's been that much use so far. You've faced about everything BUT enchanted weapons.*

"You will scry often for that whelp Rabyn?"

"I will."

"And you will use strong sorcery from the first?"

Anna nodded. She and Jecks had already been through the points he raised, but she knew he was worried. "I can't afford not to."

"So long as you recall that . . ." Jecks shook his head with an expression that wasn't quite a rueful laugh. "Still . . . much as I must hold here . . . would that I could accompany you."

"I know . . . but you can't. Someone has to hold Falcor."

"That . . . that I must accept. I like it not." Jecks forced a smile. "I will be most happy when you return." He paused. "And take care to eat and drink often."

"I will." Her fingers touched the small food pouch that was on the other side of the saddle from the shield case. She smiled. "I need to check with Liende." With a last smile and a nod at the handsome lord, she eased Farinelli around Rickel and his mount to where the chief player stood beside her mare.

Liende looked up, then gestured to the players, each waiting beside a mount. "We are ready, Regent."

"Let's go, then."

"Players, mount up," Liende called.

"Himar." Anna pitched her voice to carry across the low hub-bub in the courtyard.

"Mount up!" ordered the overcaptain.

". . . mount up!"

". . . up!"

The chain of orders repeated and echoed away from the over-captain like ripples in a pond. Before long, the column began to move from the rear courtyard past the stables and toward the north gates of the liedburg.

Anna looked northward as she rode out through the gates, taking in the city. Mist rose from Falcor as the sun struck the dark roofs. To the west, the sky was clear, except for a line of white clouds just above the horizon.

"How far will we get today?" Kinor turned in the saddle and asked Liende.

"It took us almost four days last time, but Lady Anna will ride harder, I think," replied the chief player.

"She rides hard all the time," added Jimbob.

"Even the lancers say she rides like a war leader," Kinor said.

Other voices rose over those of the young men.

". . . hope it doesn't rain . . ."

". . . late in the year for fighting . . ."

Anna had to wonder, if common wisdom were so against military actions in the late fall, why Rabyn had chosen to invade Defalk. Just because she wasn't nearby . . . or as a pre-text to lure her into a Darksong trap?

Her left hand brushed the top of the spelled shield once more, but she wondered what new threat Rabyn had developed and whether her sorcery could again prevail. *And how many times you can do this.*

75

The rain that had fallen on Falcor had extended less than a day's ride to the west. By early morning of the second day, the land and the road were dry, and the hoofs of the lancers' mounts were lifting thick red dust from the roadway. Anna's boots and the part of her green trousers below her knees were coated with red, and she was sneezing more than infrequently. Farinelli's legs were red as well.

The sun had warmed the day enough that it felt more like late summer than late fall, and Anna found herself drinking more and more water, blotting her forehead all too frequently, and fanning her face occasionally with the floppy hat. She still struggled to remind herself to eat, but the pouch before her knee helped.

Every so often, she reminded herself to touch the shield at her knee, but it remained quiet, indicating no active sorcery nearby.

The fields to the north of the road held stubble, or a few scattered tan stalks—all that remained from the maize harvest, or in some cases, small potato fields that had not yet been harvested. The slightly hillier ground to the south had fewer cultivated fields, and more woodlots, orchards, and meadows or pastures.

A line of trees wound out of the southwest, marking a stream course that angled in a general way toward a low spot in the road about a dek or so ahead of the vanguard. Anna saw a single scout perhaps half a dek ahead of the main column, midway between Anna and her guards and the vanguard. The scout continued to ride eastward. As he neared the first lancers directly ahead of Anna, Himar rode forward to meet him.

The scout reined up, as did Himar. After a brief interchange, Himar turned his mount from the head of the column and rode back, easing his mount around in order to ride alongside the Regent. "The scouts report that there is a stream ahead, Lady Anna, one with a gentle but firm slope to the water."

"You'd like to water the mounts and give the lancers a rest down there?" Anna gestured toward the patch of green that surrounded the bend in the trees ahead.

"And their mounts."

"I can use the time to check and see where we should be going and what Rabyn's forces are doing, and where we should be going once we near Denguic."

"Do you know how far into Defalk the young Prophet has come?" asked the sandy-haired overcaptain.

"Last night, he was almost two days' ride south and east of Denguic." *You think . . . too much of western Defalk looks like the rest of western Defalk.*

"More toward Fussen?"

"I think so."

"I will pass the order to water the mounts." Himar inclined his head to the Regent before riding past her and her guards. "Stand down for water at the stream ahead. Water by companies, blue company first. . . ."

Anna turned in the saddle. "Jimbob, Kinor . . . Liende . . . I'd like you to join me." She paused. "Kinor, would you find Himar and ask him as well—once he's got the watering organized?"

While the lancers watered their mounts, Anna gathered Liende and Jimbob under an oak whose yellow leaves had begun to fall. She propped the travel mirror between two raised and gnarled roots, then began a series of vocalises.

"He sees theeee. . . ."

Perhaps it was the drying oak leaves, or the residual road dust, but she began to cough immediately and had to stop and cough her throat clear.

Himar and Kinor arrived before she began the actual scrying spell, and Anna motioned for them to join her almost directly before the mirror. "You need to see this," she told the overcaptain.

Himar nodded.

Anna cleared her throat and lifted the lutar.

> Show me now as clear as it can be,
> the Neserean forces I would see. . . .

The image in the travel mirror centered on a rickety bridge across a narrow gorge. On one side were hundreds of lancers, stretching back along the curving road, under both purple and blue banners. The lancers were taking the bridge cautiously, in single file, with no more than two mounts at a time on the span.

"Fussen, I'd wager," murmured Jimbob.

Anna nodded, smiling. Hanfor was certainly obeying orders, and using the lands of Fussen as the area from which he harassed Rabyn. Anna almost would have laughed at the scene, had she not seen young Rabyn's use of Darksong . . . and the thoughtlessness with which the young ruler had already used it.

Anna sang the release spell, then blotted her forehead before half squatting to retrieve the mirror and replace it in the leather case. As she straightened, carrying the mirror, she glanced toward Liende.

The chief player brushed back hair that had gotten progressively whiter since Anna had come to Liedwahr, so that now only thin streaks of pale red remained. "He will use more Darksong."

"I know. That's why we need to keep riding." *If you can get there in time . . .*

"You have tried to do much," said Liende. "We will stand ready." She stepped back and walked toward the tree under which the players waited.

"Thank you." Anna lifted the lutar and mirror.

Had it been that necessary to help Hadrenn? To stop Bertmynn? To keep the Sturinnese from getting a foothold in Liedwahr? Had it been worth Gatrune's death? The deaths of scores of her lancers and thousands of others? And yet, what else could she do now—except ride westward and try to stop the Nesereans?

Then what? Even if you win, you don't have the lancers to take over Neserea. So . . . will that mean letting the Liedfuhr annex his grandson's land? She shook her head as she strapped the lutar and mirror behind her saddle, and mounted Farinelli. She'd think of something.

She had to.

76

NORTH-NORTHWEST OF FUSSEN, DEFALK

The dark-haired Prophet of Music paces across the cream-and-blue carpet that comprises the floor of the tent—six paces one way, an abrupt turn, and six paces back the other way. The wall panels of alternating blue-and-cream silk billow in the evening breeze, but the chill wind is not strong enough to flicker the flames of the pair of candles in crystal holders and clear crystal mantles set upon the blue linen of the camp table. Rabyn rips a single large grape from the bunch in the carved wooden bowl beside the nearest candle.

Nubara watches the thin-faced young man, waits and shivers under his heavy cloak of maroon wool.

"We could take them like this!" Rabyn holds the large golden grape up, almost pointing it at Nubara, then crushes it and tosses it aside before licking his fingers clean. "Yet they will not let us near them. Why will they not stand and face us? Because they cannot without the power of the sorceress! Yet Overcaptain Relour cannot seem to bring these cowardly dogs to bay. Nor have you been any help, Nubara."

"I might add, honored Prophet, that we have twentyscore fewer armsmen—"

"Cowards! All of them! Just because she used Darksong to make them fear her . . . and now they can't—or won't march against her. Some of them were Prophet's Guards! And you let that happen." Rabyn glares at Nubara.

"I was not there. I could have done nothing."

"It doesn't matter. They can fight against that Defalkan lord. That shows how little she knows. She spent herself on a Darksong spell that is almost useless. We still have thirty times the forces she does, and my Darksong is far stronger."

Nubara shivers.

"There is no reason we should not destroy her and her handful of armsmen. We have more men, and stronger sorcery." The thin-faced Rabyn lifts a vial from his wallet. "If we do not engage the Defalkans before the day after tomorrow, Nubara . . . you will receive no more of this."

Nubara blots his pale face, damp despite the chill wind that has strengthened, almost as if in response to Rabyn's angry tone, and now whips across the camp, fluttering the silk walls that surround the two. "I cannot order the Defalkans to meet you where you will, Lord Rabyn. What you do to me will not affect their commander. Nor will it hinder nor hurry the sorceress. You have told me of how mighty your Darksong is, and displayed to all the world how you can bring down great forests to speed our way across gorge and stream and marsh. The sorceress will come to you, because only she can face you." Nubara forces a shrug. "Arrange your forces where your Darksong will be the mightiest. Then use it to destroy her. When she is gone, nothing can stand before you, o mighty Prophet."

Rabyn raises the vial as if to throw it. "You will not mock me, Nubara."

"I am not mocking you, honored Prophet." The voice of the Mansuuran officer is thick, ragged, and tired. "You are the mightiest darksinger of the ages, but your sorcery cannot reach beyond the sound of your drums. So the sorceress must come to your drums. I cannot change that. You cannot change that. You can watch me die, and it will change nothing."

Rabyn lowers the vial, not quite pouting. "You will address me with respect. You *will*, or nothing will save you."

"Yes, honored Prophet."

"You will send scouts to determine if the sorceress will soon arrive, and from where."

"Yes, most honored Prophet."

"And you will find another small blonde girl for my enjoyment.

Nubara bows deeply. "As you command."

"I want one who will do *exactly* as I wish."

"I will endeavor to find such, lord Prophet." Nubara shivers, drawing the cloak tighter about himself.

"I knew you would, Nubara. You may go." Rabyn smiles,

and his white teeth shimmer like the icebergs of the far south. "Do not keep me waiting."

"I will do as I can, lord Prophet." Nubara moves slowly from the tent, shivering more violently as he steps into the cool twilight wind.

77

Anna finished the vocalise and glanced around the hilltop clearing that lay less than fifty yards to the south of the road they had traveled from Falcor. To the east, the morning's white puffy clouds had turned darker and begun to climb into thunderheads. To the west, the skies still appeared clear, and the midafternoon sun was pleasantly warm, if with a hint of chill in the breeze out of the west. Before her, propped against a fallen tree, was her traveling mirror. Absently, she adjusted and tuned the lutar once more.

Himar, Liende, Jimbob, and Kinor stood slightly behind the line of her shoulders, waiting for her to begin. Anna cleared her throat a last time, then began the scrying spell.

> Mirror, mirror, on the ground,
> show me lancers to be found,
> those of Rabyn whom I seek. . . .

The glass of the traveling mirror silvered over. The shimmering surface slowly evaporated to reveal a narrow stream that had cut a gorge perhaps three yards deep and ten yards wide. Yellow- and red-leafed bushes were scattered along the sides of the streambed at the bottom of the gorge. On the left side of the stream two companies of lancers had reined up. As Anna and the others watched, arrows arched over both the stream and gorge. Yet, after the sprinkling of arrows, only a single lancer in maroon clutched his arm. Another flock of arrows followed, but Anna could not see any but the single casualty among the Mansuurans. *Hanfor told you that his bowmen weren't that good without your spells.*

The maroon-clad lancers wheeled away from the gorge by the stream, leaving a score or so of riders in blue. Abruptly, a large pile of planks appeared beside the gorge, raising gouts of dust.

Anna, Himar, and the others continued to watch. A stack of wide planks appeared. She blinked. Had the stand of pines behind the lancers vanished?

"Darksong . . ." murmured Liende. "He is using Darksong."

"Darksong," Kinor repeated in a lower whisper.

Jimbob looked from Kinor to Liende, and then to Anna, but the heir did not speak.

Anna nodded to herself. Of course, to make planks from trees meant handling living things, and that was Darksong. *How long can he use Darksong?* The answer came quickly enough. *Long enough to use it against you, and anyone strong enough to level forests, young as he may be, is someone to worry about.*

She sang the release spell, then lowered the lutar, leaving the mirror propped against the tree stump.

Himar cleared his throat, firmly, if quietly.

"Yes, Himar?"

"Might there be any way to determine exactly where the Nesereans are?"

"Of course." *Of course . . . how else will you figure out what you need to do?* She was tired and not thinking as clearly as she should have been, despite her efforts to eat and drink regularly. "Let me think about how to phrase that."

"I will get my sketching board." The overcaptain turned and began to extract the rough brown paper, the grease marker, and a polished oak board from his overlarge saddlebags.

Anna slowly figured out how to change the spell, but slow as she felt, she was finished and waiting for Himar to nod before she tried again.

> Mirror, mirror on the ground,
> show us where might be found
> the lancers in maroon and in blue
> with a map that's fair and true. . . .
>
> A map that shows our men as well,
> and how to reach the enemy we must fell.

The mirror obligingly offered what appeared to be a detailed topographical map, almost like the ones she'd studied so many years ago in geography. The Defalkan forces appeared to be represented by a pulsing purple dot on the left side of the depiction. Those of Rabyn appeared in maroon and blue, with a larger blue-and-maroon dot closer to her forces, and a smaller blue dot to the north.

Himar began to sketch, and Anna tried to figure out the geography. While she couldn't determine from her crude maps exact locations, Rabyn's forces were in three locales—some around Denguic, providing Jearle the excuse not to take any action; some to the north of Fussen, as if holding the main road between Falcor and Denguic; and a larger maroon-and-blue dot pulsed to the southwest of Fussen—probably about due west of the small town where Ustal's brother had established himself— Sudborte, was it? Except that Anna had to guess about that because the mirror "map" didn't show holds or towns. Then her spell hadn't mentioned holds or towns. Or Hanfor's forces, and she hadn't mentally concentrated on thinking about them either.

"The Nesereans are to the southwest, my lady Anna, and I would say he is near-on a day away." Himar continued to sketch with rapid strokes of the grease marker.

Anna's head was splitting by the time Himar finished sketching and looked up. The overcaptain opened his mouth.

Anna spoke first. "I know," she said tiredly. "We have to find Hanfor and his forces. I need some water, and some time to come up with a better spell." *No wonder fantasy novels on Earth talked about books of spells—and those fictional characters didn't have to juggle words and match the music.* She straightened. *But they weren't real singers, either.*

It took several wedges of cheese, a half a loaf of bread, and half a water bottle before the worst of the headache subsided. Then it was nearly another half-glass and well into twilight before she had a spell she thought would do.

When she lifted the lutar and began her voice cracked. Dryness, dust . . . something was aggravating her allergies and asthma, and those were one thing Brill's youth spell hadn't helped, probably because she'd had the allergies when she'd been young the first time, and youth spells didn't take way what had been there before.

She cleared her throat and started again.

The mirror image was on a larger scale, less detailed, and showed not only Hanfor's forces, but a blue dot near what Anna felt was Denguic—the twentyscore Nesereans with their nominal siege of Jearle's hold. *Twentyscore for a nominal siege, and you're bringing a third of that against what—two hundred fifty–score?*

She forced her eyes back to the map image. Hanfor was southeast of Fussen, positioned in a way to move to harry either group of Rabyn's forces. But to join up with the arms commander's forces would entail at least a half day's ride on the part of either Anna or Hanfor.

Anna almost shrugged. Did it matter now? She and Hanfor were well positioned to block any eastward advance by the Nesereans. *That's assuming that Rabyn's forces and his Darksong don't flatten you.*

She rubbed her forehead, concentrating on holding the last map image, and waiting for Himar to finish sketching out his maps—or adding to the ones he'd already drawn. She motioned to Liende, Kinor, and Jimbob.

"We might as well make camp here. There's a stream below, and there's no point in pushing on today."

"I will tell the players," Liende responded in a low voice, nodding. "You should not be traveling farther if you do such laborious scrying."

That had occurred to Anna. Had Jecks accompanied her, he certainly would have let her know that. *As well as a few other things.*

She forced herself to take another deep swallow of water.

78

Encora, Ranuak

You summoned me, Matriarch?" The tall and thin woman stands in the doorway of the formal receiving room, a room empty except for the round-faced Matriarch, who yet wears black, rather than her more customary bright colors.

The Matriarch stands by the clear blue crystal chair of the Matriarchy, upon the low dais, but makes no move to seat herself. "I did, Abslim. If you would close the door and join me?"

Abslim steps forward, bows once, not quite perfunctorily, and shuts the carved ebony door without a sound. Against the sea-blue of her tunic, the sheaves comprising the golden pin on her collar radiate a light more than a mere reflection from the sunlight streaming in through the clear glass of the closed windows that flank each side of the hall.

"I am here at your request, Matriarch. Again."

"I do appreciate your patience, Abslim." The Matriarch extends the scroll in her right hand toward the head of the Exchange. "If you would read this . . ."

The tall and dark-haired director of the Exchange takes the scroll and unrolls it, slowly, deliberately, before beginning to study the words. After a time, she looks up. "It appears to be a request to you, asking you as Matriarch to provide for someone to assist and mediate in setting up a government by the free-women of Elahwa. He calls it a free state, if under his rule. How that might be free . . . that I would not hazard."

"That was how I read it," confirms the Matriarch. "Rather remarkable, considering how badly the freewomen were treated by Bertmynn."

"You always have had a gift of understatement, Matriarch." The dark-haired and younger head of the Exchange once more peruses the scroll. "From Lord Hadrenn of Synek, save that he styles himself Lord High Counselor of Ebra . . . now. A shade pretentious for one so young, do you not think, Matriarch?"

"What do you really think of that title, Abslim?"

"Rather pretentious. I did say that, did I not, honored Matriarch?" Abslim offers a slight smile, continuing with a voice that becomes increasingly silky. "The title, we could accept, I would think, given that we have received more from young Hadrenn than ever from the sorceress-Regent."

"Hadrenn has offered that, yet he made no move to deal with Bertmynn until the arrival of the sorceress." The Matriarch's voice emphasizes only slightly the last word.

"He let her work for him. She has often worked for men. So that is scarcely passing strange."

"Abslim . . . young Hadrenn has not the wit to offer such. Had you considered that?" The older woman's voice is low, but scarcely soft.

"Then he must have good advisors, and the wit to listen to them. For that, the SouthWomen will be grateful."

"I did not take you for such a fool. When will you see what is, and not what you wish to see?"

"Most revered Matriarch, I have asked that question myself, though not of myself."

"I do not engage in wagers and wordplay, Abslim. Will you step down as Exchange ruler, or do I remove you?"

"Remove me? I think not." A long silvery blade appears in Abslim's hand. "You have frittered away the gifts of the Matriarch and refused to act, even when it was clear to the dullest man in Ranuak that action was needed."

A blue-crystal blade appears in the hand of the older woman, though she does not speak to the Exchange ruler. The Matriarch's deep voice begins a chantlike spell.

> For the good of one and all,
> for the course of large and small . . .

The blue crystal chair begins to hum, as if to accompany the Matriarch, and a higher humming issues from the blue blade as well.

The taller and more slender woman eases forward, her feet balanced, and thrusts the glowing silver blade toward the older woman.

Though the Matriarch does not move, the blade of blue crystal *flickers*, and the point and top third of the silver blade fall to the blue-stone floor.

The Matriarch's deep song-chant continues.

. . . for harmonies of earth and skies,
for lives less strife and lies . . .

Abslim glances at the flickering crystal blade, seemingly longer than moments before, then at two pieces of metal, one on the floor, one in her hand. She backs away, her eyes widening, her mouth opening. She takes no more than three steps before she crumples to the floor, but the older woman's contralto voice continues to sing the spell, and those words do not soon cease.

When the Matriarch finishes the last words and notes, the chair's humming dies away, and there is no indication that another person has ever been with the Matriarch. She takes several slow deep breaths before she sinks onto the blue cushion that covers the seat of the crystal chair, a cushion that is the sole softness within the formal receiving room.

There is no sign of a blue-crystal blade as the Matriarch holds her head in both hands for a long time, until the sun is nearly overhead, and no sunlight streams into the chamber. Then she rises and walks slowly toward the door Abslim had closed.

79

Anna stood in the predawn light outside her tent, feeling almost guilty as she thought about the collapsible canvas cot she had slept on, while her players and lancers had to lay their bedrolls on the ground. Even though tent and cot, as well as other supplies, were carried by a single packhorse, the sorceress sometimes fretted about having those comparative comforts.

She took a last bite of the bread baked the evening before, then a mouthful of the white cheese that was growing ever stronger, before washing it down with water from one of the bottles she kept filled with orderspelled water.

"Lady Anna?" asked Kinor, as he and Jimbob approached.

"Yes?"

"Will we be heading south today?" asked Kinor.

"If we want to join with Hanfor's forces, we will." She frowned. "Himar and I don't want to travel too far, because that would let Rabyn's lancers use the road to get behind us." She turned as one of Himar's scouts rode toward where the cook-fires had already been banked, since all the baking had been done in coals and embers the night before. Himar walked toward the mounted scout, who leaned forward in his saddle toward the overcaptain.

"The scouts were out early," Jimbob noted. "I could hear one leaving when it was still dark."

So . . . Himar is more worried about leaving the main road than he's letting on. "Thank you," Anna told the shorter red-head. "That's good to know."

A puzzled look crossed Jimbob's face. Kinor merely nodded.

All three watched as the scout turned and galloped out of the campsite and then off down the road to the west. Within moments a company of lancers mounted hurriedly and followed, but Himar strode across the campsite toward them with long steps.

"You look like you have good news," suggested Anna. "We could use some."

"Lady Anna . . . there are twoscore armsmen who would join you." A smile crinkled Himar's lips above his beard. "They were less than two deks to the west and will be here shortly."

"Who are they?"

"The scout said that they are being led by a redheaded young man named Falar."

"More redheads?" Anna grinned at the two before her as she spoke. "I'm already surrounded."

"Falar?" questioned Kinor quietly.

"He's the younger son of Lord Vlassa, is he not?" asked Jimbob. "You saw him on your last journey to Fussen, Grandsire said."

"That's right," confirmed Anna.

"Grandsire didn't say much, but I thought he cared more for the younger son than Lord Ustal."

Anna decided not to comment on that directly. "We met with both of Lord Vlassa's sons. Ustal is but a few moments the elder. He is supposedly quite accomplished with a blade."

"It takes more than a blade and a strong arm to be a lord." Himar gestured in the direction of the road. "Here they come."

Flanked by Bersan, Fielmir, Blaz, and Rickel, Anna and Himar waited as the riders, escorted by the purple company, rode toward her tent.

"More than a score, maybe almost two, Lady Anna," offered Kinor from the right of her guards.

At the head of the line of armsmen in leathers of mixed—or motley—colors was a slender figure in blue. Immediately upon reining up, Falar bowed in the saddle, almost bending as low as the base of his saddle—or so it seemed. "Regent and sorceress." His eyes twinkled as he straightened, and the hint of an amused smile played around the corners of his mouth.

"Falar . . ." Anna wasn't quite sure what to say to the younger brother of Lord Ustal. "I was surprised to hear that you were on your way." *That's safe enough.*

"I am not a lord, Lady Anna," said Falar, "but our land is in danger, and my older brother has not seen fit to bring his armsmen against that enemy. I have too few to engage the Nesereans by myself. So I have brought my few armsmen to offer what assistance I can to you." His arm swept toward the armsmen mounted behind him. "Ruffians, all of us, but loyal ruffians."

Despite the charmingly calculated appeal of the would-be lord's offer, Anna remained touched. "I appreciate your offer, Falar, and I will accept it." She smiled, and added, "In the spirit in which you have made it."

Falar grinned back, then said, "I also have sent a messenger to Arms Commander Hanfor, letting him know where you are. I trust you will not find aught in that amiss?"

"Not at all. Although we know where he is, it might be better if we waited for him. I can use my mirror to see if he follows the directions of your messenger."

Standing beside Anna, Himar nodded. "That will rest the mounts and the players—and you, Lady Anna."

"And give me more time to scry exactly what the Nesereans

plan," she added, looking back at the deliberately guileless-appearing Falar. "How long did it take you from Sudborte?"

"We left two glasses before dawn." Falar yawned, if almost dramatically. "We also could enjoy a brief rest."

Himar nodded. "Let us get your men settled."

"Regent." Falar bowed once more, with yet another roguish smile, then turned his mount to follow Himar.

Anna stepped back.

Besides scrying, what else could she do? *For one thing, you can make sure you've got bread and hard crackers handy in your pouch . . . and that you eat it before any battle so that your blood sugar doesn't totally crash . . . and remember to drink lots of water before you do sorcery . . . and keep checking the spelled shield.*

She also needed to see if she could determine exactly how the young Prophet was creating his Darksong—and see if she could find or compose a counterspell of some sort.

80

MANSUUS, MANSUUR

Konsstin listens quietly, from behind the desk in his private study, as Bassil finishes his report.

". . . and the seers have found that he has set up an encampment well within Defalk, on the main road to Falcor. And the sorceress has but a fraction of the armsmen as Rabyn does, and no lancers to compare to those you have furnished. Other small groups may join hers, but even should they do so, she will still have fewer than fifteenscore lancers."

"So . . . my grandson the viper has slithered into Defalk. And Nubara has allowed this? I had hoped better of him." The Liedfuhr leans forward, his eyes fixing more intently upon the black-haired Mansuuran officer.

"Nubara looks most unwell, sire," offers Bassil. "He has a heavy winter cloak wrapped around him while the others wear but tunics. He stays close by the young Prophet, but yet remains the one to offer orders to the armsmen."

"Poison—alamarite. One cannot taste it." Konsstin shakes

his head. "That was one of Cyndyth's favorites. The lizard is being destroyed by the viper, and a half-grown viper at that. He will not reach full growth, that one."

"Then you can make Neserea part of Mansuur."

Konsstin raises his bushy eyebrows. "You assume much, Bassil. What if the sorceress should defeat him?"

"She has won every battle she has undertaken, but yet she has fewer lancers and armsmen than she did a year ago. Even with the small numbers of lancers required to protect her while she performs her sorcery, she cannot take a land as vast as Neserea. If she does, she will not hold Defalk. Four lords have revolted in the last year. Those we know about. There may have been others." Bassil clears his throat, then continues. "If Lord Rabyn defeats the sorceress, you can wait."

"That much is true." Konsstin fingers his beard. "But if she defeats my grandson the snake . . . ?"

"Then you propose a partition of Neserea, so that order may be maintained."

Konsstin stands. "We will not dwell on what might be. I cannot send more armsmen and lancers in time to change what will be. So we wait."

Bassil nods.

"You may go, Bassil."

"Yes, sire."

After the door of the private study closes, the Liedfuhr of Mansuur turns and walks to the wide window behind the table-desk and looks into the distance where the mighty Toksul River flows eastward from Mansuus. "An Empire of Music, but who would have thought it might be wrought by a sorceress? By a woman older than you who looks young enough to entice your grandson?"

There is a knock on the door, and he turns, letting the official smile return to his visage before he acknowledges the summons that will be to the afternoon audiences.

81

In the sunlight of an early afternoon warmer than that of the past few days, Anna, Liende, Jimbob, and Kinor stood under the yellowing leaves of a tree that Anna didn't recognize, waiting for Himar to join them. Anna's tent was another ten yards westward, guarded by Fielmir, while Blaz and Bersan stood directly behind the Regent.

Perhaps thirty yards south, Himar, with his sketch board in hand, was sitting on a fallen log, sketching and listening to a scout who had just returned to the encampment. The redheaded Falar stood at his elbow.

"If you had more sorcerers or sorceresses, you wouldn't need scouts, would you?" asked Jimbob.

"You'd still need scouts," offered Liende. "Sorcery . . . you need names, that sort of thing."

Jimbob looked at the Regent.

"Liende's right," Anna said. "Sorcery will let you display a map of something—if you know who or what you're looking for. The more you know before you start, the less sorcery it takes. I knew that there was a darksinger somewhere in Defalk, but all the trouble we had was because we didn't know enough soon enough. . . ." She let the words die away as she saw Himar walking past the cookfires toward them, trailed by Falar. Their dusty riding boots swirled the few handfuls of leaves that had already fallen from the trees on the gentle downslope to the west of the campsite.

"What have your scouts discovered?" Anna asked the over-captain.

"The Nesereans have begun to build defenses. They have set a firm perimeter line," Himar said. "There are even small trenchworks for sentries."

Standing at Himar's shoulder, Falar nodded in affirmation.

"In the middle of nowhere?" If Rabyn—or Nubara—had decided not to move his forces, but was apparently waiting for Anna to come to him, Anna wanted to know why.

"It would appear so," responded Himar cautiously.

"We'd better try the mirror." Anna ignored the nudge that Jimbob gave Kinor as she stood and returned to her tent to retrieve the lutar and the traveling mirror. Once inside, she paused, then ran through a set of vocalises. Sometimes—most times—they were easier without other people standing by and listening.

Then, she reflected, she'd gone from a singer struggling to get an audience on Earth to a sorceress and Regent everybody watched, seemingly all the time. She wondered how many watched to see if she would fail.

Anna brought the lutar and mirror out from the tent and set the mirror in a shaded spot not quite under the tree. Then, the sorceress began the spell, trying to ignore the all-too-many people watching the mirror. Among them was Falar, who stood almost behind the taller Kinor, as if the would-be lord were trying to be as inconspicuous as possible.

> Mirror, mirror on the ground,
> show the earthworks scouts have found
> those of Rabyn and his men. . . .

While the mirror displayed eight different small images, of sentry posts with piles of dirt and deadfall logs, all those images did was confirm what Himar's scouts had already reported.

"You see?" Himar nodded sagely.

"I see." Anna let him nod, releasing the image almost immediately while she considered how to reword the spell to get a better view of the Neserean camp as a whole. "They're definitely dug in and waiting."

"What if we do not come to him?" asked Falar.

"Then we wait, and Defalk falls apart. He knows that," Anna responded. In fact, Rabyn seemed to know far too much.

"Defalk is strong," protested Jimbob.

"Not strong enough to allow two hundred–score armsmen to fortify a camp in its Western Marches," Anna answered, her tone of voice dry.

"And how long will those in Dumar and Ebra heed her if she allows such to remain?" asked Liende.

Kinor nodded, barely, at his mother's observation.

"Let's see if we can get a better view." Anna thought for a time, a time long enough that those around her were shifting their weight from foot to foot and clearing their throats before she lifted the lutar once more.

Mirror, mirror on the ground . . .

A second image filled the oblong of the mirror's surface, this one a half-aerial view of an encampment set to the east of a hill that commanded the main road.

"You see?" Himar pointed. "These are the highest hills for deks along the road." He frowned. "But I would not have set my men with their back to that bluff there."

Anna followed his finger, trying to see what he was pointing out while concentrating on maintaining the image in the mirror. A large tent with a peaked roof and alternating blue and cream panels stood before a rust-colored cliff or bluff. Anna studied the area. The tent seemed to be on the easternmost edge of a broad shelf of grassy land, almost stagelike, below the cliff, which curved slightly so that the top projected more than the base.

Raw boulders sat near the base of the bluff. Anna squinted. The first fifty yards from the base of the cliff was smooth and bare rock. Then within a yard of the clear rock, nearly immediately, the grass began.

"Darksong." She nodded. "It's like a shell there." *That barely grown boy did that? He had to have shaved away the hillside.*

Himar's eyebrows lifted in puzzlement.

"That's a curved hard surface that throws the sound farther."

"It is a pity that you have nothing that will do the same."

Nothing that will do the same . . . the words echoed in her mind . . . nothing that will do the same. Something nagged at her, but she couldn't pin it down, and the more she tried to concentrate on the idea, the more elusive whatever her thought was. That would have to wait; it would come to her. *You hope.*

"We need to see one more thing." Anna sang the release couplet for the second image, and reached for the water bottle that Kinor extended, much as Jecks had usually done. She wondered if the white-haired lord had taken Kinor aside. "Thank you, Kinor."

"My pleasure, Lady Anna."

After drinking, Anna glanced around, then repressed a sigh. If she asked anyone to leave, those feelings would be hurt. "It's going to take a little while for me to get ready for the next spell. If you want to walk around, that's fine, but anyone who stays near me will have to be quiet while I think."

Kinor nodded at Jimbob, and the two young men stepped into the sunlight and walked toward the nearest tieline, where Farinelli and their mounts were tethered.

Himar nodded. "I will be back, Lady Anna."

Liende stepped away and into the sun, as if to get warm. Anna half smiled. She'd forgotten how much cooler Earth had been, so much that mildly cool weather was chilly to many Defalkans.

Coming up with the spell she wanted for the drums took even longer, but she wasn't a composer or a poet.

Once she picked up the lutar again, though, people appeared as if by sorcery, including both Lejun and Rickel, and she waited until her audience had gathered and quieted before beginning the spell.

> Show us those singing drums so strong
> that raise the Prophet's coming Darksong. . . .

The mirror obediently displayed three drums, each under an awning of sorts, each bound with copper strips.

At first, Anna could see nothing unusual about the drums, except that each was mounted in a wooden frame that allowed it to swivel. Then she saw the wagon in the background. Each drum had to have taken an entire wagon to transport it. Admittedly, the wagon beds were small—no more than a yard and half wide—but any drum built like that had to have a lot of volume and carrying power—and when set before an angled cliff of hard stone . . . She nodded. Young as Rabyn was, cruel as the stories reported he was, stupid he was not. He—or someone—had thought out both his abilities and the logistics to support them. And that worried Anna.

"Those are large drums," Himar announced.

"Very large," Anna agreed. She sang the release couplet, then blotted her forehead before squatting to replace the lutar in its case. Kinor gently packed the mirror in its case. Anna stood and picked up the lutar.

"Pale . . . she is," murmured Bersan to Lejun.

"Sorcery be hard, hard work, friend," answered the more experienced guard. "Seen enough I have that it's a guard I'd rather be."

Bersan's comment about her paleness prompted Anna to walk toward her tent and the food pouch that was waiting there. Would she spend the rest of her life worrying about her blood sugar and energy levels? *Probably, and if you don't, that life will be a short one.*

Kinor followed with the mirror in its leather case.

A golden leaf fluttered down in the cool and light breeze, curling almost into a cone shape before dropping to the dusty ground.

"A megaphone . . . you idiot! That's it." *And you could make it out of copper or something that wasn't living.* She shook her head—a megaphone wasn't it, because she'd end up squeezing her voice, but why couldn't she build her own shell—something parabolic behind her and the players. She didn't want to exhaust herself with sorcery to make it, and it had to be light enough to go on the handful of wagons they had. Aluminum? She had the feeling that aluminum took too much energy. *Another idea that seemed great at first.*

"Ah, Lady?" asked Kinor.

"Oh, I'm sorry. I'll take the mirror now. Thank you. I was thinking."

Kinor smiled, then handed her the mirror case before bowing and returning to the others.

Inside the small and increasingly dingy tent, Anna reached for the hard crackers and harder yellow cheese, hoping she could think through things after she ate. Or think through them more clearly.

82

The alternating blue and cream silk panels of the tent flutter in the afternoon breeze, then subside. From where he sits beside the small table covered with blue linen, Rabyn sips from the silver goblet, then sets it down and delicately lifts a single candied nut to his lips. A second nut follows the first, handled equally delicately.

Because there is but a single chair, Nubara stands on carpet that serves as the floor, his eyes looking at the interlocking design of blue and cream triangles.

"The accursed sorceress knows where we are, yet she has not moved since the night before last." Rabyn's lips move into an expression not quite a pout. "She has a scrying mirror. She uses it, but she will not move."

"She is gathering her forces—those of her arms commander and the handfuls of armsmen offered by those few lords loyal to her." Nubara swallows, then continues. "Overcaptain Relour inquired about the screams last night. He suggested . . . ah . . . temperance."

"I *was* temperate, Nubara. I let the girl go. I would have whipped her, were we still in Esaria or most places in Neserea. Here . . . I but slapped her and gave her a gold. That stopped her wailing quickly enough." Rabyn sneers. "Golds always quell the objections of the peasants, even the pretty ones."

"That was most . . . appropriate." Nubara nods. "Had you whipped her or slain her, honored Prophet, the lancers and armsmen would have been angered, for they would have seen that as a waste."

"There are always more peasants." Rabyn's voice is matter-of-fact.

Nubara opens his mouth, then closes it.

"They talk about their women, but they care far more for their animals and golds. Or even their ale, poor as it is. Why should I care when they do not?" Rabyn's laugh carries a shrill overtone.

"Peasants expect more from their leaders than from other peasants." The lancer officer barely finishes the sentence before he is racked by coughing that continues for some time.

Rabyn ignores Nubara's discomfort, finally speaking once the Mansuuran officer has straightened up. "The sorceress is east of us, on the high road. Will she move closer? What if she does not?"

"She will." Nubara coughs, then shudders. "You can afford to wait. She cannot, not when every week brings yet another lord who would rebel against her." He readjusts the heavy wool cloak, his eyes darting toward the open door panel of the tent. "More of her armsmen have died at the hands of her own lords than by the arms of her enemies."

"I would not put up with such."

"By all accounts, she has not. That is why so many of her lords dislike her. And why she cannot wait. Overcaptain Relour has suggested she will attack within days." Nubara manages to control the trembling that afflicts him and nods. "The heights and the way you employed sorcery to send the sound farther east gives your drums greater range. You cannot use the drums while they are being carted elsewhere. Moving would not improve your position, and the sorceress could catch us less prepared."

"Sometimes, one must wait," concedes the dark-haired prophet.

"This is one of those times, honored Prophet."

"We shall see."

83

The afternoon was chill, damp, and the gray clouds moving in from the north suggested a cold rain was likely.

Anna glanced from where she sat on the cot just inside her tent, puzzling through the latest scrolls and messages sent by Jecks, out across the campsite. Hanfor's messenger had said that the arms commander would arrive by midday, but it was already approaching early afternoon, and Hanfor had yet to appear. Anna's eyes dropped to the scroll before her—the second one from Lord Hulber of Silberfels.

> ... trust you will give the matter of recompense your earliest consideration once you conclude your expeditions and return to Falcor to deal with the more urgent matters of governance ...

In short, get back to Falcor and give me a share of the gold you mined through sorcery because the lands once belonged to my grandfather. Anna set Hulber's scroll in the pile to her left and picked up the next one. It was from Beltyr—even worse.

> ... continue to administer the lands of Synope ... waiting for your instructions and confirmation of succession. ...

That got a snort before she set it aside for the next one. She couldn't do anything until she dealt—hopefully—with Rabyn. The next scroll was from Lord Ebraak of Nordfels. Anna frowned. In over a year, she had heard nothing from Ebraak. The lord had paid his liedgeld, through messengers, without requests. She unrolled the scroll, gingerly, and began to read, skipping through the flowery salutation and opening sentences.

> ... we of Nordfels were pleased to learn that the Corian lineage would be restored and maintained by the Regency ... yet we have not heard of any plans for the installation of the lord Jimbob. We would like to suggest that the most proper course for the Regency would be such an installation, with, of course, the young lord being advised by a council of lords headed by one such as his grandsire, Lord Jecks of Elheld ... in this manner, Lord Jimbob would come to know and understand the contributions and needs of each lord. ...

Anna set Ebraak's scroll aside and rubbed her forehead. *You haven't been a good little girl. You didn't do things the right way. It was nice of you to save our precious heritage, but please be so kind as to restore the mess that got us in trouble.* She took a deep breath and reached for the water bottle on the ground by the corner of her cot.

At the sound of horses, Anna looked up and out through the open door panel of her tent. She smiled, broadly, as she saw Hanfor at the head of the column of lancers. She took another swallow from the water bottle, then stood and slipped out of the tent and through the misty afternoon. Blaz and Fielmir followed her.

As if he had been looking for his Regent, the grizzled veteran turned in the saddle and raised his left hand in greeting and in salute. "Lady Anna."

"Hanfor—I'm glad to see you."

"Lady Anna . . . I received your messenger and one from the noble Falar as well." The veteran's weathered and gray-bearded face displayed a lopsided smile. "They agreed, and I am here."

"We're all glad that you are." She half turned and gestured toward her tent. "We need to meet—once you have your men settled. Himar is with me; Lord Jecks remains in Falcor to hold the liedburg."

Hanfor's smile vanished. "I can tell there is much we have to talk over. I will be quick."

Anna nodded. "If you would bring Himar?"

"We will be there."

The Regent turned to walk back toward the players. She needed to find Liende. The meeting in her tent would be small—just the four. There were some things she didn't want discussed everywhere, not immediately, although nothing could be kept secret for long in Defalk.

The players were practicing before a blackberry thicket that blocked the breeze from the north. Anna listened to the long flame song, nodding as the ensemble finished.

"Liende?" Anna asked. "Would you join me?"

"Yes, Regent." The chief player nodded to Anna, then addressed the players, although her words seemed to go directly to Palian. "While I am gone, you will practice the short flame song and the arrow spell. Then the building spell."

Palian inclined her head in acknowledgment.

Jimbob and Kinor angled toward Liende and Anna as the two women neared Anna's tent. Farther behind them was Falar. Anna stopped and turned. "Jimbob . . . Kinor . . . I have a favor to ask. While I'm meeting with Hanfor, would you two tell Falar everything that happened from the time we left Loiseau—everything in Ebra and on our trip back to Falcor, and then until he joined us." She smiled as warmly as she could.

"Ah . . . Lady Anna," began Jimbob, "we have—"

"Of course, Lady Anna," Kinor said smoothly, but strongly, his deeper voice riding over that of the heir's. "We will make sure that he knows all that happened." Kinor stepped back and half turned to face both the Regent and Falar. "Perhaps we should retire somewhere less . . . obvious." An apologetic but winning smile appeared on Kinor's face, one somehow reminiscent of someone, but of whom Anna couldn't have said at that moment. A quizzical look flitted across Jimbob's face, but vanished almost immediately as he and Falar followed the taller Kinor away from Anna's tent.

"Your son is quick," Anna murmured to the chief player. "I wish there were more like him."

"You are kind," Liende replied.

"No . . . he's a young man you should be proud of." Even though Kinor was not at all like Anna's own son Mario in appearance, both were sensitive to nuances and situations. She couldn't help wondering how Mario was doing in Houston. *If he were in trouble, Elizabetta would have said something. Wouldn't she?* Anna held in a sigh as she stopped before her tent.

"I am proud of him . . . but I worry that he will attempt too much too early in his life."

"We'll try to keep him from being a hero." Anna winced inside as she said the words. Once she had promised to keep Liende from battles.

"At times, my lady, our choices are few," Liende reminded Anna gently.

"I know." *Lord, do you know.*

The two stood silently for a moment. Lejun and Rickel silently replaced Blaz and Fielmir. Then Himar and Hanfor approached from the south side of the camp.

Once the two officers had joined Anna and Liende, the four entered the tent. With only one stool, Anna remained standing and gestured to Himar. "Why don't you tell Hanfor what we've found out?"

Himar nodded almost stiffly to the arms commander. "Ser . . . Rabyn has consolidated his forces, except for those around Westfort. We think the lancers there are all from Neserea. There are twentyscore or so at Westfort. The young Prophet holds the hills on both sides of the main road fifteen deks to the west. The south road to Fussen is five deks to our west."

"We took that road. Following young Falar, no doubt," replied Hanfor with a laugh. "Our scouts saw no Mansuurans and no Nesereans. For weeks their scouts have followed us." A second laugh followed. "We have tried to make sure they saw us." His face sobered. "Lord Ustal did not attempt to join forces with us or leave his hold. The Mansuurans left him alone."

"I wonder why," mused the sorceress. "They left lancers at Westfort."

"Those were the Prophet's Guard. You may recall that you did use spells on some Nesereans."

"You think that all the armsmen at Westfort . . . ?"

"The spell was to fear and respect you, not all Defalkans," Hanfor said.

And it was Darksong, though you didn't know it at the time. "The good news is that we have to deal with twentyscore fewer. The bad news is that we still have to deal with close to a hundred and fifty–score lancers, and another hundredscore in other armsmen."

The other three nodded soberly, and Anna realized that the good news/bad news humor didn't cross cultural boundaries, not so far as Liedwahr anyway. "You did not travel with many lancers, lady," Hanfor ventured.

"We did not have that many to bring." Anna's mouth quirked. "A lot's happened since you left Falcor."

"I presume that all went well in Ebra, else you would not be here."

"That went fairly well. . . ." Anna went on to describe the ride to Ebra, the battle against Bertmynn, the terms with Hadrenn, and then the return, with all the associated problems and disasters. "Oh . . . and I did repair the ford at Sorprat. But . . . you already know that."

"It is sad, but to do what you have done and to have lost less than tenscore lancers . . . most rulers would be hailed as workers of miracles." Hanfor fingered his beard. "Still, we must defeat this Rabyn quickly. We have heard the mighty drums. How will he use them in battle?"

"He's waiting for us to come to him," Anna explained. "He's set them up just below the hilltops in a way that the hard face of the cliff will amplify the sound. . . ." At the blank expressions surrounding her, she paused. "Hard and smooth surfaces reflect sound better—like an echo in a large building. Rabyn has used his sorcery to smooth the cliff face, and the drums are set up below them. That will strengthen the sound and send it against anyone approaching his camp from the east. There's a marsh or a swamp to the south, and with the hills set the way they are, the road is the only way to get there, with lancers and horses, anyway." She shrugged. "If we wait, or try to wait him out, then every lord in Defalk will be at each other's throat, or mine, and everything will fall apart." *Or is that what you want to think? Would waiting really hurt that much? Or do you just want to deal with Rabyn quickly?*

"Must you attack him so?" asked Hanfor.

Liende and Himar exchanged glances. Himar raised his bushy eyebrows. Neither spoke.

"We can't circle around and attack from behind. The way that he's sliced up the hills won't let us. If we try to reach them from behind, we can't get down. If there's any wind, then the players' instruments and my voice will get blown away." Anna paused. "What would you suggest?"

"Can you play in the darkness, chief player?" asked Hanfor.

"Yes, if need be," Liende replied cautiously.

"Lancers and armsmen only need protect you and the players, Lady Anna. What if you wrought your sorcery well before dawn?"

"I could do that." *Except you're still not a morning person.*

"Can you afford to allow the young Prophet to use his Darksong sorcery?"

"No." *Once again, it's not wise to be honorable or chivalrous or whatever.*

Hanfor bowed his head, but did not speak.

"Ah . . ." intruded Rickel from the door opening of the tent.

"I would not trouble you, Lady Anna, but Lord Nelmor is approaching."

"Let me think for a bit after this." Anna slipped from the small pavilion tent and walked forward to wait for Nelmor as he rode alone toward the Regent. The three that had been in the tent stepped out, following Anna.

The tall and rangy Nelmor was a towering figure in the saddle, especially in a saddle set upon a raider mount even taller at the shoulder than Anna's Farinelli.

Nelmor dismounted and bowed, not too deeply, but more than perfunctorily. His eyes fixed on Anna. "If I might have a word with you, Lady Anna, on a more personal matter, before we talk of the invaders."

Anna feared she understood. "Of course." She gestured toward her tent, then added to Hanfor and the others. "If you would excuse us for a bit?" She felt like she were an usher, moving people around. Then, that was something Jecks had handled in the field, and he was in Falcor, keeping another mess from occurring, and Kinor was keeping Jimbob and Falar occupied. *You hope.* She was hoping all too much these days.

Fielmir stepped up and took the reins of the raider beast, and Nelmor followed Anna.

Inside the grimy silk tent, she turned, waiting for Nelmor to speak.

"I received your scroll about my sister." Nelmor stopped.

"I'm sorry," Anna said softly. "I know you were close, although you did not speak of it."

"I do not fault you, but I am angry. Most angry. How did this occur?"

Anna looked straight into the cold eyes of the tall blond lord. "It occurred because a young man in Pamr decided to use Darksong to bend the will of the men of Pamr to his uses. He did not wish to be ruled by any lord, but he especially objected to the rule of a lady."

"Did you know this?"

"I suspected it, but when I came to Pamr, the chandler fled. I warned your sister, and I warned her captain. They thought that I was too alarmed."

Nelmor snorted. "Regent . . . when you speak . . . when you

warn, best all listen. That even I have learned." His eyes chilled and refixed on Anna. "You said that you had destroyed all the rebels. Might I inquire as to how?"

"I used sorcery. I had all of them flogged to death with fire whips from the sky." Anna kept her voice cold as Nelmor's eyes.

"All of them?"

"Every last man and boy in Pamr who followed the chandler. I also burned the chandlery to the ground. Then I used sorcery to restore the holding—except for the furnishings. That would require Darksong."

"Some have called you soft upon the peasants or the trades-folk. That I have never seen." Nelmor shook his head. "Last summer, Lord Birfels sent me a scroll warning that you were fair, but that you were vindictively just. He was most emphatic. I have begun to see why." The tall lord paused. "I cannot fault your actions. I had thought it would be so, but . . . I had to know." A grim smile followed. "I have no objections to Herene holding Pamr, nor to Ytrude warding Sargol's offspring." The smile softened. "Nor to my son's affection for the lady Lysara. He says that she bore a blade in her own defense. Be that so?"

"She used a blade for herself and to protect Lord Hryding's heir Secca. Secca's just ten." Anna added, "So did Ytrude. Both Lysara and Ytrude did well. Ytrude was slightly wounded, and refused to admit it. She just got a light slash on the arm, but it didn't stop her. She's fine now."

"You are changing Defalk, lady." Nelmor laughed softly, humorously, before again looking directly at Anna. "Tiersen worries about his love. Has he cause?"

"He has cause. I have done what I could. I *think* she will recover."

"And her strength after?"

Anna knew where Nelmor was headed, but her voice was level. "If she recovers, she'll be as healthy as Tiersen. He guarded her room until my guards could relieve him." Anna smiled. "They would make a good match."

"With your blessing and that of Lord Birfels—and my son's devotion—have I much choice?" Nelmor's smile was ironic.

Anna returned the expression. "Probably not, but I doubt that either he or you could do better."

Nelmor laughed, but the laugh faded quickly. "You know I have chased and harassed the Nesereans?"

"I do."

"We have slain perhaps twoscore. I would do more, but I dared not hazard my men too greatly."

"I understand," Anna said. "Dubaria doesn't have the riches of Synfal or Lerona." She offered a smile. "It has more courage than either."

Nelmor flushed. "Now that you are here, I offer my forces to your service."

"I accept them gratefully. We will try to defeat Rabyn with as few injuries as possible, and as soon as practical." *With effectiveness and no honor . . . even if you haven't quite worked out the spell you need.* "I was meeting with Arms Commander Hanfor and my chief player on that when you arrived."

Nelmor offered a smile, if a wintry one. "You knew of my concerns."

"I know you and your sister were close. I'm sorry."

"In these times . . . well . . . one hopes, but hopes are not always answered." Nelmor inclined his head. "I will settle my men."

"Then perhaps we can talk," Anna said.

"I am at your command, lady. At your pleasure."

"Thank you." Anna forced a smile. "I need to find Hanfor and my chief player."

Nelmor bowed a last time before leaving.

Anna did not have to look far. Even as she stepped out of the tent, Hanfor, Himar, and Liende stepped from under the nearest tree and began to walk toward her. From a spot midway between where the players continued to practice and the tree watched Kinor, Falar, and Jimbob. Anna noted their presence, but did not look in their direction.

Once the de facto council had regrouped in the tent, Anna once again addressed Hanfor. "When would you attack Rabyn?"

"Tomorrow at dawn would be best, save we have too many arms leaders who have but arrived."

"The morning after?" questioned Liende.

"If the sorceress feels she will be ready." Hanfor looked toward Anna. "Regent Anna?"

"I guess I'd better be ready." *Tomorrow will be another long day.*

84

Anna sat on the stool in her tent and dipped the quill into the inkstand on the too-small camp table. Despite the coolness of the morning, a droplet of perspiration fell onto her brown drafting paper, leaving an irregular circle and blurring the first two letters of the word "turn" into a black blot. She looked at the words on the paper once more.

> Turn to fire, turn to flame
> all Nesereans who revere Rabyn's name,
> turn to ashes, turn to dust,
> all those in blue . . .

Now . . . how was she going to end that spell? She put the quill in its holder and concentrated. After a time, she picked it up and wrote.

> . . . turn to ashes, turn to dust,
> those in blue Defalk can't trust. . . .

She winced as she reread the words. Besides the poor language, she didn't like the idea of a spell where a country was the one "trusting." *You have a very long morning ahead of you.* Even after she got the words of the spell completed, she'd have to use the lutar to check to see if the words and the note values matched. Sometimes, the sung words didn't work out the way she thought they would.

A dark slash went through the last line, and Anna set the quill down once more, trying to think of another way to word what she needed.

"Lord Nelmor to see you, Lady Anna," Kinor announced. The young man seemed to be taking over as a sort of chamberlain in the field, for which Anna was grateful.

Anna rose from the paper-strewn table and stepped to the front of the small tent, gesturing toward the tall blond lord. "Please come in." She remained standing, since the only places to sit were on her cot and the stool.

Nelmor bent to enter, then straightened, his head almost touching the silk roof panel. He glanced around the spare tent. "You travel light, Regent, especially for a woman."

Anna forced herself to smile. "Everything I don't bring allows more supplies or faster travel."

"Arms Commander Himar said that you would have to tell me how long before we might see battle," Nelmor ventured.

"The Nesereans have dug in on the hills. Did Hanfor tell you that?"

"He did."

Anna gestured toward the papers stacked not quite haphazardly across the camp table. "I've been working on the necessary spells. Once they're done, we'll attack. Rabyn's not about to move."

"The Prophet has far greater numbers of lancers."

"That's true," Anna admitted.

"Also . . . if your spells defeat the Liedfuhr's lancers as well as the Prophet's, will the Liedfuhr's honor not require him to attack Defalk?"

Anna smiled wryly. Nelmor had figured out quickly enough another part of her dilemma. If she were going to destroy the Nesereans, and if her spells worked, she'd also need something to stop the Mansuurans—and a fallback spell for them if her ways of halting them without killing them failed. "That could be a problem. I'm working on that, also. It seems like everything I try to do to make Defalk secure upsets *someone*."

"A weak neighbor invites conquest. A strong one creates fear. Rulers who see a weak neighbor becoming strong will try to stop that."

"I'm already being criticized by many of the Thirty-three for spending too much time and too many golds on foreign adventures."

"All northern lords, no doubt. They have not watched two

armies from the west pour through the Mittfels." Nelmor snorted. "They have not seen the Evult destroy all the lords of Ebra and then start to do the same in Defalk."

"Lord Ehara also sent lancers into the south, and then refused to admit he had," Anna added.

"Much good it did him." Nelmor's laugh was mirthless.

Anna let the silence draw out, then asked, "Would you consider accepting the title and duties of the Lord of the Western Marches?" She smiled. "And the one-third reduction in liedgeld that accompanies it?"

"The Lord of Westfort and Denguic has traditionally been the Lord of the Western Marches." Nelmor's tone was cautious.

"That may have been true, but Lord Jearle has made no effort to defend those marches. He avoided Lord Behlem's forces and Rabyn's," the sorceress stated.

"He could not attack twentyscore Neserean lancers—or more," Nelmor said.

"I believe the Lord of Dubaria had more to lose, and yet he made an effort," Anna pointed out with a smile. "And he didn't have the title of Lord of the Western Marches. Or the high walls and the golds from fertile lands."

"Lord Jearle would scarce take that well."

Anna nodded. "He would not, and I won't say anything to anyone until I've resolved matters with Lord Jearle. If he has no strong objections, would you consider it?"

"I would be honored, but I would not accept such an honor if it brought greater strife to Defalk."

"I appreciate your thoughtfulness and concerns, and I won't put you in that position." *Especially not after what my failures cost you and your sister already.* "We can't do much, anyway, until after we fight Rabyn."

"That is most true." Nelmor bowed. "I appreciate that you think so highly of me and of Dubaria." He laughed. "Though such an honor may come more dearly than one might wish."

"All honors do," Anna riposted, "including being Regent of Defalk."

Nelmor smiled. "By your leave, Regent."

Anna nodded, waiting until she was sure that the tall lord was well away from the tent. Now . . . for Falar.

Stepping out into the chill mist that had remained although it was approaching midday, she glanced around. "Lejun . . . Bersan . . . have you seen Kinor?"

"He was here but a moment ago," answered Lejun.

"Lady Anna?" Kinor trotted up from behind the tent. "Were you seeking me? Jimbob and I were studying the maps with Overcaptain Himar."

"I was wondering if you could find Falar for me?"

"He was down by the south tielines, above the stream. I can see if he is still there." With a smile, the redhead was off.

Anna went back to trying to recraft the defective spell, but had only managed to write and cross out the last line twice before Falar was announced by Lejun.

"You sought me, Lady Anna?" Falar peered into the tent.

"I did." Anna stood and motioned for him to enter. "You know that we'll be attacking the Nesereans before long. Certainly, within a few days. Have the arrangements that Hanfor has made worked out for you?"

"Your arms commander is very thorough, and we have benefited from his advice and from his armorer."

"Without Hanfor, strengthening Defalk would have been much harder." Anna hadn't even known that Hanfor had found an armorer, but she didn't smile at her arms commander's resourcefulness.

"I can offer but twoscore armsmen, not all proper lancers, even," Falar said. "We will all fight." He paused. "Hanfor has suggested that I act as one of your captains, between him and Himar."

"If Hanfor asked, he feels you can do the job," Anna said.

"It is foolish." Falar inclined his head. "Yet wisdom is foolish, too."

"At times," Anna agreed. "Lord Hanfor has suggested that your brother has remained within his walls even though the Mansuuran lancers ranged across his lands." The regent waited for a response.

"Worse than that." Falar snapped out the words. "The pigs have seized near-on a half-score of girls to pleasure that beast—and burned the dwellings and shops of any who opposed them. Yet Ustal has done nothing. He has not even recompensed the tradesmen for their losses."

Anna forced herself to ignore Falar's priorities. At least, the young man had some sense of outrage for the fate of the poor girls. "No one told me this. Not about the girls." From what she'd known of the young Prophet's parents, she wasn't surprised at Rabyn's actions, but she could feel her anger rising. *But this world gets you angry all the time.*

"My brother the lord remains behind his walls. He will do so until he can sally forth and triumph without danger."

Put that way, Ustal's actions made sense—for Ustal. "That would seem prudent," Anna said. "It's hard on the people, but it's prudent."

Falar glanced at Anna strangely, as though he could not believe her words.

"Is it prudent for me to plan an attack against nearly two-hundred–score armsmen with twentyscore?" asked Anna dryly.

"If you are a sorceress, lady." Falar bowed.

"If I am a successful sorceress," she corrected.

A smile crossed the would-be lord's face. "Success makes wise men of fools, and failure fools of wise men."

How true, and which will you be? Anna inclined her head. "Thank you again for coming, Falar. I will find some way to reward you and your men." She paused. "I may not change the succession of Fussen, but I do repay loyalty."

"All have said that." He grinned. "I cannot say I hoped for aught else."

Anna returned the infectious smile. "You may go, you scoundrel."

"By your leave, sorceress and Regent."

"You have my leave."

She shook her head after he departed. Falar was a scoundrel, but she usually read people right, and he was an honest scoundrel, and that was a great improvement over his brother. *And most of the lords of the Thirty-three.*

Her eyes fell to the stacks of brown paper, and the spells she had yet to finish adapting. With a long deep breath, she pulled up the stool and sat back down at the camp table.

85

NORTH OF FUSSEN, DEFALK

The Prophet of Music sits on a gilded straight-backed chair set before the table covered in blue linen. Nubara stands at Rabyn's left shoulder. To the left of the cloaked Mansuuran overcaptain and to the right of the Prophet are guards in blue, two on each side. All four guards watch as a slender brown-haired overcaptain in the maroon of Mansuur enters the large pavilion tent.

After brushing his boots, Relour steps forward on the carpet, then stops, and bows. "You requested my presence, Prophet Rabyn, and Hand of the Liedfuhr." With the last words, his head inclines to Nubara.

"We did," Rabyn replies. "The sorceress gathers her forces. She will attack soon. She has never been slow to act. The Dark-song drums are ready. How have you prepared?"

"We stand ready, but it is most unlikely that the Regent of Defalk will soon press an attack. Half those lancers rode in yesterday, and their mounts are tired, sire."

"She has been in her camp several days. So have many of her lancers. She doesn't need lancers and mounts for sorcery," Rabyn says, an edge to his voice.

"Nor do you, sire, but should sorcery prove wanting, or take longer, you need the lancers to hold the lines and take the fight to the enemy. You seek the best from your wiser officers, and so does the sorceress. She is known for that. Her officers will not wish to fight with tired mounts."

"You *may* be correct, but it will go ill with you if she attacks soon, and your lancers are unprepared."

"The Mansuuran lancers have yet to be caught unaware, sire. The Sorceress of Defalk will not do so."

"Good. You may go."

"As you wish. Good day, sire . . . Hand of the Liedfuhr." Relour bows and retires.

When the tent flap is closed, Rabyn turns in the gilded chair. "Have you found another wench, Nubara?"

"Not a willing one, honored Prophet." Nubara shivers within the heavy maroon woolen cloak. "The guards had to use your potion. She is in your tent, tied to the camp bed, as you requested."

Rabyn's eyes glitter. "Is she clean?"

"She has been bathed, massaged with rose oil, and anointed with perfume."

"Is that a scratch upon your neck, Nubara? I trust you did not pleasure yourself before your ruler enjoyed himself."

"No, most mighty Prophet. The girl's body is as we found her." Nubara laughs bitterly. "Your *other* potions have assured that you have no fear from me."

"That is as it should be."

Nubara's eyes turn hard and glitter, but Rabyn has already turned his attention to the goblet of amber wine he has poured.

"I wonder if this one will choose to do as I wish," muses the young Prophet. "Or if I will have to enjoy her in other ways." He turns his head in Nubara's direction. "What do you think, Nubara?"

"It would not be for me to say, honored Prophet." Nubara's eyes do not meet Rabyn's. "I would suggest that you leave her gagged until you are certain of her . . . inclination."

"You are so delicate, Nubara!" Rabyn laughs, cruelly. "I will take care not to let her upset your Mansuuran lancers. Or anyone else." He lifts the silver goblet.

86

The walls of the tent rippled in the cool wind, and Anna glanced up from where she sat on the camp stool, studying the spells, again, trying to ensure that she had the words firmly in her mind. She'd still carry the written words in her belt wallet just in case, but she thought she had them down. *You'd better. Just try to read them in the dark by candlelight.*

She'd used the mirror twice, but the Neserean camp remained the same, and she certainly didn't want to look at

Rabyn again. At the thought of what she'd seen, she could feel her heart racing, and her anger rising. *No wonder people got angry at absolute monarchs!* That a youth barely past puberty could be so sadistic with a girl!

She made a deliberate effort to unclench her jaw, then rubbed her forehead. She massaged the back of her neck with her right hand, concentrating on relaxing her breathing. After a time, she stood, deciding against snuffing the single candle in the short glass mantle before slipping from the tent. She stopped immediately outside the tent, between Rickel and Fielmir. The cool breeze was calming.

The earlier clouds had lifted into a high haze, and the twilight was already chill. Most of the lancers around the cookfires wore their tunics and wool jackets. The sorceress wore a jacket, but it wasn't fastened, and she wasn't cold, despite the stiff breeze out of the north. Kinor and Jimbob stepped toward her from the nearer cookfire, which served Anna and the officers.

"Have you eaten, Lady Anna?" asked Kinor.

"I ate a little while ago." She'd had to force down the fatty mutton, and it had taken nearly half a loaf of heavy bread, but she had imagined Jecks telling her to eat more, except the handsome lord would just have looked at her and gotten the idea across without a single word.

"It's greasy," said Jimbob.

"Everything cooked in the field is probably greasy or charred or too hot or too cold," suggested Kinor.

Anna smiled faintly. "Not always, but often." She looked at Fielmir. "Is Kinor right?"

"The food here is better than in many camps," answered the guard.

"But it's less than wonderful," Anna responded with a laugh.

She found herself walking away from the tent, realizing that Rickel followed and Lejun appeared from somewhere to join Rickel. She shook her head, and turned back. *You're nervous, that's all.*

"How soon will we fight the Prophet?" asked Jimbob.

"We'll have to be up early tomorrow. Very early." Anna eased back toward her tent, stopping close enough that the guards wouldn't be following her every step. "Then we'll see how things look."

"Have you seen anything in the mirror, Lady Anna?" Jimbob pressed.

"The Nesereans aren't moving. Not yet, anyway." She offered a smile. "Tomorrow we'll see."

Anna could see Hanfor walking from cookfire to cookfire, inspecting each, talking briefly to the cooks or subofficers, and then moving on. She knew where Hanfor had to be headed, but the deliberation with which he inspected each fire and talked with those there made his approach seem almost as if it were happenstance and a part of some elaborate and long-established procedure, just another routine. She appreciated the calming impact of his efforts, wishing she felt as calm as the veteran looked.

As Hanfor left the nearest cookfire, Kinor nudged Jimbob, then took the younger redhead's arm. "Let's see if there's more."

Anna smiled as Kinor hurried Jimbob away, watching as Hanfor eased toward her tent.

"Lady Anna." Hanfor bowed, then stepped up toward her.

Anna motioned for him to enter the tent, then stepped inside. She would have held the entry panel for him, but Hanfor—like Jecks—just would have taken the panel from her to allow her to enter first.

"Are we ready?" she asked.

"All your lancers stand prepared. Have you scried anything new?" His eyes went to the cased mirror resting on the end of the camp cot, then back to Anna.

"Nothing's changed." Her mouth twisted. "Except that . . . pervert . . . is abusing some poor girl. . . . It makes me want to attack now."

"Do you think such is his scheme?" questioned the arms commander.

Anna shook her head. "That's the way he is."

"Poor Neserea . . ." Hanfor smiled sadly. "Never would I have thought myself better off serving the ruler of Defalk."

"Maybe things will change after tomorrow."

"Not if the Liedfuhr would have his way." Hanfor stopped, as if cutting off all thoughts about the Liedfuhr. "I will lead the most skilled lancers to support you. The rest will remain two deks back on the road. Himar will hold those."

"What about Falar? Can his men be trusted?"

"He and half of them will be beside me, but I did not tell him the plan. I told him that we would start early and that you had requested that he and the best half of his armsmen accompany you and me."

"How did he take that?"

"He seemed pleased."

"And Nelmor?"

"The same. I asked that he hold the north flank so that it not be turned." Hanfor smiled. "He would perish rather than let that so happen."

Anna returned the smile, but the expression faded. "I'd like Kinor with me—Jimbob should accompany Himar."

"Kinor has a head on his shoulder, and that would be best, if the chief player agrees. As for young Jimbob, should aught happen . . ."

"If . . . the worst should happen, Himar needs to get the heir back to Falcor."

"I will tell Himar—tomorrow."

That also was probably best, Anna reflected.

"You know, Lady Anna, that many of the lords of Defalk will look askance at your attacking in the night." Hanfor laughed— one short bark.

"If we succeed," Anna pointed out.

"You will succeed. No matter the cost, you will succeed."

That was what Anna was almost afraid of. She couldn't afford too many more losses like those she'd been taking. *How about none?* "Let's hope it isn't too costly this time."

"I would hope that also, but the lancers will be deployed so they can ride to us quickly, if they are needed." Hanfor fingered his beard. "We do as we must in these days."

After Hanfor left, Anna glanced at the camp table where she had already set out the water bottle, the late blackthorn apple, the bread, the wax-coated cheese, and the knife. Whether she wanted to or not, she'd need to eat it all if she were to do sorcery even before dawn.

Then she moved the mirror off the cot and next to the side

panel of the tent before sitting on the cot and pulling off her boots. After a sigh, she leaned forward and blew out the candle. Then she slowly stretched out on the cot and pulled the woolen blanket around her. She hoped she could sleep.

87

Anna turned slowly on the narrow cot and her eyes opened into the darkness. Was it just after she'd gone to bed? Or later? How many glasses? She could hear nothing but the rustling of leaves beginning to fall to the grasp of the cold wind that presaged winter. Even that rustling died away . . . and then returned . . . and died away.

She turned over, carefully, because the light cot wasn't anchored that well, and a quick movement could upset the cot and dump her and her single blanket right onto the dirt. She'd discovered that before—several times. Then she closed her eyes and drifted once more into an uneasy sleep, waking up in the darkness again . . . and again . . .

It was almost a relief when she heard steps and voices outside her tent.

"Lady Anna?" Kinor's voice echoed through the darkness and into the Regent's tent. "Lady Anna? It is four glasses before dawn."

Anna groaned in spite of herself. Her throat was dry, and her head was pounding from allergies or asthma, and the memories of a dream she wasn't sure she'd even had—a girl she'd been unable to rescue from Rabyn, or someone like him.

"Regent?" Kinor's voice expressed concern. "Are you all right?"

"I'm fine. It's the hour that isn't . . . the glass, I meant." She rolled into a sitting position. "I'll be out in a bit."

"Ah . . . do you want me to check back?"

"You can if you want." Anna smiled to herself, but even that effort left her feeling like her face would slide right off her skull. Then, waking anytime much before dawn had always left her feeling that way.

Her feet felt too large even for her well-worn riding boots, or maybe her hands were just numb, but it felt like it took forever to pull on both boots. She had to fumble with the bread and cheese she had set out the night before, almost cutting her fingers instead of the heavy wax on the cheese. At that, she stopped, and took a long swallow of water from the bottle, then scraped the striker together half a dozen times to light the candle.

In the dim candlelight, she cut the cheese and broke off a chunk of bread. The dry ryelike stuff was already stale, but making softer dark bread wasn't possible without molasses, and carrying barrels of molasses wasn't exactly the best use of wagons and horses in the kind of war she was waging.

After she ate, she began the vocalises. She had to be partly warmed up before they were anywhere close to Rabyn's encampment.

"Heeee seees theee..." She doubled over coughing, straightening up slowly. The stomachache told her in no uncertain terms that the asthma was worse than normal. *Stress... that always makes it worse.*

It was still pitch-dark when she stepped outside the tent into a darkness and a near silence broken intermittently by shuffling boots, murmurs, and a very few hardy insects. The wind was colder than the night before, but lighter, barely a breeze. All her guards were mustered and waiting, from Rickel to the newest, Bersan.

So was Kinor. "Lady Anna?"

Who else? "Did you eat anything?" she asked Kinor.

"Ah . . . no."

"There's some bread and cheese left on the table. Finish it. I'll need your eyes to be sharp."

"Yes, Lady Anna."

Anna thought she saw a guilty look as Kinor slipped into the tent, but in the dim light cast by the torch held by Fielmir, she wasn't sure. Maybe it had been hunger. She shook her head, realizing that she had left both lutar and mirror in the tent. *Morning is not your time of day, not this early.* She ducked back into the tent, where Kinor was already finishing up the last wedge of the cheese.

"I forgot the lutar and mirror. And the pouch there."

Kinor swallowed hastily. "I'll take the mirror."

"Thank you." Once she had the lutar and the emergency food pouch with hard crackerlike bread and cheese, and the redhead had the mirror, Anna blew out the candle.

Hanfor and Himar had appeared by the time she and Kinor were back in the darkness outside the tent. She glanced heavenward. Clearsong had left the sky, but the small red disc that was Darksong was rising, just above the horizon. Anna wasn't sure she liked that. *Darksong rising? Where the moons are—that's just superstition.*

"Lady Anna, the lancers stand ready," offered Hanfor.

"As do your players." Liende stood so close to the two officers that Anna had missed her slight form initially.

The sorceress nodded, then realized that nodding wasn't that clear in the flickering light of the single torch. "Let's go—as soon as I saddle Farinelli." Once again, she was slowing things down, and she found herself walking quickly through the darkness toward the tieline that held the gelding. After a moment, there was a scuffle of feet and Bersan appeared beside Anna with a torch, leading the way.

Anna set down the lutar case and patted Farinelli on the neck. "I know it's early, but you don't mind it near as much as I do."

The big gelding didn't bother to answer, by *whuff*ing or whickering or any other sound, just standing there almost stolidly as Anna saddled him and adjusted the girths, then fastened the lutar and mirror behind her saddle, and the food pouch and water bottles in their holders. She mounted quickly, and eased Farinelli toward the torch that illuminated Hanfor.

Bersan followed her, still bearing the torch in one hand.

"As we planned, Regent, fivescore lancers will go all the way with us. The rest will be on the rise about two deks back to the east from the Prophet's camp."

Nelmor and Falar led their mounts toward Anna.

Politics again . . . at this time of night . . . She offered a smile, not sure either could see it, and reined up Farinelli. "Lord Nelmor . . . Falar . . . Hanfor has told me of your offers and your courage in facing the prophet of Darksong. I appreciate your being here, and your support for the Regency and Defalk. I will not forget it." *And that is true.*

"Lady and Regent," began Nelmor, "I am here because you have not stinted doing what must be done, and because you have faced the enemy as a warrior, first in the line of battle." The tall blond lord bowed his head.

"I, too, though no lord am I."

"Thank you both."

Kinor and Jimbob had quietly ridden up, but remained several yards back, almost lost in the darkness, especially Kinor on a dark mount.

Anna waited until Nelmor and Falar stepped back and mounted before she gestured. "Kinor . . . you will accompany me. Jimbob, I'd like you to accompany Himar. If anything should happen to me, you are to order him to escort you back to Defalk."

Surprisingly, Jimbob nodded. "I appreciate the honor of accompanying the overcaptain."

Was the heir finally beginning to understand? Anna hoped so.

Jimbob inclined his head and turned his mount, disappearing into the darkness, while Kinor flicked his reins to ease his horse closer to Anna's left side.

Another rider neared.

"The players are mounted and ready, Regent," Liende reported.

"Good." Anna coughed and cleared her throat. Even after the early warm-ups, her cords didn't feel totally clear.

"Not a sound once we leave camp!" ordered Hanfor. "Not one!"

The column moved slowly, deliberately, through the darkness, with only a bare handful of torches. The torches added little to the starlight, a starlight brighter than on earth, Anna thought, but perhaps augmented slightly by the reddish light of the moon Darksong.

Anna tried another set of vocalises, ones that weren't too loud. Her throat and cords were a little better, but she still worried. Hanfor's idea of a night attack directed at the Nesereans made more sense to Anna than another sorcery-based pitched day battle when Rabyn would have the drums waiting. Still, they'd have to be ready for the drums.

"Hanfor," she called.

After a few moments, the arms commander seemed to appear on his mount to Anna's right.

"If things don't work as we planned, I could need archers . . . bowmen . . . at any time. We talked about that, but . . ."

There was a soft chuckle. "Matters in battle never work as planned. Those lancers with bows ride directly behind the players, and I have told them to be ready to nock and lift shafts at my command—or at yours."

"Good. I hope we don't need them." *But you probably will.*

The sounds of mounts and hoofs seemed preternaturally loud to Anna, loud enough to tell the entire world that lancers were riding toward the Nesereans and Mansuuran lancers. She knew that the sounds didn't carry that far, and the wind was neutral, light and coming out of the north, rather than from the east behind them, so that it was unlikely to carry sound or the scent of horses toward the Prophet's camp.

Anna tried another soft vocalise, then coughed some.

Kinor leaned toward her, reaching across and lifting out her water bottle. She took it and swallowed. She started to put the bottle back, then reminded herself of the need to avoid dehydration, took another long swallow before replacing it. "Thank you."

A rider appeared out of the darkness, making his way toward Hanfor, then sliding his horse alongside the arms commander's mount. "The Prophet's camp remains silent. We are about one dek from the first rise. Birtol remains there, as you ordered."

"Himar will be by the other torch halfway to the rear. Tell the overcaptain that, and then return here."

"Yes, ser." The messenger disappeared into the darkness with the sound of hoofs on the road clay dying away quickly.

Anna peered into the darkness as the column rode slowly westward. While the shadows shifted, and the shapes rising out of the dark changed, she still felt as though she were riding nowhere.

After something less than a glass, another scout and his mount slipped out of the darkness and rode toward Hanfor. "Ser . . . the ridge is along the left of the road."

"Column halt." Hanfor murmured to the torchbearer, who dipped the flame twice. Hanfor seemed to stand in his stirrups, as if studying the night—or very early morning. He turned to Anna. "I will be back in a moment."

As the arms commander rode eastward along the barely defined shoulder of the road, Anna could see but faint blurs of darkness beyond the vague forms of horses and their riders. The air smelled of fall, damp leaves, somewhat moldy, even if most were still on the trees.

Several mounts *whuff*ed; others *whuffle*d; and low murmurs rose in the darkness.

Anna guided Farinelli back toward Liende. "How are you and the players doing?"

"We will be ready when summoned, lady."

"Thank you." Anna eased the gelding back up beside Kinor.

Shortly, Hanfor reappeared. "All is set. We go forward." He stood in the stirrups. "Douse the torches. Now."

In the darkness, Anna felt even more alone as she and Hanfor led the smaller group of lancers away from the supporting troops—along the road to the east. Were there fires or lights ahead to her left?

"We have but a half-dek before you begin," Hanfor whispered. "His sentries are four hundred yards to the east of the picket posts."

"So . . . it's more than a dek from here to his camp?"

"I would guess so."

Anna turned in her saddle. "Liende, we'll need to do the short flame song here, and then the players will have to remount and ride about a half dek before we do the main spells. The sentries are too far out for us to use the long spells effectively on the Prophet."

"We stand ready."

Anna wanted to sigh. She could understand Liende's reluctance, but without large armies and trained armsmen and lancers, what was a regent supposed to do?

"The short flame song, as soon as you can," she told the chief player. Then she dismounted gingerly in the bare illumination afforded by the bright stars—and Darksong—and handed Farinelli's reins to Kinor.

"Players into position," whispered Liende from behind Anna.

Standing on the road, on a clay that felt damp and a little slick, the sorceress squared her shoulders and took several deep breaths as the players arranged themselves.

Anna cocked her head. Were those voices?

". . . hear something out there?"

". . . swear there was a torch out there . . . gone . . ."

". . . who'd be out this time of night . . . ?"

"Now!" hissed Anna.

"The short flame song. On my mark. Mark!" ordered Liende.

The first bar was awful, but Anna had always insisted on having three bars as a standard before the song part of the spell began, and that foresight once again proved helpful, since, by the time she began the spell proper, the players were together.

> Silence in death, silence in fear,
> the sentries who watch for us to near. . . .

A dozen blue-white spears of flame flashed across the sky, even before Anna's last words. She didn't wait to see if the effect was as she'd hoped. Either way, they needed to ride forward to enable her to use sorcery.

"Mount up," Anna ordered, taking Farinelli's reins and climbing into the saddle, urging the gelding onward.

"Forward!" Hanfor's command conveyed urgency despite the low voice in which he had issued it.

The Regent couldn't even tell exactly when they passed where the picket posts or the sentries had been beyond that, except that she could sense . . . something . . . looming ahead. The feel of so many armsmen? The presence of Darksong sorcery?

"See . . . there are the low cookfires—the red glow," said Kinor from beside Anna.

She almost started in her saddle; in the darkness and her self-absorption, she'd forgotten that the young man had been riding beside her. She thought she saw figures moving before the campfires, although they were still a good quarter dek away.

"We need to hurry," Anna told Liende and Hanfor as she swung out of the saddle. She still had to hold on to the saddle rim for a moment to steady herself in the gloom. Handing Farinelli's reins to Kinor and stepping forward, she cleared her throat once, and then again.

Behind her, as each player dismounted, a lancer eased up and took the reins of that player's mount.

"Players into position," whispered Liende. "One note . . . tune . . . now!"

The single note wavered into the darkness, then strengthened.

"The long flame song, as soon as you can," ordered Anna.

"The long flame song, on my mark." Liende's dim figure moved closer to Anna. "When you are ready, Regent."

Anna cleared her throat, facing toward the dull mound that was the hill where Rabyn's camp lay. "Now."

"On my mark . . . mark!"

Anna concentrated on the music and called up the words.

> Turn to fire, turn to flame
> all Nesereans who revere Rabyn's name,
> turn to ashes, turn to dust . . .

> . . . bring down the Prophet with that flame,
> So none will e'er recall his name.

The sorceress found herself breathing heavily after the last notes died away. For a long moment, the night was hushed, totally silent.

The faintest shimmer of redness flowed from the star-speckled skies. Then the unseen chords of harmony vibrated through the cool air, chords felt only by a handful of people, Anna knew—mostly the players and those sensitive to sorcery.

Another timeless instant of silence followed.

Abruptly, a single set of drumbeats echoed into the night, just as arrows of white-hot flame cascaded from high overhead, down across the Neserean campsite, but near Rabyn's tent the arrows veered into a pyramid—leaving the tent and the drums untouched.

"Bowmen, stand ready with shafts!" ordered Hanfor.

"He's got his own sorcery," Kinor said.

Great! Anna tried to think. What could counter that Darksong sorcery?

The arrows of flame continued to fall across the upper part of the Neserean camp, and the invisible pyramid was illuminated in flame, but those flames fell away from the tent, whose blue and cream panels were revealed by the flow of flames.

The thunder of a single drum continued to boom into the

darkness. A second, deeper tone, joined the first, then a third, and the darkness flashed with sparks of light, as glowing black shieldlike globules rose from the Prophet's tent. Each shield smothered an arrow of flame, and both dark and light points of sorcery vanished, casting an eerie flickering of dark and light across the open space and the trees, erratically illuminating the hill behind the camp.

Yells and screams rose from the camps, and some of those screams were not from men, but from their mounts. Anna winced.

From the south, farther from the sorceress, Anna could hear orders being shouted. Before long, the Mansuurans would be ready to counterattack.

Waves of pressure, like sounds that had taken on the force of a slow-moving wind, began to press at her. Her ears felt as though she were far, far underwater, slowly being crushed. She could feel something like static electricity crawling along her arms.

You've got to come up with another spell—quickly. But what? Rabyn's triple-toned Darksong was blocking her flame arrows, and the darkness was creeping away from the tent toward her, with the increasingly stronger rhythm and volume of the Darksong drums.

Think! You've got to do something.

Anna shook her head against the pressure that enfolded her, that slowed her thoughts. She had a plan. She had spells. *What are they? Where are they?*

Her head throbbed, and her eyes blurred.

88

NORTH OF FUSSEN, DEFALK

A single unheard note wakes Rabyn, and he stumbles from his silk coverlet onto the smooth wool of the carpet that covers the ground. It is not dawn, and the cookfires should still be low coals for glasses yet, but he can sense an unseen chord nearing the tent, like a slow arrow frozen within the scope of a fraction of a glass.

He stiffens, then yanks on trousers alone and hastens to the front of the tent. Outside, the night remains dark. Rabyn shakes his head and steps out and around a lone Prophet's Guard.

"Sire?"

"Shut up!" His eyes traverse the darkness. A torch? Something? "Nubara! Get the drummers!" Rabyn runs barefooted toward the drums behind the tent. "Fools! You're all fools." He reaches the first of the man-high massive drums and pulls off the oiled cloth protecting it. " 'She won't attack so soon, honored Prophet' . . . fools!"

Nubara appears with his cloak wrapped over his bare chest as Rabyn yanks the oiled cloths off the second drum, and then the third. "Rabyn! What are you doing? Why—" A racking cough chokes off the remainder of his hoarse-shouted question.

"The bitch sorceress! You fools! You're all fools!" The young Prophet turns to the bare-chested and black-haired youth barely older than the Prophet himself and thrusts the carved wooden mallets into the drummer's hands. "The first rhythm! Now!"

Rabyn takes the second set of mallets in his own hand and climbs onto the high stool by the second drum. "Follow me!"

The first uneven rumbling rhythm rolls slowly into the darkness, creating an initial cacophony that quickly smooths into a more even flow, just as a pattering or hissing that calls up rain rains down from above the tent, but the air is cool and dry, not damp.

Rabyn does not look up from where he mans the second drum as flashes of fire flicker against the alternating blue and cream silk panels of the tent.

Nubara is frozen in place beside the tent and looks skyward, incredulous at what he sees in what should have been darkness overhead. Hissing lines of fire drop out of the sky, all across the camp of the Prophet. Like a sleepwalker moving to the beat of the drums, Nubara edges along the side of the tent.

The area around the drums seems like dawn or dusk, lit by fires falling from the sky, but veering away from the tent area. Beyond the tent, screams have begun to fill the camp area, its expanse a mixture of light and shadow created by the arrowlike flames that descend from the dark heavens.

Amid the flashes of light, darkness has begun to flare as well as fire, dark bolts of sound, not quite dissonance nor yet harmony, rising from the drums with each blow of the mallets. For several moments, the drumbeats merely create a low thunder, but that mounts to a rumbling greater than the volume of the drums themselves and continues to build into a deafening roar. Overhead, the flame arrows flicker, seem to dim, and there are fewer that flare across the night sky.

"How . . . did . . . she get so close?" gasps Nubara.

Rabyn ignores the question, handing the mallets he has wielded to the last drummer to appear. "Keep it up! Rhythm the first!"

Then the slender Prophet stands before the drums, facing eastward, and begins to hum, trying to find a note or pitch suited to employing the triple-toned drums whose rumbling beat has begun to shake the ground and vibrate the skulls of all within hearing distance. His clear if thin tenor rises over the shivering beats of the massive drums.

> Find, find, find where her sorceries abound.
> Break, break, break the harmony of sound. . . .

Blue fire creeps from the ground, from everywhere, and clothes the Prophet of Music as he melds his voice into the driving rhythm of the triple drums. Slender as he is, Rabyn appears taller, more solid, than the massive drum behind him, and darkness wells out from his chanting singing figure.

Clutching one of the exterior poles supporting the tent, Nubara looks at the shining figure of the young Prophet, cloaked in a shimmering nimbus of flickering blue, then at the three drummers, also shimmering in blue, if less intensely. Slowly, the Mansuuran officer draws the unadorned iron blade from his belt. He takes one step toward Rabyn, then pauses, trying to catch his breath. He takes a second step, then a third.

Nubara stands less than a yard from the Prophet, gasping, slowly raising the cold iron knife. He lurches forward, like a bent old man, but his grip on the knife is firm, even as his steps are not, and he thrusts the blade toward the darksinger.

Half-turning, as if warned, the shorter Rabyn lashes out with an arm cloaked in blue flame, flame that wraps around Nubara's arm. Nubara falls, toppling forward in those blue flames, a self-consuming pillar of blue fire that flares skyward, then subsides into glittering dust that flames for a time.

That intrusion is enough for Rabyn to momentarily lose his concentration, for his voice to falter over a mere handful of notes. And though his voice falters and for but an instant falls behind the rhythm of the triple drums, in that instant, the web of darkness that has protected the tent and drums shreds under the assault of golden arrows from the heavens.

Rabyn's eyes widen as the flames cascade down around him.

A dull *thud* announces that one of the drummers has fallen across his drum.

More arrows flash downward, and these bear heavy iron shafts, iron that glows and sings as it falls from the darkness.

One slashes through Rabyn's shoulder, and a second through his neck—and yet another pierces his chest.

". . . bitch . . ." His words gurgle to a halt in the rain of fire.

Beneath his twitching body, the ground groans, and shudders, and the clashing chords of Darksong and Clearsong rip even through the ears of those who have never heard the sounds of dissonance and harmony.

89

Anna stood in the alternating waves of light and darkness, trying to recall what she was supposed to do next. Unseen dark waves of sound—with the feel of something dank and evil—pawed at her as she stood motionless. Behind her, her players were equally frozen.

What can you do when his sorcery blocks your flame arrows? The question pounded through her head.

Her sorcerous arrows were *only* flame arrows. Perhaps the weight of real iron-headed arrows, boosted by sorcery, would be enough.

"The arrow song! The arrow song. Hanfor! Now! Have them loose the arrows, all they can!"

She could direct that sorcery and the arrows at the drums

themselves. Then . . . she'd need another spell . . . but that would have to wait. The drums . . . she had to destroy them, first. "Liende, the arrow spell!"

"The arrow song! On my mark . . . Mark!" called Liende, her voice strong, if slower than usual.

The players' first notes were shaky, but better than with the first spell, and melded together almost seamlessly within a bar. As before when she had faced the drums, Anna felt beaten down, depressed, and as though she were crawling out of a hole, and each word of the spell was forced. She kept her focus on the spell, just on the spell.

"Loose shafts! Toward the fires! Loose shafts, now!" ordered Hanfor, his voice carrying now that the element of surprise was gone.

As she began to sing, Anna concentrated on the image of the heavy arrowheads bursting through whatever barrier Rabyn had laid, and smashing through the drumskins, the iron glowing with glistening light, searing through the darkness.

> Heads of arrows, shot into the air,
> strike the drumskins, straight through there,
> rend the drums and those who play . . .
> for their spells and Darksong pay!

Anna held her breath, watching, then coughed, and tried to clear her throat, her eyes still on those lines of glowing red iron as the arrows climbed and then arched over the fires toward the tent of the Prophet and the heavy beating of the Darksong drums.

Eiiistttt!

Like they had become sparklers, each shaft began to sizzle with light as it neared the Prophet's tent. The first shafts, like the earlier flame arrows, winked out, but suddenly more than a handful seemed to accelerate.

A brilliant line of blue fire erupted from the Neserean camp, outlining in detail the alternating blue and cream panels of a large pavilion tent.

As the blue fire died, the heavy shafts loosed by the bowmen took on a brighter and more golden glow, then a sunlight incandescence as they dropped toward the drums and the tent of the Prophet.

Got to get Rabyn . . . can't let him do another spell like the last ones.

"More arrows! More arrows . . . the arrow spell again . . . !" Anna shouted.

She swallowed, then timed her entry to the spellsong, and directed her voice westward, toward the again dark tent and the Prophet who had to be there.

> These arrows shot into the air,
> the head of each must strike Lord Rabyn there—

The sorceress could hear the *thrum* of bowstrings and sense the release of the arrows.

> —with force and speed to kill him dead,
> for all the treachery he's done and led.

She staggered for a moment at the end of the spell, trying to catch her breath.

One more set of fire lines arched across the Neserean camp, and the lowest-pitched drum fell silent, then the others. The lower camp—that of the Mansuurans—continued to bustle with mounts and men.

While the light breeze continued out of the north, Anna could still smell a hint of charred flesh, and her stomach turned.

"Now what, Lady Anna?" asked Hanfor.

The sorceress swallowed. "We ride back to where the rest of the lancers are, and we get ready, if we have to, to wipe out the Mansuurans, if they decide to attack. That will give the players a little time to rest." She turned in the darkness that had again fallen across the road and the hillside. "Chief Player?"

"Yes, Regent."

"Have the players mount up. We'll rejoin the rest of the lancers. Once we get there, though, have everyone ready to play the long flame song. That's just in case." Anna rubbed her forehead, trying to massage away the pain in her eyes, ignoring the throbbing in the back of her skull.

"We will be ready." After a pause, Liende called out. "You heard the Regent. Pack your instruments and mount up."

"Green company! To the fore!" Hanfor's voice rode through the darkness.

After mounting, Anna took the water bottle Kinor extended, swallowing half of what was in it before turning Farinelli away from the still-burning Neserean camp.

". . . form a rear guard here until the Regent and the players are well away. Then you follow slowly, and rejoin us and the rest of the force. . . ."

Anna nodded at the sense of Hanfor's orders. He was always crisp and clear. She felt she muddled through everything.

"Are you all right, Lady Anna?" asked Kinor.

"Well as I can be." With her free hand, she massaged the back of her neck for a moment.

"Will they come after us?"

"I wouldn't, but who knows?" Anna eased her mount next to Hanfor's as the column rode at a fast walk back eastward along the road. Behind them, the company of lancers Hanfor had left as a rear guard formed darker shadows on the road, barely outlined by the coals and few flames of the Neserean camp.

"Hanfor . . . when you came to serve me, you said you would not lead armsmen into Neserea. Would you consider them leading you?"

"What might you mean?" Anna could hear the frown in the arms commander's voice.

"I don't want to spend the rest of my life fighting battles between Defalk and its neighbors. Rabyn had no heirs—not that anyone knows. I'm asking you to consider becoming High Counselor and ruler of Neserea."

The veteran swallowed, loudly even in the darkness, for the first time since Anna had known him. "Lady Anna . . . I am not a ruler. . . ."

"You've seen enough to know dishonesty and scheming, and you're honest enough to try to do a good job. And you are from Neserea. If they don't attack us, I'm going to ask the Mansuuran lancers to support you. And it may be that the Nesereans who are besieging Westfort might also be agreeable to that."

Hanfor laughed. "Those at Westfort are the Prophet's

Guards you bespelled in Falcor last year. They can do nothing against you, but whether they would follow me is a different question."

"Would you consider it?"

Hanfor bent his head. "I cannot say that it would not be good to return. Yet . . . will either the Mansuuran lancers or the people accept me?"

"We'll know about the lancers shortly. As for the people . . . most of the time, they haven't been the biggest problem in Defalk." *It's only in a democracy where people are the problem . . . because they have some power, and people with power always get into trouble? What about you?* Anna didn't want to deal with that question, not yet, anyway.

"We shall see, lady, but I do not think that many will see matters as you do," prophesied the arms commander.

Anna nodded in the darkness and reached for the cheese and stuff in the small food pouch. Perhaps that would help.

The faintest hint of gray was appearing in the east, and by the time the column rejoined Himar's forces, the predawn light was strong enough that Anna could turn in the saddle and study the players. Several, like Palian and Delvor, were clearly pale, but no one was about to fall out of the saddle.

Himar rode out to meet the column, his eyes surveying the riders nearing him. "How went it?" asked the overcaptain. "We saw the fires in the sky."

Hanfor looked at Anna.

"The Nesereans and those who followed Rabyn are dead. So is Rabyn, and his drums—he used Darksong—got burned up. The Mansuuran lancers . . . we don't know what they'll do yet."

Himar frowned.

"I didn't want to kill them and get the Liedfuhr ready to take over Neserea. Not yet, anyway. I'd like to try something else first."

That got a slow, if reluctant, nod from Himar.

"Can I borrow one of your grease markers and the sketch board? I need to send a message to the head of those lancers."

Hanfor said nothing when Anna dismounted and handed Farinelli's reins to Kinor. She walked to the lower side of the road and propped herself against an oak that still held most of its leaves. As the dawn brightened, she used Hanfor's grease marker and his sketch board as a desk while she slowly wrote out the message she wanted on the brown drawing paper.

Once done, ignoring the looks from Liende and Kinor, and even Hanfor, she read over the text once again.

> ... The Liedfuhr has pledged not to enter Defalk any-
> more, although he could not countermand orders from
> the Prophet Rabyn. I have spared you and your
> lancers—my price for sparing you is this. You will assist
> Arms Commander Hanfor—who loyally served Neserea
> until he was betrayed by the Prophet Behlem. Hanfor
> will be the High Counselor of Neserea, under the sup-
> port of both the Liedfuhr and the Regent of Defalk.
>
> The people of Neserea should not have to pay. ...

And what if the Mansuuran commander refuses? She took a long deep breath and rolled the scroll, looking at Hanfor, who had not dismounted, but continued to study the road to the west.

"Are they headed this way?"

"I think not, and the scouts have reported that they are sal-vaging what they can and packing their remaining mounts and wagons."

"I've finished this." Anna held up the scroll. "Will they respect a messenger?"

"Now that the Prophet is dead, I would say that they would." Hanfor shook his head. "We can send him under a parley flag."

"Would you?" She handed the scroll to Hanfor.

"If it means fewer men who die, the attempt is worth some effort."

"Thank you." Anna remounted Farinelli and rode the gelding to the tree-lined part of the hillside where the players had dis-mounted and were resting, instruments near at hand.

Liende glanced up inquiringly.

"So far, it looks as though they aren't coming our way." Anna cleared her throat. "We've made them a proposal."

Liende waited.

"I'm proposing a Neserean as regent of Neserea under both the Liedfuhr's and my protection. If they accept . . . then we work out the details." Anna moistened her lips. "If they don't, we'll have to work out another set of details."

And she needed to talk to Nelmor and Falar, to let them know about what she was proposing, or they'd feel slighted as well. At least, she suspected Nelmor would.

The sorceress took a deep breath. All she wanted was a nap . . . but she wouldn't get that, not for a while. She rubbed her forehead again.

90

Sometime before midmorning, a maroon-clad messenger under a pale blue parley flag rode slowly eastward along the road toward the Defalkan lines. His whole body posture bothered the sorceress. His eyes surveyed the purple-clad Defalkan lancers, and his shoulders were slumped. The parley flagstaff was jammed into his lanceholder, and the banner drooped in the clear windless morning air.

The steps of his mount slowed as he neared the Defalkans.

Anna mounted Farinelli and rode up onto the road to watch from almost half a dek away, and she found all of her guards mounted and surrounding her, as well as Kinor and Jimbob.

The wind had shifted to where it blew out of the northwest, carrying not only the faint odor of moldy leaves, but also the odor of fire and charred meat. Anna swallowed quietly, watching intently as the Mansuuran messenger rode toward them, each step of his mount seemingly slower than the last.

Rickel and Bersan brought their mounts forward, their shields high, partly screening Anna from any surprise attack. Kinor stationed his mount to Anna's left.

Hanfor nodded at a Defalkan lancer Anna did not recognize, and the Defalkan rode forward alone to meet the Mansuuran and to accept the scroll carried by the Mansuuran. After handing over the scroll, the Mansuuran saluted and turned back westward, spurring his mount into a slow trot.

"He's not happy," observed Kinor. "I'll get it."

"We won't be either. Thank you." Anna waited as the red-head rode to meet the lancer and take the scroll. When he returned, she accepted the scroll, unrolled it immediately, and began to read.

> Honored Regent of Defalk, Most Powerful Sorceress, Protector of Lands, Overlord of the East . . .

The compliments went on for three lines before the message became clear.

> Much as I would like to avoid unnecessary blood-shed, I am a loyal Mansuuran overcaptain and the arm of the Liedfuhr. I am not so empowered and cannot accept your request that I use my lancers to support a turncoat or to turn the Prophet's land over to one not of his lineage.

The signature was: "Relour, Overcaptain and Arm of the Liedfuhr."

Anna sighed. *Here we go again. Another stubborn male who would rather stick to his procedures and beliefs and have his troops killed than use common sense. Does he really think I'm going to allow lots of Mansuuran troops to stay in Neserea after all this?* "They're not interested."

"Will you destroy them?" asked Jimbob, who had eased his mount up beside Kinor's.

"I think I have to give them a chance."

"They would have given you none, lady," offered Hanfor.

"It doesn't matter. We'll still have to follow them for a while, at least until they're almost out of Defalk." She nodded to herself, half-smiling. There was no reason to kill the Mansuuran lancers. Not if she didn't have to, but there was certainly no reason to spare Relour. Loyalty didn't excuse stupidity—or arrogance. "I wonder what he was really thinking."

Hanfor laughed. "I would wager that Relour would be regent and ruler under the arm of the Liedfuhr. Like Nubara."

"You would attack them now?" asked Himar.

"No. We'll follow for a time. They're inside Defalk. I'm not

going to attack all of them, anyway." *Just Overcaptain Relour.*
"Not yet. Not until I've tried one other thing."

Hanfor nodded, and Kinor nodded in return. Jimbob merely
looked puzzled.

Anna did not shake her head, although she wanted to do just
that.

91

Ignoring the sounds of conversation and cooking coming
from outside the ever-dingier small silk tent, Anna looked
from Liende to Hanfor.

"You wished to talk with us?" asked Hanfor.

The walls of the tent rippled in the momentary breeze, and
stopped moving. Anna cleared her throat, then took a long
swallow from the water bottle. "Sorry. My throat gets dry with
all the road dust." She cleared her throat a second time. "Yes, I
did. I wanted to talk about the Mansuurans. If we leave the
Liedfuhr's lancers in Neserea, we'll have the same problem in
another year. Two at the most."

"You wish to destroy them after all?" asked the veteran, fingering his gray beard as he did when thinking or nervous. "You
destroyed near-on a hundred fifty–score of the Neserean
lancers and armsmen Rabyn raised."

"That leaves almost a hundredscore lancers, and that makes
them more powerful than the armsmen left in Neserea."

"Are they not better trained?" asked the chief player.

"Far better," Hanfor acknowledged.

"Tonight, we'll try something," Anna said.

Hanfor raised his eyebrows.

"Do you have two or three lancers who can send a heavy
arrow farther than the others?"

"A half-score would be better."

"We'll get as close as we can, and I'll use the lutar to enchant
a few shafts."

"You would kill the overcaptain? That will not persuade the

captains under him," Hanfor predicted. "They would regard that as cowardice."

"Then, I'll remove them one by one until some idiot gets the message."

Liende smiled sadly. "There will be many you may remove, and before you get that far, one will order the lancers to attack us."

Anna felt like throwing up her hands. "What am I supposed to do? I spared the Mansuurans because they didn't start this mess, and because I wanted to make a gesture to the Liedfuhr. But they aren't exactly helping things either."

"They would regard that as treason . . . unless they had no choice."

"Then . . . maybe, we won't give them any choice," Anna said.

"If you attempt this, do not essay it too often," suggested Hanfor. "Or they will attack, and you will not be prepared to destroy them, for there is every chance that is what you will have to do."

"Can we try this once?" asked Anna.

Hanfor smiled. "Once . . . they will not expect, not after you have let them escape."

"And then what?"

"They will turn and attack, tomorrow morning."

Anna sighed, then looked at Liende. "Can you have the players ready with the long flame spell and the arrow spells?" *Always the flame spell, and always the innocents die because of the arrogance and stupidity of their superiors. Including you . . .*

"We will be ready. Like you, I would wish otherwise, but I do not see such." Liende offered the sad smile that Anna had seen too often.

"Neither do I." The Regent looked at Hanfor. "Do you?"

"As I said, Regent, they will not accept aught you offer that does not leave them in control of Neserea, and that you and Defalk cannot accept."

"Tonight then. They get one chance." *Which is more than people have usually given you.*

92

WEI, NORDWEI

"You summoned me, honored Counselor?" Gretslen's voice is low, and she bows deeply as she approaches.

Ashtaar remains standing, but gestures toward the straight chair before the flat table-desk. "You may sit."

Gretslen sits, her eyes darting nervously from the black agate oval on the flat polished wood to the spymistress, then to the window, and back to Ashtaar.

Ashtaar still does not speak, but walks to the wide window that is open, the hangings drawn back to reveal the sunlit hillside that overlooks the river, and the rebuilt bridges above the port itself. After a time, she does speak. "What is Wei, Gretslen?"

The hard-eyed blonde seer moistens her lips, once, twice, before she finally replies. "It is the capital of Nordwei. It is a great trading city."

"No." Ashtaar's voice is cold. "Wei is an idea. All cities are ideas. They exist because people believe that being in a city is better than not being in a city. What is the idea behind Wei?"

"That . . . all can benefit by free trade among all cities?"

"You remember that from lessons. Nonetheless, it is true. Wei is more than that, but that is one idea on which it is based. Now . . . why is the Sorceress and Regent of Defalk so dangerous?"

Gretslen frowns, and her brow wrinkles, but she does not reply. She moistens her lips once more.

Ashtaar turns from the window, her eyes on the seer, waiting.

"Because she will unite the south of Liedwahr, and will have the power to invade and destroy Nordwei?"

Ashtaar closes her eyes, then opens them. "You can do better than this, Gretslen. If you cannot, I will make Kendra the head of the seers."

The blonde licks her lips again. "I do not understand. I have worked hard. I have reported faithfully."

"You have done all that, and more. What you have not done is think." Ashtaar turns back to the window. In time, she turns once more and faces Gretslen. "Tell me exactly what has happened in Defalk."

"The sorceress has ignored the rebellious lords in Defalk. She has used her powers to destroy Lord Rabyn. She has not destroyed the Mansuuran lancers, but she follows them westward."

"Now . . . does the sorceress have the power to destroy the Mansuurans?"

"Yes, honored Counselor."

"Is the sorceress stupid? Or mad?"

"No, honored Counselor."

"Then why did she not destroy them when she could?"

Gretslen's hands curl into fists. She does not answer. Finally, she speaks. "I could not say, honored Ashtaar."

"That is certainly correct. You cannot."

Gretslen cringes at the scorn in Ashtaar's voice.

"You cannot," the spymistress continues, "because you cannot or will not understand. What is dangerous about the sorceress is not her power alone. Nor is it what she believes. It is that she believes and that she will use her power to accomplish what she believes. Now, why did she not destroy the rebels in Defalk first? Because she is intelligent enough to know that they cannot match her face-to-face and because Rabyn and the Sturinnese were the greater threats. Why does she not destroy the Liedfuhr's lancers?"

"Because she wants something more?"

Ashtaar finally nods. "You must find out what she plans. In Dumar, she molded the succession to support her. In Ebra, she used her power to elevate Hadrenn—but under her control. There is no succession in Neserea, and logically, she should have wiped out the Mansuuran lancers to send a message to the Liedfuhr. She did not. She is not like Behlem's Cyndyth, toying with folk. So . . . she has a deeper reason. You must find it, and before it is too late." Ashtaar laughs. "Or the Council will have to consent to any reasonable agreement she proposes."

"To the sorceress?" blurts Gretslen.

"Certainly not to Konsstin. The Liedfuhr is shrewd, but his ideals are limited. Hers, I fear, are not." The spymistress gestures. "Go. Think upon what I have said, and discover what she seeks beyond victory."

Gretslen stands, bows, and backs out, as if pleased to escape Ashtaar's wrath so easily.

The spymistress returns to the window, where she surveys the city that is Wei, the city built on one ideal.

93

Farinelli *whuff*ed once, tossing his head, when Anna flicked the reins to begin the evening's journey from the encampment and the torches that marked it. The sorceress glanced overhead, but the only stars visible were to the south, beyond the slow-moving heavy clouds that had moved across the sky from the northeast earlier in the day. The wind was cool, but not as chill, and there was a dampness in the air that suggested mist or rain.

According to the maps and the images Anna had been able to call up in the traveling mirror, and from what Hanfor's scouts had seen, the Mansuuran forces were camped literally on and around the road to Denguic, not more than twenty kays east of Denguic. The camp itself was on both sides of the road, with pickets more than a half-dek from the center, and scouts stationed farther out.

So Hanfor and Anna had looked for one of the side and back roads—and found one that wound within a quarter dek of the south side of the Mansuuran camp. It wasn't patrolled, probably because there was a steep and wooded gully that separated the lane from the camp, clearly impassable to mounts and lancers. Since Anna had no intention of trying to ride into the camp, the side road would suffice for what she needed to do.

"The ride there will take two glasses, I think," Hanfor said from where he rode on Anna's left. "By then, most lancers will be sleeping."

"And it will take half a glass to get from where the road splits to where we'll release the arrows?" Anna glanced back behind Kinor to see how close her guards were, but Rickel's eyes were on the road.

"Perhaps longer."

In the darkness Anna nodded and shifted her weight in the saddle, deciding that late evening was far better than dawn for a sorcerous raid. She reached back behind the saddle with her left hand and touched the lutar case to make sure that it was there. She had tuned it earlier, but whether the instrument would retain any semblance of tuning after the ride ahead was another question.

For a time, the sole sounds were those of horses breathing and hoofs striking the packed clay of the road, with the only direct light coming from the torches held by every tenth lancer or so.

"Lord Jimbob wished to come," Kinor volunteered.

"Did you suggest it would not be wise?" Anna asked Hanfor.

"I told him that for both the heir and the Regent to be riding toward an enemy in the darkness was unwise." Hanfor chuckled. "I also said that it was possibly unwise for you, but that I had no desire to be called to task for losing both of you. Especially by Lord Jecks."

"How did he take it?"

"Well enough. I let him accompany me as we prepared, and I explained all I could. I also asked for his trust in not revealing the plan to others."

"Good," Anna replied. "That's the sort of thing he won't learn around Falcor or any lord's hall." She smiled to herself. "We could do with a hall ourselves, right now."

The column continued westward, the silence renewed.

"Why do you not quarter yourself with one of the Thirty-three?" asked Kinor quietly, as if to break the silence. "Do they not owe you that?"

"The three closest lords to where we are, if I can read the maps correctly, are Jearle, Ustal, and Klestayr," replied Anna. "Jearle's to the west of the Mansuurans, and Ustal's too far south. Klestayr—it's not that convenient. . . ."

"And you trust him not?"

Anna wanted to laugh. The number of lords she trusted could be counted on fewer than two hands. Still, that was up from less than one hand a year earlier. "Let's say I'd rather not put my fate—or Defalk's—in his hands."

"Menares says that such has always been the curse of Defalk," ventured the lanky redhead.

"Ambition has been more the downfall of realms than poor ruling. Leastwise, from what I have seen." Hanfor eased his mount forward, as if to avoid the appearance of crowding Lejun, the guard riding back and to the left of Anna.

"I'm not sure anyone has ever been able to rule Defalk," Anna quipped in return. "Most of the lords I've met don't want a ruler. They want a figurehead to let them do what they want."

"You are not like that, Regent," said Kinor.

"I'm also the least popular ruler in generations . . . least popular with the lords, anyway." She frowned to herself. Was it just the lords? The rivermen hadn't cared much for her decisions, nor had the chandlers in Pamr, nor the crafters of Falcor. Was there really anyone who liked what she'd tried to do?

"A wise armsman trusts the most popular rulers not at all, lady," offered Hanfor. "The mob and the lords are bought with armsmen's blood, more oft than not."

"That's true in other . . . lands as well." Anna had almost said "worlds." Hadn't Kipling, that great British poetic exponent of imperialism, said something like that? She tried to remember. She'd heard Michael York give a reading of Kipling once, and it had been interesting, truthfully trite, and sometimes most depressing, especially "The Gods of the Copybook Headings." Did it have to be true that people always forgot the hard lessons once the troubles were past? That they always went back to the leaders that beguiled them with warm fuzzies and comforting nothings?

The silence dragged out once more, as Anna retreated into her own thoughts.

"Lady . . . you have been silent . . ." Kinor ventured after they had ridden a good dek farther westward, toward the side road and the sorcery she hoped would avoid greater slaughter, and that she feared would not.

"I'm just thinking." That was true enough.

Neither Kinor nor Hanfor spoke again for a time.

Anna listened, but winter was definitely approaching, and the insect twitters and night birdcalls of the summer and early fall had died away to nearly nothing. The only consistent sounds were those of the mounts that carried her lancers westward.

Hanfor cleared his throat, easing his mount closer to Farinelli and Anna. "Regent Anna, here is the turn . . . where the backup lancers will wait." Hanfor had insisted on bringing two backup companies of lancers, to leave them where the side lane split off from the main road, just in case.

He was probably right, reflected Anna, but it was getting as though she had to have a small army to go *anywhere*. Then, she probably did. "All right. Then we stop for a moment?"

"Yes." Hanfor nodded, then called, "Lancers halt!"

The command was relayed through the darkness.

"Weylar!" ordered the arms commander.

"Ser." A blond-bearded captain rode out of the dimness toward Hanfor and reined up, offering a half bow from the saddle.

"You hold the fork here. If the Mansuurans should come with all their forces, ride after us. If a small force should come, make sure none return. Otherwise, wait for us. We may be as long as three glasses, and as brief as one."

"Ser. As you command."

"As the Regent commands," Hanfor added.

"Yes, ser. Yes, Regent."

"Thank you, Weylar," Anna added. "I appreciate it, and we'll try to be quick."

"We'll be here, Regent."

"Thank you," Anna said again.

"Green company, forward!"

The sorceress felt even more alone as the smaller group pressed on. Alone? *Would you ever have considered being with twenty men alone? Then, would you ever have thought that you would be riding along a dark lane to rely on your voice alone to protect you against more than two thousand men armed with lances and sharp blades?*

"Lady . . . we should burn no torches from here on."

"I agree."

"If you will escort the Regent for a few moments." Hanfor addressed the request to Kinor, and his words were more order than question.

"Yes, Arms Commander."

Anna glanced back, and could almost see Hanfor's progress as torch after torch winked out. Rickel and Lejun eased their mounts forward until they rode before Anna and Kinor. Both guards had unstrapped the protective shields and now carried

them on their forearms, but partly supported by their lancehold-
ers.

"Dark it is without torches or stars," observed Kinor.

"It's not too bad," Anna replied. "At least, if we don't run
into anyone."

Hanfor returned, easing his mount back into place on Anna's
left. "It will be slower this way, but safer."

*Safer from attack, but let's hope there are no huge potholes
in this lane.*

Anna began a series of soft vocalises, trying not to be too
loud, but knowing she wouldn't be able to sing a spell, even a
single one, without at least some warm-up. Even so, it was a
good thing it was evening and not morning.

The riding was slower along the side lane that wound away
from and yet paralleled the main road, and Anna found herself
straining her eyes to look past her guards and into the dimness
ahead.

"They do not know that this lane winds within a quarter dek
of their camp, because of the wood," Hanfor said quietly. "Still,
once you have done what you must, we need to ride quickly.
They will be most angry."

Anna suspected that was an understatement. Still . . . she had
to try to get the message across that she was willing to be reasonable—and that those who wouldn't see reason would see
force.

"Regent." Hanfor's voice was low.

"Yes."

"To the right, just above the trees."

Anna followed Hanfor's directions, looking uphill. They
hadn't been able to tell elevations from the mirror scrying, but
it was clear that the side road was a good twenty yards or more
lower than the low rise on which the Mansuurans had camped.
There were several widely spaced points of lights, fires, and
other smudges of light wavering in the darkness. "That looks
like their camp. It's a good thing we put out the torches."

"Very good." The hint of an ironic laugh colored Hanfor's
words. "Green company, halt." His words were low, but
intense.

Anna dismounted and handed Farinelli's reins to Kinor, then
took the lutar from its case and checked the tuning, fumbling

more than she would have liked in the darkness. Rickel and Lejun remained mounted, flanking her on each side, but leaving her a clear path toward the Mansuuran camp.

"Bowmen . . . string your bows and stand ready," Hanfor ordered. "Aim your shafts high and toward the fires beyond the trees. Nock your shafts when the Regent begins to sing, and then release them after you count to ten in a whisper. Remember, nock when she sings. Count to ten and release."

Anna faced the fires that suddenly looked all too close, despite the trees, the gully, and the hill. Then, she took a deep breath and released it, lifted the lutar, began the chording, and then the spell itself.

> These arrows shot into the air,
> the head of each must strike proud Relour there—

As the sorceress heard the *thrum* of bowstrings, she concentrated on the images and the last words of the spell.

> . . . and turn to fire, turn to flame
> Overcaptain Relour, for all his fame.

The chords of the lutar and Anna's voice died away. She slipped the lutar into its case, fastened it in place, and climbed into the saddle.

Was there a flash of light to the northwest? Anna wasn't certain, but there was no reason to try to find out until they were back with her own forces, and with the players. Either they would face the Mansuurans on the next day—or they wouldn't.

"Are you ready, Regent?" asked Hanfor.

"I'm ready. Let's go."

"Green company, forward!" Hanfor's voice carried tension, tension Anna could well understand.

She kept glancing back over her shoulder at the fires of the Mansuuran camp, but so far as she could tell, nothing changed. If it did, she could not see it. As she rode, she groped for the food pouch, stuffing some squares of cheese into her mouth, and then some of the hard cracker-bread, which she had to moisten with swigs from the water bottle in order to soften the stuff enough for her to chew and swallow it.

But she had looked back often enough that, by the time they rejoined the other lancers at the main road, her neck and shoulder were stiff.

"Weylar?" Hanfor called.

"Ready here, ser." The subofficer rode forward into the light cast by the torch carried by the lancer accompanying Hanfor and Anna. "Not a soul came down the road. Didn't see a torch. Not one."

"Good. Have your companies fall in behind. Send a messenger up to me if you see any torches or hear any riders."

"Yes, ser."

Rickel and Lejun had dropped back behind Anna and Kinor. They had strapped the big shields behind their saddles. Anna wasn't sure how they managed to hold the shields for so long as they did, but none of the guards had ever voiced a complaint.

"Do you know . . . if . . . ?" Kinor finally asked.

"I think so. I don't know. We'll have to check in the mirror when we get back." Anna yawned. Youth spell or not, she was tired, and she probably wasn't going to get much sleep. Not if Hanfor happened to be right.

The ten-dek ride back to her own camp had taken forever, or so it seemed, and Anna kept wondering when the sun would rise.

She slowly dismounted from Farinelli, removing the lutar and food pouch, and the water bottles. Then she unsaddled the gelding, rubbed him down too briefly, and picked up the lutar and pouch. She walked slowly back toward her tent, between Kinor and Hanfor, with Lejun and Rickel following.

"We need to see what we'll face in the morning."

"That would be best," Hanfor agreed.

"All went well?" asked Liende as she approached the three, but with her eyes upon Kinor.

"So far as we know." Anna had no doubts that the chief player was at least as concerned about her son as about the results. "Join us. We're going to find out."

Fielmir and Bersan were on guard, waiting.

Anna nodded to the two, then stepped past them, into the small tent. "Let's see." She lit the candle on the camp table, then opened the case and removed the traveling mirror, setting it on the table. Next came the lutar, which she had to tune once more, slowly because she was tired.

She glanced around at the three other faces, each as fatigued as she felt, before she started the scrying spell.

> Show us now, in place and frame,
> he who bore Relour's rank and name. . . .

The mirror silvered and then reflected the candle beside it on the camp table, before darkening and revealing another scene. A single man-shaped length of black lay stretched on the ground beside a tent. Four guards formed a square around the corpse. Flickering shadows crossed the area lit by a half-score of lancers bearing torches.

Anna sang the release couplet and sighed. "You were right. We'd better be ready early, you think?"

"I already sent out scouts, and they will watch through the night," Hanfor said. "Their lancers are tired, and many were asleep. If they attack, it will be early, but I doubt they will wake their lancers tonight. If they do, we will be warned."

"I have made sure the players slept close together, and close to their instruments," Liende said.

"Thank you."

Anna turned to Hanfor. "If they do not attack, I'll send another scroll, asking that they support you."

"They will not." Hanfor nodded slowly. "They will all die before they would surrender Neserea."

"They don't have Neserea," Anna pointed out. "And they certainly won't if I have to kill off all their lancers."

"They will not accept that, for all they have seen, until it is too late."

"Why? Because they're more afraid of the Liedfuhr than me."

"He is a man, and you are a woman. This is Liedwahr." Hanfor shrugged.

"So I have to be twice as ruthless?" Again, she wanted to scream, but refrained. "And then, because they won't listen, I'm the bitch of the east, or the evil sorceress of Defalk?"

"You ask of me what I see, not what I wish," Hanfor said reasonably.

"I know." Anna took a deep breath. "We'll just have to see what tomorrow brings."

After the other three left, Anna sat on the middle of the cot, holding her head in her hands. *No matter how or what you try . . . it always comes back to force. Machiavelli was right.*

She took a deep breath, then bent farther forward and pulled off one boot, then the other.

94

With the cold sunlight striking her tent, Anna woke with a start. *What time is it? Are the Mansuurans coming? Why didn't someone wake me?* Her eyes were gummy, her mouth dry, and her head was pounding.

Dehydration—you didn't drink enough water last night. She forced open her eyes and groped for the water bottle she kept near the cot. With her lurch, the cot began to tilt, and she had to scramble up to keep from being tipped onto the dirt.

"Lady Anna?" The voice was that of Blaz.

"I'm fine," she lied. "Just clumsy. Has Arms Commander Hanfor been up here yet?"

"He came up a while ago. He said to tell you when you woke up that nothing had happened yet."

"Thank you." She paused. "Would you have someone tell him that I'll be ready in a while?"

"Yes, Lady Anna."

Anna drank all that was left in the water bottle that had been by the cot—about two-thirds of it—hoping that the headache would subside before long. She wolfed down the few fragments of bread and cheese left in the pouch, not caring much that the cheese was hard and stale and the bread even harder.

Then she retrieved the bucket of water one of the guards always set outside her tent, and splashed off the worst of the dust and grime, and completed all the other necessities before pulling on her clothes and boots. She brushed out her short hair as well as she could, trying to ignore the headache and clogged sinuses that bedeviled her almost every morning.

"Lady Anna?"

"Yes . . . ?"

"I have some breakfast," ventured Kinor.

"Come in. I'm decent." She tried not to growl. It wasn't Kinor's fault that she wasn't at her best in the mornings, especially in the field on short sleep and continuing worries.

The redhead entered with a basket—with warmish bread and cheese wedges and a battered apple. "After last night, lady, with sorcery needed this morning . . ."

Kinor looked so apologetic that Anna laughed before speaking. "I won't take off your head. I'm not at my best in the morning, and it's worse when I'm tired. But it's not your fault." She paused, then took a large chunk of bread from the basket. "You take some, too. Your eyes are pinkish, and that means you haven't had enough to eat."

"Ah . . ."

"Take some," Anna insisted.

Kinor broke off a small portion. He tried not to wolf it down, then looked up almost guiltily.

Anna grinned, but not widely or she would have had crumbs falling all over her shirt and purple vest. She set the basket on the corner of the camp table and took out the wedge of cheese, slicing it into thinner sections. She took two sections and motioned for Kinor to have some. "Go ahead."

The redhead hesitated, but Anna gestured a second time. She didn't have to insist a third time, and they both ate. Anna and Kinor had almost finished both bread and cheese, and it hadn't taken long, when she heard someone nearing.

"Lady Anna?"

She recognized Hanfor's voice. "Come on in. I'm trying to gulp down some food."

"Regent." The weathered warrior stepped into the tent and bowed. "The Mansuurans—all of them—are riding toward us. They will be here in a glass. I have ordered the men onto the road and ridge just to the west of here.

"You could have awakened me earlier," Anna suggested, after taking another large mouthful of bread and cheese.

"There was no need." Hanfor bowed, apologetically. "The chief player and I wished you to be as rested as you could be."

"Thank you." *Do you look that bad?* "I'll be there in just a bit. I'll warm up here, and then ride over." Anna paused. "Did you tell Lord Nelmor and Falar?"

"I informed them that the Mansuurans had rejected your terms and were attacking. Both stand ready to hold with us. I thanked them for you."

Anna sighed. That was something she should have done. "Thank you. I should have done that, but I appreciate it."

"You needed the rest, and even those two see such." Hanfor glanced at Kinor, bowed, and slipped out of the tent.

Kinor straightened, brushing crumbs from his face, and looking even more guilty than before. "Best I get the mounts ready."

Alone in the tent for a few moments, Anna tried a vocalise. "Holly-lolly—" The coughing was especially bad, and she doubled over, struggling to hold her bladder against the violence of the spasms.

"Damned asthma . . ." Slowly she straightened up and tried to clear her throat without triggering another coughing attack. She glanced around, but the water bottles were all empty. She'd been too tired to do a spell to get herself clean water the night before, and too forgetful.

After another vocalise, she decided she could risk a small spell, the one to clean the water, and picked up the lutar.

Cool clear water in this pail . . .

She managed to hold off the tickling in her throat and the gunk in her lungs long enough to complete the spell. After more coughing, she drank some of the cool clean water, then refilled all four water bottles. After one more vocalise, she pulled on her battered brown felt hat, swept up the water bottles and the lutar, and stepped into the cool hazy sunlight outside the tent.

"Ah . . . Lady Anna, I could carry the bottles," offered Blaz.

"Thank you."

The walk to the tieline and Farinelli was less than fifty yards. The big gelding *whuff*ed as Anna neared.

"No, you won't be left alone. And you will get ridden." She saddled him with a deftness she wouldn't have believed possible for her two years earlier.

Kinor came running, bringing a bulging food pouch. "Here, Lady Anna." He tendered it to Anna, then mounted quickly.

Preceded by Rickel and Lejun, and followed by Kinor and Jimbob, and then all the rest of her guards, Anna rode slowly to the slightly higher ground where Liende had already gathered the players.

"We are ready, Regent."

Anna nodded. "It will have to be the long flame song." *To destroy more innocent armsmen for higher goals . . .*

The chief player, whose red hair had become mostly white in the few years since Anna had come to Defalk, did not quite meet the Regent's eyes.

"I've tried, Liende. But we can't lose any more armsmen," Anna said. *And any spell that would enchant them would be Darksong and probably kill you and the players with the back-lash.* She wanted to shake her head—another example of ignorance. If she hadn't used Darksong so often and so unwittingly when she had first come to Liedwahr, then she might have been able to use it now.

Anna dismounted slowly, then began another vocalise— carefully. "Heeee sees theeee . . . he sees . . . thouuu . . ." She had to cough, but her reaction wasn't as violent as before. Still, her eyes teared slightly, and she blotted the dampness away, clearing her throat and looking westward. She saw neither horsemen nor dust.

". . . nothing easy in this world . . . even for sorceresses . . ."

". . . looks so thin . . . high wind take her . . ."

". . . might be . . . you want to face her?"

Anna pushed away the murmurs, not even sure whether they came from the newer guards or some of the players, so low were the words. She concentrated on the words of the spell she would use—it had to be the flame spell, much as she had come to dislike using it.

Kinor walked toward her, extending one of her water bottles.

"Thank you." Anna took several swallows. She glanced westward where a scout in purple rode toward the center of the Defalkan lines of lancers, toward Hanfor. Behind the rider in the distance appeared a smudge of something—dust. She nodded. The Mansuurans were coming, but they were two hills away.

Because she wasn't as clear as she'd have liked, she tried another vocalise. "He . . . sees . . . theee . . ." She nodded—a little better.

Hanfor rode toward her, reining up. "They will be here in less than a quarter of a glass. What do you need?"

Anna offered a crooked smile. "Just keep them off me until we can finish the spells. That's all."

Hanfor nodded. "I wish this were otherwise, Regent."

"You and me both."

Rickel and Lejun stepped forward—on foot—bearing the oversize shields. Each stationed himself on one side of Anna, slightly forward of her. They let the shields rest on the dusty ground, but their eyes remained on the dust cloud rising behind the crest of the nearer hill, less than a dek away.

"Have them finish tuning!" Anna called to Liende.

"Stand ready to play!" ordered the chief player.

Anna swallowed, trying to keep her body and cords relaxed as the Mansuuran forces poured over the hilltop, along the road, and hundreds of yards north and south of the road proper— their speed increasing from a quick trot to almost a gallop, looking like a wave of maroon surging toward the thin Defalkan line that held a slightly higher crest on the road.

"Liende! Have them start—the long flame song!"

"The flame song," Liende ordered, loudly, but with a quaver in her voice.

Anna pushed back the doubts. With more than two thousand lancers charging her force of perhaps three hundred, she had no choice but to use a spell that left no survivors.

> Turn to fire, turn to flame
> all those who do oppose Defalk's claim,
> turn to ashes, turn to dust . . .

Even before the music died away, the ground rumbled and shivered, and three forked spears of lightning flashed from the clear sky. A pillar of flame flared momentarily on the adjacent hilltop, and the sky began to darken, clouds forming from somewhere near instantly.

The sun dimmed.

Tears poured from Anna's eyes, and she bent forward, hanging on to Farinelli and practically hugging the gelding, trying not to let the massive sobs shake her.

Why . . . why? Was Liedwahr so alien? So alien that an over-captain of lancers who weren't even from Neserea felt he had to sacrifice everything because he refused to admit . . . what? That a sorceress had as much right to declare terms as a liedfuhr? That the lives of his armsmen were worth more than his honor? *Careful there . . . you're saying that your terms are worth more than their lives. . . .*

Thunder—the natural kind—rolled across the sky, then echoed back under clouds that had become almost black.

Anna shook her head. There was honor, and there was honor, but she'd never see that there was much honor in insisting that you had the right to subject another country to a set of rules that it didn't want. *Except that's exactly what you're doing in Defalk.*

But it wasn't. *You're upsetting the ideas of those who rule, not those who live there. Those who live there don't want their daughters to have to submit to any noble who wishes it. They don't want taxes and tariffs levied willy-nilly. They don't want to have to scrape and bow because they'll get killed if they don't. . . .*

It's still a fine line . . . and you know it.

But the sobs still came.

And so did the odor of death and fire, and charred brush and bodies.

Then came the wind—cold and empty, metallic, bearing the memory of another kind of death—moaning across the road and the hills.

With the wind came the rain, rain that was more like liquid ice, colder than anything Anna had felt in Liedwahr, hard drops to pelt both body and soul, cold as a damned soul in Dante's inferno's lowest level.

Slowly, the Regent-sorceress walked toward Farinelli, sensing, rather than really seeing the gelding, feeling that through the cool downpour, Kinor and Jimbob, and all her players and lancers watched . . . and waited . . . waited for the sorceress of destruction to leave the field.

Even tall Nelmor sat motionless on his mount. *Appalled . . . no doubt.*

Chill, ice—and guilt—poured over her.

95

The mixture of ice and cold rain rattled and pattered against the tent. Anna sat on the stool, slowly sipping water and chewing on cold bread and colder cheese. Her head still throbbed. Her eyes were blotchy, and her voice was shot.

Liende stood just inside the tent, looking at the bedraggled Regent.

Idiots! They invade another country, and then they think that they've been insulted after their allies have been destroyed when they're asked to do something reasonable—like let somebody with experience who's a Neserean run the place. Was she being unreasonable? Anna shook her head. *Was it just because you're a woman who had the temerity to suggest something different? All those men killed . . . every time you try to avoid killing, somehow you end up having to kill more people. Is any form of compromise or common sense considered weakness unless you scorch the earth first?*

Another line crept into her thoughts: "unlettered lads as mad as the mist and snow." But the lords and officers of Liedwahr weren't lads, even though they behaved like spoiled brats. Then, maybe there was more of an Irish heritage in Liedwahr than she knew. Or had the Celts stayed Germanic in Liedwahr?

And how soon before some of them understood what her sorcery could do? She shook her head. *People don't like to believe what they haven't seen or felt, and you haven't left a lot of survivors . . . and communications here aren't the most rapid or reliable.*

"Chief Player? Regent?" Hanfor peered into the tent, water oozing down his face and into his beard.

"Come in, Hanfor. You can take a moment and get dry."

The arms commander stepped out of the rain and shook himself slightly, then wiped the water off his forehead to keep it out of his eyes.

"We need to send a messenger to the Neserean forces at Denguic," Anna said. "Or get there quickly."

Hanfor raised his eyebrows.

"There's a good chance those lancers and armsmen are the ones I spelled, and that means they have to listen to me. But I don't want to chase them all the way across Neserea."

Liende and Hanfor looked at Anna.

"You are but skin and bones, Lady Anna," Liende finally said. "Better you eat and rest, and ride more slowly."

"If we can ride at all tomorrow," said Hanfor.

"We can leave now. This rain isn't good for the lancers. I've got a tent. They don't," Anna pointed out. "Besides, if we wait . . . the roads will just get worse."

Liende walked to the mirror case on the camp table and eased out the scrying glass. She walked back to Anna and held up the mirror. "If you would but look . . . ?"

Anna looked. She tried not to wince. Her face was drawn, with her cheeks almost sunken below the cheekbones. Deep black circles ran under both eyes. Her eyes were bloodshot. Even the slightly bubbled silver behind the glass could not disguise the combined pallor and flush that suffused her face. Her collarbones even jutted out under the shirt and vest. How had she gotten so thin? Was she that obsessive? *Yes . . .*

Liende lowered the glass.

"I'll eat more. Now," Anna added. "And we'll ride slowly." She looked at Hanfor. "I can't let them freeze. Not Nelmor's or Falar's men, either."

Liende and Hanfor looked at each other.

"Nor the players," Anna insisted.

"That might be best for them," Hanfor agreed. "It is not good for you."

"We can always stop if I fall apart." *But I won't.* "And I'll eat more." *You have to. . . .*

96

Shifting her weight—and her soaked trousers—in the saddle, Anna looked through the cold mist that had replaced the icy rain. In addition to being tired and underweight, she was going to have legs and a rear that were going to be badly chafed. The once-muddy road had turned back into damp clay—slightly slippery, but not a sloppy mess. The rain had turned first to drizzle, and then to mist, as the Defalkan force had struggled westward. Now the mist had gotten finer, but the process had occurred slowly over almost ten deks of muddy and slippery roads.

The lower legs of the mounts were mud-splattered as well, and Anna knew that grooming Farinelli would be a long chore. The sorceress peered more intently at the indistinct light that had to be the sun trying to break through the clouds. Then she smiled. "See . . . there's a rainbow! We're almost out of it."

Riding to her right, Kinor laughed.

Beside him, Jimbob murmured, "I'm ready for the rain to end. I was ready for it deks back."

"We might get somewhere dry before it gets dark." Anna remembered to take another swallow of water, and more of the cheese from the food pouch. She *had* to keep eating, because there was still far too much left undone, and it would remain undone unless she did it. That was becoming all too clear. She managed to push down another mouthful of cheese, swallowing with difficulty, despite her memory of the mirror image Liende had shown her.

Shortly, another scout trotted through the mist from the west to report to Hanfor. Even from ten yards away, Anna could see the arms commander's smile.

"Hanfor looks pleased," observed Kinor.

Anna nodded, waiting as the arms commander turned his mount and eased his way toward the sorceress, and Kinor and Jimbob.

"The scouts say that the Nesereans remain encamped where

they have been. The ground is dry another two deks ahead. Denguic is almost ten deks beyond where we would stop. Everyone is tired—you most of all. To go on would risk danger to all." Hanfor's eyes were intent on the sorceress as he spoke.

Anna surrendered. "As long as it's dry—that's fine. We can manage another two deks." She had to admit that even her cot sounded wonderful, and she wasn't sure she'd felt that tired in a long time. "And as long as it will be all right for the lancers."

"Everyone will be better just ahead than back in the rain," Hanfor said. "But we all need rest."

That Anna definitely knew. She nodded soberly.

97

Anna woke bolt upright at dawn, at the first hint of grayness coloring the dingy silk of her tent, mumbling to herself. "Have to get to those lancers . . . have to . . ."

She found herself shivering—and that hadn't happened very often in Defalk. Her breath steamed in the tent, and she shuddered from under her blanket into her clothes and her jacket. Then came the boots, but donning them took longer because her fingers were cold, and the leather felt stiff.

When she did stand up, her shoulders and neck were sore. After stepping over to the camp table, she slid out the traveling mirror and looked down into it. Her face was still pale, but without the sickly flush of the previous day. And the circles under her eyes weren't quite so pronounced, but her cheeks were still hollow. "You need to eat more."

Eating more was always a problem, first, because Avery had always been on her about her weight, and, now, because field rations were always short, she always feel guilty about stuffing herself. Putting off the eating question, she slipped toward the entry panel to the tent to reclaim the bucket of water. Outside, in the predawn grayness, a thin rime of frost covered everything, but there wasn't a film of ice on the water, anyway.

Bersan and Lejun were the duty guards. "Regent."

"Good morning," she said as she reclaimed the bucket.

"Good morning, Lady Regent. Commander Hanfor, he didn't expect you'd be up so early," Lejun said.

"I'd like to see him and the chief player in a bit, if you'd get word to them," Anna said.

Someone else had been watching her tent. Kinor came charging with a basket, the same one he'd been bringing every morning, except this one was clearly overstuffed. "Mm—the chief player said you needed to eat as much of this as you could."

"I'll try, Kinor." Anna managed to keep from smiling at the young man's almost inadvertent mention of the chief player as his mother. The sorceress slipped the bucket inside the tent, then took the basket, noting that besides two loaves of bread, there were several apples, two wedges of cheese, and two hard-looking biscuits.

She began with a chunk of bread and some cheese, and a bite of the firmer apple. Then she washed her face, wincing at the chill of the water, but deciding against any sorcery that wasn't absolutely necessary. The recollection of the hollowness of her cheeks strengthened that resolve. Alternating food and her minimal field toiletries, she found she had finished a loaf and a half of bread, both cheese wedges, and an apple by the time she was halfway presentable.

She had no more pulled back the tent flap to signify that she was ready to see people when Hanfor appeared, followed closely by Liende.

"How are the lancers?" Anna asked Hanfor, gesturing for both to enter, before inclining her head to Liende, "And the players?"

Hanfor stood by the camp table and waited for the chief player to speak.

"The players are better, except for Yuarl. She struggles with a fever."

Anna felt guilty. She hadn't even known that the thin violino player had a fever.

"It was better that we found a drier place for her. She slept well," Liende continued.

"I'm hoping that we won't need the players for a few days," the sorceress said. *Or longer.* "We might . . . but I'm still hoping. Can they ride?"

"Even Yuarl will ride."

"We need to get to Westfort before the word spreads," Anna said. "Before the Nesereans decide they can leave."

Hanfor raised his eyebrows. "Who might tell? None of the Mansuurans survived. Nor did any of the Nesereans who were with Rabyn."

"Jearle or the Nesereans might have a seer." Anna moistened her lips. "You both know what I have in mind. I don't want to fight another war, especially this year. I want to talk to the Neserean captain before he understands he has the largest force of armsmen left." She frowned. "That's probably the largest body of armsmen in one place south of Nordwei and east of the . . ."

"The Westfels," supplied Hanfor. "But they could not stand to your sorcery."

"No armsmen can," Liende added. "Not while you can sing and we can play."

"If they would support Hanfor, it would make life in Liedwahr a lot more pleasant," Anna said. *And life in Defalk as well.*

"They may not," demurred Hanfor.

"You just don't want the headaches you've seen me face," Anna suggested, with the hint of a smile.

"No armsman of judgment would, lady." Hanfor snorted.

"Still . . ." mused Anna, "we have to get it across that they've got a choice between a civil war or an invasion by Mansuur if they don't support you. Do they want that?"

Hanfor shrugged. "I would say not, but seldom do armsmen make such choices."

"All we can do is ask." Anna glanced through the open tent flap toward the tielines where Farinelli was tethered. "How soon before we can be ready to ride?"

"A half-glass, perhaps a bit longer."

"Then let's get started." Anna paused. "I'd better talk to Lord Nelmor and Falar, too. I've probably been neglecting them."

Anna packed up saddlebags and mirror and was taking apart the cot when Nelmor and Falar arrived. She motioned both inside.

"I'm sorry I haven't been more careful to keep you both informed of what has been happening." She looked apologetic. "Sorcery takes a lot out of me, and I don't always consider how others feel. Especially people like you, who have been very supportive and helpful."

"Regent," Nelmor began, "you and your arms commander have been most courteous."

"Most courteous, and with the strain you have faced," added Falar, spoiling the serious words with the hint of his smile.

"Thank you both." Anna paused. "There is one last group of Nesereans in Defalk. They're besieging—or camped around Westfort. That's where we're headed. It's not even ten deks from here."

Nelmor nodded. "I had known we were close, but with the mist and the rain . . ."

"I'm going to try to persuade them to leave peacefully," Anna said, "but I'd like you two to accompany me, if you would."

"For ten deks . . . to see the end of this war? After this whole season?" Nelmor shook his head. "I would scarce miss that chance, especially saving that the journey back to Dubaria lies that way as well."

Anna looked to Falar.

The redhead grinned. "Fussen and Ustal would not welcome me any sooner."

"Thank you both." Anna inclined her head. "We'll be riding out in less than a glass. I'm sorry I didn't let you know, but I didn't know for sure until a bit earlier myself."

"We will be ready, Regent, and glad of it," said Nelmor, smiling broadly.

Falar nodded.

As she watched the two walk away from the tent, Anna wanted to shake her head. She was usually good at reading postures, and both men had seemed pleased. Why, she wasn't certain, but it was better to have done something right and not understood all the reasons why than the other way around.

She looked at the remaining food in the basket and groaned, but she broke off another chunk of bread and slowly chewed her way through it. "You can finish the bread . . . you can."

The sun had barely risen when Anna guided Farinelli back onto the road westward. Rickel and Lejun rode before Anna, while Hanfor rode beside her. Kinor and Himar rode behind them, and Anna's remaining guards rode between them and the players. The mounts' hoofs echoed dully on the partly frozen road clay, and the light and chill wind blew out of clear northern sky, so clear that it seemed as much green as blue.

"It will be a long and cold winter," predicted Hanfor.

"Let's hope it doesn't start too soon. There's a lot I need to do before snow or freezing rain starts to fall."

"Regent—I fear there will always be more for you to do than glasses in which to do such tasks." Hanfor shook his head. "Two years I have known you, and yet you find there is more that you must do, for all that you have done, yet all Liedwahr is changed."

Not near enough. "I haven't done that much."

Anna ignored the barely concealed snort from Jimbob, riding behind her.

"Some would say that you have all too much," Hanfor responded, "those such as Lord Ehara, Lord Behlem, Lord Bertmynn, Lord Rabyn . . ." A lopsided grin appeared.

"The names change, but not much else does," countered Anna.

"More than you think, I would venture."

"Much more," came a murmured assent from one of the two young men riding behind Anna. Jimbob, she suspected.

As the sun struck the frost that coated the grass and the trees, mist began to form and rise, giving the land an almost-surreal look. Anna took in the beauty, leaning forward in the saddle and patting Farinelli on the neck. "We don't see many mornings like this," she whispered, just looking out silently as the gelding carried her onward.

The mist and the apparent stillness before her reminded her of New England, in the days when she had been married and much younger, and far more innocent. For a moment, she had to close her eyes. Then she straightened and looked westward.

The lands around Westfort still lay in darkness when Anna reined up on the road crest and looked out over the valley at the keep, standing like a sunlit isle above the long morning shadows.

Anna turned in the saddle. "Liende! Have the players ready. The long flame song. I hope we don't have to use it, but I'm not trusting anyone right now."

"Yes, Regent." The white-haired player turned in her own saddle. "Dismount and prepare to play. The tuning song."

"Raise high the Regency banner!" ordered Hanfor.

The Regency banner rose on the ridge to the south of where the Nefereans were camped. The discordant sounds of violinos, woodwinds, and the falk-horn rose around Anna, but she continued to watch the camp below.

"There's a banner being raised over the keep gate," announced Jimbob.

"And on the tower," added Kinor.

Anna glanced at the two Westfort banners. She could not make out the details of either, but the gates of Westfort remained closed.

A rider in blue spurred his mount toward the tent in the center of the Neserean camp. Within moments, he turned and rode up the hill, bearing a white banner. The Neserean camp began to bustle, with riders seeking mounts and armsmen scurrying into formation.

Behind Anna, the tuning grew.

Lejun and Rickel eased their mounts forward. They had unstrapped and now bore the oversize shields they used to protect Anna.

As the sole rider neared the Defalkan force, Hanfor nodded to Himar. The overcaptain and a pair of lancers rode forward toward the scout or messenger who bore the white banner.

Himar spoke to the lancer but for a moment, and then gestured in the direction of Hanfor and the sorceress.

Anna turned. "Jimbob . . . Kinor . . . if you would wait here . . ."

"Yes, Lady Anna."

"Let's see what they want," Anna suggested.

"Their lives," Hanfor responded, "else the banner would be blue."

"I hope you're right." Preceded by her guards, Anna and Hanfor rode along the road to where the messenger waited. Anna reined up a good eight yards from the messenger, and Rickel and Lejun closed in front of her, leaving just a narrow opening with the shields.

"Lady . . . sers. . . ." the messenger stammered, "my captain begs of you your wishes . . . and your mercy."

"We'd like to meet with him here—alone," Anna announced firmly. "Immediately."

"Yes, lady . . . sorceress . . . Regent . . ." The Neserean swallowed. "Be there aught else to say?"

"I will not use sorcery if we reach an agreement," Anna said. "Unless his armsmen leave their camp. If they move, then I will destroy them if I must."

"I'll be telling him all that . . . quick as I can, great Regent." The scout turned his mount and started downhill with his mount moving at a gait faster than a walk and slower than a trot.

"They know something," Anna said as she watched the Neserean scout ride back down to the camp, where ranks continued to form. Her eyes went back uphill, where her players went on with their tuning.

"They fear you, and they fear the worst," Himar said.

"You have appeared out of the mist," Hanfor laughed and gestured eastward, where curtains of fog rose into the clear sky. "No force has ever stood against you—"

"That's not true. The Evult's force ran right over me at the Sand Pass, and Sargol's big crossbow damned near killed me. So did Bertmynn's Darksong—that was too close, and I think if you hadn't come up with that night attack against Rabyn, we'd have been in big trouble." Anna shivered.

"They do not know such," Hanfor pointed out.

The three, and Anna's four guards—Rickel, Lejun, Blaz, and Fielmir—watched the camp below as the Neserean scout rode back to the central tent. Within moments, it seemed, two Nesereans were headed back up the gentle hillside.

A single officer accompanied the lancer with the white banner back up the hillside to where Anna and the others waited.

The ginger-bearded officer with silver clips on his collar reined up and bowed in the saddle. "Regent, I am Yerril, captain of the Prophet's Guard. You would not be here, save the Prophet is dead or vanquished."

"He is dead. So are all those who were with him," Hanfor affirmed.

"All of them?"

"They would not accept terms, even after the deaths of the Prophet and the overcaptain of the Mansuuran lancers. They attacked us, and the Regent had no choice but to destroy them," Hanfor explained blandly.

"What terms did you demand?" The captain glanced from Hanfor to Anna. Despite the chill, his forehead was damp with sweat.

Anna did not answer immediately, but glanced down toward the valley. The Neserean forces were formed into ranks, both of lancers and foot armsmen, but the ranks had not moved. She looked back at the Neserean officer. "Captain Yerril, you may recall Hanfor?"

"Yes, Regent. Yes, ser."

"Hanfor is from Neserea. I have a choice for you, Captain. A simple one. The same one I offered the Mansuuran lancers. I didn't think it was unreasonable, especially since Neserea and Mansuur invaded Defalk."

"Regent?"

"You have a choice. You can leave Defalk and go back to Neserea to tell everyone that the Prophet is dead, and that you couldn't do anything about it, and that you still haven't, which will probably mean that the Liedfuhr of Mansuur will take over Neserea in the next year, *or* you can support a Neserean to be Lord High Counselor of Neserea. Which do you want—a Neserea governed by a Neserean, or a civil war leading to a land ruled by the Liedfuhr?

The sweat beaded on Yerril's forehead. "I'd not wish to displease either the Regent . . . or the Liedfuhr, either."

"If you will support Hanfor, who was an overcaptain, was he not, then I will support Neserea's independence from the Liedfuhr."

"Beggin' your pardon, Regent . . . why do you need us? Why put a choice like that on a poor captain?"

"I don't need you," Anna said. "Neserea does. I don't want to rule Neserea. I didn't want to rule Dumar, and I haven't. I didn't want to rule Ebra, and I haven't. I have enough to deal with in Defalk—but I can't if I'm always fighting some idiot who wants to invade us. So I want Hanfor to rule Neserea and be friends with Defalk—and I'll support him against the Leidfuhr." *If you have to.*

Yerril frowned.

"You don't have to believe me." Anna nodded toward Hanfor. "I'm leaving Hanfor to talk to you. He'll let me know your choice." She smiled. "I *will* support Hanfor against the Lied-fuhr. I may not support any other ruler that appears in Neserea."

Yerril's swallow was audible, but Anna did not offer a response. Instead, surrounded by her guards, she turned Farinelli back toward the Defalkan lines. Rickel and Blaz kept the shields high until they were a good hundred yards up the hill and away from the two Neserseans.

Kinor and Jimbob urged their mounts toward Anna, but the sorceress motioned for them to stop, and called to Liende. "Have the players stand ready with the long flame song."

"Standing ready, Regent."

"Have them do a short tune," Anna added.

"Yes, Regent." Liende grinned.

Anna hoped that message would be clear to Captain Yerril.

"Regent?" ventured Kinor.

Jimbob raised his eyebrows, but did not speak.

"They're considering whether to support Hanfor for Lord High Counselor of Neserea," Anna said blandly.

Kinor looked sideways at Anna. "Will you destroy them if they refuse?"

"No. They can't fight against me, and destroying them would make things worse in Neserea. But I want them to think I might. If they don't back Hanfor, that will leave Neserea without a ruler, and probably create a civil war there, just like there was in Ebra. I hope it doesn't happen that way, because we don't have enough armsmen to go into Neserea." *Not with idiots like Tybel and Beltyr stirring up trouble in Defalk.* "And I'd just have to leave Neserea alone right now, and then go back next year or the year after. Or sooner, if the Liedfuhr decided to invade." Anna shrugged. "If they decide they want Hanfor, then that would make it harder for the Liedfuhr." *There's certainly no guarantee of common sense here, but maybe armsmen will be brighter than lords.*

Kinor nodded.

"Hanfor's coming this way, lady," Jimbob broke in.

Himar remained with Yerril as Hanfor rode uphill toward Anna. The arms commander was smiling, not an open smile, but one more rueful.

"He agreed?" asked the Regent as Hanfor reined up.

"Captain Yerril has one condition, Lady Anna," Hanfor said with a laugh. "You will not find it onerous."

"What condition?"

"He wishes you to commit to a scroll your support of Neserea against the Liedfuhr if they accept me as their . . . Lord High Counselor."

"How did you get him to agree?" Anna asked.

Hanfor shrugged. "I told him the truth. That you had restored Lady Siobion in Dumar and Lord Hadrenn in Ebra. That you would oppose either Sturinn or Mansuur, and that you had given the Mansuuran lancers the choice of leaving Neserea independent of Mansuur or dying, and that they would not release their hold on Neserea so that you destroyed them." The weathered veteran laughed. "He was far more accepting when he learned that there were no other armsmen left in Neserea, save his command."

Anna frowned. "These are the Prophet's Guard. What ever happened to their commander? He was in Falcor."

"That was Gellinot. Young Behlem had him removed because he retreated from Defalk. He was executed, later, very quietly."

The sorceress shook her head. She hadn't cared much for Gellinot, from what she recalled, but to kill a man for retreating when there were no options and nothing to gain . . .

"And Rabyn, he put his cousin Bertl in charge . . . but somehow in the siege here, one of Jearle's arrows went through his throat." A grim smile crossed Hanfor's face. "From behind him."

"Congratulations, Lord High Counselor," Anna said.

"I did not ask for this, you know." A wintry smile crossed Hanfor's face.

"I know." Anna's smile was half-sad. "I didn't really ask to come to Liedwahr, either."

"Came you did, Lady Sorceress, and this poor world will not be the same. Better, I think, but not the same." An ironic laugh followed. "The ruler of Neserea . . . or counselor . . . a common armsman. Who would have thought it?"

"An armsman," Anna countered, "but scarcely common."

"I was in great disfavor, you know," Hanfor continued. "I was being punished when Lord Behlem assigned me to work with you against the Evult. He hoped Alvar, Himar, and I would be killed."

"Hanfor?" Anna eased her mount closer to the grizzled veteran.

"Yes, Regent?"

"You don't have a consort, do you?" she asked in a lower voice.

"No." A look of puzzlement crossed the veteran's face.

Anna grinned. "Two will get you three that you'll have offers waiting you, and one will be from the Liedfuhr."

Hanfor returned her grin with a wry smile. "That wager I would not take. Not against your scrying."

"You will have to take one," Anna pointed out. "So take the one that will make you happiest."

Hanfor nodded. "And you . . . lady . . . what of you?"

"Sorceresses don't get consorts. Not in Liedwahr. Not if they want to put everything back together."

"Do not . . ." Hanfor broke off, then resumed in a voice not much above a whisper. "I would not be presumptuous, lady . . . but there is one who loves you. . . ."

"I know," Anna said softly. "I know. I did not say that I couldn't seek happiness. Thank you."

Anna and Hanfor both smiled, ignoring the half-bemused expressions on the faces of the two young men.

98

Seated on Farinelli with the late-morning sun warming her back, Anna watched as the last of the Neserean lancers rode westward, back toward Elioch—and eventually toward Esaria. She'd miss Hanfor, his quiet competence, but Neserea needed him. And so did Defalk—in Esaria. She wished she'd had more time to say good-bye, but that wouldn't have altered things, and the sooner the Nesereans were out of Defalk, the sooner she could deal with her other problems, hopefully before they became insurmountable.

She turned in the saddle, looking at Himar, who had watched

with her. "You don't mind being the arms commander of Defalk, do you, Himar?"

The sandy-haired and clean-shaven veteran laughed. "No armsman with aught between his ears would believe what you have bestowed. In two years, you have made a junior overcaptain a ruler, and two lowly captains arms commanders of entire lands."

"That's because you were all good." *The ones who weren't are gone or dead.*

"A ruler who rewards skill, lady . . . we armsmen know how rare that is."

Anna hoped she rewarded skill, but she knew she wasn't the best judge of her own judgment. "We're running out of armsmen again, and we're running out of officers," mused the sorceress. "Do you think Jirsit is ready to come back from Pamr as a captain?" She brushed back strands of blonde hair that the light gusty winds had tugged from under her brown felt hat.

"He would do well, I think."

Anna glanced at Rickel, speculatively. On the other side of Himar, the nearest guard was Bersan. Blaz, Lejun, and Fielmir were reined up a good ten yards away, behind Jimbob and Kinor.

"If you please, lady," replied the blond guard, shifting uneasily in his saddle. "I would rather remain as I am." Rickel paused, then lowered his voice. "Lejun and Blaz—they would make good subofficers, I think."

"Are you sure you wish to remain as a guard?" asked Anna, her eyes straying toward the keep on the lower hill, watching for a messenger.

"I am guard captain, in all but name . . ." ventured Rickel.

Anna grinned. "That we can fix, Guard Captain Rickel."

Jimbob, Himar, and Kinor, seated on their mounts, half-facing Anna, all grinned as well.

"What do you think about Lejun and Blaz?" Anna asked Himar.

"They have seen you through many battles, and none has lost his head," Himar said. "We should see—if they are interested."

Anna and Himar watched as a lancer in purple rode forth from the now-open gates of Westfort—the messenger she had sent earlier to inform Jearle that the siege had been broken, though she had her doubts about how tight a siege it had really been. "I wonder what response we'll get."

"He will welcome you, Regent, no doubt. Whether he does feel welcoming or not," suggested Himar. "I would not be so charitable toward him."

"It's his trying to show he's being charitable toward me when he's not feeling that way that bothers me," Anna admitted. Her eyes crossed the hilltop to where Falar and Nelmor sat astride their mounts, looking toward her. She did not acknowledge their glances, but she would have to talk with them, shortly. *There's always somebody ... and if you don't, they get their feelings hurt, and that leads to more trouble.*

The nine of them—Himar, Anna, Jimbob, Kinor, and five guards—waited silently for the lancer to reach them and rein up.

"Lord Jearle bids you welcome, and to enter Westfort, bastion and keep of the Western Marches of Defalk."

Even though the words were Jearle's, and repeated faithfully by the lancer, Anna bristled at the message conveyed. "Thank you," Anna said.

"If you would wait over there," Himar suggested politely to the messenger.

"Yes, ser." The lancer eased his mount away, not reining up until he was a good thirty yards from the group.

"Is it wise to enter his keep, Lady Anna?" Kinor asked from her left.

"I can't very well incinerate one of our own lords because I don't like him. I can't just march away either. And we need supplies. We have enough problems as it is." *And more than enough lords who are problems.* Anna smiled crookedly. "But I will insist on all my guards, and I'll carry the lutar."

"Perhaps I should enter first," suggested Himar.

"What about an undercaptain you trust?" Anna suggested. "A very cautious one who will inform Lord Jearle that we have, say, tenscore lancers who will need food and quarters, and Lord Nelmor and the brother of Lord Ustal."

Himar nodded.

"Might I go also?" asked Kinor.

Anna frowned, thinking about what Liende might say.

"Kinor has the graces, Lady Anna," Himar pointed out. "While Lord Jimbob does also, it would be less than wise to send the heir until we know how matters stand."

Anna considered the options. Finally, she looked at the tall redhead, more wiry than when they had begun nearly a season before, and less boyish. "Be careful, Kinor. Tell him that I didn't wish him to be surprised, which is why you're there with the advance party. If you notice anything strange, ignore it, and tell Lord Jearle you have to come get me. Then get out of there."

A half smile cloaked Kinor's face. "I understand, Regent and lady."

"If you will excuse me, lady?" Himar eased his mount across the hilltop toward the nearest formation of Defalkan lancers.

Anna turned to Jimbob, reflecting upon how quiet the youth had been for most of the campaign. "You may come with us, Jimbob, but I'd rather not announce to Lord Jearle who you are. Not in advance, anyway."

"That I understand, Lady Anna." The younger redhead offered a surprisingly shy smile. "I thank you for letting me accompany you. I have seen what I had been told. I did not see before, but I think I might see more now."

Why? Because you've finally seen how real the killing and the deaths are? The pain that goes behind ruling? Lord . . . I do hope so . . . and that it sticks. "Sometimes, you have to see things," she temporized.

Jimbob nodded. "I am not so good at hearing words and understanding."

At least he understands that. Maybe there's some hope there, yet.

Himar reappeared with a squat and swarthy figure riding beside him, an officer even darker than Alvar, who had served Anna so well and now was Arms Commander of Dumar.

Both officers reined up, then bowed in their saddles, waiting.

"This is Dutral, Lady Anna. He has been serving as the captain of the purple company these past weeks." Himar nodded in the direction of Kinor. "This is Kinor, Dutral. He is an aide to the Regent, and has been tutored by her. He will be going with you to inform Lord Jearle of our needs." Himar laughed harshly. "You will take the purple company, and you will see what you can, and return to escort the Regent."

"Yes, Regent . . . Overcaptain . . . Arms Commander." Dutral offered a knowing smile.

"Thank you," Anna said warmly. "And you, too, Kinor."

Once the purple company had left, Anna dismounted to stretch her legs, looking to the north, where a fringe of low clouds had appeared on the horizon. She hoped that they didn't herald more rain or snow.

Once again, she was waiting, but at times waiting was far better than rushing in. The problem was that she didn't always have the time to wait.

She had remounted by the time Kinor and Dutral returned.

"You are bid welcome," Kinor said, "but there are many armsmen, and all I saw wear two blades, both the shortsword and the longer battle blade."

"That is true," affirmed Dutral. "Yet we saw no archers. Nor any crossbowmen."

"How many armsmen?" questioned Himar.

"Threescore, perhaps four, that we could see."

Anna thought. *Might as well do this right.* "Kinor . . . if you would send a messenger to Lord Jearle saying we will be there presently."

"You have a plan?" asked Kinor.

Anna nodded. "But I need to talk to your . . . to the chief player."

This time Kinor was the one to conceal a smile at Anna's near slip in referring to his mother.

"And to Lord Nelmor and Falar . . . and Himar and I need to work out a few details."

Kinor bowed his head. "I will send a messenger." Then he rode back to where the purple company had reined up.

Anna flicked the reins, and Farinelli stepped easily across the brown grass. The sorceress went to find Liende first.

The chief player and the other players were standing by their mounts a hundred yards east of where Anna had been viewing the keep.

"Lady Regent?"

"Liende." Anna paused. "I will need a spellsong just before we reach the gates. Can you have the players ready to dismount and play? The flame song. It'll be a different spell, but the same tune."

Liende frowned.

"This one is not for killing, but for disarming. Lord Jearle has welcomed us, and double-armed his men."

"Does he think you blind?"

"Probably. I'm only a woman, and I did nothing when we visited him in the fall."

"The more fool he." Liende snorted. "We will prepare to play just before the gates." She walked toward the players. "Here! We have a task!"

Still flanked by her ubiquitous guards, Anna rode Farinelli westward across the hillside to where Lord Nelmor and Falar stood, also holding the reins of their mounts.

"Lady Anna."

"Regent."

"Lord Nelmor, Falar," Anna looked at both—the lord and the would-be lord. "I would like your support one last time on this campaign. I have to ask, here, not order, and if you're not comfortable with this, I understand." She paused. "Lord Nelmor, we had once discussed the duties of the Lord of the Western Marches. One of those duties is to bid one's Regent welcome." A cold smile crossed her face. "While we have been bid welcome, all the armsmen in Westfort carry double blades."

Nelmor's face paled.

Falar frowned.

"I intend to use sorcery to disarm the keep, but I will need armsmen to hold it while I look into what has occurred. . . ."

"You will not use the fire spells?" asked Nelmor.

"Not against any armsmen who do not attack me—and not at first."

The tall blond lord nodded. "We will ride in with you."

"And so will we," seconded Falar.

"Himar will order the riders," Anna said.

"We will follow."

Anna inclined her head. "Thank you." She turned Farinelli back toward Himar and Jimbob.

Himar was waiting at the head of the ranks forming up— with Kinor and Jimbob—when Anna and her entourage returned. "What will you?"

"We'll enter Westfort," Anna said, "as if nothing were wrong."

"We will lead with two companies," Himar proposed.

"Then the players . . ." Anna added her own spell strategy for disarming Jearle's forces. "This will happen once those companies hold the courtyard."

Himar nodded. "That is best—before you enter the keep. And it will leave our lancers safer as well. If there is a problem with the spell, you remain outside."

Anna nodded. *But there shouldn't be.* As the lancers formed up, she went over the spell in her mind, time after time.

The sun had finally reached midday before the column started downhill toward Westfort, but the chill winds made white steam of some mounts' breath.

The gates to Westfort were open.

Anna watched as the purple company swept through them, three abreast, then the green company. Farinelli was less than ten yards from the open gates, and the guards in red and black when Anna reined up and turned to Liende, who, with the players, rode right behind Kinor and Jimbob.

"Now!" ordered the Regent.

Alarm crossed the faces of the two guards at the gates, but neither said a word as a pair of lancers appeared next to each with bared blades.

Anna didn't even dismount, but sang full voice from the saddle, letting her spell flood into the courtyard and the keep of Westfort.

> Turn to water, turn to rust,
> turn each Westfort blade into dust.
> Break the shafts that fly from any strings. . . .

Holding her lutar ready, Anna watched as one of the Westfort guards in red and black tried to draw a blade, and found himself with a handful of red dust. She nodded, and called back to Liende. "That's all for now."

Himar nodded, then ordered, "Purple company! Green company! Take the keep!" He looked at Anna. "Best you wait at the gates."

Surrounded by her guards, Kinor, and Jimbob, Anna waited. She held the lutar, her eyes darting to the high walls, and then into the lancer-held courtyard. Farinelli sidestepped once or twice, almost as if to say that he was ready for a stall and some grain.

In less than half a glass, Himar rode back across the courtyard and out through the gates to Anna. "The hold is ours."

"Was anyone hurt?"

"One lancer was stabbed with a kitchen knife by an armsman in red. That armsman will not stab another. Other than that . . ." Himar shook his head. "Lord Jearle awaits you in the entry hall."

Anna dismounted, but kept the lutar, and let Rickel and Lejun, using their shields, lead the way through the open double doors into the dimly lit entry hall.

Jearle stood, flanked by Defalkan armsmen, just inside the great entry hall of Westfort. His face was flushed as she stepped toward him, and his jaw seemed to quiver. A pair of armsmen in red and black stood behind Jearle. Both wore twin scabbards, empty.

Carrying the already-tuned lutar, Anna stepped forward, accompanied by Rickel and Lejun. Kinor advanced beside them, and Jimbob remained several paces behind the older redhead.

"I have invited you into Westfort, and this is how you have mocked me!" Jearle blustered. "The Thirty-three will hear of this. They will, and they will strip your Regency."

"I was invited into a hold where all armsmen wore double blades," Anna countered. "I was invited into a hold that made no effort to break its siege while other lords hazarded all that they had to help Defalk."

Jearle studied Anna. "You knew Rabyn would invade Defalk. You knew he would attack Westfort. Yet you took your forces into Ebra, and left us to fend for ourselves. You abandoned the Thirty-three."

Doesn't he understand anything? "No," Anna said quietly. "I did not abandon the Thirty-three. I returned, and your lands are safe, and will be for years to come. You made the decision two years ago to allow Lord Behlem through your lands to save your soul and your lands and your golds. Don't condemn me for letting his son come into Defalk so that I could save it."

"You play with words, lady." Jearle's face turned from red to almost purple.

Anna nodded. "Blaz, Fielmir. Tie up his lordship."

Jearle lunged forward, coming up and in low toward Anna with a thin shining dagger.

Although Rickel and Lejun closed shields, another figure was quicker.

"No!" Kinor crashed into the older lord, and both dagger and lord went down. The dagger slid along the stones, leaving a trail of dark liquid.

"Poison!" snapped a voice from somewhere.

Blaz and Fielmir yanked Jearle to his feet. Bersan held a bright blade at the lord's throat.

"Do your worst, bitch."

"I intend to." Anna lifted the lutar.

> Jearle, lord, Jearle, lord the same,
> with this spell turn to fire and flame,
> fire flay you from flesh to ash to dust.
> the end of all unworthy of a Regent's trust.

With the line of fire searing from above, the guards threw Jearle to the stones.

This time, the brief screams did not even bother Anna. *Are you getting that callous . . . or did you dislike him that much?*

When the entry hall was still once more, deathly still, she turned, holding the lutar. "Kinor . . . would you come here?"

Kinor glanced at the gray dust on the stones, then at Anna.

"No matter what occurs, will you be loyal to Defalk, to Lord Jimbob as heir, and to me so long as I am Regent?"

"Lady . . . I only thought of your safety. . . ."

"That's loyalty." Anna paused. "Do you swear loyalty to Defalk, Jimbob, and the Regency?"

"Yes . . . of course . . . how could I otherwise . . . ?" The young man was clearly flustered.

"Good." Anna turned to Himar and Jimbob, then motioned to Liende, standing well back at the end of the hall.

Liende approached warily, her eyes darting from Anna to her son and back again.

Anna waited until the chief player had neared before continuing. "Westfort needs a strong, and intelligent, and loyal lord, and one young enough to support the Regency and Lord Jimbob for many years." She smiled at Liende. "What do you think about Lord Kinor?"

Kinor's mouth dropped open. Liende appeared poleaxed. Jimbob grinned. Himar nodded slowly.

"Lady . . . I did not . . . I never meant," Kinor stammered, for the first time since Anna had known him.

Anna shook her head. "That's exactly why you are now Lord of Westfort and Denguic. You will not be Lord of the Western Marches. At least not for many years. That will remain with Lord Nelmor so long as he wishes it and can maintain it." Anna motioned for Nelmor to step forward. "As you will note, Lord Jearle has no objections, Lord Nelmor. You are the Lord of the Western Marches."

Nelmor bent his head.

"You have earned that right by honor and by your support of Defalk and the Regency."

Anna raised her voice. "All those in Westfort who don't wish to serve Lord Kinor will leave, and they will depart within the week. Lord Jearle's heirs must leave Westfort today, and Defalk within the week. Otherwise, their lives will be forfeit."

"Never!" The broad-shouldered man at the top of the stairs drew a short blade, a wide-bladed dagger, and began to charge down the steps, drawing it back as if to throw it.

Anna lifted the lutar and began to sing.

> Jearle's heir, lord he'd name,
> with this spell turn to fire and flame,

Lejun flung up the shield.

Thunk! The guard staggered back with a heavy short blade embedded in the shield frame.

The sorceress concentrated on completing the spell.

> . . . fire flay you from flesh to ash to dust.
> the end of all unworthy of a Regent's trust.

A single pillar of fire flared midway down the stairs.

A woman screamed from the upper landing, and Anna stood in the hall, finding herself shaking . . . and amazed that she had managed the spell, even if it had left her with a splitting headache.

Lejun lowered the shield and looked at his shoulder, also astounded that the blade had gone several spans through the shield itself but missed his body.

Blaz stepped up to take Lejun's place, blade bared, and Fielmir held a blade to Lady Livya, standing on the foot of the stairs.

Anna turned and walked forward toward Livya.

"You have taken everything . . . you outland . . . creature . . ."

"Your consort gave me few choices," Anna said. "I could not trust him, nor you, nor your son. He wouldn't support Defalk in its time of need. Twice, he failed. When I came and lifted the siege, he armed everyone in the keep against me. And you think I should have supported him?"

"You . . . don't . . . understand . . . don't understand . . . at all . . . haven't any children . . ." Livya kept weeping, not even really looking at Anna.

Everyone thinks that his or her problems are unique, and so many are all the same.

Anna looked tiredly at Kinor. "Lord Kinor . . . you have much to do. With honor comes grief, and the knowledge that every action taken by a ruler or a lord hurts someone. *Every action!* Never forget that. *Never.*"

Kinor swallowed.

Anna refrained from sighing. She turned to Himar. "We have a keep to clean up, and more plans to make."

Himar nodded.

Anna's eyes went to the blank face of Falar. Another problem. Falar might have made a good lord, but his history with Anna was short . . . and the last thing she needed was Falar being the lord. She offered a smile to the red-haired scoundrel. "Falar . . . I'll need to talk to you later, if you would."

"Oh . . . Lady Anna, I am at your command."

You hope so . . . and that you can wend your way through more of these intrigues. "I'm not commanding, only requesting from someone who has offered great service." *There . . . was that laid on heavy enough?* She smiled again.

III

LETZTLIED

99

ENCORA, RANUAK

The Matriarch studies the formal receiving hall, sniffs the almost-metallic air, and turns to her consort. "Dyleroy will be arriving soon, and we will begin another story in the sagas of the mistresses of the Exchange."

"The story of the sorceress is more interesting," observes Ulgar, fingering the mandolin he appears ready to play. "A most intriguing tale."

"None would believe it, above all those who would know all of it," answers the Matriarch, reaching out just short of the blue-crystal chair. Her fingers seem to shimmer, and the chair hums, but for a moment.

"Were hers a drama upon the stage in the Hall of Amusement," said Ulgar quietly, "the tale of the sorceress-Regent would end now."

"True, my dear," answers the tired-eyed, but round-faced Matriarch, who yet wears black. "For has she not vanquished all her enemies beyond Defalk? Ground them into dust? Is that not where the minstrels always end the tales, with the great victories?"

"Her hardest battles are those ahead," predicts Ulgar.

"Not the hardest. Those that will take the most persistence and win her the least renown. Those that will have the lords who will not change carping to their neighbors."

"She has an even more terrible battle to confront," Ulgar insists.

"Yes," the Matriarch sighs. "Those who love—"

At that moment, a bell rings, and the round-faced woman who is the soul of Ranuak turns toward the door of the audience chamber, then seats herself on the blue-crystal throne. "Yes?"

Ulgar slips out through the door that becomes just one of the wall panels as he closes it behind himself.

A stocky, but not heavy woman in the sea-blue of the Exchange opens the main door to the chamber and steps inside. Her eyes dart from side to side, and an expression of puzzlement appears as she sees no one but the round-faced woman in the blue-crystal seat. "Dyleroy, at your request, Matriarch."

"You may approach."

Dyleroy steps forward across the blue stones that comprise the floor of the chamber. She stops a half dozen steps short of the Matriarch. "You summoned me?"

"I did." After a pause, the older woman continues, "Do you understand why your predecessor is no more?"

"I cannot say that I do, Matriarch." Dyleroy bows her head. "Would you enlighten me?"

"The harmonies demand that like be treated as like. Abslim did not wish to understand such." The Matriarch studies the middle-aged face, one with lines radiating from the eyes, but not across the cheeks. Finally, she speaks again. "The harmonies do not care what we wish, nor what we believe, nor what we would like to occur. Abslim wished the sorceress-Regent of Defalk to act according to Abslim's own desires and beliefs as to how Abslim herself would have acted had she been Regent of Defalk." The Matriarch smiles. "There is no harm in wishing. But when Abslim instructed the Exchange to treat Defalk and its traders as though they had violated the harmonies, when they had not and had acted in honor, that was her first step against those harmonies. When she diverted funds from the Exchange to the SouthWomen—yes, I know you are a SouthWoman, and that you urged her to do so—that was her second step. When she defied me and the harmonies, the balance had to be redressed."

Dyleroy looks evenly at the Matriarch. "Knowing that, you would accept me as Mistress of the Exchange?"

"You are said to be intelligent and honest. You are also said to be willing to learn. I can always hope that you learn from your mistakes and those of others." The Matriarch nods vaguely in the direction of the harbor. "The Free State of Ebra now needs your assistance; it would have needed far less had my daughter Veria and Abslim let the harmonies and the sorceress run their course."

Dyleroy looks at the blue-stone tiles of the floor.

"Both my daughter and Abslim failed to understand that I have no hesitation in acting. They did not understand that the

Matriarch only acts when the harmonies require, not when my whims or wants would wish it so." After a pause, she adds, "Perhaps someday you will understand what wisdom is necessary to determine when to act, and what great will and courage it requires *not* to act, when all around you are urging such."

Dyleroy looks into the Matriarch's cold eyes. Although the new Mistress of the Exchange continues to meet the gaze of the older woman, Dyleroy shivers, even in the sunlight of the formal receiving hall.

100

Anna's eyes dropped to the flat table and the pile of parchment Kinor had asked his new staff to round up for her. So many messages to write, and she couldn't really afford to stay in Denguic long—just long enough to give her lancers and players a little rest, to resupply, and to ensure Kinor had a firm enough hold on the keep—and that meant leaving Dutral and the purple company for a time, at least.

She could have used—again—a secretary, but, besides her fosterlings, whom she already used at times that way, who else was there? Fluency in written language wasn't exactly common outside the aristocracy, and she'd already coopted most of those flexible enough for such a position.

She laughed to herself, then wrinkled her nose.

Despite the sorcery she had used, the large guest chamber of Westfort still smelled faintly of mold, but she'd killed and removed all the vermin in the oversize bed with the dark walnut headboard that was carved with yet another hunting scene that she disliked even looking at, with its dying stags and boars.

She'd already penned a scroll to Jecks, outlining the events of the weeks since she'd left Falcor and asking him for a report from Dythya on the progress of liedgeld payments from various lords. The next step was a missive to Konsstin, the Liedfuhr of Mansuur. She couldn't imagine the Liedfuhr being pleased, not with the loss of a hundredscore lancers and assorted captains and overcaptains. And he certainly wouldn't be pleased with the death of his grandson, even if Rabyn had been a perverted little bastard.

With a deep breath she reseated herself at the table, taking a chunk of bread from the platter on the edge of the wide table, following that with a swallow of water. *You've got to get your weight back up.* Then she sharpened the quill and began the draft of the letter to Konsstin, knowing it would likely take her several attempts and more time than she wanted to spend on it.

> Most Puissant Ruler of all Liedwahr, Liedfuhr of Mansuur . . .

Anna wondered what other flowery titles she could attach to the scroll, then added, "Ruler of the West." She left a blank area and began on the body of the missive.

> . . . you had stated in your last message that your lancers were not meant to invade Defalk. Unhappily, they were persuaded to do so, either by their commander or by the former Prophet. I initially spared these lancers out of consideration for you and for the people of Mansuur . . . and in response to your earlier communications and gestures . . .

Anna swallowed hard. At least she didn't have to *say* the words. Writing them was bad enough.

> . . . but their commander insisted on being less than reasonable. Overcaptain Relour not only refused to recognize the Prophet's successor, but also refused to return to Mansuur. Again, I tried to spare your forces, and called down sorcery just upon Overcaptain Relour. His successors immediately attacked my forces—*in my land* . . .

Anna underlined the words with two bold lines.

> . . . and left me no alternatives but to destroy them and their lancers. I wish it had not been so, but Defalk is not rich in skilled lancers and armsmen, and I could not

afford to be generous with a commander who had not
listened to reason or to the orders of his own
Liedfuhr . . .

The sorceress paused. *Now what?*

Because the Prophet Rabyn left no heirs, I have taken
the liberty of suggesting that the ruler of Neserea be the
most senior officer left to that poor land—one Overcaptain Hanfor. I also suggested that he adopt the title of
Lord High Counselor, since the title of Prophet of Music
would not be appropriate under the current conditions. . . .

I believe Neserea should continue to be ruled by Nesereans, and I have offered my support to Lord High Counselor Hanfor in the most unlikely event that he should
face an invader. I would hope that you would see fit to
also extend an equally generous offer to Lord High
Counselor Hanfor, so that he and his people will understand that both Defalk and Mansuur are friends and
trusted neighbors.

Anna smiled, and then began to think of what sorts of flowery conclusions she might be able to pen, not that they would
soften the impact all that much, but what else could she do?
Konsstin had to understand that she wasn't about to allow Mansuuran lancers to run loose east of the Westfels.

She finally scrawled out a florid conclusion, wincing as she
did.

She replaced the quill in the holder, then stood and walked to
the narrow window, framed by old and dark gray stone blocks,
roughly dressed. She looked out into the cool but sunny midmorning. After too brief a glance, she returned to the table, and
the endless pile of scrolls.

She had finished nearly a dozen and thought it was close to
midday when there was a knock on the chamber door.

"Arms Commander Himar," announced Bersan.

"Have him come in." Anna stood and glanced across the
piles of scrolls set on the table that had belonged to the late
Lord Jearle, then at Himar.

Himar bowed, and his eyes went to the scrolls. "You have been busy, Regent."

"There was a lot I set aside to take care of Rabyn." She shook her head. "It didn't go away. I need these sent."

"As you wish." Himar nodded and took out his ubiquitous grease marker and a folded oblong of the crude brown paper.

Is that the standard issue Defalkan officer's writing tool? "This pile goes to Lord Jecks in Falcor."

Himar scribbled out something.

"This goes to Lady Herene in Pamr, and this to Ytrude in Suhl." Anna paused. "This is the one that we have to get to the Liedfuhr. What would be the quickest way?"

"With Hanfor, I would guess, Regent, and then by ship from Esaria."

"We'll send a messenger to catch up with him."

"We can do that." Himar offered another nod.

"Oh . . . and this one goes to Lord Ustal." She paused once more. "Could you let Falar know that I'll need to talk to him tomorrow. He hasn't left yet, has he?"

"No, Regent." Himar smiled. "He had hoped you would see him."

"He's a scoundrel, but trustworthy as scoundrels go."

"I know him little, except by watching, but I would say his word is good."

After Anna had bundled Himar off with the piles of scrolls, she stopped to munch on bread, actual dark bread. *Where did Jearle get molasses if he was under siege for almost a season?* She frowned, then cut another wedge of cheese from the platter on the side of the wide table, following that with water from the bottle beside it.

As she ate, Anna looked at her "problem" list:

Flossbend(Beltyr)
Arien(Tybel)
Silberfels(Hulber)
Fussen(Ustal)
Wendell(Genrica)
Issl(Fustar)
Mossbach(???)

She was forgetting someone. Klestayr—the lord of Aroch. But she didn't know what he was plotting, only that he was.

Eight holds, out of Thirty-three. Some were problems she didn't have to address immediately, like Ustal and Hulber. Some she couldn't until she knew more, like Klestayr. And the possible power grab by Fustar probably wouldn't happen until Genrica died, which might be a while. So that left deciding what to do about the succession in Mossbach, and righting the problems in Flossbend and Arien.

"Arien and Flossbend, first . . ." she murmured.

There was another knock on the door. Anna turned over the sheet with her list. "Yes?"

"The chief player."

"I'll see her." Anna rose and waited.

Liende stepped into the guest chamber and bowed, deeply. "Lady Regent."

Not knowing exactly what to say, Anna smiled.

Liende looked at Anna, then down, then back at the regent. "I cannot thank you . . . not enough."

"What? For giving your son more headaches than he'll ever be able to get rid of? For ensuring that I have a loyal lord on the border so that I don't have to worry every time I leave Falcor? For putting him so far away that you'll seldom see him?"

Liende laughed, softly. "All those would happen were he lord or blade or player. Did you know . . . once I had hoped he might receive some small plot or a cot from Lord Brill. But it would have been a gift. My gift. This . . ." Liende gestured around her. "This he has earned and will earn with every day he lives, and that I could never have provided."

"But you did," Anna pointed out. "You raised him well and taught him. What you helped him become is why he is Lord of Denguic."

Liende smiled and shook her head. "He was not certain when he came to Falcor. He watched you." The smile turned sad. "At first, he saw a beautiful girl, and I think wanted you for little less than your form, and did not understand. Alseta— she saw you from the first, and she was not kind to him. But Kinor is not without wit, and he watched and learned. And you were kind to let him accompany you." The chief player shrugged. "He will do aught that is necessary to keep this hold and your faith."

Anna nodded. "I would hope so, and I would hope he can win the loyalty of the people. That will not be easy."

"It may not be so hard. Already . . . there are tales, now that the lady Livya and her daughter have left."

Were there tales in every hold? Anna took a long slow breath.

Liende bowed, her eyes taking in the table with the scrolls. "You have much to do, and I would not hold you. I did wish to thank you."

"Liende . . ." Anna's voice was soft. "You have supported me and saved me when you didn't want to. I took youth from you, and I probably caused Brill's death. I didn't mean to, but . . . I didn't help there. I'm grateful to you. I won't say it often, but I am. I still need you, and your skills. I'm just glad that it worked out this way."

"You are honest, and you are beautiful, and you see women as they should be." The chief player looked Anna straight in the eyes. "You are a sorceress, and at times, you ask much. At times, you are cold. You must be, and I know that. But you essay to be fair and to care for those who support you as much as is possible for any ruler. We—and I—cannot ask more." She dropped her eyes. "Perhaps . . . I am getting old . . . I say too much."

"You . . . you are the honest one," Anna replied. "I'm glad you are. Thank you."

"I need be going." A brief smile crossed the chief player's face. "Know you when we travel?"

"I'd guess you'll have another day or two to enjoy Lord Kinor's hold." Anna smiled. "Maybe longer, but I don't know yet."

Liende bowed, then departed.

Anna had scarcely looked at the problem list again before there was another interruption.

"Lord Nelmor," announced Bersan.

The tall blond lord bowed as he entered.

"How is the Lord of the Western Marches today?" asked the sorceress.

Nelmor smiled shyly, almost uneasily. "I must confess, Lady Regent, that when first you told me of your intent, I had som concerns that you had spoken too hastily." The tall lord looked down at the worn carpet for a moment before meeting Anna's eyes again. "Yet my sister, may the harmonies keep her, and my daughter, they oft said that a wise man never stood against your word." He laughed, not quite ruefully.

Anna wasn't quite sure how to answer that. After a moment, she replied, "I do my best. It doesn't always work, but I try." She added quickly, "Is there anything . . . ?"

"You have given much . . . yet I would beg yet one favor. . . ." Again, Nelmor looked down before continuing. "It is said you can see whether another lives and where. . . ."

"You would like to see Lysara and Tiersen?" Anna hoped that was what the blond lord wished.

"Ah . . . if that be possible . . . or Tiersen . . ."

"We can try." Anna pulled out a sheet of paper that she'd scratched up on one side in trying to draft her scroll to Jecks, and stood by the table, drafting, trying to adjust the simple scrying spell. After a short time, she looked up. "If they are together this will show it. If not, the glass will show two images, one of each."

She sang a short vocalise, then lifted the lutar for the scrying spell.

> Show us in this glass, even from so far,
> Tiersen and Lysara as they are
> Show us bright and show us clear. . . .

As the notes died away, the mirror silvered, and the mist swirled. Then another mist filled the glass. Anna wondered, momentarily, before the south tower of the liedburg at Falcor appeared. With a heavy fog behind them, Tiersen and Lysara, her red hair shimmering, stood looking out at the city. Tiersen's arm was around Lysara's shoulder.

Although he said nothing, Nelmor swallowed slightly, his eyes on the pair in the glass.

Anna, not wishing to spend much energy, sang the release couplet, then turned to the lord. "You see? They're fine." She was worried about the fog. Did that mean they'd face more rain in heading eastward, not that she had any intention of going directly to Falcor, not with her other problems.

"They appear happy."

Let them, Anna wanted to say. *Let them . . . they'll have enough worries before long.* "They do."

A wistful look crossed Nelmor's face, then vanished, and he bowed. "You have been most kind, Regent, and most fair, and I thank you. We will hold the Marches and serve your bidding." He bowed again.

"Thank you, Lord Nelmor." Anna inclined her head, then waited.

After Nelmor left, the sorceress walked back to the window. She'd have to return to writing scrolls and calculating, and all the things she hadn't done while she'd been preoccupied with the Nesereans and the Mansuuran lancers.

For a time, she stood and looked out the narrow window into a day warmer than the one before, recalling other warm days, days with tender graces that were dead to her and would never come back.

101

MANSUUS, MANSUUR

A low fire burns in the central hearth, and the windows are tightly closed against the northwest wind that whistles around the palace of the Liedfuhr, bringing the chill polar air from distant Defuhr Bay and beyond.

"Sire . . ." Bassil bows low before the polished table-desk, behind which sits Konsstin, fingering his brown-and-silver beard as he studies a scroll before him.

The Liedfuhr looks up abruptly. "That extreme deference means all is not well, Bassil. What calamity has occurred?"

"Sire . . . I would not say it was a calamity."

"I would. When you bow and scrape so . . ." Konsstin purses his lips. "Will you tell me, or must I drag it from you, with each word making me less patient?"

"The sorceress . . . she has destroyed your grandson and all his forces. As if they were less than ants."

"We had discussed this." Konsstin frowns. "That is not necessarily irredeemable."

"So it seemed. The seers watched the battle, and Rabyn used the triple drums and threw Darksong at her. He was strong. Strong enough to cast a shield over much of his camp, despite the fires falling from the heavens. In the end, though, she broke his shields and prevailed, and destroyed utterly all the Neserean armsmen with him."

"That surely is not the problem."

"She spared your lancers."

"The more fool she."

"She asked for some terms from Relour. He refused. She destroyed him in the night with lightning. The captain next in command—I think that would have been Donbrin—he attacked nearly at dawn. She was waiting, and turned them all into ash."

"All hundredscore?"

"Yes, sire."

"That is war. I will not have it."

"Sire . . . there is more."

"More? How can there be more?" Konsstin stands, towering over the desk. He glares at the black-haired lancer officer. "More, you say?"

"She spared one force of Nesereans, those besieging Denguic."

"She spared them, and not my lancers, when I had sent her golds in good graces?"

"Her own arms commander rides with the Nesereans, with but a small company of Defalkan lancers, and all are returning to Esaria, or so it would seem."

"They turned and left, when she had but a handful of armsmen?"

"Would you not were you in their boots?" asks the lancer officer. "She has destroyed whole holdings' worth of lands in both Dumar and Ebra. She has brought the fires of heaven against every force sent to bring her to bay. She has destroyed two Prophets, and two lords of Ebra, and the Lord of Dumar. Would you not retreat, given the chance?"

"So . . . Bassil . . . she has flouted my power, vanquished my grandson, defeated and destroyed my lancers, and rules another land, this time over my daughter's and grandson's land." The Liedfuhr's hazel eyes flash like lightning, turning black momentarily. "And now her arms commander rides in triumph to Esaria?"

"No, sire. Less than a single company rides with the sorcer-ess' own arms commander, and the remainder of the Prophet's Guard. The sorceress remains in Defalk."

"How might that be?" Konsstin's voice turns lazy, not quite indolent.

Bassil swallows before he speaks. "It may be that he is the new Lord High Counselor of Neserea, as Hadrenn is of Ebra," Bassil suggests, finally blotting the sweat from his forehead.

"Worse and worse . . . you said this could not happen. A pup-pet ruler over the lands of my daughter and grandson?"

"This ruler is no puppet, your seers say."

"Oh . . . some young lord of Defalk, no doubt."

"No, sire. An older officer, her own arms commander, one of those from Lord Behlem's forces. He is from Nesalia, they think."

"And how would they know such?"

Bassil shrugs. "There are messengers coming to you, also, sire. From the sorceress."

"Summon the overcaptains, all of them. We must prepare our forces for the march to Esaria."

"Do not destroy yourself, sire. Do not destroy Liedwahr."

"You presume! This witch has but a handful of lancers left, and no armsmen. I will not be swayed by words. She cannot work spells without lancers to protect her."

"Yes, sire. I presume. If you wage a mighty battle against the sorceress, she will defeat you. She will destroy your forces as she has destroyed all the others. And who will rule Mansuur, then? She cannot. No one could have stopped her from ruling Dumar. Or Ebra. Yet she has let the Lady Siobion rule in his late liege's place. She has restored the old line of Ebra, if with the new free port of Elahwa, and she has apparently placed a dis-tinguished Neserean arms commander on the throne of the Prophet."

"What does the woman want?"

"Security . . . peace, sire." Bassil wipes his forehead again. "You should wait for her messengers. Should you then wish war, you will know what she wants and how best to oppose it."

"Go!" Konsstin frowns, and his lips are tight. "I will consider your fair words, Bassil." As the lancer officer bows deeply, the Liedfuhr adds under his breath. "Foul as they may be."

102

A nna glanced out the narrow window of the guest chamber, to the south, but the late-afternoon sky was clear, although she knew from her earlier inspection of the hold that clouds were gathering to the northeast.

"Arms Commander Himar," announced Fielmir.

"Come on in." Anna turned from the window.

As always, Himar bowed after entering. "All the lancers and the players are prepared to ride tomorrow." He raised his sandy eyebrows. "You have not said what you plan, Regent."

"We're riding straight to Arien. That's why we need to get moving. We still have a lot to do before the full winter closes in. We'll take the trading road directly to Cheor, and we'll stay at Synfal. Then we'll take the Synor River Road east. All the lancers will come with us—except the purple company—as far as Synfal. Then one company will go north to Falcor along the Falche River Road."

"That will leave you with but fivescore lancers." Himar frowned.

"I think I can persuade Falar to accompany us."

"You have something in mind for him?"

"We'll see," Anna temporized. "He's a young scoundrel, but an honest one, and I have a thought he might prove useful."

"He has near-on twoscore with him, and some are most experienced armsmen." Himar laughed.

"I shouldn't ask about their past lives."

"All one has to do is look."

"That's what I thought, but they seem loyal to him. Will they be loyal to me?"

"So long as you offer hope to him."

"I'll offer to pay them." Anna nodded.

"That is even better."

"On your way out, would you have one of the guards summon the scoundrel? And Kinor. I have a few things I need to discuss with them—individually."

"That I will."

Anna stood behind the table, then bent and took a long swallow of water from the scratched but clean goblet.

What would she do about Mossbach? The Regent shrugged. That depended on what Jecks had found out about heirs. She hoped an answer would be waiting for her when she reached Synfal. Jecks had been right about not saying anything before she'd dealt with Rabyn, but that had left yet another loose end trailing. Then, all Defalk was loose ends. Was that because she'd done everything backward, by dealing with the outside threats before the inside ones?

She shook her head. Hitler and a lot of tyrants had done the same thing, except that they'd never gotten around to the inside problems, not the real ones. *You have to be different. You have to be.*

"Falar to see you, Regent."

"Have him come in."

The door opened, and the slender redheaded man stepped inside, bowing.

"You had summoned me, Lady Anna?" Falar smiled, not quite a rogue's smile, but close.

"I did." Anna wanted to get to the heart of the matter. "I have considered several things. First, the succession of Fussen." She tried to be thoughtful. "I have seen your brother, and I have seen you. It's fair to say that I like you better. It's probably fair to say that you'd make a better lord. But . . . unlike Lord Jearle or Lord Dannel, your brother has not lifted arms against me. He hasn't done anything that other lords would find offensive."

Falar nodded, thoughtfully. "And many lords remain who bridle at the Regency. You wish to make no enemies you need not make."

"I think you understand." Anna smiled. "There is one other thing. I can only suggest, Falar, but I'd like to suggest that you and your armsmen accompany me. We will be traveling to Synfal, and then to Arien, and then to Flossbend. If you choose to come, I will supply your men, and I will pay them."

"Do you expect many battles within Defalk?"

"I do not plan to fight any battles. I may employ sorcery, and it would be good to have lancers and armsmen. I can promise nothing, but I'd like to learn more about you." Anna laughed wryly. "There's definitely a shortage of people who are able and whom I can trust." *Are you being too blunt? Probably.*

Those words got a thoughtful nod. "From another I would suspect merely the use of hope to obtain hired blades. Too many speak of your honor." A crooked smile crossed the young man's face. "And you have rewarded fairly those who have served you longest."

Thank heaven that got across. "I try . . . and I try to see where people can do what they can do best."

"We will come with you. Mayhap my accompanying you will turn my brother's vaunted good digestion. And curdle his thoughts."

"You have an evil mind, young man," Anna said, not quite succeeding in keeping a straight face.

"My brother deserves to have his thoughts curdled, but," pointed out Falar, "if my serving the Regent sours them, then the fault is his."

"You have a point there." Anna added, "I will also pay you what a captain gets. That's only fair, because that is the job you'll be doing."

"Then I can honestly write my brother and tell him that I have taken paid service with the Regent." The boyish grin reappeared. "That will sour his thoughts further."

"We leave in the morning. You answer to Himar."

"Yes, Regent." Falar bowed, spoiling the gesture with yet another roguish grin.

Anna managed—barely—to keep a straight face.

The next person waiting to see Anna was Kinor, and he bowed twice on the way into the guest chamber.

Anna looked at Kinor. As much as he had aged over the campaign, he was still painfully young for what Anna had thrust upon him. But he was perceptive, intelligent, and loyal, and there were few indeed among the Thirty-three who met those criteria.

"Kinor . . . I think you know. I've given you a lot to handle. It's going to take everything you have to hold Westfort. I could give you a lot of advice. I won't. I'll tell you the three things that I think are most important. First, if something seems wrong, or people seem to be doing something in a strange way . . . before you do anything or order anything or change anything, find out *why* they're doing it the way they are." She paused.

Kinor nodded.

"Second, if you don't know about something . . . ask. And ask quickly. People will often forgive what you don't know when you first start something. They won't later. And last, don't give the impression of being indecisive. If you're not sure about something, ask for opinions, then say you'll think over what everyone has said. Then do something. Either announce that matters won't change, or that you want it done a certain way, or, if you have to, say that it's my problem, and send me a scroll, and tell everyone you have." Anna laughed. "Just make sure it *is* my problem."

"Yes, lady."

"Dutral and the purple company are here to support you until spring. That's about a third of a year." Anna paused. "I wish I could offer more, but I can't."

"That is much, Lady Anna. I know how few lancers you have, and you can ill spare even those."

"I can ill spare losing Westfort, either," Anna pointed out. "If you have any questions for me, you'd better think of them between now and tomorrow morning. That's when we leave."

Kinor did not protest. "I had thought so when Himar summoned me." He paused. "I thank you for all you have done. Though it would be ill done, I would ask one last favor."

Anna nodded.

"Should aught happen to me . . . I would think Alseta is much like you, and could well run a keep. And she is my closest heir."

"I don't want you to think about that," Anna replied. "I will consider your request . . . if I have to, and not before."

"That be all I could ask."

Anna was touched by Kinor's request—thinking about his younger sister, and probably as a way to provide for Liende. Would Mario have done the same in Kinor's boots? Anna hoped so, but she wouldn't ever know.

Kinor bowed.

"And Kinor? You'd better work on building up your own force of trusted armsmen. I wouldn't rely completely on those who served Lord Jearle."

"Dutral and I have talked about such."

"Good. I'll see you at dinner."

Anna stood silently as the young lord bowed a last time and departed.

The door clicked shut, leaving her alone.

Anna hoped she hadn't leaned too hard on Kinor about the armsmen, but Defalk wasn't exactly the most peaceful of lands. She laughed to herself. If it had been peaceful and medievally oppressive, she'd never have become Regent, and probably nothing in Liedwahr would have changed. She was making some changes . . . and if she could hang on, there would be more. *And more sorcery and destruction.*

Violence has been the sire of all the world's values? Who had said that? Anna shook her head. Another line she did not remember—only those she had sung seemed locked with their authors inside her thoughts.

Her lips curled. If she were a character in one of Avery's novels, her problems would be all over. She'd defeated all the enemies outside of Defalk, and everyone would fall at her feet worshiping her for her power and skill. She snorted. Life didn't work that way, not even in strange worlds where there was magic. There were always people intriguing, and others with problems, and not enough money—or golds.

She glanced at the table—empty except for a few sheets of parchment she had saved in case she needed to scrawl out any last-moment scrolls. She had no doubt that she'd be writing *something* even before dinner.

103

The rain beat out of the north, mostly across the backs of the riders, but it was cold, almost like liquid ice, and some dribbled off of Anna's battered brown felt hat and down her neck. The oiled-leather jacket she had borrowed from Westfort—or been given by Kinor, who'd taken great pleasure in the act—was beginning to soak up the rain despite its oiled surface. And Farinelli was starting to *whuff* and toss his head.

You did have this idea about settling everything in Defalk before winter. Anna almost groaned. *No one will be expecting you in Arien, anyway.*

Anna wiped the water—a combination of condensation from under the hat and water from the rain—from her forehead. She tried to make out where the road went as it curved eastward past a hill covered with leafless trees. Supposedly, there was a town with stables and an inn ahead, but still several deks south, and Cheor was at least another day away, maybe longer if the roads got worse.

Riding beside her on her left, Jimbob was silent.

A taller figure and his mount loomed out of the rain, as Himar rode up beside the Regent. "The scouts say it is less than three deks, and there are two stables. It will be crowded, but we can manage."

"Good. How are the men coming?" Anna almost had to shout over the wind and the cold slapping of the rain on everything.

The arms commander eased his mount closer to Anna. "They know they will find warm beds in Synfal. That helps. I will pass the word about our stop. That will also help." Himar turned his mount back northward, and a glop of mud splattered against Anna's boots and lower trousers.

Falar rode forward from somewhere behind Anna, and leaned toward her. "Are all your journeys so eventful?"

"No. Some are more eventful," Anna managed.

The redhead laughed. "Did the arms commander say that there was a dry roof ahead?"

"He did. About three deks ahead. It'll be crowded, but it will get everyone out of the rain, and most of the mounts, I hope."

"Good. I must pass that on to my men." Like Himar, he turned his mount back along the column.

"Have you ridden in worse?" Jimbob asked loudly.

"A few times as bad as this—in Dumar when we were chasing Lord Ehara. There weren't any friendly towns or inns there."

"You said we were going to Synfal, and then Arien."

"I haven't decided whether you should go to Arien or stay in Synfal. Synfal is your keep, and the people haven't seen much of you since last spring."

"That is true. What do you think, Lady Anna?"

Anna paused. The question was the first time, she thought, that Jimbob had actually asked her advice and seemed to mean it. "I'd like you to think about it first before I say anything. What I have to do at Arien, I'm afraid, is like what I did at Westfort. Lord Tybel has poisoned his sister and her sons to hand her lands over to their brother."

"He doesn't know you, does he?"

Tybel doesn't want to, like a lot of the Thirty-three. "I don't think so."

"I have not spent much time in Synfal . . . perhaps I should seek Herstat's thoughts on that." Another pause followed. "You do not require my answer now, do you, Lady Anna?"

"Heavens, no."

A squall line of even more intense rain swept over the column, and Anna had to grab her hat to keep it from being blown off her head. More of the cold rain poured down her neck.

Anna hoped it didn't take them too long to get to the unnamed town.

104

The column of Defalkan riders rode northward from the town of Cheor along the straight road that bisected the flat fields south of Synfal itself. Anna peered through the foggy mist that had replaced the cold rain of the day before, looking for the low wall of ancient yellow bricks that would show that the keep was but a dek farther north. She had hoped that the mist would dissipate by midday, but it was already early afternoon, and the fog still remained hugging the ground, although, occasionally, she saw patches of blue overhead.

"How much farther, Regent?" asked Falar, riding on the shoulder of the road and calling past Himar, who rode on Anna's left.

"Not more than two or three deks—a dek after we reach the old brick wall."

"Less than half a dek to the wall," predicted Jimbob. "The big ditches running from the one beside the road are about eight hundred yards apart, and there are three small ones between them. I think we passed the last big one before the wall and one of the little ones. It can't be that much farther."

Almost as he finished speaking, Anna could see one of the smaller ditches branching off the big canal to the right of the road. She hid a grin as she asked, "Are all the ditches laid out like that, Jimbob?"

"Only the ones in the flat here. Herstat made me draw a map of them when I was here last."

"Why?" asked Falar, easing his mount closer to Jimbob's.

"He said that I should know every rod and furl of my lands." Jimbob shrugged. "He had me ride much of the land and draw maps."

"These are your lands, as well . . . as Falcor, I mean?" Falar's mouth opened.

"Well . . . I didn't inherit them the way I will Elheld or Falcor," Jimbob admitted. "Lord Arkad didn't have any heirs, and he tried to kill Lady Anna, and that meant that his lands were forfeit. Lady Anna is Regent, and she said that they were mine, except they're really not quite yet, not until I'm older, and she and my grandsire and Herstat think I know enough." Jimbob smiled and inclined his head to Anna. "That's about right, isn't it?"

"Yes. I thought that one of the problems Lord Barjim had was that he didn't have enough coins to be an effective lord. I didn't want Lord Jimbob to have that problem."

Falar bowed to Anna, with an appraising look. "There is much I have not heard, and more I should know."

"Much more," suggested Himar, from where he had ridden in front of the three. "The Regent is more than she seems."

"There's the wall," Jimbob said. "The old one, I mean. Grandsire said it's older than the time of the Suhlmorrans." He pointed ahead to his left where the yellow bricks of a two-yard-high wall protruded above a low hedgerow that had been trimmed to allow the top of the wall to show.

"It won't be long before we see Synfal," Anna said.

For a time, none of the riders spoke.

"The banner to the fore!" announced Himar.

The lancer with the banner rode around Falar, Jimbob, and

Anna and her guards to take station ahead of Himar and the column of riders.

Its weathered yellow-brick walls looming out of the misting rain, sitting on the isolated hill that had to have been the ruins of many earlier strongholds, Synfal looked, more than Anna recalled, like a relic of Defalk's even more violent past—old, scarred, and the site of who knew what unspeakable cruelties. *For Defalk, that's saying a lot.*

The crossed spears and crown on the purple banner were hardly visible to Anna, and she doubted that few in the stronghold would see them. The gates stood wide, and what seemed to be half the staff lined the courtyard of the keep and watched as Anna and Jimbob rode through the gates.

"Regent! Lord Jimbob!"

Anna glanced sideways, noting the flush rising in the young lord's face. "Remember," she said, "praise is fleeting. People praised your father, and then Lord Behlem."

Jimbob jerked in the saddle.

Falar gave Anna a searching look, but did not offer any words.

Anna raised an arm to acknowledge the greetings and whispered to Jimbob. "Go ahead. Show them you appreciate their greeting. You are the Lord of Synfal. Just remember that greetings can be fickle."

Jimbob smiled and waved several times, looking around the courtyard as he did. Then he and Anna rode slowly to the stables.

Bielttro, the young head ostler, stepped out from where he had stood by the stable doors, wearing what appeared to be the same dark brown trousers and leather vest as he had worn when Anna had first met him. He bowed. "Regent."

"Bielttro, how are your stables?"

"I have fixed the roof in the corner, and they are clean and dry." Bielttro grinned. "You can see for yourself, Regent Anna."

"I will." Anna smiled back, then dismounted and led Farinelli into the stable. Rickel and Fielmir followed closely, leaving their mounts with the other guards.

"You have the big front stall, as before." Bielttro studied Farinelli. "He is thinner."

"We've ridden a lot this fall, from Falcor to Synek, and back to Falcor, then to Denguic, and here. I've tried to get him grain . . . but it's not always been as much as he needs."

"He is not too thin, but I will see that there is grain here. I would give him but a third portion, and not until after you have groomed him. And only a little water at first."

Anna nodded.

"If you will please excuse me, lady, while I see to the others?"

"Please. Farinelli and I will be fine."

The old stables were dry, and smelled clean, as before, with fresh straw, and a pail of grain had been left beside the manger for Farinelli. Anna smiled, then unfastened the lutar case, wrapped in oiled canvas in addition to its normal cover, and set it beside the stall wall. Then came the mirror case, and the saddlebags, probably soaked through.

"Big stalls . . ." murmured Fielmir.

"It's a large keep," Rickel responded. "Older and bigger than Falcor."

Anna finished unsaddling Farinelli, then groomed him, and finally let him have some water, but not too much, before she poured some of the grain into the manger. The gelding *whuff*ed and tossed his head as Anna lifted the bucket. "That's enough for now. Bielttro will give you more, you pig." She patted his shoulder, then picked up the lutar.

Fielmir carried the saddlebags and mirror case, and he and Rickel followed her.

Herstat was waiting as Anna, Jimbob, and Himar stepped into the entry hall, followed by Rickel and Lejun. The saalmeister bowed deeply. "We are all glad you have arrived safely in this rain." He smiled. "Some thought you might be delayed, but I assured them that the Regent is seldom delayed."

"We try not to be late." Anna gestured to Falar. "This is Falar, second in succession to the lands of Fussen. He is traveling with us and offering us his armsmen." She gave a wry smile. "This year's been hard on everyone, especially the armsmen and lancers." Her eyes next went to Himar. "Himar has taken over as arms commander, now that Hanfor is the Lord High Counselor of Neserea."

"We have chambers most suitable," Herstat replied. "Lord

Jecks had sent several scrolls by fast messenger." After a pause, he continued, "If you would follow me . . ."

Anna still held on to the lutar as she climbed the steps behind Herstat toward the upper levels of the keep. Blaz carried the saddlebags, and Lejun the mirror case. The bricks that formed the floors had been thoroughly cleaned and covered with a shimmering varnish of some sort since Anna had last been at Synfal. The walls had also been scrubbed and repainted with a form of whitewash. The keep looked lighter, and smelled far better, although there was a lingering hint of mold still.

Halfway down the second-floor corridor, Herstat opened a polished-oak door, stepping through and gesturing. "The guest chamber that will always be yours, Regent Anna." Herstat bowed.

"Thank you. It looks much better. Much cleaner."

"There has been much done in the main keep, and much left to do."

Fielmir carried in the saddlebags and mirror, then took station outside the door, as did Rickel. As the two guards departed, Anna studied the room. On the fresh white-painted plaster of the wall hung a newer mirror. Herstat had clearly remembered what her scrying did to mirrors. There were also tapestry-covered floor screens set around a copper tub in the corner of the room away from the shuttered windows.

Anna swallowed as she looked at the stacks of scrolls set on the old oaken working table between the bed and the windows.

"The top one is from Lord Jecks. He suggested you might wish to read that first." Herstat bowed. "Is there aught else you might require, Lady Anna?"

"Ah . . . some cheese and bread, any fruit you might have, and several buckets of water for a bath."

"The tub is filled already. I took the liberty of having that done. And I will have someone bring you the food." The saalmeister bowed again, then eased back out the door.

Anna picked up the top scroll from Jecks, then set it down. She decided the scrolls could wait until she had something to eat and had taken a bath and gotten into dry clothes. She glanced around the chamber once more. There was even a large robe lying on the foot of the bed. Herstat definitely knew his business, but, then, that was why she and Jecks had selected him to run Synfal for Jimbob.

She went to the window and eased the shutters full open. The fog had become a white shimmering mist that promised the sun would burn through. Yet, as she watched, the mist dimmed into a darker, milkier white.

"Lady Anna?" came a voice from the door.

"Yes?" Anna turned.

"A serving girl with bread and cheese."

"Escort her in." Anna was probably getting paranoid, but it sometimes seemed like a lot of people wanted her out of the way.

Fielmir came in with the young woman, a girl really, whose eyes widened as she took in the sorceress. The serving girl carried a wooden tray with a basket holding two loaves of bread, several wedges of cheese, an apple, and a quince.

"Thank you." Anna smiled.

"Regent . . . the saalmeister . . ." The girl half bowed, managing to keep the tray level. "He said . . . you . . ."

"I appreciate the bread and cheese. It's been a long ride."

The serving girl seemed frozen in place, as her eyes remained fixed on Anna.

"I am the Regent," Anna said, "and I do have children far older than you, but probably most of the other tales you've heard have been exaggerated."

Fielmir stepped forward and took the tray.

"If you would put it on the bench at the foot of the bed . . ." Anna gestured.

The serving girl swallowed.

"Come, girl," Fielmir said gently. "She's the Regent. She won't turn you into ashes or ice or some such."

The girl bowed abruptly, then practically darted from the chamber.

The sorceress shook her head, afraid that such reactions would get worse the longer she was in Defalk and the more successful she was. *If you are.*

Anna ate an entire loaf of the dark bread, as well as almost all of one of the cheese wedges. Then she picked up the lutar, hoping that the spell for heating and cleaning the water wouldn't give her too much of a headache.

While the steaming water cooled enough for her to climb into the tub, she used the lutar once more, this time to dry and clean her single traveling gown. The bath helped with various aches, but her eyes kept straying beyond the screens toward the pile of scrolls. So, in the end, she washed more quickly than she'd thought, including her short blonde hair, then dried herself and dressed.

Once she seated herself at the writing desk, Anna took out Jecks' scroll, skimming through it quickly, trying to root out the important points. She'd have to read it again, and probably again after that.

> . . . Lord Dannel left two daughters, but Lady Resengna fled with them . . . northward, it is believed, to seek safety in Nordwei with them, taking more than two thousand golds. I have dispatched Gelen to take the hold under his control . . . not be my first choice, but will not disobey me . . .

Anna frowned. The same problem—not enough people either she or Jecks could trust.

> . . . Lord Genrica weakens, but will doubtless last for some seasons yet . . . and Lord Clethner paid the hold a visit, at my suggestion. . . .

The Regent smiled—that might hold off the greedy Fustar for a bit—at least until she could deal with the problems in the south.

> . . . the lady Ytrude arrived safely in Suhl . . . seems to have taken the household reins gently but firmly . . .

> . . . you will see . . . Lord Tybel claims that Flossbend must be ceded to his brother Beltyr . . . and protests the actions of the Regent in seizing and redistributing lands of the Thirty-three against custom . . .

Anna frowned. So far, she hadn't "redistributed" any lands, unless he meant those of Pamr, and that Anna should have given them to Dvoyal because he was the consort of Lord Kysar's half sister. *That's just an excuse to put them in his nephew's very male paws.* She'd have to look at that scroll carefully.

> ... young undercaptain Skent sent a scroll. He and Jirsit have added another score to the guards at Pamr. As you requested, I have summoned Jirsit and have taken the liberty of confirming both Jirsit and Skent as junior captains. ...

Anna smiled at that. Skent needed more experience, but if he could wait just a bit longer, then Lord Geansor might just be persuaded to allow his daughter to consort with Skent. *You hope* ...

> ... several missives from Lord Hadrenn ... has secured an envoy from Ranuak and reports that the freewomen have set up a city guard in Elahwa and a council ... like that of Wei, I believe.

> ... also received scroll from the Mistress of the Exchange in Encora, informing you that all lords in Defalk will receive the favored terms of trade granted all of the peaceful realms in Liedwahr. ...

That was most interesting. Because of the establishment of the Free State of Elahwa? Anna went to the third roll of parchment.

> ... Halde sent several reports from Mencha ... have enclosed those, since Mencha is your demesne, and I felt you would prefer to review them in more detail. He does seem most careful and conscientious. ...

After reading all of Jecks' reports, and just looking at the pile of scrolls, Anna almost wondered why she was in Synfal. *Because you can't just rule this place. You have to change it, and you can't change it from Falcor.* She glanced at the scrolls again. After a moment, she began to sort through them, until she had a stack of a dozen, which she set beside the serving tray on the bench at the foot of the high bed. Then she nodded and went to the door, opening it.

"Rickel . . . if you would have someone summon Lord Jimbob for me? I'd like to see him now."

Rickel tightened his lips, as if concealing a smile. "My pleasure, Regent."

Anna closed the door—except not quite all the way—and listened.

"Regent . . . good for that boy. Full of himself until she took hold of him . . . had that look in her eye . . . bet she's going to straighten him up proper again . . ."

Not quite in that way. Anna eased the door closed all the way and returned to the latest scroll from Lord Clethner.

> . . . being that Wendell sits near-astride the border
> with Nordwei and Lord Genrica's consort is the cousin of
> one of the counselors . . .

Thrap.

Anna looked up at the knock. "Yes?"

"It's Lord Jimbob, Lady Anna."

"Come on in." Anna set down Clethner's scroll and stood behind the table, waiting.

Jimbob stepped inside gingerly.

Anna motioned for him to close the door. "You see those?" She pointed to the scrolls on the bench.

"Yes, Lady Anna."

She smiled. "You're going to get a better understanding of something else. Jimbob . . . I want you to read every one of these. Right now, while I go through some of the others." She pointed again to the stack of scrolls she had preselected. There were a few, such as those from Tybel, Jecks, and Clethner, that she didn't want him to see.

"Me, Lady Anna?"

"You were the one who told me you learned more by doing. These are what I have to deal with. I want you to think over each, and then write down two or three lines of what *you* would do if you were in my boots."

Jimbob swallowed.

Anna smiled. "Oh . . . and you'll do it here, because those scrolls aren't leaving me. You can also ask me questions, if you need to."

"Ah . . . yes, Lady Anna." The redhead pulled a straight-backed chair next to the bench and sat down. Slowly, he picked up a scroll on the side, almost as if the parchment were fire that might burn him.

Anna searched to find the scroll from Lord Tybel. After she read it, she was seething. She took a deep breath, and a swallow of water, then studied it again.

> . . . while it is most commendable for a female Regent to attempt to maintain the lineage of the lords of Defalk from father to son . . . under the ancient and honorable traditions of Defalk, all lands must pass from fathers to sons, or nephews or brothers. Otherwise and one might as well say that Defalk is no more. . . .

The sorceress-Regent forced herself to take another slow breath.

> . . . first you as Regent have let women hold lands for sons, and now you would have women hold lands for daughters . . . the Thirty-three cannot accept such a perversion of what has always been and what must be for Defalk . . . I will raise the entire south against the Regency should this continue. . . .

She shook her head. Was Tybel an idiot? Hadn't he heard what had happened to Dannel? Or was he so isolated that he couldn't believe it? Or did he truly believe in some sort of harmonic divine right of primogeniture? She slowly rolled up the scroll. Somehow, she had the feeling that Tybel wasn't going to back down, that his beliefs justified the murder of his daughter and her children. *So your beliefs justify his death?*

She didn't have the armsmen to force him to submit, and she couldn't risk those she had, and she couldn't risk another attack like the one that Dannel had led. *And that doesn't leave a lot of options.*

She looked helplessly at the wall for a long time before picking up the next scroll.

After more than a glass, Jimbob set down the last of the

scrolls he had been poring over and looked at Anna. "These are not all, are they?"

Anna set down the goblet of water she had been sipping. "No. You'll see some of the others as you get more experience. Now . . . remember, you have to draft a short suggestion on each for me."

Jimbob nodded.

Another knock sounded on the door. "Lady Anna . . . the saalmeister would like to inform you and Lord Jimbob that dinner will be ready in a quarter glass . . . unless you would like it later."

"No . . . we'll be ready." Anna looked at Jimbob. "You can think about the scrolls tonight and write up your suggestions in the morning. I'll be writing most of the day, I suspect." She stood. "We shouldn't keep the others waiting." *Most of them didn't get snacks . . . .*

Jimbob stood. "I am hungry."

Anna smiled. She hadn't known many thirteen- or fourteen-year-olds who weren't hungry. "Let's go."

105

In the gray that preceded sunrise, Anna looked at the lutar case on the bench at the foot of the high carved bed. One full day in Synfal really hadn't been enough, although the red-headed young Lord of Synfal who had just stepped into her chamber had probably thought so with all the scrolls Anna had pushed at him.

She studied Jimbob, but he looked back steadily.

"I wanted to talk to you again before I left," Anna said. "Do you understand why I don't think you ought to be on this journey?"

Jimbob nodded, and his longish red hair flopped over his ears. "You don't think I should be involved when you have to decide who inherits lands?"

"Whoever does what I'm going to do isn't going to be popular for a while. It's better that people look forward to your rule than feel that you won't be any different from me."

"Grandsire says you're the best ruler Defalk has ever had."

"I appreciate his words, and his support. But you have to remember that what people feel isn't necessarily the way it should be. Sometimes, when you do what is right, it's not very popular, especially with the Thirty-three." *Is that ever the truth.* "I think you'd do fine on the trip. You've done well so far, but you need more time with Herstat, and more time here to learn about Synfal and so that the people will come to take you as their lord in their hearts as well as their heads."

"Their hearts as well as their heads . . ." Jimbob smiled shyly. "Sometimes, your words . . . they sound . . . well, I wish I could talk like you do."

"You have time to learn. Just listen. Words help, but actions speak as well, sometimes better." Anna cocked her head. "Any last questions?"

"I can't think of any."

"I need to saddle Farinelli. You can come with me if you'd like."

"I'd like to." Jimbob picked up the saddlebags and the mirror case. "I can carry these down."

"Thank you." Anna glanced at the saddlebags that held the two sets of riding gear, the single gown, and only the scroll from Jecks. The one from Tybel she had folded into her belt wallet.

Bersan and Fielmir followed them down to the stable.

There Bielttro was waiting. "Lady Anna . . . here are two sacks of grain, and they fasten behind the saddle with these loops. They're not heavy, and you can feed him one tonight, and one tomorrow night."

"In short, you're telling me that he really ought to stay a few more days under your care and feeding?" Anna grinned.

Bielttro shifted his weight and looked down at the straw, then at Anna. "Mayhap your care and my feeding, lady?"

"We'll try to do better, Bielttro."

"You do better than many, Regent . . . but he is a good mount."

Anna accepted the reproach. "I know."

Bielttro nodded, then smiled. "Will you be back soon?"

"I hope so."

The ostler glanced toward the courtyard.

"I understand, Bielttro. You can deal with the other problems."

"Thank you, lady." The young ostler slipped away from the stall.

"He told you that you should handle your mount better," Jimbob said.

"He was right," Anna pointed out. "And he was tactful about telling me. He is a good head ostler, and he will get better. Treat him with respect, and listen to him, and he'll save you horses and coins."

Jimbob nodded. "Many would take umbrage."

"Just because I'm Regent doesn't mean I'm always right. People will tell you you're right because you're a lord. You have to know which are telling you the truth and which are flattering you." *You're probably laying it on too thick, but he needs all the reinforcement he can get on that point.*

"Grandsire said that, too. But an ostler never told him—"

"Your grandsire is far more experienced with horses than I am. He wouldn't make a mistake like that. I've heard Dythya and Herstat correct him on coins and numbers, though."

"Oh . . . I had not thought . . ."

You'd better . . .

"I need to get moving, Jimbob," Anna suggested as she finished tightening the girths and adjusting the saddle.

"I know." The young lord handed her the saddlebags, the small grain bags, the mirror case and then the lutar. "I'll watch from the hall door." He stopped. "You be careful, Lady Anna."

"I will." She watched as the embarrassed young man bowed and darted out of the stall.

Once she had led Farinelli out of the stable, Anna mounted and surveyed the courtyard, her breath steaming in the cold morning air. Himar was already mounted, and lining up the lancer companies. Falar, with his men along the east wall, flashed a roguish smile, one that Anna returned with a nod.

"Lady Anna, the players are ready," offered Liende.

Anna turned in the saddle. The chief player and the other players were mounted, and waiting, behind her guards. "Thank you."

"As are your guards," added Rickel from behind her right shoulder.

Anna turned and offered another acknowledgment. She'd wished that they'd been able to leave the day before, but just going through everything that Jecks had sent had taken two full days. Then, three nights with solid food and dry beds and stalls had probably been worth it to all the lancers and their mounts. *You feel better, too*. And . . . she'd had time to adapt the spells she'd need at Arien and Flossbend.

Jimbob had crossed the courtyard and stood on the mounting block by the carriage entrance to the hall, looking toward Anna. Herstat waited on the steps several yards behind the young lord.

Himar rode toward her. "All is ready. The gold company will stay here today, if you approve, and then leave for Falcor in the morning."

"Playing it safe, I see," Anna said. At the puzzled expression that crossed the arms commander's face, she added, "You want to make sure nothing happens on our way out of Synfal and through Cheor."

"Yes, Regent. And I know Finsul will ride hard to Falcor, no matter what order I leave with him." A crooked smile crossed Himar's lips.

Anna returned the smile. "That's fine. Let's go."

"Van forward!" Himar slid his mount around beside Anna.

The sorceress had the feeling that Jimbob watched until she was well out of the gate, but she didn't look back.

106

As she tried not to bounce in the saddle, Anna unfastened her jacket to avoid sweating under a clear sky and a midday sun that was almost summerlike. She reached for a water bottle and drank deeply. After replacing it, she stripped off the jacket, glad of the slight coolness remaining in the late morning.

"The mist worlds must be chill indeed," said Falar, riding to her right, still wearing his heavy leather jacket.

"Compared to Liedwahr, they are . . . or mine was." Anna peered eastward, but the road looked the same, winding around rises too low to be proper hills.

The Synor River Road had gotten more rutted and less traveled after they had passed the south road to Suhl, but when they had turned south on the trade road that led past Arien to Sudwei, the way had smoothed out again. But another day later, when they had turned eastward toward Arien, the road had quickly degenerated into a hole-filled and rutted country lane. Anna had checked the mirror twice to make sure they were headed to Arien, but the aerial view in the glass had confirmed it.

So she swayed in the saddle, with their progress slower than she would have hoped.

"Even my brother keeps better roads than these," offered Falar, "and I thought his efforts poor indeed."

"Fussen's roads are much better." Anna grinned. "I'm not so sure about its bridges, though."

"My sire always said that bridges should be strong enough for wagons and weak enough to be removed in case you wanted to deny an enemy a crossing."

"That didn't stop the Prophet," the sorceress pointed out.

"He didn't think about sorcery. There haven't been many sorcerers or sorceresses in the west since the lady Peuletar, and that was many, many years ago." Falar added, almost conversationally, "They say that she was beautiful, too."

"You're very gallant," Anna replied, half-pleased at the indirect compliment, but wanting *that* to go nowhere. "But you're my son's age, Falar."

"My eyes do not see that, lady."

"I said you were gallant, you rascal." Anna watched as one of the scouts rode down from the long hill that they approached, then stopped to talk to Himar, who had ridden ahead of the main column with several lancers, if behind the vanguard. "The scouts have seen something."

"Let us hope we are nearing our destination."

Anna wasn't certain about that.

Himar rode back from the head of the column, where he had been talking to one of the scouts. "Lady . . . once we reach the hills ahead, Arien lies in the valley beyond. How would you wish to proceed?"

"We'll try the mirror again, once we get to the hilltop and can check what it shows us against what we can see and the maps." She paused. "They didn't see any armsmen, did they?"

"No, Regent."

"Good."

Once they had reached the hillcrest, Himar led the column about a third of the way down the steeper hillside before he brought them to a halt by a browning meadow, where a small stream crossed the road at an angle, leaving a muddy ford of sorts.

"They can water their mounts while you scry, if you would not mind."

"That's fine."

Followed by Falar, Liende, and Himar—and Rickel and Blaz—Anna took the glass to the top side of the sloping meadow, setting it on a rock that was halfway flat. Then she lifted the lutar and began the scrying spell.

> Show us now and show us clear,
> how the ways to Arien do appear. . . .

Anna studied the mirror, then out eastward, and then back to the mirror. Just as Dvoyal, who had approximated a brother-in-law to Gatrune, Anna thought, had told her, Arien indeed lay in a valley, but unlike Stromwer there was no real barrier to approaching the keep, which lay just east of the small town. Rolling hills surrounded the gentle valley on all sides, hills partly forested and partly in brown-grassed meadows. There were few fields showing cultivation, and far larger grassy areas with dark shapes that appeared to be cows. A dairying region? Cheeses? Cheese kept, unlike milk, at least if you had cool cellars.

"Is Arien known for its cheeses?" she asked Falar, standing behind Himar.

"I could not say." The redhead shrugged, apologetically.

"The best hard white cheeses come from Arien," Liende finally said. "Some prefer the light yellow. Lord Brill bought the white."

Anna forced her thoughts back to the most unpleasant

prospects of the action soon to be required of her and concentrated on the mirrorlike map. There was a knoll to the south of the keep—or a rise. Anna pointed, as Himar sketched, and asked, "Could we hold that hilltop for a little while if Lord Tybel sent lancers after us?"

"With your arrow spells . . . and if he has fewer than tenscore armsmen."

"What if we circle to the south from here?"

"Word will reach him," Himar observed. "There is little real cover."

"He's not expecting us."

"And that will alarm him greatly." Himar paused. "He may know already. The scouts saw riders hastening toward the keep."

Anna suspected her arms commander was totally right about that.

When she finally released the spell, she took a deep breath, then picked up the lutar again.

> Show us now and show us clear
> Where Lord Tybel does appear. . . .

The mirror obligingly displayed a keep's courtyard where armsmen and lancers in armor and with shields milled into a rough formation. In the center of the armsmen was a square-bearded and broad-shouldered man wearing what Anna would have called glittering half armor.

"This one will not wait behind walls," Falar said. "Would that his brains equaled his courage."

Anna wasn't sure she agreed with that wish, either. She sang the release couplet and looked at Himar. "We'll have a glass or so before he arrives?"

"Almost two."

Neither doubted Tybel's destination.

"Where would be the best place to spellcast on him?"

"The ridge ahead, just above the bottom of the hill," Himar said flatly.

Anna turned. "Chief Player, I'll need the long flame spell and then, if necessary, the arrow spell."

Liende looked at Anna. "As the Regent commands."

Anna glanced at Falar, then Himar. "I need to talk to the chief player."

Both men stepped back.

"I will stand ready," Himar said with a bow.

"I also." Falar bowed.

Anna reached into her wallet and extracted the folded scroll from Tybel. She extended it to Liende. "If you would read this, Liende. Then I'd like to hear what you think."

The chief player's face looked like it had been chiseled from stone when she handed the scroll back.

"Now . . ." Anna said softly, "do you see why I don't have any choice? If I let Tybel dictate how Defalk is run . . . nothing will change."

Liende shook her head. "You would have taken nothing from him. He has sons. Even his grandsons would have held Flossbend . . . is that not so?"

"I wasn't happy with them, but I wouldn't have changed that," Anna admitted. "Just like I didn't unseat Ustal." *As big a chauvinist as he is.*

"Because you would allow a few women to hold lands . . . he would torch all Defalk?"

Anna gestured eastward toward the distant keep. "He's certainly acting that way."

Liende fixed Anna with intent eyes. "How will you use the spell?"

"To kill anyone who supports Tybel and who also believes that women should be slaves."

"Not to kill them all?"

"Not unless they keep attacking. Then I'll have to use the full flame spell."

Liende exhaled slowly. "You are as fair as the harmonies allow. I will have the players make ready once we reach the ridge."

"I'm sorry."

"They will be sorrier still, the hapless fools." Liende's eyes were bright with unshed tears.

Anna and her guards followed the player back toward their mounts, Blaz carrying the scrying mirror.

The area overlooking the road that Anna had picked was more like a bench protruding from the gentle eastern side of the hill than a true ridge. The lancers, each beside his mount, were arrayed in an arc that flanked Anna and the players. Anna's guards remained mounted.

The sorceress watched as the dust rose from the road leading from the keep beyond the town toward their position. She had picked a slight knoll in the benchlike meadow, one not quite in the center of the open space overlooking the road from Arien. Standing behind her were Liende and the players.

The sound of tuning overrode the intermittent whispers of wind in the dry grass of the hillside field.

"The first warm-up song!" ordered the chief player.

Anna launched into the third vocalise. "Muueeee . . . ooowee . . ." Her cords and throat were clear for a change, perhaps because the night frosts had reduced the amount of pollen and molds in the air, and perhaps because the winds had been light and carried little dust.

After the vocalise, the sorceress stepped forward to the edge of the knoll and looked eastward again. Rickel and Blaz, shields out, rode forward to cover her.

The black-surcoated riders slowed almost a dek away and began to re-form from a column into a broader formation, at least several riders deep, from what Anna could tell. Two outriders with black banners bearing some sort of silver device took station before the formation.

At the sound of hoofs, Anna turned to watch as a scout rode up to Himar. Then she turned and walked back toward Liende. The sorceress waited until the players finished the second warm-up tune.

"Yes, Regent?"

"Lord Tybel's armsmen are forming up. It won't be long."

"Stand ready!" Liende ordered.

Both women turned as Himar rode toward them.

"Regent . . . Chief Player. The scouts say that Lord Tybel has near-on thirtyscore armsmen." Himar looked eastward for a moment, then back to Anna.

"Thirty? That's more than any lord in Defalk." Anna looked at the slowly advancing riders and the dark lances with tips that glittered in the cool afternoon light. As she watched, the formation halted once more, and a rider with a blue parley banner rode forward from the lines of black-surcoated riders and up the gradual incline of the road.

"Birtol! Go hear what he has to say!" ordered Himar.

"Stand ready," Anna said quietly to Liende. "I think Tybel will make some impossible demand, and when we reject it, he'll have everyone charge us and try to overwhelm us before I can sing anything. So the players have to be ready to go as soon as their herald or messenger or whatever he is turns." She paused. "Or if I signal sooner."

"We are prepared."

The herald with the parley banner guided his mount to a position a hundred yards below the Defalkan lines. After reining up, Tybel's herald declaimed. "These words are for the sorceress and for all to hear. Lord Tybel would have naught said in secret, naught hidden." After a moment, he continued, his voice ringing across the late afternoon. "The most honorable Lord Tybel of Arien demands that the Regency be turned over to him to preserve the heritage and honor of Defalk. He further demands that the false sorceress be stripped of her powers and executed. . . ."

Anna turned to Liende. "Have them play. Now!"

Liende pivoted on one foot, her face grim. "The flame song—on my mark. MARK!!"

The first introductory bars of the players drifted downhill, past the sorceress and toward the herald and Tybel's armsmen.

Anna began the spell, trying to maintain both her composure and her images while she projected full concert volume across Tybel's forces.

> Turn to fire, turn to flame
> all those under Tybel's claim,
> those who hold women as does he,
> those who will not honor the Regency.

As she sang, she concentrated on an image of a curtain of fire, white-hot, descending from the cold, clear sky.

"Charge the bitch!" came the order from below, even before the herald had finished his words of challenge to the Regent-sorceress.

The drumbeat of hoofs began, as the black-clad lancers charged toward the knoll. Anna kept her mind and voice on finishing the spell.

> Turn to ashes, turn to dust,
> all Tybel's lancers we cannot trust. . . .

The chords of harmony strummed once, heard but by Anna and the few of the more sensitive players, then a second time. Those twin chords were clear, but unstrained, unlike other recent efforts by the sorceress.

Whhhhsssttt! Instead of lines of fire, there was an intense sheet of white flame, brighter than the sun that dropped like lightning.

The hillside was silent, deadly silent.

Anna blinked, her eyes watering profusely. White stars flashed before her eyes, the aftermath of the strobelike white fire wall.

"Dissonance . . ."

"Mother of harmonies . . ."

"What happened . . . ?"

The sorceress blotted her eyes, trying to clear her vision, hoping that the spell had been effective, because she wasn't seeing anything. Except for murmurs from her guards, the silence drew out.

When her eyes stopped tearing and she could finally see, Anna looked downhill. She shook her head. There were five . . . maybe six men on their mounts in black surcoats. There were no other black-clad figures—or mounts. Beginning about fifty yards below the Defalkan lines, the ground was black, and not a trace of vegetation remained—just a swath of charred ashes three hundred yards deep and almost half a dek wide.

Anna looked at the devastation blankly. Never had one of her spells destroyed a foe so completely and quickly. *Your sense of frustration and anger?*

The sorceress turned.

Liende looked at her. ". . . I wanted that . . . so much . . . after what the herald said. . . . May . . . the harmonies . . . forgive me."

Anna touched her arm. "I guess . . . maybe I did, too."

Himar had turned his mount and rode slowly toward Anna across the browned grass, with the faint hint of the orange redness of twilight falling across his face. Seated in his saddle looking down at her, he appeared to be looking up. His voice was hoarse as he asked, "What would you have us do?"

"I couldn't do it any other way," Anna said raggedly. "Look down there . . . how many are alive? The spell would have spared anyone loyal to the Regency . . . anyone who thought women were people. . . . What was I supposed to do? Too many people have died because I tried to be forgiving and understanding."

Himar swallowed. "There are some few who live."

"I'd . . . like to see . . . them."

For a time, Anna leaned against Farinelli, not quite clinging, before she finally fumbled out the water bottle and drank. She had just about finished when a squad of lancers escorted a man on foot toward Anna. The man's hands were loosely bound, and his scabbard was empty.

Rickel and Lejun stepped forward, shields on their arms, blades out, barring the way to the sorceress. Beside Rickel were Bersan and Fielmir. Blaz flanked Lejun. All five focused on the captive.

"This man remained among those still living," Himar said.

The man before Anna wore a silver pin of some sort in his black collar, and he stared defiantly at her.

"How many were there?" Anna asked.

"A half-score, all older lancers except this one."

Anna studied the man with the slightly frizzy henna-colored hair. She should have recognized him, but her mind wouldn't come up with a name or from where she knew him.

"Will you slaughter me as well, lady?" he finally asked.

The voice was familiar as well. Yet she could not place him. "Why should there be any more killing?"

"So that you can dispose of my uncle's lands as you please."

Zybar . . . the younger brother at Gatrune's.

"Did he fight?" Anna asked Himar.

"He rode and he had his blade. He was wise enough not to use it after the others fell."

Anna shook her head at the irony.

Zybar flushed. "You mock me as well!"

"No . . . I'm not mocking you, Zybar. You didn't think what your uncle and your father did was right, did you? But you didn't want to cross them? Or you feared them?"

"I stood with them."

"That is not what I asked."

"Best you answer the Regent," suggested Himar.

Rickel and Lejun raised their bare steel blades slightly.

Zybar shifted his weight, and his eyes finally dropped from Anna's level gaze. "You had given Lord Hryding's lands to his consort for his heirs. That was right. I would not, held I lands, have wished it otherwise. Better even a daughter hold her father's birthright than an outsider or a distant cousin." Zybar flushed. "I like you not, Regent, but with the lands have you been fair."

Anna nodded. "I'm glad you think so, Lord Zybar."

Zybar looked directly at Anna. "You say you do not mock me, yet you call me lord, after you have slain even my brothers and my father and uncle with your sorcery."

"I used a special spell, Zybar—it only killed those who opposed the Regency. Why do you think you're alive?"

"Yet you have shamed me, for I did not stand in my heart with my father." Zybar lifted his head, but his eyes avoided Anna's.

"You stood for what you thought was right," Anna pointed out.

"The more fool I. For I will die later as sooner."

Anna shook her head, waiting. "You say that you think lands could go to daughters as well as sons."

"Aye. What of Lord Hryding's lands?"

"His daughter still lives," Anna said. "Lord Dannel attacked the liedburg in Falcor. His men tried to kill several daughters of lords who were their father's only heirs. They failed. Lord Dannel is dead. I did seize his lands for that, and that attack was partly why I came to Arien. The other reason was the strange death of Anientta and her sons."

Zybar's face paled. "My uncle . . . he . . ."

"The 'illness' that killed Anientta and her sons was a little too convenient, wouldn't you say?"

"You have shamed my family . . . yet . . . I feared such." Zybar lowered his eyes once more.

"Look at me," Anna said quietly.

Zybar raised his eyes.

Anna's eyes were like ice as she addressed him. "You can worry about shame, or you can get on with redeeming your family's honor by supporting the Regency and what you know to be right. What will it be, Lord Zybar? Will you be Lord of Arien, and support the Regency and the rights of daughters?"

"Altyr has two boys living, and they are in the hold at Arien," Zybar said slowly. "The oldest is but five. Altyr's older son died of the flux two years ago."

"Tybel's older son may have children, Zybar, but two generations of treachery is enough for me. If you wish to be their guardian, you may do so, but only with the condition that they will never be lords in Defalk. Nor will their children, and you must ensure that. Nor the children of any others except for you."

"If I cannot undertake such?" questioned the henna-haired man.

"I'll have them fostered somewhere in the far south or north, as far from Arien as possible."

"I will foster them myself, save that you allow it." Zybar's voice was hoarse.

"I will allow it." Anna continued to study the young man. "Will you swear fealty to the Regency?"

Zybar lowered his head for a moment, then raised his pale green eyes to Anna's. "In honor, I have no choice. You have acted with greater honor than my own kin." He laughed hoarsely. "Yet, so far removed was I that I have no consort, for none . . ." he shook his head.

"I doubt you will have trouble with that now," Anna said dryly. After a moment, she added, "You and your remaining armsmen may return to Arien. You can tell your brother's consort and your cousin's consort and anyone else that, if *anything* happens to you, I will exile every living relation of Tybel's and will use sorcery to destroy whoever lifts a hand against you.

You are your family's sole hope, Zybar. You'd better make good on it."

Zybar's eyes met Anna's. "Dare I do otherwise?"

"No." Anna glanced toward Himar. "Escort him back to his mount and his men. Then untie him, and let him go."

She watched the young man walk slowly downhill in the twilight, his steps uneven.

"You are hard, lady," offered Falar, who had slipped up beside Anna's guards.

"Hard? Not as hard as Tybel would have been."

"He must atone for two generations of wrongs, and know that you could destroy him in a moment." Falar shook his head. "He must change everything his sire and his uncle believed in. He knew they were wrong, and he was not strong enough to stand up to them, and you did, and you are a woman."

"That's because I have some power, and he didn't."

"From what I hear, you had little enough power when you came to Defalk. Yet you would not turn from what you saw to be true. You have shamed him." Falar laughed, almost lightly, "Not that we all could not use shaming at times."

Including you . . . but what else could you have done—except let people keep getting slaughtered. What you've started is like an avalanche . . . you either stay ahead of it or get swallowed in it.

Her eyes burned as she turned and walked out to the end of the knoll, looking eastward at the distant keep of Arien. Zybar and his ten lancers had already vanished into the twilight.

108

Under the morning sun, Anna turned in the saddle and looked back over her shoulder at Arien. While some had wondered at her refusal to enter Arien, and her insistence on making a camp above the battlefield, after what she had done, she could no more have stayed in the town or the keep than . . . physically touched Elizabetta across the gap between worlds. Or worked sorcery on Earth.

Her face turned to the road that would lead to Synope and the keep of Flossbend, but she saw nothing. After a restless night's sleep, her eyes watered and burned with the questions that ran through her mind. *What have you become? All you wanted . . . was a few more rights for women . . . a little more justice . . . and it's as though you were . . . some sort of monster. Even Himar looks sideways at you.*

She twisted in the saddle, then reached for the water bottle, not sure she was thirsty, but knowing she couldn't afford to get dehydrated, either. The water was cool, tasteless, and she swallowed, then replaced the bottle in its holder. The wind was cool, but not cold, on her face, and the air carried the mold of autumn. She found herself coughing, leaning forward in the saddle for a time before she straightened. Stress always had made the asthma worse.

Liende rode up beside Anna. "You are troubled, Lady Anna." Her voice was soft, sympathetic in a way Anna had not heard from the older-looking woman in weeks, if not seasons.

"Does it show that much?" *Stupid question.* "I'm sorry. Yes . . . I'm troubled." *More than troubled . . . very troubled.*

"You did not wish to destroy Lord Tybel that way?" Liende glanced ahead toward Himar and the vanguard. Except for Liende and her guards, Anna rode very much alone, with wide spaces between her and the lancers.

"It's not that. I mean, it is, but it isn't. All I started out to do was to survive and then to make sure Lord Jimbob would have a country left to inherit, and then I tried to make sure that women weren't treated as slaves. But I kept having to use sorcery against other countries to keep them from invading . . . mostly, except for Ebra the second time, but Bertmynn was killing all the women in Elahwa because they didn't want to be slaves anymore." Anna swallowed. "And somehow, almost half the lords in Defalk are or were against me. And most of Defalk's neighbors. It's like a holy war, and all the old lords want to kill me and stop what I'm trying to do. Some of the old crafters like the chandler in Pamr, too. So I either give up, and that doesn't seem right, or I kill a lot of people, and that's not right, either. When I tried to talk, no one listened, and when I used force they all thought I was terrible."

Liende nodded. After a time, she spoke. "Lord Brill treated women well, but he would do nothing beyond his own lands. He died, and nothing changed."

"If I died tomorrow," Anna said, "nothing would change."

"It has already changed, lady, and if you can but survive a handful of years, it will never change back." The chief player continued more softly. "Never would I have paid as you pay," Liende said. "You have given my son lands, and my daughter hope and dignity . . . and others as well, but few will thank you. You have begun to change this land so that it will survive and prosper, but few will thank you for that."

"I guess I just got tired of being the good little girl."

"Ah . . ."

Another expression that doesn't quite translate. "Women are supposed to listen to men and take their advice. They're not supposed to be too assertive, even if they're regents. They're not supposed to use sorcery to wipe out brave strong armsmen. It's all right for that brave strong armsman to use his blade or lance, or to take an unwilling woman with his strength, but good girls don't point those embarrassing things out. Good girls don't say, 'You're not going to keep doing this, and back it up with superior force.' Good girls don't . . ." Anna broke off the monologue. "I guess I'm just not a good girl. Maybe I never was . . . Now I'll have to hold the Thirty-three—or many of them—under an iron fist." The sorceress shook her head. "I never wanted that."

"Perhaps not . . ." There was another long silence, before Liende continued. "Were there another sorceress to follow you . . ."

"Another sorceress?" Anna laughed harshly. "I'm not sure that one isn't too much for Defalk."

"Power must be balanced by power, and women cannot lift blades as heavy as do men."

Anna wasn't certain about that. She'd seen Ytrude and Lysara carrying blades. *But how many Ytrudes and Lysaras are there in Defalk?* "Another sorceress . . ." Maybe that would help balance things out. *But whom do you choose—and trust? Secca? She's young, and will she have the insight after her hormones kick in? Clayre—Birfels' other daughter, who had once expressed interest and might be coming to Falcor?* Was there anyone else? Would there be? Could there be?

Anna frowned. Why did everything just get more complicated?

109

Under a cold midday sun that foreshadowed winter, Anna sat upright in the saddle and looked across the low valley, finally catching sight of the white structure that, as she had recalled, resembled a Mediterranean villa as much as a Defalkan keep. Flossbend stood on the low rise to the northeast, across the Synor River, linked to the main road by a winding lane that climbed the gentle slope to the hold.

"There, that's Flossbend." The sorceress pointed for both Liende and Himar, reined up beside her. "Both the holding and the town are on the other side of the river, but the town is upstream—east—of Flossbend."

"The walls are low," observed Himar.

"It's not designed for a siege."

Farinelli sidestepped, and Anna bent forward in the saddle and patted his neck. "Easy . . . easy . . ."

"What do you plan?" asked the arms commander.

"I'd like to get as close as I can, and then cast a spell over the keep to kill the handful of people, especially Beltyr, who are guilty of murdering Lady Anientta and her sons and who oppose the Regency."

"After that?"

"We try to organize the keep before we head back to Falcor." *You make it sound so simple . . . and it won't be.* She looked at Liende, reined up beside Himar. "The players may have to dismount and perform quickly."

"We will be ready," the chief player confirmed.

The sorceress took another long and studied look at the white-walled hold before nodding to Himar.

The arms commander raised his arm, and the lancers followed the vanguard and the players downhill on the road to

Synope. As Anna reached the bottom of the short incline, the light and cool breeze died away, and she found herself using the square of worn gray cloth to blot her forehead.

Anna began the first vocalise after they had traveled another dek across the western end of the valley. "Holly-lolly-pop . . ." She coughed, but the amount of mucus she brought up was minimal, and she continued vocalizing.

"Lady?" Himar's voice interrupted her concentration.

She looked up, following his gesture. Puffs of dust marked the four riders headed westward on the road from Synope—toward Anna.

"They all wear green surcoats."

"How far is the hold?"

"Two deks, perhaps three." Himar stood in his stirrups. "Green company! Forward, arms ready! Bring forth the banner!"

The lancers of the green company used the shoulder of the road to make their way around the players and Anna. The sorceress coughed as the dust rose around her. The standard-bearer did not follow the green company, but led the main body of the column.

As the score and a half lancers rode eastward, the four armsmen in the pale green of Flossbend reined up on a high spot on the road, less than half a dek away, looking at the approaching lancers and the purple banner. Then all four turned and spurred their mounts eastward, raising a far larger cloud of dust in returning to Flossbend than they had in leaving it.

"I think they will be telling Beltyr that the sorceress is on her way to Flossbend," Liende said.

"Will you need the lancers to attack?" questioned Himar.

"I'd rather have them ready to protect me and the players." Anna looked back at the chief player. "There's no point in losing lancers in an attack. We'll have to plan on the flame spell, the long one."

"The one that singles out the traitors?" asked Liende.

Anna nodded. "I wish I dared to try something else, but this fall I've lost tenscore armsmen. Where we'll get more, I don't know. Beltyr has seized these lands, and he and Tybel killed every heir but Secca. They tried to kill her." Anna took a deep breath. "I can't just turn my back on Beltyr."

"None of us chose this." Liende's smile was both warm and wintry. "What we chose far earlier led us here."

Is that true! Anna coughed, then continued to watch as the four lancers turned their mounts up the lane that led to Flossbend.

"There is little cover, and no hill or knoll near the keep," Himar pointed out. "To defend the players will be hard if Lord Beltyr sends forth lancers or armsmen."

Anna shifted her weight in the saddle before replying. "When I was here before, Lord Hryding didn't even have twoscore armsmen left after the mess at the Sand Pass. Nearly a score of those left with Markan. Most of them are with Ytrude at Suhl. I'm sure Beltyr brought his own armsmen, but he was the younger son, and with all those that Tybel had . . . I can't believe he has any more than we do."

"If that be so, then I would judge less."

"Far less," added Falar, who had ridden up past Blaz and Fielmir to join the other three. "As a younger son, I know what coins it has taken for my poor score and a half of armsmen."

At his rueful smile, Anna laughed. "You would know."

"You think this Beltyr will not attack?" questioned Himar.

"There's no movement outside the hold." Anna gestured toward the lane and the keep above. "And your scouts haven't reported anything. We could get attacked—like Tybel did—but I don't think that will happen. I'd say that Beltyr would hole up in the keep." Anna frowned. "He might do that because we don't have that big a force. Not enough to storm a keep, not even Flossbend." *And none of these people seems to believe in your sorcery until they've experienced it.*

The green company had reined up and waited at the base of the lane that wound up toward the white-plastered building. Anna and the players kept riding until they neared the green company.

"Riders, halt!" Himar ordered before turning his mount back to Anna and Liende.

Anna could see the roof of the stable for travelers, where she'd first tethered Farinelli when she had met Lord Hryding. *Is Calmut still around? Unpleasant as ever?*

"I would not ride more than to the midpoint of the lane,"

Himar suggested. "Could you work your sorcery from below that small cot there?" He pointed.

"That's a small stable for travelers, and I think that my voice will carry—if the wind doesn't pick up."

Liende glanced westward, toward the few scattered clouds that hugged the horizon. "There will not be more wind in the next glass or so."

"Let's go halfway up," Anna suggested. "The sooner we do this, the less chance Beltyr will have to come up with something."

"A moment, Lady Anna?" requested Rickel, as he unstrapped the large shield from behind his saddle.

Anna nodded, as did Himar. There might be archers.

Once their shields were in place, Lejun and Rickel eased their mounts ahead of Anna.

"Riders, forward!" ordered Himar.

Anna tried another vocalise, and was relieved to find that her cords and throat were clear. Not even halfway up the lane, Anna could see that every window was shuttered, every door barred. Not a soul was in sight, and the only sounds were those from her lancers and players.

"They fear you," murmured Liende.

"Not enough to have done what was right," Anna answered quietly. *Not nearly enough.* She rubbed her forehead. *You've defeated two enemies, one to the east and one to the west, and are trying to negotiate something lasting with the Liedfuhr, but you're still dealing with backward lords at home. Then, your foreign enemies know more about you than do half the lords of the Thirty-three.*

"Riders, halt!"

At Himar's command, Anna nodded to Liende.

"Dismount and stand ready to play!"

Anna waited until the tuning died away before she dismounted. Flossbend remained silent, without even a single head appearing above the wall, not a single shutter moving. *Let's hope Beltyr doesn't have any nasty surprises . . . been enough of those this year.* She stepped forward, still flanked by the shield-bearing Rickel and Lejun, then inclined her head to the chief player. "Now."

"On my mark . . . the long flame song!" Liende called. "Mark!"

After the first three introductory bars, Anna began the spell, her voice open and free and cascading across the white-plastered stone walls of Flossbend.

> Turn to fire, turn to flame
> all those against the true heir's name
> turn to fire, turn to flame,
> who stand against the Regent's claim.

While fire hissed from the sky, that fire came in arrows, rather than in a solid sheet, as had happened at Arien.

As Anna stepped back, Rickel and Lejun stepped forward, raising their shields to guard the sorceress. Anna watched as the last of the flame arrows died away.

Almost expectantly, Liende glanced at the Regent, waiting but not inquiring. Anna stood, studying the walls and the few crenellations irregularly set in the upper walls, but the keep remained silent.

Abruptly, the barred doors on the lower level were flung open, and an armsman in a pale green surcoat stepped out, carrying an irregular square of white cloth tied to a pole. He glanced from side to side, his head darting in one direction, then another, as he waved the makeshift white flag.

Anna turned, remaining behind the shields. "Arms Commander . . . if you would send a company to see if those who remain will accept the true heir to Flossbend?"

"Green company, forward!" ordered Himar.

"Have them ready with the short flame song—just in case," the sorceress told Liende.

"Stand ready for the short flame song!" ordered the chief player.

Anna and Liende watched as the green company lancers rode up the lane, past the small guest stable, until they reached the armsman with the banner. After a moment, a single rider in purple turned his mount and rode down the lane, finally reining up before Anna and the still-mounted Himar.

"The hold surrenders, but begs mercy," announced the lancer.

"We will secure it, Regent," Himar promised. "I would that you remain here until we have done so. Captain Falar and his men can guard you."

Falar's face was blank for a moment, before he nodded.

"If there's *anything* strange, bring all the lancers back, and I'll use more sorcery," Anna said.

"That I will, Regent." Himar barked a short and humorless laugh. "That I will." He guided his mount around Anna's guards and uphill, another company of lancers behind him.

"You value your armsmen highly," Falar observed.

"Good armsmen are hard to find and train," she replied. "It took over a year to build up a force of twentyscore, and I've lost half of them in a season."

"You destroyed a hundredfold of what you lost, mayhap more," the redhead countered.

"That still leaves only a few more than tenscore. Not very much for a ruler or a regent. Lord Jimbob will need ten or twenty times that."

"Because he will not be able to rely on sorcery?"

Anna nodded.

"Players . . . you may rest, but stand ready to play," Liende ordered.

She and Anna—and Falar—watched as the two companies of lancers opened the lower doors, and then the double doors to the inner courtyard.

"They did not fight," Falar said.

"How could they?" asked Liende. "The sorceress would have slain them all."

Anna did not comment.

When Himar emerged from Flossbend and remounted, Anna climbed back into Farinelli's saddle, but waited for the arms commander to ride to her.

Himar's face was grave as he reined in his mount, short of Anna. "We hold the keep. Beltyr had but threescore armsmen. More than half died under your flames. Beltyr himself is dead, as is his consort . . . their children live."

"His consort?" *Another scheming woman?*

"Ah . . . yes, Lady Anna."

So much . . . again . . . for so-called innocent consorts . . . and more children, another focal point for future dissension.
"The children will be fostered in Dumar. Lady Siobion, I'm certain, will aid in that. So will Alvar." Should she have spoken so quickly, so openly?

"Dumar?" blurted Falar.

"We'll talk about the details later," Anna temporized. "And we will sleep in Flossbend tonight. The men and their mounts deserve some rest before we head back to Falcor."

"They will appreciate that."

"They are *not* to molest any of the women. This is Secca's hold, and she doesn't need that kind of trouble." Anna's eyes were hard as she glanced from Falar to Himar.

"I will let all the men know what you have said, lady," Himar said mildly. "There will be no trouble."

"Nor from mine," added Falar.

"Good." Anna flicked the reins, and Farinelli started up the lane. Rickel and Lejun flanked her, shields still at the ready. The sorceress-Regent reined up outside the door she had last entered more than a year before. *What a difference a year makes* . . . Her thoughts were cribbing from somewhere, but she couldn't recall from where. Abruptly, she turned.

"Falar . . . ?" Anna looked at the redhead. "Would you see if you could find the saalmeister. Or whatever assistant is left?"

Falar bowed suavely. "I will see who I can find."

"I'll be up on the top level."

Rickel and Lejun led the way, and Blaz, Bersan, and Fielmir followed.

As she passed the first landing, Anna could hear whispers.

". . . that's her . . ."

". . . said she'd be back . . . can't keep secrets from that one . . ."

". . . Lady Anientta . . . scared of her . . ."

"Fat lord Beltyr should have been . . ."

Once she reached the top of the stairs, Anna walked slowly across the tiled roof pavilion where she had once played Vorkoffe with Secca. A long charcoaled form lay sprawled by the wall, surrounded by several smaller forms. Beside the tall blackened corpse was a hand-and-a-half blade, as if it had been drawn and dropped.

The sorceress tried not to breathe deeply. She turned to Rickel. "Ah . . . could you have someone . . . from the hold staff remove those?"

Rickel gestured to Blaz, who headed down the steps.

Anna stepped toward the eastern wall, the one overlooking the entry and facing toward Synope. *Does it end like this everywhere?* She shook her head. It hadn't ended in death in a lot of holds—not in Dubaria, or even Fussen, nor Abenfel, or Lerona, nor Sudwei . . . *But at times it feels like it has.* In the near-twilight sun, the lands to the east of the hold were bathed in a rose glow. Anna just looked. Looked until she heard boots approaching and turned to see Falar nearing, escorting a thin-faced man with graying hair.

Rickel and Fielmir stepped forward to block the two from moving any closer to Anna than about three yards.

Falar smiled and tapped the man on the shoulder. "This man says he was saalmeister. The other saalmeister died under the fire arrows," said the red-haired de facto captain.

The older man bowed into a near grovel on the tiles of the floor. "She is the sorceress! The same one that promised to keep young Secca. Sorceress . . . be merciful. This was against my will. I could do nothing."

"Secca is safe," Anna said. "She is well and safe in Falcor. Who are you?"

"I am Gylun, Regent-sorceress . . . I was saalmeister . . . before . . . Lord Beltyr came." Gylun remained on his knees, but looked up at Anna.

"Why did you let him poison Anientta?" Anna asked bluntly.

"Lord Beltyr . . . he sent me to the fields . . . me . . ."

"For now . . . Gylun . . . your job is to work—if you would not mind," Anna asked the redhead, "to put Flossbend back in order. Back in a state appropriate for the lady Secca. Falar will get you started."

"I would like to be of service to Lady Secca," answered Falar with his roguish smile. "And I will do my best."

"She's too young for you," Anna said with a laugh, "you smiling devil. You can start things, but I'd like you to come with me. But don't worry. I always reward loyalty and skill." *Who else can you leave? You'll have to talk to Himar about that. You still need Falar under your thumb. What about Lejun and one of the captains?*

"That she does," murmured Liende, standing at the top of the stairs.

Falar bowed.

"Have you got the players settled?" the sorceress asked the chief player.

"We are settled. Will you need more playing?"

"Not that I know." Anna paused. "Thank you. I know it's been hard on you . . . and on them."

"They will all remember these days, lady and Regent, and few players can say such. Few indeed."

Few indeed . . . but how will they remember them? Anna smiled sadly in yet another twilight. She walked slowly along the wall, looking down as her boots kicked a Vorkoffe stone that skittered along the floor tiles. *A tile Secca might have used on a day past, a more innocent time.* Had those times been better? Or merely more cruelly innocent?

The sorceress turned and looked westward. Another sunset . . . the clouds almost bloodred. Her lips curled into an ironic smile as she watched the red sky fade.

110

MANSUUS, MANSUUR

Sire . . . sire . . ." Bassil stands barely a yard inside the carved door to the Liedfuhr's private study. Outside the windows, rain patters against the shutters, and a cool dampness seeps into the room.

"What? Bassil . . ." There is a long pause. "Don't tell me. You have even worse news from Esaria or Defalk?" Konsstin stands up from behind the desk.

"Worse? I . . . ah . . . perhaps you should read it . . . I mean, them, yourself, sire." Bassil extends a scroll, still sealed in wax and bound in purple ribbon. A second follows, sealed with severe blue wax and wrapped with a strip of dark blue felt.

"You have not opened them?"

"They were addressed to you, and brought by the same courier from Neserea. There are two scrolls. One from the sorceress-Regent and one from one Hanfor, Lord High Counselor of Neserea."

"Two scrolls . . . both filled with trouble." Konsstin snorts. "As if I had no other difficulties." His eyes fix on the dark-haired officer. "Why did I ever listen to you? Why?"

Bassil swallows.

"Why? Answer me!"

The officer squares his shoulders, then meets the Liedfuhr's blistering scrutiny. "Because I have given my best judgment, whether it later proved wrong or not. Because I have never lied to you, and because that is greater loyalty than flattery." The lancer officer swallows, and the sweat pours down his brow and cheeks.

Abruptly, the Liedfuhr nods. "And you have the nerve to tell me so." He sighs. "Best we read these." He breaks the purple wax seal and unrolls the scroll.

Bassil watches.

The Liedfuhr's frown deepens as he reads. Silently, he finishes the first scroll, then breaks the seal on the second, a much shorter length of parchment. Near the end of the scroll, suddenly, he laughs, and shakes his head. "Things could be worse . . . far worse."

"Sire?" blurts Bassil.

"She has appointed a professional armsman as Lord High Counselor of Neserea, and she has gone back to Falcor—or somewhere. She has also suggested that I support the new regime in Neserea, and rather politely suggested that she'll forgive my sending lancers into Defalk, but that she'll do the same to them again if I send any there or into Neserea." Konsstin pursed his lips. "She'll probably live longer than I will, and that means Kestrin will have to deal with her for a time as well."

"But the second one?" prompts Bassil.

"Oh . . . that is from the armsman. He was quite short, if most circumspect. He just said that Neserea regarded Mansuur as its friend, and Defalk as its protector, and hoped that I would understand why it must be so." The Liedfuhr drops both scrolls on the shimmering polished wood of his table-desk. After a moment, he begins to pace back and forth. "What to do . . . what to do . . . ?"

Bassil holds his tongue, waiting.

Konsstin straightens, nods to himself. "It might work. It will work."

The lancer officer leans forward, as if encouraging the Liedfuhr to explain.

"Aerlya . . . she's sixteen," Konsstin says. "If he has no consort, and I'd wager he does not. Is he not the one who was her arms commander?"

"Who?"

"This Hanfor."

"She had an arms commander of that name. That was what your envoys reported."

"Aerlya . . . she needs a consort, and what would be better than the new Lord High Counselor of Neserea?"

"Sire?"

"Bassil . . . if you are going to say something trite about Aerlya being too sweet . . . that's the point. The envoys—I remember their report—they said this Hanfor was honorable. If he's survived in Defalk and if he survives in Neserea, he'll be most intelligent as well—his scroll shows that. If the sorceress trusts him, he'll be a good man. A bit hard, perhaps, but good, and he will not treat women badly. Not after what the sorceress has done, he couldn't have survived. And . . . he'll know treachery. What an honorable man is most influenced by is by honest respect and, in a woman, sweetness. Aerlya is strong, but she's not a schemer. Not too much, anyway." Konsstin laughs. "And this Hanfor, he will have to balance between us, and Aerlya, she has seen enough scheming to respect honor."

"She may not love him."

"She may not. But he cannot afford to turn her down, and she cannot afford to turn down being the consort of a ruler. And her being his consort will ensure both his rule, and the succession of their children. So . . . Kestrin's heirs will have a chance. While the sorceress lives, no one else will take Neserea." Konsstin shrugs. "Even if that doesn't work out, I'll have grandchildren ruling both lands."

"Yes, sire." Bassil's face bears a faintly puzzled expression.

"You'll see," predicts the Liedfuhr. "You will."

111

Anna looked over the lane leading to the house—not really a hold—that now belonged to Lady Herene. The trees beside the packed clay were bare, and the cold wind out of the north-east swirled fallen leaves along the ground. The scars in the plaster and timber of the outbuildings had been painted or oiled over, and the air smelled merely of damp leaves and fall, unlike the odors of her last visit.

Just two figures stood on the lower steps that led up to the dwelling Anna had rebuilt with her sorcery—Skent and a tall blonde woman.

Skent bowed as Anna reined up at the foot of the steps, still trailed by Himar, Falar, and guards. "Lady and Regent."

"Captain Skent, Lady Herene." Anna smiled at the dark-haired young captain, then looked at Herene, who stood behind him.

"Regent." Herene bowed. Her blonde hair had been cut shorter than the one time before when Anna had met her. Now it was not much longer than Anna's.

Anna dismounted, then gestured to the redheaded Falar, who quickly dismounted as well. "This is Falar. He has been serving as a captain for me, but he is also second in succession to the lands of Fussen."

"For now." Falar smiled engagingly at Herene. "My brother but recently took a consort."

Anna gestured at Himar—still mounted. "Lady Herene . . . Arms Commander Himar."

Herene inclined her head slightly. "Arms Commander."

"Lady Herene," answered Himar. "Lady Anna, if you would excuse me . . ."

"Of course." Anna watched as Herene's eyes flicked back to Falar for a moment, then centered on the Regent.

"Your messenger said you had come from Flossbend?"

Anna nodded. "Another unfortunate duty. You may have recalled Lord Hryding?"

Herene nodded.

"After his death, his consort Anientta was holding the lands for his sons. She died rather suddenly. So did her sons. Then Lord Dannel attacked Falcor and tried to kill young Secca. After that, Lord Tybel's younger brother Beltyr took over the lands. Tybel attacked us on our way to Arien to look into the matter." *Shading the truth a little there, you are.* Anna shrugged. "So . . . now young lord Zybar, Tybel's nephew, holds Arien, and Secca is the heir to Flossbend."

Herene shook her head. "Did they think you would allow that?"

"They did not think," Skent suggested.

"That may be." Anna shrugged, then belatedly handed Farinelli's reins to Blaz. "But Defalk has to change, and they didn't want to see that." Anna smiled, half-sadly. "I am sorry that you have had to bear the grief of your sister's death and the burden of restoring the hold, but I am glad to be here. You and your family have been encouraging from the beginning."

"You are always welcome. Always." Herene returned Anna's smile with one of her own. "You have given me a hold and a home to make, and though it comes from sadness, so does all of worth and value."

The sorceress couldn't help but notice that Falar continued to watch the new lady of Pamr as she spoke. *You hadn't thought about these two. . . .* She refrained from shrugging. *If it's meant to be . . .*

In the meantime, she had a tired gelding to unsaddle and groom . . . and yet a long journey back to Falcor. She forced herself to keep smiling.

112

WEI, NORDWEI

The oil lamps on the Council Chamber wall cast a low light, but one strong enough that the faces of the five counselors are reflected in the black-polished and gemlike surface of the long table around which they are seated. Chill seeps from the stone walls as leader Tybra raps the ebony hammer on the ebony striking plate. Several darts of light flash from the black-and-silver seal suspended from Tybra's neck.

"The Regent-sorceress has once more done the unexpected. Counselor Ashtaar, would you explain?" Tybra turns to the spymistress. "As we have all received your scroll outlining the actual events, please confine your remarks to explaining *how* this occurred."

Ashtaar looks to her right and then to her left. "Before I explain, I would like to suggest that we consider building more warships." She ignores the frowns and continues. "The real problem we have faced with the Regent and Sorceress of Defalk is that she is truly strange." Ashtaar shrugs. "She looks as we do. She can be injured or wounded as we are. But she is not as we are. We thought she was merely after power, like Lord Behlem or his son, or the Liedfuhr. So did the Evult, Lord Ehara, Lord Rabyn, and many of Defalk's Thirty-three—"

"She is clearly after power. She has destroyed close to a third of the Thirty-three," responds Virtuul. "She has replaced those lords with others and ladies who support her."

Ashtaar's smile is cold. "No, I said that we thought she was *merely* after power. Unlike the others, this one sees power as a tool. Think . . . most rulers consolidate their power at home first. They eliminate rivals, force consortships, raise taxes and armies—and then they strike at their neighbors and seize lands and goods. Some engage in foreign campaigns as a way to pacify their people with either excitement or loot, or use the campaigns to place rivals in places where they may be more likely killed by enemy blades or shafts. Has she done any of that?" Ashtaar's eyes rake those sitting around the long polished table.

". . . not that we know," comes a whisper from the end of the table, "or you would not have asked the question."

Ashtaar nods toward the figure cloaked in black and shadows. "No . . . she has reformed the way Ebra is governed—and destroyed all the lords and armsmen who could protest—and gone home. She has eliminated all the Liedfuhr's lancers east of the Westfels, and most of the armsmen in Neserea, and then placed a good and honest man as ruler over that land. She did not invade it, though she could have swept all the way to Esaria. She destroyed Lord Ehara—and the Sturinnese fleet and all the

Maitre's lancers in Liedwahr. After placing Ehara's widow on the throne—with her own arms commander to watch—she went home.

"She has used her sorcery to mine gold and mint coins—and little of that has gone into warfare or luxuries. She has begun to send couriers with messages to every lord. She has begun to teach the heirs in Falcor, and she has been replacing those lords who are rebellious or stupid with others who are intelligent and loyal. She is no softhearted girl who would let the poor or the mob rule, either. Witness her actions in Pamr."

Ashtaar pauses, but no others speak.

"How many lords in Defalk will stand against her? Five years ago, every one of the Thirty-three in Defalk was a man. Nearly a quarter are women today, and she controls more than half the lords outright. Has Defalk ever been so strong?"

"If she lives . . ." suggests Tybra.

"Why would any in Defalk wish to kill her? Any of sound mind? She rewards those who rule both well and fairly—and destroys those who oppose her. Were you a lord in Defalk, would you oppose her? She uses her sorcery to determine who plots against her. Would you risk such, Leader Tybra?"

"She will not live forever," says Virtuul, his deep voice almost lazy.

"If she lives but a handful of years longer, will it matter? Already she molds the heir and all those around her." Ashtaar laughs. "Besides . . . what if she teaches what she knows of sorcery to another?"

"Kill her," comes the whisper from the shadows.

Ashtaar smiles sadly. "Do you not see? Every ruler south of us has said that—except the Matriarch. Where are they now? The sorceress will never attack us—unless we attack her. So . . . do we accept the changes she will bring . . . or do we attack her and destroy Wei now?"

"We have those with poison . . . those with stealth . . ."

Ashtaar glares at the shadowed figure. "If . . . if we succeed, then we would turn all of Defalk except Wei and Ranuak over to Mansuur. Do you wish that, Lady of Shadows? Do you wish Konsstin on our southern borders?"

"You had said we should build ships, Counselor," Tybra interjects quickly. "Why would golds spent on ships help?"

"Liedwahr will never be the same. Sturinn will be. The Lied-fuhr has more than enough armsmen to defeat the Sea-Priests—and Mansuur needs little trade. Ranuak will trade more and more with the sorceress and her allies. What will we do?"

"You suggest that our fleet must contest the ships of the Sea-Priests, and from where will come the coins?"

"From trade. Defalk will return to prosperity, and there is much it does not produce. We will trade more, and gain coins, and those coins will build more ships, stronger ships. We need not worry about our borders," Ashtaar points out. "The sorcer-ess makes a good neighbor but a deadly enemy."

"One woman and all is changed . . . changed utterly," Virtuul says quietly.

"One might even call hers a terrible beauty," suggests the spymistress.

Neither the Lady of the Shadows nor Tybra speaks, and the Council Chamber falls silent.

113

In the grayness preceding dawn, Anna sat at the writing desk in her chamber, quill in hand. Her breath steamed faintly in the chill air, as did the vapor drifting through the archway from the tub in the adjoining chamber. The two candles on the desk cast an uneven light, despite the polished-brass reflectors behind each.

Although she had arrived in Falcor late the night before, too exhausted from making a day and a half journey in one to talk to anyone, she had found herself awake and tossing before dawn. A hot bath had only made her more alert—and restless. Her eyes went to the rectangle etched in black on the stones of the outside wall. *Elizabetta*. She could send a scroll to her daughter, and she would, but what more could she say—or do? Her daughter was growing up a world away. *How do you tell her that you love her without it sounding trite? How can you tell her what you're really doing? Can you say that you're killing people to create a little more fairness for women—and*

*generally privileged women at that? Or to keep a land together
that might be better falling apart? Or that you're tired of fighting the same battles in Liedwahr that you fought on Earth—
except that you can force people to listen now?*

Awake as she was, she was too emotionally tired to write and
send Elizabetta a message, and her daughter still wouldn't get it
any sooner.

Finally, Anna looked at the scrolls beside her and the rough
paper before her.

Lord Hulber of Silberfels and the gold issue . . . more grain
for the grasslands riders of the north . . . and whom to name as
the next Lord of Mossbach. Should she seek thoughts from the
Thirty-three as a political move? Or have Jecks feel people out?
Or name Falar? *But if Falar's interest in Herene is real . . . ?*

After a time, she sharpened the quill and dipped it into the
ink, slowly writing out the list . . . name after name . . . Arkad,
Sargol, Dencer, Hryding and Anientta, Gatrune, Dannel, Ustal,
Jearle, Tybel, Beltyr . . . and Brill. *Don't forget Brill.* Almost a
third of the Thirty-three—dead in the two years since she'd
come to Defalk.

*Lord . . . even the Reign of Terror wasn't that sweeping, was
it?*

Thrap! She jumped at the single sharp knock on her chamber
door.

"Lord Jecks . . . if you will see him."

"I'll be happy to see him." She watched the door open.

"Lady Anna." Jecks bowed. His eyes sparkled as he looked
at the sorceress. "I was not sure you would be up this early after
so long a ride, but Lejun said you had been moving around for
some glasses. "I took the liberty . . ." He gestured to the serving
girl bearing a large tray filled with two small loaves of steaming bread, eggs scrambled with cheese, white cheese wedges,
and a large red apple. Jecks carried a pitcher. "This is hot
cider."

"Thank you." Anna didn't have to force the smile as she
cleared a space and moved some of the scrolls to the bench-
chest at the foot of the bed. The girl set the tray on the table-
desk and bowed. Anna directed a second "Thank you" to the
server as the girl left.

After filling Anna's goblet with the hot cider, Jecks pulled up the straight-backed chair and sat across from the sorceress as she broke off a chunk of bread.

Anna stopped eating after bolting two bites of bread. "Aren't you going to eat anything? There's plenty here."

"I had one of the loaves out of the oven," Jecks admitted. "I was up early, and Dalila was baking."

Dalila—another indirect casualty of your sorcery. "If you're still hungry, please have some." She smiled. "Please."

Jecks smiled, the smile she enjoyed so much. After a moment, he took his belt knife and sliced off a small section of the hard white cheese. "Perhaps a little cheese." Then he sliced several more sections. "And for you."

"Thank you. I'm sorry I didn't want to talk last night," Anna apologized. "I was exhausted."

"You rode two days in one."

"A day and a half, I think, but it felt longer." She took a sip of the cider—better than water, but what she wouldn't have given for coffee. "I couldn't even think by the time I unsaddled and groomed Farinelli."

"You looked tired—and worried."

"I'll always be worried." She forced a laugh. "That seems to go with being Regent." After a pause, Anna asked, "You got the scrolls from Synfal?" She took another mouthful of cheese and bread.

"There were two."

"I sent just two before we left for Arien." She swallowed more of the bread, then took another sip of cider, conscious—very conscious—of Jecks' eyes resting upon her. "So much happened."

Jecks waited—with far more patience than she would have shown—for her to tell him what had happened.

"Lord Tybel . . . somehow he'd raised nearly thirtyscore armsmen. He staged a phony parley and was going to attack. . . ." In between bites, Anna began to fill Jecks in on the details of her efforts since leaving Falcor, first what had happened at Arien and then at Flossbend and Pamr, and finally the bits that hadn't been in her scroll from Synfal.

"So . . . young Zybar is now Lord of Arien, and your little Secca is truly the Lady of Flossbend?"

Anna nodded. "I left Lejun and half a score armsmen with

one of Himar's older captains there. It was the best I could do. And Herene seems to be rebuilding both her hold and the town. Falar begged my leave to stay there for a time. I told her she was free to accept him as a consort, and equally free to reject him." She laughed. "He can be *very* charming, but she's stubborn."

"Some men are charming." Jecks nodded. "Others are not."

Anna sensed the meaning behind the words, and could feel the closest thing she would ever hear to a plea from the white-haired lord. *Lord . . . I'm not ready for this.* "What do you think about Kinor as Lord of Denguic?" Anna glanced up after swallowing another mouthful of bread and cheese, not quite looking at her lord high counselor. "He has a lot to learn, and we'll have to keep a rein on him . . . but I wanted someone young, and someone who would stand up to Jimbob."

"He will do both. I like Lord Kinor." Jecks laughed. "So long as he is not made Lord of the Western Marches, or not for many, many years."

"No. Lord Nelmor has earned that. He fought when no other lord did, and because he thought it necessary." Anna grinned. "He did fight most cautiously, but I didn't mention that. Anyway, we need cautious fighters."

"The others of the Thirty-three cannot fault that you made him Lord of the Western Marches."

"There's plenty that they can fault. They can fault the dreadful sorceress." Anna shook her head, recalling other words, other times, and how those words had a different meaning. *Be not proud, for though some have called you mighty and dreadful, you are not so. . . . Donne hadn't meant the words that way, but you certainly have no reason to be proud . . . not after this season.*

"Too long a sacrifice can make a stone of the heart," Jecks said quietly. His eyes were warm and deep—and fixed on her.

"What?" With the intensity of Jecks' words, Anna looked closely at her lord high counselor.

"You said that . . . you spoke of . . . but that was before you went to Arien. The words are yours, but you do not take them to your heart."

The words belonged to a true poet, one she'd sometimes wished had seen more of his work put to the music she'd once sung. "We all make sacrifices . . . and sometimes they go on. You've left Elheld to come to Falcor for Jimbob."

"I did not come to Falcor just for him, my lady."

Anna knew that, somehow welcomed and dreaded the words at the same time. "I know that. I've known it for a long time. I'm glad you did." *You said it . . . you are glad.*

"Lady . . . would you return to the mist world . . . if you could?" Jecks' voice was soft, deep, concerned.

Would you return if you could . . . would you . . . The words seemed to spin through Anna's mind . . . over and over. Would she return? Her mouth was dry, and her hands trembled. She clasped them together tightly. "That's an impossible question. I can't. I can barely send a message once a season, and I risk my life doing that."

"You know you cannot," Jecks persisted. "But would you if you could?"

Anna swallowed. *To see Elizabetta and Mario again . . .* A colder, harder voice appeared. *And then what?* And then what? *Do you want to go back to struggling as an untenured professor? How would you even get a job . . . or explain two years' absence? And what would you do when Elizabetta graduates and starts living her own life?*

Would you if you could? The words rattled through her like an ice-edged blade.

Jecks sat, patiently, a man of action, yet one who had stood by her, helped her, reined in his nature, even changed who he had been. His eyes were bright.

Anna swallowed. *". . . and we are here, as on a darkling plain . . ."* Another poet, another set of words. *But our armies aren't that ignorant . . .* "They don't have to be . . ."

Jecks raised his eyebrows at her murmured words.

The softest of unheard chords echoed through her mind, and she rose and stepped around the table-desk. As he stood, she took his hands.

Those strong weathered hands and muscular arms slipped around her, and Anna's arms went around Jecks, the lord who had always been there . . . and who always would be, through the seasons . . . through Darksong and Clearsong.